By B. S. H. Garcia

The Heart of Quinaria

<u>Novels</u>
Of Thieves and Shadows
Of Love and Loss

<u>Novelettes/Novellas</u>
From the Ashes
From the Depths

From the Ashes is free to mailing list subscribers at bshgarci a.com/subscribe*

OF LOVE
AND LOSS

Of Love and Loss

The Heart of Quinaria:
Volume Two

B. S. H. Garcia

Lost Relic Publishing

Cover design and illustration by Jeff Brown Graphics

Interior design by B. S. H. Garcia

Map and interior illustrations by Jared Garcia

First edition: September 2024

ISBN 979-8-9913473-0-3 (hardback)

ISBN 979-8-9867208-9-0 (paperback)

ISBN 979-8-9867208-8-3 (ebook)

www.bshgarcia.com

For Grandma Herold.
Forever loved and never truly lost.
March 16, 1939 ~ July 30, 2023

CONTENTS

A QUICK NOTE

Before you return to Quinaria, I'd like to make you aware of two things:

1. I've included a cropped version of the map in the following pages; however, I highly recommend pulling the map up on my website to view a full-sized, scalable PNG. This version is easier to read and shows the scope of Quinaria. You can find it at bshgarcia.com/map.

2. The back matter of this book contains some helpful resources, such as a volume one recap, inhabitant list, race list, and glossary. Please reference these sections prior to/while reading if you'd like clarity on any characters or world-building.

Thank you,
B. S. H. Garcia

TU
MT. KELDARA
MOROTOK
GREATER QUENTARR
ATSUKUT
SKU
LESSER Q
DARUK
NORGOOS
NIPAT RIV.
ETHOOS LAKE
AGAAS
APAASUTAK
NEHAREM
NI'ANKO
LAUTEI
LAKE
RAYNOOS
MOÁKUN
SUNRISE BAY
MOATIWE
KAHALOÁN
SKYE
BANAXA
YUSTANO
DIAN SEA
TANGEESH
PUETALA
STRAIT OF ITASO
S
AMIREN
NISHAPAR
TARMEHK
RAHEPTUS
KHORSAR
ORILLON
ZOHARAAD
VASHI
MUNSKAHAN
AMENKAH
DESERT
TETH

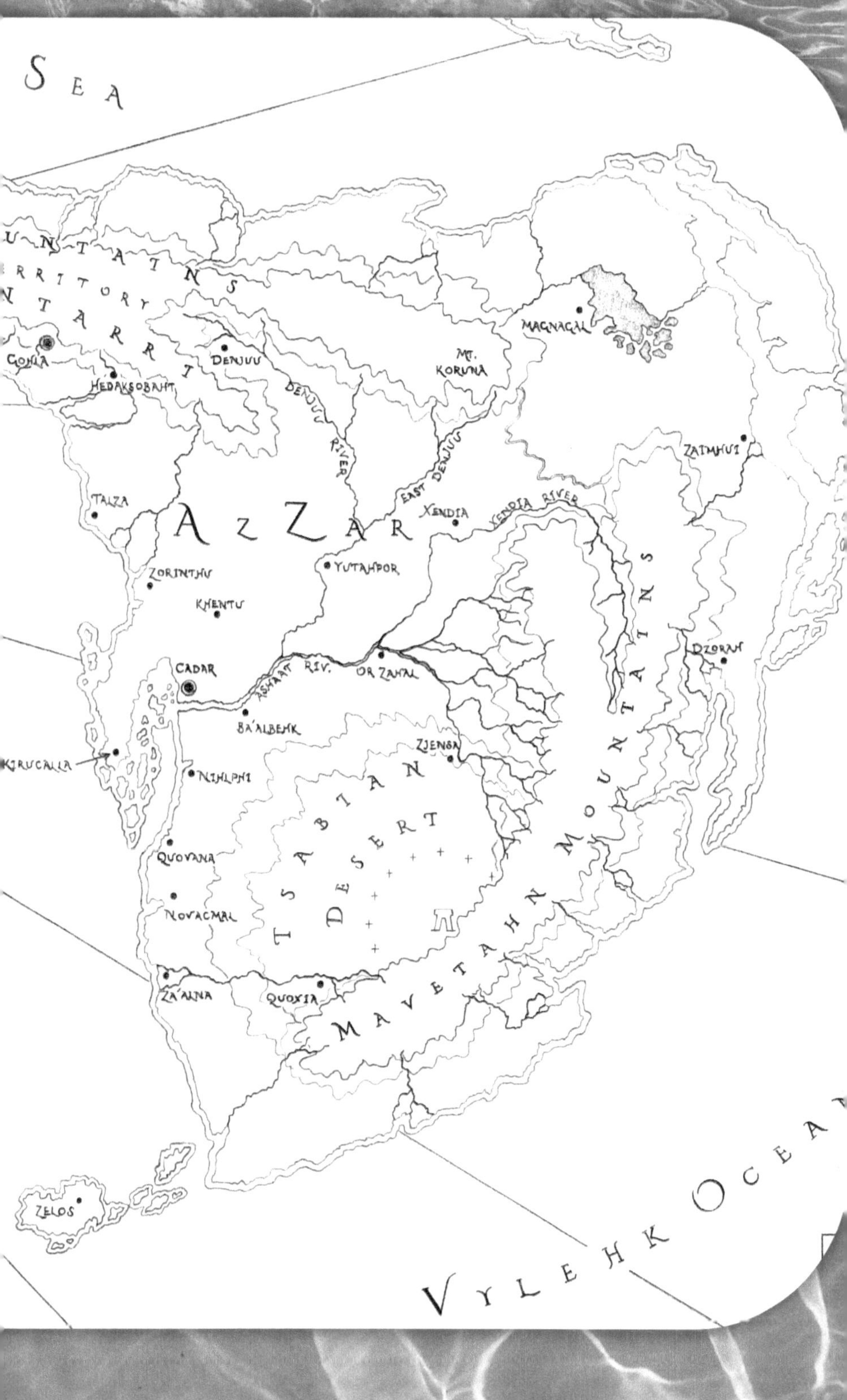

SEA
MOUNTAINS
TERRITORY
NTARRI
GONIA
HEDAKSOBAHT
DENJUU
MAGNACAL
MT. KORUNA
DENJUU RIVER
EAST DENJUU
ZAIMHUI
TALZA
AZZAR
XENDIA
XENDIA RIVER
ZORINTHU
YUTAHPOR
KHENTU
DZORAN
CADAR
ISHAAT RIV.
OR ZAHAL
MAVETAHN MOUNTAINS
BA'ALBEHK
ZJENSA
KIRUCALLA
NIHLPHI
TSABIAN DESERT
QUOVANA
NOVACMAL
ZA'ALNA
QUOXIA
MAVETAHN MOUNTAINS
ZELOS
VYLEHK OCEAN

Ignorance is the womb of monsters.

–Henry Ward Beecher

Don't walk behind me; I may not lead. Don't walk in front of me; I may not follow. Just walk beside me and be my friend.

–Albert Camus

PROLOGUE

R ykahl's footsteps echoed down the corridor as he fled, his lower back and buttocks still throbbing from the twenty-six lashings inflicted by a reed pole. It was all he could stand before delivering a swift kick to his eudna's genitals and making his escape.

Louder, more erratic footsteps pounded after him. "I sentenced you to fifty!" the emperor bellowed. "Come back here and face your punishment like a man."

Rykahl didn't slow down. He ducked around the corner just before a wine glass shattered against the wall.

"You're weak as your eumma and unworthy of my bloodline. One more son. That's all I need to be rid of you." The emperor's voice grew distant, and the footsteps fell silent. "I'll fuck a million whores if it means I get to scrub you from the Zal Drusa lineage."

Paintings of ancestors raced past Rykahl in a blur as he tore down one nevethium lit hall, then the next, wending his way through the deserted palace. His eudna's words stung worse than the lashings, but he wouldn't let a single tear fall. Not for him.

Not for anyone.

When his lungs could no longer draw smooth breaths and his sides seized up with sharp, pulsating pains, he halted. Listened. The emperor had given up chase, likely tantalized by the prospect of the latest vintage—whether that be wine, women, or weaponry.

Most of Eudna's evenings consisted of all three.

After scouring for guards, of which Rykahl found none, he tiptoed across the marble hall and stopped before an arched door framed by pillars embossed with golden, web-like patterning. A pair of nevethium sconces lit the entryway to his sanctuary.

The library.

But tonight, there were voices coming from within. Soft. Accented. Rykahl pressed his ear to the door, but its make allowed no more than muffled whispers to escape. He stepped back, a wrinkle forming on his brow. The emperor never allowed visitors free rein of the palace, and as far as he knew, none were present. No one used the library besides Rykahl and his late eumma.

Mavet keep her soul.

Rykahl darted down the hallway, tattered strands of his silk robe streaming behind him, and pushed aside a painting of a gnarled-looking forefather. A small indent lay within the wall. He pressed it. The wall retracted and slid to the left, revealing a dark tunnel marred with cobwebs and dust. The corner of Rykahl's mouth quirked as he sealed it behind him. He knew the inner workings of the tunnels better than anyone. Knowledge of the palace layout required exploration and reading, neither of which the emperor cared to sacrifice time for. It had provided escape from his eudna's beatings on more than one occasion, not to mention allowing him unrestricted access to the palace regardless of day or hour.

He didn't need the glow of nevethium to proceed. Hands extended before him, he walked ten paces ahead, then turned a sharp right. A staircase. Thirty steps to the top. The sixteenth was missing a chunk of stone. The twenty-second contained an abandoned skirvin nest on the far right. He paused at the top and steeled himself with a breath before heaving open the door.

Murky light spilled into the tunnel. Rykahl stuck his head out, looking both ways before creeping onto the balcony. The scent of old parchments and musk tickled his nostrils. A woven rug imported from Orillon ran the length of the platform, fringed in tassels with fabric so clean it looked to have never been trod upon. Row upon row of scrolls and bound books filled the length of the walls and stretched up to the level of the balcony, many of which had been acquired after Ashaat the Victor decreed that all written knowledge—save for modern religious texts and laws—belonged to the empire.

Above it all, a stained-glass dome filtered the moonlight, casting ghostly shadows on the giant globe at the center of the room. Founded by ancient Vysilliam philosophers, the library had once been the center of public learning and a temple for the pagan gods of old. Many considered it the first (and only) Sanctum of the Arcane in Quinaria, and it was indisputably the birthplace of scholars. It flourished for many ages until disagreements over classism and racism arose. Wars decreased desire for knowledge, and the rise of Mavism sought to obliterate any opposing views on the newly ordained scriptures. Statues were torn down. Scrolls burned. The library and surrounding temples were combined and converted into a palace. Education became a novelty for the powerful and wealthy, and Nyzar deteriorated into a nation of single-minded fools and the highborns who led them.

So said one of the newer parchments in the restricted section, one Rykahl speculated had been inked by an enemy of the empire hoping to seed an insurrection. It was currently stowed away in his chambers for safekeeping—Eumma's dying request.

The emperor didn't entertain such treasonous theories.

Rykahl crept toward the balcony's lyvium cross-hatch railing. Below, two figures huddled over the curved countertop encircling the globe, a scroll unrolled between them. Threadbare cloaks shrouded their faces as they whispered in the heavily accented and slang-laden language of Zelos, Az Zar's southern-isle province rife with criminals, pirates, and other scum (according to the emperor). Their kind rarely frequented Cadar, and most certainly weren't welcome in the palace.

Shadows engulfed Rykahl as he descended the staircase at the far end of the balcony. They wouldn't know of the secret entrance and had no reason to spare a glance in his direction.

But when he slipped off the last of the winding steps, they were gone.

No voices. No scroll. No sound to signal their departure. Which meant, of course, they were still there.

Panic gripped Rykahl's throat as he backed toward the stairs...

...and into a knife. The cool prick of the blade against his back was undeniable.

"You breathe louder than a beast in labor," his assailant hissed. "Don't climb many stairs, do you?"

Rykahl squirmed in his silks. An inaudible plea left his lips as the blade encroached a hair deeper.

"Don't hurt him," another voice chimed. "Do you have any idea who this is? What punishment awaits should we get caught?"

Right. His only bargaining tool.

Rykahl cleared his throat and pressed the remainder of his resolve into his shoulders. "Unhand me at once if you wish the emperor to spare your miserable lives."

Murmurs rumbled behind him. The blade pricked his back, breaking the skin, then retreated. Rykahl winced as he turned to face the intruders. Then his eyes widened. Standing before him were a boy and a girl who looked close to his ten years. The boy, a touch older, had ebony skin, bright violet eyes, and a stern mouth beyond his age. The girl, maybe two years Rykahl's junior, bore a similar complexion, though her eyes were even more vibrant and danced with some tantalizing secret. White, roped locks tumbled from both their hoods. Fellow nyrians. He could justify conversing with them.

At least for an explanation.

Filled with a renewed sense of superiority, Rykahl folded his arms. "What in Mavet's name are you doing in my eudna's palace?"

The boy and girl exchanged glances, then the former fell to his knees. "Forgive us, Prince. We are new servants in the palace and got separated from the others before sundown. We didn't want to appear foolish and tried to find our way back to our quarters, but we came across guards and took shelter in here."

Rykahl swore the girl smirked as the boy spun his tale.

"Please, have mercy," the boy continued. "If you could just point us in the direction of our quarters, we'll be on our way."

The boy nudged the girl, and she fell to her knees without a hint of piety. "Yes, please, oh great Prince. Search the depths of your heart for Mavet's kindness." Her words came out in a monotone rush, eyes darting about the room as if desperate for something interesting to settle on.

Rykahl folded his arms. He wasn't so naïve, even for a pampered palace brat. "The palace is large, but if you are new enough to get lost, you'd still have a shadow servant assigned to you. That servant would've notified the head of the guard of your absence. And since when do servants carry knives?" He paced in front of them, hands clasped behind his back as the emperor often did in such situations. "Care to try again?"

The boy fingered something in the sleeve of his oversized tunic while restraining the girl with his free hand. "If I give you the truth, will you swear upon your god to spare our lives?"

My god? A flicker of a history lesson came to Rykahl, one of the southern islanders clinging to their old, pagan ways. Though under the jurisdiction of Az Zar as one of its provinces, the islands were a constant thorn in his eudna's side. Too unruly to govern; too useful to obliterate.

"I swear." The lie triggered only a small twinge in Rykahl's chest.

"We *are* servants, and still new to our duties." The boy touched the girl's arm, and the pair began strolling around the globe. It was a casual motion meant to induce a sense of familiarity and ease, but Rykahl tensed as they made their way toward the side nearest the doors. He stayed rooted to his spot, allowing them the upper hand.

"Assigned to the stables?" he asked, having noted the distinct scent of manure and sweet straw emanating from their clothes. "I haven't seen you around the palace."

The girl scowled. "They make us sleep in empty stalls, do you know that? We don't even know anything about horses." The knife still dangled at her side. She tightened her grip.

Rykahl wished he had his practice blade. "Doesn't explain why you're in the palace after hours. In the library of all places. I didn't think servants could read."

The girl reacted as he'd hoped. She wrenched herself away from the boy and stomped toward Rykahl, knife extended. "My bretata and I speak many languages and read well beyond our years. Our parents refused to let us become victims of the world your ancestors created."

The boy grunted, but he didn't move to restrain her.

Rykahl pressed his chest to her knife, hoping his bluff would caution her bravery. "And where are your parents now?"

The girl's hand faltered. "Your appa had them killed for piracy." Her lower lip trembled, and for a moment, she looked her age. An innocent, orphaned girl.

The boy slipped his arm around her shoulders, eyes fixated on Rykahl's. "The emperor traded directly with them for years, happy to overlook the manner in which they attained their goods for the discounted rate they gave him. He even sent them on a special mission to uncover an item your priests would undoubtedly consider pagan."

"Impossible." Goosebumps prickled Rykahl's flesh. "My eudna would never—"

"He did," the girl said through clenched teeth. "They spent the final moons of their lives recovering something for him. A scroll of great power. But when they realized the cost of the exchange, they refused to deliver it until your appa granted them equal payment and amnesty." They'd backed away as she spoke and now lingered a few steps from the door. "And when they made their demands, he killed them. We were sentenced to a life of slavery."

The boy kept his gaze on the ground as she spoke, fingers twitching at his sides. Something was fabricated within the girl's story, but what? And how much?

Rykahl searched his memories for any snippets of conversation that might have bled out from his eudna while he drank, or during his morning bragging sessions to whatever unfortunate girl had ended up in his bed the night prior. Anything about pirates or scrolls. There had been that public execution Eudna forced him to attend one or two moon cycles prior, but he couldn't for the life of him recall *who'd* been the victims. He'd always done his best to block such events out. But, as Eumma had always said, it wasn't who or when that mattered.

Only the why.

"They told you something before they died." Rykahl meant to process the thought in his head, but out the words slipped, bared for his enemies like whores lined up for the emperor's nightly selection. He wasn't used to anyone listening when he spoke. "That's why you're here researching in the library. You're trying to get to the scroll before my eudna." His eyebrow arched. "What were you reading? Give it here."

"Goodbye, Prince. We'll remember your kindness." The boy tugged on the gilded handle, but Rykahl lurched for the door and shoved it closed.

The girl brought her blade to his throat. "Let us pass."

Rykahl bared his teeth. "If you do anything without my consent, I'll scream with my dying breath. Guards will be on you before you make it halfway out of the palace. You'll die a worse death than your parents, and they'll never be avenged."

The boy's lips thinned. "What are you suggesting?"

The girl began to protest, but the boy silenced her with a glance.

Rykahl lowered her blade with a steady hand and rested his opposite elbow on the door handle. "I won't tell my eudna, and I'll see to it your services are no longer needed in the stables. The old woman who tends to my chambers has recently taken ill. Perhaps you could better serve the palace inside."

The boy's eyes narrowed. "Seems generous."

"In return, we'll keep this scroll business to ourselves, and I want to be a part of the research and exploration. If we locate it, we'll share in its wealth or power—whatever you believe it possesses."

"We can't trust you," the girl spat.

Rykahl feigned indifference. "I don't see that you have a choice."

They exchanged whispers. Rykahl circled the globe, tracing his hand over the nevethium-flecked pedestal. His finger came back coated in dust. He dared a glance over his shoulder every so often, all too aware of the excitement bubbling in his stomach. Adventure and a chance to get back at Eudna? He couldn't have dreamed up a better scenario.

Footsteps padded up to him. The boy and girl wore somber expressions, but he sensed truth in their eyes.

"We'll work with you," the boy said, "but you must promise to never go back on your word like your eudna."

"Fine." Rykahl shrugged.

"And you'll swear it in a blood pact to the First Amma." The girl dug her finger into his chest, nostrils flaring and jaw set. "If you should waver and betray our trust, they'll strike you dead."

An itch tickled Rykahl's throat. He swallowed it back and nodded, bowing his assent. "As you wish."

They kneeled there on the marble floor, and each pricked their palms with the blade until it drew blood. The prayers the girl offered gave Rykahl only a slight sense of unease. He hardly cared for Mavet's blessings. It was Eudna's religion; not his. When they held hands, however, forming a tight circle, palm on palm, blood on blood, Rykahl fought to keep his rising gorge at bay.

Something shifted in the room. A flicker of the sconces. A wraith in the moonlight. A rustle in the parchments.

Rykahl shivered and smeared the blood on his robes. He'd burn them tonight in his room. No one would be the wiser.

"I'm Konar," the boy offered after they finished. "This is Karliah." The girl dipped her head but regarded him with weary eyes.

"My pleasure. I'm Rykahl Zal Drusa, heir to the throne and future ruler of Az Zar. If you stay true to me, I will raise you up by my side and see no harm ever comes to you." He rose and beckoned them up the stairs, back to the secret passage. "Now, tell me everything."

PART ONE

KONAR

"That's close enough."

Konar halted mid-stride at Elaysia's command, toes curling in the sand. The scene about to unfold was long overdue. Years upon years of lies stacked like the layers of Quorath's core, each built upon the last, waiting for the weak foundation to crumble. It was a miracle it'd held for so long.

He extended a hesitant arm, shivering as the sun disappeared beneath the waves. "Elaysia—"

"Don't touch me." Her eyes glistened. Pools of fire seething a deep, festering hatred. "I *never* want you to touch me again."

Onitus raised his plumage in response to his rider's distress. The stormbird's wings flared the width of a loft, his midnight blue feathers radiant in the fading light. A massive talon arced above the sand.

Konar retracted his arm and sat cross-legged on the beach. "How much do you know?"

"Enough to justify killing you. Too little to find peace." She took a step toward him. "Can you give me that much?"

"I'll do everything in my power." He gripped his knees and kept his gaze on the rolling waves.

"There's one thing, really. One small thing." Elaysia uncovered a shell with her toe, its exposed ridges as red as freshly spilled blood. "Davier betrayed me for growth. For luxury and riches. For his family. For a future. But you, Konar..." Her voice broke, fists trembling at her hips. "You had everything. Influence. Security. Love. What did you have to gain?"

She wasn't ready for an answer, so he didn't give her one. Just the space to unload all the venom he deserved.

"At first, I thought it was power," Elaysia continued. "But that didn't explain why you left me alive. Why leave a loose end? Jealousy didn't seem a strong enough motive, nor hatred." She crouched before him. He couldn't meet her gaze. "Then I realized *he* was right. Only from some convoluted premise of control could you devise such a plot."

"He?" Konar whispered.

Elaysia gathered the shell into her palm and traced its spine with her thumb. "I hate you so much. But I loved you more than anyone, even my family. You were everything to me." Her tone darkened. "You were supposed to protect me."

Tears welled in Konar's eyes. Intense pressure rushed to his face, his nose, his throat, like a dam ready to burst. "I won't dare ask your forgiveness."

"And you'll never receive it."

A bone-chilling breeze rippled off the ocean, cutting through Konar's robes. "I'm so sorry, Ellie. I thought I was making a choice for the greater good. I've spent most of my life keeping the peace in Quinaria, and your parents threatened it. The power they sought could never be used for good, or so I thought." A sob rattled his chest, but he withheld the tears. "I'd take it back if I could. I've regretted it every night since. I never sleep."

"I hope you never do."

He raised his gaze to meet hers. One moment of staring into them was a punishment worse than death. "And how will you seek retribution?"

"I'm putting you in the cliff holds until I confer with my council." She left a cold shadow in her wake as she strode toward the sea. "I've conjured many hateful things. Lain awake at night dreaming up ways to make you suffer as I've suffered. But you're not like the rest of us. Your heart died long ago, and your spirit with it." The water lapped at her feet, soaking the train of her crimson gown in a fringe of sea foam. "Tell me it isn't so."

A gulf widened between them. It spilled secrets too deep for words, exposed feelings Konar had long since buried, cutting to his core in a smooth, killing stroke. This time, no manner of speech would save him. No gentle cadence or logic-laced argument could come to his rescue.

He couldn't interpret Elaysia's expression as she tossed the shell at his feet. "I trust you won't run, and if you do, I'll assume you'll take care of things yourself." She jutted her chin toward the tree line across the beach. "An escort awaits you. If you go quietly, I'll reserve a place in my heart for the shadow of the man you once were." She whirled toward the forest, Onitus strutting behind her like a guardian statue come to life.

Konar rose. "Elaysia." She halted but didn't grace him with a glance. "Annonitus wasn't…that wasn't me. I never intended for him to…"

"I know," she said, voice cracking. "Control is an illusion, after all."

She hurried across the beach and disappeared into the trees. Konar's will to live vanished with her.

Two warriors awaited Konar, where sand mingled with soil. He would've been offended at the number if not for the selection of escorts: Jakki, for humility, and Yerakai, to wreak further havoc upon his conscience.

Their stormbirds accompanied them. With nearly identical markings (broad black bands across their upper breasts, separating their gray heads from smooth, cream stomachs), their defining difference was that Jakki's female was twice the size of Yerakai's male.

Konar offered a weak smile in greeting. Four pairs of eyes glared back at him, ranging from disappointment to revulsion. All were void of compassion.

Yerakai dared a step toward him. White locks framed his sharp features, making his ashen violet skin appear a shade darker in contrast. "This way, High Elder. We are to take you directly to the cliff holds. I must ask you to surrender your staff."

Konar ran his hand over the leather binding. It'd served him since he departed Az Zar all those years ago, been a way to carve out a new future not built upon the selfish desires of youth. It was appropriate it leave him now. His final chapter had begun.

Before he could surrender his staff to Yerakai, Jakki snatched it from his hand and jabbed it into his stomach. "Move. Now."

Yerakai winced as if he'd been the one jabbed. "Jakki, he's—"

"He's a monster. Or have you already forgotten what Elaysia told us?" Jakki stared Konar down, muscles taut and staff raised in a defensive position.

Konar cleared his throat. "I won't challenge anyone's loyalties tonight, nor will I resist imprisonment."

"Part of me wishes you would." Jakki drew her staff back, though she refrained from striking him again. "Walk. You know the way."

No one spoke the rest of the journey.

The cliff holds were constructed from naturally occurring cutaways on the rock face overlooking the ocean. With a sheer drop below, a steep climb above, and harsh weather berating the doorless cells, few dared an escape. In the times of the stormbirds, convicted parties had been flown to the holds in the Great Beasts' talons and deposited with little more than a blanket and some rations. Some didn't survive the sentence back then.

Survival had since become a rarity.

In the absence of stormbirds—they'd been assumed extinct until Elaysia had recently proved otherwise and, even now, were still too young to bear riders—prisoners were lowered to the holds on ropes, and rations were scarce, for few cared to make the hike to the top of the cliffs with any regularity. Konar doubted anyone would make an exception for him.

Yerakai cinched a rope around Konar's waist and another beneath his buttocks, while Jakki brooded in the background. They supplied him with no food or drink, and he didn't beg any of them.

Jakki shoved Konar toward the ledge. "Tug the rope three times when you've reached a vacant cell. Don't take your time. We aren't staying here all night."

"Understood." Konar nodded to Yerakai. Pursed his lips at Jakki. "Take care of Elaysia. Her enemies are great, and they'll only grow in power and number before this is through."

Jakki raised her staff in warning. "She's no longer your concern."

Konar drew a sharp breath, then lowered himself over the edge. Wind billowed his robes like a sail, pulling his body away from the rock face. He let go.

He half expected them to let him fall. It was the least that he deserved. But whatever their personal qualms, they valued Elaysia's will over their own—which was more than he could say for himself. The rope tightened as he pushed its bounds. He swung back into the rock face, feet first, and began his descent. Five feet. Ten feet. Twenty. He nearly missed the cell, as fast as they lowered him. Catching the edge at the last moment, he heaved himself inside and slipped out of the rope. It slithered back up the rock face before he could give it a tug.

Konar surveyed his new lodging. Not enough room to stand or fully extend when lying down. No more than five feet from the cave wall to death's ledge. Of all the holds, of course this one had chosen him. Maybe he'd chosen it.

A breeze laced with brine tingled his face as he lay upon the frigid, jagged stone. Dampness crept into his clothing, nosing its way through the threads until it clung to his skin like a wet blanket. He hadn't summoned the scroll's magic in a moon cycle. With luck, he'd fade away long before Elaysia reached a decision. Or perhaps he'd roll off the edge in his sleep.

Maybe that's what she hoped for, deep down. A clean, blameless break for both of them. A guiltless death.

Konar rolled onto his left side and flinched as a lump beneath his robes pressed into his hip. With a trembling hand, he withdrew the doll. Held it up to the sky. Its beaded, violet eyes caught the moonlight in a cheap imitation of its original owner. A small hide tunic shrouded what remained of its sand-stuffed torso, and thin strands of bleached leather hung from its head. He pressed it to his chest. Countless years had passed and he still couldn't let it go.

Let her go.

Karliah would've likely laughed if she knew he still clung to a version of her she'd fought to distance herself from. A young girl, tenacious and outspoken, mature beyond her years with a knack for finding trouble in the unlikeliest of places. But he was no longer there to dig her out. The fated night of his departure, there'd been no goodbyes, no kind words or fond memories recalled, nor acknowledgment of the bond they'd shared, the Haeshol they'd fought through to make the ghosts of their parents proud. Only forlorn glances and shattered hearts.

"I'm sorry, Setata," he whispered to the doll. "I should've stopped you while I had the chance."

Konar didn't fall to his death that night, nor the next, no matter how carelessly he positioned himself near the cliff. His lips dried long before his stomach growled, despite the condensation he licked from the cave's crevices, despite the air heavy with humidity. When a storm blew in with shrieking gales and needle-sharp rain, he almost jumped. He crawled to the edge and imagined his body splattered below, food for the seahawks and fish, life exchanged for life, his essence finally of use. But even as he played out the scenario in his head again and again, Konar knew it wasn't his time. Something was still unresolved. Until he achieved his life's purpose, he'd find no peace in death.

The third morning came as gentle as a mother's kiss with glowing rays and a hint of warmth in the wind. Konar rubbed the crust from his eyes and propped himself up on an aching elbow. Before he heard the clatter of stone or saw the first pebbles fall, he knew someone was coming. His heart quickened the way it always did before something upended his life. A slight tensing of the muscles. Widening of the eyes. He sat cross-legged, facing the sea, and folded his hands in his lap, trying his best to silence his raging headache.

Several angsty grunts later, Zavik dropped into the cliff hold. Or past it, rather. The lad missed the ledge and, with wide-eyed horror, thrust his skinny, white arms into the air like a fledgling thrown from its nest. Konar grabbed his wrists and wrestled him inside.

Zavik sat up, panting, and drew his knees to his chest. His seers had fogged up with the ocean's moisture and his own exertion. With twitchy hands, he used his tunic to clean them, then placed them back on his face, gaze sweeping over the horizon, the cramped quarters and, finally, Konar.

"Sorry to drop in on you like this. Literally."

A twinge of amusement found its way to Konar's face. "I'm a bit occupied at the moment, but I'll make an exception for an old friend."

A breeze tousled Zavik's curls, revealing wrinkles on his freckled brow. He unfastened a waterskin from his hip and passed it to Konar. "Brought you this. And these." Bruised berries stained the palm of his hand.

"Thank you." Konar took a hesitant sip. If he was too greedy, his stomach might reject it, leaving him thirstier than before. "I'm surprised they let you see me."

Zavik's forefinger picked at the cuticle of his thumbnail, gaze shifting from Konar's chest to his feet. "They don't exactly know I'm here."

Konar popped a berry into his mouth to hide his surprise. It was almost too sweet. "Who lowered you to me?"

"T'Vak. He's following me around like a duckling until I serve up a platter of nevethium. Haven't found the right time to bring that up to Elaysia with all...this."

"Understandable."

A seahawk shrieked in the distance. Zavik shifted uncomfortably on the stone floor and fixed his gaze on Konar. He must've had some faith in his old mentor to risk a visit, but disappointment hardened his eyes, tainting whatever thread of hope he clung to, whatever explanation he sought.

Konar didn't blame him. Part of him wanted to tell the lad off and destroy what little chance he had for redemption. The other part wanted to glean a scrap of sympathy. Neither was what he needed to say, nor what the friend awaiting his response needed to hear.

"I've done it this time, Zavik."

The lad's eyes widened into pools the same blueish green as Skyfall Sea. He blew air through pursed lips. "That you have. And I want to understand why."

"Elaysia hasn't told you?"

"She told me your motives behind...back then." Zavik shrugged, had the grace to allude to what they both already knew instead of beating him over the head with it. "But your logic eludes me. There are holes. You've not told her everything." He leaned forward, eyes narrowing. "It has to do with the scrolls, doesn't it? I think you know far more about them than you let on."

Konar didn't confirm. Nor did he object.

Zavik gripped his knees with pale fingertips. "Tell me everything."

Konar's body tightened in response. Where to begin? The ill-fated treasure hunt that consumed his parents, spurred by a greedy ruler? The moment he first held a scroll—worse yet, when he first took part in a ritual that changed his life forever? Or the decades spent searching for the remaining scrolls, only to realize they held the power to destroy Quinaria, to corrupt the best of people? It was a chance to clear his conscience in the presence of someone who mattered. Pass on his legacy.

But he didn't. Not all of it, at least.

Not yet.

"The scrolls contain the powers of gods, or what some might call magic, or the essence of life itself," Konar said in a voice like a receding tide. Zavik's brow furrowed, but he didn't object to the claim. "I sought them when I was young and blinded by pride and revenge. I made the mistake of entrusting my discoveries to the wrong company. The world pays for my blunders to this day." He closed his eyes, trying to wish away the painful memories. "When I learned the errors of my ways, I searched for the remaining scrolls alone, with every intention of destroying them so they couldn't wreak havoc on the world. But when it became clear I was incapable of such a feat, I set my sights on preventing the discovery of the remaining scrolls."

The rope around Zavik's waist went taut. He gave it one tug back. T'Vak was growing impatient up top, apparently.

"Why didn't you just tell Elaysia's parents that?" the lad asked.

"I tried. Elishon wouldn't heed my reasoning." Konar traced the worn fringe of his sleeve. His ceremonial garments would need mending before they were passed onto his successor—assuming Elaysia dared to salvage the corrupted cloth.

"The scroll translations." Zavik's hands went to his chest as though he still stowed the scrolls beneath his tunic. "Were you sabotaging the process?"

Konar shook his head. "I'll admit I've been hesitant to share everything I've translated thus far, but my intentions are pure. I meant it when I said I had a change of heart. The scrolls want to be found. That's why they were created." A vision of the great bear entered his mind, hulking and ethereal, coated in midnight blue, with a roar that would weaken the strongest of warriors. He blinked it away, forcing his attention back on Zavik. "If we can secure the rest, we can put an end to all this. I'm certain of it."

Zavik inched toward the edge and rested his hand on the cave wall. His shoulders heaved with unseen burdens. "You've lost everyone's trust. Elaysia should never have to see you again. One betrayal is enough for a lifetime, but you were her second within a matter of days."

And she'll see more before the end. The thought crossed Konar's mind like a shifty gwanei darting through the jungle back home in Tongura. There one moment, gone the next. But always lingering close by.

"I still need you, though," Zavik admitted. "I can't finish the translations on my own." He faced Konar, determination etched into his stubbled jaw. "If you want redemption, be ready after the sun sets tonight."

"You've convinced them to spare me?"

"No." Zavik gave the rope two hard tugs. His body lurched into the air as soon as he leaned out from the cliff hold. "The council voted in favor of your execution tomorrow at dawn," he called down. "But I'm stupid enough to risk my life on Elaysia's behalf. Again." A pause. "Tonight, Konar. Be ready. Don't make me regret this."

Konar squeezed the doll. He'd spent practically his entire life in a state of regret, wishing away poor decision after poor decision. But while he couldn't change the past, perhaps maybe, just maybe, there was a glimmer of hope for the future.

ZAVIK

The door to the high chieftain's quarters had faded to a weather-beaten gray over the years, but it had not lost its majesty. Ferns bordered the edges, carved with great attention to detail on the leaves, and moss dangled from the antlers of two nytak stags rearing on either side. A stormbird soared above it all, lightning bursting from its outstretched wings. The woodgrain itself gave the illusion of rain—a gift from nature, or the gods, depending on who you asked—and the subtle staining of mold nipped at the corners, accenting it.

Zavik was aware of such intricacies because he'd been standing outside the high chieftain's quarters for at least ten minutes.

As he raised his hand to knock, the door swung open. Elaysia stood in a sand-colored shift, hair tangled about her breasts. Red lines tainted the whites of her eyes like veins, and dark shadows bruised the skin beneath them, betraying the emotional beating the past few days had taken out on her. She'd maintained composure around citizens and in council meetings—far more than he knew her to be capable of—but then she'd shut herself in her quarters after sunset, refusing to surface until the next day's duties demanded it of her. He should've approached her sooner, but he hadn't been certain what to say.

He still wasn't certain.

Elaysia's fingers lingered on the handle. "Oh," she said, taking him in, as if trying to place who he was for the briefest moment.

"Oh." Zavik took a step back, finding himself no longer sheltered from the mist-like rain. He shouldn't have come without a speech prepared. "It's early, isn't it? I'll come back later. Or meet you elsewhere. Actually, we don't even have to—"

"Zav." Elaysia gave the faintest smile, but it was genuine. "It's never too early for you. Come in." She backed away from the entrance, then hesitated. "I just remembered I need to check on something. Walk with me?"

Before Zavik could answer, she disappeared inside and returned with a cloak, closing the door firmly behind her. She either assumed his compliance or had altogether forgotten she'd invited him, because she walked right past him, her cloak doing a decent job of masking her ever-growing belly, and hurried through the High Tree courtyard.

Zavik considered letting her go. She clearly wasn't in a conversational mood, and to be honest, he still didn't know how to approach her with topics of urgency. The role of high chieftain indisputably belonged to her now, and between that and everything she'd experienced in Az Zar, he felt a gap between them. And it was growing.

But then he thought of Konar. How terrible it was going to be to smuggle him out of the cliff holds and frame it as—

Hmm.

Surely, he could come up with something, should it come to that. But he'd rather make Elaysia understand, to see why they needed the former High Elder Lightfoot around just a little longer. All without admitting *he* needed Konar to aid him in translating the scrolls. Because...well, pride. His own damn pride.

Brilliant, Zav. Just brilliant.

He caught sight of Elaysia halfway across the High Tree bridge, just beyond two armed watchers who'd been recently positioned at every entry point in Agaas. The high chieftain had acted quickly after reclaiming her seat by doubling their numbers and patrols. There wouldn't be a repeat of the Igtheos Tree massacre under her watch.

A Daruk watcher, identifiable by his thick beard and pale skin, gave Zavik a semblance of a nod as he passed by—and not in a negative way. It was almost…respectful?

Zavik returned a confused stare. He wasn't exactly used to people regarding him positively, if at all.

"That was odd," he muttered when he caught up with Elaysia on the other side.

She didn't slow her pace, nor glance over her shoulder to assess his expression. "What?"

"That watcher acknowledged me. They never do; at least, not like that."

Elaysia pressed on in pursuit of her mysterious quest without a word, and Zavik instantly regretted bringing it up. Why would she care that some random Daruk gave him two seconds of recognition when she literally carried the weight of Neharem on her shoulders?

"It's nothing," he added, quickening his pace to catch up. "I'm just over-scrutinizing, as always."

"You're not. I've named you Konar's replacement." Elaysia gave a careless shrug, as though she'd told him they were having venison for dinner instead of fish. "I informed all the watchers to ensure you are well protected and allowed access wherever you deem necessary."

Zavik halted as a herd of children thundered by, caught up in a game of hunter and prey. He was grateful for the interruption. Multiple emotions vied for control of his being. Excitement, because becoming a high elder was one of his greatest aspirations. Sadness, because although he'd always hoped to replace Konar, he didn't expect it to be under such circumstances, or so soon.

And fear. Fear because this was a dangerous time to step into a position of power in Neharem, let alone Quinaria.

All these thoughts and more circled his mind, but all he could manage in response was, "When were you going to tell me?"

Elaysia's gaze was lost on the children, her full lips pinched together as she studied them, one hand on her belly. Zavik wasn't certain when her time was, but ever since she'd defeated

Rajar a few weeks prior, she seemed to grow every night. As far as he knew, the baby could arrive any day, but something told him it would be a while still; that she'd get larger, deal with more stress, and eventually transition to that final phase where those with child were all shuffles and groans. Assuming the execution of her father figure didn't send her into early labor. Something he needed to address promptly.

Zavik cleared his throat. "I'm honored you'd consider me, but—"

"It's not under consideration. It's decided."

"Doesn't the council need to vote?"

"The high chieftain chooses one high elder, and the other two are voted into place by the council. I theoretically could've replaced High Elder Lightfoot when I first assumed leadership, but I wasn't aware of his treasonous past, nor well enough versed in the laws." There was a harshness in her features as she regarded Zavik, though it wasn't directed at him. "I won't make the same mistake this time."

Elaysia had neglected to draw her cloak's hood over her head, and her hair and face had the appearance of petals covered in morning dew. On the outside, she looked healthier and more confident than ever, but inside, something bitter and malnourished had taken root, and it showed through her eyes. She'd changed a lifetime in little more than a year.

"I've already announced it to the council," she continued, "after we voted on what to do with your predecessor."

Zavik rubbed anxiously at his ink-stained fingers. "I imagine it wasn't well-received."

"There was some pushback due to you not being of Neharem birth, but most acknowledged you were trained for this. Besides"—she raised her hand as an elderly woman with a toothy grin hobbled past—"I need trustworthy people by my side. Those who find themselves in disagreement with me should leave now rather than later."

Zavik removed his seers and wiped the mist from the lenses. "Aren't you worried about the Banaxa? There's a chance they're only lingering in Agaas and remaining part of the council to glean information for the Lautei. If they're part of a plot to avenge Rajar—"

"I'm certain they are, and I'm preparing an argument to ban hoksanu because of it. In fact, next time you're in the library, see if you can find any information pertaining to its origins, or any special circumstances that might negate their right to invoke it. Gods know I'd never beat a challenger now." She pulled her tangles of black and white streaked hair atop her head and secured it with a leather cord, then strode toward the nearest ramp.

Once again, Zavik found himself unsure if he should follow. He'd decided against it, on the grounds of not wanting to be intrusive, when she cast a glance over her shoulder and used her chin to gesture for him to accompany her.

He followed.

Elaysia led them down and out of Agaas, through base camp, and—thank the scholars—avoided that damning trail through the woods leading to a cliff she'd grown too fond of lingering at when chaos threatened her life. They took a well-trodden route through the hulking, red-barked trees and outstretched ferns with their long tendrils gently brushing Zavik's ankles as he trudged through the mossy undergrowth, the ground soft beneath his boots. The mist hung heavy and low, making the air seem alive, as though it and the water had sanctioned their surroundings holy.

Maybe they were.

They didn't speak as they walked, and they didn't need to. Something about knowing someone so well and for such a long time made it alright to linger in that awkward stillness, in that space where people truly experienced one another without embellishment, without pretense. Without fear. Perhaps, that's when a genuine connection was born. When you could sit with another being in silence and enjoy it, truly enjoy it, for all its simplicity.

Was that not love at its purest?

When they reached the spot where fallen coniferous needles intermingled with sand, Elaysia removed her cloak. The wind slapped against her thin shift, hugging all her new curves with surprising tenderness. She set off across the beach, and Zavik followed, feeling somewhat like an intruder, until she kneeled and retrieved a small crimson shell in the shape of a spiral.

"Help me find two more like it?" she asked, holding it up.

Zavik immediately set to searching. Within the hour, they'd located three perfect shells, all roughly the same size and shade, and laid them atop a large piece of driftwood. He noted the relevance of the number and quietly matched each one to a family member Elaysia had lost.

She gathered beach grass, some dark gray stones smooth as newborn skin, and made a small nest for each shell in the sand. Zavik looked on as she kneeled before the shrine, offering silent prayers and kissing each shell before laying it in its commemorative resting place. When she finished, she took his hand and led him to the cool sands dampened by the waves. Tear tracks snaked down her cheeks, but that was the only evidence of sadness that remained. Now, she looked fierce as a warrior, yet as hardened as an old man.

"I needed to say goodbye." Her voice was scratchy and monotone instead of rich with its usual deep melody. "Now that I know what really happened to them and why, I feel I can finally move on and lay them to rest."

Zavik squeezed her hand gently. "Does it hurt any less?"

"It hurts more." She drew a steadying breath as she wiped her cheeks. "But I can't linger in mourning any longer. It's taken too much out of me. I hope by offering them to the gods, I'll finally be at peace. As at peace as I can be, anyway."

Zavik's hand was beginning to sweat holding onto hers—and not because he was warm—but he held tight. "And will you..." He struggled for the right words, the best way to present a suggestion that would surely sour her mood. "Still be at peace after you see Konar's sentence through?"

Her two-toned eyes darkened, and she removed her hand from his. "Do you not think my family deserves justice?"

"Of course, they do, it's just—"

"Just what?" She backed away from him, toward the sea.

Just that I think you'll never find peace if you go through with this, he thought.

But aloud, he said, "Maybe it would be best to wait until after the baby's born? Maseeya says the stress isn't good for—"

"I think we've known each other long enough to sense when one of us is lying." She smiled—though it didn't reach her eyes—and rubbed her temples as she returned her gaze to the ocean. "So please, don't pretend this is about my health or the baby's. I'm sorry if my decision hurts you, but Konar knew what he was doing all these years, and he knew eventually he'd have to pay for it. You'll feel better about it after it's done."

Elaysia retrieved her cloak from the sand and trailed across the beach until the forest swallowed her form.

This time, she didn't look back to make sure Zavik followed.

"Should we have tied a note to it or something?" Zavik asked as he dared a glance over the cliff. Moonlight cast an eerie pall over an ocean smooth as glass. "Is this even the right spot? Maybe one of us should've gone down first, you know, to make sure he's alright."

T'Vak joined Zavik at the ledge and spat over it. "Be my guest."

Zavik drew back. He was *not* going down there again. His first—and, hopefully, only—visit to the cliff holds had nearly given him an anxiety attack, and he'd told Konar to be ready by nightfall, so if that scheming old nyrian missed the rope, it wasn't Zavik's fault. Nope. He'd done his part, risked his life.

And he was straight out of luck if Konar refused to comply.

A chilling wind ripped through Zavik's clothes. What if Konar *had* died? Zavik had left him water, given him a few berries, but the man was ancient. Or, overcome with hopelessness, he could've accepted his fate and surrendered his body to the sea.

Zavik's pulse quickened. Fine. He'd go down one last time to confirm.

But before he could formulate the words, the rope jerked taut against the tree T'Vak had fastened it to.

Zavik jumped with an audible squeal. "T'Vak!"

The backhander shooed him away as he took a swig from his wineskin. "I see it, I see it."

"Pull him up! Pull him up!" When T'Vak didn't move fast enough for his liking, Zavik gave the rope a little tug himself.

Nope. No way he was hauling six plus feet and at least two hundred pounds of nyrian up the side of a cliff.

T'Vak rolled his eyes and pushed Zavik away with the flat of his hand. "Give the old man a moment to secure himself, eh?"

He let out a resounding burp, tossed his wineskin toward the woods, and began pulling the rope back up. Within moments, his breathing gave way to heavy drags. The moonlight accented the sweat glistening on his brow. T'Vak wasn't small, especially for a human, but Zavik guessed he was just barely the same size as Konar, if not a touch shorter. It had taken both Jakki and Yerakai to lower the former high elder down.

"Do you want any—"

"Fuck off," T'Vak wheezed.

Zavik raised his hands in defense as he backed away. "I'm here if you change your mind."

Zavik passed the time pacing, daring a glance at T'Vak every so often, which occasionally earned him a nasty glare. Twice, the rope slipped, and his heart skipped a beat at the prospect of losing his knowledge and protection in a single instant. He was about to offer his assistance again when T'Vak made a grunt-worthy heave and shouted a slew of expletives into the night.

"If all you're going to do is pace, then get over here and help, for fuck's sake," T'Vak spat. "Can't concentrate with you scurrying around like a wraith."

Zavik gripped the rope and found it slick with sweat. He resisted the instinct to remove his hands and wipe them on his tunic. T'Vak was relying on him, and together—well, mostly T'Vak—they heaved and pulled until Zavik feared his arms were going to rip straight from their sockets.

"Almost there," T'Vak said between grunts. "Three more pulls. Three." *Heave.* "Two." *Heave.* "One." *Heave.*

An arm shot over the side of the cliff, then another. Zavik let go of the rope and, only distantly aware of T'Vak cursing behind him, grabbed one of Konar's arms and pulled.

Konar collapsed on the ledge, panting as though *he'd* been the one to pull another man's body weight up a cliff side.

"That'll go on your tab," T'Vak muttered as he unwrapped the rope from the tree.

Zavik ignored the comment and directed his attention to Konar. "You didn't jump."

"Didn't have much choice." Konar's teeth shone bright as the moons. He studied Zavik's face, then dropped his smile. "I must pay penance. As tempting as it was to take my own life, I would've found no peace in death."

Zavik dropped to a knee before Konar, holding the nyrian's gaze. "I need you to promise me something."

The former high elder's attention was wholly his.

"I will provide you with safety, anonymity, food, drink, and shelter," Zavik said, his voice just above a whisper. "In exchange, you will tell me everything you know about the scrolls, and I mean *everything*. You'll also agree to answer all questions I have regarding translations."

Konar stroked his beard as he nodded slowly, considering.

When Zavik sensed no pushback, he dropped his last, and biggest, request. "And if the opportunity presents itself, you will confront Elaysia again to see if you can provide her with the peace and closure she so strongly desires."

Konar took longer to reply than Zavik would've liked, but he eventually gave an affirmative nod, brushed his hands on his robes, and extended one.

"You have my word. I swear it before you, our gods, and"—Konar eyed T'Vak with the same suspicion he'd first shown him the day they met in Agaas—"I have no reason to lie, Zavik. Not anymore."

Some part of Zavik still didn't trust him, but he couldn't tell if it was his own intuition or Elaysia's overbearing opinions swaying him, as they often did. Even so, he needed Konar, and he didn't have to trust him. Just keep him close. Use him when required.

The thought struck him with a wave of guilt.

"I'm giving you the benefit of the doubt, High—" Zavik bit his lip, stared down at his feet. "Konar."

A flicker of recognition flashed across Konar's face. "I see." He shrugged it off, but Zavik noted the hurt in his tone. "And who has she appointed? Nanotsuk of the Morotôk? Kelsia's celibate daughter? Maybe Gibrund's half-wit of an elder?"

Zavik laughed nervously.

"Ah." Konar didn't need further explanation. But was that pride in his eyes? Or mere acceptance?

As if reading his thoughts, the former high elder patted Zavik's shoulder and said, "It makes sense. Good for you, lad. I'd offer my expertise, but I'm not sure you'd want it."

Zavik bit his lip. "Not sure Elaysia would want it."

"Not sure I want to wait around here for some watcher to learn we helped Agaas's greatest enemy escape from his cliff hold," T'Vak called out, holding his blade to the sky as he examined its glinting edges in the moonlight. "Mayhaps we move this party elsewhere, like this criminal's new lodging?"

Konar glared at T'Vak but gave a reluctant nod as he addressed Zavik. "He's right. Where did you have in mind?"

Zavik didn't suppress his giddiness. "Oh, just an ancient structure overlooking the beach. It's infamous, but practically no one knows it's there or ventures to visit it. Not even Elaysia."

A smile creeped across Konar's face. "The sanctuary Igtheos built for his people when they first sought refuge here. It's been a long time since I've set foot in that place."

T'Vak forced an exaggerated yawn. "Well, ain't this a night for making memories? Zavvie boy's first time committing a crime punishable by death, the ex-high elder's"—he squinted at Konar—"what's this, your third chance at life? And me, well…" The backhander drained his second wineskin and hooked it back onto his belt. "I'm getting richer every day."

Zavik considered feigning illness when Elaysia called a gathering of the Stormriders at the summit lodge the following morning, but that would've only further incriminated him. He was grateful she'd at least kept it from the council.

For the time being, anyhow.

They'd neglected the oversized table and gathered near the fire, their positions varying from seated to pacing. Zavik had chosen to stand, hoping it made him appear alert yet concerned. T'Vak hadn't been allowed to attend, and he was surprised at how vulnerable he felt without the backhander's presence, even among friends.

Probably because you're the only guilty one here, you fool.

Zavik chased the thought away with a forced smile at Mardus, who, to his credit, received it with tightly drawn lips and raised eyebrows instead of a frown.

The rest of the riders didn't so much as acknowledge him. Yerakai reclined beside the fire, whittling away at a piece of wood that was starting to resemble a nytak. Elaysia squatted nearby, making a show of attentiveness. Anahi and the beridians carried on a hushed discussion he couldn't quite make out, and though their gestures remained calm, their faces were anything but. Xaren sat cross-legged in the corner, eyes closed in a meditative state.

And Jakki...

Zavik just hoped she wouldn't show.

As if reading his thoughts, the double doors to the summit lodge swung inward. Jakki stormed across the room, neglecting to close them. Zavik hurried to remedy her negligence, happy to have something to do other than sit around and look guilty. It didn't last long. As he shoved the second door closed and returned to the fire, he could make out the end of Jakki's tirade.

"...searched every bit of the surrounding forest. There's no body." She planted her hands on her hips and cast a scowl over the room. "Someone freed him. I'm certain of it."

Warmth filled Zavik's cheeks. He took a seat on the edge of the roughly formed semi-circle and angled his face away from the flames as Elaysia turned to face them.

"He'd lost everything," Yerakai said, setting aside his whittling. "Can we be so certain he didn't jump?"

"There was no sign of a body on the rocks beneath the cliff hold," Jakki snapped. "No blood, no seahawks. Nothing."

Mardus rubbed his jaw in the way he did when assuming responsibility for a situation. "Maybe he landed in the water and swam to freedom."

"He was in no condition," Grokhion said, giving his mane a shake. "Even if he avoided the rocks, he would've drowned."

"Someone helped him," Jakki said through clenched teeth. She pointed at the doors. "He's probably strolling about Agaas as we speak."

Anahi's warm brown eyes flashed as she clenched her fist. "Who would've dared to go against the high chieftain's command?"

"Someone who attends council gatherings," Mardus suggested, as if everyone hadn't already deduced the obvious.

Elaysia didn't turn away from the fire as she spoke. "Someone who didn't want him dead."

Zavik felt eyes on his back and glanced over to find Jakki scowling at him. His stomach turned in response. Soon enough, he wouldn't even have to feign illness.

"Only a few of us know Konar well enough to care," she said, eyes narrowing into slits. "And even fewer have reasons to overlook his wrongdoings." She took a few graceful steps toward Zavik, then faced Yerakai at the last moment. "You seemed apprehensive about lowering him to his cliff hold to begin with," she accused her fellow nyrian. "Couldn't stomach the thought of his death, could you?"

Yerakai folded his hands in his lap. "I can rarely stomach the thought of needless death."

Elaysia cocked her head, but Zavik still couldn't make out her expression.

"Did you do it?" The question came from Lumira, who seemed fairly unconcerned about the ordeal, all things considered.

"No," Yerakai answered, crushing Zavik's hopes of escaping scrutiny. "But perhaps we should consider what it means. If the gods gave him the opportunity to escape—"

"This was not the work of gods." Elaysia whirled around, eyes hot with rage. Zavik swore she glared toward, but not directly *at*, him, meaning only one thing.

She knew.

And of course she did. Who else? Why else? Konar might've been respected by the people, but he certainly wasn't loved. Zavik was the only one who needed him, really needed him.

He tried to pull together the words for a confession, one that might cast him in a somewhat redeeming light in the eyes of the Stormriders. But before he could do so, Grokhion cleared his throat.

"We have a saying back on the Isles," the great beridian said in his impossibly deep yet soothing voice. "'The wind blows when it will.'"

Tears filled Elaysia's eyes. She didn't let them fall. Despite her fury, Zavik swore he saw the faintest hint of relief on her face.

"What are you getting at?" Jakki said, folding her arms.

Grokhion heaved his large shoulders. "That this situation, like the wind, is outside our control. All we can do is work around it."

"If I may be so bold, High Chieftain," Yerakai said as he made for the gathering table. "We have greater concerns than a former high elder evading his punishment." He stopped at the section reserved for the Banaxa, his face solemn. "More council members have departed Agaas despite not seeing the punishment—or the celebration of your induction—through. I fear conflict is on the horizon."

Elaysia gave a curt nod as she chewed her bottom lip. "Your concerns are well-founded." She swept her gaze over the room, looking at everyone but Zavik. "The stability of Agaas and Neharem are the priority. We will speak no more of the former high elder, and hope he has met his end. If anyone happens across him, he is to be killed on the spot."

Everyone nodded and muttered their agreement as Elaysia marched to the door. A confession rose in Zavik's throat. Maybe he could follow her outside; speak to her in private.

He started after her, stopping in his tracks as she glanced over her shoulder.

"And should anyone come across him and not heed my command," she said, her gaze finding his, "their own life will also be forfeit."

PART TWO

The fifth of Onelar, year 3039, N.W.

DECLARATION OF WAR

WHEREAS the current High Chieftain of Neharem has no claim to the role due to tainted blood AND has wrongfully claimed it by use of foul play during an ill-timed competition brought on by invoking a tradition she had no right to;

WHEREAS the very sovereignty of Neharem is at risk, her people are subjected to the whims of other nations due to reliance on trade, and the collective wealth of the people is wrongly distributed by an unjustly formed capital with no regard for the nation's ancient traditions;

NOW THEREFORE, I, Raynar, Chief of the Lautei, along with Paska, Chief of the Banaxa and Senei, Chief of the Atsukut, declare that a state of war exists between those loyal to the Lautei, and therefore Neharem, and those loyal to the imposter High Chieftain, and therefore Agaas;

IN WITNESS WHEREOF, I have written this declaration by my own hand and provided my seal, along with the markings and/or seals of those loyal to me, including but not limited to Paska, Chief of the Banaxa, and Senei, Chief of the Atsukut. This was completed on the 5th day of Onelar, year 3039, N.W., in Lautei territory.

-Raynar, Chief of the Lautei, High Chieftain of the Lawful Dominion

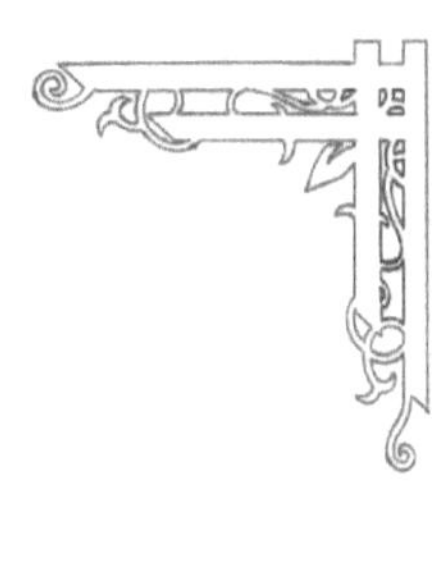

ELAYSIA

"It's too soon."

Elaysia distantly registered Maseeya's voice as another surge formed within her. She clung to her cot for support, bunching the woven blanket between her fingers until she could no longer make out the stormbird pattern, only its vibrant colors. Her body wanted to tighten up, to fight the sensation as it intensified. Contracting. Squeezing.

It's not pain, she told herself, repeating the birth keeper's mantra. *My body is doing what it should. I'm...it's—*

Air hissed through her teeth as the surge reached its peak, then ebbed to a dull ache.

And this isn't the worst of it. Not even close.

She didn't dare speak her fears aloud. No need to give them voice when they already grew more powerful with each passing minute of labor.

When her body reached its brief hiatus of relaxation before the next surge, Elaysia slowly unclenched her fingers and searched for Maseeya. Her mother figure—gods, she was practically her mother now—forced an encouraging smile, but her deep brown eyes told another story.

The eyes always did. They weren't capable of deceit like the rest of the body because the soul shone through them. At least, that's what some ancient proverb said, spoken into existence by some ancient elder, back when the world was a simpler place.

Elaysia lay back on the cot, awaiting the next surge with nightmarish dread.

"The body does what it will," the birth keeper whispered to Maseeya. "If it's saying she's ready, then she's ready. And she's measuring near full-term."

"She can't be more than eight moons along," Maseeya insisted, voice rising. Elaysia imagined the Az Zarian woman balling her petite fists and pinching her face in a way that subdued even the most rambunctious of adolescents.

"There's nothing I can do to stop it." The birth keeper sounded affronted. "I've given her teas to aid the surges and wine to ease the tension. Now, it's in the gods' hands."

"Her surges have been waxing and waning for days now. Surely there's something you can do to—"

"In the gods' hands," the birth keeper repeated.

Footsteps padded away. A door opened and closed. Another surge began, and Elaysia gritted her teeth through it, lying on the cot with her eyes squeezed shut. When the pain ceased, she opened them to find Maseeya gazing down at her, her soft features overflowing with compassion.

"The birth keeper thinks it's truly happening this time."

"I overheard," Elaysia mumbled. "It's early. Is it of my doing?"

She recalled the physical and mental trauma she'd endured while imprisoned in Az Zar. The training to prepare for hoksanu. Racing through the forest, climbing the tallest tree she'd ever climbed. Battling Rajar. To the death. And now the utter mess that was Konar.

There was no doubt in her mind. She'd brought this early labor upon herself.

Maseeya was kind enough to tell her otherwise. "Of course not, Elaysia," the older woman said, squeezing her hand. "These things are rare, but they can happen. Most likely, the baby will be fine. He or she just can't wait to meet you."

Most likely was another way of saying no, things weren't alright, weren't guaranteed, and perhaps she should worry quite a bit.

But she didn't voice that opinion aloud, either.

As Maseeya busied herself about the room with things that didn't need tending to—menial tasks like refreshing the water basin for the third time in an hour or stoking the fire when it didn't need stoking—Elaysia tried to recall if her mother experienced difficult labors. Had they ever discussed such things? She'd been awfully young when Annalee died, so it was unlikely.

"Maseeya, did my mother..."

She didn't need to finish. The Az Zarian woman raised her pale face from the pile of linens she'd set to refolding and came to sit on the edge of Elaysia's cot. Her eyes told an entire story in a moment, one that spanned far beyond childbirth. The story of two women who'd been inseparable since childhood, who'd given up everything for each other and kept every secret their lips ever uttered.

Not that Maseeya had ever shared such stories. She didn't need to. The love on her face was evident every time she mentioned Annalee's name. It radiated when she gazed at Elaysia, when she poured out every last drop of her devotion in the way only a parent could. For nurturing a child was the bond of spirit, of dedication. Not blood.

Elaysia promised to love her child the same.

Maseeya's face lit up as she spoke. "She was the fiercest warrior when it came to labor, Elaysia. A sandcat would've trembled to behold her might."

"And they both went well?" Elaysia grimaced as another surge swelled. "Annonitus's birth and mine?"

"They went beautifully, as yours will."

Elaysia studied the ceiling as she had nearly every night since her family passed. The wood grain seemed to come alive, the streaks moving into one another like a dance. She couldn't remember the last time everything had looked so vivid.

Then the babe inside her kicked. Hard.

"Alright, little one," she whispered. "I'm ready for you. Come."

She wasn't ready, and neither was the baby.

Her fleeting moments of empowerment were shattered again and again, whether by pain, exhaustion, or looks of worry on the birth keeper's face.

She was hot, then cold. Wanted to be touched, then wanted everyone out of the room—couldn't they see she wanted to be left alone?

Gods be cursed.

The walls shrunk as the hours passed. She had a loose grasp on time, but it was still strong enough to recall her labor began when it was dark.

It was dark again.

If the surges had once ebbed and flowed like waves lapping upon the shore, they now raged against her, abrupt and harsh, like the first gusts of a storm.

She hadn't left her room in hours. Or was it days? Everything hurt. She just wanted to sleep. Close her eyes for just a moment.

A dull, swelling pain destroyed her dreams of rest. She screamed. Grabbed the edge of her cot and clenched her jaw until it throbbed.

"I'm going to check again after this one has passed," the birth keeper said, no longer bothering to whisper.

Elaysia moaned. No words would come.

Maseeya helped ease her back after the surge dissolved and blotted her head with a cool cloth. Tears stung Elaysia's eyes as she opened her legs for the birth keeper to inspect. She'd long since given up on modesty and lay there as naked as the day of her own birth. What others thought of her body was the least of her worries.

The birth keeper, an older nyrian woman of Apáasutai descent, laid a wrinkled brown hand on Elaysia's belly. "Can I have a look?"

Elaysia nodded, her gaze boring into the ceiling. She tensed as the fingers entered her, probing against her inner walls, reaching back farther, higher.

The birth keeper slowly pulled her fingers out, and Elaysia glanced at her just in time to catch a worried look shared between her and Maseeya.

"Just tell me," Elaysia whispered. She scarcely recognized her voice, hoarse as it was from her groans and cries.

The birth keeper glanced at Maseeya again.

"I am your high chieftain," Elaysia commanded. Another surge was building, and she channeled its intensity into her voice. "Tell me what's happening to *my* body."

The birth keeper tucked a loose white strand back into her braid and wiped her forehead with her shawl. "The babe is ill-positioned, High Chieftain. I've been trying everything I know to help you turn it, but it's a stubborn one. You're fully open, and it should come, but something is stopping it from descending."

Elaysia grasped at her throat. It tightened like the rest of her body, restricting her air flow.

Breathe. Just breathe.

"What can be done?" Elaysia asked, though she sensed the answer coming.

Nothing.

The birth keeper's brow furrowed. "We can pray. If the gods will it—"

"I will not leave her fate to the gods," Maseeya snapped. She grabbed Elaysia's arm and helped her sit up. "Can you walk?" she whispered. Her deft fingers combed Elaysia's hair back, and she began fastening it into a braid. "I've heard it helps. Some fresh air might reinvigorate you."

Elaysia wasn't certain she could, but she was certain she couldn't spend another moment in her prison of a room, eyes on her, worrying, watching, waiting for whatever bad thing was going to happen next. If she couldn't get the babe out, they'd...she'd...

No. There was no option but to get the babe out, whatever it took.

She struggled to her feet, waving off the birth keeper's out-stretched hand, and wrapped a woolen blanket around her naked body.

"I don't think this is a good idea," the birth keeper said, moving between her and the door.

Elaysia stared her down. "I'm no longer in need of your guidance," she gritted out.

"High Chieftain—"

"You heard her," Maseeya said, grabbing Elaysia's elbow as if she sensed the oncoming surge about to take her.

The birth keeper moved just in time for Elaysia to grab the doorframe. Maseeya rubbed her back and encouraged her to breathe as she worked through the pain—no, sensation, she was supposed to call it.

Fuck that. It hurt like nothing she'd ever experienced.

Maseeya offered her a sip of water. "Where would you like to go?"

"The beach," Elaysia rasped, exhaling the last of the pain away. "I'm going to the beach."

Maseeya didn't protest as Elaysia shuffled down the hallway, unsure of her own decision until she opened the exterior door and stumbled out into the night.

The air was bone chilling, and the moment it hit her, Elaysia felt herself come alive. All other sensations faded, making room for the luscious, refreshing breeze. She let the blanket fall open so the cool air could kiss her bare skin. And for the first time in days, she smiled.

The descent from Agaas was endless, filled with short, uneasy steps and long, painful stops. But every time despair threatened to take her, every time the weight of her body fought to drag her down, she looked up at the stars winking through the branches and found hope. It was a mercifully clear night, fogless and calm, rare for the season, with not a drop in the sky.

When they reached the end of the ramp, arriving at the cluster of lodges and livestock pens that made up base camp, Maseeya bade her stop and rest. The surges were becoming more frequent and, gods be cursed, getting even more—

A scream tore its way out of Elaysia's throat. She got down on her hands and knees in the pine needles beside the stable and moaned. A mare with a coat like sunset approached, lowering her head over the pen to nuzzle Elaysia's cheek. Something stirred inside her, as though her insides were all turned about. She looked down and saw a bulge in her stomach, pressing against her skin like a caged beast.

More movement. More pressure.

Elaysia fought it.

"What's happening?" Maseeya whispered as Elaysia's breathing steadied.

"It's moving down. It feels so heavy. But it's not right yet. I must keep walking."

Elaysia struggled to her feet, neglecting the blanket and the stares of curious watchers patrolling around base camp. Maseeya called after her, but Elaysia couldn't quite make out the words, nor did she want to expel any energy trying.

Everything inside her body was racing, thrashing, yet the world slowed around her, as if time wanted to magnify the sensations she was feeling.

She pressed on, bare feet sticky with sap and crusted in soil. Down the path. Not her path, but the other. Her mother's path to the beach. To the shells.

By the time Elaysia felt sand between her toes, there were scarcely any breaks between the surges. They came on like a herd of buffalo: unstoppable, loud, fierce. She couldn't make out the scenic seascape she knew lay just ahead, but as she fell to her knees from another surge, she could see every grain of sand. So many particles. So many colors.

So much life.

Her eyes closed. She crawled until her fingertips sank into the moist sand at the edge of the water, then she curled up into a fetal position and sobbed.

The pain deepened. She wanted to distance herself from her body, yet she was more in tune with it than she'd ever been. She thought about wading into the sea and disappearing forever.

So she did.

The waters grabbed her ankles, her thighs, and finally, her stomach. And then something bore down inside her. She couldn't stop it. She was helpless against this force. Everything in her body screamed *push*.

"I can't," she moaned. "I can't, Eumma."

"You can."

Maseeya, like the goddess she was, suddenly appeared in the ocean beside her and grabbed her hand. Her touch gave Elaysia strength. When the next surge came, she surrendered to its call and pushed.

The birth keeper had said the last part wouldn't hurt, that it was the best part.

Liar, Elaysia thought as tears streamed down her face. Still, she pushed again.

"Good, good," Maseeya murmured beside her. "Just trust yourself. You know what you're doing."

"My body is going to tear open," Elaysia screamed, tensing. "I can't."

Maseeya pushed on Elaysia's lower back to ease the pressure. "Loosen your jaw. The rest of your body can't relax when it's tight. Breathe, Elaysia. Breathe."

Her jaw *was* tense. Taut as climbing rope. When the next surge came, she forced herself to keep it open by making a low, groaning sound. Something about it felt right, and she did it again, pushing harder, growling louder.

"Is it coming?" Elaysia sobbed. "Maseeya, check."

"The babe is coming. I don't need to look. I trust you. I believe in you. Keep doing what you're doing."

By some miracle, the pushing grew easier, or she grew stronger. The babe descended inside her. But it was so big. She could feel it pulling, stretching.

There was no way in Haeshol it was coming out.

"I hate this," she screamed.

"You don't have to love it. You just have to beat it."

Maseeya pushed on the small of her back again. Hard. It helped.

Two surges later, Elaysia disappeared beneath the waves and screamed.

"Curse the gods for making birth this way!" she shouted when she resurfaced. Pain blurred her vision. "I can't do it any longer. Make it stop, Maseeya. Make it fucking stop."

Maseeya grabbed her shoulders and spun her so they were face-to-face. "You can handle this. The force is you. You create it, you control it, you ride it. Find that light, Elaysia. You are a flower opening and blooming. Reach for the light, let it take you, let it pull you. Don't fight it. Become it, dear heart, because you are that power you feel within."

Elaysia closed her eyes.

I am a flower opening and blooming. I am the light.

And this time, she saw it. A warm glow surrounded her. Beckoned her. She sank into it, and when the surge came, she felt no pain. Intense pressure, but almost blissful, as though it could be a distant cousin to love-making.

Become it. I am the power I feel within.

I am enough.

Elaysia wasn't even certain she pushed the next time. Something inside her moved on its own, as though she commanded it, and warmth released between her legs into the chilling ocean water.

She reached down. A small head covered in something wispy.

You have hair, she thought to herself. And that little detail suddenly made it real.

A final surge came, and she reached down to pull the babe out. Waddling out of the water, she brought the babe to her chest. It was warm and writhing, and by the time she reached the shore, it screamed.

"Khiev-Tatamic keep you," she whispered, staring into its smushed little face. Moonlight draped them in an ethereal glow,

and in that moment, all pain was forgotten, replaced by a pro–
found love reaching into her soul. It was as though her heart
had been ripped from her chest and placed in the fragile hands
of this foreign, wrinkled little creature.

"It's a boy," Maseeya said. She was crying, laughing, and
Elaysia realized she was doing the same.

She tried to bring the child up to her breasts, but the cord still
tethered it to her.

Then another surge started.

"It's the afterbirth," Maseeya explained. "You'll push it out the
same way, but with much more ease. Here, I'll cut the cord and
take the boy while you finish."

But it wasn't easy.

It hurt just as bad, felt just as intense. Elaysia didn't fight her
body as it worked, though. This time, she knew what it was
capable of. What she was capable of.

And it wasn't the afterbirth. She sensed it the moment it
began its descent.

Five minutes later, she held another babe in her arms.

A girl.

Elaysia kissed her face and wept.

LUMIRA

The boy gazed up at Lumira, his eyes reflecting the same radiant gray hue as lyvium. Wisps of ashen hair framed his tiny face, accenting the faintest points cresting the tops of his ears. The girl's hair was warmer, like bleached wood, but her eyes were a deep crimson with only a touch of luminescence. She, too, had a subtle point to her ears, but that was where her nyrian resemblance ended. Once their hair grew in, they'd both pass as human with ease.

So small, Lumira thought, as she examined the babes nestled in the basket, the boy wrapped tightly in a thin blanket and the girl flailing free in her miniature tunic. It was hard to believe every being she'd ever crossed paths with had also started out so fragile and incapable. So innocent.

The boy continued to stare at her, and a small smile spread across his face. Lumira reached for him, feeling a sudden urge to stroke his cheek.

She retracted her hand at the last moment.

"Sorry," she muttered to Elaysia, distancing herself from the basket. "That's probably not something you want people doing without your permission."

Elaysia couldn't have appeared less concerned. "I wouldn't have summoned you to my quarters if I didn't want you around them." She gestured to the basket with an open hand. "Go ahead, please. I need all the help I can get."

When Lumira hesitated, Elaysia scooped up the boy and placed him in her arms.

Lumira stiffened, suddenly aware of the value entrusted to her. "I'm not very good with cubs—er, babies."

"Neither am I."

Elaysia emitted a nervous laugh. Dark rings hung beneath the high chieftain's eyes, and the hair she'd piled atop her head was a far cry from her usually ornate braids. The girl started fussing, and Elaysia groaned as she retrieved her from the basket.

"Mind if I—" She touched her breast with her free hand. "If they're not sleeping, they're eating."

Lumira shook her head. As if she'd tell a new mother to starve her baby on account of her presence. She averted her gaze as Elaysia slipped the tunic off her shoulder.

"What's his name?" Lumira asked, stroking the boy's silky, downlike hair. It wasn't all that different from Anadu's baby feathers a few moons prior.

Elaysia looked up from the happily nursing babe, her brow wrinkled. "The council haven't announced their names?"

Not to me, Lumira thought, bristling. But the last thing Elaysia needed was more to fret over.

"Maybe I missed it," she said with a shrug. "Don't always focus so well when people get to rambling."

Elaysia's eyes narrowed. She looked ready to slit someone from navel to neck. "They've held gatherings without you, haven't they?"

"It's probably a misunder—"

"I informed the council you were to act as my representative," Elaysia snapped. Her harsh reaction triggered a wail from the girl. "They knew that well before my labor." She began soothing the baby with gentle pats and hushing sounds, but her face was unfettered rage.

Lumira gave her as much space as she could in the small room. The fire faded to coals as Elaysia paced with the girl, and, eventually, Lumira found herself doing the same with the boy. The longer she held him, the more her sense of attachment grew, as though she had to protect his tiny life at all costs.

It awakened a primal fear within her.

"His name is Elaron."

Lumira tore her gaze away from the boy and glanced at a tired but proud Elaysia. "Elaron." She said it slowly, as though turning over a word from a new language in her mouth.

"Do you like it?"

She gave a nod of approval. It sounded strong and regal, yet just. "A family name?"

"Of sorts." Elaysia chewed her lip. "It means light-bringer in Nyrinian."

"And the girl?"

"Dytana. Don't ask what it means. I made it up. Her name is unexpected, much like she was." Elaysia lifted the girl off her shoulder and beheld her with a mixture of wonder and worry. "But the best things in life are unexpected, and perhaps that is what her name means."

"They're beautiful, Elaysia."

The tip of Elaysia's chin raised. "Thank you." She wrapped a loose-knit shawl about her shoulder and waist, then tucked Dytana inside.

Elaron began to squirm, and Lumira held him out awkwardly for Elaysia to retrieve. The high chieftain sat on the edge of her cot as she popped him on her breast, then looked longingly out the window, where a dreary rain pattered against the High Tree platforms.

Feeling she'd overstayed her welcome, Lumira started for the door.

Elaysia's voice halted her mid-step. "I assume you've read the declaration."

It wasn't so much a question that rolled off Elaysia's tongue as it was an acknowledgment of a shared irritant. Lumira faced her with a grimace. She hadn't read it, only been relayed the information by Zavik after his personal backhander lifted the parchment from High Elder Sower. But the intent was clear enough.

Rajar's son wanted war.

Unsure whether she wanted to sit or stand, Lumira crouched. "I assume that's why you really called me here."

Elaysia didn't respond, didn't look up. Her fingers scrunched the loose fabric of her already wrinkled tunic. Lumira cursed herself inwardly for not addressing the threat sooner. The poor woman was probably stressed out of her mind with the babies and terrified at the prospect of war.

"Have you had time to give any thought to your next steps?" she asked in a voice that probably sounded more demeaning than calming. How did Konar have such a mastery of tone?

"I've had all the time. I'm awake all hours of the day and night with nothing to do but think. They aren't exactly gracious loft mates." Elaysia cast an irritated glance at the babes, one still at the breast, and one in the sling.

Lumira sensed the love in it.

The high chieftain retrieved a wooden cup from the table adjacent to her cot and took a long drink. Lumira detected the faintest scent of wine.

"I've had turosses sent to the tribes excluded from Raynar's declaration," Elaysia said between sips. "So far, the Apáasutai, Moákun, and Daruk have answered with their allegiance. It's early on, so I expect more will follow."

You hope. Lumira fought to contain her bluntness. Given the general leanings of the tribes, she didn't expect more than a third to side with Agaas—especially the declared pacificists, such as the Ni'anko and Kahaloán. And the tribes that would side with Elaysia, well...

Their numbers combined wouldn't measure up to the Banaxa and Lautei.

"You think we've lost this war before it's begun."

Lumira blinked. Elaysia was rarely so forward, and it was more than the wine in her cup emboldening her.

"I know we lack the numbers," Elaysia continued, setting her empty cup back on the table. "Even with the Yustano, we are still greatly outnumbered. Several tribes—the Tangeesh, Ni'anko, and Kahaloán—will likely not take sides until absolutely forced.

The Moatiwe are unpredictable, and the Morotôk will likely side with the Atsukut if pressured."

"They may join still, High Chieftain."

"Lumira." Elaysia gave a longing look at the empty wine cup. "Let's be honest, you and I. Can you promise me that? I feel as though you're the only one who will do so if I ask it of you."

Lumira nodded. She wasn't here to child-tend a high chieftain, nor was it her prerogative to coddle.

"I don't know what I'm doing," Elaysia admitted as she tried to lay a sleeping Elaron down on the cot. Dytana fussed at the motion, awakening him. "I finally embraced my duties as high chieftain, something I once believed to be the most arduous task of my life, and now look at me. I can barely keep these children alive." Agitation crept into her voice as she repositioned the babes. "How am I supposed to lead a war? I knew it was coming, but I thought it'd be far later and against Az Zar. I'm not ready for this." She lay down on the cot, a babe in the crook of each arm, and sighed.

Lumira knew she needed to say something, but what? Lie to her high chieftain? Everything Elaysia said was true. The youthful optimism she'd spouted when Lumira first met her was long gone, replaced by the skepticism of someone who'd been cheated and used. A friend might, in such a moment, offer words of wisdom, rub her back, or tell a lighthearted story to take her mind off things.

None of those came naturally to Lumira.

"Get smarter," she said, echoing the best advice her mama had ever given her.

Elaysia regarded her with a steely gaze. "I'm sorry?"

Moons be cursed.

Lumira scrambled for an explanation. "It's a beridian saying. It means that if you find yourself knee-high in shit—whether that's your own fault or just bad luck—you have to get smarter. Grow beyond it to beat it."

A smile tugged at Elaysia's mouth. "Is this your attempt at comforting me?"

"Is it working?"

"That remains to be seen." Elaysia motioned to a rolled parchment resting on the far corner of the table against the wall. "Open it."

Lumira did. It was a map of Neharem, the most detailed she'd ever seen, complete with the basic layout of each tribe's territory and important landmarks. It also included trading ports, naturally occurring fortifications, and hideaways.

"It's the only one of its kind," Elaysia said, peering over Dytana's head. "Take it. Study it. We need to assess our weaknesses and know theirs. We won't be the first to attack, but we will be ready for them. I've called an official gathering of our allies a fortnight from now, and in the meantime, I'd like you to learn enough to brief them."

The hairs on Lumira's back raised. Such tasks weren't what she signed up for. But she had sworn to never abandon Elaysia again, especially not in her time of greatest need.

"I'm not putting this all on you," Elaysia added, her voice carrying the strain of worry. "You can assign tasks to others, seek insight—whatever you need. I'm not going to be sitting idle, either. Maseeya said she'll start watching the babes, maybe incorporating goat's milk into their—"

"I'm honored, High Chieftain," Lumira reassured her. She rolled up the parchment and brought her fist to her heart. "Time to get smarter."

Unruly was an understatement when it came to describing the stormbirds.

Lumira wasn't certain at what point they decided they had little need for their riders' insights, but it likely had to do with the first time they took flight. As soon as Onitus had spread his wings and disappeared into the horizon, the others were on his tail feathers. Literally. Gone was any trace of their baby down. They still accepted treats, but mostly hunted for their own meat, often sourcing directly from the ocean, and occasionally picking off smaller fowl. Lumira didn't doubt they'd seek larger land animals soon, especially if they had a treeless area to hunt, like Banaxa territory. Maybe even snatch up some Banaxa—if it came to that.

And it would.

As if confirming Lumira's prophecy, Anadu swooped down from the sky and landed on the beach beside her with a thud. She was more graceful than some of her nestmates, but still struggled to adapt to her rapidly growing body. At over a year old, she stood the height of a stallion with a wingspan double that, and Lumira wagered her thick talons could crush the skulls of most land-dwellers with ease. Her feathers had settled into a dusk blue with a light gray underside speckled in black. And her eyes were equally as captivating as they were terrifying: the color of the sea on a cloudy day, with the slightest hint of nevethium green.

Lumira approached her and nodded at the still-wriggling fish in her talons. It was some sort of bass, large enough to feed seven to ten mouths. Anadu fluffed her plumage, perhaps out of pride, then bit off the fish's head. Its mouth continued to gape. She dropped the body at Lumira's feet and cocked her head.

"It's a big one," Lumira said, eyeing the tears in its skin where Anadu's talons had penetrated it. "But go ahead, keep it. I don't have the stomach for eating much today, and you're still growing and all."

Anadu blinked once, then hopped forward to collect the fish. The way she ripped its flesh apart told Lumira it had been a courtesy offer, and probably a good thing she'd declined. Still, even though she wasn't in a place where she needed to rely on the bird's charity, it was good to know such a relationship existed between them, should the time come.

Lumira sat on a petrified log a few feet from the waves and dug her toes into the sand. "Where are your kin?" she asked, searching the cloudy sky.

Anadu continued ripping the fish apart and throwing her head back to gulp chunks down.

"I suppose I can interpret your silence several ways," Lumira continued. "You don't want to tell me?" Nothing. "You don't worry yourself with keeping track of them?" Still nothing. "Or maybe you simply don't understand what I'm saying."

This time, Anadu stopped mid-tear. A chunk of flesh dangled from her black beak.

Lumira suppressed her excitement. But did Anadu truly understand, or had she simply picked up on Lumira's intonations? Stormbirds couldn't speak, at least not in the conventional way, but according to the mainlanders and their lore, all the Great Beasts of Old communicated as well as any other intelligent being. Some considered them to be even more evolved, even more intelligent, for they no longer required conventional language to communicate with one another.

It was likely just another fireside tale passed down from one generation to the next. Still, one of Yerakai's stories crossed Lumira's mind, one regarding his time with the nazrath, the ancient giants of the north. He'd said they communicated similarly.

In silence.

"Will you teach me how to communicate with you?" Lumira asked as Anadu swallowed another chunk of fish.

A small chirp came from the stormbird's throat. She hopped over in one smooth movement and nestled beside Lumira in the sand.

Lumira placed a hand on her back, only for a moment, and in the way one would touch a friend's arm. "I'll hold you to it."

The woods rustled behind them. Before Lumira could leap up, spear in hand, Anadu had already risen, her wings and plumage flared.

Grokhion emerged, followed by Roth, who appeared somewhat irritated by the naturally occurring obstacles that were the trees. The stormbird broke free of the woods and locked gazes with Anadu, then took to the sky with a piercing screech as he disappeared into the horizon.

Anadu glanced at Lumira. She wasn't asking permission; merely letting her partner know she was departing.

That much Lumira could understand, secret Great Beast language or not.

As Anadu followed the same path across the sky Roth had taken, Grokhion joined Lumira on the log. His fur smelled of smoke and salt, as though he'd been cooked over a fire alongside the salmon. He wasn't brandishing *Belzaith*, nor did he wear his usual ornate belt and Ni'anko silks. With a simple loincloth around his waist and two lyvium rings in his right ear, he looked more beridian than ever.

"I keep thinking I'll stop being in awe of them one day, but it's not looking like that's ever going to happen," Grokhion mused, stroking his bearded chin. "Especially once they come into their powers."

Lumira leaned her spear against the log. "Part of me still doesn't believe it, even after seeing them. Ancient beings are one thing, but I can't help but think their powers are stories people told themselves because they were inspired by the Great Beasts and searching for an explanation for things they didn't understand."

"Does that make it any less magical?"

Lumira considered his words. "Guess not. They can still tear people to shreds. I'd call that magical."

Grokhion snorted. "Anadu looks ready to take down half an army. I knew the females were larger, but Roth looks like a fledgling beside her."

Pride flared inside Lumira, as it always did anytime someone complimented her bonded bird. Still, she felt a need to negate some of the positivity. "Siren's even larger, though. And with Jakki's temper to boot."

Grokhion made no reply, but his mouth turned downward into the subtlest of frowns.

A chilling wind rolled off the waves. The sky responded by darkening a deeper shade of gray as the moons materialized behind veils of clouds. Raindrops began kissing Lumira's head. The stormbirds hadn't returned, and there was never a guarantee they would. Once they discovered the freedom of their wings, they spent most of their days hunting, sometimes carrying on well into the nights. Lumira thought of her own beridian appetite and could only imagine how much work it took to satiate theirs. The only stormbird who seemed to stick around with any sort of regularity was Onitus. Elaysia's bird was fiercely loyal and spent every night with her and the twins.

"Do you think they're summoning this storm?" Grokhion shouted as the wind started blowing rain sideways into their faces.

"I think we need to get out of it, regardless of how it started."

Lumira ducked into the shelter of the trees, and Grokhion followed, belting an old beridian lullaby she hadn't heard since she was a cub. It was an eerie tune, melancholy and melodic. She resisted for a moment, then joined in with him.

> *Come, my child, hear a tale of*
> *a warrior queen*

> *Who carved this very world*
> *from clay at the beckoning*

> *Of goddesses fierce as night,*
> *three moon sisters were they*

That when betrayed by his
hand, the traitor sun they
slay

Buried deep and dark was he,
no air for his light to shine

Until he seduced the stars
with whispers of wealth
sublime

They rained down from the
sky like fire upon the land

And returned all life back
into dust from where it once
began

"Maybe I'll teach that one to Elaysia's children," Lumira said when they'd finished. "Tales of betrayal and the world ending are always the best songs to fall asleep to."

Grokhion let loose one of his deep belly laughs. "It worked well enough on us."

They walked in as much silence as the forest allowed between the wind rustling leaves and the night creatures carrying on with their shrieks and chitters. It was only when she saw the first firelight from base camp that Grokhion caught her shoulder.

"Lumira." His green eyes narrowed. "I am here to help you with whatever you need. I know you're unlikely to ask for my assistance, so I'm offering it now, and I will do so again and again until we've seen this war through. Do you understand?"

Lumira shrugged and directed her gaze upward to the spattering of stars peering down through the branches. "Understood. I'm fine, though. Really. The fighting hasn't even—"

She gasped and spun out of his grasp, toward the sound of crackling debris.

Four large figures approached, all of them nyrian. At least two were watchers she'd patrolled with on more than one occasion. Their presence in the forest wasn't necessarily abnormal, but something about the way they approached, in formation with weapons at the ready, set her on edge.

Lumira rooted herself to the ground. Her claws extended instinctively.

She didn't retract them.

"Out for an evening stroll?" she asked in the calmest voice she could muster.

A stocky female with tattooed arms stepped away from the group. Her name was on the tip of Lumira's tongue. Ashana? Shay?

"Lumira of the Isles, you are to appear before the council at once," the tattooed watcher commanded.

Lumira's jaw clenched. "The gathering is tomorrow. Or has a special session been called?"

"You've been accused of treason and will face the council without delay," the woman repeated. "Hand over your spear and come quietly, or we'll escort you by force."

Grokhion stiffened beside her. The other watchers moved in, spears and staffs brandished. Lumira thought back to her first time in Agaas when she'd found herself in a similar situation. Surrounded by hateful mainlanders who wanted her disarmed, bound, and thrust into the cliff holds.

Only this time, she wasn't guilty.

JAKKI

Murmurs drifted like smoke through the summit lodge as members of the council took their places around the gathering table. Many tribal representatives were absent, but their spaces were occupied by the overflow of various elders and esteemed warriors of those present. In Jakki's case, she wasn't certain if her opinion mattered all that much, or if her mother just finally felt she'd earned the right to represent the Yustano, given *she'd* been the one in servitude to Agaas and the high chieftain all these years. Not Chief Jattai Rain-Bringer, whose time was better spent overseeing every menial aspect of daily life on their island.

Until recently.

Jakki glanced at Elaysia, hoping to catch her gaze, but the high chieftain looked to be one blink away from making the gathering table her new cot. She'd thrown a robe over her tunic and piled her hair atop her head—a style that, since birthing the twins, had replaced her more intricate braids. Despite the exhaustion weighing heavily on her face, she was beautiful. Physically softer, yet mentally sharper. More seasoned. The dusting of maturity suited her, and so did her enlarged breasts from feeding the babes. Zavik sat on her right, his long, pale fingers fiddling with the table, his tunic, his hair. A touch of pink adorned his cheeks. *He* caught Jakki's gaze and returned an awkward smile.

Jakki rolled her eyes. Zavik wasn't the best choice for Konar's replacement, in her opinion, but there was no way in Haeshol

Elaysia would've selected anyone else. She was short on trust, and Zavik, for all his faults, was trustworthy.

Not honest, though. Someone hadn't wanted the former High Elder Lightfoot dead, had something to gain by freeing him, and Jakki's suspicions pointed to the bumbling redhead seated beside Elaysia, one whose heart often overwhelmed his otherwise logical mind.

Not that the high chieftain had dignified Jakki's accusation with any sort of action. Gods forbid she implicate her replacement high elder. And perhaps, deep down, she hadn't wanted Konar dead either, at least not with every fiber of her being. Otherwise, she would've murdered him there on the beach that fateful day. Fuck the council trial.

But maybe honesty was overvalued. Not everything said or done deceitfully was bad or driven by ill intent. Sometimes the truth hurt people, and sometimes one needed to help others along with whatever motivated them to act in a way that benefited the whole. Or at least the important ones.

Besides, honest people often ended up dead before their time.

Elaysia sucked in a breath, and Jakki looked over just in time to catch her clenching her fists. "I hope the reason behind this gathering requires the utmost urgency," she called out, her voice raspy with sleep. Or, in her case, lack thereof.

The room fell silent in response.

"Indeed, it does, otherwise we wouldn't have disturbed you amid your child-tending. I imagine it takes a great deal of your efforts, and I hate to trouble you with the grievances of the council."

The reply came from High Elder Sower, the only remaining high elder from the original trifecta since Strong-spear had defected with the Lautei and Konar had been sentenced to—rather, evaded—his punishment.

Elaysia glared back at the elderly human but gave no further indication his backhanded comment had pierced her armor. She whispered something to Zavik, and he rose from Konar's old spot, his eyes alive with whatever task she'd thrust upon him.

It triggered a twinge of jealousy in Jakki, but before she could decide what to do with it, the summit lodge doors groaned open. A harsh wind barreled in, teasing the fire and ruffling hair as though it, by sheer force, had blown the doors open with no mortal aid. The room fell silent as all gazes fixated on the darkness that lay beyond.

Two watchers appeared first, soaking wet, followed by Lumira, Grokhion, and another pair of watchers to escort them from behind. Both the cats' ears were pinned down, their eyes narrowed and constricted, but only Lumira's lips pulled back to reveal the slightest bit of fang. Jattai made a *tsk–tsk* sound loud enough for everyone in the summit lodge to hear.

Jakki lowered her gaze.

"What in Khiev-Tatamic's name is this?" Elaysia said, her tone just shy of a shout. "Unbind them immediately."

"The reason for the gathering." High Elder Sower's voice sounded like he looked: weathered, tired, and cunning. "I'm afraid we have a traitor in our midst."

"That you do," Lumira muttered.

Jakki kept her face solemn and studied her hands, but she felt her mother's gaze boring into her.

"I'll be the judge of that," Elaysia said.

"*We* will judge," High Elder Sower clarified. "All of us, with Khiev-Tatamic's guidance."

"And *I* am still the high chieftain." Elaysia planted her palms on the table, raising herself from a seated position in a show of dominance. "I order you to unbind Lumira and Grokhion while we weigh the charges brought against them."

One of the watchers pulled out a dagger and, with a look of contempt, sliced through the rope restricting Grokhion's hands. When it was Lumira's turn, she uttered something in Hispen that had an undeniably negative connotation, then rubbed her wrists as she swept her gaze over the room like a ryptan on the hunt.

"Please, have a seat," High Elder Sower offered, sparing no benevolence.

Lumira directed her glare at him. "I'm good."

She came to stand a few feet away from Elaysia's spot at the table and crossed her arms. Grokhion followed, positioning himself a few inches over and behind to her left, as though the beridians attended the gathering as the high chieftain's protectors and not the accused.

Zavik returned from wherever he'd scampered off to, taking a seat on the cushion beside the high chieftain's. He nodded at the cats in greeting, then whispered something in Elaysia's ear.

She nodded, then tapped lightly on the table. "Who would like to tell me why two of my Stormriders—one of which happens to be my appointed war chief—were brought before me bound?"

Jakki glanced at her mother. The chief's aqua eyes burned with intensity. She wanted Jakki to speak her piece now, to weave the tale as they'd planned, but whatever ambition Jattai tried to sow within her had yet to take root. Maybe if she didn't speak, the situation would sort itself out.

Elaysia took her place beside the beridians as she furthered her argument. "Lumira has proven herself again and again to be loyal to Neharem. To me." She placed her hand on her chest as she shot accusatory looks at one council member after another. "And Grokhion has been with the Ni'anko for decades. Tell me what crimes they are said to have committed, or I will end this gathering without further discussion."

"Tell them, Jakki," Chief Jattai said loudly as she elbowed her daughter. "Tell them what you uncovered this morning."

Jakki's stomach twisted as all gazes fell on her. They weren't looks of adoration as she preferred, as she'd come to expect from a life of beauty and skill, but the anticipatory looks people cast when they sought the downfall of others. It was the look one might have when watching another being killed for entertainment; the kind of look that bared the darker side of a soul.

And Jakki didn't like being at the center of it.

She fingered the back of her waistband where she kept the old man's parchment, the one she swore every day to destroy, but still it remained with her like her dagger. For like her dagger, it was a form of protection, should she need it. That's what she told herself when she felt its magic pulling on her as it did now, in moments of uncertainty.

"It's with great sadness I share this information with you, High Chieftain," Jakki said finally, her voice weaker than she intended. Jattai nudged her under the table, and Jakki straightened her back to make up for her poor delivery.

Elaysia's fists clenched at her sides. "What information?"

Jakki rose and removed a small, folded piece of cured leather from between her breasts, the one her mother had forged earlier that day. She slid it across the table to Zavik.

"Read it," Elaysia said through clenched teeth. "Aloud, for all to hear, please."

Zavik shot her a side-eyed glance as he adjusted his seers and unfolded the parchment. "It's written in Nyrinian and signed, 'A Friend of The Empire.'" He looked back a final time and, receiving an affirmative nod from the high chieftain, proceeded to read. "It says, 'The birds are a force to be reckoned with. Every day, the illegitimate high chieftain sees to it they're trained, better prepared to go to war against Az Zar. She's out for blood, for revenge, and will stop at nothing to overthrow the All-Sovereign. I fear she's coming for the Beridian Isles next. Below I've listed the locations of their stores, weaknesses in their defenses, in exchange for amnesty and citizenship—'"

"Enough." Elaysia seized the parchment and buried it somewhere in the folds of her robe.

"It's not the first," Chief Jattai shouted over the growing bustle of voices. "Just the first we've been able to intercept. Jakki witnessed her sending at least eight other turosses since you returned from Az Zar."

Lumira extended her claws as she glared at Jakki. "I'm honored you've dedicated so much of your time to stalking me."

Chief Jattai shot from her cushion, planting her hands on her curved hips. "No one's given you permission to speak, ca—"

"Lumira will speak her piece now," Elaysia interjected sharply. "I'll have silence in this room at once."

"So defensive of her pet," Jattai hissed in Jakki's ear, loudly enough for those seated nearby to eavesdrop. "She should be worried about outsiders communicating with the nation who imprisoned her, especially an outsider who ran instead of coming to her aid when things took a turn for the worse."

"It's true, High Chieftain."

Jakki's head jerked up at Lumira's confession. She had, in fact, caught the beridian sending turosses out a handful of times, but she'd only brought one down successfully. And the letter, while destined for Az Zar, said nothing of treason or usurping. It merely asked questions regarding one person's whereabouts, a person who, in his own right, was scandalous enough.

Lumira sauntered forward until her shins brushed the low table. "I have sent several turosses east, and without your consent. The one meant to incriminate me, however"—she gestured to the Yustano representatives with disgust—"is not mine, though it's made to sound like it by referencing the Isles. But I'd never use phrases like, 'a force to be reckoned with,' or, 'in exchange for amnesty.'"

She paused, maybe for emphasis, but also maybe to read the room. Jakki met her gaze, channeling the anger she felt toward her mother into the beridian. Neither of them broke away until High Elder Sower jabbed his thumb in Grokhion's direction.

"What about him?"

"Grokhion has nothing to do with it," Lumira said with a growl. "He's as ignorant as everyone in this room. Though, perhaps not as ignorant as some." She directed the last remark at High Elder Sower, and the nyrian further creased his already wrinkled brow.

Elaysia grabbed the cord securing her stormbird pendant around her neck and twisted it into tight spirals. "Who were the turosses sent to?"

"An old... I was hoping maybe..." Lumira kneeled beside the table, gaze lowered. "We left a member of our original party back in Az Zar, and I thought there might be a chance he lived."

Elaysia's nostrils flared. She stormed to the fire at the opposite end of the room and spent a long moment in silence. Jattai squeezed Jakki's knee and gave her a victorious wink.

Jakki could not share in it.

"That was not your choice to make," Elaysia said, returning to the gathering table. Her demeanor and tone were calm, but there was a wildfire in her eyes. "We can't risk any messages being intercepted by the wrong people, no matter your intentions. Besides"—she swallowed, adjusted her robe—"his death was all but confirmed. Even if he survived, I never wish to see him again. I will have him executed if he ever steps foot in Neharem." Her jaw ticked as she regarded Lumira. "Do you understand?"

Lumira gave a subtle shake of her head as she retreated from the table. "Understood."

High Elder Sower rose and tapped the floor with his staff. "If the beridians didn't write this, then who did?"

"We have a traitor among us," Chief Arkuun of the Apáasutai said, leveling a stern gaze over the room.

Kelsia, chief of the Ni'anko, folded her slender, dark blue arms. "There are always traitors among us, and rarely do they expose themselves at the beckoning of an outburst."

A Moákun elder pointed his finger at her. "If Az Zar learns of our civil dispute, then—"

"Civil dispute?" Gibrund, the towering Daruk chief, bellowed. "It's a fucking war. Rajar's bitch of a son has already cut off friendly trade and travel in his territories, and there have been multiple reports of attacks by bandits on outlying settlements." He took a swig of mead from his drinking horn. "I think we all know they aren't bandits."

"Be at peace, Gibrund," Kelsia said, her silken voice like water over flames. Jakki admired the ease with which the Ni'anko chief calmed the room.

"I'm more concerned that someone, likely someone in this room, has tried to get Lumira removed from my service. Maybe even killed." Elaysia touched her breasts, wincing, as she strode around the table. "These accusations are no light matter. If you have problems with my decisions and the people I recruit to make them, you will address them with me directly. The last thing we need is more dissent in our council."

"And are you hearing complaints now, High Chieftain?" The question came from Chief Jattai. "For I have several concerns I'd like addressed, namely how long we're going to let this rebellion writhe and breed like the underling it is. I, for one, am not content to sit idle until they make the first move."

Orandus, chief of the Moákun and Mardus's father, made a face suggesting he agreed with her, although he took no pleasure in it. "I fear they are receiving foreign aid. The dagger Zavik found after the attack last year all but confirms someone in Az Zar was working with Rajar. His death doesn't mean the relationship is over."

"What action do you all suggest we take?" Elaysia stopped beside Orandus, though her heated gaze was locked on Jattai. "We only have a fraction of the council present, and not everyone agrees with taking the offensive."

"I suggest we finalize allegiances here and now," Jattai said. Her plan to replace Lumira with Jakki may have been thwarted, but the Yustano chief never missed an opportunity to take advantage of a situation. "My people and Orandus's have pledged, and so have Gibrund's. But there are others in attendance still unspoken." She tilted her chin toward Kelsia.

If the Ni'anko chief was ruffled, she didn't show it. "Taking part in a war goes directly against our beliefs. We can offer aid by means of food, shelter, and medicine, but beyond that, we must refrain from violence. There are no warriors among us, anyhow."

Someone in the room snickered, and everyone stared at Grokhion. Gibrund grumbled and muttered something about needing another drink.

"I understand," Elaysia said. Her tone suggested she didn't. She finished her walk about the table and returned to her spot.

She didn't sit.

"I can send turosses to the chiefs who haven't responded," Zavik offered.

"Tell them they have a fortnight to reply," Gibrund said. "If nothing by then, then they get nothing from us."

"I don't think we should allow non-allies to be a part of council meetings during war time either," Jattai said, directing her words at Kelsia.

"Neutral parties can attend gatherings in hopes of better serving the peace." Elaysia rubbed her eyes and yawned. "Gods know we'll need negotiators."

"But not war councils," Orandus suggested, and others nodded in approval. "It's safer for all parties if they aren't aware of our plans."

Elaysia nodded. "Fair enough. Now, if everyone's satisfied with the outcome of this trial, may I suggest we reconvene tomorrow, as originally planned, to discuss our next moves?"

Jattai surprised Jakki by not objecting. Gibrund burped, evidently excusing himself and everyone else from the gathering, tipped his head to Elaysia, and heaved open the doors.

As the room emptied, Jakki approached Elaysia with the best oblivious look she could conjure. "Sorry about my mother. Believe it or not, that was her on a good night."

A hardness settled over Elaysia's mouth. "Where did you get that message?"

"We brought the tuross down early this morning, like my mother said." Jakki crossed her arms. She felt herself sliding into the defensive, her kindness shriveling along with it. "I handed it directly over to her without opening it."

Elaysia's eyes flooded with hurt. "Why not bring it to me first?"

"You were busy," Jakki lied. "Besides, Chief Jattai is right that we need to be more careful and less trusting of outsiders than ever." She placed her hand on her friend's shoulder and squeezed. "I know you hate advice, Ellie, really, I do. But for once, you need to set aside your pride and listen to those wiser than you."

Jakki winced as Elaysia's lips parted. She hadn't intended to berate her with such words, but perhaps it was better to have them out in the open instead of festering inside her heart.

All traces of softness vanished from Elaysia's face. "I'll see you at tomorrow's gathering." She dropped the letter at Jakki's feet and strode from the room.

Jakki turned the parchment over in her hands for a long while, her guilt overwhelming in the silence. When she couldn't stand it any longer, she tossed the forged letter into the fire, watching as flames shriveled the edges.

A figure emerged from the shadowed corner of the room and came to stand behind Jakki, startling her.

"Not your best attempt," Lumira purred in her ear.

"Not my worst." Jakki left the room in haste, her white hair tumbling behind her like a snowstorm.

There was no point in placing the blame on her mother. No one would believe it, and Jakki wasn't sure she even cared any longer. Even if Lumira wasn't a threat, Jattai was right. They couldn't take any more chances with outsiders.

Never again.

ELAYSIA

"Thirty-one dead, my High Chieftain. Mostly Moákun, but a few Kahaloán were caught in the fighting."

Elaysia rubbed her sleep-crusted eyes as she processed the messenger's report. The young Apáasutai nyrian was fitted with a tunic of multicolored fabrics stitched with the utmost care—a garment that had never seen so much as a snag from a branch, let alone combat. She shifted awkwardly, first scratching one shoulder, then the other, her gaze lost somewhere on Elaysia's chest, as though she wanted to give the illusion of eye contact without actually committing to it.

She reeked of travel and fear.

Kahana, Elaysia's newly appointed head of the watchers, had given the girl a thorough interrogation before allowing her access to the high chieftain's quarters at such an hour. Elaysia, however, was grateful for the timing, as night lessened the risk of drawing unwanted attention and concern. There was already more than enough fear circulating about Agaas. She strived to handle most issues herself before they could trouble the council—and therefore, the people—even if it meant sacrificing the few precious hours of sleep she procured in between the twins' frequent wakeups. Maseeya waited just down the hallway, ready to swoop in and take them at a moment's notice, as she had just a few minutes prior.

Elaysia couldn't praise the Daughter enough for such a goddess of a woman.

A furrow appeared in Kahana's brow as she studied the messenger, her strong, brown fingers tapping along the handle of her club in deft, choreographed strokes. One of the few nymans in Neharem, Kahana had taken it upon herself to abandon her Moákun clan when she learned one of her own had returned to lead Agaas. Returned *and* reproduced, twofold. Elaysia never questioned her loyalty and named her head of the watchers within a fortnight of her exceptional service. That she was Mardus's cousin only further solidified her merit.

Elaysia adjusted her oversized woolen robe that had once belonged to her father, then lifted her hand to still Kahana's fidgeting. "And them?" she asked the messenger.

The girl's luminescent eyes widened. "Them, High Chieftain?"

Our enemies, Elaysia wanted to say, but it still felt wrong to name her own people, other inhabitants and tribes of Neharem, as such. Perhaps not the Banaxa, with their history of bloodlust and violent resolutions, or the Lautei, with their nyrian-pure bloodlines set on occupying all positions of importance in the nation. But the Atsukut had never given her cause for concern before, not with their nomadic and apolitical ways. Surely, they were misled. Understandably angry, scared. Who knew what lies Raynar had woven to convince them to join his cause—or worse, what he'd threatened them with. She had to believe that deep down, they didn't want to fight either; that they could be won over with a reasonable speech and a promise of peace.

But when bodies began dropping like rain, did reason matter any longer?

Kahana cleared her throat, clearly not as concerned with the motivations behind the bloodshed. "Our high chieftain is referring to the murderous, traitorous cowards who have such little dignity that they stoop to attacking neighboring tribes at the whim of an infantile tyrant."

The fire crackled in the corner of the room and sent a spark flying onto Elaysia's bare foot. She hardly noticed the sting.

"I'm not certain," the messenger stammered, "but I believe our loss was greater."

Our loss. By that, she meant the allies, as people had come to call tribes loyal to Agaas. An official title hadn't been given to their opposition, but Elaysia had heard a phrase murmured around fires and in the hushed, private debriefings after council gatherings.

The Lawful Dominion.

"That will change soon," Kahana muttered, placing a hand on her hip to show off a well-sculpted arm.

The messenger cleared her throat as she inched toward the door. "If you have no further need of me, High Chieftain..."

"You're free to go," Elaysia said, rising from her cot. "Kahana will see to it you are fed and rested."

Kahana cast a glance over her shoulder as she escorted the messenger out of the room. She lingered in the doorway and tapped the frame as she had her club, waiting, it seemed, for Elaysia to beg her to stay, or at least inquire as to her thoughts on the matter.

Elaysia had no intention of doing so.

"Kahana, I look forward to discussing this with you tomo—"

The piercing, rasping cry of an infant drowned out her voice. For once, a surge of relief washed over her, as opposed to the typical onset of grimace-worthy tension at such a sound.

Kahana brought her fist to her heart. "I'll find you tomorrow after we break our fasts, High Chieftain. Until then, may your sunrises always hold promise, and may your sunsets always hold peace."

"And yours."

Elaysia waited until Kahana's footsteps faded down the hall-way, followed by the familiar *thud* of the main door shutting. She dropped her robe, exposing a milk-stained shift. The shrill cry grew in volume, and before she made it to Maseeya's room, another joined it, creating a cacophony of shrieking destined to keep her awake for the rest of the night. Only this time, she didn't mind. Let them keep her up, let the minutes drag into hours.

She wished the dawn would never come.

It came all the same. A harsh wind slammed into the living trees, snapping off small branches and rustling the thatched roofs of the lofts. Most of the people sheltered indoors, and the few who dared to venture out, whether for love or duty, skirted the thick trunks, their robes and hoods pulled down tightly about their faces like shields. Angry clouds marred the sky, promising a storm.

It won't be the only storm of the day, Elaysia mused as she stole across the High Tree platform toward Zavik's loft.

She didn't expect him to be there. In fact, she was counting on his absence. The watcher she'd assigned to observe him reported his near-nightly excursions down to base camp and into the woods. She never let the watcher venture beyond that; she didn't want him to uncover what she already suspected. There was only one place outside Agaas Zavik would have reason to visit with regularity, and only one person who would prompt him to do so. She'd known for nearly four moons, but despite her rage, she hadn't been ready to face it. To face *him.* Between her pregnancy, delivery, and the declaration of war, it never seemed the right time to add more turmoil to her already tumultuous life. Maybe it never would be. Unless the scrolls were there, too, as she feared, instead of safe in Agaas where they belonged.

It was time to find out.

Rain blew sideways into her hood and dripped down her face as she hurried along. By the time she reached Zavik's loft, puddles soaked the path, seeping through the tops of her nytak–skin slippers. From the outside, his home appeared lifeless as ever. A closed door, a shuttered window, darkness where there should've been light. No scents of a morning meal, no idle chatter or hint of a melody. An outsider would've assumed the loft abandoned.

The thought struck a pang in Elaysia's heart. She hesitated outside his door, ignoring the gnawing hunger in her stomach and the twins' phantom cries in her head, determined to convince herself that Zavik was indeed happy, in his own way.

"He'd tell me if he wasn't," she muttered, hoping that if she said the words aloud, she'd believe them a little more. And if he wasn't, well...

It was his own fault.

She raised her hand to knock, then reached for the door latch at the last moment.

It opened freely, as all Agaasian doors did—an issue, Zavik insisted during every council gathering, especially with the threat of war.

The faint light from a stub of a candle drew Elaysia's gaze to a left-leaning table positioned beside the window. A stool was pulled up beside it, and on the stool perched a lean figure hunched over the desk, its shoulders rising and falling with the slow breaths of sleep.

For Khiev-Tatamic's sake.

Elaysia held her breath as she backed out of the room, but a gust of wind slammed the door closed before she could make her escape. Zavik murmured something, raised his head a few inches off the table, then lowered it again. She glimpsed a scroll beside him. But was it one of *the* scrolls? Her heart quickened.

Before she could convince herself otherwise, she tiptoed across the room, her leather soles silent on the wooden floor. She slipped the scroll into her robes.

She was at the door again, hand on the latch, when a familiar, comforting voice stilled her.

"You could've just asked." Zavik's voice was thick with sleep. "I'd gladly share the little I have with you."

"I didn't want to wake you."

Elaysia knew neither of them believed the lie as it rolled off her lips, but was it any better to be brutally honest? To admit it was easier to steal from her dearest friend rather than confront him with her frustration, her suspicion, her anger? To tell him she couldn't fully trust him when he kept secrets from her?

Zavik brushed the tangle of curls off his forehead, then removed his seers, holding them up to the ghostly light streaming in from the open door. He did so in a casual, unaffected manner, but Elaysia saw the hurt in his eyes.

"It's not one of *those* scrolls," he said as he wiped the lenses clean. "Just some of my notes. I mean, you might find them useful, but the writing's a bit disorganized—more of my in-the-moment thoughts as opposed to an articulated argument, and some of it's...much of it's speculation." He continued wiping with vigor, so much so Elaysia feared the frames might snap. "We could look at it together. If you're not too busy, that is."

Another gust of wind slammed into the loft as Elaysia fought to secure a pleasant demeanor. It didn't use to be hard to come by with Zav, but her fingers twitched as task after task assaulted her thoughts, each one demanding to be attended to at once instead of making small talk with an old friend. She hated herself for it, and she hated herself even more for the way their conversation had begun. It was the first time they'd been alone—truly alone—in moons.

She had to make the most of it. Especially if she wanted the scrolls.

Zavik's cot lay adjacent to his table, its blanket tucked flawlessly into the corners without so much as a crease disrupting the geometric patterns. Elaysia sat. Handed him the scroll, which was really more of a thinly rolled parchment—not some work of grandeur penned by members of Quinaria's last scholarly order. He tucked it beside an ink jar on the table, then fidgeted with a quill, adjusting it over and over, as though he'd yet to uncover the secret behind its perfect placement.

Elaysia bit her lip. She owed him an apology. But he owed her one, too, and his offense was far greater.

"It's cold in here," she said, hoping her lack of friendliness would prompt his remorse.

Zavik eyed the firepit, utterly unaware of her subtleties. "I can make a fire?"

"It's fine. If you're not cold, then don't wor—"

"But are you?"

Elaysia shrugged.

Zavik clapped his hands as if the matter was settled, then retrieved the few pieces of wood stacked beside the fireplace. It was scarcely enough to last twenty minutes. She decided to forgo telling him the effort wasn't worth the wood.

"I received word of another attack last night," she said, as he struggled to ignite a flame. "They raided supplies, dug up nevethium, and left blatant messages that it's time to return to the way things were before."

"As in?"

"Before Neharem was united under Agaas."

Zavik cursed as the flint slipped from his fingers. Elaysia kneeled beside him and retrieved it, striking a spark within three swift strokes. A nervous laugh escaped Zavik's throat. He gestured to the herbs hanging above his fireplace and a pot, implying he could make her tea, but she shook her head and returned to the cot. He glanced at the spot beside her, then returned to his stool.

"What if you just grant them what they want?" he asked softly as the flames danced into being.

Elaysia's eyes narrowed. "And lose allied Neharem?"

"I think you've already lost it, Ellie."

"I refuse to accept that." Her voice rose with the flames, and Zavik scooted back as far as his table would allow. "The moment the rest of Quinaria knows we're fractured, they'll pick us off one-by-one, like wolves taking down stray nytaks. We're weak alone. Even if Raynar's tribes agreed to peace, how are we supposed to survive? If we return to the old ways and rely strictly on local yields, it won't be enough. The land isn't what it used to be."

Zavik picked at a strip of wood peeling off his unfinished table. He knew as well as she that when nevethium was removed, even in sustainable amounts, everything left in its stead suffered. Plants didn't flourish the same, the crops produced three-quarters of their old harvests, and the game slowly bred fewer and fewer offspring each year. With time, less advantaged tribes would resort to trading the precious crystals again, and even if they didn't, other nations would help themselves to Neharem's ample supply.

And Agaas would be the first to fall.

"The Lawful Dominion won't settle for a truce, anyway," Zavik said. The firelight accented the red in his hair, brought a touch of color to his pale cheeks. "Not with Raynar's vendetta against you. They're more likely to win over or scare the neutral tribes into submission, then make their way to Agaas. And when they do, we won't be able to hold our own against them."

"Thanks for the encouragement."

"I'm not trying to be pessimistic, just—"

"Realistic."

Zavik didn't counter her assumption. "I'm certain they have foreign aid. Az Zar must see some benefit to their victory, and Raynar's probably promised them things they can't refuse."

"Like my head."

"Or the stormbirds."

As if on command, a screech pierced the sky above Agaas.

Elaysia shivered. It was the typical sound the birds made when they returned home from a successful hunt. They grew more independent with each passing day, flying further, hunting longer, acting more like the adolescents they were, like the intelligent beings the stories spoke of. But no matter how Onitus and the others stretched their wings, Elaysia didn't question their loyalty. She'd never felt such an instantaneous bond.

"The birds are loyal," she said, leveling her cool gaze on Zavik.

He shrugged. "It's not my place to make judgment, but I don't think winning them over is what the All-Sovereign intends. If they're gone, the threat is gone. If the threat is gone, you're gone. If you're gone, the alliance falls apart. If the alliance falls apart…"

"They gain access to the most abundant nevethium stores, and Neharem ceases to exist as we know it." Elaysia bunched the once pristine blanket covering Zavik's cot with her hands. "I'm well aware, but I appreciate you laying out that thoroughly depressing future all the same."

Zavik's cheeks blazed bright as the flames. "Right. Sorry, I just..." He rubbed the place between his eyebrows and paced the length of the room, muttering to himself.

Elaysia tried in vain to smooth the blanket back out while she formulated an excuse to leave. "Zav, I—"

He spun to face her, his green eyes wide with wonder. "That's it! The best nevethium stores." He scampered to the chest at the foot of his cot and began rifling through it. "They're not in Neharem. They're not on land at all. If we could establish contact—I mean, it's been thousands of years, but maybe they'd be understanding of our plight."

"Who?"

If Zavik heard her question, he made no attempt to answer it. He retrieved a parchment from his chest and unrolled it on the floor, revealing a map of Quinaria. "I mean, surely they wouldn't want to support Az Zar, not after, well, you know..." He trailed off again, staring at the map, his finger hovering just below Sunset Bay.

"Zav, what in Haeshol are you talking about?"

He blinked, as though only just recalling her presence. "Oh, sorry. One of the scrolls I recovered has the locations of the largest nevethium stores I've ever heard of. They're all near—or in—myrem settlements. Allegedly." He plopped on the cot beside her, apparently too distracted by his idea to fear their shared proximity.

Elaysia let a small bubble of hope rise inside her. "Let me see."

Zavik winced. "I don't exactly have the scrolls with me at this moment."

A familiar, dull ache weighed heavily on Elaysia's chest. Rain pounded on the roof, nearly drowning out the crackle of the flames. She wanted to storm from the loft and let him wallow in fear and regret for days. But it wouldn't make anything better. She needed resolutions, not more problems.

She took several shaky breaths in through her nostrils, then drew her legs up on the cot, angling her body to face him, cross-legged, as she had when they were children. "Konar has them."

Zavik couldn't hold her gaze, but he didn't deny her. He plunged his hands into the pockets of his tunic.

The fire waned, its great sunset-toned arms diminishing into embers, drawing away the light, the warmth.

"You're hiding him at Igtheos's old refuge, aren't you?" Elaysia pressed.

Zavik peered up at her through long lashes. "Are you upset with me?"

"Often, as of late."

The rebuttal flew out with a mind of its own, though Elaysia didn't regret it. A little guilt was the least penance Zavik could serve, for he'd betrayed her, too, with his actions, even if he'd done it for her good and Neharem's.

Elaysia's words had the desired effect. Zavik retreated to the edge of his cot, shoulders slumped like a wind-blown tree. The guilt hit her then, a feeling like being surrounded by scowling faces and pointing fingers and voices calling out who she really was: an inexperienced leader driven by emotion and eluded by reason.

Desperate to make amends, she scooted alongside him, so their shoulders touched. "My wrath and longing for justice blinded me, and I suppose I might've regretted it, had he perished—at least for your sake. I just wish you hadn't lied to me."

Zavik lifted his smooth chin to meet her gaze. "You're justified in your feelings, and I'm ready to face whatever punishment you deem necessary."

"I don't want to punish you. Why else do you think I've avoided this confrontation for so long?" When Zavik didn't seem convinced, she added, "You wouldn't have been able to translate the scrolls without his help, would you? That's why you saved him?"

Visible relief washed over Zavik, relaxing the lines on his brow and around his tired eyes. "Yes. I think I could one day, given enough time and tutelage. But he's the only one I know of with that kind of knowledge. On our side, at least."

"Konar is on his own side. Always has been."

"That's fair."

Black ash surrounded the last of the embers in the fireplace, and Zavik tried, and failed, to coax any remaining life out of them.

"Do you want to see him?" he asked, his back turned to Elaysia.

Her chest constricted. A small, childlike part of her did long to see him—even throw her arms around his neck and tell him she wanted to understand, that his actions didn't negate the time he'd sacrificed on her behalf, the love he'd given her in his own, unconventional way. If she was being honest with herself, she sometimes still craved his fatherly attention and guidance.

But a far greater part of her hated him with every bit of her being. Even now, she couldn't guarantee she wouldn't lash out should they meet again. End him then and there herself, the same way he'd let Annonitus perish before her child-eyes. Monsters didn't deserve forgiveness. Nor love.

"Not yet," she croaked. "Maybe never. But I want him to know that *I know* he's alive, and that I'm allowing him to live, even though he couldn't give my family that same grace."

Zavik gave a melancholic nod. "As you wish."

Elaysia squeezed his shoulder. "I'll be better, alright? I'm try-ing to sort all this out. I can barely think most days. When I'm with the twins, I'm so tired. It's harder than anything I've ever done. More demanding than council gatherings, more physically taxing than traversing the Tsabian Desert. Sometimes I sit there holding them and wish desperately to be anywhere else, to be anyone but their mother." Once the confession began pouring out of her, it was unstoppable, like a dam broken apart.

But there was relief in it.

Zavik, too, placed his hand on her shoulder. They sat there, holding each other at a respectable distance, and Elaysia knew in that moment that nothing could ever break their bond. A tear snaked down her cheek, leaving a warm trail in its wake.

"Don't think I'm a terrible person," she whispered. "Because when I'm away from them, I think of almost nothing else. It terrifies me how much I need them. It's like my heart lives outside my body now, split between two fragile vessels. And I'm scared I can't protect them, Zav. I'm scared I'm going to fail them like I've failed everyone else, and this war is only beginning."

"You're a lot of things, Elaysia, but a terrible person isn't one of them." Zavik drew her closer, and she folded into his shoulder. "Don't let these circumstances rob you of your decency. It's alright to feel these feelings and acknowledge life isn't fair. Just don't lose the beauty in it. Don't let the darkness take you. Promise me that?"

Elaysia sniffed. "I promise."

Zavik smoothed her hair back. A small sigh escaped his lips, and she sensed he had more to say, something he didn't want to tell her but felt compelled to after her vulnerability. She pulled away, wiping the ghost of a tear from her cheek. He let her go and returned to his table, hands retreating into his pockets.

The rainfall on the roof softened to a patter. Elaysia felt a sudden urge to yank the door open and let some fresh air drown out the tepid musk of ink and dust from Zavik's loft. Instead, she rooted herself to the cot and searched for the right tone. Too demanding, and he'd clam up, but too lenient, and he'd keep his secrets.

And she was done with secrets.

"What aren't you telling me?" she asked calmly.

"I don't want to add even more to your—"

"Stop. No more lies between us. We promised."

Zavik glanced over his shoulder, not quite meeting her gaze. "The scrolls in our possession might provide solutions to turn the war in our favor."

Elaysia held her breath. "Go on."

"I'm still not sure I believe everything the authors claim in their writings," he added quickly. "And even if the rituals work, their outcomes may not be worth the price. I suppose that's your decision to make, though."

A sudden craving overwhelmed Elaysia, not unlike the random hunger pains she'd experienced since nursing the babes. But this time, it was deeper, more desperate than the need for satiation, more primal than the desire for lovemaking. She tensed, not wanting to give in to the pull of the scrolls. She'd yet to touch them—even lay eyes on them—and yet they'd made their way into her dreams and beckoned her with their power.

It was time.

"Konar is proof the rituals work," she said, advancing on a shrinking Zavik. "I don't doubt the severity of the price. It makes monsters of men. But we're up against an imminent war that we stand no chance of winning. Even if we did, it's only the first of many."

Zavik studied his feet intently, his face painted with an incriminating mixture of fear and regret.

Elaysia lifted his chin. "My father believed the scrolls were the answer to our salvation. So, tell me what he sought and paid for with my family's lives, what Konar paid for with his honor, and what you paid for, though you've yet to tell me the cost."

Zavik grimaced. "That remains to be seen." He fished beneath the desk and came up with a wineskin and a poorly carved cup—no doubt his handiwork. "You want to discuss the details now?"

"Or never."

He shook the skin. Liquid slapped loudly against the empty spaces.

"We're going to need more wine."

JAKKI

The sky was a canvas smothered in ash and the off-white of dirty snow. It saturated the meadow in darkness, bringing out the undertones of the grass and the deep violet of the wild-flowers billowing against the somber backdrop. The silhouettes of trees faded into the mountains, making it difficult to decipher where plant ended and mineral began. Despite the tight braid Jakki had woven her waist-length hair into, the wind showed no mercy as it tugged strands free, whipping them about her face. She pushed through the knee-high grass, still wet with rain, each blade soft as silk, and relished the calm.

For another storm was on the horizon.

A forceful gust slammed into Jakki as Siren swooped by with an unsettling shriek. The stormbird flew with smooth, broad strokes of her black and white wings, propelling her higher into the air as she cast a faint shadow over the meadow. She clutched the limp body of a nytak fawn in her scythe-shaped talons, her black eyes narrowing as she glided down to land beside Jakki. The air surrounding the stormbird reeked of the coppery scent of blood and the musk of drenched foliage. Jakki acknowledged her partner with a nod, not daring to approach the magnificent bird until she'd finished devouring her prey. No matter how strong their bond grew, Siren was a being who commanded respect, not a tamed mutt to be forced into a life of servitude.

Jakki watched with fascination as the stormbird tore off a strip of the fawn's flesh and threw her head back to swallow it whole. They were the first to arrive for Elaysia's impromptu gathering, but it wasn't long before a cluster of figures crested the hill above the training grounds where they waited. Soon after, the silhouettes and cries of other stormbirds filled the sky above their riders. Siren continued to make quick work of the nytak, but she cocked her head ever so slightly to the sky—whether in greeting or warning, Jakki knew not. Hers was the largest of the birds, even superior to Lumira's Anadu, who was impressive in her own right. But the cat's bird lacked the cunning Jakki sensed within Siren, and for that, her bird was the survivor.

The victor.

As the figures descending the hill morphed into discernable individuals, Jakki counted nine in total. All the Stormriders (save for herself), then Zavik and his bodyguard. The Orillon man clung to Zavik as much as the new high elder clung to Elaysia, creating a chain of overly dependent people.

Jakki rolled her eyes and drew her water-resistant leather hood over her head. Elaysia had ordered them to the training grounds under the guise of actual training, the true purpose of the gathering apparently so important and secret that it couldn't be held in the summit lodge like usual. Jakki, who'd spent the better part of the afternoon seducing a new watcher into her cot, nearly slammed the door in Zavik's face when he pounded on it relentlessly, then demanded they depart within the hour and journey to the ancient training grounds in the dead of the Resting Moons.

If whatever they were about to discuss wasn't something *she* deemed important, he'd be the first to pay.

Yerakai reached her before the others, a look of unmistakable calm on his flawless face. "Have to beat the rest of us to every-thing, eh, Jak?" he said with a smile.

Jakki's lips pulled thin despite his genuinely playful manner. "Just eager to learn what required our immediate attention."

Yerakai gave a knowing nod and kneeled on the grass beside her, his ashen-violet skin rivaling the beauty and hue of the wildflowers. The others joined them, sectioning themselves off into pairs as if they'd been ordered to go patrolling: the beridians, Mardus and Anahi, Zavik and the backhander, and Elaysia and her surrogate younger brother, Xaren. The Az Zarian boy's dark eyes crinkled at the corners when he saw Jakki, and despite her mood, she softened her face to him. He seemed to think they'd formed some bond after their duties in Cadar, and to his credit, he was far more tolerable than most of the riders. She gave him a here-we-go shrug and sauntered toward Elaysia.

The high chieftain greeted Jakki with a traditional fist to her heart. "I hope you haven't been waiting long. I told Zavik to give everyone an hour after notifying them."

Zavik caught wind of the conversation and cast a worried glance in her direction. Jakki held his gaze long enough to let him know she could twist the blame onto him but would let it pass this time—though he better remember it—then flashed an alluring smile at Elaysia.

"He gave me plenty of time," she said, stroking her nevethium pendant. "I choose to leave early. Wanted to make sure I could track down Siren."

"She's hard to miss," Xaren said, eyeing Siren the way one might assess a hungry bear. "Is that a…"

Jakki nodded. "She prefers the woodland kills over seafood."

Elaysia grimaced as Siren gulped down the last of the fawn. "They won't be able to access the woods much longer."

"Shadow will be able to for a while still," Xaren said with a laugh. "He's so small that Siren could practically swallow him whole.

Jakki waved him off as she searched for the little black terror in the sky. "He's not *that* small."

He was, though. At barely a third of the size of Siren, Shadow's primary advantage was his discreetness—at least as much as a stormbird could be discreet. He emerged from the cover of clouds, spreading his wings slightly to slow his descent as his glossy feathers reflected the meager daylight. Upon landing, his amber eyes scanned the meadow with no shortage of caution.

"They are all formidable, in their own way." Elaysia concluded the debate with a whistle, awakening Onitus from his solitary perch a hundred yards away.

The stormbird flared his wings, his fire-tipped edges stark against the midnight blue adorning the bulk of his feathers. Siren perked up as he glided toward them. Only to Elaysia's and Lumira's birds did she pay any mind, and Jakki expected it had to do with attraction and competition, respectively. The rest rarely solicited so much as a glance from her stormbird.

Elaysia beckoned the birds and their riders to the arena where she'd defeated the former Lautei chief, Rajar. She'd likely chosen the location for its logs and rich, grassy patches that provided ample seating, but it didn't hurt to remind the Stormriders of her recent victory. *I've won once,* her face seemed to say. *Do not underestimate me.*

Jakki strived not to.

Everyone quieted once gathered. There was no need to hush them, to remind them of the severity of the looming war. Elaysia motioned for Zavik to join her at the edge of the arena, and the new high elder shuffled to the front, his hands jammed into the pockets of the ridiculous long-sleeved, high-collared tunic he'd acquired in Orillon. A snide remark danced on the tip of Jakki's tongue, but one glance at Elaysia stifled it. It was not the time for jesting.

Zavik cleared his throat, then took a hesitant step toward the riders, hands clasped behind his back. "The high chieftain would like me to give you a brief, of sorts, regarding where we stand with the rebellion, what options are available to us, and—"

"I've been thoroughly briefed," Mardus interjected gruffly. "Chief Orandus has dealt with the brunt of the attacks, and my people are the most ill-positioned for Az Zar's wrath, should it come." He tightened the leather cord holding his dark hair in place atop his head, simultaneously giving his muscled arms a flex for good measure.

Before Zavik could respond, Lumira butted in with her crude beridian accent. "I've kept everyone informed to the best of my abilities. Unless there's something I haven't been told." Her tail twitched.

"It's safe to assume you don't know everything." Jakki gave her head a slight shake at the cat, then returned her attention to Zavik. "So, perhaps we should let the high elder continue."

Lumira said something presumably vulgar in Hispen, prompting Grokhion to lay a massive paw on her arm.

"I mean no disrespect to anyone, it's just…" Zavik's cheeks puffed as his gaze darted around like a trapped rodent.

The wind picked up again, stirring the branches and leaves of the surrounding trees in a cacophony of whispers; it smelled of ocean and wildflowers. Elaysia tapped her fingers on the arena railing, her nostrils flaring wider with each passing moment. She looked ready to take over Zavik's failed speech, but before she usurped him, High Elder Talab (Jakki was fairly certain that was his surname) shook his curls with fury and assumed a stance not entirely laughable.

"Look, we're all aware of the less-than-ideal predicament Raynar's put us in," he began. "As it stands, we don't have enough allies to hold a candle to his numbers, and he's already taken aggressive action. Unless the neutral tribes agree to join us, we'll have lost this war before it even takes off. And new allies aren't looking promising, are they, Yerakai?"

The Apáasutai looked up from the arrow shaft he'd been carving and frowned. "I returned from my journey to the south-western territories not two days past. None of the neutral leaders will stand with us. They mostly agree with us, but refuse to take aggressive action, whether out of fear or personal beliefs."

"Did you remind them they'll be forced to take aggressive action when the Lautei and Banaxa burn down their homes and sell their children to Az Zar?" Jakki demanded.

Elaysia held up her hand. "Yerakai's job wasn't to frighten them into allying with us, merely to remind them of their options should they have a change of heart."

Jakki held her tongue while Yerakai elaborated on the neutral tribes' excuses. She should've been the one to go. Yerakai may have been known for his persuasiveness, but only she could've scared the outliers into submission. And as long as they joined, did it really matter how?

"So, to put it in the simplest of terms, we're fucked."

Everyone looked wide-eyed at the origin of the blunt observation.

Grokhion.

Not only was the language crass for the great cat, he was also rarely so pessimistic, especially with grave matters. He shook his formidable mane and bared his gleaming white fangs in a yawn.

"But that's not all, is it, lad?" the beridian continued. "Otherwise, why the urgency of this gathering?" He fixated on Zavik, his green eyes wide, pupils narrowed into slits. "Let's waste no more time on the knowns. What have you learned that may alter the course of our future?"

Zavik's mouth wasn't the only one hanging open, but it certainly was the widest.

"The scrolls," he stammered.

Jakki straightened, grasping her staff.

"I've recently finished translations, and while I don't think using them is the best course of action, Elaysia feels it necessary to share the information with you all, seeing as how the circumstances—"

"I thought you said the scrolls' power was metaphorical."

The rebuttal came from Anahi, and while there was no spite in her remark, Zavik visibly crumpled all the same.

"I did say something to that effect, but I didn't yet understand them, nor was I familiar with testaments of the scrolls' power."

Jakki leaned forward. "Such as Konar's abnormally long life."

Elaysia flinched at his name, then rubbed her forehead with vigor. "Just tell them what the scrolls can do, Zav."

"Right." Zavik shoved his seers further up the bridge of his nose and looked Jakki straight in the eyes. "There's a lot of information to unpack—literally, the majority of the scrolls are exposition and historical documentation—but, like Konar's extended life, they claim to reward those willing to trifle with the powers of gods."

"More of Mavet's lies," Mardus huffed.

A tingle ran down Jakki's spine, up her arms, and across her legs. She didn't doubt the scrolls' powers; not after multiple uses of the magic parchment she'd acquired from the old man in the woods. But someone like Mardus would never understand such a gift. He was too frightened of the unknown.

Zavik glanced at Elaysia, prompting the high chieftain to step forward with a determined set to her jaw that even Jakki didn't dare challenge.

"I will have no more interruptions until Zavik has finished speaking. Do I make myself clear?"

Rain began to sprinkle on the training grounds. It tasted like the ocean, each drop carrying a hint of salt and tide. No one offered further protest. Jakki chewed her inner lip and stifled the questions bubbling inside her.

"In case anyone was otherwise distracted in previous gatherings," Zavik said as he refastened a button on his tunic. "I recovered two scrolls in Orillon. One is myrem in origin; the other shaktar. In the event we locate other scrolls, and referring to them by their languages no longer provides clarity, I've taken the liberty of naming the two in our possession. I will hereby refer to the myrem scroll as The Scroll of Crystals going forward. The scroll written in Shaktari is likewise now called The Scroll of Persuasion."

Zavik paused, as if waiting for a protest. A look of surprise flicked over his face as he observed the Stormriders' silence and drew his hood about his head.

"Alright then," he said, seemingly to himself. "The Scroll of Crystals' author—I should clarify there could be multiple authors, or at least contributors—had a deep fascination with nevethium and uncovering its potential and limitations. I won't bore you all with the details, but one intriguing claim is that Quinaria's greatest nevethium stores are, in fact, not on land.

Which I find to be perfectly logical, given we must mine or dig for it as is. Oh, and it also comes with a warning about exploiting said stores."

Anahi uttered something breathy in Westmun, her doe-like brown eyes wide with wonder.

Zavik, a fellow speaker of the unrefined Orillon language, acknowledged her with a knowing look. "Yes, according to the scroll, myrem stand guard over the greatest nevethium hoards. But we should keep in mind this information is at least a few thousand years old." The fire-haired high elder removed his seers and wiped the rain off the lenses. "Aside from that, the most outrageous claim the scroll makes is a ritual bestowing the gift of foresight."

Foresight? Jakki's brow furrowed. She hoped another Storm-rider would ask for further clarification so she wouldn't have to.

Xaren's hand shot into the air. "Pardon, High Elder, but many people claim to have foresight. What makes this special?"

"I'm not talking about speculation of future events based on an educated analysis," Zavik said with a hint of irritation. "The scroll claims to give actual visions of what will occur should things remain on course."

"Messages from the gods," Grokhion mused. "We have diviners back on the Isles who've cultivated the ability to receive such visions."

Zavik shrugged. "It could be something like that, but the author was adamant that these are fully tangible visions of soon-to-transpire events. They seemed to believe that, if used effectively, these visions could alter the future of Quinaria. Maybe even all Quorath."

Yerakai steepled his fingers together as he gazed into the distance. "And what is the cost?"

"The invoker of the ritual must go blind in exchange for the visions." The answer came from Elaysia, who'd drawn her robes so tightly about her frame that only her face peeked out. "And there's no telling what they'll be about. It could be something entirely unrelated to what the invoker desires."

The rain fell harder, each drop cool and sharp against Jakki's hands, like shards of glass. She decided enough people had spoken up that she wouldn't seem too eager. "How frequently do they occur?" she asked. "Giving up your sight in exchange for one or two visions seems extreme."

One of the stormbirds screeched, and Zavik flinched away from the sound. "It doesn't say. I doubt many people volunteered to do it, making it impossible to create a consistent account. The author hinted they planned to personally partake in the ritual, but there's no record of what happened to them, or even any details regarding the visions. It's almost as though it was intentionally omitted."

"Or they died because of it," Anahi offered.

Everyone began talking at once. Jakki caught snippets of speculation, of skepticism. Despite the lofty claims, no part of her doubted the scroll's promises. She sat silent amid the chaos, pondering, reaching for the parchment that wasn't tucked into its usual spot in her waistband—she'd hidden it in her loft—until she sensed eyes on her. She looked up and met Elaysia's unwavering gaze.

"You're quiet, Jakki," Elaysia said, loud enough to draw everyone else's attention. "I'm always eager to hear the thoughts of those who won't freely give them."

Jakki braced her foot on a log so she could rest her arm on the adjoining knee, hoping the stance would give her an air of aloofness. "I think it's safe to assume the scrolls are genuine and that one of the Prophets sacrificed themselves for these visions. I dare suggest that's even where they gleaned knowledge that had evaded the races of land for millennia. Such knowledge would surely benefit us, especially in a time of war." She'd made eye contact with each rider as she spoke, but now returned her attention to Elaysia. "Imagine if we could see our enemies' moves before they make them."

"Imagine if we never uncovered their moves at all and only hastened our pending destruction," Lumira said as she dragged her claws across the log she and Grokhion sat upon. "Imagine if we all went blind, and it benefited no one."

Jakki glowered at her.

Elaysia watched their interaction with curiosity, but did not intervene.

"All excellent points," Zavik offered. "You both show great insight."

"It's common sense, not insight," Jakki said. "We could benefit from these visions."

"Are you volunteering to go blind?" Lumira hissed.

Jakki's grip tightened around her staff. "I'm one of our best warriors. You, on the other hand…"

Lumira rose, but Grokhion held her back with his trunk of an arm.

"I can't afford to lose any Stormriders," Elaysia said, raising her voice to combat the wind. "And neither am I ready to trust anyone outside this gathering. If you're all in favor, I suggest we postpone the use of this scroll until we can agree on a worthy candidate."

"We have a say in this decision for once?" Jakki bit her lip as soon as she spoke, but she didn't regret the jab, or the way Elaysia looked a little less certain, if only for a moment.

Onitus hopped over to Elaysia and fixed his predator gaze on Jakki. In response, Siren swooped down a few feet away, her plumage raised to add to her already immense height.

"And the Scroll of Persuasion," Zavik shouted, his voice cracking at the end. "It promises a power even more alluring, but at a much greater cost."

"A greater cost?" Anahi sounded suspicious, as though she couldn't imagine a sacrifice worse than losing one's sight.

"I think so." The wind blew more rain into Zavik's seers, and he ripped them off in frustration. "We don't have much time before this meadow turns into a swamp, so refrain from further questions, if you can."

A smile crawled across Jakki's lips. She could get used to this emboldened, irritated Zavik.

"There's a prophecy of Mavet's imminent return alongside what the Prophets believed to be the scope and limitations of a Caman's power, but we don't have time for that right now. What you want to hear most is this scroll's power, so here it is: control of another being."

Yerakai stood up and summoned Wind Chaser. "I've heard enough. I don't care what the cost is. Nothing will ever convince me it's right to exact control over another being."

"You think Az Zar would hesitate to use it against us, or that Raynar is above such actions?" Mardus asked. Keera fluttered to his side, her red eyes standing out against the white of her feathers, like blood on snow.

"The All-Sovereign would control everyone in Quinaria if he had the opportunity," Xaren added, retreating to the shelter that was Shadow. "He already does, in a way."

Grokhion roared, demanding silence. "The price, lad," he asked Zavik. "What is it?"

"Translated literally, it says sacrifice of self. I'm still uncertain of the details, but it's something like forfeiting part of your life to control someone else's. Time for time." Zavik had given up on his seers and dangled them limply at his side, eyes squinting for clarity. "But it's not a clean exchange. The loss is far greater on the ritual invoker's end. You might lose several days—even moons off your life—in exchange for temporary sway over someone else. Like the power of foresight, I don't think this one was utilized enough to give a consistent account."

"I don't like it," Grokhion growled.

"How does it even work?" Anahi asked.

"That part is a bit..." Zavik swallowed. "Dark. The ritual invoker needs a piece of the person they wish to control."

Anahi's eyes widened even further, as if that were possible. "Like part of their body?"

Zavik laughed nervously. "It could be more metaphorical, like something significant to them. It's hard to say without actually performing it."

Yerakai approached Elaysia and spoke in a hushed tone, though Jakki was close enough to make it out. "Are you suggesting we use these malevolent artifacts? To do so is to sacrifice our humanity."

"I suggest nothing," Elaysia snapped. "I merely wanted to be honest with you all and to put it to a vote." With that, she pushed away from the railing she'd been leaning against and marched to the center of the circle. "All in favor of attempting, or at least considering, the use of the scrolls' powers, raise your hand."

Jakki waited for the other supporters to show face, those willing to do what it'd take to win. Lumira raised a cautious hand, but she was the first all the same. Xaren raised his next, followed by Elaysia. When it was clear no one else intended to show support, Jakki snaked hers into the sky. She wanted to appear cautiously supportive, not overzealous for power.

Elaysia frowned as she eyed those with lowered hands. "I'll assume the rest of you are against."

"We aren't desperate enough yet," Mardus offered, stroking Keera's beak. "Perhaps we can reconsider, should our situation become dire enough."

If we make it that long, Jakki mused.

"I think we should destroy them." Yerakai brought his fist to his heart and gave Elaysia a nod of respect. "But I appreciate you being forthright and considering our counsel. These scrolls are dangerous, and using them will only bring us pain."

Elaysia forced a smile that didn't reach her eyes. "Well spoken, Brother. I shall consider your words."

Lumira marched to the edge of the arena, her golden-striped tail flicking out from beneath her cloak. "Morality is a privilege," she argued, and Jakki found herself in agreement. "At the very least, we need to better understand how these scrolls can help us. Need I remind you all, we're in the same place we were an hour ago: outnumbered and ill-equipped. We need outside intervention."

"She's right, and I think I know where we can find it."

The affirmation came from Anahi. The armor-clad Orillon woman turned to face the mountains just as the ghost of a sun began its descent, painting the meadow a shade darker. Corvax, her stormbird, took to the air with a cry.

Elaysia hurried to her, almost giddy. "Who? Where from?"

Anahi fixed her with a sad smile. "Orillon. I have contacts back home who are more than capable of lending us aid."

"Why would anyone in Orillon want to help us—even listen to us, for that matter?" Jakki asked as she joined the women, forming a small circle. "What contacts could a pit fighter possibly have?"

Dark lashes shielded Anahi's eyes as she studied the crumpled grass beneath her sandals. "I'd wager just about anyone would be willing to help if it benefited them. Regardless, I can guarantee they'll at least hear me out."

Jakki leaned forward. "Why?"

"Because I'm nobility."

KONAR

"**Y**ou have to swear, Konar. Otherwise, I'm not leaving."

Konar pulled his nose out of the journal and gave Zavik the benefit of his full attention. The lad stood in front of the door, a travel sack slung over his shoulder and a knife strapped to his hip. It could've just been the dim lighting of the old Igtheos refuge, but something about his features seemed hardened, a little of the boy chiseled away to make room for the man. It had happened overnight, as it had with Elaysia, as it had with the countless other children he'd watched come of age, but a select few were special, a genuine pleasure to watch grow.

And Zavik was one of them.

The lad put an impatient hand on his hip. "Did you hear anything I just said?"

"Was it something along the lines of, 'Don't do anything stupider than you've already done in your waste of an extended life, Konar'?"

Zavik's stern demeanor cracked. He let his shoulders fall to their usual relaxed state and dropped his sack on the floor, then joined Konar at the table, pulling out one of the chairs nested around it. Konar's own chair creaked as he adjusted his weight.

It wasn't the finest handiwork; Igtheos had done little to flesh the place out besides ensuring minimal seating and lodging for his rebellion survivors all those years ago, but they had turned it into a livable commune until modern Agaas came about. The furniture, like the refuge itself, had been constructed from driftwood sourced from the beach a few hundred feet below with the tools their Apáasutai allies lent them. It still smelled of the sea. The refuge could sleep a few dozen inhabitants spread between three rooms filled to the brim with stacked cots, and it centered on a common room with a rectangular firepit and a sturdy table. Nothing adorned the wood, save for a phrase carved into the center of the table in Nyrinian:

There is only rebirth.

Konar had stared at those words every day since Zavik gave him yet another chance at life. Igtheos had lost a wife and daughter in his fight against Ashaat the Victor, so perhaps the words had been a comfort to him; a hope that he'd be reunited with his family in death, or at the very least made anew and given a second chance. But Konar liked to think it was more comprehensive, that no matter how bad things got in Quinaria, it could be remade. That all people could be remade whenever they so choose. He had to believe it.

Zavik nudged the charred wood in the firepit with the toe of his boot. "So, will you promise me?"

"I will protect the scrolls with my life," Konar answered. And he meant it.

"And you won't approach Agaas—especially Elaysia—under any circumstance until I return?"

Konar reached for his pipe, kindled it. Scratched an irritated spot on his forearm where the rough knit robe Zavik had given him had rubbed against his skin; it was nowhere near the quality of his old robe, but then again, he was no longer of such quality himself. He eyed the lad's clothing, noting the lack of ornamental attire. Perhaps Elaysia was ushering Agaas into a new era, after all.

"Konar." Zavik leaned across the table. "Unless they're coming here *for* you, you must remain. She doesn't want to see you, and I can't promise they won't kill you should you attempt to enter Agaas."

A warm, gentle hum settled over Konar as he inhaled smoke from the kinawa leaves. "I promise."

Zavik closed his eyes and chuckled darkly.

Konar lowered his pipe, only slightly on edge. "What amuses you so?"

"I'm just finally realizing that I can't ever trust you again. Not fully." Zavik collected his things from the door and cracked it open, ushering in a wet breeze laden with salt and the murky light of a gray morning. "I guess this will have to be comfort enough. Farwell, then, old friend."

Something in Konar stirred. A dull ache in his chest, a clamminess about his palms. He wiped his hands on his scratchy tunic and took another deep inhale from his pipe to calm his nerves. He was no stranger to the sensation. It had happened only a few times in his life, and the result was always the same.

He never saw that person again.

"Before you go, lad," he said as he rose, his voice thick with emotion. "I also need you to promise me something."

"Oh?" The look on Zavik's face was one of suspicion. "And what could I possibly owe you in that regard?"

Konar tightened his hands into fists to hide the shaking. "This isn't for me. Nothing is anymore." He swiftly blocked the door, noting the brief flicker of apprehension in Zavik's eyes. "You must promise me you will always stay true to her, and that you will protect her at all costs. Even if that means lying to her."

Zavik scowled. "I think I've already proven I can do so on all accounts."

"Please forgive my presumptions," Konar said, wincing. "I'm in no place to question your judgment." He cursed himself silently as he wrestled with what he wanted to say. "It's just that you're the only trustworthy one, Zavik. A dying breed. I hate to thrust my responsibilities upon your shoulders, but you are the *only* one capable of carrying them. I realize that all this time I've been waiting for you, my replacement, a stronger, purer version of me. I..." Konar swallowed the lump in his throat. "I fear our paths will only diverge from here, and that mine is rapidly approaching a cliff."

Zavik's lips parted, but for once, the lad uttered no response. They stood, toe-to-toe, as the breeze yanked at their clothes, their hair, smattering their faces in a fine mist.

"There's something else," Konar pressed, fearing his successor's inevitable escape. "Something you haven't told me, and I don't blame you for it. But if you open up to me now, I might be able to provide you with some parting insight." When Zavik didn't protest, Konar went on in the calmest, most non-threatening tone he could muster. "I tried more than once to gain entry to the Shaktar Caverns. So have others. Yet they revealed themselves to you. Gave you two scrolls. What are you not telling me?"

The lad's green eyes widened. He dropped his head, but not before Konar noticed the guilt burdening his face. "I have to leave now."

Konar stepped back. "Go on then, but don't doubt your significance, lad. Protect Elaysia. Protect yourself. And find the rest of the scrolls."

Zavik nodded, stuttered a few words that resulted in no coherent thoughts, then stepped outside. Only a few steps, however. And not ones filled with intent. He lingered just outside the refuge, his back to it, droplets forming in his fiery hair.

Konar tried his best to encourage him. "This journey is yours now. Trust yourself above all else, and if you have to, break the rules. They're only a construct created by mortal beings. You must choose what your heart tells you is right."

"Because that's worked out so well for you." Zavik turned his head enough that Konar could make out the cut of his nose against the yawning woods ahead. "Tell me, do you really believe each person is capable of discerning good and evil with absolutely no guidelines?"

"Good and evil don't exist as separate entities. They are opposite ends of the same being, just as how a river is still the same river, no matter where you step into it. Some may think it's cold and thrashing; others find the spot a few feet down to be tepid and calm." Konar gripped the doorframe, rooting himself to the moment, to the feel of the woodgrain beneath his fingertips. "All you must concern yourself with is what's true. If you're true to yourself and true to others, you'll find most things happen as they should."

"I'd like to believe that," Zavik whispered. "Really, I would. But I fear others don't care to concern themselves with truths and therefore prevent things from happening as they should."

He pivoted to face Konar head-on, a mixture of grief and respect plastered on his face. "I appreciate you, High Elder, for all you've taught me. Your evil deeds aren't enough to make me regret the time we've spent and the lessons I've learned. In a way, I understand it—rather, I can see why someone in your position would feel the need to resort to such..."

Tears welled in Konar's eyes, blurring his vision.

"I'm not condoning it," Zavik concluded. He crossed his arms like a defiant child. "You ruined lives that day, and many days since. I just want you to know, were I to remove biases from my heart, that, well, you're not the power-hungry monster people are making you out to be."

Konar wiped his face with the rough edge of his sleeve. "I accept your consolation with a humble heart. Now, go. Go and fight for the little good left in this world."

Zavik offered a frown of a smile, gave Konar one last nod, and trudged into the woods with short, dragging strides. A shadow emerged and followed him into the darkness. The Orillon stray, always lingering just out of earshot, if not closer, ever armed, ever alert, keeping Zavik in reach the way a wolf waited for its targeted prey to wander from the safety of its herd.

Konar's eyes narrowed. Deceit surrounded that one. He'd sensed it the first day the backhander appeared in Agaas, breathing down the back of Zavik's neck and studying the city layout with an aloof interest that only made him all the more culpable.

"Better wise up to the company you keep, lad," Konar murmured, though Zavik was long gone.

A gust of wind slammed the door shut behind him, as clear a sign as any that he needed some fresh air himself. He followed the overgrown path around the refuge and popped out on the side of the structure overlooking the ocean. A crude bench stood sentry, bleached by the sun and weathered by gods knew how many nights of raging storms and heavy mists. He sat. Plucked an insect's dried remains off the wood.

No. If he saw the boy again, which he very much doubted, he would not be the same. But Zavik was important, especially to Elaysia, and she needed to be reminded of it before it was too late. No one could better fulfill that duty than Konar. She needed the wisdom he'd withheld, insights only he could share, and a reminder of the scale and gravity of the situation.

Even if it meant his death.

Konar waited a fortnight before breaking his promise to Zavik. Enough time to convince himself he'd tried to uphold it, but not so long that it weakened his resolve to do what needed to be done. He wended his way through the deepest part of the woods, where the cool air was heavy with must, and one could wear the scent of moss like perfume. By the time he reached the edge of base camp, dusk had fallen. There, he waited, as he had every night since Zavik departed. And soon, she appeared.

Elaysia descended the ramp from Agaas under the cover of darkness, her hooded cloak shrouding her figure. It likely fooled the average passerby, but Konar recognized the way she moved, spotted the mended tear in the fabric from one of her late-night escapades years prior, when the cloak still trailed well past her feet.

Back when she trusted him.

He burrowed further into the shrubs as she skirted the base camp barrier, drawing his own hood about his face. His mouth craved the taste of his pipe, the calm of its leaves.

You will confront her with a clear mind, he chided himself.

He drew a steadying breath, then glanced back up to locate Elaysia.

Only there was no one to locate.

Unlike the nights prior, where she'd darted through the woods with a nytak's grace on the same route to the old Igtheos refuge, halting at the tree line overlooking the cliff to spy on *him*—or so she thought—she'd vanished.

Konar's feet were doubling back to the refuge before he even made the conscious decision to retreat, over sprawling ferns and fallen logs sinking into the forest floor. He wasn't as nimble anymore, not since he'd resorted to using beasts exclusively in his rituals, but his legs were sturdy, his footing strong.

Until it wasn't.

The root must've been disguised beneath the carpet of greenery smothering the ground, and it'd found its way over the tip of Konar's nytak-skin slipper, netting his foot like a salmon as the rest of him went hurtling forward into the darkness. A branch scraped his cheek as he fell, though it was mild compared to the final impact. Skull met stone with a sickening *crack*.

Konar lay there for a moment, stunned, his face smothered by the mossy ground. His first thought was how terribly ironic it was for his head to locate the one rock within the immediate vicinity. The second was that his right hand was *in* something and, worse, that something was crawling on it. He pushed himself up with his left hand, simultaneously jerking his right hand free from the confines of its rotten prison: a fallen log smothered in fungi. The moons withheld much of their light in the forest's belly, so Konar squinted into the caved-in log to confirm he'd removed the culprit. Before he'd finished his investigation, however, something pricked his hand. A small, red spider skittered down his leg and back into the safety of the log.

It moved fast, but even in the scant light, Konar still registered the dark crossed-bone marking on its back.

A widow-maker.

He drew the trembling hand to his chest. The only signs of assault were two small pinpricks, just below his middle knuckle. For the time being, it looked like any other spider bite, but within minutes, there'd be muscle cramps and spasms, followed by chills, fever, nausea, and vomiting. He'd get headaches. Likely go into shock, if not a seizure. Assuming he didn't pass out before all that.

And in a few hours, he'd be dead. For someone his age—rather, someone his presumed age—it was almost a guarantee. The widow-maker venom targeted the heart.

Already, the skin around the bite burned. There was a cure, a paste concocted from a local weed that when mixed with part of the spider and aided by nevethium increased the likelihood of survival. But the spider was long gone.

Unless there was a nest hidden somewhere in the rot, a favorite place of the females. He reached his hand back inside the log and tore away a chunk of bark as long as his forearm. All manner of insects spilled out into the night, wriggling on the carpet of decay. Ants, grubs, beetles. A shudder seized Konar as he peered closer. There, tucked in the shadows of the log and guarding a sizable nest, was a widow-maker, much larger than the one that had bitten him. It raised its barbed front legs as if taunting him.

Konar kept his gaze on his antidote as he felt along the inner layer of his cloak for something to trap it with. His hand swelled with heat, and he blinked to clear his blurring vision. The spider waited, motionless.

"I thought you'd given up creeping."

Konar tensed at the sound of Elaysia's voice. He glanced over his shoulder—a motion that required far more effort than it should've—and was surprised to find only one pair of boots.

She hadn't come to kill him, then. How fitting he'd already taken care of that for her.

"I thought you'd given up late night escapades." It was the wittiest response he could manage with his muddle of a mind laced with venom, and probably his last.

"We never really change, do we?" Elaysia moved into his line of sight, stopping just out of reach, her stance guarded, her cloak pulled back enough to expose the dagger strapped to her hip. "Just become more or less ourselves."

"Or better at stifling the parts of us that don't adhere to moral guidelines."

"I don't think that's one of your strengths."

"I don't suppose it is."

Konar started to rise, but his head swam, obscuring his vision. He returned his gaze to the spider who, by some miracle, remained. Actually, there were two of them now, creeping toward the ring of faint moonlight. Or were there? They blurred together. One moment, two spiders, then the next, only one.

"You don't look well, Former High Elder." The words rolled off Elaysia's tongue free of venom, as though she merely stated a fact.

Konar winced all the same. He drew his legs beneath him and crossed them. It took all his focus to sit upright, hands on his knees, his gaze attentive.

"My diet's been lacking, of late," he said, taking extra care to ensure his voice remained steady. If she knew he was dying, she'd probably wash her hands of him without another word. But if he could pierce her hardened exterior, just for a moment, perhaps she'd stay long enough to hear him out.

"Harder to come by innocent souls when you're isolated." This time, there was an undeniable bite in her tone. "But does it give you the same thrill to carve out fish hearts?" She kneeled beside him, a curdled expression on her face, as if she could smell the stench of death festering inside his hand. "Not going to defend yourself?" she whispered. "Did you not come here to beg for my forgiveness one last time?"

The pain in Konar's hand ceased as numbness set in. A glance down confirmed it'd already swelled to twice its regular size, and now the sensation spread up his forearm, teasing the edge of his elbow. He instinctively tucked it behind him. Despite the cool night air and the breeze tugging at his clothes, a line of sweat trickled down his forehead and collected in his beard.

The spider. Where was she? He peered into the log and found no movement, only evidence of former residents. A maze of webs with little skeletal carcasses dried up inside.

Elaysia rose with a snort. "I don't know what I expected. Even now, you can't humble yourself."

Konar caught the edge of her cloak. He tried to speak, but his throat began to swell. All he could manage was a groan.

She glared at him as she tugged her cloak free, but then her eyes widened in recognition, her malice slowly giving way to frustrated pity. "What is it? What ails you?"

He used the last of his strength to make a weak gesture at the log with his infected hand.

Elaysia gasped, took his hand in her own. "A widow-maker? Honestly, Konar, there were better ways to get my attention." She thrust his hand back onto his lap like the lifeless slab it was. "The spider, where is it?"

He shrugged. At least, he thought he did. He wasn't sure his body listened to his commands any longer. Shadows ebbed at the edge of his vision.

Something stung his cheek like a dozen hornets. He traced the sensation to Elaysia. Her hand was raised, ready for another slap.

"I swear to Khiev-Tatamic himself, if you die *this* way after everything..."

Konar leaned against the log, distantly registering the rot caving beneath him.

"Where's that fucking spider?!"

Everything was warm. So warm. If he shut his eyes for a moment, just to rest, it would be...just a moment...

"Never mind. Zavik might have some antidote left in his loft. If we..."

Slap.

Slap, slap.

"Stay with me, Konar, dammit! Stay!"

The forest faded, and Konar with it.

Light raged against Konar's eyelids. He scrunched them tighter together and raised his hand to shield his face.

Instead of receiving a moment of reprieve, however, the light still penetrated. A chain of fear coiled around his heart, but he silenced it, lowered his arm, and told himself he was oversensitive to the light. He would need to wait a moment to open his eyes anyhow, given the layer of crust covering them.

He drew a shallow breath, then another, repeating the motion deliberately, as though it wouldn't occur on its own as it had for centuries. The air smelled of ink and smoke, with a hint of sweet wine. Voices carried on outside of whatever room held him, then they floated away, leaving only the sound of a nearby crackling fire in their place. He sensed another presence in the room, and though they didn't seem threatening, he didn't like the way they continued silently observing after he'd come to.

Konar cleared his throat. His right arm weighed heavy on his stomach, but not heavy enough, not as heavy as it had been, not enough to silence the war drum pounding in his head. He tried to curl his fingers around the blanket weighing him down. They refused to comply.

"It helps if you acknowledge it isn't there before opening your eyes. At least, that's what my eudna told me when he came back marred from battle."

A knot formed at the base of Konar's throat. Maseeya. He'd not heard her voice in moons, not seen her face in what felt like an eternity. The sting of tears pooled in his still-closed eyes, and he clenched his eyelids tighter, as though he could squeeze the drops out of them like wringing out a wet cloth.

"It's alright, to be upset," Maseeya continued, her voice drenched in pity. "I'm sorry for your loss, though part of me thinks you deserve it." She inhaled sharply, and Konar could perfectly visualize the regret on her face. "I shouldn't have said that. Wishing ill on others only poisons oneself." A pause, then, "You should try to open your eyes now."

Konar gave a reluctant nod. The first thing he registered was a blur of orange, which soon crystallized into a fire roaring in a pit that wasn't his own. It was too small, unevenly stacked with sharp edges from stones that'd never been polished or secured in place, and a thick, gray layer of dust covered the meager stack of wood piled beside it. The feel of the blanket against his skin was rough with vibrant colors, not the softened wool he'd taken for granted in his old quarters. Beside the fire, a table with uneven legs and dangerously sharp corners leaned leftward. Atop that, a dried-up jar of ink void of a quill, and a cup of water.

Konar blinked slowly as he processed his surroundings. He was near certain he resided in Zavik's loft. At least, it once had been—the lad had likely been relocated to the High Tree since obtaining his new position. How appropriate to store the former high elder in his replacement's humble loft.

But that also meant Elaysia hadn't let him die in the forest. She'd not just spared him, but tracked down the anti-venom, secured the talents of a healer, and discreetly stowed him in Agaas so he could recover. And, according to the roaring fire, along with his relatively fresh linens and Maseeya's presence, someone had been assigned to attend to him all hours of the day and night.

Did Elaysia again care for his well-being? A wave of shame rolled over him, a sensation he'd once silenced with a shift of his mindset. Now it commanded him.

But no. He supposed it wasn't care. It was caution. Criminals such as him couldn't be left unattended, crippled or not.

He snaked his right hand into the folds of his robes, searching for the comforting familiarity of Karliah's doll. It was halfway inside when he registered a throbbing heat blooming up his forearm. He stiffened in hopes it'd stop the pain, then slowly withdrew his hand...no...his...

"Konar."

The fire cast a warm glow over Maseeya's face, softening her already round features. She'd wound her long, dark hair streaked with gray tightly atop her head, accenting her wood-carved earrings in the shape of sun-blood blossoms. A gift, he recalled, Annalee had requested of Elishon for her dearest friend. Maseeya stroked one of the earrings, as if reading Konar's mind. Fine lines etched in her brow even as she stared at him motionless, face at rest, her lips gently parted.

Konar forced his gaze down to his injury and was grateful to find it wasn't as gruesome as he'd built up in his head. A stump where his right hand had been, wrapped tightly in clean linens, no blood seeping through, no foul odor assaulting his nostrils. It felt like his hand was still there, though, as if he could summon it back into existence by sheer willpower.

An illusion, like much of his life.

"It *is* the least I deserve," he whispered. He swung one leg out of the cot, then the other, taking care to balance tenderly on the edge should his head rebel against him. "What does she want from me?"

"I don't think she knows." Maseeya retrieved the cup from the table and brought it to his lips. Tea, much cooler than he usually preferred, but a gift from the gods on his tongue, nonetheless. "She never really wanted you dead. I know that much. Perhaps the question is what do you want from her?"

Konar drained the cup and thanked her with a nod. For a moment, he sensed a tenderness between them, one that could've been more, should've been more, had he ever acted on it. But then it was gone, replaced with the protectiveness of a mother whose child was threatened. Konar respected her for it. In all his years, he'd yet to come across another woman as wise as Maseeya.

"I need to share the rest of my knowledge with her," he said finally.

"Just tell me. I will pass it along."

Konar shook his head. "It's more than a single conversation. The information can't simply be repeated or even condensed onto ink and parchment. I need to show her, Maseeya. She's running headstrong into a battle that she *will* lose without guidance."

A spark flew out of the fireplace and landed at the foot of the cot, charring the blanket.

Such a short life, Konar mused. *As it should be.* Everything was made to be renewed, reborn, but not prolonged.

A sigh escaped Maseeya's lips as she left his side. "I'll talk to her. If she agrees to meet, it will be on her terms. Do you understand?"

Konar nodded, not daring to tarnish his chance with unnecessary words.

A chill seeped into the room as Maseeya cracked the door. She lingered in the entryway, small wisps of stray hairs dancing around her face as she clutched the door handle.

"I know why you did it," she said, voice thick with emotion. "But I must know this. If you could go back in time and stop it, would you? Annalee was a good person, Konar. The fiercest and kindest woman I ever had the pleasure of knowing. And Elishon, he loved you like a father." Her eyes glistened with unshed tears. "Surely, you can see the error of your ways."

"I..."

Konar pushed aside the lies, the simple responses curated to achieve optimal results, and looked inward. Yes, he regretted it, had every moment since he'd received confirmation it'd happened as he ordered. He hated the nightmares, the pain, watching Elaysia grow up with a burden he could've prevented, knowing that, had he been more aware, he could've prevented the unnecessary death of Annonitus.

But Konar had also come to accept that things happened as they should. If someone had to play the sinister role in events that would unfold regardless, then it should be *he* who carried the guilt, who lived with sleepless nights, whose every waking moment was bombarded with the regret of his own existence.

For who was to say some other chief wouldn't have acted similarly? There was dissent in Agaas even back in Elishon's time, and he had no shortage of enemies. It could've transpired then, far before the players aligned as he'd intended.

Things happen as they should. He had to believe that.

Konar returned his attention to Maseeya. "Who am I to rewrite time, to speculate what the gods have willed? I regret it every day. I always will, and I don't deny there's a special form of Haeshol awaiting me. But I can't promise I would change it, Maseeya. We are where we are today because—"

The door slammed.

No tears would grace Konar with release, so he turned to the fire and begged it to consume his soul.

ZAVIK

"**P**recisely how many cocks does one need to suck to gain permanent residence in one of these palaces? I'm not saying I'd do *anything*, but I'd wager the view from that balcony would be worth suffering a fat lord or two." T'Vak let out a shrill whistle for emphasis, just in case the past ten minutes he'd spent glorifying every single 'palace' they'd passed by wasn't confirmation enough. "Whaddya say, Zavvie boy? Between you and me, we ought to satisfy most anyone's fantasies."

Between you and me, how about never? Zavik's mind screamed as his insides constricted. But all he managed to get out was a clipped, nervous laugh.

He could forgive his friend's lack of discretion under such circumstances, though. The golden-domed roofs of the nobles' homes were a sight to behold, stark against the flawless blue sky like painted flames and shimmering where the spiral-patterned gems caught the sunlight. Latticed shutters adorned the windows, and every home was at least two stories high with wide, rounded balconies. Kuza guarded the courtyards—every home had at least one of those, too—their uniquely colored head wraps and embroidered patches signifying the great houses or individuals they served. The air was rich with the fragrant aroma of snap flowers alongside the sweet, spiced char of cooking meats. And it was quiet. So quiet. Only the occasional chatter of passing nobles and the trickle from a fountain in the adjacent courtyard.

Zavik loved it, and he hated that he did.

Anahi placed a hand on both Zavik's and T'Vak's shoulders, steering them back into a cobbled street that was marvelously clear of feces. "You two act as though you didn't grow up in Munskahan."

"Oh, we grew up in Munskahan," T'Vak said, shrugging her off. "Just not your version of it." He spat dead-center in the street, much to a passing noble's dismay. "Which of these humble abodes belongs to your family? The one with ten kuza stationed out front? Or are you the unfortunate sort who could only afford two?"

"Do you miss it here?" Yerakai cut in, saving Anahi from another volley of T'Vak's sarcasm. The Apáasutai nyrian stood out more than Zavik in Munskahan, and he'd exercised little effort in hiding his features, which resulted in a slew of eyes on them at all times. The nobles, to their credit, looked on more out of fascination than disgust.

Anahi lifted her shoulder in a half shrug. "It's home."

Zavik fell in behind the members of his party, happy to be ignored and left alone with his thoughts. So far, the walk had been quite pleasant. The heat was forgiving—for Orillon, anyway—and the vibrantly colored canopies provided shade on the right side of the street. They'd avoided the main thoroughfares of the city by utilizing an exclusive gated entrance Anahi gained access to with the flash of a ring she'd never displayed prior. She'd popped the dazzling specimen out from her armor, showcased what was presumably her house seal to a perturbed kuza, and then they were through, traipsing down streets Zavik had only dreamed about as a child. The ease of entry almost made the journey from Neharem to Orillon by boat worth it.

Almost.

T'Vak stopped abruptly, shattering Zavik's contemplation. It took grinding the heels of his boots into the ground to avoid slamming into the backhander's backside.

"Excuse you," Zavik began, but Anahi silenced him with a glare.

"*This* is your dwelling?" Yerakai asked, his mouth agape.

Zavik looked up and drew a sharp breath. The home towering above them was a palace in every sense of the word, a sprawling splendor that made the buildings they'd strolled past on the way appear little more than the residences of common folk. Its towering spires, adorned with nevethium and other precious jewels, pierced the sky, casting a dazzling array of colors on the street. The ten-foot walls encasing the courtyard were covered with intricate mosaics, depicting scenes of epic battles and mystical beings like a winged ox and a goddess with six arms. Vines grew up over the walls and intertwined themselves in the lyvium gates.

T'Vak let out his most obnoxious whistle thus far, one that drew a look of irritation from an otherwise understanding Yerakai. "Holding out on us, eh?" he asked Anahi with a wry smile.

"No one asked." Anahi's attention was wholly fixated on the handful of kuza guarding the palace perimeter. She marched a few steps closer, then, catching the eye of a tall, muscle-hardened man missing his left ear (and what appeared to be most of his good humor), hesitated.

"Halt in the name of House Undali," the kuza commanded. His voice had the cadence of a calculating man, one who'd remain calm in the face of chaos but chop off your head without delay, should he deem it necessary. "Speak your business or vacate the premises."

Anahi lowered the silken shawl covering her head. "It's me, Hallahd."

The kuza's brown eyes narrowed in suspicion as he marched away from his post, then widened upon drawing nearer to Anahi. "Ani? Is that you?"

"Still swinging," she said, closing the distance between them. "Looks like all those lessons were worthwhile."

A grin broke across the kuza's— Hallahd's—face, revealing an assortment of white and gold teeth. "I told your faja you needed protection from no man. You'd have your taste of the world and come back when you were ready, I said." He looked her over with a gaze that was both brotherly and protective. "And look at you, strong and alert as ever."

Anahi reached for his hand, but he drew her into a bone-crushing embrace. To Zavik's awe, she didn't resist. When she pulled away a moment later, a seriousness had settled over her face. "How is he?"

Hallahd stroked his thick beard as his gaze meandered upward. "He's well in health. His spirit weighs heavy with affairs, but your presence will lighten it." His nostrils widened as he took in Zavik and the others, the way a predator might assess if certain prey was worth expending energy on. "These are your companions?"

"Partners. They are good people and welcome in our home."

Hallahd's down-turned face suggested they were, in fact, not welcome, but he motioned for the other kuza to open the gate.

T'Vak nudged Zavik forward with an elbow to the ribs. He hurried after Yerakai and kept his gaze down as they passed through the gate and into the courtyard. Manicured grasses flourished on either side of the pathway with golden snap flowers clustered throughout, their toothy petals twitching ever so slightly as flies buzzed around their sweet nectar. Ahead, the path curved around a mosaic-tiled fountain in the shape of a star.

Zavik hesitated as the others followed Hallahd up the palace steps. It felt wrong to be surrounded by such finery when he'd spent the earliest years of his childhood begging for scraps and stealing things alongside the other ferrets for Lanston just a few miles away. He took a seat on one of the benches surrounding the fountain, deciding he'd just as well enjoy a moment of solitude while waiting for the reunion to conclude. Being back in Orillon still gave him chills. No matter how hard he worked to block out the painful memories, ghosts of them would surface: fleeting memories of his father's raised fist, his mother's chest-rattling coughs, digging through the refuse bins for scraps. Or the other ferrets attacking him on his way to deliver goods to Lanston, making him even more unworthy in his benefactor's eyes. Something deeper and darker clawed out from his most repressed depths, but he refused to acknowledge it.

The sooner he could leave the city, the better.

"Zavik!" Anahi called from the top of the stairs, looking anything but pleased.

With a final glance of longing at the bench, Zavik bounded up the path. Hallahd leveled his own glare of disproval, then ordered the two kuza on guard to heave open the massive palace doors adorned with more mosaics, this time depicting Quorath's three moons.

Inside, Zavik found himself caught in a cool breeze laden with the sweet fragrances of honey and spice as he trod marble floors lined with plush, rust-colored rugs. Tapestries adorned the wall, mostly with geometric patterns, but a few depicted well-endowed men and busty women, or fields ripe for the harvest.

Zavik blushed and followed the others deeper into the palace. It was a veritable labyrinth of corridors and chambers, and he took note of their path in case affairs soured. He didn't fear for Anahi, but his last adventure in Orillon had taught him he was a target for, well, whatever sort of bad people preyed on innocent folk, be it thieves or ancient Vysilliam. He stuck close to T'Vak us they wound past countless rooms—rooms for feasting, rooms for relaxation, rooms for meditation—each more opulent than the last, filled with the finest silks, the softest cushions, and the most sumptuous of furnishings.

They all paled in comparison to their destination: the throne room. Towering columns lined the walls, and a breathtaking mural of the stars and moons ornamented the ceiling. In the center of the room, sparkling like a multi-colored sun, sat two thrones embellished with an array of gems, some of which Zavik had never seen. The spiky black, spidery-looking specimens were particularly eye-catching, but even they were overshadowed by the flawless nevethium crystals glittering at the top of the headrests. A gray-haired man with bronze skin sat erect in the larger throne, his arms positioned stiffly on the armrests, stoic enough to imitate a child's figurine. A woman of the same age and similar coloring sat in a smaller, though no less ornate, throne to his left, and a wall of kuza streamed across the great hall on either side of them.

Zavik cleared his throat; he winced as it bounced off the walls, drawing all the attention he most certainly didn't want.

Brilliant, Zav. Just brilliant.

"You have visitors who wish to pay their respects," Hallahd said, his baritone voice resounding through the hall.

The man on the throne leaned forward, though not enough to disturb his headdress—a rigid cylinder with a crenellated decoration that was at least as tall as his head. He descended the marble steps leading to the thrones, the curved sword strapped to his waist swinging from the motion.

Anahi broke free from the group. As she and the ruler drew near one another, Zavik noted a similarity in their posture, the way both their feet turned out as they strode. They stopped an arm's length apart and stared.

"It's good to see you, Faja."

At Anahi's words, the woman on the throne rose but waited atop the stairs, hands clasped together, hope brimming in her eyes.

"I didn't think you'd ever grace us with your presence again." The man remained rigid and controlled, though emotion choked his words.

"I'm sorry, I—"

Anahi didn't get to finish, for the man pulled her into a fierce hug. The woman ran down the stairs, sobbing, and Zavik took several steps back even though he was already a respectable distance away. A sigh of relief escaped his throat, loosing the tension bottled inside him.

Now for palaver.

"So." Anahi's father, Saya Undali, raised a steaming beverage to his lips. He sipped, nearly set the finely painted ceramic cup down, then took another drink, his golden gaze surveying the visitor sprawled out on his fine cushions. "You don't intend to stay long."

Anahi added more sugar to her tea, swirling the jade spoon with the same delicacy she exhibited in her sword fighting. "The high chieftain expects me back within a fortnight. Our presence and the birds will be missed."

As if summoned, a screech echoed outside. Corvax and Wind Chaser had returned from hunting not long past, much to the displeasure of a nearby cattle raiser who'd lost several of his prized specimens. Saya Undali paid the man double the beasts' worth and required that Anahi's and Yerakai's birds remain in the courtyard for the duration of the visit. Zavik doubted their compliance would last long.

Warm rays filtered into the room through the geometric patterning of the windowless shutters spanning the length of the western wall. An ornately woven golden rug lay beneath the cushion Zavik reclined against, and atop its moon-patterned center rested trays of honey-dipped insects, flaky nut, and sunkiss rolls, and a variety of spiced teas and moskuto. The latter was an Orillon specialty made from roasting the beans of the mosku plant, which resulted in a bitter and acidic beverage. Zavik hadn't had the luxury of trying it prior (he'd only been eight when he and his mother stole away to Neharem in hopes of a better life), but he immediately took a strong liking to its rich profile. Given the antsy feeling overtaking his legs and the jitters in his heart, he could easily fight through deepest exhaustion to study with a cup or two by his side.

Anahi's mother, Sayetta Undali, sat cross-legged on a cushion beside her daughter, her finely sculpted eyebrows bunched together. Kohl accented eyes of the richest brown. If not for the fine lines sketched across her face and the fog-colored hair hanging in ringlets around her shoulders, Zavik wouldn't have assumed her to be much older than Anahi. She reached for her daughter's hand and gripped it fiercely.

"Why come back if you don't intend to stay?" Saya Undali said as he dabbed his face with a napkin embroidered with golden thread, careful to not disturb the finely braided beard that ran the length of his neck down to his chest. It alone was thicker than all the hair Zavik could grow on his scalp and face combined, and that said nothing of the saya's hair, which was twice as thick and nearly as long.

Anahi's free hand crumpled the fabric of her cushion. "Must I have a reason to visit my loved ones?"

Saya Undali snorted. "Apparently. That's why you've refused to grace us with your presence for over a decade, is it not?"

T'Vak hiccupped, divulging the wine he'd been sneaking sips of when gazes were drawn elsewhere. He tucked the wineskin back into his tunic with no attempt at discretion.

Yerakai rebuked him with a look, then faced Saya Undali. "If I may have the honor of addressing you, Saya, I'd be more than happy to discuss the ways Agaas could compensate you, should you aid our cause."

Saya Undali frowned. "There's only one way you could repay my temporary—or potentially permanent—loss of kuza, and I doubt your high chieftain is willing to part with it."

A servant crept into the room to replenish the food and drink, keeping her silk-wrapped head bowed as though she could sense the simmering tension. Yerakai bit his dark violet lip and sought Zavik's gaze, to which Zavik offered a weak shrug. Nevethium was no longer something to be negotiated with. There was no chance Elaysia would condone sacrificing it, thereby giving up something Agaas fought to protect in the first place.

"Am I not entitled to some of the family's wealth?" Anahi asked, her voice rising. "I'll pay for the use of your men, Faja. Take it out of my inheritance."

"Does a coyote relinquish its alpha status to a long-lost pup when another has stayed by his side, learning his ways?" Saya Undali made a *tsk* sound with his tongue. "Your brother will inherit your share, unless you care to dedicate the rest of your life to House Undali's affairs."

"I am the eldest," Anahi said through clenched teeth.

"Then act like it."

Anahi shoved a roll into her mouth and chewed it with no shortage of aggression.

"Besides," Saya Undali continued, "your inheritance is irrelevant. I'm aware of events unfolding in the north and east. Unless nevethium is part of the exchange, you will find no help here."

"Then we're done here." Anahi sprang up from her cushion and motioned for Zavik and the others to follow. "There are other houses." She bent to kiss her mother's cheek. "Be good to yourself, Maja."

"You'll sooner fly than find aid elsewhere," Saya Undali muttered, fixing her with a scowl.

"I'll find myself doing both sooner than you think, and without your help. Thank you for the nourishment, Faja. It's the one thing I can always count on you for."

"Anahi, wait." Sayetta Undali rose, her hands fastened in a plea. "There is a way to satisfy both parties without nevethium."

Saya Undali's and Anahi's heads snapped to face her. "How?" they asked in unison.

A hopeful smile spread across Sayetta Undali's face. "Your brother's betrothed has perished from the desert bite."

A silence fell over the room as Zavik stitched a theoretical story together in his mind. Anahi was the ruling heir, who'd run off for...personal reasons not yet obvious to Zavik...and her younger brother had stepped up in her place. He'd likely been betrothed to another great house's heir to secure a powerful union. Logical.

Desert bite, however, was rare among nobles. Zavik hadn't heard of the fatal disease spreading into the well-to-do districts, which raised a myriad of questions not relevant to his situation. What *was* relevant was the fact that this younger brother of

Anahi was now without a betrothed, and the only union better than joining with another great house was joining with a great nation. And Elaysia wasn't spoken for.

From an unbiased, rational perspective, it made sense. From a subjective, emotional one, his heart told him she'd sooner die defending Agaas alone.

"Where is Vahid?" Anahi remained rooted near the door, her body angled toward it with her head cocked to face her mother.

Sayetta Undali twisted a honeyed insect thoughtfully in her fingers. "He will return from his former–betrothed's burial this evening. What say you, Saya Undali?" She studied Anahi's father as she popped the insect into her mouth. "Surely, such an allegiance would benefit both our house and Agaas?"

Before he could respond, T'Vak rose in a yawning stretch and said, "I say lovely plan, and where, in such a fine palace, can one take a piss?"

As a disgruntled servant led T'Vak from the room, Anahi caught Zavik's gaze and raised an eyebrow, her lips drawn into a thin line that seemed to question whether such an arrangement would work.

Zavik forced a nod before his conscience could get the better of him. Agaas needed allies, and he had to believe Elaysia would do anything to save it. Even this.

Maybe.

"If Vahid will consider it, so will we," Anahi told Saya Undali. "Though, I can't speak for our high chieftain. Zavik will send a tuross to her tonight, if we receive Vahid's consent."

Saya Undali's down–turned face appeared oddly pleased. "He should have little reason to refuse, unless some disfigurement plagues the girl."

As the room cleared, Zavik wrestled with the sinking feeling that he was once again the bearer of bad news, and that he'd yet again failed Elaysia.

At least this time it stung a little less.

LUMIRA

Lumira couldn't shake the chill coiled around her muscles.

The southernmost tip of the forested Apáasutai territory wasn't as deep or dense as the old growth surrounding Agaas, but it was still cooler and more foreboding than the tropical forests she'd once called home. She padded silently across a moss-covered log, the footsteps of her companions deadened by the hum of insects and the occasional scurry of small animals through the brush. A ceiling of branches loomed above, reaching out to her like skeletal fingers, casting strange shadows that danced with each whisper of wind. They blocked her view of the sky and gave the forest air a stifling stagnancy that altered her perception of time. And without the stars, she felt all but directionless. If not for the Apáasutai trackers accompanying her party, she likely would've led her warriors astray, though she was no longer certain that would've been the worst scenario. She couldn't shake the feeling that something was watching her, waiting to pounce from the shadows. Every fiber of her being screamed at her to leave.

And a year past, she would've done just that.

"But then you got attached," she muttered, dancing around some nytak droppings.

"I did what?"

Lumira's ears flattened as she glanced over her shoulder at Xaren. The little sneak had crept up beside her—not the easiest of tasks—meaning he'd caught her off guard. Meaning she'd sacrificed her superior senses to wallow in her inferior feelings.

Meaning she needed to snap out of it or else she'd bring their moon-cursed mission to an end before it even began.

"Did I begin that sentence with, 'Listen closely, dear slaver child?'" she hissed.

Xaren blinked, his deep brown eyes far more amused than hurt by her sarcasm. A smile revealed the dimples in his cheeks. "You're rarely so eloquent."

Lumira bared her teeth and pressed on, the ground spongy and damp beneath her feet as she stirred up the sharp scent of coniferous sap mixed with the musty smell of decaying leaves. She had no vigor for banter. It was as though the mission literally weighed on her chest, making it hard to breathe. Every sound she made seemed amplified, clumsy and stupid for her kind, from the crunching of leaves underfoot to the scrape of her spear against stray foliage. She sought Grokhion's monstrous frame in the line of the four dozen warriors that trailed her and Xaren, allowing a hint of a smile to grace her lips when their gazes met. He raised his war ax, *Belzaith*, like a chalice in a toast. Her heartbeat slowed as the reassurance of her kin settled over her.

It would be alright. As long as they were together, they were unstoppable.

"You think the birds are faring well?" Xaren asked as he fought to keep pace with her, his shorter, wiry legs working up to a slow jog. "I know Shadow understands me, and I think he'll listen and stay back with the others, but there was a look in his eyes. It was the same look my mother had when they drafted me into the All-Sovereign's army. Like she..." The boy's nose wrinkled, as though he couldn't locate the proper Nyrinian word.

Lumira touched the arrowheads adorning her necklace. "Like she hated that she couldn't walk with you every step of your life."

Xaren's eyes brimmed with understanding. "Your mother looked at you the same?"

"Never." A lump formed in Lumira's throat. She swallowed it, then forced her mind to the task at hand.

Until recently, Elaysia had practiced leniency, ordering her warriors to the defensive, sending Raynar and his allies pleading tuross messages, offering to give more, compromise more, be more—all with hopes of securing an armistice. But a moon cycle's worth of assaults against the innocuous Kahaloán and the hard-pressed Moákun had hardened the high chieftain's heart, and the near-annihilation of a small Apáasutai village—the one their mission centered on—was the final shove over the cliff that was Elaysia's empathy. When the northern Lautei clan responsible for the attack agreed to hold a peace conference, she ordered Lumira's band to travel under the pretense of accepting whatever outlandish demands they made. For before their departure, Elaysia pulled Lumira aside and gave her one command: kill the Lautei clan leader. Send them the message Agaas would no longer stand by waiting for more innocents to be slaughtered. No longer were they above retaliation.

An ember of Lumira's conscience stirred, recalling the details.

She crushed it. The backhander in her took over, the way a storm usurped the sky.

As the trees became more dispersed, exposing a small clearing ahead, Lumira held up her hand to warn the rest of her party to stay put. She waited for Jakki to shove past her, angling for an opportunity to spite her or impress Elaysia or moons knew what, but the nyrian held her position without offering so much as a look of disdain. Lumira recalled Jakki's similar disposition the night of the temple assault. The night they'd failed—she'd failed—and nearly lost Elaysia forever.

Tonight wasn't like that. Not half the risk or stakes. Just a simple gathering with the clan leader to arrange a fake peace treaty and maybe recoup some wounded captives before she slit his throat. But as Lumira stepped out from the concealment of the tree line, her heart skipped a beat all the same.

The path to the village was well worn, a mashing of dead grass and mud with some footsteps still visible from the recent rain. No fence encircled the settlement, but its boundaries were clear enough. Roughly fifteen huts surrounded a communal building, and from a distance, it would've looked to the average human or nyrian as though it were merely a community at rest.

A beridian's vision didn't allow for such erroneous judgment. Lumira's sapphire eyes widened as her pupils dilated, taking in the singed walls and charred thatched roofs, some of which leaned drunkenly, as if a malevolent force had twisted them. She hesitated a few feet outside the village, tail twitching, nostrils widening. Amid the musty scents of the land, she detected remnants of smoke, of decay. Any other signs of struggle had been long since cleansed, the weapons repurposed, the bodies disposed of, the blood scrubbed away by sheets of rain. Still, the unmistakable ghost of death lingered about the ruins, its gnawing silence eating the memories of the unfortunate souls in its grasp, never again to dance in the moonlight.

The fur on Lumira's back raised. An abandoned village only meant one thing. She'd expected a trap, but not prior to discourse. She'd warned Elaysia before departing Agaas that the violent attack on a bordering village was simply a means to lure them there, but she hadn't pushed the issue. Ever since her spineless escape to Talza after the high chieftain's capture, she'd done everything in her power to redeem herself in Elaysia's eyes, in her own, and reining in her naysaying seemed the best way to show support.

And now she paid for her silence.

Her gaze flicked to the opposite end of the clearing, to a dense cluster of logs the villagers had likely once stockpiled for firewood. A shimmering pair of eyes the color of embers stared back at her, just beyond the logs, nestled in the dark of the forest, peering through the anonymity of the branches. She adjusted the grip on her spear, ready to attack if provoked, but the eyes just continued to stare, unblinking.

A tickle stirred in her throat, though she didn't dare swallow. Whatever loomed beyond the log pile wasn't a beast, as clever as its eyes were, and the way it waited, locked onto her presence, but with restraint, almost as though toying with her, beckoning her closer, sent a chill down her spine. Despite their concealment, the eyes betrayed no fear.

Then they vanished.

Lumira cut through the clearing, hugging the perimeter of the village as she went, as though the shadows might mask her painfully exposed approach. She was a spear's throw away from the logs when she halted. Her body reacted to the threat long before her mind, and her claws dug into the soil like a tree stretching its roots to strengthen its foundation. She crouched, body tingling with anticipation, tongue salivating from some ancestral tendency to associate extreme tension with an impending meal.

Thwack.

An arrow lodged itself in the hut not two inches from her head. She sank even lower, thanking the moon goddesses for giving her a body that cared more about her well-being than her heart did. Another arrow whirred past, and this time a scream followed, though she couldn't decipher if it was a cry of pain or anger. They were often the same. She dove behind the opposite side of the hut and cast a glance back toward the woods where her party waited.

One of her warriors—she couldn't assess his tribe from the distance, but the moonlight accenting the nyrian white of his hair was unmistakable—kneeled just beyond the perimeter of the village, his hand clutching his stomach. An arrow protruded from his back like a blood-soaked spine. Mardus raced out from the tree line and began dragging the warrior back to safety until an arrow to the calf brought him down with an agonized yell. The stocky human shielded his nyrian ally with his body.

A snarl scraped Lumira's throat as she abandoned the safety of the hut. Mardus was closer to the sanctuary of the forest than she was to him, but she ran anyway, narrowly evading another arrow, this one flying in from the left instead of behind her.

Lovely. And I bet they're on the right, too.

The next projectile came from straight ahead, soaring over Lumira toward the other end of the clearing. Her gaze went to a cluster of warriors peeking out from the branches like fowl ripe for the taking.

"Stay there!" she shouted as she bared down on Mardus. She scrabbled for commands more fitting of a war chief as she flinched from arrows both real and imagined. "Hold back or you'll meet your gods sooner than you'd—"

The words died on her tongue as her warriors poured out of the woods like a herd of nytak pursued by a ryptan. She didn't have to wait long to see the motivation behind their reckless abandonment of shelter: Atsukut warriors stampeded out on their tails, brandishing giant toothed clubs and other two-hand-ed weapons only those of their superior stature could swing. Some rode out on mounts twice the size of a nytak buck, some-thing not too distant from that bloodline, but far fiercer. The enormous stags had thick, muscular necks that sloped down to equally powerful chests. Long, sturdy legs plowed forward with incredible speed and agility, some running Lumira's warriors down with ease and trampling them beneath the bulk of their massive frames. One met her gaze as it stomped an Apáasutai human into the ground with its serrated hooves, its eyes a deep, blood red, glowing in the darkness with breath-taking intensity.

Lumira reached Mardus just before one of the monstrous stags gored him. She yanked him out of the way, but the nyrian he'd tried to save wasn't so lucky. The stag lowered its jagged antlers at the wounded warrior, piercing his chest with sharp, hooked barbs that ripped apart more flesh upon their exit. Lu-mira sucked in a breath as the warrior's stomach tore away, leaving a gaping hole of exposed innards and gore. The stag emitted a guttural bugle and turned toward its next victim, which—thank the moons—was not in their direction.

Mardus struggled against her grip, straining toward the disemboweled warrior whose spirit no longer inhabited their world. She slapped him in the face.

"Save your strength," she hissed, gripping her spear. "Stay close to me. We'll fight our way out of this."

Mardus's brow furrowed, but he heaved himself up, taking care to place less weight on his wounded leg, and raised his club.

Lumira spun just as a Lautei charged from the woods, two warriors on his tail. She threw her spear at the nearest, pinning him to the ground through the stomach like a speared fish, then lunged to meet his allies with claws to their throats. The first one crumbled, his long, moss green fingers grasping at his throat, but the second, a woman, tucked and rolled, coming up behind Lumira with a club to the back. Lumira dove away, but not quickly enough to avoid the impact. Air caught in her lungs. She doubled over, grasping for clarity as Mardus clashed clubs with the woman. The battle raged on around her, arrows whizzing past her head as stags let out unsettling howls.

As she struggled to her feet, she caught sight of a blur darting through the clearing, taking down their enemies with astonishing speed and skill. The ghost warrior slowed for a moment to lock onto her next target, and Lumira recognized the thick, snowy braid cascading down the nyrian's back.

Jakki?

A sharp sting in Lumira's side realigned her focus. Her heart pounded as she dodged the second blow and delivered a swift kick to her opponent's chest. The sound of cracking ribs echoed in her ears, and she couldn't help but smile viciously. She followed it up with a swipe of her claws, and this time, she didn't fight the tingle down her spine or the way the scent of blood and sweat filling her nostrils awakened her.

A cry rang above the battle. Lumira spun to find one of her warriors, a pale, red-haired Daruk man, limping away from a cloaked figure wielding a sleek Az Zarian sword. The ominous figure closed in on the Daruk with swift strides and, before Lumira worked her dry throat into a scream, lopped off his head in a single stroke.

Fire raged in Lumira's chest as she raced toward the cloaked figure, and as she drew nearer, she caught the fiery glint of eyes beneath its hood. The eyes from behind the log pile. The cloaked figure didn't flinch as she approached. Not so much as a twitch of the hand or a shift of the leg. Whomever it was stood a good head taller than her six-and-a-half-foot frame, far taller than the average human or nyrian. She hurled her spear. It hit the sword-wielder in the heart...

And sailed right through.

Lumira's throat constricted. An otherworldly shriek poured out from the hood with an intensity that rivaled a rupturing fire mountain. The figure closed the distance between them with a leap and arced its blade toward her neck. She flipped back, landing on her hands, then sprung back even further, nearly colliding with an Atsukut wearing the yawning, fanged mask of a krizah, one of the solitary feline predators of the north. A dive between his legs swiping up with her claws ended his fertility. Someone drove a staff into his skull before she could finish him off, and she looked up to find Jakki, wide-eyed and panting, standing above her in a stance that was almost protective.

Almost.

Jakki glared and yanked Lumira up by the arm. "We're fucked," she snarled, using her dagger to open the Atsukut's throat. "A few of us can escape and bring word to Agaas, but only at the cost of everyone else's lives."

Lumira cast a weary glance over the clearing. Atsukut and Lautei surrounded her warriors, and for every one of the Lawful Dominion's dead, she counted at least three of her own. Soil clung to her feet, a stomach-riling mixture of dirt, blood, and loosened bowels. A memory pulled at her consciousness, momentarily paralyzing her with the inability of action she felt whenever she—

No. Not now.

She roared, shattering the memory before it could crystalize, and drawing all eyes to her.

She grabbed Jakki by the shoulders. "Go. Take the survivors nearest to you and make for the northwestern corner. It's the least guarded. I'll create a distraction—"

"And let you steal all the glory?" Jakki pointed to the woods with her spear. "You go. I'll hold them back." It wasn't unlike her to want to claim victory, no matter how unlikely the circumstances, but was that a hint of concern in her voice as well?

Still, Lumira refused to surrender her responsibility as war chief. "This isn't up for debate."

Jakki's eyes flashed, and for the briefest moment, a black abyss replaced her golden irises. She shook her head and raced toward the woods, calling warriors to her as she sprinted.

Lumira retrieved a spear from the fallen and drove it into the chest of an incoming assailant. She moved with intent, quieting her emotions, drawing her strength inward as she navigated the battlefield of corpses. Dodge, lunge, swipe. Retrieve another weapon. Use it.

Repeat.

A blade sliced her shoulder. She sunk her teeth into its wielder, ripping away a chunk of flesh just as someone swung a club at her torso.

Crack.

A sickening pain echoed throughout her ribs. She dropped to her knees, taking her enemy down with her. There was no remorse in her heart as she drew her claws over his throat, his eyes, his mouth, over and over, until his entire face was shredded beyond recognition. She rolled onto her side to avoid another incoming blow and glimpsed a small band of her warriors fighting their way out of the clearing. An armored Lautei closed in on an unassuming Jakki, who was already struggling against four Lawful Dominion warriors.

Lumira dragged her aching body toward an abandoned spear. She let it fly, and it hit its target with perfection, dropping the Lautei mere feet from Jakki's exposed backside.

Another blow to the spine all but robbed Lumira of her consciousness. She crawled through the trampled grass, the moon goddesses looking on as she weakly thwarted attacks. When an Atsukut approached wielding a spiked club, Lumira had no fight left to give. She extended her claws in a last attempt at protection, just as an ear-shattering screech pierced the night. A shadow fell over her. Massive talons snatched up the Atsukut as he raised the club to end Lumira's life and bore him deep into the sky.

Anadu.

Lumira's nostrils widened, drawing in dewy air tainted with blood. The stormbird climbed higher, holding the squirming Atsukut captive. Then, when she was a good eighty feet above the clearing, she let go. The Atsukut plummeted with a shriek. He met his end somewhere in the village, beyond the range of Lumira's superior vision. Anadu plucked another victim, this time crushing his skull in her talons and tossing him aside like an unwanted doll.

Her spirit reignited by Anadu's aid, Lumira limped back into the fray, bringing down as many enemies as she could as they fought to prevent her warriors' escape. At least five more Lawful Dominion scum fell prey to her claws. But despite her determination, her body continued to rebel against her, stiffening her movements and shortening her breath.

She crumpled beside a cluster of bodies. Grokhion roared somewhere in the distance, a desperate, angry sound that brought tears to her eyes.

Go, she thought, some part of her hoping he'd sense her words, or at least feel her intent. *This is for you. For them.*

The white hair of the fallen nyrian beside her stirred as Anadu flapped her massive wings and landed beside them. The stormbird locked gazes with her.

"Get on."

Lumira swore she heard the words in her head, though the voice was not her own. She pressed up on her elbows and peered between Anadu's legs. The cloaked figure with the ember eyes was racing toward her with shocking speed. She needed no further prompting.

With a groan, she flung herself onto the stormbird's back. Her muscles spasmed, and she began to slide back down when

Anadu's beak jabbed into her side, nudging her to a balanced position atop her back.

"Hold on."

An arrow sailed overhead as Anadu flapped her wings, silken feathers shining in the moonlight. Lumira wrapped her arms around the stormbird's neck with all the strength she could muster.

And then she flew.

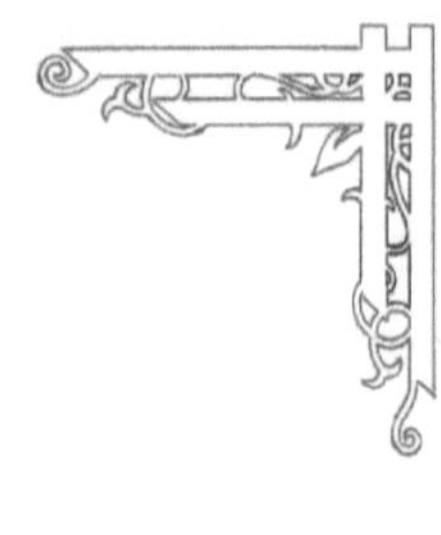

ELAYSIA

The library-door hinges groaned as Elaysia shoved it open, spilling murky afternoon light across the dusty shelves and worn flooring. Memories hit her as soon as she crossed the threshold. The countless lectures, the late nights spent roleplaying council gatherings, the warm days devoted to learning new languages while the other children played—of all her positive moments with Konar, the library held very few. Maybe there weren't even that many to begin with.

She hadn't wanted to meet here, in *his* domain, but he'd insisted he was ready for his first excursion, despite the fact it'd only been a few weeks since his deadly dance with the widow-maker. Kahana had witnessed him leaving Zavik's old loft nearly an hour prior, and Elaysia didn't doubt it had taken him nearly that long to make the journey. She almost pitied him, but the strain he'd put himself through was self-inflicted. And, in a way, the spider poison was, too.

Perhaps there was some justice left in the world.

"Ellie?" he called out from below. "Is that you?"

She slammed the door shut behind her in response.

"I'll be right up." He sounded weary.

She wouldn't let herself care.

The sound of a chair sliding echoed from the twisted stairwell beneath the open trapdoor, followed by the *thunk* of a journal closing. Elaysia took a seat at the table closest to the main door and crossed her arms. A staleness hung over the library and its grimy shelves, clinging to everything it stored. She'd once loved the smell of it, had long ago found pleasure in the yellowed parchments, in the way the ink stained her fingertips. But now it smelled like him. He'd become the staleness in her life, clinging to her.

And she hadn't the courage to shake him.

A creak on the stairs announced Konar's approach shortly before his head peeked above the trapdoor. Elaysia eased her bow off her shoulder and laid it gently on the table, creating an extra barrier between the two seats. As if there wasn't already enough of a barrier between them.

"You're soaking wet," Konar observed as he struggled up the remaining steps. "I have an extra blanket downstairs, let me—"

"You barely made it up here as is. Don't waste my time with any more of your frivolities."

A thorn of shame latched deep into Elaysia's chest after she spoke, and she did her best to ignore it. She was the high chieftain. He was a traitor. None of their past mattered, nor the authority he once held over her, nor the sway she'd allowed him to have over her decision-making.

Yet, it did.

Konar tripped as he neared the table, grabbing the edge of it just before he went crashing to the ground. Elaysia's hand shot out instinctively to help him. She was glad when he refused. He managed a polite nod as he lowered his trembling body into the seat, then assumed a formal posture, as though they attended a council gathering. He probably couldn't fully shed the demeanor. The position had been his for Khiev-Tatamic knew how long, and even stripped of his title, robes, and beads, he still carried himself as such. She noted the way he covered the stump on his right forearm with his left hand and felt another surge of pity.

This time, she allowed it to linger.

"I've been training again," Elaysia said, wringing some of the excess water out of her braids. "Onitus is almost ready to carry me, and I want to be able to fight alongside our warriors, should the war come to Agaas."

"You're smart to prepare. Always assume the worst." Konar kept his tone neutral, though there was apprehension in his eyes. "Is the training going well?"

"Well enough." There was no point in telling him how difficult it'd been to regain her strength, having only given birth to the twins less than three moons past. The look on his face suggested he knew, anyway.

Konar cleared his throat. "I presume you didn't want to meet with me to discuss something as trivial as your training."

Elaysia gritted her teeth as she retrieved a small, bound parchment from her leather tunic. She tossed it across the table. Konar draped his fingers over it one by one, slowly tightening his grip the way Onitus did when he played with his prey.

"A tuross message." He withdrew his pipe from his robes and set it on the table beside the parchment, then retrieved a piece of flint and lyvium. "Do you mind?" he asked, not quite meeting her gaze. "It helps with the pain."

Elaysia lit the pipe in silence.

Konar inhaled and released a cloud of green-tinted smoke over the table. He eyed the parchment warily. "I'm uncertain whether my involvement in council matters is appropriate any longer. If the chiefs learn of—"

"Just read it," Elaysia snapped.

"As you wish." Konar's eyes widened as his gaze darted over the small strip again and again. When he finished, he pressed it face-down on the table beside Elaysia's bow. "That's quite the offer."

Elaysia couldn't interpret his expression. She snatched the message up and shoved it back into her tunic without bothering to roll it. "Is it enough?"

Konar's brows knit together. "Enough?"

"Don't play games with me." Air hissed out between Elaysia's clenched teeth. "Will my acceptance of this proposal create enough of an upper hand to win this war? You know far more about the great Orillon houses than I do."

"Zavik seems to think so."

"I'm asking you."

The floor creaked as Konar rose. He limped over to a shelf sparsely lined with gems and arrowheads, staring beyond them as if the shelf were a window. "Forgive me for not being caught up with current events, but have we won the last few skirmishes? Where do we stand with this war?"

Tendrils of fear wrapped around Elaysia's spine. "We've lost as many as we've won. And winning is an overstatement. Lumira's band barely survived the last assault. It wasn't even a full-scale battle. When that happens—and it will—we'll…" She fought to keep her mind from spiraling into bad outcomes, each worse than the last. "If they attack with the full strength of their forces, we'll be outnumbered ten to one."

"What of the stormbirds?" Konar adjusted one of the arrowheads, then faced her. "The healer tending to my bandages this morning mentioned Lumira flew. She couldn't stop talking about it."

Elaysia gripped the wooden stormbird pendant hanging from her neck. "They're still too vulnerable to take into battle. Anadu shouldn't have intervened. They haven't even come into their powers yet."

"If Lumira has fully bonded with Anadu," he said, returning to his seat, "then it won't be long before the others follow. If all eight of you took to the skies, you'd be able to target your enemies' weaknesses, pick off their leaders, destroy large weapons—"

"They aren't ready."

"Perhaps you aren't."

Elaysia rose, snatching her bow from the table and slinging it over her shoulder. Why had she even come? Had she really thought he'd give her the answer she so desperately needed?

Her fingers were wrapped around the handle, ready to open the door, when it hit her. She hadn't wanted to meet with him for answers. No. What she sought was something the rest of her advisors couldn't give her.

A parent's approval.

Some part of her still craved his acceptance of her decisions, still wanted him to look at her with that half-smile he so rarely relinquished.

And she hated him for it.

"I'm surprised you aren't in support of the union," she said, releasing her grip on the handle. "The Konar I knew would always suggest practicality over comfort."

"Your comfort has nothing to do with my hesitation." He peered down his still-smoldering pipe at her. Despite his furrowed brow, there was a hint of a smile on his weathered face.

She couldn't help but return it. And it felt good to stop hating him, if just for a moment. Clinging to bitterness was like using the last waterskin in a desert to douse an enemy's campfire. Somehow, the embittered one always suffered more.

Konar used his pipe to gesture to Elaysia's tunic, where she'd tucked the parchment away. "I would ask myself not how happy this arrangement would make me, nor how it might benefit me, but what they'll expect in return. This proposal is more than a union of bodies. It's a union of armies, of wealth, and of nations. They might come to our aid, and we might turn the tides of this war yet. But what will it cost? Not just you, but Neharem?"

A lump formed in Elaysia's throat. The familiar tightening of her chest paralyzed her; the same sensation she always got when hit with an opinion she disliked but couldn't invalidate.

He was right. Of course, he was. He was always right, him and his pessimistic, defeatist, suspicious way of looking at the world.

But...

"What else can I do?" she whispered. The certainty had fled her voice, replaced with the frightened speculation of a child. "The neutral tribes won't take sides, and this is the only way outsiders will put themselves at risk."

Konar twirled the pipe in his left hand with surprising dexterity. "The union is your wisest and only move, High Chieftain. But I think you already knew that. If you still care for my approval, I give it. Just be aware of what spores this fungus will breed."

Elaysia offered a clenched-jaw nod and left the library without another word. She slammed the door behind her, welcoming the rain as it kissed her cheeks in a mist as fine as silk.

"What an utter waste of time," she muttered to herself as her boots slapped the water-slick platform of the High Tree.

But deep down, she knew it wasn't.

And deep down, she felt just a little better.

The mouth-watering aroma of nytak stew drew Elaysia to the gathering table as soon as she cracked the summit lodge doors open. She smoothed back the flyaway strands of hair the rain had plastered to her face as she approached Maseeya, who balanced a twin on each hip and didn't seem the least bit upset by the inconvenience. Kahana stood watch a few paces to her left. Her long whalebone club hung from her belt, the nevethium eye of its stormbird-head handle beaming back at the larger crystal lodged in the gathering table. It had once been customary to leave all weapons outside the summit lodge, but those peaceful ways had fallen victim to ever encroaching war. More and more Agaasians carried protection with them as they went about their daily lives, fearful of unexpected attacks, but also of each other. Agaas was a stew of races, tribes, and loyalties. While Elaysia wanted to think those who remained did so because they believed in her and the Neharem she represented, it wasn't outlandish to assume Raynar had allies in one of the living trees—maybe even in the High Tree. It was why she'd welcomed Kahana's pledge of loyalty.

And why she never unstrapped her grandfather's dagger from her hip.

Elaron fussed as soon as Elaysia took a seat on one of the cushions beside Maseeya. His head bobbed unsteadily on his neck as his eyes widened, his lips working in a sucking motion. Dytana didn't make a sound. Her pudgy fingers clenched into tiny fists, arms moving with the awkward jerkiness of an infant.

Elaysia felt an overwhelming desire to scoop them up in her arms and bury her face in their sweet-smelling heads. Another part of her wasn't ready to have them back. She'd only been away two hours, and there were endless tasks unfinished, gatherings to be held, trades to approve, wounded to visit—gods, she had only visited Lumira once since the beridian flew in, broken but alive thanks to her magnificent bird. And what of her own bird? Onitus hadn't been home in almost two days. Had he finally grown tired of—

Dytana let out a shriek that drowned out Elaron's whimpering. The familiar tingle of milk descending awakened Elaysia's breasts. As usual, the matter had been settled for her. Even as the leader of her nation, she still rarely had true power over her decisions.

"Shh, shh," she whispered, dropping the ties of her tunic. Maseeya had designed special clothing for her to make feeding the twins more accessible, as if she hadn't already done enough by assisting with the night wake-ups, securing milk from other mothers to supplement Elaysia's own, and setting aside nearly all her former duties to be a full-time child-tender.

Elaysia popped a twin on each breast and gave Maseeya a tired smile. "I'd embrace you to thank you, but..." She used her chin to gesture at the infants nestled below.

"Cuddling them is like embracing you ten times over," Maseeya said warmly. "They smell better, too."

Kahana snorted, then masked her slip of demeanor by studying the edges of her club.

"Your sleepless nights have helped you find your humor, I see." Elaysia accepted the shawl Maseeya draped over her shoulders with a kiss on the older woman's cheek. "You must tell me your secret."

"My secret is knowing that children and animals are here to remind us there is good in this world, no matter how terrible things get. They embody divinity. Inspire enlightenment. Only by nurturing them and honoring the innocence lost in ourselves can we find healing. And"—she returned to the cushion beside Elaysia and gave her a wink—"it doesn't hurt that yours are beautiful."

Dytana looked up at Elaysia from beneath long eyelashes as she suckled, then broke away just long enough to coo, as if echoing Maseeya's musings.

"Not everyone will think they are," Kahana said bitterly. She didn't expound further, and she didn't need to. They all knew how parts of Quinaria perceived nymans.

Elaysia better than most.

As the twins' eyelids fluttered between waking and sleeping, Maseeya retrieved Elaron and laid him down on a makeshift cot she'd assembled near the fire. Elaysia placed Dytana beside him, and they curled in toward each other, falling into a slumber with their limbs intertwined.

"Is it unavoidable?" Elaysia whispered as she tucked a thin blanket about their waists.

Maseeya broke off the tune she'd been humming. "Is what?"

Elaysia kissed each babe's downy head, then trudged to the gathering table, where she gathered a handful of cushions and collapsed on a makeshift cot of her own. "War. Or rather, the greed that incites it." She eyed the bowl of stew and found her hunger pangs had vanished, replaced with the twists and cramps of tension. "Are we destined to fall prey to our most primal instincts? To want more and more, driven by the fear of lack, even when there's no threat, thereby causing the very scarcity we dread in the first place?"

Maseeya's warm fingers draped over Elaysia's forearm and gave a gentle squeeze. "Greed isn't primal. The tulek bear doesn't think itself better than the nytak, nor does it seek to eat more than all its kin. It knows what it needs, gets its fill, and goes on as such until the end of its days. It doesn't know greed. Somewhere along the way, we—humans, nyrians, and the rest of our evolved kin—lost sight of that." She scooted the bowl closer to Elaysia and tucked a wooden spoon into her hand. "But we can find our way again, and no one is better suited for the task of guiding us there than you."

A warmth enveloped Elaysia as though she'd already consumed the soup. She lifted the spoon to her lips and took a small bite. The savory notes of meat hit her tongue, followed by the bite of herbs and the buttery texture of mushrooms. "Sometimes I wonder what you see in me," she said between bites, "though I'm glad for it."

"I see your mother's strength. Your father's determination. Your brother's wit. But mostly, I just see you." Maseeya took a sip of her wine. "You're all that and more. And you know what else?"

"What?"

"You're a survivor."

Elaysia slurped the end of her soup, fighting the urge to lick the bowl clean. "And who do I get that from?"

Maseeya's eyes danced as she raised the wine cup to her lips. "That"—she took a drink; smiled—"you get from me."

"I don't doubt that." Elaysia grasped Maseeya's hand in her own, drawing strength from the woman she viewed as a mother. "Do you think I should go through with the union?"

"What does your heart tell you?"

"That I'm miserable either way." Elaysia laughed darkly. "Might as well be miserable with someone who commands a large army."

Maseeya's smile dissipated. "Don't succumb to misery, Elaysia. You are stronger than that, and you have much to be grateful for. Every day is a new opportunity for you to decide who's going to rule: your heart, or your emotions."

"I think they're one and the same."

"A strong heart allows emotions to pass through it, over it, feeling and bending to them, but not breaking. You are a tree rooted beside a rising river. You can't let yourself get carried away. Spread your roots, dig deep, stay strong. Promise me this."

Elaysia forced a smile. "I promise."

Whatever Maseeya needed to hear. Whatever anyone needed. She'd be the leader, say the right things, bind herself to a man with the resources to help her win the war.

But her heart would buck and rear every step of the way.

JAKKI

The last rays of sunlight painted Norcoos Lake in a golden glow, casting a near-flawless reflection of the coniferous trees that hugged the edge of the water. Despite the crisp bite to the air, the unhindered sunlight blanketed Jakki in warmth. With the sand beneath her cradling each curve of her body, and the gentle kisses of waves on her toes, a small sigh found its way to her lips. She closed her eyes and breathed in the rich, woody fragrance of the evergreen forest, combined with the subtle mineral tang of the lake. The effect was paradisal. Just as good as the little nazrath clearing, and, in fact, better because said nuisances weren't around.

Then again, she'd merely traded them for newer, arguably far more irritating, nuisances.

"Hate to disturb your peace," a deep voice purred, "but everyone's here, and I'd like to get this over with."

Jakki's eyes drifted open. She rolled onto one side and propped herself up with an elbow, leveling a glare at the cat. "No, you don't." Sand clung to her legs and arms as she rose from the impression left by her body. "Lucky for you, I'd like to get this over with, too."

Lumira's ears twitched back, not quite flattening against her head but communicating hostile intent all the same. The beridian muttered something in Hispen as she hobbled toward a crude firepit the others had dug in the sand a few yards away. A wave of sympathy washed over Jakki, softening the muscles in her previously hardened lips as she noted the pink patches of flesh where Lumira's fur had been ripped out or shaved to attend to her wounds. She had no love for the beridian—and likely never would—but Lumira had proven herself loyal in recent moon cycles, and that was more than Jakki could say for some of her fellow Neharem-born.

Besides, if anyone was going to put the cat in her place, it'd be her. Not some backstabbing buck playing at chief or his band of blood-thirsty traitors.

Jakki waited until the fire was kindled to saunter toward the others. She reached for the parchment tucked into her waistband and, savoring the surge of comfort that arose when her fingertips traced it, smiled. She didn't need to read the words any longer. They were seared into her mind like a tattoo, their effects forever imprinted on her soul. Though, she wasn't certain if the magic would work the same—if at all—without the parchment nearby, nor was she keen to find out. Hopefully, it would never come to that.

"Jakki." Xaren raised his hand, and a clay bottle, in greeting as she approached. "In case you need any persuading to join us." His charcoal hair fell over his face, masking one eye and reaching down past his chest; visible evidence he'd fully abandoned his former soldier's life.

Jakki squinted, studying the bottle's double-handled neck and the fine details of the pottery. A trifecta of brown, blue, and black with geometric patterning woven in. "What are you doing with toi, slaver?" she asked, though the amusement in her voice betrayed the harshness of her words.

"Agaas received several crates of goods from the Tangeesh this morning," Mardus cut in with his usual monotone. "They wish to support our war efforts."

"I suppose sending supplies is a decent enough alternative to, you know, fighting alongside us to win the war." Jakki sat in the sand beside Xaren, indifferent to the gazes fixed on her, and popped the cork off the bottle of toi. "You can all stop gawking," she said, raising the fermented plant drink to her lips. "I'm just saying what no one else wants to."

The fruity notes of toi danced on her tongue and warmed her belly. She took two more sips, then passed the drink to Xaren, who sniffed cautiously from the mouth of the bottle.

"It's good," she told him, dropping her voice just above a whisper. "Sweet. Light. About as strong as a cup of wine."

Xaren thanked her with his eyes before taking a sip. He passed the bottle to Lumira, but the beridian shook her head, then offered it to Grokhion, who passed it on to Mardus without drinking, though his demeanor was more apathetic than resistant. Jakki almost commented on Lumira's sudden sobriety, but thought better of it. She'd already made her snide remark of the evening at the expense of the Tangeesh. Besides, Lumira was now a war hero, and judging by the way the others looked on in awe as she recounted her first flight for the dozenth time (at Xaren's request), she might as well have been divine. Just in case Jakki needed any other reasons to detest her.

As if privy to Jakki's thoughts, Anadu soared over the tree line and glided across the water, her fire-tipped feathers skimming the surface with the utmost precision. Her curved beak arced toward the water. With a flap of her wings, she plunged her feet beneath the surface, emerging moments later with a fish squirming between her talons. It was a sizable bass, one that could've easily satiated their small gathering, but Anadu tossed it up in the air and gulped it down in a single swallow before resuming the hunt.

Jakki waved at her bird and searched the horizon for the others, but none were nearby. It wasn't terribly uncommon. Though they'd developed a kinship, their bond was far from a flock mentality, and only the closest of the birds hunted together. And Siren didn't appear to be close with anyone. Jakki wasn't sure if that was something to be proud of or concerned about.

"Jakki."

Lumira's voice was unmistakable. Jakki returned her attention to the flames flickering before her, to the four pairs of eyes studying her intently. Maybe it was the toi swaying her perception, but they all seemed irritated—save for Xaren, who drew his knees to his chest in a childlike manner she couldn't help but find endearing.

"Sorry, just…" Jakki gestured to the stormbird disappearing back over the tree line.

Lumira's ears were fully flattened now. "Can you, or can't you?"

Jakki snagged the toi from Mardus and took a swig, not wanting to admit she hadn't been listening. She shrugged, then took another to erase any remaining hints of unease.

Xaren glanced at her, his deep brown eyes as wide as a nytak fawn's. A spark landed on Jakki's exposed knee, and she made a show of brushing it off as she braced herself for whatever gods–cursed request was about to be demanded of her.

"I understand you may not want to venture north again. It just seemed like you established good standing with the Morotôk during our last visit." Lumira scratched the bare skin around the notch in her ear, lingering for a moment on the cuff earring attached beneath it. "And you're more likely to sway them, given your…" The cat's claws flexed. "The message would be best received from your kind."

"And what message am I to deliver?" Jakki allowed herself another drink, fairly certain she knew what was coming, and even more certain she could handle another sip with more grace than the humans seated on either side of her.

Mardus emitted an unnecessarily loud grunt as he leaned forward, elbows on his knees. "The same one we've been sending all the tribes since the start of Raynar's rebellion: join us or die."

"Though not death by our hand," Grokhion clarified with a shake of his auburn mane.

Jakki nestled the bottle into the sand, freeing her fingers to work through tangles in her hair so she could braid it. "If previous messages weren't enough to sway them, I don't see how a visit is going to suddenly change their minds."

Lumira's tail flicked behind her, casting shadows on the sand. "The high chieftain hopes the encroaching threat from the Atsukut is enough to persuade them."

"And what's preventing them from siding with the Atsukut?" Jakki replied. "They are few in number and isolated up there, with nothing and no one preventing an Atsukut attack. They'd be foolish to ally with us."

"The high chieftain has promised them sanctuary in Agaas." Lumira spoke with a forced optimism usually absent from her tone.

Jakki shook her head as she tied off the braid and slung it over her shoulder.

Mardus scoffed beside her, the information apparently new to him as well. "Agaas can barely support the influx of warriors assigned to protect her because of the trade cessation. The Morotôk will find no livelihood this far south, even if we could find them lodging."

"We either find them lodging or add them to our ever-growing list of enemies. Surely, having a few more mouths to feed is better than decreasing our odds of victory."

The response came from Xaren, who'd reclined in the sand, his gaze fixed on the stars and fingers interlaced over his stomach, accenting the gentle rise and fall of his breath.

Mardus glared at him, at Jakki, at Lumira, allowing Grokhion the privilege of being the sole survivor of his death stare. "The Moákun lent aid without benefits. We understand the value of—"

"Your self-righteousness isn't changing our predicament," Jakki interjected, shoving the bottle back into his hand. She jutted her chin at Lumira. "Why me, though? The truth. Did Elaysia order this?"

Lumira exchanged glances with Grokhion. The elder beridian leaned forward. "If you have reservations, I'm sure we can come to an—"

Jakki held up her hand. "Not you. Her. Our *leader* in our true leader's absence." She narrowed her eyes at Lumira. "Is this your idea, or Elaysia's?"

The beridian's eyes almost appeared gray, their twinkle gone, replaced with the cool, calculated disregard of a killer. "Mine."

Jakki nodded slowly. She could accept such a sentence from the cat, especially after the stunt her mother pulled with the forged tuross message. As long as it wasn't of Elaysia's making, she could live with it—even welcome such a command in the spirit of rivalry.

"I'll leave within a fortnight." She lay down next to Xaren, a sense of calm softening the tension in her muscles and allowing her to sink further into the sand. The boy looked at her with lively eyes and a quirk of his lips. There was nothing romantic or lustful about it. Just pure admiration. Jakki's initial instinct was to ignore it, to keep him at a distance like her mother had demonstrated her whole life, even with her own daughter.

But the attention inspired her.

"No objections." Lumira's tone was that of a statement, as though she spoke the words aloud for her own clarity.

The fire crackled and danced, competing with the lapping water and chirping insects for their attention. A seed of bitterness nestled into Jakki's thoughts, and she buried it, as she often did, tucking the feeling away until it sprouted into untamable passion.

"None," Jakki said with a tight-lipped smile.

Lumira cleared her throat. "It's mainly because of Siren, you know. She's the most impressive of the birds. I thought you two would stand the best chance of convincing them."

Jakki rolled her eyes. "Scaring them shitless, you mean."

The following silence confirmed what she already knew: everyone—even Grokhion—sanctioned using fear as a tool in such dire times. And if she had to be the bearer of bad tidings, so be it. At least it stung less than her previous assignment. Where her prior journey north felt like a punishment, this time they wanted her to go because they needed her, because she was strong enough, skilled enough, and boasted the resource of the best ally.

And yes, being nyrian was rarely a disadvantage in Quinaria.

Xaren pushed himself into a seated position, then stretched his arms up and to the side. "Let me know how I can help prepare for the journey," he said, fighting back a yawn. "The longer we delay, the more likely it is the Atsukut will get to them first."

Jakki raised an eyebrow. "We?"

"Yes." Xaren flashed a toothy grin. "Shadow and I are coming with you."

No one spoke up to contradict him.

Jakki waited beside the lake, water washing over her feet, sending little bumps prickling up her limbs and down her neck. She waited while Mardus stormed off huffing, while the beridians made their gruff goodbyes shortly after. She waited while Xaren sat beside her, happy to carry on the entire conversation himself, clearly exhilarated by the adventure they were about to embark on. She waited until he yawned, bid her goodnight. She waited until the flames faded to embers, no longer stoked by Xaren's deft hands, the skin on her back cool in its absence. She waited until she was the water, and the water was her: ever-flowing, ever-changing, and ever-powerful. She waited until it hurt, until the ache inside her writhed and stretched like a butterfly escaping its cocoon.

And then she whispered the words. The parchment rustled in her waistband, perhaps because of the wind. And perhaps not.

It was a little easier to handle each time, the magic. She'd adapted to it the way one might grow a tolerance to alcohol, and like alcohol, she found it demanded more with each use. More consumption, more often, more of her. But unlike alcohol, every time she spoke the words, it felt like the first time, as though it grew with her. As though it knew exactly what she needed.

And what she needed tonight wasn't dexterity of movement or unnatural speed. She needed answers, no matter their source.

Jakki didn't hear him approach. Instead, the air surrounding her grew even colder, as though she'd drifted into a deep pocket in the woods. It was thin, hard to breathe, and she drew long, steady breaths to still her throbbing heart.

"Have you summoned me to die?" a crackly voice said. "Or are your threats as empty as your heart?"

"You're certainly making that outcome increasingly desirable." Curiosity overwhelmed her intent to remain defiant, and she drew her chin over her shoulder, allowing her gaze to fall on the figure seated a few feet behind her.

He looked the same as he had that first night in Daruk territory: a bony, shriveled figure with tangled white hair and a beard that ran well past his knees. The gleam of his eyes competed with the glow of the gem nestled atop his staff, and when he caught her staring at it, a cruel smile slithered across his face.

"Not for you," he said, waggling his finger. "Not yet." He wedged his staff into the sand between them, never taking his gaze off her.

"I don't give a shit about your imposter nevethium," she lied. "I'm returning to the north tomorrow, and since you won't leave me alone, I have some questions I want answered."

"What am I that I won't leave you alone?"

"A ghost. A spirit trapped between realms, probably serving penance for the terrible life you led." Jakki had never spoken her speculations aloud, but what else could he be? With his ability to appear after the untimeliest summons—or completely of his own accord, as with their first meeting—he was no mere mortal. Yet, he lacked the dignity of a god. If he was indebted to servitude, better it be to her than someone who would yield his power for personal gain.

"And if I don't have your answers?" he asked in his disinterested way, with his yawning speech and the aloof arch of his wiry eyebrows.

"I'll burn your parchment."

The old man made *tsk* sounds and shook his head. His antlers cut dark patterns in the starry sky as he rose, his ancient limbs cracking with audible *pops* and groans. He waded into the water until it washed over his loincloth and above his belly button. A gasp of pleasure escaped his lips. Jakki looked away, finding herself, for once, uncomfortable with someone else's indecency.

"Ask your questions, but expect only lies. Within the lies are truth, for what is a lie, but the truth reimagined?"

Jakki retrieved her staff from the sand and waded into the lake after him, only distantly feeling the cold bite of the water. She wanted to disappear beneath the waves as she had the first time she used the parchment. The darkness below promised peace, promised sanctuary.

She pointed her staff at the old man. "Your endless riddles don't make you seem wiser, you know. Just more insane."

"Insanity and wisdom are two sides of the same coin." His eyes flickered, and Jakki's heart raced in response. "You can't have one without the other."

"Does the magic work without the parchment nearby?" she blurted before a wiser, more selfless question could take its place.

The old man leaned back into the water, drawing his legs up until he lay as gracefully as a leaf on the lake's surface. "The magic doesn't work at all. It merely exists, and those who think they can tame it are its slaves."

Fear coiled around Jakki's heart. She plunged into the water until the panic subsided and inhaled the muddied scent of the lake, drawing its essence into her core like a calming salve. Inhaling water was purer than air; almost nourishing. When she reemerged, the old man was nowhere to be seen. The lake's surface was unbroken, the surrounding air as still as the library in Agaas. She spun to face the shore, half expecting him to be there, sitting cross-legged with that diabolic grin on his face.

You may ask one more question, a voice within her said. Part of her hated the way he seemed to invade her body when she used the parchment.

But the magic—the feeling of relief, of release, the momentary dance with unfettered power—was worth even that.

Does any of this even matter? she returned. *Even if we save the essence of our world in this lifetime, who's to say it won't be unraveled in the next?*

A familiar cackle vibrated through her body. And then, pure ecstasy.

It was getting more delayed each time, or she grew better at controlling it. She swam further out, each movement effortless, her mind sparking and growing with such clarity that nothing else seemed to matter. Not the war. Not herself.

Not even Elaysia.

Does it? she pressed.

No, the voice replied. *None of it matters because it all matters. And when everything matters, nothing really does.*

Then I'm already dead. Jakki exhaled sharply and sank back into the water, allowing the weight of her body to carry her to the lake's silken floor.

And more alive than I've ever been.

ZAVIK

V ahid was less pompous than Davier, so he had that working to his advantage. Zavik distinctly recalled wanting to
both punch and cower before the ex-soldier when he'd first appeared in Neharem, but Elaysia's new life partner didn't inspire
either reaction. Not for lack of size (Vahid was comparable to
Davier in that regard, if not larger), but because of his disarming
smile that seemed to radiate genuine kindness. Still, smile or no,
Zavik wasn't eager to befriend him, except for where protection
was concerned. Which, given the circumstances, was the primary benefit Anahi's younger brother offered.

Vahid stood over a table, his back to Zavik, inspecting a tray a
servant had just placed before him. Zavik couldn't see over his
towering frame, but the steam curling about the air filled the
room with the nutty, smoky aroma of moskuto. Vahid inhaled
deeply and released a sigh. Half of his hair was gathered into
a bun at the back of his head, the rest of it hanging free in
thick, black waves that reached down past his shoulders. He
turned to acknowledge the servant's efforts with a brief dip of
his head, and Zavik caught sight of a nevethium stud earring
adorning his left ear. It was the only obvious sign of affluence
Vahid displayed. The rest of his clothes were simple—if not
finely stitched—layers of linen, with silk sashes accenting the
belt securing his tunic. Perhaps Vahid was not so unlike Anahi
after all.

"And how do you take your moskuto, Zavik?" Vahid's voice
was deeply rich and pleasant, the sort of tone suited to lull chil-

dren to sleep with tales of valiant gods and eternal paradises. Or for seducing lovers.

Zavik wrinkled his nose at the thought.

"My faja ensures our household is always stocked with the finest array of sweeteners," Vahid continued. "We have sunkiss paste, raw honey, moon dust imported from the Beridian Isles..." He glanced over his shoulder, his amber eyes wide with anticipation, as though he could assess the kind of man Zavik was from the way he took his drink.

The realization sent prickles of panic rippling through Zavik's stomach. The straight moskuto he'd consumed the other day was a bit bitter for his liking, but that seemed to be the way most of the men in the household preferred it. "Uh..."

Vahid gave a knowing nod. "I, for one, like a little moskuto with my milk and honey." He chuckled as he split the entire milk jar's contents between their cups and added two heaping spoonfuls of honey to each. "Give my recipe a try and tell me it's not the best thing you've ever tasted."

Zavik received the gilded cup from Vahid, his attention momentarily captivated by the lyvium ring on the middle finger of the future saya's right hand. It featured what appeared to be some sort of winged deity, though not one Zavik was familiar with.

Vahid raised his cup to Zavik's. "To my new union, eh?"

Zavik's lips stretched into thin, hard lines. He nodded to mask his displeasure at the thought, then raised the drink to his lips. A sweet medley of flavors danced on his tongue, carrying only the slightest hint of the moskuto's acidity. He fought the urge to down the warm beverage in one gulp as Vahid watched, amused, from the cushion opposite him.

"That's surprisingly pleasant," Zavik said, setting the half-emptied cup aside.

The corners of Vahid's eyes crinkled. "I won't tell if you won't."

Well, there went Zavik's attempts at disliking the man.

Vahid traced his thumb and forefinger over his finely trimmed beard as his gaze drifted from one latticed shutter to the next. They reclined in the room Zavik had first met Saya and Sayetta Undali in a little over a fortnight past, only this time they were alone, and Zavik was tasked with the superfluous duty of preparing Vahid to meet Elaysia. Yerakai had suggested it, thinking it might soften the blow of an arranged union should both parties have a better understanding of one another. Anahi agreed, saying no one knew Elaysia better than Zavik; though he had his suspicions it had more to do with making *him* fond of Vahid, so he could convey that sentiment to Elaysia. He hadn't brought attention to their scheming, of course.

"Care to take a stroll with me?" Vahid said, slapping his hands on his knees as he rose. "I know why they've forced our company this morning, and I understand it must be done. But should it matter whether it takes place in here or outside while we sample the bounty of my faja's orchards?"

"I don't see why it should." Zavik came to stand beside him, desperately wishing the silk tunic he wore to uphold his hosts' standards had pockets to jam his hands into.

"Then it's settled."

Vahid grabbed his linen-wrapped headdress and wrestled most of his hair inside it as he secured it atop his head. Zavik did the same with the one he'd been loaned, taking extra care to wrap another layer around the back of his neck until most of his skin was protected from Munskahan's unrelenting sun.

As they made their way through the palace's marbled halls and towering pillars, Vahid stopped to acknowledge every member of the household who crossed their path, and everyone from the crustiest kuza to the most weathered maid stopped their duties to return his smile and converse. And it wasn't just superficial nods or greetings he spared, but prolonged eye contact and specific inquiries.

"Is your husband's fever on the mend?" he'd asked one.

"Only three days until your stallion enters the races," he reminded another.

To an older woman cleaning the steps: "Anya, I hear you were blessed with another grandchild! Take the rest of the day off to help your daughter, please."

As he left each person, they seemed to glow from within, their outlooks brightened by the interaction. Unlike Anahi, Vahid had more the look of his mother than his father, not to mention her temperament, and while those similarities certainly weren't doing him a disservice, there was more there, too: a sincere compassion untainted by an ulterior motive.

Dammit. Now Zavik really couldn't hate him.

When they finally escaped the palace walls, Vahid led him along the side of the building to a smaller, but no less ornate, gate than the one barring entrance to the property. A kuza heaved it open as they approached, revealing striking rows of green breaking up the otherwise rocky landscape. Golden mountains loomed in the distance, speckled with smatterings of the rugged shrubs and naked trees that accounted for most of the local flora. The air carried the sweet notes of sun-ripened fruit among the more dominant stenches of dirt and manure, and for a moment, Zavik forgot he was in a bustling city at all.

"It's breathtaking," he said, and he wholeheartedly meant it. He'd rarely witnessed such greenery in Orillon, especially in Munskahan.

"Our yield declines every year. We had four times this acreage when I was a boy, and now its upkeep nearly outweighs its profit." Vahid crossed his arms, his gaze lost in the fields and some unseen memory. "But you're right. Breathtaking she still is, and I have much to be grateful for."

Zavik toed the dirt, kicking up a miniature windstorm of dust. A question still nagged at him, and it was time to get it over with.

"I overheard some of your household offering sympathies for your recent loss, and I wanted to offer mine as well." When Vahid didn't respond, he added, "Were you close? You and your betrothed?"

Vahid fidgeted with the lyvium deity ring on his finger, slipping it off and back on.

Zavik assumed his host's prolonged silence meant he'd overstepped his boundaries. It wasn't his place to ask such questions. If Vahid and his betrothed had been in love, he'd likely just reopened an unhealed wound. And if they hadn't been, then he'd put Vahid in a place where he might feel pressured to lie to maintain an appearance.

Brilliant, Zav. Just brilliant.

Zavik was about to transition the conversation to something dull, like the weather, when Vahid escorted him down the hill and into the orchards. They walked row after row, occasionally stopping to examine the roots of a sickly plant or to taste the fruit of another. Zavik thought the misstep of his ill-timed interrogation was all but forgotten when Vahid suddenly turned to face him with glistening eyes.

"She hated me," Vahid said, his voice steady but somber. "My betrothed was a child, and she loved a stable boy in her family's employment. And who could blame her? She hadn't seen more than fourteen name days. I'm more than a decade her senior." He snapped a branch off a palano tree—the sacred bearer of sunkisses—inspecting its insides for health. The action didn't mask the tremble of his lip.

"It wasn't your fault, though. Desert bite is—"

"Desert bite?" For the first time since Zavik had met him, Vahid's manner took a bitter turn. "That's a lie her family weaved to keep their reputation untainted. They'd rather the public believe their daughter succumbed to a commoner's disease than admit she tied a rope fastened to a rock around her neck and flung herself into the sea."

Zavik's mouth gaped open. He knew he needed to say something, but none of his consolations felt worthy enough to expel.

Vahid worked the branch between his fingers, caressing it as though he had the power to coax life back into it. "If I'd known how much she feared the union, I could've eased her mind—broken it off, even. I never wanted it in the first place.

I was just trying to appease my faja and keep our lineage…" A huff escaped his lips. "Never mind."

He tossed the branch aside and strode to the end of the row, where a crumbling stone bench stood out like a beggar among nobility. He sat, then motioned for Zavik to join him.

"I refuse to be the cause of someone else's sorrow," he said after they'd sat in silence for an amount of time Zavik deemed uncomfortable. "I will end this engagement before it takes another life, should it come to that." He scrutinized Zavik with sincere curiosity. "You are your high chieftain's primary advisor, yes?"

Zavik blinked. It felt odd hearing it from someone else's mouth, as though it finally made his new role of high elder official. He nodded.

Vahid's gaze intensified. "Is she going to be alright with this arrangement?" A servant passed by with pruning shears, and the future saya smiled warmly and waved. "I'm not asking if she will love me," he whispered as the servant strolled out of earshot, "but I need to know that our union won't break her."

"Um…" Zavik removed his seers to wipe away the sweat building on the bridge of his nose, taking his time so he could formulate a response.

He considered the power in his hands. No matter how good of a man Vahid was, Elaysia surely didn't want to be traded like a rare spice in exchange for an army. But he had a feeling deep down that she would do anything for Neharem, and if she had to commit to a union to secure an alliance, she wasn't likely to find another highborn half as kind as Vahid. Assuming any of the other great houses would even consider them. Anahi's bloodline was the only reason they'd been allowed to even set foot in the wealthy districts.

"I think you'll find Elaysia is beyond breaking, at least regarding menial matters like a union," Zavik said, choosing his words carefully. "If you treat her well, she'll have very few reasons to hate you."

The tension vanished from Vahid's face. "She sounds like a woman to be reckoned with. I hope I can lessen whatever pain she carries."

"As do I." Zavik rose, staring beyond the orchards in the direction of the Shaktar Caverns. It must've been at least a year since he'd set foot in their domain, trading a vague promise for the scrolls. Did the ancient, winged Vysilliam know he'd returned? Could they sense him this far away?

He is worthy, they'd said just before giving him the scrolls. *The blood tells true.*

And when he'd asked what it was they wanted in exchange, he'd received riddles.

It remains to be seen. But you must pay it when demanded of you, no matter the cost.

The nagging fear of what they might demand of him coiled around his heart like a snake made of ice. The sooner he left Orillon, the better.

"Anyway," Zavik said with a nervous laugh, trying to shake the memory. "You should rest easy knowing you're doing for Neharem what we cannot. Countless lives will be saved thanks to your family's aid."

Vahid nodded, though a heaviness pulled at his features. "And countless more lost."

Zavik spent the days leading up to Elaysia's arrival busying himself with personal affairs. With no pressing Agaasian issues to address and no desire to wander the streets of Munskahan (and potentially cross paths with merchants he'd robbed as a child—sorry, ferret, as Lanston so coined his fledgling criminals), he dedicated his free time to research. Even with the union nearly secured, he still had his doubts about Neharem's longevity post-war, and nevethium, in his mind, was the answer. Not abusing it as Az Zar had, but not letting it sit idle either, as Neharem had allowed it to for so long. Surely, there was a way to preserve the crystals while using them to one's advantage, perhaps by powering some sort of weapon in a sustainable manner.

And Zavik was going to be the first to find out.

He yawned as he reached for his third cup of moskuto of the day. Since he'd begun sweetening it the way Vahid had shown him, he found it pleasant, if not downright addictive. He'd been awake for nearly two days, though it scarcely felt like more than a few hours had passed. After their heart-to-heart in the orchard, Vahid had given Zavik his secondary bedchamber to use as his own. A kind gesture, but also, Zavik wasn't entirely sure why a second bedchamber was needed for one person in the first place. He kept such comments to himself, however, happy with his new quarters furnished with two feather beds and a bathing tub the size of a fishing boat. Aside from servants knocking three times a day to offer food and drink, he was afforded complete solitude.

Well, almost.

As if privy to Zavik's thoughts, T'Vak belched from where he dangled off one of the beds like some ill-intending street cat, a wineskin loosely clutched in one hand, and a few pieces of aspar jingling in the other. The backhander had taken it upon himself to move into the room with Zavik—*There are two beds after all, Zavvie boy, enough space for someone even as prudish as you*—for his 'protection,' and while he was glad T'Vak wasn't causing scenes around the palace without his knowledge, he'd just as soon have had a zaka-zaka hopping about the beds for all the distractions T'Vak caused. At least the two-legged marsupials could remain sober and provide transportation.

Zavik drained the last of the moskuto dregs from the cup and set it back on the sun-blood desk without a sound. House Undali was wealthy indeed to import the rare Az Zarian wood, which was sacred in its home nation and prized for its fine grain composition and crimson coloring. In fact, after visiting

the kuza barracks located on the property just south of the orchards near the river, Zavik was feeling more confident in their
new arrangement than ever. During the tour, Saya Undali had
claimed the ones stationed at the property were only one-third
of those in his employment, that some were home on rotation
and others utilized for labor or lent out to other houses as gifts
or to settle various debts. Even with just a third of the Undali
forces, Agaas stood a strong chance at winning the war. Assuming all Raynar's allied tribes never attacked simultaneously,
anyway. Not that Zavik expected a full-out battle in the middle
of some clearing, but one could never be too prepared. Hence, the
parchment unrolled before him.

Not that his work would matter if Elaysia never consented to
using the crystals for violence—even if he found a way to do it
sustainably. Still, he'd rather be prepared for the worst possible
outcome, should things sour. And a deeper part of him couldn't
deny the exhilarating bumps dotting his forearms whenever a
new idea occurred to him.

"What's that then, lad?"

T'Vak's wine-soured breath was hot on his neck, meaning the
backhander had slunk off the bed and over to his desk, stooping
close enough to—

Zavik turned the parchment over, wincing as he imagined the
still-wet ink smearing onto the crimson wood. He scowled at
T'Vak, who stood just behind him, slouching over crossed arms
with an unwitting grin plastered to his face. Zavik believed the
ruse less and less, as of late.

He'd been foolish to ever believe it.

"Nothing that concerns you," Zavik snapped. "And can you
please stop calling me 'lad'? You've maybe seen three more Sowing Moons than me at most."

T'Vak's eyes no longer danced, but his smile grew wider.
Toothier.

Predatory.

"You're awfully busy for someone whose job here is already
done." T'Vak drew a knife from the folds of his sashes—one

of at least five in his possession, from what Zavik had counted—and began picking grime from his unkempt nails. "Hope it has something to do with my pay. As much as I enjoy our time together, I don't fancy myself returning to Neharem this time around."

Zavik's nose wrinkled as T'Vak wiped the gunk from his knife tip onto the silk bedsheets and moved onto the next finger.

Neither do I.

"I'll send another tuross to Agaas to see what the high chieftain can arrange," Zavik said, peeling the parchment off the desk. The staining was minimal—nothing a little sanding couldn't fix—and the drawings on the parchment were mostly unmarred. He rolled it up gently and tucked it into his robe.

"You do that." With that, the backhander patted Zavik's shoulder and strode from the room, slamming the gem-embossed door shut behind him.

A chill seized Zavik's spine as he stood in the empty chamber with nothing but the humid breeze drifting lazily through the lace curtains to distract him. It'd been brief, only the faintest flicker of change in T'Vak's wily eyes, but it was enough to unsettle him. It was the look an Apáasutai huntress gave before she slit a nytak's throat, combined with the look of a mother handing her child off to a great house for indentured servitude.

Pity. Guilt. A blood-curdling combination of the two.

And Zavik didn't know why.

KONAR

The graying mist of dawn greeted Konar like an old lover as he snuck out from Zavik's loft, cloaked in a woven blanket and nytak-skin slippers. A smooth-headed watcher stirred from her post by the bridge as he approached, but she didn't interfere with his crossing—even though her narrowed eyes and the set of her jaw suggested she very much would've liked to. Konar raised his hand at her in greeting, then hurried across the bridge before he could witness her response.

He didn't blame her for distrusting him. He didn't blame any of them. He'd lied to and betrayed them, taken advantage of their politics, and removed non-compliant leaders. He'd killed for his own gain again and again. And for what?

For her, he told himself.

But that wasn't really true. Not until recently, and even then, how much of it had still been for *his* desires, for the vision he had for the world? Maseeya had asked if he'd go back and change things, given the chance, and he still couldn't say with complete confidence that he would. Meddling with fate was a dangerous game. Someone had to play the role of villain, and Konar would wish it upon himself a thousand times over to spare the more innocent or weaker, more easily manipulated beings from sabotaging the good he'd sifted from the bad. The order he'd arranged amid the chaos.

Let them hate me that they might love her.

"High Eld—Konar," the watcher's monotone voice cut in, interrupting his thoughts.

Konar halted, his hand clinging to the damp wooden railing. It was soft with rot. Needed to be replaced soon. He should speak to Cosar about infusing the—

No. No longer his duty. He could have someone pass along his concerns to Zavik upon the high elder's return, but the state of Agaas's infrastructure was no longer his to address.

"Sister," Konar replied, keeping his back to the watcher. Sweat saturated the fabric beneath his armpits, and his legs trembled beneath him. He'd only journeyed outside Zavik's old loft a handful of times to regain his strength, and though the venom had long since left his body, it had taken its toll. It didn't help that it'd been over a moon cycle since his last...revival.

A problem soon to be remedied.

The bridge creaked under the weight of the watcher's footsteps. "Do you need an escort? The high chieftain said to ensure you lack nothing, be it sustenance or assistance."

The high chieftain said to not let me out of your sight, you mean, he thought bitterly.

"The high chieftain is generous; may her sunrises always hold promise." He started walking again, albeit slower. "I'm only stretching my legs, though. No need to abandon your watch."

"May her sunsets always hold peace," the watcher said, echoing the refrain, but not bothering to mask her suspicion. "If you say true, then I'll leave you be."

"I do." Konar held up the stump where his right hand had been as a parting gesture, but also as a reminder. How much of a threat could a battered old man be?

No one else stopped him as he made his way to the library to collect a ration of ground kinawa from his hidden stash, nor as he departed there and descended the ramps leading down to base camp and the woods beyond. It was ironic, he realized, that the one time he wasn't trying to, well, get away with anything, was the time no one seemed set on interfering with his plans. Truth be told, Konar wasn't even certain where he was going or why, just that he needed to get away from the confines of Agaas and the charming prison that was Zavik's old loft. He supposed he should take to calling it *his* loft. Zavik wouldn't inhabit it again. Elaysia had reassigned him to the high elder loft in the High Tree, one of the best chambers in Agaas, and closest to the high chieftain. It stung a little, being replaced by his apprentice while he still lived on.

But it was what he deserved.

As Konar trudged through the woods, the first rays of sunlight illuminated the dew-drop speckled moss hanging from thick branches like clusters of ratted, green hair. Though Agaas still slept, the forest was alive with the skitters and chirps of those who called it home, and he found comfort in their presence, in their tolerance, and even in their apathy.

"Perhaps I'll settle down here with you, if you'll have me." He directed the comment at a snake with scales the same fiery tones of Gathering Moon leaves, but it slithered beneath a fern without so much as a pause.

Konar sat on a log, careful to avoid the decomposing section and any potential widow-makers, then fingered his pipe with longing. He waited several minutes before giving into his urges, slipping one foot out of his slipper, then the other, wincing as the coastal damp soaked deep into his bones. With the caution of one committing an act of great indecency, he set his pipe on a trampled bit of fern, filled it with kinawa, and drew a piece of flint and lyvium from the folds of his blanket. He muttered an unintelligible prayer as he tucked the flint between his feet and secured the lyvium with his remaining hand.

"Please," he murmured, readying his hand.

The first strike sent the flint clattering against his pipe, spilling some of the kinawa onto the fern. Konar rescued as much of the ground leaves as he could and, after nesting it back in the pipe, jammed the flint between his feet. The second time, he held onto it, but the effort birthed no sparks. The third time knocked it free again, turning the pipe upside down and dumping the entirety of its contents into the fern.

A scalding, writhing rage shot through Konar's body, tightening his muscles and accelerating his heartbeat. He half growled, half yelled as he kicked the pipe across the path and hurled the fire-starting tools after it. So be it. Another part of his life had ended, along with so much else.

"Oh, Konar, you always were so dramatic."

Konar startled at the voice that, though it came from within his own head, was not his. He would've known it anywhere, recognized its deep notes and subtle rasp, the clarity and intent with which each word was spoken.

"Karliah?"

He waited for a reply, not really believing one possible. And when the only response was the creaking of trees against the backdrop of the distant waves, he pinched the bridge of his nose and exhaled a groan.

"First you lose your position, then your hand, and now you're losing your mind, you ancient fool," he muttered to himself.

Threatened with the pain inflicted by his own mind, Konar hobbled into the forest and searched through ferns and loam until he located his means of relief.

It took the sun fully rising and bloodied feet from holding the flint in place to finally create a worthy spark, but as soon as the kinawa hit his lungs, he forgot his troubles. His stress melted away as euphoria took its place. He drew deep breath after deep breath, chasing oblivion.

Just let me forget everything for a moment, he prayed as he reclined against the log, grateful that its rot made for a comforting headrest. *And when I wake, I'll make it alright.*

I'll make everything right.

"You should really consume something. And I don't mean a cluster of berries or a hunk of dried venison—or that bark you grind up for pain relief and sprinkle liberally into your teas. At the rate you're going, you'll strip the entire forest by moon cycle's end."

Konar opened his eyes and tried to blink away the darkness, but it only set in heavier, pressing on him like the weight of a pile of skins. The voice speaking to him was muffled and distant, with some feminine undertones despite its deep register. He turned his head left, then right, gaze piercing his surroundings for any hint of light, any ghost of a form.

There was none, which was just as well. He knew better what happened when one consumed too much kinawa, especially in his state.

He'd closed his eyes to sleep it off when a cool breath kissed his cheek. His right hand shot out instinctively, his fingers brushing up against nothing but more air.

His fingers.

He held his breath as he curled them into his palm one by one, letting each one nestle there with tenderness as he relished the warmth of flesh against flesh. He didn't dare believe it, but he cherished it all the same.

"Don't get used to it," the voice said. It was closer now, more alive, its tone mocking. "The spirit-scape allows you to behold yourself in the form you most strongly identify with. You will return to your mortal form when you leave."

Konar tightened his fist. "Perhaps I'll never leave."

The laugh that followed was shallow and sharp, coated in a lifetime of pain, its owner someone as learned and jaded as he. And there were only so many of those people in Quinaria.

"I'm afraid that's not possible for you, Bretata. Even I can only conjure sanctuary here for brief intervals."

Prickles rippled down Konar's limbs, raising the fine white hairs that covered them. "So it was you earlier in the woods," he said to the darkness. "It's been a long time, Karliah."

Another laugh echoed through the darkness. When his sister spoke again, her cloaked monotone had transformed into the voice of a child. "And whose fault is that?" she replied.

It would've been torture enough, just hearing her voice come back to haunt him after hundreds of years. But then a gray light appeared, highlighting first a bare foot, then another, then two thin but strong little calves that butted into the frayed edges of a worn sleeping gown issued to Az Zarian slaves. Konar knew its rough-spun make well, for he'd worn one identical to it. He recalled how little warmth it'd provided on Resting Moon nights.

He shut his eyes, refusing to see anymore—he'd vowed never to relive those moon cycles again, that time spent in servitude to the palace stables, when they were freshly orphaned and hope had ceased to exist. But instead of vanishing, the vision increased in clarity, bypassing his closed eyes and taking root in his mind. Or maybe it'd been there the whole time.

The child was only an arm's reach away, tiny hands fidgeting with holes in the oversized gown. Konar recognized the scar on the knuckle of her right forefinger. It had been there since the day she'd stuck her hand in a gwanei nest to rescue an abandoned baby—only the two-legged reptile hadn't needed rescuing. Just a meal. It assumed Karliah's hand was there to serve that purpose and bit down with its razor-sharp teeth. Then its jaw locked. It dangled there, a wild look in its eye as Karliah ran through the jungle back to the family hut where Appa had made quick work of it.

Konar's hands trembled, yearning to hold his sister's ghost, to stroke her hair and whisper the words every child yearned for.

You're always safe, always loved, with me.

But they were just lies. The gods-cursed lies.

"Still can't look me in the eye, even like this?" Young Karliah planted her hands on her hips.

Konar averted the question with one of his own. "This is the form you most strongly identify with?"

"This is the form *you* most strongly identify me with. I've allowed you control of our spirit-scape. Provisionally." The edge of her mouth quirked up slightly, not unlike the way their amma's used to when she was letting them get away with something.

Warm air encircled Konar. He didn't doubt for one moment it originated from her, its source whatever scrap of goodness she'd held onto despite the trauma life had thrown her way. And for the first time in countless moons, a flicker of hope sparked within his soul.

"And how do you see yourself now?" he asked, settling himself into the cross-legged position he used for meditation. He felt an odd sensation of being cradled, despite no tangible contact with the ground beneath him. "A timeless ruler? Empress of Quinaria? I can't imagine you'll need Rykahl much longer. He's long outlived his usefulness."

Young Karliah tittered in an older woman's voice. "Call me sentimental." She sat across from Konar, imitating his posture from the fold of her legs to the placement of her palms on her knees. A begrudging sigh blew through her lips. "He *is* becoming more trouble than he's worth. How about I give him to you? You can torture and execute him to lift your spirits. I hear tell your old apprentice got promoted."

Konar winced. He'd assumed she had spies in Neharem and was likely behind the attack on Agaas the day of Elaysia's induction—and he still had strong suspicions regarding Rajar's motives. And while Zavik's former apprenticeship and recent advancement to high elder weren't hidden from the people, Konar had the feeling she was among the first to hear of it.

He needed to warn Elaysia before it was too late.

"I keep an eye on you, Bretata," she said, watching him intently. "Family first, after all. Except for the Brunes. Amma and Appa saw to that." Hurt crept into her eyes, but she blinked it away almost as quickly as it came. "No, for our family, I believe it was fortune first. Or was it fame?" Another laugh, albeit forced. "Matters not. One breeds the other, and we weren't strong enough to shake our familial pursuit of them."

Konar's breath shortened. "I seek neither."

Young Karliah lifted her shoulder. "Call it what you like. Your desire for knowledge and control manifested into fame and fortune of a sort, didn't it?"

He ignored the accusation and gestured to the vast nothing-ness cocooning them. "So, is this how you gather your information? Malicious rituals to invade people's minds?"

"Malicious rituals?" Her eyes widened in genuine surprise. "My, my. Grown judgmental in your old age, haven't you? Ironic, seeing as how we have the same worldview." She picked at her nails, allowing his suspense to build.

He took the bait. "Which is?"

Young Karliah grew solemn. "Do whatever it takes to reach the most favorable outcome."

Konar wouldn't deny it, but neither would he grace it with an affirmation.

"In the off chance your inquiry was sincere," she continued, "this isn't anything like *that* ritual." She braced herself with her hands as she reclined back, basking in the darkness as though it were sunshine. "This is one of Amma's old tricks, actually. She and her awskada setatas were forces to be reckoned with. It's a shame they never realized their true potential." A disingenuous frown, then, "Some of their ways are lost to me because I was never made kindred, but much of their gifts were simple spells and incantations. Turns out you don't really need Amma's order around at all. Just their books and their blood in your veins."

The smile that crept across her lips made Konar's blood run cold. He knew most of the awskadas in Zelos had long since perished or gone into hiding. Az Zar's holy crusade to eliminate all illegitimate gods and heathen practices from their nation and those they occupied had been long and bloody. But he never would've dared to believe Karliah was behind it—gods, even the reason for it.

"You didn't answer my first question," he said, fighting to keep the emotion from his voice. "How do you see yourself?"

"Always so forward, Bretata." Young Karliah closed her luminescent violet eyes, and when she reopened them again, they'd aged a lifetime. "I see myself as a goddess awakened, a healer divine, the restorer of worlds." She didn't continue until Konar held her gaze. "So cease prolonging the inevitable. Enjoy what remains of your life—or better yet, join me. You can't stop what's in motion any more than you can stop the sighs of the seas and the cycles of the moons. Deep down, you know it's all futile."

"Why have you brought me here?" Konar asked hoarsely. "If the world dances at the snap of your fingers, what purpose could I serve?"

Her eyes took on a childlike vulnerability. "What purpose? Are you not still my bretata? The only family I have left?" She reached for his hand; he took it and squeezed it firmly. "You broke your promise to me all those years ago, but I've returned to offer you one last chance to redeem yourself. I never gave up on you, nor our promise. We said we'd always be together. You and me against the world." She gripped his other hand, nails digging into his flesh. "It's not too late to do this together like we've always dreamed. The journey has been long and rife with heartache. Our hands are bloodied, our souls stained, but it's not without purpose unless you make it so. The scrolls are our destiny, Konar. Remember what Amma said. Ours."

"Setata—"

"Shh." She shook her head fiercely enough to free her corded strands of moon-white hair from the loose knot at the nape. "Will you not fulfill your oath to me? No one knows better than us how to make Quinaria whole again. With our knowledge and power combined, it could be quick and painless."

"For us," he corrected.

Young Karliah raised a delicate eyebrow. She tried to pull her hands free, but Konar gripped them tighter.

"I'm no longer certain the world we dreamed of is what's best for Quinaria," he said. "We've spent our lives trying to make things better, both together and apart, but the circumstances have only worsened. Deny it if you'd like, but we are to blame for much pain and heartache."

"But with purpose," she said coolly. "If it wasn't us, it'd be someone else. Someone with a monstrous vision."

"Those who harbor ambitions to rule the world, regardless of their motives, become monstrous in their pursuit." Konar loosened his grip, and she immediately ripped her hands free. His palms felt empty and cold in their absence, and his heart echoed a similar sentiment.

"Then my bretata is long dead."

She rose and put several steps of distance between them as a charcoal mist swirled around her, obscuring Konar's view. When it dissipated, a towering woman stood in the girl's place, her lean figure swathed in great lengths of white silk with crimson-stained edges at the hems and sleeves. Her violet eyes had faded into a milky gray void of pupils, but he could still trace her gaze to him.

It seethed with anger.

"This is the last time we speak," she hissed. "Should we meet again, I'll have no love left in my heart for you. Only pity. And that's not enough for me to spare you."

Konar walked toward her, intending to offer comfort, his mind scrabbling for the right words to strengthen a bond that was about to be severed forever. But before he reached her, she held up a forbidding hand. Powerful wind spiraled toward him, knocking him onto his back.

"I see now that it was never me who needed you, but you who needed me. And I'm sorry for the little girl who wasted her love on a family who didn't love her fully in return. I'll never make that mistake again." With a parting look of sorrow, she turned her back to him. "I'll remember you as you once were, if it's any consolation. My brave, smart bretata who died searching for truth and justice."

Konar grew lightheaded as his vision flickered in and out of focus. His head swarmed with thoughts, all bumping into one another like fish spawning upstream. All he could manage was a simple, "I love you, Karliah, no matter what you've become."

And they were the truest words he'd ever spoken.

With that, he drifted into a deep and dreamless sleep.

ELAYSIA

I f it ever rained in Orillon, it had been at least a fortnight since drops last kissed the ground. Everything from the people to the architecture was adorned in a fine layer of dust and grit, and Elaysia found herself constantly blinking to keep her eyes moist. That said nothing of her sore throat and dry skin. The babes weren't taking well to the climate change either. Dytana's tiny nose wrinkled as she squirmed in protest, and Elaron's face was fixed into a permanent frown.

If the arid heat afflicted Maseeya similarly, she didn't show it. In fact, Elaysia couldn't remember the last time the woman's eyes had shone so brightly. She hummed an Az Zarian lullaby Elaysia's mother used to sing as she strode down the stone path, Elaron strapped to her chest in the sling she'd fashioned for him out of woven hemp inlaid with silk. Dytana rested in a similar sling nestled against Elaysia's breasts, her tiny hands gripping the edges of her mother's neckline so she had the comfort of skin readily available.

"Is this the first time you've journeyed outside of Agaas since coming to Neharem?" Elaysia asked as they rounded a corner to a street hemmed in by buildings with teardrop-shaped roofs. A pleasant aroma of sweet and savory spices filled her nostrils, and from within one of the courtyards hidden by stone walls, the bright, soft melody of an unfamiliar stringed instrument calmed her nerves.

Maseeya looked over her shoulder and offered a sad smile. "Annalee was going to take the three of us on a grand tour of Neharem and Orillon when she felt you were old enough for such an adventure, but then she and your father decided to go back to Az Zar, and..."

Elaysia busied herself with consoling Dytana, even though the babe was perfectly content. Ever since the twins arrived, her yearning for her long-dead parents had increased tenfold, and she didn't need such emotions weighing on her as she approached yet another of life's unpleasantries.

As they walked, Elaysia quickly lost count of the gilded archways and well-armed kuza stationed outside them. The Orillon guards were more akin to Az Zarian military than Neharem watchers, though their air of brutish intimidation was more pronounced. Most of them regarded the two women and babes with disdain, if at all, but when Maseeya lingered in front of one to refasten her sandal—an arduous task with a baby strapped to one's chest—he muttered something insulting in Westmun. Elaysia was near-fluent in the Orillon language, thanks to Zavik, but much of the slang was still a mystery to her. Not that he'd been the type to toss about derogatory verbiage, anyway.

Praise the Daughter for that.

"Shouldn't we have arrived by now?" Maseeya asked as the sun inched its way higher in the sky.

Before Elaysia could respond, Elaron let out a wail. Dytana squirmed upon hearing her brother's distress, her face scrunched up and signaling she was only a trigger away from doing the same.

Elaysia squinted at the road before them. The gated entrances to the grand homes were growing larger, but fewer and farther between as the fields and orchards in the interim stretched wider and wider. They had to be close. Unless they'd missed it.

The mere thought of backtracking with the babes during the scorching heat of midday was enough to make her curse.

It didn't help that she had no idea what to look for. Zavik's last tuross had promised someone would be there to greet and guide them when they'd docked in Amiren three days prior, but no one had looked eager to assist the two foreign women and wailing babes weary from sea travel. It'd taken them the better part of that night to find lodging, and nearly double that time the next day to find someone willing to take them by cart to the capital. In other circumstances, Elaysia might've found the endeavor exciting—freeing, even—but seeing as she was on her way to a less than joyous union with two babes still waking through the night, clawing for the teat, well...

It wasn't Az Zar. Things could always be worse. At least in Orillon, she and her offspring were just a nuisance, not an abomination.

"Elaysia." Maseeya caught her by the elbow. "We need to get the twins out of the heat. Maybe we could speak to one of the guards. I'm sure they'd let us indoors long enough to—"

"No." Elaysia dug her heels into the ground as she glanced at the nearest kuza. He glared back with wary eyes. "It's further ahead. I'm certain of it. Anahi said her family is extremely wealthy. They probably live somewhere like that."

Maseeya followed Elaysia's outstretched finger, pointing to the rolling hills ahead. Half a mile up the road, a smaller path branched off and disappeared beneath the shade of broadleaf trees. It reemerged atop a hill, and at its end waited a home that could only be described as a palace. Though not as large as the All-Sovereign's structure in Az Zar, it was arguably even more ornate, with glittering roofs and skillfully laid murals. It was the home of the wealthy and powerful, and Elaysia instantly felt a bristling of wariness deep in her chest.

"I," Maseeya said, with a little pout to her lips, "would not run away from my family residence if it looked like that."

Elaysia continued down the road, albeit at a slower pace. "I'm sure she had her reasons."

Dytana cooed as a shadow engulfed them, momentarily offering respite from the sun. Elaysia glanced skyward, catching the fringes of Onitus's tail feathers as he soared toward the palace, emitting shrieks as the form of another stormbird appeared on the horizon. Another outline appeared soon after, and Elaysia loosed a restrained breath at the sight and sounds of Corvax and Wind Chaser in good health. No matter how magnificent and good-willed a creature, there was always someone seeking to harm it, whether out of ignorance, fear, or downright greed. Or, according to Zavik's tuross messages, out of retribution for vanishing livestock. The stormbirds' rarity only protected them if people felt their value outweighed their destruction.

And Elaysia's trust in people dwindled with each passing day.

They were still a good distance from the palace when a cloud of dust kicked up on the path ahead of them. Zavik was the first to emerge, followed by his protector-turned-stalker, T'Vak. Elaysia broke into something akin to a sprint, moving as best she could with the weight of the babe attached to her torso. She was far from her prime in terms of mobility and agility, but the training sessions she'd dedicated herself to for the past few moon cycles showed. Her lungs ached less, her limbs moved faster, and strength was returning to her deep core.

When she reached Zavik, warm faced and panting, she nearly felt giddy with exhilaration. According to Zavik's expression, he felt similarly. His cheeks shone a deep pink, and his seers had slipped off the bridge of his nose and dangled from a thin lyvium chain around his neck. Elaysia didn't think twice before embracing him (cautious of Dytana caught between them), even in her sweaty and ill-rested state. There were only two people she could be the truest version of herself around, and she counted herself among the gods blessed to have both Zavik and Maseeya supporting her in her time of need.

"What are you doing here?" Zavik said as he pulled back from—but not fully out of—her embrace. "I thought you weren't arriving until the ninth of sub-Vynar. Your last message said so."

Elaysia studied the lines of his furrowed brow for a moment before bursting into laughter. "It said the *fourth*. But I suppose my penmanship could use some work."

Zavik's frown dissipated. "No, the mistake is mine. These things and all." He slid his seers back onto his nose.

"What's this?" Elaysia asked, fingering the lyvium chain.

"A gift." His tone was a little embarrassed, but even more resigned; the way someone spoke when congratulating the winner of a game they'd lost.

"From?" she pressed.

"Your betrothed."

"Oh."

They stood there until both Maseeya and T'Vak caught up. Maseeya's cheeks were flushed with exertion and heat, and T'Vak's from drink—at least according to the stench rippling off him like a sour perfume. Behind T'Vak lumbered a mountain of a man with skin as weathered as well-worn leather. He was missing an ear. And his sense of humor.

"House Undali is eager to welcome you," the man grunted in Nyrinian, though his Westmun accent was so thick, it made his words near indiscernible. "You're early, but we will make accommodations."

"Thank you?" Elaysia began, but the man was already walking away at a much quicker pace than the one he'd used to arrive.

"Don't mind him," T'Vak slurred. "Hallahd's personal goal is to see to it that everyone has a shit-stained day. Keeps us peasant folk humble, lest we forget our place among the worthy." He slipped a wineskin out from the leather belt holding his deep-neckline tunic in place and tossed it back with a wink.

The look Maseeya fixed T'Vak with had no limits to its disgust. She raised a hand before Elaron as if to block the babe from witnessing such indecency.

"Well." Elaysia inhaled deeply as she locked one arm with Zavik's and the other with Maseeya's. "Let's get this over with. Take me to what will become my people's salvation."

Elaysia rolled the sunkiss between her thumb and forefinger, further tenderizing the oblong fruit that already had a fleshy texture to its wrinkled, golden skin. Regardless of the servants—and Zavik—singing its praises, she couldn't work up an appetite for anything but wine. She glared at the rug beneath her feet, staring at the vibrant colors and each symmetrical shape long enough to steep her hatred into it. The glittering candle holder hanging from the ceiling only added noise to the chaos, casting flecks of shimmering light every which way about the room. Everything from the marble pillars to the ornate wooden carvings masking themselves as window coverings screamed wealth, and she wanted no part of it.

"Just try one," Zavik whispered, popping a sunkiss into his mouth. His face radiated genuine bliss. "I've eaten at least a dozen of these a day since arriving here. Believe me when I say you've never tasted something so sweet and smooth. Sunkisses were a rare delicacy when I was a child, but here in House Undali"—he inhaled another, making quicker work of it than the first—"they're as commonplace as flies." He lowered his voice and added, "And your daily calls of nature will be as punctual and smooth as ever."

"For Khiev-Tatamic's sake, Zav." Elaysia dropped the sunkiss back onto the filigreed platter with a groan of disgust.

She leaned back in the cushioned chair, her body tight with discomfort despite its luxurious stuffing. Its embroidered geometric shapes within geometric shapes must've taken some poor soul the better part of a year make, and it was probably worth more than they received for their efforts. The windows in the room they'd been abandoned in—of which she took its sole purpose to be for lounging—were left partially open, as if the cross breeze was enough to make the suffocating heat bearable.

She tied her hair in a disorderly knot atop her head, and while it helped some, sweat still collected around her breasts and everywhere else her body made contact with itself.

"So," Zavik said, still whispering, even though they'd been left alone in the room long enough for the shadows to shift. "What do you think of it?"

Elaysia grimaced as she reached for the water vase to the right of the platter on the hexagonal table. It made a scraping sound as she slid it across the mosaic tiling and poured the liquid into a translucent chalice adorned with a single band of lyvium stamped with some crosshatching patterns.

She set the vase down with a clatter. "It reeks of excess."

Zavik pursed his lips. "I know you hate this. You deserve better, and if there was any way I could take your place, I'd—"

"You can't," she snapped. Then quickly, grabbing his sunburned forearm with gentleness, "But it's alright. I know you would, if you could." She swept her gaze over the room once more, trying to view it in a positive light, as Maseeya so often did. "I suppose all this excess benefits us. If they can toss around rare goods and expensive tableware like fodder, how much more can they help Neharem?" Saying it aloud invigorated her resolve. She'd already been through Haeshol and back. How much trouble could some pompous, rich man's son truly be?

The door groaned open, and Elaysia assumed a rigid posture as she shot Zavik a final look of agony. Seven people entered the room; two of whom, clothed in matching silk tunics, immediately positioned themselves on either side of the door with the butts of their spears firmly planted on the ground. Out of the remaining five, Elaysia recognized two. Hallahd regarded her with a look caught somewhere between suspicion and curiosity, and Anahi exuded discomfort as she positioned the great lengths of her gown's train to drape over the crook of her left arm. Its make was unlike anything Elaysia had seen, alternating silk and some other, heavier fabric with patterning similar to the rug she stood upon.

The woman beside Anahi wore similar attire, and though she bore more delicate, hyper-feminine features, Elaysia could still place her as Anahi's mother. That left two men of similar height—both on the taller side, for humans—but that was where their similarities ended. The elder, upon closer inspection, wasn't nearly as tall as the younger man, and gleaned some fictitious height from his cylindrical headdress. He made up for it with his thick, ornamented beard and a commanding gaze. He wore a thick, white tunic with deep blue embroidery, the pattern of which resembled constellations.

As for the younger man, it was easy enough to presume his identity. Dark, wavy hair like his father's. Warm eyes laced in thick lashes like his mother's. A glimpse of discomfort beneath the confines of his formal attire, like his sister's. But when his gaze caught Elaysia's, the genuine compassion on his face overwhelmed her with a rush of diffidence. She drew a long, soft breath and studied her dirt crusted boots, suddenly regretting not taking Hallahd up on his offer to cleanse herself prior to the meeting. Then again, what did it matter? She was only there to secure help for her people before they found themselves on rationed food and stuffed into cramped shelters.

Or dead.

Zavik leaned closer, just a light brush of his shoulder against hers, but it was enough. A glimpse of starlight between the thick branches of a great forest. A caregiver rushing into the room after a nightmare. A skin of water after a day in the unrelenting sun. Drawing from the strength offered, she strode across the marbled floor, her every step exuding confidence.

"Elaysia Moonrider, high chieftain of Neharem, daughter of Elishon and Annalee, and a Stormrider bonded to Onitus," she said, bringing her fist to her heart as she stopped in front of Anahi's father.

The man's stoic expression turned into a frown as he cast a sideways glance at Hallahd, who shrugged, absolving himself of what Elaysia now realized was her impropriety.

She looked to Zavik for support, but his flared nostrils and thinly drawn lips told her she'd ventured beyond rescue with her boldness. Gritting her teeth, she readied an apology that would undoubtedly be perceived as insincere. Before she could deliver it, though, Anahi's brother stepped forward and offered his hand. Elaysia accepted it, ensuring her grip was as firm and intentional as his own.

"Vahid," he said, still holding tightly to her hand, "and my title is not half as worthy of a mention." A warm chuckle rumbled in his throat as he offered a bow. "We express our utmost gratitude for the privilege of hosting you for as long as you deem suitable, and we eagerly anticipate the fruit our potential future alliance might yield."

Vahid's speech snapped his father out of his embittered musings. "Saya Undali," he offered without a hint of his son's charm. "However, the alliance is surely more than *potential*, isn't it? After all, why else would you make the journey?"

Fair enough.

Elaysia turned her attention to Saya Undali, forcing a smile that would've made even Konar proud. "Thank you for allowing us an audience, Saya, and even more so for your consideration in lending us aid. Neharem has never in its history seen such trying times, and—"

Saya Undali flipped his fingers in a dismissive gesture and motioned for the kuza to open the doors. "Yes, yes. We'll have plenty of time to discuss. Forgive me, for I have pressing matters to attend to. Sayetta Undali will see to it that you are properly situated in your temporary chambers, and we can begin discussing the arrangement and ceremony plans during the evening meal."

Anger flared in Elaysia's chest, shortening her breath and straining the muscles in her neck. She guided her mind away from the room, from the palace, from Orillon, and back to the dew-soaked branches of Agaas's high trees. And despite the many negative feelings still surrounding their relationship, she considered Konar's relentless dedication to his goals, no matter the cost.

This is a sacrifice I must make, she told herself. *And I'll do it with every shred of dignity that remains within me.*

She forced another smile, allowing a little extra toothiness for a predatory effect, and bowed her head in agreement. "The honor would be mine. I look forward to this evening's meal."

Saya Undali wrinkled his nose. "Sunset. On the veranda. Anahi can show you the location. Don't be late."

Elaysia glared at the procession as they left the room in single file, only softening her gaze when Anahi glanced up with remorseful eyes.

Just before the doors slammed shut, however, Vahid peered back in, offered an exaggerated roll of his eyes, and said, "I'll be there early, if you want to speak before a certain someone's presence spoils the evening. Prepare a great many of your tales, for I'm in need of a good story that's not some old man's fabricated embellishment of his past."

Elaysia only offered Vahid a stiff nod. But we when he left the room, another smile crept across her face.

And this time, it was sincere.

"And then he asked me to come to the evening meal early, that I might entertain him with tales of my adventures in Az Zar." Elaysia glanced at Maseeya as the older woman replaced Elaron's soiled loincloth with a fresh wrap given by the sayetta herself. It was made specifically for infants incapable of holding their bowels, sewn to fit snug and lined with silk atop the more absorbent layer beneath.

Maseeya regarded her with crinkling, knowing eyes as she brushed Elaron's wispy hairs with her fingers. One would never know the twins were born early by looking at them now. They were both chubby, with wide, bright eyes, and their gums hinted at the arrival of their first teeth.

"I'm not going to, of course," Elaysia clarified as she freed a lock of her hair from Dytana's remarkably tight grip.

A golden, late-afternoon sun trickled in through the latticed shutters of the room she was to share with Maseeya and the babes, illuminating the crimson rug with a fiery glow. Elaysia placed Dytana directly onto the rug on her stomach, and Maseeya joined her, positioning Elaron beside his sister. As the babes pushed away from the ground, fighting to raise their oversized heads on unstable necks, she sat on a stool behind Elaysia and began running a comb through her tangled hair.

Maseeya's tone was unsuspecting as she asked, "Whyever not?"

Dytana pressed up suddenly, her little arms straining as her face glowed with pride at the impressive feat. Both women cheered her on, and Elaron, wanting the same reaction, struggled to do the same.

Elaysia shrugged. "I didn't think it proper, not yet knowing their customs and what they deem acceptable. They seemed affronted enough by my introduction." That wasn't the only reason, nor the primary cause of her hesitation, but she wasn't of the proper mind to discuss it with Maseeya, a woman who, given a bottle of wine and an afternoon, could unpack a lifetime of trauma from a stranger.

"I see." Maseeya approached the room's most visually arresting element: an ornamental, gilded imitation glass that stretched floor to ceiling. She studied herself in it, smoothing flyaway hairs and pinching color into her cheeks. "I'm glad that's all. For a moment, I worried you found him intimidating."

Elaysia shut her eyes.

Don't fall prey to her baiting. Do. Not.

When she opened them again, she caught Maseeya watching her just before the older woman's gaze averted. Those deep brown eyes didn't stop smiling, however.

"I'm *not* intimidated." Elaysia joined her at the imitation glass, unable to resist the implication any longer. "Especially not by anyone in this palace. I've far greater issues back home and abroad to concern myself with. I just don't care to waste my time, is all."

Maseeya faced her, arms crossed over her stomach. "You have urgent matters to attend to right now? You've already fed the twins, and they'll be needing to rest within the hour. Unless you need rest, too, there's little else to do before the evening meal." She sighed as she squeezed Elaysia's shoulder. "It might be wise to get to know your betrothed outside the confines of his reputation."

Elaysia slouched in resignation. "Why are you always right?"

"Woman's intuition." The edges of Maseeya's sunset-red lips turned up. Her gaze roved over Elaysia from head to toe, brow wrinkling. "But you shouldn't wear that."

The muscles in Elaysia's throat tightened. "Because it's not customary here?"

Maseeya laughed. "Because it's covered in at least ten layers of dirt. Here, I'll watch the little loves while you draw yourself a bath, and then I'll see if I can't track down something breath-taking for you to wear."

The towering pillars and yawning ceilings threatened to engulf Elaysia as she walked alone through the hallways of House Undali. Comprised primarily of marble and stone, the building exuded an ambiance of sophistication, with its diverse range of white, gray, and tan shades. There was a subtle vibrancy, too, amplified by ornate rugs and meticulously crafted vases, which housed an assortment of plants and miniature trees in a myriad of colors. Elaysia bent over to smell one particularly welcoming flower with petal layered over petal in a spiral formation. It was more yellow at the base, closest to the stem, but as it stretched out, the coloring transformed to a rich orange, then finally a red fringe the color of fresh blood. It smelled sweet, yet slightly acidic, almost like wine.

"These are my favorite," someone said behind her—a little too close for comfort.

She flinched, straining in the stifling, over-layered dress Anahi had loaned to her. It looked similar to the one Sayetta Undali wore during their first meeting, only it exposed Elaysia's ankles and clung far too tightly to her milk-endowed breasts.

She gathered the surplus fabric in the crook of her arm as she stole a glance at the intruder, fully expecting a frowning kuza to inform her she'd broken some rule by gazing upon the sacred flowers. Instead, a kind pair of warm eyes looked down at her with curiosity.

She tried to return the warmth. Truly, she did. But the charming countenance of an attractive stranger no longer held the same sway it once had. Besides, it was all for show. The man standing before her had a duty to perform, as did she. It wasn't time for playful banter and long walks through orchards, for foreplay and discussions of dreams.

It was survival. It was an exchange. And the second she stopped seeing it as such was the second she opened herself up to more pain.

Vahid offered his arm to escort her—presumably—to the feasting hall.

She rejected it.

"After you," she said, sweeping her arm before him.

If her betrothed took offense, he didn't show it. He just kept smiling that damned smile, utterly unvexed.

Their footsteps fell silent on the marble, slippers padding in unison, though his were far more elaborate with their pointed, up-curled tips and shimmering gold embroidery. They passed innumerable rooms dedicated to lounging and hosting, leading Elaysia to believe that their kuza, storehouses, and other un-sightly things were situated elsewhere on their extensive land stretching to the foothills. As they drew closer to the feasting hall, the scent of sweet spices and oiled meats enveloped them. Her traitorous stomach growled in response. She'd always had a healthy appetite, but with the twins deriving all their nourishment from her, she maintained the food intake of a man twice her size.

However, when they reached the double doors of what Elaysia took to be the feasting hall, Vahid marched past it toward a spiraling staircase where he took the steps two at a time.

"I thought you wanted to have a conversation prior to your family arriving?" she asked, hesitating at the foot of the stairs. Although he didn't give off the impression of someone with malicious intentions, Az Zar had imparted a crucial lesson to her: everyone was capable of vile deeds. All they needed was the right motivation.

"Oh, I do. I just think you'll prefer this ambience over the feasting hall." His gaze softened as he once again offered his arm. "Trust me?"

Elaysia stiffly linked her arm in his, though she maintained minimal contact as they climbed the polished steps. It was just another arm. Just a courtesy.

A large wooden door awaited them at the top. It was stained a deep amber, and carved in the center were three moons: one waxing, one full, and one waning. She traced her fingers along the outlines, then pulled away abruptly when she remembered Vahid standing watch beside her.

"After you," he said, echoing her prior refrain and sweeping his hand in the same manner.

Elaysia fought to hide her annoyance as she lifted the latch and eased the door open. Once inside, however, all irritation vanished from her mind. Shelf after shelf lined the walls of a room three times the size of Agaas's library. There were scrolls and journals, small statues and rare gemstones, dried herbs and skulls—all positioned with an eye for aesthetics in a space made for both awe and comfort. A single, arched window glowed at the far end of the room, casting a pinkish light onto a giant cushioned chair large enough to be a cot. Beside it stood a single-legged table adorned with a spiky plant.

"My sanctuary," Vahid explained, running his fingertips across the spines of some books. "Ever since Anahi left, I've spent much of my free time here. It was once my grandmaja's tearoom, but I like to think I've made it my own."

He slipped a book free from the shelf and handed it to Elaysia, who cradled it as though it were one of her babes, tracing her thumb over the forest-green leather, inhaling the dusty, woodsy scent.

"I'm told you can read a great many languages, so consider this my union present," he continued. "What's mine is yours and all that, as unions, at least here, go." A nervous chuckle escaped his throat as Elaysia offered her first genuine smile. "This is something sacred to me, but you seem fully deserving of it. I hope it brings you happiness."

A tight ball formed in Elaysia's throat as her eyes burned with the threat of tears. For Khiev-Tatamic's sake, she needed to say something, to express her gratitude.

No words would come.

Vahid briefly touched her shoulder on his way out of the room. "I'll give you some time to yourself. I'm sure a great leader—and mother—like you rarely gets enough of it. And don't worry about impressing my family or saying the right things at the evening meal. My faja is permanently unimpressed, and the rest will see you for who you are."

The door closed softly behind him. Elaysia tucked herself into the oversized chair and drew the book close to her, as though her life depended on it, determined to feel nothing and everything all at once.

But she wouldn't let the tears fall.

LUMIRA

I cy wind bore into Lumira's yawning fangs. She laughed through the discomfort, relishing the freezing air as it entered her lungs, offering a natural high more exhilarating than any intoxicant. Anadu's glossy feathers rippled beneath her as they climbed higher and higher, soaring beyond the clouds into the grayest voids of the sky.

She wanted to keep going, wanted to break the barrier between gods and mortals and witness what lay beyond the boundaries of Quorath. But, as always, Anadu dove right as Lumira's breathing began to constrict.

"Just a little further this time," Lumira pleaded, but Anadu continued her descent.

"It's not safe for you."

The words pattered into Lumira's mind like a soft rain. It remained a mystery to her how quickly she'd grasped the unspoken language of the stormbirds. Though all the Stormriders had fully bonded with their birds through flight—at least the ones constrained to Neharem—no one else had experienced unadulterated communication yet.

Must be the beast in me, she mused, to which Anadu gave a sharp shriek.

The stormbird tucked in her fire-edged wings, hurling toward the unusually placid sea, the wind yanking tears from Lumira and plastering her whiskers to her cheeks. She shut her eyes and clung to the spot on Anadu's neck where the light gray feathers deepened to a midnight blue. Though she trusted the bird to guide them safely to land, she didn't like the feeling of flying blind. When they launched their first stormbird-led assault—which would be far sooner than she liked—the riders would need something to protect their faces from the wind and any other elements that might weaken their battle prowess.

And maybe some protection for you, she thought, pressing herself tightly to Anadu's careening body.

"I need no protection."

The stormbird's wings splayed out moments before colliding with the water. Anadu glided just above the surface, then arced right without warning, plunging her talons into the sea. The abrupt change in movement nearly threw Lumira into the waves. She regained her balance halfway down the magnificent bird's back and flattened herself there as Anadu made for land. Curiosity won over, and she risked dangling her head over the stormbird's side to peer down at the still-writhing animal locked in her talons. Anadu had captured some sort of eel as girthy as Lumira and easily three times as long. It squirmed and whipped its serpentine head back and forth as it bared its serrated fangs.

Lumira had never seen a seaserpent, but assuming they existed at one point, if not presently, she imagined they resembled Anadu's soon-to-be-meal. To hear some of the more learned beridian sailors back on the Isles tell it, the aquatic Great Beasts grew large enough to engulf ships with one fell snap of their massive jaws. Meanwhile, a second set of jaws emerged from their throats, making quick work of all aboard while it dragged them down to a watery grave. And if the tales of Igtheos spun by Elaysia and her people were true, there'd been at least one time in history when they'd snatched full-grown stormbirds out of the sky.

"No sea beast would catch me unwitting," Anadu interjected as she perched atop a rocky, moss-covered cliff just outside the forest.

That's the kind of thinking that will get you caught. Trust me. I know from experience.

The stormbird didn't offer a reply as she waited for Lumira to dismount and move a safe distance away. She then snatched up the eel with her beak, bashed its head against the cliff until it stopped wriggling, and plucked out each of its four eyeballs before inhaling the rest of the meat in long, stringy strips. When she finished, the feathers that adorned her ever-lengthening crest ruffled, and she took to the skies.

"Cassonith haya," Lumira whispered in her native tongue as Anadu's form faded into the horizon.

The stormbird's response rushed through her mind like the wind. "*And may the moons watch over you as well.*"

"Don't tell me you haven't had to shut your eyes while riding Roth," Lumira pressed. "We can't afford to be blindsided while fighting."

Grokhion offered an aggravatingly relaxed grin in response to her prodding and clasped his monstrous hands behind his back. They were making their rounds about Agaas, assessing the structure of the living trees and inspecting the platforms for weakness, should war find its way to the holy city.

Which it most certainly would. It was simply a matter of when, whether the council wanted to admit it or not.

"Honestly, Grokhion, of all the Stormriders, I thought you'd be the most concerned with—" Lumira halted at the foot of the bridge connecting the Zaria Tree to the Elize Tree, sensing her brethren no longer strode beside her. She glanced over her shoulder and let out a low growl.

Grokhion had stopped to retrieve an anderberry that had tumbled out of an overflowing basket balanced atop a crimson-skinned nyrian's head. Unbeknownst to the woman, he placed it back in its vessel with the elegance of a dancer, then motioned for Lumira to join him at the entrance to one of Agaas's many communal gardens.

Lumira begrudgingly complied.

"You seem vexed," Grokhion said as he examined a large squash coated in a brilliant green the same color as his eyes. His beard, contained in three thick strands, brushed the vines woven around the gourd like a cage.

"I seem to be the only one who thinks we need protection," Lumira repeated. She shook her head when Grokhion moved aside for her to inspect the squash.

The elder beridian wove all eight feet of his frame along the narrow path separating the gourds from the herbs. "I trust Roth, not only to protect me, but to value his own life as well." He inhaled deeply of a long-stalked plant laden with tiny yellow flowers, then gestured for Lumira to do the same.

She took a reluctant whiff and found herself calmed by the minty aroma. "I'm not implying he'd deliberately put you in harm's way, but he can't foresee everything, no matter what moons-blessed sight he's touched with. Are you comfortable sacrificing one of our most valuable skills while in flight?"

Grokhion stroked his braided beard. "A beridian without sight is a fish without gills."

Lumira cringed at the proverb, but nodded. "We need masks. Or better yet, helmets. Before Zavik left, he mentioned sketching plans for just that, and we can use our new Orillon connection to import glass at cost."

"For the eye lenses." Grokhion stopped perusing the plant life and met her gaze. "You've thought this all through."

Lumira shrugged. "It's sort of my job now."

"So it is." He brought his forehead to hers, and she swallowed to loosen her tightening throat. The gesture still summoned the ghost of her father, the last beridian she'd exchanged such affection with. "The moons are with you, Lumira. They are proud, as I am proud."

A plant guardian on the verge of manhood slipped around them, muttering sheepish apologies under his breath as he reached a russet arm to strengthen a stalk with a stick and some twine. Lumira seized the opportunity and pulled away from Grokhion, slinking down the path and over the length of rope enclosing the garden. Once free, she crossed the bridge to the Elize Tree, investigating the series of lofts that made up the central platform. Their layouts were identical, from the thatched roofs to the single, unlatched doors preventing nothing but the elements from walking inside.

Lumira cringed as a memory of her first time in Agaas took hold of her mind. She'd entered loft after loft, looking to exploit unassuming people, and received unmerited compassion in return. Recalling it triggered a wave of shame.

The citizens of Agaas did not deserve the war looming over them. If she could stop it, could do something important with her life for once, she would. Regardless of the council's malicious gossip or the haunting memories of her past, she would persevere.

She descended the ramp to the lowest level of the living tree, where she kneeled to inspect a ladder. The rickety old things were reserved for catastrophes, in the event the ramps were compromised. But, like much of Agaas, they were a weakness that could be easily exploited if there were not proper patrols stationed all around base camp.

"It would require great effort on our enemies' part and great blindness on ours to let an entire army ascend without our knowledge," Grokhion said, kneeling beside her. The last streams of light speared down through the thick branches of the living tree, highlighting sections of his auburn fur with gold.

"It's not an entire army I'm worried about." Lumira lowered half her weight onto the first rung, wincing as it creaked. "It only takes one person with a well-placed strike to compromise Agaas's integrity. Just ask the high chieftain about her induction day."

Grokhion's brow furrowed. "The Lawful Dominion won't be encroaching on Agaas anytime soon, but should our forces fall, we can station what remains of our armies at base camp."

"It'd be a deathtrap." Lumira's whiskers twitched as her ears flattened against her head. She leaped back onto the platform. "The citizens would be poultry in a pen."

"They'd never abandon the holy city." Grokhion's trunk of an arm gestured to the living tree. "They'd never leave the nevethium hearts to certain destruction." As if he sensed Lumira's brewing rebuttal, he raised her chin with one clawed finger, then lowered himself onto the ladder. The rungs moaned beneath him, but they held firm. "Still, it's wise to prepare for the worst, and I don't fault you for your suspicion. There are some adjustments we can make to both watchers and fortifications, starting with these ladders." He winked, then fixed his attention on the rungs as he slowly lowered the hundreds of feet to base camp.

"Some?" Lumira called after him. "Agaas is as vulnerable as a virgin in Amiren."

A whisper of Grokhion's laughter trickled up to her.

At least someone understands, she thought as she lowered herself down after him.

Elaysia had left Lumira in charge of Neharem in her stead, namely of Agaas, and she'd do whatever was necessary to fulfill that oath, even if it meant going behind the councils' backs or upsetting the people. Perhaps, in that way, she truly was the best for the job. She didn't have a reputation left to uphold.

Thank the moons for that.

Rap. Rap.

Lumira's eyes shot open. She scented the air for blood, ears twitching and straining to capture any sounds of distress.

Rap, rap, rap.

She sprung out of her cot, landing lightly in front of her loft door, claws extended. A growl rumbled in her throat.

"Shadow Chieftain, are you in the dream world?"

Her claws retracted. She recognized the voice, and while apprehension stained it, there was no fear and little urgency. Moonlight spilled into the loft as she swung the door open. A pair of mossy-green, vaguely luminescent eyes stared back at her.

Kahana.

Lumira motioned for Elaysia's recently appointed head of the watchers to come inside. "I told you not to call me that," she said as she secured the door behind them.

A look of confusion crossed Kahana's face. "But it's your title. The person the high chieftain appoints in their stead is their shadow, also known as—"

"I know. You don't have to bother with it. No one else does."

"Then they mean you dishonor."

"I..." Lumira couldn't summon a rebuttal in her sleep-deprived state. She collapsed back on her cot with a groan. It was Agaasian custom to offer one's guest refreshment, but glancing about her loft, all she located was a bowl of fishbones and skins.

Moons curse it.

The Moákun nyman shifted uncomfortably, gripping the handle of her club. "I come bearing bad tidings."

A dark cloud bloomed in Lumira's heart. Her hand snaked up to rub the notch in her right ear, then found the cuff earring below it. "Go on."

"We received a tuross from the Ni'anko." Kahana held Lumira's gaze with bravery as she whispered, "They've been conquered."

Lumira's thoughts rushed to Grokhion, to the people he swore forever changed his life by embracing him with compassion. She didn't know exactly how long he'd been with the Ni'anko prior to joining Elaysia's Stormriders, but she had a feeling he more strongly identified with them than his clan back on the Isles. And they'd been the only Neharem tribe to truly welcome beridians among them.

"Why?" she demanded. "They're a neutral tribe without a fighter among them. They're not a threat to the Lawful Dominion, they're—"

"A nuisance." The truth of Kahana's words stung Lumira like a slap. "And they occupy land adjacent to the Apáasutai, to Agaas."

Lumira's claws extended again, unbidden. "Give it to me."

Kahana retrieved a small, rolled parchment from the beaded belt securing her tunic and handed it over. Lumira turned to give herself the illusion of privacy as she slowly unrolled the strip. The broken seal was that of the Ni'anko, the figure of a pregnant mother nestled inside a star, a reminder of their beliefs that all life came from the stars, and to the stars it returned. The words were scrawled elegantly in Nyrinian, the language of correspondence used among all tribes to avoid discrepancies in the numerous dialects of Neharem. Just below the seal was a dark brown stain, a different shade from the ink used to inscribe the note.

A lump formed in Lumira's throat as she read.

The Lawful Dominion has taken our lands, but they will not take our hearts. Many of our people have returned to the stars, and the rest now come to you, seeking refuge. I will not abandon my home until all my children still awake in our world have found fires to warm their bodies and food to nourish their souls. Please, embrace them. Please, do not force them to take sides in a war they never wanted. They will serve Agaas in other ways, and the Ni'anko will be bound to you for generations.

With stardust,

Kelsia, Chief of the Ni'anko

Lumira crumpled the parchment in her hand, rage suffocating her grief. "Has anyone else read this?"

"I've ordered all tuross messages to be brought to me first." Kahana's gaze didn't leave the crumpled parchment.

"And you trust that?"

Kahana crossed her arms. "I trust the people I have on post at the receiving nests. They're all Apáasutai or Moákun."

Lumira retrieved her spear from the foot of her cot. "Gather the Stormriders, and tell them to summon their birds, if they can."

"No additional warriors, Shadow Chieftain? Only Mardus and Grokhion remain in Agaas."

"I'm aware," Lumira snapped. She closed her eyes and inhaled deeply through her nostrils to calm the storm inside her. "We'll get there quickly on our stormbirds if no other warriors are slowing us down. We won't engage the enemy."

"As you wish." Kanaha stepped out into the night, club swinging at her hip. "I will ready a few trusted watchers, but we won't depart Agaas without your word."

"Good." She followed the Moákun onto the platform, not caring if the door latched behind her. No latch could protect the things she cared most about, anyway.

And that scared her most of all.

The largest Ni'anko settlement was nearly two days' ride on horseback, but the stormbirds cut that time down to a night. Lumira, along with Grokhion and Mardus, departed Agaas within an hour of receiving word and followed the coastline under the glaring light of the full moons.

They exchanged no words; not that the circumstances would've welcomed it. And even if they'd flown under better tidings, the Stormriders still couldn't hear each other over the wind howling through their ears, their faces buried deep into the bird's necks.

Masks, Lumira thought as a chilling gust cut through her. As soon as Zavik returned, she'd have him make his sketches a reality. Maybe see if Maseeya could work her magic on some uniforms and light armor for the nyrian and human riders, too. Their naked bodies could only withstand so much.

"I can communicate with my kindred." Anadu's voice flooded Lumira's mind like the vibrations of a beridian singing bowl, releasing the same calming waves as the favored instrument of her people. *"If there's something you want to say to your brethren, tell me."*

Lumira considered the offer. Because of Anadu's superior size and speed, they were well ahead of Mardus and Keera, and even further ahead of Grokhion and Roth. But passing messages along could cause delays, and delays were detrimental in urgent situations.

Can I learn to speak to them as you do with your own kind? Lumira asked.

Allowing her thoughts to flow into Anadu's mind grew easier by the day. Was it so outlandish to suppose they could communicate non-verbally without the birds? Surely, the feat couldn't have been exclusive to Great Beasts and northern giants.

Lumira sensed the uncertainty in Anadu's thoughts as the bird replied, *"It is more than learning a language. It is a relationship with the essence of Quinaria, an ability to harness the power flowing through all living beings and channel it into thought."*

So, Lumira pressed. *It's possible?*

"Everything is possible"

Anadu cut right without warning. In a desperate attempted to stay on, Lumira sunk her claws into the thick feathers coating the stormbird's neck.

"You're hurting me." A harshness overtook Anadu's tone, and it throbbed in Lumira's skull like a headache. *"Let go."*

And die? Lumira retracted her claws and wrapped her arms around the bird's neck. If there was a balance to be achieved of keeping Anadu uninjured while still preventing her own death by a fall, she was doing a poor job of finding it.

"We'll have to see about harnesses, too," she muttered, burying her face as Anadu increased speed with her descent.

When Lumira dared a glance a few minutes later, the sun peeked over the horizon, bathing the ocean in crimson and gold. Its hues were reminiscent of hot coals; the heat almost tangible. A few hundred yards from the shore sprawled the Ni'anko settlement, home to more than half their people.

There were no obvious signs of habitation in the region, at least not from above. It wasn't until Anadu glided parallel with the settlement that Lumira caught the first hints of dwellings. Caught between the deciduous trees and rolling hills of the lush terrain of the Ni'anko were oval wooden doors emerging from the land itself. Single walls, consisting primarily of stone and sod, were the only mortal-made parts of their dwellings, the rest of the structures sealed naturally by the hills they fed into. Some had the added feature of a smokestack, but even those looked like little more than cairns from a distance.

Towering in the heart of the settlement was a magnificent hundred-foot tree, its expansive roots intertwining with the shimmering waters of the lake beneath it. Compared to the size of the living trees of Agaas, the tree the Ni'anko reverently called Akaesho was nothing to marvel at, being only a couple of feet taller and broader than other pocoaon trees. But while it bore the same long, flowing branches and leaves that hung down in canopies, like the pocoaons found throughout Northwestern Neharem, its coloring was otherworldly: a myriad of luminescent blues, greens, and purples. The last (and only) time Lumira had visited the settlement, Grokhion had explained the Ni'anko believed it was gifted its unique coloring by the stars, and that its name—loosely translated—meant 'star seed.'

It was sacred, a deity, and treated as such.

But when Anadu landed in the clearing beside it, the warmth drained from Lumira's face.

Dangling among the limber branches of Akaesho were the bodies of countless Ni'anko. An elderly human woman wrapped in a vibrant robe embroidered with constellations. A young nyrian male, who could've been a formidable warrior, had he been born to a different tribe. A nyman girl, her black and white streaked hair so reminiscent of Elaysia's it made Lumira's chest ache. She tried to distance herself from the scene by counting the corpses, but she gave up after a few dozen, unable to escape the haunting display of bloated, lifeless faces, of stiff limbs and wind–tattered hair. Except for a few, they were not bound, meaning they'd willingly sacrificed themselves for the belief they cherished most.

Peace.

Lumira hated and loved them for it. She wanted to rip one of their bodies from the tree and shake it back to life only to scream at it, *why*? Their silent protest was surely lost on anyone loyal to Raynar, the son of a bloodthirsty chief who'd spent his entire existence seeking war. They could've at least run, could've—

The breath caught in Lumira's throat. Scattered around the tree's great white trunk were fallen slippers and plant–based shoes that hadn't been able to withstand the force of the thrashing incited by hangings. And hidden beneath a pair of well–trodden sandals was a small doll, beridian in make. The tail gave it away, a long, silken thing made with real fur probably shed by the cub's parents. Its two jadestone eyes were identical to the one Lumira's mother had made her all those years ago. It meant somewhere in the tree was a cub, young enough to still carry a doll, its own tail stiff, its whiskers to never twitch with excitement, its fur never again to be ruffled while frolicking beneath the moons.

A sob formed in Lumira's throat as her chest heaved with irregular breaths. She collapsed to her knees and sunk her claws into the loam.

She didn't glance up as Roth and Keera landed on either side of Anadu, their mighty wings stirring up a cascade of fallen leaves. Only when Grokhion's gut-twisting roar disturbed the silence did she flinch. Even then, she could not bring herself to look upon his face. If her heart ached so to behold the massacre, how much more would it affect him, who called the settlement home?

The *thud* of Grokhion's frame vibrated the ground as he leaped from his mount and sprinted toward Akaesho with a rage Lumira had only witnessed him unleash once before. Back in Az Zar, the night they took Elaysia. He ripped off his tunic as he ran, a finely stitched leather dyed blue and embroidered with constellations beloved by his tribe, leaving him in nothing but a loincloth. As if determined to remove any ties to civility, he charged on all fours and leaped into the tree's lowest hanging branch. A swipe of his claws severed the first rope. He caught the body as it fell: a young woman, her skin a lusterless, lifeless blue. Grokhion sprang from the tree, the woman still in his arms, and laid her gently at the base of the trunk.

Lumira's mouth opened to cry out his name, to offer her help, her condolences, but all that emerged was a choked mew. She clenched her fist, her posture rigid as stone. Grokhion descended with the cub next, then a third body. A fourth. A fifth. She padded to the base of the trunk, then hesitated.

The look on his face told her to stay back. The seething, animalistic rage. The pupils dilated enough to render his emerald eyes black. The fangs that had yet to disappear behind a usually pleasant mouth.

Even she was unwelcome in his rage-filled grief.

"We should help him."

The nearness of the voice sent Lumira whirling to face it, her claws poised at its bearer's throat. Only when she recognized Mardus's startled eyes did she retract them.

"No," she breathed.

The Moákun raised an eyebrow, his square jaw twitching as though he meant to defy her.

Lumira made her body a barrier. The faint sound of rope snapping and branches quivering echoed behind her as Grokhion persisted in his efforts. "He's taking responsibility for their deaths," she whispered when Mardus wouldn't retreat.

"That's foolish." Mardus crossed his arms in the same disgruntled manner his father displayed at most council gatherings. "He couldn't have known the Lawful Dominion would lay waste to a neutral tribe."

"But he'll always feel he should have."

Lumira marched past Mardus, uncertain of her destination but desperate to escape the heap of corpses amassing by the shoreline. There was no point in trying to convince him. Mardus wasn't Ni'anko, and more so—and perhaps most importantly—he wasn't beridian. He didn't understand that the worst thing a beridian could do was abandon their clan with a looming threat. It didn't matter that the Ni'anko didn't hold those beliefs, for Lumira doubted Grokhion had ever fully shed the ways of the Isles. Back home, being absent from battle wasn't simply shameful.

It meant banishment.

Lumira prowled around the Ni'anko settlement, peering inside dwellings and clinging to the hope of survivors. And though the warmly furnished and somewhat cluttered homes of Grokhion's adopted tribe were a far cry from the minimalistic dwellings of the Morotôk, she couldn't help but notice the similarities. An unprovoked attack. An eradicated settlement.

And no sign of nevethium.

Lumira lingered inside a dwelling, captivated by a detailed painting of two nyrian men and a small human child, until Mardus's voice dragged her back to the harsh realities of the present. Words flew from his mouth in some Moákun tongue, and though she'd done her best to pick up phrases from the tribes that frequented Agaas, she was far from fluent in any of them.

She turned from the painting, one hand still pressed into the rough edges of the canvas. "I don't understand."

Mardus's eyes were nearly as dark as Grokhion's. "Come with me," he said slowly in Nyrinian.

Lumira followed him into the unrelenting sunlight of midday, shielding her face as she walked. The stormbirds had abandoned the clearing, but she didn't give their absence a second thought. It wasn't uncommon for them to return to the skies as soon as possible. On the ground, they were vulnerable. In the clouds, they were gods. Grokhion, however, had ceased his retrieval of bodies and sat crumpled at the base of the tree, his face buried in his massive hands.

"Leave him," Mardus said gruffly. "What I'm about to show you will only worsen his grief."

The Moákun's lyvium-plate earrings clanged together as he strode down a path of trampled grasses and wildflowers, leading to a generously sized dwelling fortified with stone walls. Greenery hung down from the sod roof to help blend it into the natural surroundings, but its form was unmistakable. Lumira scoured the region for anything Mardus might've deemed notable. If he'd dragged her over to inspect kicked in doors or traces of blood coating the entryways—

She stopped mid-stride, the pad of her foot pressing on something metallic. A shiver coursed through her body as she kneeled to inspect a small lyvium casing no larger than a berry. She held it to her ear and tapped lightly with one claw.

"There's a—"

She silenced Mardus with a growl and prowled forward, snatching up another casing, then another. After collecting more than she could carry, she shoved a few into the pouch fastened around her waist and entered the oversized dwelling. Several long wooden tables filled a room the size of Agaas's summit lodge, leaving only a narrow space at the far end for a large canvas exhibiting a range of constellations. Against the wall was a collection of looms, and beside those, various stringed and percussive instruments—some of which Lumira had never seen—and finally, a station for woodworking.

"The Ni'anko believe in the collective learning of many skills to better the community," Mardus said, running his fingers across a loom. "Structures like this are made to host many children at once so they can bring in masters of various crafts to instruct them."

Lumira detached herself from any thoughts of children sitting innocently inside a center for learning while monsters brandishing weapons broke down the door. She was certain of little in life, but she knew beyond a doubt that harming a child was the point at which someone lost their last shred of goodness. She took a cautious step forward, startling as another lyvium casing clattered across the floor.

The room spun around her. She gripped the back of a chair to steady herself, only to find it tacky with blood. Darkness encroached at the edge of her vision. Her tongue went dry, and suddenly she was pulled from the room and back into a hut on the Isles.

The sun seeps through the cracks in the hut, casting warm, crimson stripes onto Lumira's back. She's little more than a cub, just a mewling kitten, her ears not fully developed, her claws extending and retracting without her command. Outside, there are roars and snarls as her clan fends off another. She doesn't know why they've come, only that she's been stashed in this hut at the center of the village with the rest of the young, their bodies tangled in a giant mass of tails and limbs.

The screams are getting closer now. Lumira watches through the cracks as one of the warriors meant to protect them collapses. His hooked fishing knife clatters to the decking. There's a dart in his neck. His face swells to twice its size until she can no longer recognize it. She shrinks back into the mess of cubs, hating herself for the tendrils of fear snaking around her heart. A clawed hand tears off the siding and—

"Lumira?"

She gasped, unable to draw a full breath. Mardus gripped both her shoulders, his face etched with lines of worry.

"I'm fine." She shrugged him off and worked her way to the far end of the room. It'd been a long time since the memory had sprung on her, and it was not the time or place to dissect it.

"Are you sure you're alright? You look ill."

Despite the concern in Mardus's voice, she ignored him, leaning in to closer inspect the canvas. It was marred with countless holes. Beneath it, a pool of drying blood. The Lawful Dominion had worked to remove the bodies, likely stringing them all up in Akaesho. But they'd wanted the evidence of their massacre to remain.

She held one of the lyvium casings out to Mardus, who responded by retrieving one from his own beaded pouch fastened to his belt.

"The weapons from Az Zar," she murmured. "What did Xaren call them?"

"Shieum." He spat the words as if they were poison.

Intense, stabbing pains seized Lumira's stomach. "Az Zar is supplying Raynar's rebellion with weapons."

Mardus slipped the casing back into his pouch. "That was my assumption, also. But if so, why haven't they used the new weapons in battle with us? They're far superior to anything we have."

"They didn't want us to know yet. Now they do." Lumira hurried from the room before another memory could assault her.

Mardus followed her outside, allowing a few moments' silence as they walked before stating the obvious: "This is a message."

"What else?" She swallowed her rage. The last thing Grokhion needed was for her to lose herself to her emotions. "They want us to know they have powerful allies and weapons, and that they're not afraid to exercise both against even the most innocent of people. If they could do this to the Ni'anko, how much more could they do to Agaas?"

They stayed until nightfall, bringing the bodies down one by one and preparing them for death in the way of the Ni'anko: simple holes in the ground with naked bodies nestled inside. Since the Ni'anko believed all life came from the stars, it was to the stars they'd return. But as their mortal bodies were no longer needed, their shells became a gift to the soil, similar to how they composted what little food waste they made into food for their gardens. Even in death, Grokhion told her, there was life. A gift.

The stormbirds knew when to return, as they always did, arriving shortly after the last body was planted. There were three hundred and sixty in all. Roughly half that number in Akaesho, and the rest fished out from the lake below. Those had been even worse to retrieve, the bodies far more grotesque, swollen and waterlogged, riddled with abrasions and wrinkled skin. Lumira only made it through the ordeal by telling herself the spirits were long departed. They were just carcasses. Nothing more.

Mardus took to the skies first, eager to get word back to Agaas. When it became apparent Grokhion had no intention of leaving, Lumira started a small fire, then scooted as close to him as she dared.

At least an hour passed. The sky glistened black and silver, and Lumira's stomach growled with a ferocity she'd not experienced in moons. But her hunger was a mere whisper compared to the deep sorrow she felt for the now abandoned settlement and the people who'd once occupied it. She was about to nod off to sleep when Grokhion loosed a mournful roar.

"When I first arrived here," he said, emotion choking his voice. "I was searching for a fresh start. A place to right all the ways my life had gone very wrong. The Ni'anko embraced me without question, without judgment, and without expectations. Kelsia herself saw to my rehabilitation..."

His shoulders heaved with silent sobs.

Lumira placed her hands on either side of his massive head, drawing his forehead to hers. "It's not your fault."

Grokhion pulled away. The look he gave turned her insides to water.

"I know. But vengeance will be mine."

ZAVIK

"**Y**ou gonna finish that?"

Zavik glanced up from the parchment in a daze. T'Vak leaned over the desk, knotted strands of hair from the unshaven side of his head nearly dipping into the inkwell. The object of his desire, a wooden bowl of sunkisses stuffed with sun butter and lightly sprinkled with salt, rested to the right of Zavik's ink-stained hand, mostly uneaten.

"I suppose not," Zavik mumbled, sliding the bowl over to the backhander. The sweet, savory, and salty combination of the Munskahan staple was a newfound favorite, but he had neither time nor appetite for mindless munching.

He sighed and reached for the cup of moskuto that had long since gone cold. No flavor registered on his tongue as the liquid slipped down his throat, only a note of bitterness and the accompanying zing of vigor. Satisfied, he set the empty cup aside and dipped his quill in the inkwell.

He'd only made it a quarter of the way through his latest sketch for an aquatic vessel—more speculative than systematic—when the sound of smacking lips triggered a twitch in his left eye. He peered over his shoulder and found T'Vak reclining on the windowsill, licking the sticky sweetness from his fingers.

Zavik tried a subtle clearing of his throat. When that didn't work, he tried it a second time, much louder. But T'Vak continued sucking and smacking to his heart's content, then wiped his hands on his borrowed silk tunic. As if that wasn't offensive enough, he retrieved a wineskin from his hip and chugged at least half the contents before releasing an unnecessarily loud burp and closing his eyes.

Gritting his teeth, Zavik carefully positioned his quill over the parchment.

Then the humming started.

He pressed a finger to his still-twitching eye. "Do you think you could afford me some solitude today? Saya Undali is expecting this union contract tonight, and I'm not even halfway through the conditions."

That the saya expected the union contract was true.

That Zavik actively worked on it was not.

"You're good at bullshitting and saying things the way wealthy folk want to hear them. Always have been." T'Vak slipped down from the window and sprawled out on his bed, limbs stretched out like a sea star. "You'll eke something out, and no one besides me will know how much agony it cost you." A snort, then two hiccups, followed by another snort-laugh likely triggered by said hiccups.

Zavik dug his forefinger into his thumb's cuticle. He never knew whether to take the backhander's compliments as genuine. As he returned to his work on the navigation mechanism, however, something T'Vak said lingered in the back of his mind.

"Always have been," Zavik repeated, keeping his gaze on the parchment to appear distracted. "That phrase connotes a long-term relationship. Something of substance."

"Telling me we aren't close, Zavvie boy?" Another laugh followed, but it had a hint of unease. "Our relationship that's stretched well beyond a year isn't 'substantial' enough to you?"

A hot, stinging sensation arose from the spot on Zavik's cuticle where he peeled a sliver of dead skin away. "I'm not saying that. We've been through some real shit, as you'd say."

T'Vak grinned at that, though his eyes remained closed.

"It's just…" Zavik plucked the seers from his face and massaged the bridge of his nose.

It's just what, Zav? Odd that something about him has seemed off ever since your chance meeting in the desert?

Strange that you feel like you know him—rather, knew him—prior to said chance meeting?

But he wasn't going to say any of that. Not until he was certain and, ideally, not alone with the man he needed to confront.

"Just what?" T'Vak's tone suggested he didn't care, but Zavik knew he did. Otherwise, he wouldn't have fished for an answer.

Zavik let out a groan, implying his frustration with the union contract he pretended to work on. "Just this that contract is jumbling all my thoughts together. Maybe I'll go for a walk to clear my head."

A deciding thumb shot up from T'Vak's hand. "You do that. The closer we get to that ceremony, the closer I get to my payment, eh?"

"Something like that."

Zavik grabbed the head wrap from his bed and a thin scarf for his neck, then slipped out of the room, closing the door softly behind him.

His head *was* all a jumble, constantly playing tricks on him, planting unwarranted suspicions and fear. Maybe he imagined more to his relationship with T'Vak because they'd scarcely left each other's side. He'd sort things out with a walk, and the world would make sense again.

As much as it ever did, anyway.

The days and nights butted into one another as Zavik and the rest of House Undali's inhabitants prepared for the grand ceremony. He completed the contract, much to the liking of both Saya and Sayetta Undali, and at least with terms acceptable enough for Elaysia to concede signing.

The essential agreement (which took two and a half sheets of parchment to formally express) was simple: in exchange for the union of Vahid and Elaysia, House Undali promised to lend its resources—be it wealth, soldiers, or nourishment—to Agaas, and Agaas promised to do the same, until one party perished or both agreed to a severance of the union, and therefore the contract.

It wasn't exactly the loving sort of agreement most couples vowed to abide by on such a momentous day, but perhaps it was more commonplace among the wealthy than Zavik knew. Regardless, it was prepared and verbally agreed upon, and all that remained was the day itself, which rapidly approached.

The palace seemed to diminish in size with each passing day. New pots and plants began filling the corners, more livestock grazed in the fields, and piles of brightly colored blankets and jars of incense covered the tables—all anticipatory union gifts from other great houses. It grew increasingly hot with the influx of guests, and servants bustled around with flushed faces and sweaty brows preparing chambers and coordinating provisions. Even the kuza multiplied overnight. Saya Undali had called them in from their previous assignments to prepare for the war in Neharem, in case they were among the one-third chosen.

The ongoing chaos left even the riders ill at ease. Anahi had been cranky since returning home, so there was little change in her, but Yerakai exhibited behavior that made Zavik increasingly worried for him. He'd come across the soft-spoken Apáasutai tucked into corners of the palace, clutching his throat, his cheeks flushed, face covered in a sheen of sweat. Zavik assumed it was a reaction to the heat at first, but after witnessing it several times, coupled with Yerakai sneaking away every chance he got to tend the stormbirds or mitigate whatever trouble they'd caused that day, he feared the Stormrider was not as well-adapted to Orillon as they thought.

And Ellie? She spent much of her time locked away in Vahid's tower chamber, reading or meditating or cursing the world, and when she wasn't there or forced to attend the frequent feasts House Undali hosted to show her off, the twins claimed ownership of her remaining hours. Zavik mostly saw her in passing or when he was lucky enough to be the bearer of some trivial message. She looked well; healthy as ever. The death of her innocence had awakened something fierce beneath, but along with her newfound resilience came an almost unhealthy dose of skepticism. He tried to pull her away in between dress fittings, rehearsals, and walks through the orchards with Saya Undali to 'better understand the family she was about to be adopted into,' but those moments were rare and the contact superficial. She'd always tell him she was fine, and he'd never press further.

Until one afternoon, the ceremony only a few days away, Zavik received a curled piece of parchment slipped beneath his chamber door. The wax seal was House Undali's: the winged deity from Vahid's ring. The handwriting and language were not.

Z,

Meet me in the courtyard tonight after the kuza's fourth round.

East gate. Dress discreetly, and bring your friend, if you must.

–E

"Whatcha reading?"

Zavik yelped and crumpled the note in his palm. He glanced over his shoulder and found T'Vak eyeing him with a knowing look. His disheveled hair made it look as though he'd just woken from a nap, but Zavik could've sworn there was no one in the room when he'd opened the door moments prior.

"It's, uh..." He shoved the crumpled parchment into his pocket. "Are you busy tonight?"

A shrill whistle escaped T'Vak's lips. "Oh, always busy, Zavvie boy. Always more wine to drink and love-givers to pursue and delicacies to filch from the Undali's kitchen." He studied the pocket Zavik had shoved the note into as he gave his stubbled jaw a massage. "Could make an exception, if the pay's right."

"Just add it to what I owe you." Zavik maneuvered around the backhander to peer through the lattice shutters. The sun was well into its descent, giving him just enough time to finish the calligraphy on the guest list and arrange payment from House Undali to House Dessaton for the livestock losses caused by the stormbirds. Again.

They'd gotten better about pursuing wild game or eating meat procured by Yerakai, but there were still times they went too long between hunts and got bored with already dead food. Saya Undali would only tolerate so many more of those times before that bulging vein in his forehead finally burst.

"So," T'Vak said, joining Zavik by the window. "What's the mission?"

"Assisting the future sayetta of House Undali on what will probably be her final escapade as a free woman." Zavik tucked his seers into the neckline of his tunic and splashed his face with some water from the basin beside his bed. "Or something of the like. Just be discreet when we leave tonight. She only wants you along for protection."

"And what purpose do you serve?"

Heat flashed across Zavik's cheeks as he dabbed his face with the cloth folded atop the stand. "Entertainment, obviously."

T'Vak snickered and slapped his back. "That, my friend, is the cleverest remark you've made all week."

The crescent moons smiled down on Zavik as he slipped into the courtyard under the cover of a relatively dark night—at least as dark as it got in the clear-skyed, ever-awake city of Munskahan. T'Vak trailed behind him, not half as concerned with maintaining anonymity, especially since he'd befriended the kuza on patrol. And to be fair, there wasn't a genuine need for such deception. House Undali placed no restrictions on the comings and goings of their household and guests. Still, Elaysia had wanted it kept discreet for a reason, and the least Zavik could do was try to uphold that wish.

"Are you armed?" Zavik asked as his boot dislodged a pebble and sent it skittering across the path and into the shelter of a sculpted shrub.

T'Vak sauntered past the fountain, pausing long enough to run his hand through the water as it shot out in a wide arc, shimmering in the moonlight. "When am I not?"

Zavik shrugged, scolding himself internally for the foolish question.

While House Undali's east gate was not as grand as the other entrances, it still had its share of ornamentation. Intricate winged deities and zaka-zaka motifs adorned its brilliant blue tiles and served as a testament to the craftsmanship and religious significance of Munskahan architecture. But, like all the other gates, it remained locked after sunset.

Which could pose a problem, Zavik thought, assessing the sheer wall. He was about to consult T'Vak's scaling expertise when icy hands covered his eyes from behind.

"You came," Elaysia whispered. She uncovered his eyes, careful to avoid knocking off his seers.

"Couldn't refuse the future sayetta of House Undali," Zavik said, turning to face her.

A cloak the color of midnight covered her from head to calf, and beneath it were leather leggings tucked into her old Agaasian riding boots. It harkened back to her favored attire in Agaas, at least prior to her induction. The leather gloves and high velvet collar were new, however, and looked to be Maseeya's handiwork.

Zavik gestured to her ensemble with a thrust of his chin. "I don't suppose you're intending a night full of scandal dressed like that. Are we breaking into other great houses and stealing their rarest gems?"

A warm laugh bubbled up from Elaysia's throat. She withdrew her hood, revealing streams of small braids woven into a massive one, the great lengths of which were secured by multiple leather cords to prevent any strands from escaping. "Right on the first account, wrong on the second." She surveyed the courtyard beyond him, her smile dissipating. "Did T'Vak not come?"

Before Zavik could answer, the backhander sauntered from the shadows cast by a line of palano trees, dragging one of their fallen fronds behind him.

"At your service, High Chieftain Sayetta, Rider of Great Beasts and Bearer of Unforetold Offspring," the backhander said with impeccable, and rarely exercised, enunciation. He used the frond to accentuate an already extravagant bow, then flashed her a grin that wasn't entirely unbecoming.

Elaysia threw Zavik a look to assess T'Vak's sincerity, and when he reacted with a shrug, she brought her fist to her heart in a traditional Agaasian greeting. "I know Agaas owes you a great deal, and I personally want to express my gratitude for your continuous aid." She looked at Zavik again, then hurriedly added, "After the ceremony, we should have enough to repay you twice over."

"Just the agreed-upon amount between me and Zavvie boy's fine, High Chieftain. The twice over bit you can keep as a union present." The way T'Vak glanced at the ground as he shoved his hands into the pockets of his robe made him appear almost bashful.

Zavik knew better.

"I'm honored," Elaysia said, feeding off the backhander's demeanor.

T'Vak, glancing up just in time to see Zavik's eye roll, eased back into the tactless way in which he preferred to conduct himself. "And in what way might I best honor you tonight? It might not be the sort of amusement you're—"

"The high chieftain is short on time," Zavik said, intercepting T'Vak's soon-to-be crass comment as he moved in to examine one of the crystal handles adorning the gate. "Speaking of which"—he yanked on the handle, which didn't budge, then faced Elaysia—"were you intending to scale this wall? I mean, I'm not opposed to working up a little sweat, but..."

His nervous laugh that followed didn't do him any favors.

Something flew from Elaysia's hand as stealthy as a hawk. Zavik surprised himself by catching it, his fingers wrapping around a cool, light metal that could only be lyvium.

Of course she had a key. She was the future sayetta and had full access to the property. What an entirely pointless thing to get worked up over.

"Well played." He turned the key over in his hand as he looked between her and the gate. "What, exactly, are your plans for the evening?"

The luminescence of Elaysia's eyes betrayed her nyrian heritage. Her lips curled into a smile almost as devious as T'Vak's, but there was also childlike anticipation aglow on her face. "I'm going to ride Onitus for the first time tonight, and I want you to bear witness."

Zavik couldn't put the key in the lock fast enough. He shoved the gate open, allowed Elaysia and T'Vak to walk through, and secured it behind him.

As he turned to follow them down the road, a faint flapping sound drew his attention upward. A silhouette of a winged creature hovered above him. His stomach twisted, and he made a mad dash for his friends.

He never reached them.

Zavik awoke to darkness.

A cold, dull ache clung to his bones. The metallic scent of blood tingled the hairs in his nostrils, and his heart quickened in response. Somewhere close by was the gentle trickle of flowing water, but the sound was muffled and distant. He tried to open his eyes and found them held shut by a rough cloth pressed against them. The same fabric dug into the corners of his mouth, gagging him, and the rest of his body fared similarly: limbs bound, torso stiff, cheek resting on the cold stone beneath him. But his head was the worst. It throbbed, the pain radiating from the base of his neck, intensifying as he came to his senses.

Zavik attempted to calm his churning insides by drawing slow, steady breaths while he recalled the preceding events. A note from Elaysia. Prowling through the courtyard with T'Vak to meet Elaysia. Getting the key. Opening the gate. Securing the gate. Unnerving silhouette descending from the sky. Then, then...

Nothing.

But he knew that silhouette. Even without his previous shaktar encounter, he would've recognized it from the old tales and songs. No Orillon child went to bed without hearing of the bloodsuckers, the flesh-eaters that flew through windows at night, singing mischievous children to sleep before whisking them away to their cavern lair. It was said they absorbed the innocence of youth, deriving from it their immortality. But based on what Zavik saw in the infamous caverns, they just ate people.

The thought was no less unsettling.

Frigid fingers touched the place on his neck just beneath his jaw to check his pulse. Fingers like leather, yet slick, as though they'd just been oiled. Zavik's skin crawled.

The blindfold slipped off his face with an unexpected gentleness. A cavern ceiling loomed several hundred feet overhead, the dust-caked redness of its walls illuminated by a sizeable nevethium crystal lodged in an altar-like structure that rose from the ground. Long, jagged spears of rock cradled it like the fingers of a gnarled old woman, casting eerie shadows among the stalagmites.

One of them moved. A chill slithered up Zavik's spine as it unfurled into the shape of a wing. Another shifted beside it, its form undeniably that of a shaktar. Zavik shut his eyes again, wishing the creatures away.

"Greetings, Zavik of Az Zar."

A single voice addressed him this time, unlike the ensemble that had overtaken his mind the first time he'd met the winged Vysilliam moons past. Zavik tried to keep his thoughts focused on the present, hoping to shield what little information he possessed from the shaktar.

"You abducted me," he croaked, his throat raw from dehydration.

The shaktar betrayed no remorse as its hollow, sobering tone reverberated through Zavik's mind. *"We have refrained from interfering with your affairs or inflicting harm on those closest to you."*

"I suppose you'd like me to thank you for your tact," Zavik muttered, his irritation subverting his fear. "Do you have someone following me all hours of the day and night, waiting for a moment of vulnerability? How did you even know I'd returned to Orillon?" He tried to raise himself to a seated position, then froze when he felt a cool breath on his neck. Something growled behind him, akin to a raspy purr, then there was a tugging at his wrists and the tear of cloth ripping. Freedom. He drew his hands to his chest and rubbed the raw flesh, not daring to turn around.

"We require no thanks. Only compliance." More voices joined with each word as the walls rippled with an ocean of flared wings, shifting in the darkness like phantom sails. *"Your payment is due."*

"You could've just sent a tuross," Zavik mumbled as he hurried to unbind his feet, a task that was exceedingly frustrating until he remembered the knife tucked into his boot.

Unless the bastards had removed it.

He slipped a cautious finger inside, sighing with relief as it grazed the handle. They hadn't bothered to disarm him. Then again, they hadn't at their prior meeting, either.

Don't be dense, Zav. They're ageless bloodsuckers with a hive mind. What could they possibly be afraid of?

A sallow gray figure shuffled into his peripherals, bringing with it the putrid scent of decay. The upraised nostrils of the shaktar's flattened nose flared, and Zavik began to fear he'd upset them. He winced as it lowered its face to his, the rotten fangs that jutted from its lower lip nearly brushing his face. It extended a long, grimy claw and touched it to the base of his neck. An icy venom pulsed through Zavik's body, intensifying his pain until he could no longer bear it. Then it vanished. His headache, his thirst. Any hint of discomfort.

"The poison will leave no trace on your physical form," the voices said.

"Uh..." Zavik rubbed the spot on his neck, searching for a wound. There was none to be found. "Thank you?"

The shaktar retreated to the shadows until Zavik could only make out the contrast of its stocky frame against the crystal's glow. *"You will fulfill your oath now."*

"And how might I do that, exactly?" Zavik's gaze frantically searched the cavern, landing on what appeared to be a tunnel. He backed toward it, only for his boot to catch on a protruding slab of stone, which sent him crashing to the ground.

The walls shrieked and flapped in response to the outburst. *"You must comply,"* a single voice whispered. *"The blood tells true."*

That cursed phrase again. It had haunted Zavik nightly since they'd first surrendered the scrolls.

"The blood tells true," more shouted. *"The blood of time."* More and more joined in until Zavik's ears rang with their cries. *"His blood, his blood, his blood!"*

His limbs were stone. He tried to speak, but no sound would come out.

"Only you can retrieve it," a single voice said. *"North it lies in mountain depths, from the tallest peaks one must not rest, until dusk is dawn and dawn is night, the world like fire all alight."*

The hairs on Zavik's arms raised as his mind wrapped around the words, phrases so foreign, yet they triggered an innate resonance. It was beyond reason.

And he was beginning to loathe things beyond reason.

"You will retrieve it," the voices said. *"The blood tells true."* The shaktar that had healed him flapped to a ledge, joining its kin. *"Find the scroll and bring it to us, Zavik of Az Zar, or you shall find yourself forever alone."*

Zavik forced a strained laugh. "I find myself alone more often than not." When it became evident his humor was lost on them, he added, "I'll need some time. There's a war brewing in Neharem, and I have pressing responsibilities as high elder that—"

The voices struck him like a physical blow, forcing him to drop to his knees to brace himself. *"There is no time for a life as fleeting as yours. The scrolls are awake. They summon. They hunger. The one we seek requires your blood. Bring it to us, or your clan will suffer."*

Zavik's stomach dropped, bringing with it a sickening sensation. "Why me? I don't even know where to start."

"We have shared all we know. Make use of it. Now, sleep."

An eerie chant filled the chamber with a reverberation unlike any Zavik had ever experienced. Before he could rise or make any final protests, he drifted off to sleep with dozens of black eyes bearing down on him, peering into the depths of his soul.

"Zavik? Are you awake?"

He thrashed, determined to leave the shaktar's lair at any cost. But when he blinked his eyes open, an almost ethereal glow greeted him. And at the center of it, Elaysia.

"Ellie?"

Her eyes danced upon hearing her name. "Khiev–Tatamic be praised." She brushed his cheek with the back of her hand, and despite his throbbing headache, he blushed at her touch. "You've been asleep half the day. What happened last night?"

"I..." Zavik pushed up to his elbows to better take in his surroundings. He was back in the palace, in the chambers he shared with T'Vak. No sign of the backhander, though. Just an increasingly concerned Elaysia and a servant preparing him a cup of tea. "Where did you find me?" he asked, not wanting to reveal any details regarding his whereabouts unless pressed on the subject.

She frowned. "Just outside the main gates. You reeked of alcohol and looked far more disheveled than usual." She took the tea from the servant and brought it to his lips.

"Oh." He managed a small sip of the bitter concoction. How lovely of the shaktar to portray him as a drunkard.

"Why did you run off last night?" she pressed as frustration usurped the relief on her face. "I thought you'd be excited to witness my first flight, but then you disappeared. We spent the rest of the night looking for you."

"I was—I am. Something caught me off guard, though." He rubbed the back of his neck, wincing at the pain. He did feel hungover. And without a good time to show for it. "It's regarding a surprise? For your union ceremony?" he said in a desperate attempt to ease her displeasure. He couldn't burden her with the shaktar. It was his to carry, and his alone.

"If you say so." Elaysia patted his hand, then departed with a look of utter disbelief.

It hurt worse than the shaktar's poison.

JAKKI

Jakki glared as the Morotôk elders, their bodies wrapped head to toe in furs, mounted their sleighs and urged their cloven-hooved steeds across the tundra. The air was cold enough to freeze the fine hairs in her nostrils, and it felt unnaturally thin, making her lungs work twice as hard to take it in. And as if failing her mission and enduring the biting chill wasn't enough, fresh snow had begun to fall.

Damn fucking north.

"I'm never returning to this desolate slab of ice again." She dropped her hood for long enough to wrap a woolen length of fabric around her nose, mouth, and ears, then tugged it over her head again, leaving only her eyes exposed to the elements. "Remind me why I even agreed to this in the first place?" she asked Xaren.

The corners of the Az Zarian boy's eyes crinkled, betraying the smile beneath his own face coverings, a smile that seemed to never fully abandon his face, except in the direst of circumstances. "Because you're a good person."

The reply caught Jakki off guard. She sifted through her thoughts for a snarky rebuttal, but it was as if she'd never been quick of tongue. The wind picked up around them, tugging the few strands of hair that had escaped her braid out from her hood. There was nothing but ice and snow for miles, save for the foreboding peak of Mount Keldara to the west and the Greater Quentarri Mountains to the south.

"We could return to the village," Xaren said, tucking his gloved hands into his armpits. "At least until Shadow and Siren return. Chief Amkah said we were welcome to stay until—"

"Chief Amkah," Jakki said through clenched teeth, "is no longer our ally, therefore she and her people cannot be trusted."

Xaren arched his neck toward the sky, catching snowflakes in his long, dark lashes. "They treated us well and heard what we had to say. I don't think she means us ill. She's just doing what's best for her people."

"And what's best for her people is allying with a tribe intent on overthrowing Agaas. We will clash weapons with these people before the moons shift to another cycle." Jakki huffed and started in the direction the stormbirds had flown to hunt. "Don't be fooled by their illusions of hospitality."

"At least she was forthright with us," Xaren called after her. "Agaas can prepare accordingly." His voice drew closer, accompanied by the heavy-footed steps of boots crunching through the snow. "I don't think they want to fight us. They're just afraid of the Atsukut and feel they don't have a choice."

"Neither do we."

They hiked north toward the Tulek Sea, despite the shore being more than a day's walk away and the journey itself being pointless. The stormbirds would soon return from their hunt and bear them back to Agaas. Still, the weather proved too unrelenting to sit idle, and Jakki couldn't stomach the thought of lounging in one of the ice huts of their soon-to-be enemies.

Onward it was.

"What's our next destination?" Xaren asked. There was a cheeriness to his voice despite their predicament, and it made him both endearing and vexing.

Jakki reached for her water skin and found it frozen. No matter. The wine would do. She took a sip and shoved it at Xaren, encouraging him to do the same. "We walk until the birds find us, then go home."

"Oh."

Jakki stopped trudging through the snowdrifts, which now reached halfway up her booted calves. Her burning muscles expressed their gratitude. "Oh?"

"I'm just surprised you want to go back to Elaysia and the others bearing only bad tidings." He sighed and slipped the wineskin strap over his head without taking a drink. "But we've already wasted several days here, and we're in enemy territory now, as you've said. Returning to Agaas is the wise thing to do. Forget I spoke up."

The gleam in his eyes suggested otherwise.

"Spit it out, slaver. I'm not in the mood for fishing cryptic messages out of your bloated little head."

"Ouch. Bloated?"

"You've got one more chance before I continue north until Siren retrieves me. Then I'm not speaking to you the rest of the journey to Agaas, if ever again."

"No pressure," he muttered. Still, he danced his lithe frame across the snow and extended his arm southeast. "What lies over there?" he shouted.

Jakki rolled her eyes. "The Greater Quentarris."

"And beyond them?"

"Atsukut territory, Daruk territory, skulmor territory."

"Two of which are our enemies," Xaren added.

"Do you have anything of actual value to share?" Jakki heaved her leg out of the snowdrift that was making itself too familiar with her body and marched north.

Xaren hurried after her. "The stormbirds provide us an exclusive vantage point. We'd be fools not to utilize them."

She faced him, and the wind, wincing as icy kisses flecked the tender skin around her eyes. "An unsanctioned scouting mission? Because that worked out so well for me last time."

"But...didn't it?" Xaren's brows knit together. "You secured knowledge we never would've gained otherwise, and you ended up coming to our aid in Az Zar. Who knows how we would've fared if you hadn't disobeyed orders."

Despite her attempt to prohibit it, a warm smile creeped across Jakki's face. She reached a gloved hand to her chest and pressed until the parchment hidden beneath her furs crinkled against her skin.

"We could make a map of the Lawful Dominion's camps," Xaren continued. "Assess their numbers, maybe even fly close enough to inspect weapons and other resources. I know Elaysia doesn't want to risk the birds in battle yet, but if we're merely scouting, the risk is minimal."

Jakki graced him with a look of approval. "You know, Xaren, you're not a complete idiot. For a child."

"Thanks?" he replied, raising a skeptical eyebrow. "So where to first?"

Another sip of wine called to her. She slipped the skin off Xaren's neck and took a long drink as she warmed up to the idea of venturing beyond her orders. "Where would you set up camps in a terrain like this to hide your warriors from both the elements and prying eyes?"

Xaren thought for a moment. "The mountains? In the foothills, not the peaks. Caves a plenty, and fewer exposed borders to patrol."

Jakki nodded, took another drink, and passed him the rest. "To the mountains we'll go."

As the crystalline whites and glimmering silvers of Morotôk territory gave way to the reddish-brown tundra of the Quentarri Mountains, Jakki's heart soared. The hints of greenery concentrated around the rivers broadened into blankets of forests, and within a day of setting off on the backs of their stormbirds, they were well into Atsukut territory. Unlike the Daruk and Morotôk, she knew little of the largest northern tribe's ways, save for their massive statures and preference for nomadism.

The latter made them difficult to locate. And, if she was being honest with herself, she wasn't exactly eager to track them down, given the latest skirmish involving their monstrous stags and whatever otherworldly being led the attack. She wasn't certain if it was more akin to her ghostly old man or the Caman present the night Elaysia was taken in Az Zar, but whatever it was, it'd given the Atsukut an advantage, and it had likely yet to abandon them. Jakki could still feel those eyes like embers boring down on her as the towering, cloaked figure they belonged to maneuvered about the battle with unmatched grace, almost as if it glided instead of walked. While Jakki never got close enough to attack it, Lumira swore the being was immortal, its body impenetrable, that her spear had gone clean through it and pierced the ground, free of gore and blood.

Next time, she'd find out for herself. She had the parchment, after all. More than one could play at magic and immortality.

Shadow soared dangerously close to Siren, drawing Jakki out of her reveries. Though Xaren's stormbird was the smallest of the bunch, and Jakki's the largest, it didn't stop his spectral form from locating turbulent air pockets and using the currents to boost his speed. It allowed him to keep pace with Siren, often outshining her with quick bursts. And, given the way Xaren gushed about it every time they landed to stretch their legs, he didn't mind the irregularity of Shadow's flight patterns.

The Az Zarian boy momentarily freed a hand to wave at Jakki—which she took for an apology for flying so close—then melted back into Shadow's back, both bird and rider shrouded in midnight.

If only you were half as discreet, she thought, pressing her face into Siren's silver feathers to take respite from the wind.

"If only you had a shred of humility."

Jakki's lips quirked at the insult. She could admire the bird's quick wit.

Learning to attune to Siren hadn't come easily. At first, she'd only been able to discern intense feelings, those so strongly tied to the bird's physical posturing that she doubted the accuracy of her perception. But then she'd catch the more subtle emotions, things like irritation and apathy, and from there, simple words and phrases that didn't originate from her mind manifested in it. Although there were moments when Jakki couldn't fully understand Siren or grasp everything the stormbird was trying to communicate, she believed their connection was powerful enough to conquer any obstacle. With Siren, she was complete.

And unstoppable.

"They want to land." Siren's words made Jakki's head tingle with a clarity not unlike the parchment. *"Shadow saw movement on the timberline."*

Disregarding the need for approval, the stormbird dove after the other pair, folding her wings inward to create a sensation of freefall that made Jakki's stomach churn. She held her breath for most of the descent, only daring a shallow inhale as Siren's wings and talons flared, slowing her pace for a skilled landing atop a ridge on one of the smaller mountains.

With shaky limbs, Jakki slid off Siren—an act that became riskier as the bird grew—and joined Xaren at the edge of the ridge. The cloud cover blanketing the peak caused a snowfall of great enough magnitude to mask their arrival from anyone searching the mountains from a lower vantage point.

"What do you see?" she asked, kneeling beside Xaren. Though her nyrian eyesight was far superior to that of most humans, Xaren was an exception to his kind, nearly as keen-sighted as his bird.

He removed one of his gloves and pointed at a thick cluster of conifers roughly a mile below. Jakki watched the spot intently and without exasperation. She'd learned not to question Xaren after their palace infiltration in Cadar. The boy wasn't cocky, and he only spoke when certain of his words. Mother Itaso—she'd come to trust him more than nearly all the Stormriders, despite his limited years. Instinct wasn't something to be taught, anyway. One was either born with it, or they never got it at all.

Jakki didn't have to wait long to discover what Xaren had observed. A shadow spilled out from the forest and disappeared into the mountainside, far too quickly for a human or nyrian. And it moved on all fours.

"Skulmor," she whispered.

Xaren nodded, not taking his gaze off the mountainside.

Jakki sought refuge beneath Siren's wings. Once nestled, she ran a hand over her leather, fur-lined leggings, lingering on her scarred thigh. It was a permanent reminder of what happened when one crossed the wolven monstrosities.

"They shouldn't be here," Jakki said as Xaren approached. "We haven't entered skulmor territory. I know you drove them out of their lands, but—"

"Az Zar drove them out," Xaren corrected. "And that was before my time." His stern face made it clear he no longer wanted to be associated with the All-Sovereign's military.

"Sorry." Jakki shrugged. "The point is their raids on Neharem villages have ceased. I assumed they'd been killed off, or maybe fled to the uncharted north to try their hand against the nazrath. Maybe it's just a lone wolf."

Xaren shook his head. "I saw at least three others before you landed."

"All going into the mountains?"

"No. The first two were leaving."

A growl rumbled in Jakki's stomach. She retrieved some dried rabbit meat from her pouch, grateful (if not begrudging) for Chief Amkah's parting gift. "You think they have a settlement down there?"

"At least a cave to keep warm in." Xaren shyly stretched his hand toward Jakki's pouch. She grumbled, but tossed some to him.

"What do you think they're doing in Atsukut territory?" she asked, as he nibbled away.

"Must've allied with them." He swallowed, his deep brown eyes probing her own. "At least that's what you're thinking."

Jakki crossed her arms and burrowed deeper into the soft feathers of Siren's belly. "Let's wait until nightfall. We'll have the birds drop us off in a clearing a good distance away, then sneak our way in."

Xaren's hand froze halfway in the pouch. "Little bold, isn't it?"

"This was your idea. Don't turn craven now." Jakki snatched the pouch away and reattached it to her belt. "If the skulmor are truly allied with the Lawful Dominion, we'll need to bring evidence to the council. Our mountaintop speculations aren't enough. We can ask the stormbirds to stay nearby in case we require assistance. I, however, don't plan on being seen."

"No one plans on being seen," Xaren said with a shrug. "That's why they get caught."

Despite thick layers insulating Jakki's body, the cold still found its way in like minnows through a fishing net. The tips of her nose and ears had gone numb shortly after nightfall, and she'd all but lost feeling in her toes and fingers. Even the water-resistant sealant applied to her boots was weakening from constant exposure to the snow, and she understood why the Morotôk coated their feet and legs in seal fat before a long trek. She could survive a few more hours, though. Just until dawn. Until she had her proof.

Then she'd never go north again.

Xaren peered around a trunk twice his width, waiting for her signal to advance. She held him off with a hand as she crouched to inspect the ground. The skies had cleared, but not before the snow did its job of eradicating any sign of skulmor prints. An annoyance, but not a hindrance. She was no Yerakai when it came to tracking, but she'd hunted enough to know what signs to look for. The snapped low-hanging branches, the places where the snow became more compacted, leaving a hidden layer of ice beneath, and—as undeniable confirmation they headed in the right direction—rare patches of yellow snow.

She motioned for Xaren to follow, then moved ahead herself. After he took her place, he'd scour behind them, ensuring no one followed, then give her the go ahead. They'd already been at it for over an hour, working their way from the clearing the birds had dropped them in all the way to the timberline. As Jakki finally approached the break in the trees where they'd witnessed the skulmor, however, a fiery rage flushed her cheeks.

"Where is it?" she hissed, her voice rising above a whisper. Nothing but rock face and snow-crusted soil loomed before them.

Unwilling to wait for Xaren, she darted along the timberline, keeping to the trees and searching the mountain for a cave entrance. Her breath fogged the air as she sprinted, and eventually, her pace slowed to a jog. Frustration bubbled inside her, her desire to locate the skulmor hideout overwhelmed by her need to find shelter. They had no food left, hardly any water, and she'd cut a hole in the gods-cursed mountain herself before spending a night shivering against a boy who'd no spare body heat to offer.

When she returned to Xaren an hour later at the place they'd parted ways, she was pleasantly surprised to find he'd passed the time searching in the opposite direction—albeit to no avail. A shadow glided over them, disappearing over the mountain.

"At least the birds are close," Xaren offered. His chattering teeth chopped his words. He wasn't made for the north any more than she.

"That cursed cat sent us up here to freeze," she grumbled, hoping to offer some levity.

Xaren smirked. "Should we summon Shadow and Siren?"

Jakki glared at the mountain. Moonlight glinted off its snowy peak, giving the illusion of it winking, as though it mocked them. She wanted to keep searching, but she could hardly feel the staff in her hand. Their time was up.

Hoping to get a glimpse of Siren, she emerged from the tree line, then froze, a rock-like knot forming in her stomach. Not a foot away from her were fresh tracks in the snow, tracks that hadn't been there an hour past. Tracks not laid by any human or nyrian. She felt eyes crawling over her and knew before turning that they already had Xaren. Otherwise, he would've been right behind her, studying the prints himself.

Jakki tightened her grip on her staff and whirled, banking a sharp right to put distance between herself and whatever lurked behind her. There was no time to recite the parchment. She couldn't even recall the words, not with her heart threatening to burst from her chest while her limbs moved in the awkward, jerking motions of a newborn nytak.

Dark figures with sickly green eyes peered through the trees, but she kept running, the snow betraying her with every pace-slowing crunch. She was outnumbered, could sense the bodies mounting behind her and the swiftness of their padded steps. Even as she ran, she anticipated the blow, the bloody stink of matted fur that would knock her to the ground and rip flesh from her unmarred leg.

She saw her chance in the trees and took it. If she maneuvered well and called out to Siren, she might stand a chance.

She didn't notice the signs until it was too late. The trampled snow. The sturdy branch ten feet above. The length of rope snaking down its trunk and promptly vanishing.

A trap seized her ankle. She careened up and back, her head hurtling toward the tree. A *crack* rang throughout her skull, followed by a sickening, buzzing sensation. Her world turned upside down. Somewhere in the distance, Xaren cried out for her.

The last thing she saw before losing her battle with consciousness was a narrowed pair of golden-green eyes emerging from the shadows.

ELAYSIA

The dress was oil on her skin. Sheer layers of mesh and satin molded themselves to the contours of her body, accentuating the meticulously crafted embroidery that captured the very essence of the natural world that had inspired its design, as if the gods themselves had breathed life into it. A forest-green leather braid secured the skirt at the narrowest part of her waist, flowing out into a fan of like-colored patterns. Beadwork sewn into shapes representing the moons' many phases. Ferns reaching toward the ground, their leaves returning to life-giving soil. Stormbird feathers for power. Waves for humility. And at the very bottom, where the fabric brushed the floor, dancing around her tattooed feet, a mountain range, to ground her.

Leather cups secured her breasts, sewn into the same fabric used to make the skirt, and a braided halter woven with strips of leather, wildflowers, and hand-carved beads was knotted loosely around her neck, holding it all in place. Her hair was a storm. Wild and free, unrelenting in its beauty, strikes of lightning piercing the midnight black. It tumbled down to her waist in waves, small strands catching and twirling about the wind as she ascended the tower stairs with the elegance of a stag.

Somewhere below, a large crowd had amassed, eager to watch the unity ceremony of one of Orillon's greatest houses, to lay eyes on the outsider who'd stolen a position coveted by many—or so she'd been led to believe. Perhaps it was a lie, something to make an undesirable task not without its merit. A little honey to help the poison go down.

Elaysia glanced down at her hands, at the intricate patterns stained into them in Orillon tradition. Fine dots, lines, and curves woven deftly together to create the illusion of rings and bracelets. Some looked like the great crystal fixtures hanging from House Undali's grandest rooms. A crescent moon on one hand. A rising sun on the other.

A new life to usurp the old.

The sun lingered low in the sky, casting its glow in red and purple waves that spread across the horizon like spilled ink. It was not alone. The moons intensified, beginning their brief period of shared visibility with the sun, a unity ceremony of their own making. And so began such a time in Elaysia's life.

She paused on the stairs, clinging to the smooth marble railing. Hope trickled to the forefront of her thoughts as her curiosity regarding the looming union momentarily overwhelmed any apprehension. A similar sensation had overtaken her when she'd run from Agaas, from her duties, and discovered the stormbird eggs. It'd returned when she abandoned her role in favor of adventuring with an unconventional band of allies on a dangerous voyage overseas. And yet again, though more discreetly, the first time she'd dared to love without holding back.

The thought sent a thorn through her heart, crushing the still-vulnerable seeds of hope.

It was for the best. Love and curiosity were no longer her allies. Cunning and resilience had been her redemption, and there was no need to abandon them for fleeting feelings.

A shadow blanketed her in darkness. She glanced up in time to see Onitus gliding overhead and smiled at the memory of their first flight just a few days prior.

Her fingers grip silken but stiff feathers the color of an ocean amid a storm. Wind rushes into her lungs. It takes her breath away while concurrently refilling her body with so much air—air so pure, it's nearly intoxicating. Her hood trails behind her like tail feathers of her own. Tears slip from half-closed eyes as her hair pulls free of its braid, falling, flying, tumbling behind her. There is no past, no future. Only now. Only this feeling of nothingness, this utter loss of where she ends and Onitus begins. They share the same breath. Hearts beat in unison. Blood rushes to the same rhythm. They are the wind, the sky, the stars. The moons are their mothers, the oceans their fathers. Nothing makes sense, and nothing needs to. Just unabashed serenity. Let this never end. Please, let this—

"Elaysia."

Anahi regarded her from a few steps above, garbed in a traditional Orillon wrap dress of embroidered velvet and silk, the great lengths of fabric placed just so over her arm. It was the dress Elaysia should've elected to wear, but she could only resign so much of her life to this family, to this man. The temporary tattoos on her hands and feet would have to be enough.

She met the older woman's gaze. "Are they ready for me?"

Anahi chewed her lower lip. She descended to the step just above Elaysia. "Are you ready for this?" Her eyes narrowed, awakening the early signs of wrinkles around their edges. "Maybe I was wrong to suggest this. Gods, I couldn't even handle my own birthright, so who am I to encourage you to—"

Elaysia caught Anahi's hand in her own and squeezed it firmly. "I wouldn't be here if I didn't see the reason, and I'm glad you finally told me. It took courage for you to face your past for the sake of another nation, and I will be forever indebted to you."

"Vahid's a good man," Anahi said almost apologetically, as if she still needed to convince herself she'd done right by the high chieftain.

"If he's half as good as you, I'll have nothing to fear." Elaysia looked up the staircase, entranced by the marble infused with flecks of nevethium to illuminate an otherwise dark path. "Let us become sisters, shall we?"

"Couldn't think of anyone better."

The women linked arms and continued up the stairs. There were three hundred steps to the top—or so Zavik had said when drowning her in union ceremony advice to make up for his impromptu night of frivolity—but she'd made it well over halfway and worked up only a slight sheen.

She was almost grateful for the climb. Not only did it remind her of the winding, steep pathways of Agaas, it gave her a moment to process and shed any remaining anxiety. By the time she reached the top, she'd be almost fully present in her body, and that was what she needed to get through the ceremony. Well, that or a skin of Cyan's anderberry wine from Agaas. But she'd settle for physical exertion.

From below, the two towers used for ceremonies by the great houses looked somewhat like the headdress worn by Saya Undali. Their domed peaks with great jeweled spires stabbed the night sky, and beneath the domes stretched circular awnings to protect the platforms below. Great lengths of vines and flowers hung from the spiral staircases like jewelry, and each platform and its accompanying dome was supported by four thick pillars, the carvings of which couldn't be fully appreciated until one stood where Elaysia soon would. She stopped one last time at the top of the stairs to admire the winged deities and moon cycles adorning the pillars, then directed her attention to the faces of the people gathered atop her tower, those representing her side.

Her family.

The realization sent a tingle down her spine, and she blinked back tears. Zavik holding Dytana. Maseeya cradling Elaron. T'Vak flashing a mostly respectful grin. Anahi supporting her through their linked arms, her warm skin reminding her she was alive and loved. Yerakai waiting across the bridge to escort Vahid to her, as Anahi would deliver Elaysia to her own brother. And so many more back home, supporting her despite the distance. Jakki and Mardus. Lumira and Grokhion. Xaren. She could feel their love in the breeze, their blessings in the stars. And maybe, just maybe, her parents and brother smiling down from the moons themselves.

Dytana reached a pudgy arm for her mother as she emitted a breathy coo. Elaysia's heart surged with love as she planted a kiss on the babe's sweet-smelling head, then gave Zavik an affirmative nod.

"At least you're not fighting this one to the death," he offered, a sheepish grin on his face. He'd been nothing but accommodating since his disappearance, and tonight, she finally forgave him. There was no good to come from holding a grudge against someone she loved.

"Not yet." She winked, then strode with Anahi out from the cover of the awning and onto the lyvium bridge binding the two towers.

The bridge was wide enough for four people to walk side by side, and long enough that she couldn't make out the individuals gathered beneath the opposite tower's dome. Vahid boasted at least three times the number of supporters Elaysia had; though that said nothing of the overflow crowd spilling down the spiral staircase.

At the center of the bridge stood a simple wooden table supported by one clawed leg. On it rested a bowl of honey, along with a small vase holding two incense sticks. Per Munskahan tradition, there would've also been two small, rare birds to release, but Elaysia had infused that part of the ceremony with some Neharem flare. That, and the woven blanket the Apáasutai tribe had sent as a union blessing. Elaysia hadn't been allowed to see it yet, but Maseeya assured her it was one of the most beautiful patterns ever woven.

A resonant blast came from a horn on one of the wider, yet shorter bridges below, where the other great houses and their guests had gathered to watch the ceremony unfold. The streets beneath them were lined with commoners grateful to simply be in the vicinity of the grand affair, and cheers erupted as the horn's reverberations faded. Elaysia's heart quickened. Her hands were clammy; her stomach knotted.

Then she thought of Agaas. Pristine, sacred Agaas, its living trees aglow with life-giving nevethium, and she suppressed her worries with a sigh. She straightened her shoulders and led the unexpectedly more reluctant Anahi across the bridge, the lyvium cold beneath her bare feet, the wind a warm kiss on her cheeks.

Two figures strode from the brimming tower opposite hers. Yerakai's silken white hair hung down to his chest in two simple braids. He'd painted moons on his forehead, two crescents with a full moon in the center, the white tint accenting his deep lavender skin. He wore his Apáasutai beaded, fringed tunic and leggings, but had embellished them with satin sashes to offer tribute to the man he escorted across. The sight of Yerakai formed a lump in Elaysia's throat. He'd embraced the role of her brother without question, escorting her betrothed to the union table in Orillon tradition. She thanked him with her eyes. He responded in kind.

Elaysia's lips parted in astonishment as she took in Vahid. From the moment she set foot in Munskahan and entered the magnificent halls of House Undali, she'd been surrounded by excess. Architecture and art that took lifetimes to manifest. More food and drink than the household could ever eat. Enough jewelry to ensure one never had to wear the same piece twice. She'd expected Vahid to be wrapped head to toe in the most exquisite fabrics, gems hanging from his neck, fingers, and ears, oil slathered on his skin. Perhaps an entourage of servants trailing him, their fingers clutching at the great lengths of his robe to keep it from touching the unclean path.

He'd come with no such pretenses. His dark hair was clean but unadulterated, flowing freely in the breeze. A white tunic of woven, unrefined fabric hung loosely around his shoulders, cutting deep at the collarbone and unfolding into billowing sleeves. It ran down to his knees, meeting loose-fitting pants of the same make, and the sun's final rays cast him in an ethereal glow. He'd come barefoot, as had she, bronze feet padding across the stone, steps intentional yet relaxed, as though he strolled along the beach looking for shells. As they drew near one another, she caught the glint of the nevethium stud in his left ear.

Not completely void of his former self, she mused.

Her hand flinched, aching to reach up and rub the stormbird pendant hanging from her neck, but Anahi's arm was still interlocked with her own, preventing the movement.

Nor am I.

Her heart slowed to a steady beat. It was the plainest she'd ever seen him, yet the most beautiful. He didn't look at her with the lustful eyes of a man consumed by desire, but neither did he appear aloof. Just unwavering interest tempered with respect. Perhaps he was a suitable partner, after all, considering the circumstances.

Yet, she would've fled down the winding staircase without a second thought if told the union was no longer required of her. Because he *was* a good man. A likeable, if not loveable, man. One that could sway the heart, given enough time.

And that scared her most of all.

Elaysia approached the table and halted at its edge, her fingers gathering the fabric of her skirt at her sides and then releasing it, only to gather it again. Vahid stood across from her, his gaze lowered—whether out of his own discomfort or perception of hers, she knew not. Her mind wanted to wander to any place but that cursed bridge, another ceremony where she'd yet again agreed to give her life in service to something greater than she, because doing the right thing was expected, was what her parents would've done. What her brother would've done.

As Yerakai and Anahi took their place between the union couple, Elaysia glanced down at the lower towers and platforms filled with faceless nobles, their nevethium lanterns like firebugs in the night. The crowds of commoners beneath them waited in the encroaching darkness, perhaps not wanting their already limited view to be further tarnished by firelight. Elaysia told herself they'd gathered to see the stormbirds, and not her. Truth or not, it lessened her anxiety. She returned her attention to the table and vowed to not look out again until the deed was done.

Another bellow rang from the horn. Chatter from the crowds dissipated, and Anahi began to sing in a deep, raspy voice. Elaysia's body softened at the beautifully haunting melody leaving the woman's lips. If she hadn't known better, she would've assumed it was Anahi's profession. She closed her eyes, allowing herself to get lost in the tune.

As the sun finds harmony with the moons,

now you shall find harmony with one another.

You will suffer no heat, nor the desert chill at night,

for each of you will be the shelter for the other.

May your love be like water,

cherished and preserved,

sweet as a sunkiss,

and always deserved.

You will never know loneliness, for the seeds that
you'll sow,

and when the rest move on, you two shall still be
one,

eternal love ever aglow.

The gods brought you together, but even they can't
drive you apart,

they gave up their powers when they blessed us
with hearts,

for no matter what ravages us from above or below,

love is too great a magic to ever unknow.

Blessed be your journey; may you always find reason to dance.

Don't ever forget:

It might be your last chance.

Anahi bowed her head as she finished, then settled back into her relaxed warrior's stance, hand on her hip as if itching for the sword that wasn't currently strapped to it. Elaysia longed to lean over and whisper in Anahi's ear her appreciation for the song, perhaps tease her for having such a breathtaking voice but rarely using it, to ask if it was the same song sung at all Orillon union ceremonies. Or was it reserved for the great houses? Or just for their house specifically? But then she recalled the spectators gathered below, and she consented to wriggle uncomfortably beneath their imagined, judgmental gazes.

Yerakai cleared his throat and offered an Apáasutai blessing. Its meaning was likely lost on everyone in attendance, but Elaysia clung to every word, as though the prayer was the key to her salvation. And, in a way, it was.

Now, you are the mountains.

The wind, the sea,

You are in them, and they in you.

The nytak herds, the tuross flocks,

The storm clouds and their offspring rains,

You become a part of them.

*You are in the ferns, the forests, the nevethium
itself.*

They become you.

And now, you become each other;

For you have always been.

So it is,

So it will always be.

You are the world,

And the world is you.

So it will always be, Elaysia repeated silently to herself.

Vahid regarded her with a warm smile. She tried her best to return it.

Silence accompanied the rest of the ceremony. Anahi lit two incense sticks, which she and Yerakai circled about the couple to cleanse them of any past trauma that might stain the new union. Once sanctified, Elaysia and Vahid each dipped a finger in a bowl of honey, then offered it to the other person to taste, an act symbolizing the sweetness they'd bring into each other's lives. There was a shared glass of wine, blessings from other great houses, and then Anahi and Yerakai drew them both to the head of the table.

They were shoulder to shoulder now, his body warm against hers. Because of the ceremony, he smelled mostly of incense, but beneath it was a muskier scent, one that smelled of the orchards. The gifted Agaasian blanket was thrust over their shoulders, combining the two into one. And then they were unified, before mortals and gods.

In principle, at least.

Elaysia snuggled the blanket against her cheek, marveling at the vibrant teal salmon, the green nytak with vine-laden antlers, the branches of the living trees sprouting out from the nevethium trunk at the center. A deep sense of loss and longing overwhelmed her. As soon as the festivities were over with, she'd demand to go home, whether her new household approved or not.

A chorus of shrieks filled the dark skies. The crowd took a collective gasp as Onitus soared overhead, flanked by Corvax and Wind Chaser. Their magnificent wings gleamed in the moonlight, though Onitus's were by far the most breathtaking with his fire-tipped edges. They looped around the towers twice over, the second time passing beneath the bridge to give the spectators a better glimpse, before heading back to the hills.

A solitary bolt of lightning flashed as they vanished.

Elaysia exchanged glances with her fellow Stormriders. No clouds had gathered. No rain fell. One could deem it a blessing, or warning, from the gods. Something to sanctify the union. But to Elaysia, it only meant one thing. The birds neared sexual maturity, and what would soon follow was power.

Power that could turn the tides.

And that made it all worthwhile.

"Behold, the grand chambers. Not the grandest, mind you. That's reserved for the saya and sayetta. But it is the second-best House Undali has to offer. You'll find it quite luxurious if you can settle for five stained-glass windows instead of ten."

Vahid chuckled at his attempted humor as he stood at the threshold, bowing slightly and gesturing for Elaysia to enter the room first. She complied, forcing her attention everywhere but the bed. Their union chambers were at least three times the size of the room she'd been sharing with Maseeya and the twins. An archway separated the bed from the rest of the room, giving the illusion of privacy, and the space beyond was illuminated by magnificent, stained-glass windows that captured the moonlight, spilling it onto the floor in great silver beams. The domed ceiling was painted a deep, dark blue littered with luminescent stars, the effect of which had likely been achieved with mizol ink. In the center of the room sat an oversized cushion capable of seating three full-grown people, and beneath it, a gold and blue threaded rug featuring the moons and stars in unnatural patterns, such as birds and buildings. Sconces adorned the archway to the bedchamber and the space between each window. Elaysia was surprised to find them fire-based as opposed to nevethium, especially when the rest of the palace displayed no concerns about using the crystals at their leisure.

"It's lovely." She made her way to a bookshelf nestled between the windows and ran her fingers across a leather-bound spine. "I've never thought to keep books in my chambers back home. Not that Konar would've…"

Would've let me take one from the library in the first place. She bit her lip to chase away the thought and turned back to Vahid, the anticipation of the final act of their union ceremony tightening her chest.

Vahid walked over to the bed and pulled back the thin curtain veiling it. "I'm sure you're tired after the day's events. This bed is the softest in Munskahan, or so I'm told. It's good enough for me." He shrugged and drew back the blanket to expose the violet sheets beneath. "Hand stitched, stuffed with layers of wool and feathers, straw added for firmness, and satin sheets that the gods themselves would envy."

The bed became a burning pit of fury clouding Elaysia's vision. All her muscles hardened, and her throat locked up with tension, making it hard to speak. She couldn't do this part. Wouldn't do this part.

"I'm not going to bed with you." She moved sideways toward the door. "Not now. Not ever."

Vahid raised his hands in a plea. "You misunderstand me. I wasn't suggesting we share this bed, even for an act as innocent as sleep. You can have it to yourself."

Elaysia continued toward the door. There was no lie in his eyes, but maybe he was just a good liar. And even if he meant well now, he'd expect her to fulfill her union duties, eventually. It was better to remove the temptation. "It's fine. I'll go. My children must sleep near me. They still take their feeds throughout the night."

"Please, don't leave." Vahid caught her hand, his gaze boring into her, as though he could peer into her mind and all its inner workings. "I will. Your children deserve the best in this house, and I'm more than happy to surrender my share of it to them and your handmaid."

Heat flared in Elaysia's chest. "Maseeya is not a servant."

Vahid grimaced as he weighed her words. "Forgive me, I just assumed since she cared for your children that—"

"That she loves me. Like a daughter."

A thick silence sunk its talons into the space between them. He didn't relinquish her hand. And she didn't force him to.

"My sincerest apologies." Vahid smoothed his already finely combed beard with strong fingers tattooed from the ceremony. "I will do my best to amend this mistake, if you'll allow me to."

Elaysia wouldn't give him the comfort of a reply, but she signaled she'd tolerate whatever he intended to say by remaining put. It was the least she could do.

"I want to make this relationship work," Vahid continued. "Not in the traditional sense—especially not in the way my faja expects. But I desire for us to live in peace, if we can. So before you head out this door and run off to Neharem with my family's finest kuza, I want to clarify that I want the best for your people, and I"—he rubbed at his face furiously, then gestured to the large, cushioned seat—"would you sit with me, just for a moment? If your children don't need you right at this moment."

Elaysia glanced at the cushion, at the long wooden table stretched before it, at the two translucent chalices, and finally at the clay bottle bearing Cyan's mark: two wavy lines to symbolize the Nipai River, where he harvested most of his berries, and two bottomless triangles directly above them, paying homage to the white fox he swore always watched him while he worked.

A knot formed in Elaysia's throat. She hadn't noticed the wine earlier, and a wave of guilt washed over her as she considered the trouble he must've gone through to learn her preference without her knowledge *and* arrange for it to be imported.

She made her way to the table and took a seat. "I fed them shortly after the ceremony. Maseeya has extra pouches, so they should be alright for a bit."

"I won't keep you long." Vahid sat a respectable distance away on the cushion, then interlaced his fingers atop his knees. "Wine?"

Of course. Thank you for going through all this effort to bring me something that reminds me of my home. I know you didn't choose this either. You are making great sacrifices yourself, and I'm sorry I've directed my anger toward you. I've had nowhere else safe to channel it.

Such were the thoughts swirling about Elaysia's mind, but all that made its way to her lips was, "If you'd like."

Vahid didn't mask the disappointment drawing fine lines about his forehead and the corners of his mouth as he opened the bottle and poured the dark violet liquid into the chalices. He passed one to Elaysia, then held his glass up to hers. "To us."

"To our union." Elaysia took a sip. A tinge of bittersweet nostalgia washed down with the warming spices of the wine. She took several more sips before breaking the silence. "I do appreciate you." The wine made it easier to access feelings she hadn't been able to dredge up moments prior. "I know you are as much a prisoner in this as I, and I also want to make this union a tolerable one."

Vahid swirled the liquid in his chalice and took a sip. "I think tolerable is an achievable goal." Another sip. He refilled both their chalices, though they weren't yet empty. "Forgive me my brashness, but I've come to care for your wellbeing in the brief time we've shared. Enough to sail back with you to Neharem, if you'll have me."

Elaysia nearly dropped her wine. "I...don't you..." She took another sip to collect herself, hoping the liquid magic would soothe the tremors in her body. "Aren't you needed here?"

"Needed here?" Vahid snorted. "My faja barely lets me touch anything related to House Undali's affairs. He likes to lecture me on it well enough, but he prefers to carry out any and all actions himself." He rose from the cushion and padded across the carpet to the largest window, which he cracked open and leaned out of with a sigh. "I'll be needed one day, but not as long as he's living. I think I could be of better service to you." He glanced over his shoulder at her, dark eyes imploring.

Elaysia looked down at her wine.

"The kuza will want someone familiar to look up to," he continued, withdrawing his gaze. "And though I've seen no battle, I've tried my hand in the pits more than a few times, and I have lessons upon lessons of military tactics just collecting dust up here." He tapped his head thoughtfully, then sat on the edge of the sizeable windowsill.

Elaysia set her half-full chalice on the table. She could find no valid argument opposing his wishes, especially regarding the command of a foreign, private military.

He came to kneel beside the cushion and rested his hand on the armrest next to hers, close enough for her to feel the warmth radiating from his fingers. "And secretly," he whispered, "I'd like to see more of the world. I'm a bit jealous of you, you know."

"There's much to be jealous of." The quip came out with ease, the way she often jested with Zavik, and it unnerved her how quickly she'd become comfortable in his presence. "But I agree," she added, hoping to mask her vulnerability. "I think some time in Agaas might do you good, sieges and skirmishes aside."

The smile that followed made her regret every ill thought she'd ever had in his presence, spoken aloud or not. He laid his hand atop hers, lingering just long enough to convey his care, then he was at the door, opening it with courtesy, as though he didn't want to wake a sleeping babe.

"I'll have Maseeya and your children sent in," he said, closing the door. "May you all rest well. Tomorrow, we can make plans for our return."

A bow, and then he was gone.

And when Elaysia was finally alone in the vast luxury of the room, her every need attended to, her every wish met, she realized she hadn't wanted him to leave after all.

ZAVIK

T railing T'Vak through the deserted streets of Munska-han's seediest marketplace wasn't Zavik's idea of a good time. The darkness cast an eerie pall over the abandoned stalls and carts, giving them an otherworldly aura, their once vibrant colors muted by the dead of night. He winced at the sound of his footsteps crunching the grit of the road, half expecting something to jump out from the shadows. At least he had T'Vak.

Then again, the backhander was to blame for his predicament. Zavik had been happily designing plans for nevethium-based defenses for Agaas when T'Vak appeared at his desk—completely sober—his demeanor stoic, his eyes twitching. According to him, Elaysia insisted he accompany them to Neharem on the morrow to collect his payment, which was fine, because he preferred the way the air smelled and how the people looked up north. Before he departed the capital for an indefinite length of time, however, he had an important proposition to consider. And for that, he required Zavik's assistance. On that account, the backhander had been far more veiled, but he alluded to needing someone with knowledge of ancient languages and ancient objects for authentication.

Though Zavik wasn't fond of becoming a victim of spontaneity, he found himself in good spirits at the prospect of returning home. He obliged the request, surprising himself. Even more surprising was his relief upon learning the backhander wouldn't be departing his company as soon as planned. For all T'Vak's indecencies, he brought a sense of levity to even the harshest of circumstances, and Zavik couldn't deny he felt safer with him around. He'd spent enough of his life looking over his shoulder to know good people were scarce. T'Vak gave him security, and for that, he was indebted beyond the superficiality of a belated nevethium payment.

And what does he want for it?

The thought irked Zavik, but he couldn't deny its validity. He couldn't deal with it at present either, though, isolated in the middle of the city during a time when drunkards and thieves ran wild. Their heart-to-heart would have to wait until the morning, aboard the boat to Neharem. It was only a few hours away, after all.

"How much further?" Zavik asked, struggling to keep pace as he dodged a puddle of vomit. He hoped the person who'd expelled it wasn't stumbling nearby.

T'Vak stopped to take a swig from his wineskin. "Won't be long now." He took another, one that drained whatever was left, then hurled the empty wineskin into an abandoned stall.

Zavik peered over the countertop, unsure if he should bother to retrieve it. The backhander wasn't one to treat things with delicacy, but it was odd, even for him, to toss aside a perfectly reusable alcohol vessel.

"Are you sure you don't..." The question faded from Zavik's lips as T'Vak's boots crunched down the street. "Whatever is the matter with you, old friend?" he whispered. His own words struck him instantly as odd, and he couldn't for the life of him determine why he'd chosen them. Had the backhander really become worthy of such a title? Sure, the time they'd spent together the past year was considerable. But 'old friend'?

A flicker of recognition sparked in his mind, that hint of familiarity, that voice whispering he knew T'Vak from another life. There was something he'd repressed, and being back in his childhood city was awakening it. Zavik searched his memories for someone bearing the backhander's semblance. He'd encountered dozens of alcoholics and countless more unruly men looking for scuffles and mates, but none bore the face of the man he now knew.

Come on, Zav. Think. Stop fighting it.

A vision, warm and hazy, emerged in the forefront of his mind. A boy with eyes like the desert, and a smile as radiant as the moons. He didn't tease Zavik like the other boys. Not that he stopped the other ferrets from their cruelties, such as forewarning previously unaware merchants of Zavik's petty thefts. But the desert-eyed boy hadn't derived pleasure from it. He hadn't encouraged the others to yank Zavik's foreign hair again and again, to smash his seers, to send him staggering through the boiling streets to an empty house with a mother off giving love to strangers and the ghost of an alcoholic father lingering in the dented table and unhinged doors.

That boy...

"Hate to keep you from your musings, but I've got a deadline to keep."

Zavik jumped at the nearness of T'Vak's voice. "Sorry, I just...you left your..." He grasped at the boy's fading face, trying to align it with that of the man peering down at him. Emboldened by the lack of confidence in T'Vak's eyes, Zavik quieted his uncertainty and fear of judgment that so often bade him to stay silent. "I know you, don't I?"

The backhander traced his thumb over the hilt of his sword, his normally playful mouth locked in a lipless line.

"You were one of Lanston's ferrets, weren't you?" Zavik pressed. He shoved his seers higher on the bridge of his nose. "I can't recall your name. I've tried to block out so much of my life here. I think that's why I didn't recognize you at first."

The sound of drunken laughter echoed behind them. Zavik waited until two young men stumbled around them, one with his arm about the other's neck as they swayed back and forth, a scandalous tune on their lips.

"I mean, you look different," Zavik said when they'd passed from earshot. "Probably changed your name. Grew out your hair. Gained a few muscles." A nervous laugh tickled his throat.

Still, the backhander did not reply.

Zavik's hands found their way into his pockets. He tried to fight the doubt settling over him like a fog. "It is you, isn't it? You were that quiet boy. The one who didn't seem to take pleasure in humiliating me."

T'Vak's throat bobbed. He started back down the road before Zavik could assess the emotions in his face.

"T'Vak," Zavik shouted after him. He begged his own mind to bring forth whatever pain was necessary to recall the boy's name. It'd had a hardened sound to it, yes? Something like...no. No, it wasn't hardened at all. That's why the boy had always tried to appear so detached and tough. Because his name meant 'benevolent,' or something of the like. His name was—

"Paval!"

T'Vak—Paval—froze mid-stride. He didn't turn, but there was a sag to his shoulders. A tingle coursed down Zavik's spine as he hurried to catch up with the backhander. When T'Vak faced him, harsh lines cut rivers across his brow.

"Why are you doing this now, Zavvie boy?" All hints of melody deserted his voice, leaving in its stead weary acceptance. "Why do you see it now?"

"I..." Zavik stammered. His gaze drifted to the moons, to the slivers nestled against one another like spooning lovers. A mawsk skittered across the street, scenting the air with long, fanned whiskers before disappearing beneath a stall. Another group of stumbling revelers strolled along either side of them, at least two of them kuza. Another was a city official, and yet another wore the towering headpiece of the great houses.

When they were again alone, Zavik turned to Paval, who was now T'Vak. "I don't think I wanted to recognize you before. Orillon holds many memories for me, and most of them are so terrible that I've spent the rest of my life trying to banish them from existence. I immersed myself in Neharem, in Elaysia." The admission tightened Zavik's throat. "I never wanted to come back here, you know. But I guess I was meant to."

"I suppose your face was easier to commit to memory than mine."

Zavik's cheeks flushed. "Yes, yes. Flicker and all that. Lanston made sure you all remembered me, as if my Az Zarian looks didn't make me enough of a target."

"And I was just one of the boys making your shit life shittier. Hard to remember one dirty street ferret from the other, eh?"

The sadness in his voice tugged at Zavik's heart. "And we were children," he added, "young children. Maybe you can afford me some leniency?"

T'Vak smirked, and though it lacked authenticity, Zavik felt the corner of his mouth lift. "We need to keep moving. My contact won't wait around all night for us to show."

"But—"

"I promise I'll answer all your questions, but I need you to do this for me first, alright?" T'Vak slapped Zavik's back, albeit gentler than usual. "I swear it by my wineskin."

"The one you just tossed aside without a second thought?" Zavik folded his arms—not that he had any intention of putting up actual resistance.

A groan escaped T'Vak's lips. "Can you help an old ferret or not?"

"Yes." Zavik offered his hand. His questions could wait a few more hours. They could actually wait a few more days for all he cared. T'Vak being a ferret changed everything and nothing all at once, and for the first time since leaving Neharem, he felt at home. "Ferrets for life?"

T'Vak gripped his hand and gave it a firm shake. "For life."

The fighting pit T'Vak dragged Zavik to was below average in terms of cleanliness and patronage. Back in his days with Lanston, he'd been sent on enough errands to various arenas throughout Munskahan to recognize the more sordid establishments. This was one of them.

The stench of unwashed bodies assaulted his nose as he shouldered his way through the crowd. Half the occupants of the feasting-hall-sized room swayed and cheered drunkenly; the other half looked one argument away from starting brawls themselves. Zavik and T'Vak only made it a few feet from the doorway before dead-ending into an unrelenting sea of spectators, creating a natural perimeter around the fight.

Zavik raised up on his toes to get a better look at the spectacle, then squirmed his way around a toothless old woman shaking a small bag of aspar with trembling, bony fingers. She screamed insults at the fighters, spittle flying from her mouth and plastering itself to Zavik's cheek. It took all his resolve to keep from gagging.

"Sure, why not throw away what remains of your life's savings," he muttered. Most of the lot present would end up like the old woman: addicted to the violence and gambling with no place, and no one, to call home. It was what made the pits thrive, and why the great houses invested in them. And the fighters were as dependent as those cheering them on.

Honest pay for mostly honest work, Anahi had said with a wink when Zavik pried into her past amid the unity ceremony preparations. Even still, he couldn't picture her at such a place. Surely, she must've vied for the larger arenas, the ones more focused on sport and rewards. The ones folk of the reputable sort weren't above frequenting.

"Move," T'Vak shouted over the howls of pleasure that erupted after what had likely been some gruesome takedown. He yanked Zavik's collar, dragging him a few feet before Zavik wrenched himself free.

He tried to excuse the offense as he followed the backhander through small gaps in the crowd, sidestepping piles of questionable consistency and color. A leathered man with one opaque eye screamed as Zavik approached, crumpling to the ground in a frail ball of angst as he pounded his fists against his head. Zavik gave as much breadth as the space would allow and hurried after T'Vak, much faster this time, trailing alongside the poles that had once contained division ropes to separate the left pit from the right.

Pit was more a term of familiarity than an appropriate definition. The only boundaries for the contestants were the walls of spectators wedged elbow to elbow in crudely formed circles. Occasionally, the crowds would part enough for Zavik to glimpse a fight. The right pit contained two young women, one tall and wiry with a fresh gash running the length of her right forearm. Her opponent, though lacking in height, compensated with muscles to rival T'Vak's. They seemed well-enough matched, which couldn't be said for the pair on the left. Zavik wasn't even certain the man sprawled face-first on the ground was still conscious, much less living. A masked fighter towered above him, then nudged the body over with the toe of his boot. Zavik looked away as soon as he registered the concave face of the grounded opponent.

It didn't prevent the bile from rising in his throat, though.

With a fist covering his mouth, he scurried away from the scene to the opposite end of the hall, away from the strained voices and sloshing beverages. He feared he'd lost T'Vak when a bronze arm shot out from the shadows, yanking him into a dark room that reeked of stale urine. The *thunk* of the door locking into place raised the fine hairs on the back of his neck. Then his world plunged into darkness.

"T'Vak?" he stammered, suddenly fearing the company he kept.

"Ease your storm, Zavvie boy."

A warm, rough hand gripped Zavik's, and he reluctantly followed, his feet clunky and uncertain as he stuck out his free hand to fend off anything intending him harm. His fingers brushed something cold and smooth, yet hard. Then another. And another. As he pieced together the object in his mind, his blood ran cold.

A cage.

Tremors rippled through his body. He recoiled, trying to assess his instinctive reaction. After all, cages were common enough in and around the fighting pits. Though Munskahan had nowhere near the size of the venue or the number of undesirables at their expenditure, the locals tried their best to imitate the ancient arena in Cadar by occasionally importing or capturing fierce and rare beasts. Even the elusive Az Zarian sandcat wasn't above finding its way into the pits. Cages, like the ones surrounding him, were often the beasts' final resting places before surrendering to a painful, sometimes slow, pit death.

The groan of a door silenced Zavik's thoughts. A warm light bathed an entryway across the room, revealing cobwebs in the corners and uneven chunks and scratches marring the inside of the wooden door. Before he could speculate what beings had so desperately fought for escape, a voice as rich and aged as the desert broke the silence.

"Been too long again, Flicker."

Upon hearing the old merchant's voice, a wave of cautious relief washed over Zavik. At least it wasn't a stranger. In fact, it made sense Lanston would be T'Vak's connection. The merchant had a wealth of knowledge, and it stood to reason that he'd keep his favorite ferrets employed well into adulthood.

Zavik pulled his hand free from T'Vak's. For the briefest moment, he swore he felt a tug of resistance, as though the backhander didn't want him to enter the room. But he could trust Lanston, couldn't he? And if not, he could certainly trust Paval, the desert-eyed boy who never sought to harm him.

The boy who'd just struggled to release his hand.

On second thought, Zavik wanted nothing to do with Lanston or the fighting pits. He backed away slowly, bumping into T'Vak.

"Can we do this in the morning? I just remembered I need to—"

The backhander responded by shoving him into the room. Zavik's heart skipped a beat as the door, his only means of escape, slammed shut behind him. The room was no larger than the average loft in Agaas and contained a few storage closets alongside a chest overflowing with rusted weapons and armor in need of repair. In the center of the room, his feet propped up on an off-kilter table and an open wine bottle in hand, sat Lanston. The merchant occupied the only chair, his well-endowed rump barely contained by the thin slab of wood making up the seat. He rubbed his thumb across the bottle's neck, eyes brimming with mischievousness.

The stagnant, musty scent of the room sickened Zavik's stomach. Something about it felt familiar. He'd been here before, long ago. And not just once.

Again, he backed away, hoping to flee. Again, T'Vak prevented his escape.

"Come, come," Lanston bellowed, motioning him over. "There's no reason for a ferret to be afraid of its handler."

Zavik's feet remained rooted.

"Don't be like that, Flicker. Here, this will calm your nerves, it will." Lanston held up the bottle, and when Zavik refused to budge, tossed it to T'Vak, who snatched it from the air. He didn't drink, though.

It all but confirmed Zavik's fears.

"I'm told you require my expertise," he said, adjusting his stance to ensure his knife was readily available in his boot.

Except it wasn't. He leveled a glare at T'Vak, who'd likely disarmed him during the chaos of the pit fights. The backhander wouldn't meet his gaze.

"So I do, Zavik. So I do." Despite the crinkles around Lanston's eyes, his voice lowered, and his fingers tapped a steady rhythm on the table. "And I think you know what for."

A coil of dread wound tightly around Zavik's core as he connected the chains of events that were now so glaringly obvious. Lanston's knowledge of the scrolls. T'Vak's sudden appearance in the desert and unwavering loyalty despite no immediate payment. The theft of the scroll in Amiren after T'Vak sent him back into town for Beridian Moonlight. The revelation of the backhander's true identity.

Brilliant, Zav. Just brilliant.

He lunged for the door. T'Vak caught his tunic, yanking back with enough force to send him sprawling.

"Please," he whispered, hoping some remnant of Paval still survived beneath the backhander's hardened exterior. "Whatever you're about to do, please don't. We can take care of you. Elaysia will—"

"Come here!" Lanston thundered.

Zavik's shoulders slumped under the summons. He saw Lanston, but heard his long-dead father's voice: *Come here, you little shit. Come here, or I'll give you double.* Then Lanston became his father, hurling bottles and swinging furniture. Zavik buried his head in his hands.

It's not real. It's not now.

He blinked the vision away, then rose, rubbing the spot above his right eye where a sharp, throbbing pain had set in. Once again, he dashed for the door.

T'Vak caught him effortlessly. "Stop fighting it," he said under his breath, restraining Zavik's arms. "Just do what he says, and he'll take care of you, like…"

"Like a good handler." Zavik ceased struggling. "As long as the ferrets behaved. And we were good ferrets, weren't we? Blindly following his orders for a pat on the back and a scrap of food while he collected aspar and rare gems in greater numbers than anyone could ever need." The room throbbed around him as years of buried memories clawed their way to the surface. "He sent us to snatch information and treasures, no matter how dangerous. And he—"

Zavik's voice cracked. He ripped his hand free and cast an accusatory finger at Lanston. "He wasn't above sending us to places like these…to this exact room…" Tears muddled his vision. He swallowed a hard lump in his throat, refusing to let specific memories take hold of him. "His own underground love den for the wealthy when they grew bored with consenting love-givers of an appropriate age." He spun to face T'Vak. "Tell me you don't remember," Zavik whispered through salt-stained his lips. "Tell me why you still work for him after everything he's done."

"Bring him here," Lanston shouted, as he smashed a meaty fist onto the table. Red veins marred the whites of his eyes.

Strong hands secured Zavik's shoulders and guided him to the table. Suddenly, he was a child again, quaking with terror, a single sconce the only one to bear witness to—

No. With a shake of his head, he gathered all his humiliation, agony, and fear, molding them into pure hatred. And then he aimed his rage-filled gaze at Lanston. To his astonishment, the merchant looked away.

Shame, or cowardice? Either way, it was a small victory, and Zavik clung to it.

"What do you want, Lanston?" he asked, his voice unsteady.

The merchant leaned back in the chair and crossed his arms. It creaked beneath his weight. "You were always a favorite, Flicker. Foreign coloring and all." He tipped the bottle back, wine staining his beard as he drank. "Don't look at me like that. It kept food on your table after your papa died, didn't it? Believe it or not, I tried to spare you as often as I could. Wasn't more than once a moon cycle—"

"Shut your mouth."

T'Vak glanced up at Zavik's outburst, his eyes wide and cautioning.

A chilling laugh emerged from deep in Lanston's belly. "Fiery as ever. You were the only one to put up a fight, you know that? Scrawny little you, half the size of your peers, yet you clawed and thrashed and screamed till your voice ran dry."

"Enough," T'Vak croaked. "Just tell him what you want."

"Why don't you tell him?" Lanston retorted. "It's your fault he's here. Had you done your fucking job for once, he wouldn't need to be here now, reliving all this."

The backhander hung his head.

"I don't have them," Zavik said, assessing T'Vak's downcast gaze. If he could just get out of the room and through one that lay beyond it, he could vanish into the crowd. The streets of Munskahan weren't just T'Vak's, after all.

They were also his.

"Liar," Lanston hissed.

"I'm not. I left the scrolls in Neharem, somewhere you'll never find them."

The merchant set the bottle back on the table. "That's unfortunate."

"And," Zavik added, fear prickling his heart, "if you kill me, you'll never get them. No one knows where they are but me."

Lanston heaved himself out of the chair and came to stand before Zavik. He was a good foot taller, and with his bulk, he almost appeared more formidable than T'Vak. "Wouldn't dare kill a ferret. Especially not one intertwined with the scrolls' fates." He retrieved a small, rolled parchment from his brightly colored robes, the size often used for turosses. "But I'm not the only one who wants you. And the others, well..." He flashed an array of brown and gold teeth. "They aren't as kind as me."

"I doubt that," Zavik mumbled.

Lanston shrugged. "You have two choices, because I always give you choices, don't I, Flicker?"

Outside the room, beyond the chamber of cages, the crowd erupted in a cheer.

The old merchant held up a thick finger. "One, you tell me where in Neharem the scrolls are, and I hold on to you for liability purposes while T'Vak retrieves them." He raised a second finger. "Two, you be the stubborn little slaver bastard you've always been, and I hand you over to the All-Sovereign, along with the scroll in my possession, for amnesty. I've learned what I can from it, so it's of no consequence to me. And neither are you." He let his words sink in, as if they held weight with Zavik, as if they could hurt him worse than his actions years past already had.

"The All-Sovereign doesn't care about me." Zavik darted a glance at T'Vak as Lanston wiped his face with his sleeve. The backhander's arms were crossed, his attention on his boots.

He needed to act soon.

"Oh, he does now." Lanston combed through his long, white beard with his fingers. "Now that he knows you can access them. And he'll care even more when he hears tell of your recent theories on nevethium-powered weapons and—don't you dare!"

But Zavik was already bolting for the door, throwing it open, and stumbling into the dark room, his hands shielding him from a collision with the cages. His heartbeat flooded his ears. The edge of a cage caught his foot, but it only slowed him a little. And there, the ray of light beneath the door leading to the fighting pits. He was going to make it. He was almost—

Someone grabbed the back of his jacket and clamped a rough hand over his mouth. Someone who could've only been T'Vak.

Zavik struggled against the backhander as he dragged him back into the room and shut the door behind them. It was futile. T'Vak was impressive enough when intoxicated, and tonight he was the closest to sober Zavik had seen him in moons.

"What will it be, eh, Flicker?" Lanston asked as T'Vak bound Zavik's hands and feet. "Give me the scrolls? Or give yourself over to the All-Sovereign? I will say, your Neharem stands a better chance with the scrolls in my possession."

Zavik didn't allow Lanston the dignity of a glance and instead sought T'Vak's gaze, appealing to any empathy that hadn't yet been beaten out of him. "Please, T'Vak. Paval."

T'Vak winced at his old name. "I'm sorry, Zavvie boy. I'm too far in. Just do what he says, and—"

"Sands curse you both and your love-giving mothers."

Lanston drew a vial from a pouch on his leather belt and popped the cork with his thumb. Before Zavik could react, the merchant was prying his mouth open and dropping the bitter liquid in. "Your indecision is a decision, lad. Hope you enjoy the return to your homeland. T'Vak will find me the scrolls, and Az Zar will be off my ass for the foreseeable future." He ruffled Zavik's hair. "Don't say I didn't try to help an old ferret. T'Vak here will get his. Your loss."

Zavik's tongue was numb, but he managed to get out, "And you'll get yours, Lanston. You've a lifetime of wrongdoings to pay for, and I'll make it my life's purpose to see you never harm another being again."

The room faded around Zavik. As consciousness slipped from him like fine sand through fingers, the last thing he saw was a single tear snaking down T'Vak's cheek.

Then everything went quiet.

T'VAK

T'Vak nursed a bottle of Beridian Moonlight as the Az Zarian soldiers loaded Zavik onto a sand sleigh pulled by four unruly zaka-zakas. They hopped and tugged at the harnesses fastened around their chests, long ears twitching. A dreary yellow haze stained the sky, signaling the first signs of dawn, and though the temperature of the desert rose with it, T'Vak felt no warmth. He looked away as one of the soldiers, his entire body masked head to toe in a tight-fitting black uniform, dropped a pouch into Lanston's outstretched hand.

"For your trouble," the soldier said in painfully clunky Westmun. "Az Zar will remember your allegiance when the time comes."

Lanston regarded Zavik abed on the sleigh as though he were no more than a sack of grain. "Please tell your All-Sovereign I am forever grateful for his kindness. If there's anything else I can do for the empire, don't hesitate to call upon this old merchant."

"I'm sure His Holiness will have need of you yet." The soldier wrapped a hand—firmly enough to be threatening—around Lanston's shoulder. "And you will tell us if you learn the whereabouts of other scrolls."

"I swear by my left nut," Lanston began, then, apparently realizing his attempts at humor were wasted on the soldier, he added, "and by my mother herself, sands preserve her." He reached into the sleigh and brushed Zavik's hair from his eyes, a gesture that would've appeared genuine to an outsider. "Do take care of this one. I'm told no harm's to come to him."

The soldier's eyes betrayed no emotion. "He is the empire's responsibility now."

A sandstorm of nausea raged in T'Vak's stomach, and not for the first time that day. The other soldier, the one not currently exchanging pleasantries with Lanston, unsheathed one of the sleek blades strapped to his back and made a show of cleaning it while eyeing T'Vak from the slits in his face mask. T'Vak took another swig of the Moonlight, swirling the syrupy liquid around in his mouth to keep any rash words at bay.

Zavik moaned. His eyelids fluttered open for a moment, then he resumed his labored breathing.

"What I gave him ought to last ya until the sun's at its peak," Lanston said as he fingered through the pouch to inventory his aspar. "But I'd be wary of this one. He's feisty despite—"

"That will be all." The soldiers climbed into the sleigh and urged the grunting zaka-zakas forward with the crack of a whip.

T'Vak and Lanston stood there, sand blowing over their sandaled feet, until the sleigh disappeared behind one of the dunes.

"Gimme some of that," Lanston said, reaching for the Beridian Moonlight.

T'Vak's fingers tightened around the bottle. His gaze met the merchant's with chilling certainty. Only when Lanston began to squirm did he relinquish it.

After a few drinks, the merchant regained whatever courage he'd lost and jabbed a thick finger into the center of T'Vak's chest. "Don't tell me you're going soft. We've sought these scrolls for years, and there was always a risk Zavik wouldn't comply."

A shriek pierced the sky. T'Vak looked up just as the massive silhouette of a stormbird drifted overhead. The Great Beast arced its neck down to peer at them, then continued west as if registering them as allies, not prey.

The thought only made T'Vak's head ache more.

Lanston thrust the bottle back into T'Vak's hands. "You better get back to House Undali before they grow suspicious. I need you in good standing if you're going to have a chance at securing those scrolls."

"Do you honestly think they're going to let me return to Neharem without Zavik?" The thought of facing any of them, especially Elaysia, sent an icy chill down his spine. "They'll never trust me."

"Of course they will. They trusted him, and he trusted you."

T'Vak couldn't move, couldn't speak, as the merchant heaved himself onto his zaka-zaka and loped into the distance. He finished the bottle, then hurled it in the direction the soldiers had gone. He needed to rescue Zavik. If he could get his filthy mount to move fast enough...

The ground was unsteady beneath his feet, and he lurched forward, landing face-first in the sand beside his zaka-zaka. It startled the beast and sent it hopping a good thirty feet away, ears flatted against its head.

"You little shit," T'Vak groaned. Determined, he crawled after it, grains of sand clinging to his palms, scratching his eyes, and coating his tongue. But his head swam, and his stomach raged, and he collapsed beside the empty bottle. He reached for it with a trembling hand, then wedged it into the sand like a monument. With a groan, he forced himself to a kneeling position.

Then he waited for the words to come.

"I've wronged you, Zavvie boy," he whispered, lest the wind carry his secrets. "And you've been nothing but good to me since we were kids. I know I've fucked this up, but I'm going to make it right. Now wasn't the time, he would've...they would've..."

He struck himself in the chest with his fist until the sadness loosened its grip on his throat.

"Just hang on. You're safe, you hear me? They won't hurt you. I'll figure it out, I swear it. Ferrets for life, and all that shit."

T'Vak wiped his eyes and offered a silent prayer to whatever cursed gods or goddesses still gave enough of a shit about the mortal beings left to struggle through lives filled with pain and longing. He'd continue playing Lanston's game, but this time, he'd play his own, too. Before he went back to Neharem, he'd pay a final visit to the old merchant's home. Borrow some aspar, some drink, some trinkets. And one precious little parchment with Lanston's most important notes from the scroll he'd just traded to Az Zar. Wouldn't even be T'Vak's fault, really. The ferret handler should've known better than to allow a ferret around his most prized possessions, no matter how much he thought he'd broken him in.

As T'Vak urged his zaka-zaka toward Munskahan, he gave one final glance back at the bottle.

The sand always remembered.

So would T'Vak.

PART THREE

AHMARAHN

Ahmarahn winced as light stabbed the darkness. His hand jerked, instinctively trying to shield his face from the assault, but the shackles hindered his movement. He lowered his gaze instead, nose wrinkling as the growing orange beam highlighted the soiled straw beneath him. Metal clinked against metal, followed by the satisfying *clank* of a key sinking into a lock. The door groaned open, as though it didn't want to be roused from its slumber, either. Feet shuffled through the straw.

Still, he didn't look up.

"Learned your lesson, eh? Finally keeping your pride in check like the rest of us?" a nasal voice said. Rough hands yanked his head so far back he thought his neck might snap. "Behold, the great general of Az Zar. Oh, wait; never made it that far, did you, Captain?"

Ahmarahn glared into eyes so dark they could've been mistaken for black. The man they belonged to wasn't his usual warden. The grumpy but fair old man who'd treated him with much appreciated apathy had recently taken sick, leaving the bitter young man in his place, a man bent on making sure Ahmarahn didn't go a day without remembering what got him imprisoned in the first place. As if taunting could even begin to compare to the loss of his family, his dreams, his identity. The punishment had begun long before that, though.

It'd begun with her.

The warden gave him an ear-ringing slap to the side of his head. "Answer me this instant, or I'll see to it you have to be carried up the stairs."

Ahmarahn mumbled a reply, one convincing enough that the warden shoved him aside with disgust and swung the cell door wide open.

Though his legs ached and wobbled from the day's work in the mines, he struggled to his feet and assumed a passable version of his old military stance as the warden unlocked the chain securing him to the wall. Not the shackles on his hands and feet, though. By the time they reached the foot of the spiral staircase leading out of the palace's secret dungeon, Ahmarahn's ankles were raw from chafing. Normally, they'd remove his shackles for labor.

That was apparently not what his night was to hold.

A knife tip jabbed into his back, urging him to quicken his pace. He maneuvered as smoothly up the stairs as he could, careful to stay within the torchlight's glow and avoid piles of skirvin shit or crumbling bits of staircase. There were three hundred and thirty steps to the top, and he counted them as he went, as he did each morning, to give himself a sense of accomplishment. As he passed other cells filled with ballsy city officials and deceitful merchants, some gripped the bars with hopeful fingers while others cried out curses or prayers. Perhaps they were the same: a prayer, a hopeful curse; a curse, a desperate prayer.

Two nevethium sconces greeted Ahmarahn when he reached the top. The warden looked him up and down as though assessing a slave for auction, then heaved the door open, flooding them with moonlight.

Ahmarahn inhaled the night air, fresh and free of the stench of piss and shit clinging to the prison like mold. A chill rippled down his spine and raised bumps on his arms as he bathed in the light of the moons, all three of them full as a belly on Dzro Jiazin. That was how Xi used to describe them, anyway. The holiday had been his baby sister's favorite, and not because it celebrated Az Zar's foundation. Only because they'd all be together, filled with food and laughter, life's hardships momentarily forgotten. She'd beg him to lie out on their family porch, her tiny belly round with bean cakes, and show him the shapes in the stars.

Ahmarahn flinched at the thought, at his weakness. He didn't allow his mind to wander there, not ever. It did him no good to reflect on the memories of another man's life, one he could no longer claim as his. Davier was dead. He'd not appreciated his blessings, and his desire for more cost him what mattered most. But Ahmarahn was stronger than Davier had ever been. He'd nothing and no one to hold him back. He could wait moons upon moons to achieve his sole purpose in life.

Revenge.

A foot sank into his back, knocking the air from his lungs as he went sprawling to the ground. Ahmarahn he now was, but remnants of his previous instincts persisted, prompting him to turn his body as he fell, giving his shoulder the brunt of the impact rather than his face.

"Am I being punished for something?" he asked, shaking tangled locks of hair from his eyes to meet the warden's sneering gaze. "I thought my work today was satisfactory. There are plenty of others who—"

"I'll beat you if it pleases me, and it does."

The warden kicked him in the ribs to prove his point. Ahmarahn hardly felt it. He'd grown somewhat desensitized to beatings, and the warden had little strength left after heaving his substantial body up the stairs. As the larger man leaned against the wall, panting, Ahmarahn let his gaze wander about the courtyard reserved for military and servants, over its well-manicured shrubs and freshly cleaned stables. The door they'd just emerged from was tucked along the backside of some barracks, a discreet enough entry point for a prison that didn't officially exist, a place where the All-Sovereign stored criminals of...interest. Those he perceived as less dangerous or likely to escape as opposed to the ones he kept imprisoned on the island fortress. The implication of his prison assignment would've offended Davier, but Ahmarahn didn't care. A cell was a cell.

"Into the palace," the warden growled, gesturing across the courtyard.

Ahmarahn hesitated, eyeing the steps from a distance. Servants' entrance or not, it wasn't lacking in grandeur with its jade deathstalker statues standing guard on either side of the staircase. They glared down at him, stingers bared, pincers wide, their nevethium eyes both alluring and promising death. Ahmarahn's head buzzed, and he locked his knees to steady himself. He hadn't been in the palace since...

He shivered. Took a step back.

There could only be one person seeking an audience with him at such an unholy hour, under the cover of darkness. One he'd once been so desperate to please, before everything was taken from him. Now he wanted nothing but to make the man-god suffer as he had suffered.

But he couldn't. Not yet.

The warden unsheathed his blade and pointed it at Ahmarahn. "Don't keep His Holiness waiting. Meet me back here as soon as you're finished. And if you try anything"—he hovered the blade just above Ahmarahn's throat—"I'll personally see to it your death lasts moons."

"Where am I to meet him?" Ahmarahn asked, although a part of him already knew.

The warden shrugged. "He said you'd know. Something about where you received your first mission."

Ahmarahn nodded and shuffled across the courtyard before vulnerability showed on his face like a torch in the darkness. The veranda was where he'd received his first mission directly from the All-Sovereign. His first and his last. Even then, he hadn't been allowed to navigate the palace alone. His newly sanctioned independence was no doubt a ploy; a means to show him just how inconsequential he'd become. So harmless that he could be trusted in the All-Sovereign's presence without an escort.

Humiliation burned his cheeks as he approached the stairs. He tried to focus on each step as it disappeared beneath his feet, on the pain in his legs, the groans in his stomach—anything but the memories.

Visions of his family obscured the looming palace. What torture had they endured as the light vanished from their eyes? He didn't even get to say goodbye, to cradle Xi in his arms one last time—

No. The stairs. He needed to focus on the stairs. On how clean they were, even for an entrance utilized by slaves and soldiers. Or on how forgiving the night air was against his tacky skin. Or—

What if the All-Sovereign felt he hadn't been punished enough? The brand on his forehead burned as though it'd just been applied. He wanted to reach up and rub it—no, scratch it out. Burn away the rest of his flesh until—

The stairs, you weakling, he cursed inwardly at himself. *Focus on the fucking stairs. Get control of yourself or else.*

Ahmarahn didn't look up as the guard opened the palace door. He kept his gaze on the ground, on the crimson carpet sprawled before him like a throwaway tapestry for the rich. The All-Sovereign loved red. The palace drowned in it. Homage to the lives he destroyed, to the wars his bloodline had orchestrated. There were even whispers he feasted on hearts, prolonging his life well beyond its natural means.

The path to the veranda came to him like a dream, like a memory he'd buried deep but could never fully forget. When he arrived at the veranda entrance, one of the gilded doors was propped open, beckoning him to enter. He considered fleeing, throwing himself off one of the palace's many balconies, but that would mean the All-Sovereign won.

Ahmarahn would live a thousand pain-filled lives before surrendering so easily.

As he stepped onto the veranda, the first thing he noticed was the absence of the table and chairs present during his previous audience. The lattice railing had also been cleared of overhanging foliage, preventing the vines from wrapping around the pillars like elegant serpents. Perhaps most perplexing was the fine layer of debris covering the marble beneath his feet, giving the veranda, once the All-Sovereign's favored meeting place, a sense of abandonment. And the air, pure as ever and sweetened with the citrus scent of sun-blood blossoms, wasn't overpowered by the palace's usual rank incense. In fact—he ducked back inside momentarily to verify—there was no scent emanating from within the palace at all.

Something had changed. Or someone.

Ahmarahn used his thumb to crack his knuckles as he returned to the veranda. A breeze brushed against his threadbare tunic, and only then did he fully register the subtle warmth in the air. He squinted at the sky, trying to piece time together. The positioning of the stars suggested the Sowing Moons, but that couldn't be right. He'd just...it'd just...

Unless it'd been that long. Nearly a year?

"A glorious evening, is it not, Zadel?"

The blood drained from Ahmarahn's face upon hearing the All-Sovereign's voice. He lurched to the railing, bracing himself against it. His heart thudded in his ears. Chest constricted.

Just breathe.

He looked to the moons and told himself to think about nothing besides their splendor, the way their ghostly light drifted down into the garden like a gentle mist. It was all just a bad dream. He could survive another bad dream.

Breathe.

"No greeting?" the All-Sovereign asked, leaning against the railing beside him. He smelled of blood and ash. "Has your servitude robbed you of your civility?"

Even as his body rebelled against him, Ahmarahn kept his gaze on the sky.

The All-Sovereign grunted in frustration. "Address me at once. Or did I brand your balls?"

The moons became a blur, a shimmering mirage in the sky. A steady, white heat burned inside Ahmarahn, one so fierce and unruly that he didn't dare meet the All-Sovereign's gaze, lest his body act of its own accord.

There was a slurping sound, then the *clink* of a glass placed on the railing.

"I suppose I deserve this," the nyrian dictator murmured. His tone was level, his voice distant, as though he spoke to himself. "But surely you can see how you pushed me, Zadel. What was I supposed to do? Allow your public display of insolence, your audacity to betray me, to go unpunished?"

"Ahmarahn," he gritted out, facing the All-Sovereign.

"Sorry?"

"My name is Ahmarahn."

It still felt foreign on his tongue, so little had he spoken it aloud. He couldn't recall who had bestowed the name upon him, but the first time he heard it, it resonated like a finely tuned harp. A few guards continued to use it as an insult, then other prisoners adopted it, and little by little, he'd responded to it, acknowledged it. Now, it was all he knew. Ahmarahn was the key to his survival. He could live on when Davier could not.

"Enslaved." The All-Sovereign scraped the glass off the railing as he eyed Ahmarahn, a thin smile pulling at his lips. "And you undoubtedly think they call you that out of some cock-swooned measure of respect. Makes you proud, does it?"

Ahmarahn gave a curt shrug. It was not a conversation he wanted to have with anyone, much less the All-Sovereign. There was no pride left in him. Only survival and spite, and what wonderful bed partners they made. For what the All-Sovereign didn't know was the internal brand he carried consumed him more than the one of his forehead ever could. He'd been broken and degraded beyond reason, and while it had destroyed Davier, it left a stronger person in his place. Ahmarahn had nothing to lose.

And the All-Sovereign had everything.

"As pleasurable as this is, I do have actual business to discuss with you."

Business? Ahmarahn snorted. The pointy-eared prick had somehow grown more deluded over the past year. "I know you're a bit out of touch with the common people, but if you think for a moment that I'd—"

"Ah, I almost forgot." The All-Sovereign clapped, and two soldiers emerged from the shadows, carrying a small, limp body between them. Even in the moonlight, Ahmarahn could make out the rich golden coloring of the victim's hair. "Your motivation," the All-Sovereign said, his lips parted in a sickening grin.

Ahmarahn's throat tightened. He inched closer to the body, only to have another pair of guards block his path with crossed blades. One of them secured a cluster of golden hair and pulled the victim's head back, revealing her face.

No.

Ahmarahn's body lunged at the guards before he gave it permission. He fell into old rhythms as they fought to restrain him, driving his elbow into a nose with a satisfying *crunch*. Another guard grabbed his neck, and Ahmarahn brought a knee to his groin. He made it two more steps before someone kicked his legs out from under him. A blade tip found his throat.

"Xi!" he cried, rolling away from the blade. "Xianna!"

A boot connected with his stomach. Ahmarahn winced, gasped for breath. Someone yanked him up and hit him in the face. Hard. He never saw who delivered it, only tasted the blood in his mouth, felt the throbbing circle of pain radiating through his cheek.

"Enough. I need him coherent. Take her away."

The sound of footsteps receded in response to the All-Sovereign's command. Ahmarahn groaned and struggled to rise with his still-bound wrists. By the time he made it to his feet, the veranda door had closed, and a sizable nyrian guard blocked the entrance.

He turned a heated gaze on the All-Sovereign, his lower lip trembling. "Where are they taking her? What's wrong with her? Why did she—"

"I had her drugged so she wouldn't have to see you in this state. You should thank me." The All-Sovereign wrinkled his nose, then looked away with an air of disgust. "You've seen she's alive and well, so let us commence with the purpose of this meeting."

Ahmarahn lurched forward on unsteady feet. The All-Sovereign's golden eyes widened, but he didn't retreat, nor did he summon the guard posted at the entrance. They exchanged a thousand words in a glance, and for a fleeting moment, Ahmarahn swore he saw a hint of guilt. Perhaps buried beneath the nyrian's polished exterior was a simple man who'd dug himself an early grave, one he couldn't climb out of, but one that wouldn't just kill him already either.

Pitiful.

The All-Sovereign must've sensed his own vulnerability, for he withdrew his gaze and crossed his arms to establish a barrier between them.

Ahmarahn raised an eyebrow to make it clear that, yes, he'd witnessed the abject man within, and he wouldn't forget it. Ever.

"You must be desperate to call upon me, Your Holiness."

The All-Sovereign's lip curled. "Why have a hunting dog if you never use it? Your talents are wasted in the mines, and by the looks of your complexion, you could use some sunlight."

"The rest of my family..." Ahmarahn couldn't finish the thought. He didn't want to dare to hope, but with Xi alive, he had to know.

A slow shake of the All-Sovereign's head was his response. "Crawling with maggots, I'd wager." He retreated a few paces closer to the guard. "I only needed one bargaining chip, and the tiny one was the easiest to manage."

Darkness ebbed at Ahmarahn's vision. He dropped to his knees, head swimming as though he'd just heard the news for the first time. "You're a monster," he whispered.

"You know, monsters and gods aren't all that different." The All-Sovereign studied a nail on one of his long, silvered fingers, then motioned two more soldiers out from the shadows. They stood on either side of Ahmarahn, gazes probing. "Now, do as I say, like an obedient dog, and I swear upon my sovereignty that I won't touch a precious strand on your sister's pretty little head. Otherwise, she can start serving wine at the brothels tonight."

Ahmarahn's world pulsed red. He forced himself to step back, hoping the distance would keep him from doing anything rash and endangering Xi's life. "Your word is shit."

"And you're not exactly in a place to negotiate."

The wind held its breath as the All-Sovereign advanced like a sandcat stalking prey, so bold in his element, behind the protection of his walls and hired blades. But strip him of it, and he was nothing. Weaker than most, with no love in his heart. And that was how he needed to go. Stripped, alone, wallowing in his own wretchedness.

And Ahmarahn would relish every moment of it.

"Honestly, Zadel, I'm offering you an opportunity here." The All-Sovereign crouched down beside him to raise his chin. Ahmarahn almost bit his fingers off. "Do you really want to spend the rest of your days in the dark, breaking your back in the bellies of my mines for a cause you rebelled against? Do you enjoy the company of slaves who hate you and soldiers who envy what you threw away? Just look at you." He jabbed Ahmarahn's ribs, which practically poked through his skin thanks to his long hours and meager rations. "You've aged a lifetime in a year. By now, you must've accepted that you'll never escape. No one is coming for you. No one cares, save for your sister, whose life is in your hands."

The All-Sovereign rested his hands on Ahmarahn's shoulders, and bile crept up his throat. Tears waited at the threshold of his eyes, begging to be let out in a waterfall of heated, miserable rage. He looked down at the wound on his chest, at the faint bruising blooming around the cut from a cave-in just the day prior. It'd nearly killed him—had wiped out a dozen other slaves—and it wasn't his first near-death experience in the mines.

Ahmarahn dug his fingernails into his palm. Deep down, he knew the All-Sovereign was right. He could die in the mines tomorrow, or in his cell years from now, plagued by some illness spawned from his unclean living conditions. He'd never get a chance for revenge, and Xi would never be free. But if he complied, just one last time, maybe he could set things right.

If he had to become evil to defeat it, so be it. He'd gladly pay the price. He'd been stripped and beaten. Enslaved. Yet freed to be the rawest version of himself: a monster.

And monsters were governed by none.

JAKKI

J akki's head pulsated with a dull, aching throb that ran down the base of her skull all the way through her spine. Her mouth was a desert, so stale she could practically taste the stench of her breath. But the worst was the light. Blinding and cold, it barreled down onto her eyelids, antagonizing her headache, amplifying her sense of torment and helplessness. She tried to raise her hand to shield her face from the oncoming assault, only to find it tethered to something far stronger than she.

And then a flood of memories crashed into her. The mission. The mountain.

The trap.

She forced her eyes open, watering as they took in the light, shuffling backwards on her feet and free hand toward—

Her back pressed into stone. Smooth, cold stone.

"Jak?"

Xaren. He sounded nearby.

Jakki rubbed her eyes fiercely with her free hand. Slowly, her surroundings trickled into focus. She was underground. The cool, damp scent was her first clue, a refreshing mixture of mineral and fresh snowfall. Her second was the naturally occurring rock making up the walls of her prison, save for the startlingly ornate bars creating the door. They weren't made of metal, but an ice-blue crystal, far more beautiful than the glass work mastered in Orillon. She'd never seen its like.

She scooted toward the bars and pressed against one with her boot, assessing its durability. An icy bite seeped through the leather sole, chilling her toes and foot, and ascending halfway up her calf before she pulled it away. The chill lingered long after. In an effort to break it, she gave a forceful and precise kick to a twisted, narrow section where the bars appeared to be less sturdy. It sang upon impact, a resonating sound that brought her a sense of calm and—dare she admit it—euphoria. Still, it didn't break. Not even a hint of a crack or loosening.

"Jakki? Are you awake?"

Xaren again. He was undoubtedly close. With luck, in the cell adjacent to hers. She inched as close to the bars as she dared, shivering at the cold emanating from them. "Unfortunately."

The audible sigh of relief she heard in response warmed her more than she cared to admit. "I was worried about you. You've been unconscious all day."

Jakki cast a suspicious look at the skyless ceiling above her as she attempted a dry swallow. "Feels longer than that."

"They said they'd be back to collect us by nightfall."

"They?"

"The skulmor."

Glowing hunter's eyes filled her mind; the last thing she'd seen before slipping into darkness. The scar beneath her leggings tingled. They should both be dead.

Jakki shook her head—not that Xaren could see it. "Impossible. No one's ever heard them speak, let alone one of our languages."

"Maybe no one's ever given them the chance." There was a rustling sound, then his voice was nearer. "They understood enough Nyrinian to heed the All-Sovereign's threats and commands, so it's not surprising they can speak a rudimentary form of it. Even the stormbirds understand us and communicate in their own way."

"The birds." Jakki closed her eyes and tried to establish a connection with Siren. She struggled to find a coherent line of thought, but deep within her, in the realms beyond logic, she sensed the steady drum of the stormbird's heartbeat. Siren was alive and...worried?

No. She was enraged.

"I tried communing with Shadow." Xaren's shaky voice betrayed his youth. "I think he's hurt."

Jakki pressed her hand to the stone wall dividing them. She swore she could feel him doing the same. "What do you remember from last night?"

"I thought I heard movement in the woods, but before I could investigate, one of them pinned me. It was almost as big as Grokhion. I tried to fight it, but I could barely breathe, much less move." There was a long pause, and Jakki almost interjected with her own thoughts when Xaren whispered, "Its eyes were so hateful."

Jakki recalled her own encounter with the skulmor back in their former stronghold, Gohla. She could still feel the relentless weight bearing down on her, hear the snapping jaws and scrabbling claws, smell the reek of rotted flesh on its breath. She'd only survived then because of her nazrath savior. This time, she was alone.

"The skulmor dragged me bound and gagged to the clearing," Xaren continued, "hoping to lure Shadow near. I tried to warn him in my mind, but he came anyway. He killed some of the skulmor guarding me, snatching them up in his talons and hurling them into the trees. But then they threw spears at him. The spearheads were these icy blue crystals, like our cell bars." His breath seemed to catch, and the words that followed dripped with sorrow. "I think they hit him. He's in pain. He's cold, Jakki."

A white-hot heat roiled in Jakki's chest. "What happened after?"

"Siren intervened. She swooped in, carrying a small tree she'd ripped up, roots and all, and launched it into the skulmor attacking Shadow. She got him out of there, but as they flew, she kept looking back in the direction you'd gone. Then someone blindfolded me. It felt like they marched us at least a mile into the mountain. Lots of steps and ramps."

Jakki's heart sank. They'd been placed at the center of a maze, not unlike the trials favored by the Moatiwe to sharpen their logic and survival abilities. And even if they escaped their cells, who knew how many skulmor they'd have to fight through on their way out.

"Who spoke to you?" Jakki pressed. "And when?"

"They took off my blindfold after dumping me in the cell. I didn't even know if you were..." He drew several steadying breaths. "When I begged to see you, they snarled and howled. But then one came back after the others had gone. He told me our fates would be determined tonight."

Despite knowing the suffering that would follow, Jakki slammed her hand against the bars. Pain coursed through the thin, protective layer of her glove, numbing her hand in a burst of icy fire.

"Why are they keeping us alive?" she snapped. Then, louder, "What could you possibly need to know? Just kill us and be done with it." Her voice echoed in the ominous space beyond. Her head still throbbed, but now that her eyes had adapted, she realized the cell had never been bright to begin with. Only the crystalline bars disturbed the darkness, their icy-blue glow only slightly dimmer than nevethium. "I know you can hear me with those predator ears, you filthy mutts." It was the only insult she could muster.

"Don't," Xaren cautioned. "Maybe they're curious about us."

"They weren't curious when they tried to kill me last time. There's nothing we have that—"

Jakki's blood ran cold. She plunged a hand down the front of her cloak and searched beneath her tunic.

The parchment was gone.

An overwhelming sense of vulnerability engulfed her. She couldn't remember the last time she'd felt so defenseless. She gripped the bars and screamed, only for her scream to intensify as tendrils of ice climbed up her arms.

"Brondite is not to be disrespected," someone called out. The voice was vaguely feminine with a harsh accent Jakki had never encountered before. It almost reminded her of the way the Daruk spoke, but far more guttural.

Golden-green eyes emerged from the darkness, fixating on Jakki. Eyes the color of manipulated nevethium. The eyes of a killer. Jakki swore on Mother Itaso herself they belonged to the same skulmor who'd approached her the night before, as she hung upside down, struggling like a rabbit caught in a trap.

She clenched her fists, barely containing her seething rage. "But we are?"

"You hunted my pack, or do you deny it?"

"*You* took something of mine. I want it back."

The eyes drew closer, and with them came the ghost of a figure. Pointed ears. Broad shoulders. A silvery-white coat the same shade as Jakki's hair. It was smaller than the other skulmor she'd encountered, standing just a touch taller than Lumira, but it was the first one she'd witnessed walking on two legs. Still, it moved about barefoot and wore nothing but a thin loincloth and an extensive necklace covering half its torso.

A necklace of bones.

The skulmor approached the bars. "It was never meant to be yours."

Jakki summoned the most hate-filled expression she could muster. "So kill me."

"When the time comes, the right will be mine, for I claimed you. Until then"—the skulmor slid a sizeable key into the lock, turning it in nearly a full circle until a *clank* echoed off the walls—"you're to remain intact." She shoved the door open, barely giving Jakki enough time to dodge the icy blow of the brondite bars. "Come. The dominants wish to see you."

Jakki hesitated. They'd taken her staff and dagger. Her parchment. To walk next to the skulmor was to place her life in its hands. She could try to escape, might even stand a chance, but Xaren was still locked up. Her freedom would forfeit his life.

"I hope you run," the skulmor growled, stepping into the cell. "I'd love the opportunity to maim you before bringing you and your mate before the dominants."

Xaren snorted in the cell over, and Jakki couldn't help but shake her head.

"We'll appear before your pack leaders." Jakki sauntered past the skulmor, hoping it'd mask the helplessness she felt in the parchment's absence. "But you better have some sacred-ass water to offer us after."

Even if Jakki had heard tell of a thriving skulmor community rich in art and culture, even if she'd read a dozen scrolls documenting their accomplishments, even if she'd spoken to multiple people who'd encountered their grandeur, it still wouldn't have prepared her for the city that lay beneath the mountains.

As it was, she could hardly contain her awe.

The path from the cells wound up a spiraling staircase and spilled into the largest cavern she'd ever laid eyes upon. A region so grand in scope that she couldn't take it all in with a single glance. It stretched at least as high as the living trees of Agaas and diverged into countless tunnels snaking through the mountainside into only goddesses knew how many dwelling centers. Two gigantic skulmor emerged directly from the stone architecture, their statures at least five times the size of the living beings they represented. They'd been carved to make it look as though they braced the weight of the bridges and dwellings on their shoulders; as though they were born of the mountains, their stone claws and jaws ready to lunge at a moment's notice. Beyond them, a waterfall streamed down, its color a crystalline blue illuminated by the clusters of brondite gathered around the place where the mouth vanished into the cavern ceiling. The pool beneath it sparkled with life, begging Jakki to drink from its wellspring.

Their white she-wolf escort snarled, and Jakki quickened her pace, tearing her gaze from the water to ensure Xaren still marched beside her. The boy's eyes were wide with wonder, his mouth slightly agape. He muttered something in Zarith, to which Jakki raised an eyebrow.

"Did you ever think…" he began in Nyrinian, only for a cluster of luminescent fungi to steal his attention.

Still, she gathered his intent, for the sentiment was hers, too. "Never. Everything we knew was wrong."

"Now you know what the Az Zarians think about your kind," the she-wolf said to Jakki, her voice dripping with irony. "How could such uncivilized people achieve such wonders?"

A wave of shame washed over Jakki, and she knew in that moment her perception of the skulmor was forever changed. She experienced a sudden urge to apologize, to explain herself, but her pride wouldn't allow it. Not now, while their lives were still in question. And certainly not while Shadow slowly succumbed to an icy death.

She vowed not to speak again until she'd been presented to the pack leaders.

They followed the she-wolf past the statues and around the waterfall to where the cavern opened up even more, branching out into several main paths and numerous stairs. Jakki counted at least twenty levels before her eyesight failed her, each featuring sturdy stone platforms with bridges and pathways connecting them. The dwellings, like everything else, were carved directly into the mountain, some as rudimentary as caves, and others so large and with such fine attention to detail that they rivaled the architecture of Az Zar. Some even boasted sprawling balconies, multiple levels, and smaller, but no less realistic, statues acting as weight-bearing pillars. Where the icy light of the brondite couldn't reach, luminescent fungi illuminated the paths and interiors, their colors ranging from midnight blue to a vibrant magenta.

As they made their way further into the mountain, they came across skulmor of all ages, from floppy-eared pups to the docile elders minding them. Some harvested the fungi, storing it in woven bags slung over their shoulders, while others chipped away at the rock, carving new structures. When they passed by another waterfall, Jakki stuck out her tongue, relishing its spray as it provided relief (albeit minimal) from her dehydration. It was enough to sustain her until they got to their final destination: a stone bridge at least twenty feet wide and twice that long. It led to a grand foyer where four pillars the size of the skulmor statues supported a triangular gable forming the end of the roof slope. Etched into the gable were runes similar to the ones she'd come across when surveying Gohla, the village previously assumed to be the largest skulmor stronghold.

Runes similar to the ones on the parchment, actually.

Her fingers itched to hold it again. Just for a little while. Just long enough to use its magic to escape. Then she'd bury it somewhere, only retrieving it for the most desperate times. A secret to die with her. Unless the parchment had the power to prevent death.

Jakki caught Xaren staring and silenced her internal musings. There'd be time for such thoughts later, once they were free of their wolven overlords.

Large stone bowls holding clusters of brondite adorned the head and foot of the bridge, lighting the path and chilling the air. Jakki kept her distance from them as they crossed. Awaiting them on the other side were six hulking skulmor guarding doors made of brondite. They wore an array of furs, skins, and bones from various creatures, and if she wasn't mistaken, the skull masks adorning their faces were of their own race. From their glossier coats to their whiter teeth, the mountain-dwelling skulmor had a healthier look than the ones who'd attacked her warriors in Gohla. A more restrained demeanor, too. As the sentries heaved open the doors to the inner chamber, Jakki cautioned Xaren with a look, one that conveyed she'd take the lead.

Their lives depended on it.

As soon as the doors opened, the mouthwatering aroma of roasting meat wafted over Jakki, and her grumbling stomach momentarily banished her apprehension. A path unraveled before them, adorned with naturally occurring rock spires and columns that resulted in an asymmetrical, yet pleasing, aesthetic. Roughly fifty skulmor occupied a space comparable to one of the living tree platforms, most of which were gathered in clusters on the primary level. At the far end of the hall, a grand staircase, its every step inlaid with brondite, ascended to a throne the size of an Agaasian loft. It, too, was backlit with brondite, giving the being carved into it an ethereal glow.

Jakki's brow furrowed as she took in the majestic statue occupying the throne. It wasn't skulmor like the rest of the architecture, but something more akin to a withered human male, its beard curled and flowing down to its bare feet. It clutched a large staff with a brondite crystal the size of a child affixed to the top, and instead of a headdress, it boasted a rack of impressive antlers. The eyes, also fashioned from brondite, twinkled at Jakki. She could almost hear a cackle emanating from its haggard mouth. Blood drained from her face as a sickening, sinking sensation seized her stomach.

It was the old man who'd shown her the parchment. The one who'd taught her to summon its magic.

Impossible, she thought, boots digging into the ground.

But it wasn't. In fact, it made all the sense in the world. What was it the old man had said upon their second meeting, the first time she'd used the parchment? Something about how it had outgrown the skulmor long ago, that it required a bearer of strength and intelligence—at which the old man had laughed, claiming the skulmor possessed but one of those traits.

Xaren peered at her from beneath thick locks of hair that had escaped the leather strip containing the rest in a knot at the base of his neck. "What is it?"

The she-wolf prodded them forward before Jakki could respond, and she quickened her pace, grateful for the distraction. A few skulmor growled as they passed, looking up from the blue-flamed fires they'd gathered around. Jakki couldn't fathom a reasonable explanation for the color of the flames, barring the suspicion that they stemmed from the brondite, perhaps lit by some spell or reaction to another element. She drew close enough to one to confirm they still radiated heat, and did a more than adequate job of cooking the nytak flanks roasting on the spits above them.

At the center of the hall, nestled inside a ring of sconces alive with the blue fire, was an altar shaped from brondite. More runes adorned its sides, though the altar itself sat empty. Again, Jakki swore she heard it sing. One glance at Xaren made her question her sanity in that regard, however.

As the doors sealed shut behind them, Jakki cursed herself for wasting the time it'd taken to travel from their cells to the throne room gaping in awe at the skulmor city, when they could've attempted escape. Then again, what good was fleeing without the parchment, without the cure for Shadow's ailment, without a map of the cursed tunnel systems entrapping them? Their survival depended on their ability to befriend the wolven race.

At least until Jakki got her hands on the parchment.

The she-wolf ushered them to the foot of the stairs. In the shadow of the statue's throne lay two smaller ones, their back-rests composed of brondite shards, their seats lined with plush furs. In them sat the skulmor leaders, or, as the she-wolf had called them, the dominants. One male, one female. Both were broad in the shoulders and strong in the limbs, with thick fur cresting their necks. Their snouts were raised as if scenting the air, and their pointed ears twitched. The male's fur was the color of the mountains: a misty gray brushed with patches of white across the ears, eyes, and mouth, hinting at his age. The female was as black as moonless night, her fur also lighter about her face and chest. Jakki recalled the short lifespans of their kind and speculated that the dominants were inching ever closer to their fortieth year, a decade few skulmor saw the end of.

As the she-wolf approached her leaders on all fours, Jak-ki glanced over her shoulder, assessing the skulmor prowling around the great hall. At first, she was pleased to find none of them armed. The more she considered it, however, the less it mattered. They were formidable enough with their fangs and brute strength, and they undoubtedly had weapons stashed nearby. And who knew how many thrived beneath the mountain?

But also: how might an army like that turn the war in Neharem's favor?

Jakki bit her lip. It was an illogical reaction to her already desperate situation. Still, the seed had been sown.

The she-wolf spoke to the dominants in a harsh, animalistic language that Jakki would've struggled to attain fluency in even if she spent a year with them. Their ears flicked as they listened, and the female's golden eyes bored into Jakki. She met her gaze and held it. If there was one thing her mother, the great Jattai Rain-Bringer, chief of the Yustano, had lectured her about over and over, it was to never be the first to break eye contact.

If you show them you're weak, even once, her mother would say as they made their rounds through the villages back on their island home, *they'll never stop seeing you as such. Doesn't matter if it's for a fight or a trade or a turn in the cot. Don't ever show weakness.*

"We will proceed in their language," the dominant female said in Nyrinian, addressing the white she-wolf. "So there is no misunderstanding."

Jakki sensed an air of disdain in her tone. "I think you have something of mine," she said through clenched teeth.

The dominant male sprung from his throne at the accusation. "That *something* was never meant to be yours, though I will hear how it came to be in your possession before we decide how you die."

"Sit," the female dominant snarled. Much to Jakki's amusement, he complied. The feeling was short-lived, for she turned her gaze back on Jakki, motioning for the she-wolf to bring her closer. "You will tell us how you found it. It's been missing from our pack for two Resting Moons."

The she-wolf forced Jakki to kneel before the thrones, then retreated beneath one of the blue-flame sconces, bringing Xaren with her.

"How long have you had it?" The male dominant's voice was so growly and low that Jakki had to take an extra moment to turn the words over in her head. She wasn't certain she wanted to volunteer that information just yet, either.

"Long enough to know it no longer wanted to be with your kind." Jakki caught Xaren wincing out of the corner of her eye and lifted her shoulder in response.

The female dominant's ears flattened, and she bared the slightest bit of fang. "My hunters told me they pierced one of your birds with a brondite spear." She raised a hand in a beckoning motion, summoning a skulmor bearing a finely sculpted pitcher and a cup forged from the skull of some helpless creature. As the attending skulmor poured a thick, dark liquid into the skull cup, Jakki picked up the faintest scent of blood. The stain on the dominant's muzzle after consuming it all but confirmed her suspicion.

"Do you mean to threaten us?" she said, not bothering to mask her disgust.

"And people say your kind has superior intellect." The dominant female drained the rest of her cup and placed it gently on her armrest. "I'm offering you an opportunity. Tell us how you came to possess the parchment, and give us a reason to not stave off our hunger with your flesh."

"You don't seem to be starving."

Jakki awaited the punishment that would surely follow. She was well aware she'd crossed a boundary, but she'd deemed it a worthwhile risk. To her surprise, however, the dominant male regarded her with an expression caught somewhere between amusement and curiosity. The female remained opaque.

"I found it in Daruk territory," Jakki admitted. She'd give them just enough of the truth to make it believable, but not so much as to make herself vulnerable to them. "In the woods, where their land intersects with yours."

The female dominant leaned forward in her throne. "You don't have the look of the northern tribes. What were you doing there?"

"Investigating the carnage your people caused, seemingly without reason."

A growl escaped the dominant male's throat. "We've never attacked the tribes of Neharem unprovoked."

"I can assure you they did nothing to incite it." Jakki's fists balled at the memory of the massacred Daruk village, at the decapitated bodies stacked outside their longhouses like kindling. "Evidently, their mere existence was enough to—"

"Though your kind likes to lump us into one mindless horde of blood-thirsty monsters," the female dominant cut in, "our packs are independent and often feuding." Her face softened, as though she knew the pain first-hand. "We take no blame, but offer our condolences for your loss."

Murmurs circulated among the skulmor, and the atmosphere of the room seemed to shift from judgment to pity. Jakki saw an opening, a way to manipulate the interrogation in her favor.

She took it.

"I found the parchment on one of the few fallen skulmor." It was an easy lie. In fact, she didn't know for certain that a skulmor *hadn't* placed the parchment in a bottle in the pond. It could've been an attempt to keep it hidden during the attack. The more she thought it over, the more she believed it. And from the looks on the dominants' faces, they did, too.

"Have you read it?" the male asked.

A hush fell over the room, silencing any remaining commotion from those gathered around the blue fires. Jakki was most conscious of Xaren's unwavering gaze. She weighed her options, the foreseeable outcomes that could arise from each. If she lied, she'd keep her secret from Xaren and the rest, but then she'd deny her connection to the parchment, rendering her life worthless in the skulmor's eyes. But if she confessed to knowing and using the full extent of its power, they might consider her a threat and kill her anyway, to keep word from getting out.

There was the unlikely chance they'd respect her for being able to read their runes and channel a power previously exclusive to them. An even smaller chance that they'd view her as the hero for returning the parchment to its rightful place among them.

Not that it would remain in their possession while she still lived.

Jakki lifted her chin, then rose to her feet, keeping her gaze trained on the dominants. "I've channeled its magic. More than once."

Gasps rippled through the skulmor. The dominant female leaped from her throne and grabbed Jakki's throat, her snout inches from her face. "Who taught you to read our runes? Did you torture one of our kind?"

"Your god taught me himself," Jakki croaked, struggling for air. The dominant female let her fall, and even as Jakki massaged her throbbing neck, pride swelled within her. "He's appeared to me more than once."

The room erupted in murmurs. Only Xaren and the she-wolf remained silent, both of them studying Jakki with the same furrowed brows. She chewed her lip as the dominants exchanged snarls, hoping she hadn't just sealed their fate with her admission.

The male dominant let loose a bone-chilling howl that echoed through the chamber, leaving silence in its wake. He approached Jakki with fiery eyes and bared teeth. "The parchment has never allowed someone outside the skulmor to awaken it. If our god has indeed chosen you, we will give you the opportunity to prove it."

Jakki tried to maintain the appearance of confidence, even as a pit formed in her stomach. She had a thousand questions about the parchment, about this god of the skulmor, about the feuding among their packs. But for now, they'd only allow her the one.

"And how might I do that?" she asked.

The dominant male looked to his partner, and the female responded with a nod. A chorus of low growls vibrated through the room, tingling Jakki's skin and raising the fine hairs on her neck.

"Long before the parchment was stolen from us," the dominant female said, "it had stopped answering our calls. No pack member could awaken it, no matter how pious." She circled Jakki in the prowling way of a predator, drawing nearer with each pass. "Yet you claim it responds to you, an outsider. A nonbeliever." The growling intensified. Xaren looked ready to bolt. "We'll give you one chance to prove your connection to the scroll and the blessing of our god by confronting the monster that's plagued our pack for many moons. If you succeed, we'll let you and your mate leave with the knowledge required to heal the unfortunate stormbird bound to you."

Jakki's mind spiraled into countless death traps ranging from a pack of enemy skulmor to a horde of Atsukut on a rampage. The skulmor's enemies were countless, the fear and hatred of them sown deep into nearly every culture. And apparently, even within their own.

"And if I don't?" Jakki's voice was scarcely above a whisper.

The dominant female drew close enough for Jakki to smell the rich scent of her fur, an aroma of rain and musk, of ancient forests and rich blood. "Then I'll skin you alive myself, turn your shell into parchment, pour your blood into one of my fine jars, and feast on your flesh while my grandchildren teethe on your bones."

"I appreciate the meticulousness of your description." Jakki crossed her arms over her chest in an attempt to still her thrashing heart. "Consider your offer accepted, but not until I've received water and food. Or how else do you expect me to face whatever challenge you've assigned?" She pointed to Xaren. "And I demand nourishment for him, as well."

The dominants exchanged growls, then the male said something in their guttural language to the she-wolf still guarding Xaren. She guided the boy to Jakki, glaring all the while, then pointed down the hall.

"Go," she snapped. "I'll observe your last meal, then brief you on your mission."

Mission. Jakki almost laughed aloud. It was always someone else's mission. Some life-threatening command that offered her little benefit, even though she was the one risking her life. Just a pawn in the games of power-drunk leaders, those too weak to bloody their hands.

As the she-wolf led them from the inner chamber, Jakki made two promises to herself. One, it would be the last time she carried out an order she didn't agree with. And two, when she led one day, she would do the most undesirable and dangerous tasks herself.

People desired leaders who led the charge into battle; not those who hid behind their privilege. And Jakki was no coward.

She was chaos itself.

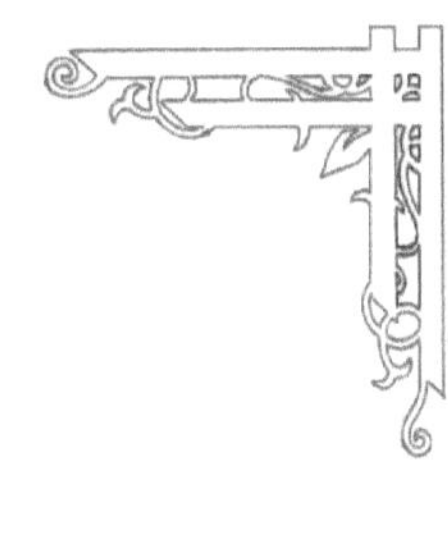

ELAYSIA

E laysia clung to Onitus as he glided just above the treetops, his otherworldly gaze searching for foes through the gaps in the branches. Wind Chaser and Yerakai conducted the same task a few miles to the south, while Corvax and Anahi guarded the boats bearing Vahid's kuza army. They'd successfully transported one thousand handpicked specimens of House Undali's private military across the Strait of Itaso and along Neharem's southern coastline. Between coordinating sand sleighs from Munskahan to Amiren and securing ships for the voyage, it'd been nearly a fortnight of travel; of rationed food and sleep-deprived nights. And even though all were eager to set foot on land when arriving at Sunset Bay earlier that morning, Elaysia had commanded them to wait. Though she had no reason to believe the Lawful Dominion had successfully infiltrated Apáasutai territory, she wanted to know with absolute surety before allowing Maseeya, Vahid, and the twins to approach Agaas. One could never be too certain, especially one with her luck.

Or lack thereof.

I should've sent T'Vak to scout on foot, she thought bitterly. *Should've made him wander weaponless through Lautei territory.*

Onitus filled her mind with a sharp, fiery hue, volatile and expansive. She hadn't learned to sift words from his emotions the way Anahi and Yerakai claimed they could do with their bonded stormbirds. The harder she pried into Onitus's mind, the more distant and blurred his feelings became. Yerakai told her it would get easier with time. That, with practice, she'd hardly be able to tell where her thoughts ended and the storm-bird's began. She wasn't so certain.

I feel the same, she replied, acknowledging the rage and suspicion consuming Onitus. *The backhander is not to be trusted. But what choice did I have?*

When T'Vak had returned to House Undali without Zavik the morning of their departure, she'd launched a full assault of prodding and incriminating questions at him, stopping just shy of full-blown accusation. He'd parried each one with the ease of a practiced charlatan.

Yes, he'd been the last one to see Zavik. No, the late-night excursion wasn't of his prompting; rather, he'd been a good backhander and accompanied Zavik to say a few parting words to an old friend, the name of whom T'Vak couldn't recall—some frail old merchant on his deathbed. Yes, T'Vak had left him there, deep in the belly of Munskahan's Pleasure District, but only after Zavik assured him his services were no longer needed. No, he had no idea what happened after that; he was a little drunk and spent the rest of the night in a love den. Yes, he went looking for Zavik the following morning.

No, he was nowhere to be found.

Elaysia had no proof beyond the shiftiness of the backhander's eyes. Zavik hadn't told her of any plans, and though it was unlike him to wander a dangerous part of the city at night to reunite with someone from a life he claimed to resent, he had been acting strange as of late. Like the night she'd set out to ride Onitus for the first time, only to have Zavik disappear without warning and not return until dawn, disheveled and reeking of alcohol. He'd offered no valid reason then, save for some unconvincing excuse about a union ceremony surprise.

A surprise he never revealed.

It all reeked of foul play. But after scouring every inn and pleasure den in Munskahan proper for several days, Elaysia had to call off the search. The birds had grown restless, their riders more so, and an urgent tuross message from Agaas made the decision final. She'd accepted blessings from the saya and sayetta, both physical and spiritual, and together, alongside the impressive army her new union had bought her, her band departed Munskahan under the cover of night.

Elaysia allowed T'Vak to accompany them under the pretense of finally receiving payment for his services. In reality, she wanted to keep her only connection to Zavik's whereabouts as close as possible because he *was* alive. She'd experienced enough death to know when that thread had been severed. Though distant, Zavik's presence still pulled at her heart. And despite T'Vak's show of apathy, she'd sensed a genuine connection between them, something that went beyond a debt owed. When she looked into T'Vak's eyes, she saw anger, sadness, and regret.

Not mourning.

Besides, if she'd learned anything over the past year, it was that everyone would betray anyone for the right price. To survive, you had to be the last one to show your vulnerabilities. As much as she didn't trust the backhander, she wanted him to trust her. It would only be a matter of time before she pried the truth out of him. For now, she'd let him think he'd won. Maybe even let him hold on to some nevethium, just long enough that he'd miss it when she ripped it away—along with his life.

Onitus let loose an excited shriek, prompting Elaysia to squint at the incoming cluster of trees, the place where the forest converged into a pinnacle of rich, thickly clustered greenery that hid the thriving community below: Agaas.

All clear, then? Elaysia asked the bird.

Thankfully, Onitus had no trouble perceiving her thoughts. He whistled, and her mind filled with a calming, golden glow.

Good. Can you leave me at my cliff? Hunt as long as you'd like, but don't go too far, please. Lumira sounded worried in her last tuross message, and I want us all to remain close by until I know more.

The golden glow pulsated into cool blue, as though he reluctantly complied.

Thank you, my friend.

She buried her face in the silken feathers of Onitus's neck, wishing she had something to protect her head from the wind and rain. Zavik had talked of fashioning unique masks for each Stormrider. In fact, if she recalled correctly, he'd already drawn up plans. When he returned, he could—

She shook her head, cutting off the thought. Better not to hope. Better not to tempt the fates.

If she didn't dare to dream, then she didn't have to risk facing the disappointment that so often accompanied it.

Elaysia reached Agaas well before the others, giving her time to assess the state of the holy city. She'd been gone for nearly two moon cycles, and in her absence, there'd been several battles, some of which resulted in the shrinking of Apáasutai borders. At a glance, base camp looked as vibrant as ever, the ramps leading up to Agaas clean, the surrounding foliage flourishing, and more watchers on duty than she'd ever seen. But as she peered into the ground level gardens, she found them harvested beyond the usual half they tried to preserve. An assortment of tents and other temporary lodgings had also sprung up around base camp's perimeter—far more than were ever present at even the most important of Neharem festivities, such as Novitae.

Elaysia approached a Daruk family of four sitting outside an abysmal lean-to, their golden hair warm against their pale skin. The youngest girl looked so like Jörd, the warrior Elaysia had lost at the Caman Altars, that it triggered an unexpected tightness in her chest. She recalled the light in Jörd's eyes fading as the Daruk warrior crumpled, her veins pulsing green from the nevethium arrowhead.

Elaysia brought her fist to her heart and hurried on, no longer wanting to engage in conversation. The little girl caught her gaze as she left, though, offering a smile that didn't quite reach her large, lake-blue eyes. Arms wrapped around her stomach, Elaysia took refuge under the overhanging roof of a watcher lodge. The burden of her people weighed harder on her than it ever had, and she didn't know why. It was as though she felt responsible for their every feeling, meal, and rest; as though she alone dictated their peace. It wasn't until Vahid appeared in the clearing, Dytana nestled in his arms, that she understood.

As much as she wished to harden her heart, to prevent herself from ever knowing the pain of loss, her journey into motherhood had torn it wide open, leaving it gaping for the world to see, compelling her to carry the burdens of every innocent being who needed someone to love them. To stand for them.

To fight for them.

Vahid approached her with a smile that could only be described as wholesome. Dytana, however, didn't even search for Elaysia until they were all but upon her, so content she was to gaze up at Vahid, babbling on in the secret language only infants knew.

"I hope I've not overstepped," Vahid said, passing the wide-eyed babe to Elaysia. "Maseeya couldn't carry both of them at once, and—"

"Thank you." Elaysia kept her attention on Dytana as she spoke, an easy enough feat, as she hadn't seen her daughter since that morning. She pressed her lips to the downy, golden-white hairs on Dytana's head, inhaling the sweet scent that arose from her. "She seems well."

"I handled...she had a movement, and I...took care of it."

Elaysia's gaze flicked back to the well-groomed man in front of her. "A movement?"

"It was rather...pungent. I didn't want her to sit in it until Maseeya caught up, so I made do." Vahid chewed his lip as he lifted the torn hem of his tunic.

"Oh." Elaysia's eyes widened. In Agaas—throughout much of Neharem, actually—it was standard for any parent to assist with all matters of child rearing, regardless of gender or position. But from what she'd experienced in Orillon, she doubted such an outlook was commonplace there. Especially not among the great houses.

"It was no bother," Vahid added quickly. "I just didn't want you to think it odd when you saw the fabric later. I might not have fastened it right, either. If you want to—"

"I'm sure it's more than acceptable." Elaysia forced a painfully awkward smile. She wanted to move away, to end the conversation and be done with all unnecessary interactions. How many more of his kind deeds could she take before accepting that he was genuinely a good man?

Good men don't exist, she told herself. *Only clever ones.*

But even as she lied to protect herself, deep down, she didn't believe it. Didn't want to. Not yet. There had to be some good people in the world, even if they were rare.

Vahid looked like he wanted to say more, maybe tell Elaysia he'd handpicked some anderberries and ground them into a violet pulp suitable for babes with two teeth, when Maseeya emerged from the forest. She wore Elaron, who leaned his plump body as far out of the sling as it'd allow to peer back at Hallahd. House Undali's head kuza refused to let both Anahi and Vahid leave Munskahan without his protection and, much to Elaysia's surprise, that privilege now extended to her and the twins. He'd taken extra care regarding Maseeya and the babes as they'd made their way from Munskahan to Amiren, and even stayed up all night guarding them as they awaited the preparation of their ships in the seedy coastal town.

Hallahd lowered his curved sword, taking in the tightly packed housing that made up base camp. His eyes widened as he arched his neck further and further back, lips parting as his gaze traced the ramps as far up as the branches would allow. Elaysia assumed he'd seen little greenery in his life, let alone trees the size of the ones in Agaas.

Wait till you see the city itself, Elaysia thought with a renewed sense of appreciation for the place she called home. Had it really been less than two years since she wanted to abandon it all? And for what? Some misplaced sense of entitlement? How ironic and fitting that it was now under threat, that the very paradise she'd once sought to flee was now the target of not one, but two enemy leaders and their accompanying armies.

"Elaysia?" Maseeya's voice strained as she pulled a squirming Elaron out of the sling. "I'm afraid I'm in need of a brief reprieve. These bones and back are no longer suited for long days aboard a cramped sea vessel."

"And the twins only add to your exhaustion, I'm sure," Elaysia said, taking Elaron in her other arm. "Go on ahead. We'll meet you shortly."

"Oh, but the twins are the only thing keeping me young." Maseeya winked before starting up the ramp. "Still, I'll accept your offer with no complaints."

Elaysia gave the older woman a parting look of gratitude, then returned her attention to Vahid and Hallahd—just in time to catch the head kuza watching Maseeya ascend the ramps with no shortage of pleasure. She fought the urge to roll her eyes. "I'm going to look into some things down here before making the ascent," she said, excusing herself. When Vahid didn't make any move to leave, she added, "You don't need to wait for me. Agaas isn't all that large, and if you get lost, just keep following the ramps and bridges. It all loops back to the High Tree."

"I can help with the twins," Vahid offered, holding out his hands. "I imagine having mobility will make your tasks easier?"

Dytana raised her traitorous, chubby little arms in response, reaching for the man Elaysia feared she'd already begun to associate as a parental figure. Elaron, however, burrowed further into her arms, looking on with a furrowed brow and suspicious, silver eyes—an expression she'd seen more than once on Davier. The resemblance twisted something in Elaysia's gut. She handed Dytana over, then hurried inside the lodge, closing the door before she dared to breathe again.

The room was mercifully empty, all the watchers likely busy with assisting the influx of refugees flocking to the holy city. She pressed her back to the door and Elaron's cheek to hers, allowing the softness of his skin to work its way through the hardening layers of her heart. The babe nestled against her, and everything she'd bottled up manifested in a single tear that trailed down her cheek and onto his dark locks.

Soon enough, she'd be forced to attend a summit lodge gathering, to reconcile the horrors of a nation at war under the scrutiny of what remained of the council. But, at least for a moment, she could hide, could be weak and broken and utterly flawed beyond repair. Because the second she set foot outside that door, such vulnerability could mean her death. For as much as people claimed to value authenticity, they didn't truly want it.

They followed those with carefully constructed composure: a stallion, broken in.

She's trapped.

Her prison is a hazy, ethereal plane, one blanketed in a fog so thick she can hardly make out her hand at arm's length. Someone calls her name, but the voice is distant and murky. She can't decipher its source.

Everywhere she runs, it's the same. More haze. More choking fog. She rubs her eyes, begging to wake up from the nightmare, but she's already awake. A sharp pain cuts through her neck. Everything's hot, so hot. Screams fill her ears, and she can't breathe anymore. It's burning; the poison air suffocates her lungs.

Because it's not fog. It's smoke.

It's fire.

It's death.

Something cold grabs her hand; yanks her free of the golden-green flames. But she's falling. Plummeting. Her limbs splay out as she screams for Onitus, but he's not there, he's not anywhere. She reaches for him, reaches for anyone.

But no one's left. They've been consumed by—

"High Chieftain?"

Elaysia gasped, clutching the wooden stormbird hanging from her neck. She blinked rapidly, trying to regain awareness of where she was and why. She could sense gazes trained on her, but she didn't dare meet them. The last thing she needed was someone to deem her crazed, unfit for leading during a time of war. There were already enough usurpers in her midst.

A warm hand wrapped around her forearm. She followed the strong fingers up a well-muscled arm to the stern but caring eyes of Kahana. Her black and white streaked hair was pulled back, as usual, emphasizing the deep brown tattoo staining her lips and adorning her chin. Elaysia glanced at the tabletop beneath her, immediately recognizing the tribal marking representing Agaas: a stormbird, much like the one she wore around her neck. She was in the summit lodge, holding her first gathering since returning from Orillon the day prior. She'd welcomed the still-loyal chiefs and their advisors, and then, then...

The haze had enveloped her.

"If you have more important matters on your mind, we can handle the gathering from here. It's nothing we haven't done the past two moon cycles."

Elaysia glared across the massive table. She knew Jattai Rain-Bringer's voice well, despite only hearing it a few times. It had a distinct and underlying tone of condemnation, and it commanded attention.

It took a moment for Elaysia to find her voice—not for lack of words, but for lack of a means to sift out the unsavory ones—but when she did, she delivered it with enough tact and confidence to make even Konar proud.

She almost wished he were there to hear it.

"All the matters on my mind are important, my chief," Elaysia replied in an equally crisp and commanding voice. "That's what it means to be a mother and a leader during wartime, for a mother and a leader aren't so different. We protect fiercely, guide with empathy, and make the wisest decisions we can for all our children, whether or not they are bound to us by blood. I think you understand that better than most."

The scowl contorting Jattai's otherwise alluring features would've set the All-Sovereign himself to cower. "I would've liked a say in the wise decisions made on my daughter's behalf, but despite being a leader and mother, no one consulted me."

Elaysia allowed her primitive defensiveness to subside before responding. She took in the faces of the chiefs and their advisors seated on cushions and blankets around the oval-shaped table. Moákun and Apáasutai. Daruk and Yustano. In Elaysia's absence, Lumira had finished the complicated task of replacing the absent tribes with members of a hand-picked war council, consisting primarily of the Stormriders and a handful of watchers who'd been around long enough to prove their trustworthiness. But there were still empty spaces; the most glaring of all being the vacant cushion that should've belonged to her high elder.

Only temporarily vacant, she reminded herself. Zavik was alive, and when she finished crushing the Lawful Dominion with her kuza army, she'd tear down Munskahan to find him.

"Jakki volunteered willingly to go north," Lumira said, answering on Elaysia's behalf. "She's been gone longer than expected, but maybe she's assisting the Morotôk with relocating to Agaas."

The Yustano chief's eyes flashed. "She would've sent a tuross. I raised no fool."

Based on Elaysia's experience, communication wasn't one of Jakki's strongpoints, but she wasn't about to disclose that to the council in front of an already enraged Jattai. "I'll send one to Chief Amkah to confirm. Actually, I plan to send turosses to all neutral tribes one last time. We need everyone loyal to Agaas within Apáasutai borders as soon as possible."

A loud burp echoed across the table, drawing all eyes to Gibrund, chief of the Daruk. "That won't take long," he said, peering suspiciously with his good eye into his presumably empty drinking horn. "Most everyone loyal to our cause *is* here, much as they can be. My people have deserted our territory.

Fucking Atsukut made sure we had no choice." He eyed Orandus's wooden cup, and the Moákun chief surrendered it willingly.

"We've already moved half our forces here," Orandus confirmed. "We had to abandon some villages along the Kahaloán border. Some of my best warriors hold our prized fishing bays and docks, but it's only a matter of time before the Banaxa move north." He rubbed the deep wrinkles set into his bronze forehead with fingers that also showed their age.

"There's no point in holding the docks if trade with Az Zar has ceased," Jattai said sharply. "They'll plow through what remains of your forces on their way to siege Agaas like they did all the tribes south of you. Better you send what remains of your people here."

"You make it sound so easy to surrender your ancestral lands for someone who hasn't offered more than a handful of warriors in service to the holy city." The rebuttal came from Mardus, rushing to his father's defense with a quick tongue he rarely displayed. A look of pride beamed on the older Moákun's face.

Jattai planted both palms on the table, obscuring the outline of Itaso, the mother of water and symbol of her people. "Perhaps you forget how much nevethium lies beneath the reefs of my isles." She looked so like Jakki, or rather, Jakki like her mother, that it was hard to believe anyone else had contributed to her conception. They could've been sisters.

Elaysia saw an opportunity while Mardus whispered something to his father, and she seized it. "Lumira, what lands remain friendly to us?"

"The Lawful Dominion has allied with or conquered all neutral tribes." The beridian leaned across the table to reference the map of Neharem carved into the center. "Aside from the Yustano—"

Gibrund muttered something in the Daruk tongue. While Elaysia wasn't as practiced in the northern languages, she interpreted enough to grasp his sentiment: the cowardly, selfish, southerners.

"—everything from here"—Lumira used her claw to trace from the Tangeesh capital of Puetala up through Banaxa and Kahaloán territory before cutting west to the lands of the Moatiwe and Lautei—"to here is under Lawful Dominion control." She continued the path northwest toward the Ni'anko, stopping just shy of them.

Though the two-dozen people gathered in the room were already silent, a deeper stillness enveloped them; a solemn respect only brought upon by mourning.

"The Ni'anko lands have been..." Lumira looked to Grokhion, who stood cross-armed near the double doors barring entrance to the summit lodge. He'd barely spoken more than a few words in the special discussion Elaysia held with the Stormriders prior to the war council gathering. Something cold and predatory lingered in the depths of his eyes.

"Let's not pretend we don't already know what befell those blissfully ignorant people," Jattai said, pulling a pipe from the folds of the white and cerise fringed skirt bunched beneath her exposed midriff. Though it was similar in cut to Jakki's usual attire, it was sheathed in a short-sleeved robe of the same pattern, adding a flair of elegance. "They've been purified of the ideology that blinded them."

Elaysia's nostrils flared. One of the summit lodge doors groaned open, and she glanced over just in time to catch the fiery orange of Grokhion's fur slipping through before it thudded closed again.

"Rash-Yaanah's ax, Jattai," Gibrund growled as he slammed Orandus's cup onto the table. Elaysia sensed grief behind the Daruk chief's display of anger; something more personal than the loss of another tribe. "Have you no decency?"

"Decency has nothing to do with it." Jattai filled her seashell pipe with ground kinawa leaves and motioned for one of the attending Yustano elders to light it. "I only speak to the way the Lawful Dominion sees it. As far as they're concerned, it's just another threat eliminated." A cloud of smoke drifted across the table as she exhaled. "My heart aches for them as though the loss were my own, but let it be a lesson to the rest of us about what happens when you refuse to fight or flee." Another inhale, another puff of smoke. "I told Kelsia this would happen. Her infantile optimism was always going to be the death of her."

A *crack* filled the silence.

Elaysia's eyes widened as she took in the splintered wood in Gibrund's hands. His expression suggested he felt similar to how the cup now looked: broken beyond repair.

"I'm sorry, Orandus," the Daruk chief said, handing over the ruined cup with tenderness. "I'll replace it with a dozen more like it."

"There are no more like it, but you are forgiven all the same." Orandus's lips were drawn into a thin line, but he took the cup with dignity and passed it to a less-forgiving Mardus, who wrapped it in a cloth and tucked it away. "These are trying times."

"Detrimental times," Jattai clarified, exhaling yet another puff of smoke.

An urge to intervene seized Elaysia, but she hadn't the time to get involved in the personal affairs of the chiefs. If she was expected to set aside all her burdens to take on the people's, so could they. "And Jakki and Xaren were our last attempt to secure Morotôk support, yes?" she asked Lumira.

The beridian stared at the doors where Grokhion had loomed not moments prior, and when she returned her attention to the gathering, a little of the light had gone from her eyes. "That's correct. But we haven't received word from anyone in the north since they departed."

Jattai dangled her pipe just beneath her lips. "So you sent my daughter on a futile—maybe even deadly—mission."

Lumira met her gaze with a patient, yet unrelenting, stare. "I presumed she was of the most qualified in Agaas at the time the duties needed carrying out."

"You presume much. Your kind always does."

Lumira's claws visibly dug into the table.

"I will search for her myself, Jattai," Elaysia interjected. "Though, I have no doubt Jakki and Xaren are alive and well. They have the stormbirds with them, if it's any consolation." She eyed the wine cup resting on the table before her, then looked away. "In the meantime, is there any circumstance under which you'd be willing to leave your isles? I don't like the thought of your people isolated, but I feel it may be necessary to restrict all travel to and from Apáasutai territory until the war has ended."

"We've always been isolated, High Chieftain, or did your cast sessions never teach you that?" There wasn't a hint of warmth in Jattai's face. Elaysia had often sensed that Jakki's mother didn't like her, but this was the first time she had verifiable proof.

And her answer.

Elaysia grabbed the wine and took a long drink, relishing its near-instantaneous calming effect. But while it dulled her physical tension, it did nothing to ease the pain of yet another loss. She'd counted on the Yustano's sizeable contribution of warriors. Now, even with the addition of Vahid's kuza army, they weren't much better off than when she'd departed Agaas. She'd simply made up for what they lost.

And she couldn't help but wonder if Jattai had planned it all along. According to Lumira, the Yustano chief had claimed she was saving her warriors for when the cause truly needed them, then proceeded to use Agaasian supplies and to stave off Lawful Dominion attacks with Apáasutai and Moákun warriors lent to secure her borders. And now, with the enemy moving north and the kuza army able to stand her warriors' stead, she could retreat to her island home, blaming Elaysia's leadership for the presumed loss of her daughter.

It was so sickeningly brilliant, and Elaysia cursed herself for not seeing it sooner.

"If the Yustano remain on their isles, how long can we sustain Agaas's current inhabitants?" Elaysia asked Yerakai. Normally, she would've directed her question to Zavik or Konar, but Agaas was short on high elders for the time being.

The Apáasutai nyrian cleared his throat quietly. "Given the fully packed lofts, the addition of the kuza, and that nearly two times our typical population now resides around base camp…" He closed his eyes while he mumbled something beneath his breath, then replied, "No more than a year until total depletion."

"Is that an optimistic guess or a well-thought-out prediction?" Gibrund snapped.

"It's sanguine," Arkuun, chief of the Apáasutai said, breaking his silence for the first time.

"If the rest of the Moákun relinquish our lands and relocate to Agaas, then we'll have little more than a few moon cycles guaranteed in the holy city," Kahana said, looking to her cousin and uncle.

"There's more than enough game in these forests and fish in the sea to sustain us all for years," Lumira contradicted. "The brunt of the hunting will be placed upon the Apáasutai and Daruk, but the Moákun can offset the burden by fishing and tending the plants."

"What do you feel is the best path for your people, Orandus?" Elaysia asked the Moákun chief. "I would never command you one way or the other, but I think the odds for survival are higher for all our people, should you strengthen our numbers. In fact"—she faced the Yustano, hoping to win some of them over in spite of their chief—"I advise it of any tribe unwilling to fall prey to the Lawful Dominion."

A melodic laugh drifted from Jattai's lips, but there was cruelty underlying it.

Elaysia rose from her place beside Kahana and began circling the table, the way Konar used to when he assessed the room. Even now, despite most in attendance having proved their loyalty, she felt like an imposter. Like a child who'd just learned the game she played at was, in fact, reality.

And there was no one coming to save her.

She caught Vahid's gaze as she walked. He'd been standing beside the fire pit, taking up little space, keen to listen and understand. He offered her a half-smile in solidarity.

It was all she needed.

She continued around the table, stopping behind the Yustano. Jattai shook her head as she extinguished her pipe, the look on her face conveying that the intrusion annoyed her.

"Consider this an official declaration," Elaysia said in a firm voice. "Whoever resides outside of Agaas and Apáasutai territory will henceforth be barred from receiving aid, whether that be in the form of food, supplies, or warriors. Anyone not within our borders by the turn of the moons will be considered an enemy of the holy city and the unified tribes of Neharem."

The silence that followed was nearly as stifling as the heat in Munskahan. Then, Gibrund had the kindness to speak up, and Elaysia had to fight back the urge to run over and embrace the hardened, bearded nyrian.

"I agree," the burly chief said, leveling a glare at Jattai. "The Daruk stand by Agaas, High Chieftain."

Orandus gave a firm nod. "As do the Moákun."

"You know where the Apáasutai stand," Chief Arkuun said with a weighted sigh. "These trees mean more to me than any alliance. I will use my dying breath to protect them and the nevethium hearts."

Jattai shrugged as she rose from the table, removing her ceremonial bronze headdress in favor of her staff. "So be it. I wish you blessings, High Chieftain." Her warriors made a shield about her as she strode to the door, not one of them gracing another soul with so much as a parting glance.

"May your sunrises always hold promise," Elaysia said through gritted teeth.

"Promises and peace are the hopes of dying elders." Jattai waited for one of her warriors to open the door, then inhaled deeply of the rich air, letting it blow her robe and skirts behind her like a goddess reborn. "I would think *you* understand that better than most."

Elaysia's hands balled into fists at her sides.

The Yustano chief gave one final look at the place she'd held at the summit lodge gathering table, as though bidding it goodbye. "Send my daughter home, should she return," she said coolly. "I will not let her die for a half-breed playing at war."

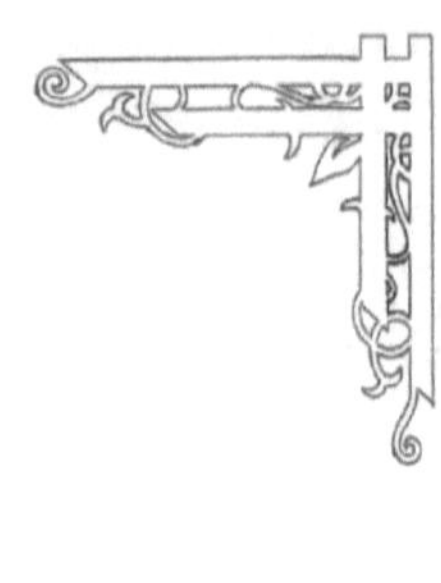

KONAR

'Neath the ancient tides, where shadows weave and wreathe,

Speak the words that ripple through realms beneath.

In the twilight's aqueous grace, by stars that shimmer, not wane,

Unveil the visions hidden, birthed from the ocean's arcane.

Whispers from the deep, on the currents of dread they soar,

Call the ages to reveal, what dark depths have in store.

By the breath of coral tombs, where echoes linger long,

Summon visions, cloaked in brine, where shadows' whispers throng.

Pearlescent sigils mark the waves, secrets woven in the night,

Enchanter of abyssal sight, grant the gift of foresight.

Yet heed the dire cost, a pact that binds the soul,

A changed existence, currents shift, as futures take their toll.

Once the veil is lifted, no unseeing what's been shown,

Life transformed, entwined with tides, a path for-
ever sown.

As the echoes of invocation ripple through the wa-
ter to the air;

See the specters of what's to come, in realms of
oceanic despair.

So mote it be, the shadowed spell, in twilight's silent
chime,

Summon the abyss beyond, as your soul com-
mences its climb.

"What are you reading?"

Konar gasped as he covered the scroll with his arms. He looked over his shoulder to find Maseeya peering down at him, the displeasure she'd displayed in their recent interactions banished by curiosity. It wasn't unlike her to creep down into his lair below the library, but it was unlike him to not be more aware.

"Is that myrem?" she asked, leaning closer. She carried the scent of rain on her like perfume, hinting to the weather without.

Konar allowed her to slide his hand off the parchment, as well as the stump of his right. She handled it with tenderness, her thumb gracefully tracing the bandages protecting it.

"Myremese, yes," he managed as he tucked his arm beneath the shelter of the table.

"It's beautiful." Maseeya pointed to a section containing the invocation for the foresight ritual—the section he'd tried to shield her from. "What does this part say?"

"I'm afraid this passage is rather uninteresting. Just a list of lineages for one of their kingdoms." Konar rolled up the scroll as casually as his unpracticed left hand would allow.

Maseeya blew air through her lips. "You still won't be honest with me, even after all these years? After everything we've been through?" She shoved some books he'd stacked on the other chair onto the floor, taking a seat. He winced as they landed with a *thud*. "You've barely said a word to me since the night Elaysia saved your life."

The pain in her eyes, complete with unshed tears, tore the scab off his heart. "I didn't think you wanted me around. The only use I am to Elaysia and Agaas is through my knowledge, so I've chosen to remain down here in hopes of uncovering something of value."

"That is the problem with you," Maseeya murmured. "Over a thousand years old, and you still make the mistake of assuming other's feelings. People aren't books, Konar. You can't just flip through them to find your answers."

"I suppose some things are beyond my grasp, no matter how many times I borrow life from those who would've done it better justice."

A burst of crimson flushed Maseeya's pale cheeks, and though she wrapped her moon-patterned shawl tightly about her shoulders, bunching the midnight locks of her hair beneath it, she didn't make to leave.

Konar offered her the scroll. She shied away from it, as though it were poison. Her gaze wandered to the pile of stained rags and oversized leaves cluttering his desk, some of which had once held smoked salmon, flatbreads, and roasted squash.

"That section that intrigued you was an invocation," he said hurriedly, as she wrinkled her nose at the waste pot he'd stashed in the corner. "I don't know how much Elaysia has told you about the scrolls Zavik retrieved, but this one claims it has the power to grant foresight."

Maseeya crossed her arms. "Elaysia tells me everything, but I don't trust these scrolls, magic or not. They've already led to more deaths than they're worth."

Konar's thoughts drifted to his amma and appa, to the quest that led to their demise and destroyed his innocence forever. "I've witnessed the havoc they wreak."

She seemed to consider this, then cocked her head, lips pursed. "Do you believe they're as powerful as everyone says?"

"No." Konar tucked the scroll into its waterproofed leather case before sliding it into the oversized pocket hidden in the lining of his robe. "I think they're far more dangerous than anyone fathoms. The scholar Elize risked her life to hide them, then sacrificed herself to ensure they remained hidden. But the powers they offer come at a cost." He gestured to himself, to the ancient bones hidden beneath his unassuming frame.

"You want to use this one, don't you?" All the warmth had vanished from Maseeya's voice. For a fleeting moment, Konar swore he saw a hunger hidden in the depths of her deep brown eyes, the same as he'd first seen in Karliah's all those years ago. Their call was getting stronger to seduce a woman as steadfast as Maseeya.

All the more reason to find them before they fell into the wrong hands.

Konar folded his arms around his stomach, shielding the scrolls within. "The power of foresight it yields is erratic, and it causes a lifetime of blindness and spasms in the wielder. I'm the only one experienced with the scrolls' effects, and the one most deserving of punishment should anything go awry."

Maseeya glanced at the journal next to the drying inkwell on the table. "You're also one of the few people alive who can translate them, especially with Zavik gone."

Konar massaged the spot between his brows to keep his remorse at bay. He should've stopped the lad from going to Orillon the moment he had a premonition about not seeing him again. How foolish he was to assume it signified his own forthcoming death instead of the lad's. He'd poured far too many years into Zavik to start anew with someone else, just as he'd poured far too many years into Kayrune, his wayward son, long before.

"Elishon received visions of the future and past, unbidden," Maseeya said, pattering across the floor to the stairs leading up to the library. "He needed no scroll. Maybe Elaysia doesn't either."

A memory of Elishon banging Konar's door, eyes crazed with lust for the vision he'd glimpsed of a foreign land and world-shattering scrolls, tightened the space around his heart. It wasn't the first or only time the gods had blessed (rather, cursed) the former high chieftain, but it was certainly the most condemning.

Konar knew Elaysia shared her father's cursed blood. It'd shown up in little ways when she was young, like how the nightmares about her family's deaths plagued her long before they met their ends. Or how she'd come to learn of the stormbird eggs—or had an inkling of where to search for Stormriders. Elaysia was full of irrational decisions. But some of them were so brilliantly auspicious that divine intervention was the only plausible explanation.

"Talk to her, Konar," Maseeya's voice echoed from the top of the stairs. "You've put it off for far too long, and she needs you now. Don't break her heart again."

The trapdoor thudded closed behind her.

Despite the fawn he'd used in a ritual the day prior, Konar's journey to base camp proved challenging enough to seek the aid of a mare before setting out toward the training grounds. But when he placed his palm on the velvety skin of her muzzle, she nipped at him, exposing the whites of her eyes.

"You can smell it on me, can't you?" he whispered in a soothing voice. "My unity with death is long overdue, so she haunts me, seeping into my pores, replacing my blood and breath with her essence until I bleed rot and exhale shadows. But it is not your time, my lady. Not yet."

The mare relaxed beneath his touch, and when he trailed his hand to her bare back, she offered no resistance beyond a shiver. Konar guided her to the gate and used the fence post to climb up. Thankfully, no one was watching closely enough to behold his frailty.

In fact, no one seemed to care that he'd gone, nor had they for some time. It was just as likely that many assumed he'd fallen to his death in the cliff holds nine moons past.

And maybe he had.

When Konar emerged from the forest and crested the hill overlooking the training grounds, he was welcomed by a gentle breeze carrying the delightful fragrance of wildflowers. The pleasure only lasted a moment before a blast of wind sent his mare into a rearing frenzy. Above, Onitus and Elaysia soared in unison as she launched a flurry of arrows from atop his back, raining down on targets set up in the field below. Onitus dove, uprooting the ones she'd left unharmed with his outstretched talons. His screech echoed through the valley, sending a flock of smaller birds swarming into the forest.

Konar steadied the mare long enough to dismount, narrowly avoiding her path as she tore back into the shelter of the trees, hooves kicking up clods of soil. He collected himself, then waved at the bird and rider as they made another pass above the targets. Onitus dropped from the sky like one of Elaysia's arrows, flaring his wings at the last moment to glide just above the ground. As he began another upward arc, Elaysia dove off his back, landing on all fours. She raised a fist to him, perhaps signifying her successful landing, and only then, after making a final pass over the field, gaze boring into the nooks and crevices of the hills, did he glide west toward the ocean.

Konar waited patiently atop the hill, not wanting to force his presence upon Elaysia. He sat cross-legged, eyes shut in meditation, as sharp blades of grass poked through the threadbare fabric of his leggings. Elaysia's frustrated shouts carried on the wind as she leveled attacks at the stationary targets with her mother's sword. She'd never learned to use the weapon. Swords weren't commonplace in Neharem. In fact, aside from the Daruk, most of the tribes still preferred weapons of wood, bone, and stone as opposed to metal.

All were laughable against Az Zar's new shieum.

Elaysia trudged up the hill within the hour, face glistening with sweat. She wore new clothing that looked like Maseeya's handiwork, a midnight-blue attire that covered her neck to toe, complete with beaded accents. Strands of hair had come free of her braids and framed her face delicately, reminding Konar just how young she still was.

Her two-toned eyes told a different story.

"You're at it early," he said, offering her a drink from his waterskin.

She shook her head and retrieved her own as she sat on the grass beside him. "The kuza and our warriors have been using the training grounds to find a sense of unity within their varied fighting styles. This is the only time of day I can avoid the masses." Her sword lay unsheathed on the grass beside her, its lyvium blade glinting in the sunlight. She looked at it and groaned. "Not having any luck with that, though."

Konar rubbed his jaw as he studied the hacked-up targets. "A sparring partner would be ideal."

"And who in Neharem is skilled with such a blade?"

"I'd say you have a surplus now, thanks to your new army."

"Never wrong, are you."

The field came alive with a few dozen warriors, followed by a kuza collective, and soon after, two stormbirds took to the skies. Elaysia frowned as she watched them, occasionally gnawing at bits of dried venison. It didn't take long for Konar to see why. Not only did the kuza have a drastically different approach to that of the Neharem warriors, there were also divisions within the tribes. Most hadn't lived through war, and the fighting styles of the Daruk contrasted that of the Apáasutai, and both more drastically so with Moákun. With the Stormriders in the mix, and the random assortment of warriors unique to Agaas, such as Grokhion and Lumira, it was a wonder they hadn't seen any accidental deaths.

"They need someone to lead them," Konar mused, eyeing the ever-reluctant high chieftain.

"They need someone with actual battle experience." Elaysia lay back on the grass and covered her face with her cloak. "Something nearly everyone down there has in greater quantity than me."

"Experience will come with time." Konar reached for his pipe, then thought better of it. "Those were some impressive shots earlier. I imagine it takes a great deal of balance to maintain mastery over your bow while flying."

Elaysia pulled her cloak away, revealing a scowl. "They'd be more precise if I had something to protect my eyes. I was hoping Zav could fashion something when we returned, but—"

Her voice cracked. Sadness only took hold for a moment before anger hardened her features. "Someone in Orillon must've known he had the scrolls. I thought they were maybe using him as leverage to get them, but it's been a moon cycle now, and no one's tried to contact us."

Konar's thoughts drifted to T'Vak. "Perhaps his abductor is already in our midst."

"Oh, I know he's involved." Elaysia pushed up onto her elbows, scouring the field for who Konar presumed to be the erratic backhander. "Part of me wants to throw him in a cliff hold until he confesses, but I think men of his ilk would sooner jump than be truthful."

"Give him to me."

Elaysia raised an eyebrow. Konar feared he'd overstepped, but the idea had come to him in a torrent of undeniable logic, as his best ones usually did.

Although, occasionally his worst, too.

"If he truly seeks the scrolls, then it's me he'll be wanting to get close to," Konar explained. "So why not let him think he's earned our good faith? I can use him for menial tasks and keep an eye on him, freeing up your trusted watchers for more important duties."

Elaysia studied him with rapt attention. "Go on."

"I'll keep him busy. Give him bits of information to let him think he's getting closer to the scrolls. With time, perhaps he'll confide in me: the jaded exile of Agaas." Konar made the final statement in jest, but it felt freeing to address a topic that had long since needed addressing. "If you trust me, that is."

"Konar"—Elaysia sat upright and drained the rest of her waterskin—"there will never be trust between us again, nor love." She didn't seem to take pleasure in the harshness of her words; rather, sorrow tainted them, along with a heavy resignation. "But I may consider us unlikely allies, should our goals align."

"I'd like that," he whispered.

They sat shoulder to shoulder, observing the dance of the miniature armies gathered below. As if the language barriers weren't enough, Konar could pick up the distinct differences in their preferred techniques, along with the issues it spawned. Where the kuza operated as one, their methods predictable but uniform, the Apáasutai spread out like a blight, listening to no one but their inner voice. The Daruk were caught somewhere in between with raging clusters of ax heads and shields tearing down the hillsides. And though bold, the Moákun were not yet comfortable in the northwest's terrain, and they appeared uncertain in their movements.

At least the stormbirds looked promising. Anadu alone was a terrible and beautiful sight to behold, and Konar hoped the fear she'd strike in the hearts of their enemies would be leverage enough.

Elaysia rose, stretching her arms skyward. "This has been more pleasant than I expected. T'Vak is yours. I'll let his watchers know when I return to Agaas."

"If I can trouble you with one more thing," Konar said, following her toward the woods. "I've been meaning to talk to you about your visions."

She stopped mid-stride to sheath her mother's sword. "What visions?"

"I know you see things, Ellie. Moments in time that you've not lived through yourself."

A scowl took over her face, but she allowed him to continue. Even had the decency to slow down enough for him to keep pace.

"Many of your people believe such visions are a divine blessing from Khiev-Tatamic." He waited until he held her gaze, then clarified, "That he allows some souls to see echoes of the past and whispers of the future."

"And?"

"I wondered if you've had any of late?"

The look in her eyes told him she had, but she wasn't ready to discuss it with him. "What does it matter? They rarely occur and make little sense when they do."

"Nothing regarding the war?"

Elaysia's jaw twitched. "Is this about the scrolls? We've decided not to use them. You yourself discouraged it."

"That's why I'm asking if you've had any revelations, like the ones—"

"My dead father had? All the crazed visions that possessed him before his demise? Is that what you're fishing for, Konar?" A bitter laugh escaped her lips. "I should've known. You always have ulterior motives disguised as concern."

Konar didn't bother to defend himself. It wasn't about him, anyway.

Elaysia tugged on her cloak as she resumed her march to Agaas. "I'll let you know if I start dreaming of scrolls and my death. In the meantime, see if you can uncover something of value in those dusty old books of yours."

ZAVIK

Z avik was drowning.

Choking. Burning. Suffocating. The world all red and black all at once.

He flailed trembling arms, trying to paddle his way to the surface of whatever watery prison he'd fallen into, but he was met with no resistance. Still, water burned his throat, filling his lungs with acidic—

Acidic?

A roll found Zavik on his side, cheek pressed to a hard, sticky surface. He coughed up the poison bile just in time for another heave to corrupt his stomach. The taste triggered another retch, then another. He lost count of the times and simply lay there, limp, until his body ceased its self-revolt. The ringing in his ears was almost as disorienting as the stench of his own vomit.

And when he dared to open his eyes, he was met with darkness.

A heavy weight pressed on his chest. He tried to draw a breath, finding it shallow and constricted. The weight pushed harder. He clawed at his throat, begging his body to cooperate.

It refused.

Air. He needed to get up. Needed space. Needed air.

He opened his eyes again, this time waiting for them to adjust. The weight of his seers was missing from the bridge of his nose, which would make whatever happened next more complicated. Zavik didn't consider himself helpless without them, but their absence would certainly affect subtleties and his depth perception. Not light, though. And the thin strip of yellow a few feet ahead called to him.

He scrambled on all fours until he connected with a wall. He ran his hand across the surface, searching for the handle.

Nothing.

His breathing became more rapid as he blindly frisked the length of the wall, fingers crawling up and down one, then another, until he'd exhausted the small space he'd been enclosed in. A tightness seized his throat and spread into his chest like deadly roots. His head spun even as he lay down. He tried to reason with himself, to breathe slowly, think wisely, act cautiously.

Then the memories came.

Lanston. T'Vak. That cursed room. Then unfamiliar voices, accompanied by snatches of conversation that felt like a dream.

For your trouble.

…tell us if you learn anything else about the scrolls.

I'm told no harm's to come to him.

He is the empire's responsibility now.

…be wary of this one. He's feisty…

Zavik rubbed his face with a vomit-stained hand and tried to blink back the tears already sliding down his swollen cheeks. His skin was hot and puffy; likely some reaction to whatever poison Lanston had used to render him unconscious. He traced the rough edges of his lips with his tongue and tried to recall the last time he'd consumed water.

It'd been moskuto, actually. Just before T'Vak asked him for…

Before he betrayed you, you fool. And you just had to go along with him the night before you were headed homeward.

Brilliant, Zav. Just brilliant.

The next time he opened his eyes, they'd adjusted enough to assess the boundaries of his prison. It was essentially what he'd calculated with his hands: an empty room roughly six by eight feet. Perhaps a storage area. But where? And why?

They didn't want him dead. He knew that much. If they did, they wouldn't have accepted whatever trade Lanston proposed to them.

Zavik could hold on to that.

"Hello?" he croaked, scarcely recognizing his own voice.

A dry cough irritated his throat, triggering a fit that left him gasping for air.

Water. He needed water.

He crawled toward the murky, golden light beckoning from beneath the closed door and knocked.

No answer.

He knocked again with fervor. "Please, I need water."

The wood was cold against his cheek as he pressed his ear to the door to listen. When no one came, he pounded again, then shouted, alternating shouts and slams until his voice ran dry and his energy waned.

He tried to stay awake, willed his body to fight, to try just one more cry.

The darkness took him instead.

Zavik awoke to a burst of light. He scrunched his eyes tighter to ward off the pain as he rose, but rough hands shoved him back, smacking his head against the ground.

"There's a good lad," a gruff voice said in Zarith. "Hold still now."

Zavik thrashed, to no avail. At least two pairs of hands held him down, while a third pair forced his mouth open. He braced himself for more poison.

But it was water.

Cold, healing water.

Zavik stopped resisting and tried to suck in the life-giving element as quickly as possible.

"Easy there," the voice said. "Too much and you'll be upheaving it on the few clean spots left in this room."

The water was gone before Zavik had his fill. It was enough, though. Enough to fight another day.

"Where am I?" he managed as he blinked his eyes open. The harsh light had abated enough for him to study the vague outlines of his three captors. Though they spoke Zarith, they had the Zelosi look about them with their rich skin tones and vibrant clothing. And the accent was unmistakable. They were probably pirates, hired by someone in Az Zar to transport contraband. Which meant...

"Are we at sea?"

A pirate with luminescent teal eyes laughed—far too heartily for Zavik's liking. "You're in a dream, my friend. Now go back to it."

Zavik raised his arms to defend himself. "No, wait!"

But the pirate was already pouring a vial into his mouth. A bitter taste assaulted his throat, and before he could fight back, he was slipping, fading...

Gone.

Zavik lost track of how many times the same scenario occurred. He'd wake, sort through foggy memories and panic, crawl to the door and demand to speak to someone, then receive just enough water to survive.

Followed by another drugging.

Every so often, they'd surprise him with a meal. It was always fish on the verge of rotting alongside a cup of questionable broth. The first time, he'd foolishly refused, demanding to be taken from the room and have all his questions answered before eating. They'd responded by taking away his food and pouring the poison down his throat.

He didn't make that mistake again.

On it went, his body growing thin alongside his hopes for survival. He began to wonder if it was, indeed, a dream—rather, a nightmare—until one drugging incident ended with new parting words from the pirate.

"'Fraid this is the last time we'll meet. Enjoy the palace life for me, eh?"

And before Zavik could ask what he meant, the poison kicked in, and back into the darkness he went.

When Zavik woke next, he was all but certain he'd died.

The ground beneath him was much too soft, the air too pure, his body void of pain. Rain pattered outside, and the sweet scent of blossoms and spices tickled his nose. His curls rested gently on his forehead—not plastered, crusted with sweat and vomit, as they'd been the last time he woke. Even his headache and sore throat were gone. But soon enough, he recalled the pirate's parting words, and icy tendrils of fear wrapped around his heart.

He wasn't dead. But something told him he'd be better off in that state.

Instead of a searing light, the gentle glow of nevethium greeted him when he opened his eyes. That, and the clarity provided by a new pair of seers. The room he lay in rivaled the luxury of House Undali, though its interior decoration was distinctly Az Zarian with crimson accents and screen partitions. Nevethium lamps hung from the ceiling, illuminating the well-padded lounge he lay upon, their glow casting shadows through the geometric cutouts carved into the extended railing of the second floor. Small sun-blood trees sprouted from gem-inlaid pots beside a gaping balcony window, their crimson-blossomed branches reaching for both the sunlight and nevethium, creating balanced growth not otherwise attainable indoors. The room was no larger than the summit lodge back in Agaas, and from what he could tell, he was alone.

Zavik pushed himself to a seated position, half-expecting a bout of lightheadedness to force him to lie back again. Beside the lounge rested a hexagonal table carved from a dark wood native to the northern lands. On it was a crystalline pitcher sweating from the cool liquid inside. It took the strength of both hands to lift it to his lips, but he was rewarded with the purest water he'd consumed since leaving Neharem. Before he knew it, half the pitcher was gone, and his stomach awakened with hunger pains.

"Wouldn't drink much more, if I were you," a gnarled voice said in Nyrinian.

The pitcher slipped from Zavik's hands and landed on the table with a thud, spilling the water onto the rug beneath. His heart raced as he searched for the intruder. In the far corner of the room, behind one of the screen partitions displaying an elaborate mural of sun-blood trees overlooking a lush valley, arose a rustling sound.

"Mavet almighty," a cloaked figure muttered, stepping out from behind the screen. "You start breaking things around here and they'll send you right down to the dungeons. Mark my words. Won't be my fault; no, it won't."

"It won't happen again," Zavik stammered, as the intruder hobbled toward the table. The thick cloak did little to disguise the petite stature hidden within, but he was still surprised to find a shriveled old woman peering from beneath the heavily embroidered hood.

"You going to clean it up?" she asked impatiently, her luminescent yellow eyes narrowing.

"Uh..." Zavik looked helplessly around for a rag or blanket.

The old woman forced a puff of air through her wine-stained lips, the coloring of which stood out starkly against her pale complexion. "If you want something done timely and properly, do it yourself." This she muttered to herself as she shoved Zavik out of the way—an unnecessary action that conveyed her sentiments well enough—to wipe the mess with the lengths of her cloak.

When she finished, she sat across the table on the lounge opposite him, fixing him with her unsettling gaze. She withdrew her hood to reveal pointed nyrian ears peeking out beneath strands of thinning, white hair that reached down past the nevethium brooch fastening her cloak.

"Get on with your questions, then." Her expression was entirely unapologetic. "We've much work to do and can't be bothered with them later on."

Zavik glanced at the ornamented double doors located just beyond the lounges, then at the balcony behind him, featuring a sky darkened with storm clouds.

As if on cue, distant thunder rumbled.

"This is Cadar?" he asked, trying to find the best way to frame his other, more relevant, inquiries. "Are we in the palace?"

The old woman continued to glare. "They said you were intelligent."

Zavik bristled at the insult. "If you'd been repeatedly drugged in a dark room aboard a ship for days on end, you might desire confirmation of your surroundings, too," he snapped. A slight sense of guilt plagued him as he took in her widening eyes. It wasn't the old woman's fault.

But neither had she proven herself to be a friend.

"Fair enough." She shrugged, leaning back in the lounge with an exasperated sigh. "Regardless, they'll be here to collect us soon, so I suggest you ask any pressing questions now. They aren't fond of us discussing personal matters in the arcanum."

Zavik straightened. "Arcanum?"

The old woman raised an eyebrow, as though he'd asked yet another ridiculous question; one she wouldn't grace with a response.

"Fine." Jaw clenched, he dug his forefingers into the cuticles of his thumbs until he deciphered the question that lay at the root of all others. "Why am I here?" He thought he did a fair job of keeping his voice calm and collected, but that could've been the residual drugs. He could use a cup of moskuto.

The old woman didn't bother to turn her sharp-featured face in his direction. "You were supposed to come *with* the scrolls—please note the plural—to help push my research from theory to action. All I got was the promise of one scroll, and you. Rather, a broken, sickly version of you they tasked *me* to revive." She groaned as she raised herself back into a seated position. "You're welcome for that."

"Thank you?" Zavik hoped the gratitude didn't read as too disingenuous.

The old woman waved him off. "Don't mention it. Ever."

As if he needed an incentive. "About the scrolls..." he began, not wanting to give away too much.

"They tell me they're all as good as the empire's, but they still want us to make progress in the meantime."

Zavik tried to steady his racing heart as the old woman began cracking various appendages, following each with a moan of relief. Even if T'Vak managed to ferret his way back into Elaysia's company, surely she wouldn't allow him near the scrolls. And Konar would die before handing them over to someone else. He had to believe that.

"What sort of progress?" he asked innocently.

The old woman ceased her movements with a final *pop* of a joint in her neck. "Posing as incompetent won't get you far here, lad. Not with what they know about you."

"What do they know?"

The look she gave told all.

Everything. They knew everything.

He strode toward the balcony on legs as shaky as a newborn nytak's, then pressed his palms onto the cool glass. "Alright. I know about the shieum, about the arkthanax, and the scrolls—obviously. I know the All-Sovereign is ancient and wants to wage war on Neharem for our nevethium. Probably Orillon, too. And the scrolls will help him win."

A shrill cackle filled the room. Zavik refused to return his attention to the sneering old woman and kept his gaze trained on the small rivers of rain forming on the window.

"The scrolls aren't a means to the end, lad," she said, the laughter dying on her lips. "They are the end."

Zavik pressed harder into the glass. He thought of the shaktar and their command, of the ongoing civil war in Neharem, of his own plans for new tools and weapons back on his desk in Munskahan. Plans that had likely already found their way into T'Vak's hands, into Lanston's hands, then been borne across the sea, like him. But not the scrolls. They were secret. They were safe.

And if the end was coming, he wouldn't be a part of it.

"I won't help you," he said, clenching his stomach muscles for resolve. "The All-Sovereign can kill me if he wants."

"So, you are a fool." The old woman groaned in protest as she made her way to the window. "His Holiness won't kill you. He needs you."

A spark of intrigue flickered in Zavik's mind. He tried to ignore it, but the old woman's will proved strong. After what felt like an eternity, he cracked.

"Needs me because I've laid eyes on scrolls he's yet to get his decrepit hands on?" he said, hoping it was enough for the nyrian to reveal her secrets.

It worked. The old woman grew visibly impatient.

"That's certainly one of your redeeming qualities," she croaked. "Your relationship with one former high elder doesn't make you less valuable either, nor does your knowledge of Neharem and its leadership."

"I suppose not."

Zavik backed away from the window, rearranging the information until it made sense. It wasn't enough for the All-Sovereign to want him strictly for his mind and the information he could provide. Surely he wasn't the only learned being in Quinaria at Az Zar's disposal, nor was he the only one capable of informing on Agaas and Konar. Davier had pretty much taken care of the latter, anyway. That left one connection. One he hadn't told another mortal being.

"You couldn't," he stammered, "he couldn't, couldn't know."

The old woman offered a sad smile. "He has eyes in every corner of Quinaria, the All-Sovereign does. He and his priestess sought the scrolls you retrieved, as did your old mentor and countless others. The Shaktar Caverns were never revealed to them. What do you think that says about you, a slight lad who strolls out of there unharmed with three scrolls?"

Zavik felt the warmth drain from his face. It was a question he'd fought to ignore since departing the Shaktar Caverns the first time. He'd been lucky, was all. There was no divine presence guiding his life. His success was the result of hard work and determination. Or maybe he'd caught the ancient Vysilliam in good spirits.

Zavik of Az Zar. The shaktars' words filled his mind.

Yes, he carried Az Zarian blood. The same blood that ran through Davier's veins: the humans of the north. But he'd been born to parents in Orillon, to a fugitive father and pleasure-seeking mother who'd fled there to escape their criminal pasts.

"I don't know why the shaktar let me take the scrolls. I'm nothing, no one. Just a fatherless bastard."

He is worthy. The blood tells true.

"Ahh, shut up!" Zavik shouted at the voices. He couldn't take any more revelations. Life needed to make sense. Everything had a logical reason for unfolding as it did.

If it didn't, he feared his mind would fall apart.

"Speak to me like that again, and I'll see to it you sleep in the dungeon after all." The old woman bared her teeth, half of them gold and the others stained with age.

"Why did they let me take them?" he whispered. He didn't wish to know the answer, but there was no room left for denial. "Because I was destined?"

"Because they had no choice." Lightning struck, illuminating the room in a flash of gold. When it vanished, it seemed darker than before, the woman's face more haunted and haggard. "You carry the blood of Prophetess Elize, the woman who traversed the deepest tombs and highest peaks of Quinaria to disperse the most dangerous knowledge the world has ever known."

"Yikos speaks the truth, however inconvenient it may be," a newcomer said.

Zavik hadn't even heard the door open, but without turning to look, something told him the voice filling the room belonged to the All-Sovereign. A figure joined them at the window on his right, and a large silver hand pressed the glass next to his.

The All-Sovereign's oily voice slipped into Zavik's ear, alighting his body with fear. "And you're the key to recovering the remaining scrolls."

LUMIRA

Dealing with civil disputes was worse than any battle. Of that, Lumira was certain.

She kneaded the tender spots behind her ears, wincing at the headache radiating through her temples. Before her stood a graying Daruk human with a tethered goat in his arms—one of the northern breeds with quad horns and a long, furry tail. Both the goat and its keeper scowled at the Moákun woman next to them. A child clutched the woman's leg and peered up at Lumira through waves of dark brown hair, his lower lip protruding in a pout.

Lumira crossed her arms as she examined the quartet. "Alright, let's try this again, but one at a time." The words grated against her patience, but if she lost her composure, no one in Agaas would let her live it down. "And no interruptions." She pointed to the Moákun woman. "You first, Lay—Liel—"

"Aleilah," the Moákun corrected, placing a tattooed hand on her hip.

"My apologies." The urge to say something backhanded rose to a pinnacle, then Lumira released it with a practiced exhale. Maybe she was getting better at—what did Elaysia call it? Negotiations?

More like ass-kissing.

"This creature," Aleilah said, pointing to the goat, "has been wandering over to my family's hut every morning the past fortnight. She climbs onto a log to chew the leaves and plants off our roof, and she terrorizes my son."

The Daruk rolled his eyes at this and opened his mouth to speak.

Lumira silenced him with a look. "Go on, Aleilah.'

She pursed her tattooed lips and returned the Daruk's glare before continuing. "I expressed my frustrations to my neighbor, a Ni'anko man living next to us. He said if the gods keep sending something your way, they want you to make use of it. I told him I wouldn't use some stranger's beast; that I didn't even know how to milk the wretched thing."

"How honorable of you," the Daruk muttered.

Aleilah stepped toward him, the boy still clinging to her leather wrapped legs. "He offered to milk it for my family. He said his people lived communally, and that it was the same in Agaas."

A flush overtook the pale coloring of the Daruk's cheeks. "So you trusted the words of an outsider?"

"How am I supposed to know whose rules stand here? This isn't your territory, is it?" Aleilah was only a breath away from the Daruk now. "My family is barely surviving on the rations."

"That is not my problem," the Daruk snapped.

"Enough!" Lumira had reached the point where she no longer cared if there was a bite to her tone. She stepped between them and pressed a claw to the Daruk's chest. "What was your name?"

He stopped glaring at Aleilah long enough to target Lumira with his animosity. "Hilför."

Both names would abandon Lumira's mind within the hour, but she would do her best to retain them for the duration of the ordeal. "Is your goat not tied up?"

Hilför set the animal down, tether in hand. "He's penned up with the rest, but our makeshift fences aren't as good as the ones back home."

Aleilah's driftwood–colored eyes flashed. "The *rest?* You have more than one, and you want to brawl with me over a few pints of milk?"

"It's the principle!" Hilför shouted. "You shouldn't take another person's livestock, especially in times like these."

"Then keep your precious animals in *your* territory." Aleilah scooped up the boy, who'd begun to wail, and pointed a finger at Hilför's goat. "If she comes back to my hut, I'll cook her. Just you wait and see."

Hilför's pale blue eyes darkened. "Why don't you just hunt like the rest of us?"

Aleilah gripped the fishing knife hanging from her plant-made skirt. "You try hunting in a foreign land with one child clinging to your leg and another growing within you, while your mate lies cot-ridden."

Remorse flooded Hilför's face. "I did not know."

"You did not ask." Aleilah sheathed her knife.

Lumira retreated a few paces, hoping it would be one of the rare times where the dispute sorted itself out. The scent of a fire tickled her nose and awakened the groans in her stomach.

"My wife and I have many children," Hilför said begrudgingly, as though coerced to make amends. "When Chief Gibrund sends me to defend our borders, she struggles to maintain the children and animals, alongside hunting, without me. Perhaps you could help her in exchange for milk and meat." He glanced from the corner of his eye at Aleilah, face contorted in shame-tinged pride.

Aleilah lifted her chin. "I would meet her before agreeing to anything, but I'm above no work. So long as my boy can come along."

Hilför's face melted into a half-smile as he regarded the boy. "I have a daughter his age. She can't keep up with her brothers and would love the companionship."

He scratched at his long, coarse beard, then extended a hand to Aleilah. At first, Lumira feared the Moákun wouldn't take it. But Aleilah's hand found his and gave it a firm shake. As the pair and their wards strolled off toward the temporary Daruk settlement, Lumira's muscles finally relaxed with the confirmation of their harmony.

"That went well," a deep voice purred behind her.

Lumira glanced over her shoulder and found Grokhion leaning against one of the makeshift huts, his gigantic frame garbed in a simple leather tunic, leaving his arms, legs, and tail exposed. There was a chill in the morning air, but nothing strong enough to push past the barrier of beridian fur.

She motioned for him to follow her, accepting his small flask of Beridian Moonlight when offered. "It's the third conflict today," she said as she stooped to pick up a child's doll. "And I haven't yet broken my fast."

Grokhion walked with his hands clasped behind his back, giving him the air of a scholar. "People transform during times of uncertainty, especially war. There's something primal about it that awakens them to fears they'd never otherwise concern themselves with."

Lumira returned the flask. "You speak as though you've lived through this before."

"More than once, I'm afraid. It never really gets easier."

"Moons be cursed." Lumira tugged the center arrowhead adorning her necklace as she regarded her fellow beridian. Though it had been over a moon cycle since the Ni'anko massacre, the cold emptiness hadn't abandoned his eyes. Eyes that once radiated as warmly as nevethium. "How are you coping with..." *The loss of nearly everyone you held dear.* But she couldn't bring herself to say it. "All this?" she said, gesturing to the ever-growing array of makeshift lodging that surrounded base camp. There were new tents, too, ones that'd been constructed solely for tending to the wounded. Lumira feared they'd need dozens more before the war was through.

Grokhion bared his fangs in a grimace. "I thought I was done with this part of my life, that I had paid my penance. Alas, our deeds, for good or ill, always find their way back to us."

He stopped to help an elderly man layer some thick fern branches over the still-wet mud of his lean-to roof. As the lodging in and surrounding Agaas had been filled beyond capacity, latecomers were left to fend for themselves with materials from the surrounding woods. Thankfully, Apáasutai territory was known for its forgiving climate, and the foliage offered ample resources. Assuming one knew how to use them, which wasn't always the case; especially for the warm-weathered Moákun and the free-spirited Ni'anko.

"And what about you?" Grokhion asked as they walked past a cluster of children making art with ground ash on the side of a watcher's lodge.

Lumira was at a loss for how to answer. She barely found the time to eat and sleep, much less ask herself *how* the war was treating her. In some ways, it was more bearable than her previous life spent thieving, running from the law, and hunting down people with outstanding debts (or those who'd just crossed paths with the wrong person at the wrong time). But she hadn't been responsible for anyone else back then.

That she missed.

"My injuries are fully healed; what more can I ask for?" she said with a shrug. "And at least for now, our borders are holding strong." A sudden craving for the ocean breeze rippling through her fur overcame her, and she realized the last time she'd sailed was their return trip from Az Zar nearly a year past. "Actually, I'd give anything for a long voyage right about now."

"Aye," Grokhion said, and the longing in his voice was tangible. "Do you remember your first time?"

"No," she admitted. "But I don't remember a time *not* knowing it. My father said he'd take me out in a canoe to lull me to sleep as a growly newborn. Years later, even as I grew too old for such spoiling, I'd still feign insomnia until he'd break down and row me out past the reef to watch the stars dance while the rhythm of the waves rocked me to sleep."

Lumira could still feel the salty-sweet air teasing her fur as she'd nestle up to her papa, the sky alive with sparks of cool light. He'd always smelled like wood smoke and brine as he'd warm her with his massive paws and say, *The stars don't have to shine, but they do so to let you know they're always watching over you.*

Then one night, she'd asked why they did that for her. She wasn't the cub of a matriarch.

Her papa had leaned back in the canoe, leaving just enough space for her to snuggle against him. *You see, long ago, I did a favor for the moon goddesses. I almost died, but when I returned triumphant, they told me I could have anything I wanted in our world or the worlds beyond.*

She'd begged for his answer. To sail the entirety of Quorath? A world of his own? A lifetime of wealth?

Better than all of those things, he'd said with the stoicism of an elder. *I asked for a daughter, a fierce warrior with a heart filled with all the passion of a fire mountain. And I wanted her protected forever. So, the moons told me they'd command the stars to watch over and protect you always. Never forget, Lumira: the world does not deserve you, but it needs you all the same.*

She'd hardly known what to make of that at the tender age of six, but she'd kissed his cheek and burrowed further into his arms.

And when I pass on one day, he'd said, pointing to the sky. *I'll live up there with them in the realm that knows no darkness or despair. Then I, too, will smile down on you.*

He just hadn't known how soon that would be.

"It sounds like he loves you deeply," Grokhion said, pulling her out of the memory just before it pulled her under.

Lumira tightened the muscles in her face to brace against the torrent of grief dragging her down. "He did."

For the first time since she'd met him, Grokhion couldn't hold her gaze. "Do you know what happened to him?"

"The clan wars were bad when I was young," she said, her own voice distant in her ears. "We weren't prepared for one of the attacks. All I remember is being shoved into a hut with my older sister and the other cubs while my father and mother ran out to defend our village. He came back badly wounded. She didn't come back at all."

Grokhion's pain was as audible as hers. "What happened after that?"

"Papa wanted to make a new life for me and my sister away from the isles. We begged him to wait; his wounds weren't fully healed. But he was determined to get us out of there as quickly as possible and no longer be a pawn in the clan wars." She snapped a low-hanging branch off the unfortunate tree in her path—hadn't even realized they'd deviated from base camp into the surrounding forest. Her pace quickened. "A fortnight later, they found his boat broken against the shore a few miles from where we lived."

Grokhion had the intuition to withhold empty words of comfort, and Lumira loved him for it. Words never helped. Just silence and support.

"My sister grew distant and threw herself into serving our matriarch. I couldn't stand being around her or anyone else in my clan. Couldn't handle the memories or my parents' ghosts. So I ran away to the southern tip of Beridia and joined another clan. I told them my clan had been wiped out, and they took pity on me." She wasn't even sure why she continued to share her story, only knew that it felt good to let it out, like airing a wound. "I learned what I could from my new clan members, especially those skilled in the ways of seafaring and fighting. By my sixteenth year, I'd fashioned my own boat capable of carrying me away from the isles. I set sail, and I never looked back."

They'd drifted far enough away from base camp to hear the shrieks of seahawks overhead. Lumira ran her claws against the rough bark of a tree, tearing it away until the light-green wood beneath revealed itself.

"It's funny," she said, voice choked with pain, "I used to think the water felt like home. I only realized after he'd gone that it had been him all along."

"Lumira." Grokhion placed his massive hand on the trunk beside hers. She didn't like the look in his eyes.

"What?"

"There's something I've been meaning to tell you."

A gnawing apprehension unsettled her. The same fear that had paralyzed her right before she'd received the report of her father's death. "Whatever you're about to tell me, it's not going to make things better." She backed toward base camp, heart racing. "I don't want to hear it."

Grokhion pursued her. "Please, Lumira. Allow me this moment of integrity."

Before an excuse found its way to her tongue, the ground came alive behind her with the *cracks* and *snaps* of hastening feet. They both turned as Mardus and Kahana appeared from the foliage, clubs swinging from their hips.

"The high chieftain received a tuross message and has ordered all Stormriders to the summit lodge," Mardus said in a rush of words and air. A grim look weighed heavily on his face. "The Lawful Dominion have Chief Kelsia. They want us to surrender a stormbird, or they'll send us her head."

AHMARAHN

Ahmarahn shot his hand up to catch the bundle of garments flying at him from across the room. Zhia scowled, as though she'd hoped to catch him off guard and poke fun at his waning reflexes.

As if he hadn't already been humiliated enough.

He glared back and unraveled the twine securing the bundle. Folded inside was a loose-fitting tunic of rough make—likely hemp—and pants of the same material that gathered at the ankles. Shoes fell out of the pants as he unrolled them. They were a size too small, but their equally poor make would allow for stretching. After spending a year in slave garments littered with holes and stains from their previous wearers, too threadbare to offer protection from any elements besides his own nakedness, anything new seemed luxurious.

"Change. Now."

Ahmarahn glanced up from the clothing at the pinch-faced nyrian standing at attention by the door. Civilian silks adorned Zhia's towering frame, everything perfectly tied, smoothed, and groomed to create the illusion of a statue. Her moon-pale skin mimicking the milky white of her hair garnished the aesthetic.

"I'd appreciate some privacy," Ahmarahn said with a shrug.

Zhia rolled her eyes with enough angst to rival a youth's, but she turned all the same. "You have two minutes. And don't try anything, unless you'd like to join the rebel cause sooner than expected. In the arena."

"Wouldn't dream of it." Ahmarahn shrugged out of the silk robe he'd been loaned after bathing. He'd soaked for an hour, but he still felt grime embedded deep into his skin, and though he'd slathered himself with oil upon departing the bathhouse, everything itched and ached as if he'd peeled a layer of his flesh off. The woman who'd shaved him—they wouldn't let him touch a blade of any sort—had done a shit job, too, and left his cheeks and head covered in nicks and still-bleeding wounds. But he was clean, and some part of him felt reborn, like a butterfly emerging from a cocoon.

A defective, jaded little butterfly. Or better yet, some species of toxic moth that would poison its enemy if ingested.

Ahmarahn smiled at the thought.

"Finished?" Zhia growled.

"Don't get too taken aback by my beauty when you turn around." Ahmarahn crossed his arms and leaned against the frame of the tri-stacked bunk nearest him. Zhia had escorted him to a barrack in the palace grounds after bathing, and he hadn't been prepared for the overwhelming sense of regret it triggered. It was a large room, meant to house at least four dozen soldiers—none of whom were present at the moment—and it smelled of sweat, piss, and naïve, youthful visions of grandeur. And part of him missed it.

Zhia's expression lacked any amusement. "Apparently even a year of enslavement couldn't dampen your arrogance." She raised a dyed eyebrow—something the highborn nyrians had adopted in Cadar to create a more striking appearance—as she studied his tattooed forehead, now more prominent than ever, thanks to his lack of hair. "Looks like it took just about every-thing else from you, though."

Ahmarahn squeezed his arms until he felt the earliest signs of bruising. "Just about."

His change in demeanor softened the firm lines of Zhia's lips. "What is your name?"

"Ah—"

"I said, 'what is your name?'" She'd drawn a sword and crossed the room before she finished uttering the last word. The cool touch of metal kissed his throat.

Ahmarahn's toes curled in his ill-fitting shoes, scrunching the fabric. "Davier."

"And what is your story?"

"I tried to overthrow the All-Sovereign. I paid for it with my family's lives and my eternal servitude. Now that he trusts me enough to once again carry out his evil deeds, I seek vengeance."

"And what is your actual mission from the All-Sovereign?"

"Expose the rebel leaders. Destroy the rebellion."

"Or else what?"

His jaw tightened as the blade dug deeper into his throat. A thin trickle of blood snaked down his neck, staining the tunic below.

"Or else *what?*" Zhia repeated through glistening, white teeth.

A lump formed in Ahmarahn's throat. He swallowed it away, and with it, the memories of his younger sister's laughing eyes and playful banter. "He'll destroy Xi."

"Good."

Zhia withdrew her sword from his neck, but she kept it brandished as a warning. Despite the risks, Ahmarahn hovered his fingertips over the sleek lyvium blade. His hands ached to hold a sword, to taste just a hint of the life stolen from him.

"Remove your filthy fingers at once," Zhia barked. She sheathed the sword behind her back and snatched the collar of his tunic. "You've been given free rein of the city, but not of weaponry. If I catch wind of you carrying anything more than a dinner knife—"

"Going to be difficult to pass myself off as a pacifist keen on rebellion."

A sharp slap flushed his cheek with heat. He'd barely registered the first offense when another, on the opposite cheek, took precedent.

"Interrupt me again, and I'll cut out your tongue."

The deep red settling over Zhia's face told Ahmarahn that she just might follow through on that, given the circumstances. "My apologies," he muttered, though he didn't lower his gaze.

Zhia smoothed a flyaway strand back into the tightly braided knot at her nape. "You have two moon cycles to infiltrate their inner circle. Each day you're delayed, I'll remove one of your sister's fingers. If you refuse to report for weekly debriefings, or if I hear tell of any conspiring on your end, I'll remove her head. Are we clear?"

Ahmarahn envisioned removing Zhia's fingers one by one, then her toes, flaying her skin, scalping her head, hanging her upside down over a pit of starved sandcats in the heat of the Feasting Moons, and then, and only then, removing her head and shrinking it down to a little novelty he could clip to his belt.

He offered his most wicked smile. "Transparently."

Zhia's lips bunched to the side, as if sensing his animosity.

Well, of course she could. She knew he hated her; that he would kill her, given the chance. She just had no idea how depraved his mind had become, how it'd stretched and bent and broken until the one he'd been born with had died along with his past life.

Zhia withdrew a wide-brimmed straw hat from one of the bunks and placed it on his head. "Go. May Mavet guide your hands and guard your heart."

Ahmarahn snatched the hat off his head and fanned it out before him as he bowed. "And may he give you everything you're due."

As he walked through the door and into a hallway lined with rooms like the one he departed from, his gaze flicked to a glowing nevethium sconce. A specter moth fluttered around it, its ash-black figure broken up only by the fluorescent green adorning its wings. A warning to its enemies. A promise of poison. Of death.

A corrupted, little moth.

"Keep to the right."

A city guard jabbed Ahmarahn's side with the butt of his spear, herding him back into the steady stream of commoners flowing down the eroded cobbles of the street. The sun still peeked out from beneath the clouds, but the moons were on the rise, challenging it for possession of the evening. The reek of sweat from too many bodies huddled together stung his nose, but it was nothing compared to the stench of the cage he'd called home for the past year. In fact, he almost welcomed it; though, being surrounded by countless people set his body alight with nervous energy, as if a million worms wriggled beneath his skin.

Ahmarahn raised his hand in apology. The guard responded by spitting a wad of mucus on the path before him.

A small part of his old self surfaced, a part that wanted to challenge the guard, perhaps spit back in his direction, on his boots, to snatch the spear from his weak, inexperienced grip. But Ahmarahn wasn't so foolish, and as he peered closer at the guard, he saw a young, human boy lacking confidence, fighting for his chance to impress the empire, to earn his right to exist in the world he'd been born into.

And Ahmarahn pitied him.

As he shuffled along the path, the ringing, hollow note of the first warning gong echoed through the streets. People responded by quickening their pace, clutching bags and children closer to their bodies as they scattered like skirvin retreating to their holes. Most of their eyes were downcast, their movements twitchy, and there was scarcely a word exchanged among them. It made him recall his previous lectures with Zhia about what to expect when he rejoined life in the capital.

Operating in near perfect order, she'd said. *Less crime. Fewer outbursts. Unsurpassed temple attendance. Food shortages mitigated from Cadar all the way to Or Zahal.*

It didn't take long to understand why. For the entirety of Ahmarahn's journey from the palace courtyard to the Old Nyzar District, he never once felt free of the watchful eyes of the empire. Since the Lord Priestess's new order had gone into effect, the city patrol had nearly doubled, and there seemed to be one soldier for every four citizens. Even the reputable, private-owned shops of the Sun-blood District favored by the highborn had closed, replaced with city-owned distributors selling mass-produced goods. The Old Nyzar District was worse, the streets lined with soldier-guarded storefronts plastered with signs stating, '*Exchange capital notes here,*' and, '*Forging capital notes is punishable by imprisonment and reduced rations.*' New lyvium statues filled prominent squares where artistic structures had once resided, some in the likeness of the All-Sovereign, but many showcasing unsettling depictions of the Lord Priestess—such as her stroking a baby deathstalker, or baring her teeth in a disturbing grin while accepting a tithe offered by a small child.

We've brought peace and prosperity to Az Zar, the statues seemed to say.

The commoners of the Old Nyzar District told another story with their thin frames and ragged clothing, with their sharp expressions and clenched fists. All the men wore the same muted, ill-fitting tunics he'd been assigned, and the women hardly fared better with their modest brown dresses masking the curves of their bodies, their hair piled atop their heads and wrapped in scarves or covered with wide-brimmed hats. Those residing in the lesser districts weren't known for their fashion, but Ahmarahn didn't recall them being quite so tasteless. Or uniform.

Something else was amiss, and as he wound his way through the main thoroughfare, gaze darting down each side street, searching for the homely but friendly faces of performers offering entertainment in exchange for aspar, it came to him.

The silence. In the absence of the gong, there was no chatter, no music, no rhythmic pattering of footsteps.

No joy.

Ahmarahn stopped outside the chipped wooden archway of his destination: a three-story inn offering the bare minimum of accommodations required for weary travelers. He hadn't made it a point to know its name in the past, and now he never would, for the sign had been removed, leaving a dark rectangle to contrast with the rest of the sun-bleached siding. Dirt covered a courtyard that he could've sworn had once flourished with grass, and the skeletal steeds tied to a rapidly declining post pawed at it, ears flicking as the crunch of Ahmarahn's footsteps alerted them. One gave a weak little tug on its rope before dropping its head in defeat.

The only sign of decoration still hinting at the inn's former glory was a single flame lantern hanging from the deathstalker-headed corbel positioned at the center of the eaves. A murmur of voices seeped from the cracked door into the courtyard, and Ahmarahn hurried up the steps, eager to speak to someone not bent on controlling or killing him. Not that any such relationship would last long.

A small marking on the last riser of the stairs caught his eye. He crouched to inspect it. Someone had used charcoal to outline the silhouette of what he presumed to be a stormbird, based on the prominent, curved crest of feathers and the way its beak hooked at the tip.

The rebels have chosen a symbol of division, Zhia had said. *They want to take us back to uncivilized times, to an age of war and survival, where fear ran rampant, and uncertainty plagued the future.*

As Ahmarahn traced his thumb over the symbol, a storm of memories thrashed at the frail fortification guarding his sanity, tearing down shoddy barriers and awakening the dusty, dark corners where he'd imprisoned his demons. He drew a ragged breath and clung to the stair tread to steady himself.

Davier had been impulsive. He'd thrown everything away for promises of opulence and destroyed the lives of nearly everyone he cared for. But Ahmarahn was smarter. He knew pain, knew that his heart wasn't to be trusted. He could learn from Davier. Use him. And now, it was time to harness his former life and be the soldier he was bred to be.

He wouldn't fall prey to another game of love and loss.

Ahmarahn leaped across the porch and pushed the faded red doors open with both hands. A hush fell over the common room as he entered. Around twenty patrons sat alongside two long tables, cutlery and cups in hand, their gazes fixed on him. They were mostly men, all human, and not a soldier among them. A slab of red meat roasted on a spit over the fire, its fat drippings making the flames dance and crackle, a sound which seemed to echo in the silence brought upon by his presence.

Ahmarahn's hands twitched awkwardly at his sides, wishing for blades he no longer possessed. A dark-haired man leaned away from a round of xyrong—a strategy game consisting of an octagonal board and hand carved tokens—and gave him a particularly appraising look. Ahmarahn returned it. The man sauntered to the counter and tossed a few aspar at the innkeeper, who busied himself with continuously drying the same cup, then approached Ahmarahn with exaggerated swagger.

"They're letting palace slaves wander the humble district of us common folk now?" the man asked, resting his ass against the edge of the table a few feet from where Ahmarahn loitered at the entrance. He rubbed a stubbled chin, his storm-blue eyes narrowing. A flicker of recognition crossed his face. "Sent you to spy on us, did they?"

Ahmarahn steadied his voice, determined to not let his general unease about the situation imply the cocksure man intimidated him. "My duties allow me a wider berth than some."

The man looked over his shoulder, his full lips pursed in a sneer. "Hear that, boys? The All-Sovereign's pet is just out for a little stroll. Back to your drinks, then." His thick brows bunched together as he inspected Ahmarahn. "You just traded one form of slavery for another, you know. Pity you don't recognize it."

Something in his diction triggered a memory of Davier's past, though Ahmarahn couldn't put his finger on it. The man had the look of a soldier. Cropped hair, a posturing stance. The general attitude of disdain that came with the need to prove oneself after giving time in servitude to another.

"Do I know you?" he asked, voice calm.

The man's lip curled upward. "Everyone knows you now, Zadel, even if they didn't have the pleasure of knowing you before."

"Ahmarahn."

"What?"

"It's Ahmarahn."

The man let loose with a hearty laugh, bracing himself against the table so he could flex the muscles in his forearms like some pompous peacock. "Right." He raised a hand and snapped twice, sending the innkeeper scurrying over to him with a bottle of kuba wine. "Don't remember me, do you?"

"Uh..."

He opened the bottle with a *pop* and raised it to his lips. "It's alright. I'm not a memorable sort of fellow." The glint in his eyes suggested he thought the opposite. "Six moon cycles' worth of initiation together, assigned to the same barrack, I might add. But everyone paled in comparison to you, didn't they?"

Ahmarahn eyed the kuba wine. He had no idea who in Mavet's eternal realms the man was. The only thing on his mind was that, besides the occasional sip from the assortment of half-finished brews gathered by the kitchen slaves, he hadn't had a proper drink in over a year.

"Third round of human initiate training. Chailar, year 3026." The man took a long pull from the bottle and swallowed it with a grimace. "You'd already impressed the sergeant at arms, but apparently felt the need to further distance yourself from your brothers."

Ahmarahn's fists clenched. Davier had been a fool. Hard-working, talented, and determined, but an arrogant fool, nonetheless. He couldn't count all the men he'd stepped on to earn his status, much less name them. "I... I'm sorry for however I may have hurt you."

Out of empathy, or perhaps some lingering sense of brotherhood, the man offered him the bottle. Ahmarahn took a long drink, every muscle in his body relaxing as the alcohol warmed him.

The man looked on with a snarky grin plastered across his face. "Seeing you like this is almost worth it, you know."

Ahmarahn passed the bottle back. "You'll have to remind me of your name." The blunt honesty was partially driven by the alcohol, but also out of curiosity. Besides, he had no reputation to maintain.

"Kymerius."

Ahmarahn waited for the connection to form in his mind. It didn't.

Kymerius laughed and took another drink before passing it back to Ahmarahn. "You and I were drafted the same cycle, though I was two years older." He bit his lip and looked beyond Ahmarahn at the courtyard. "My mother tried to hide me. They always do."

Ahmarahn nodded. His parents had never tried to hide him, but sharing that information with Kymerius would do little to gain his sympathies. "Are you from Or Zahal?"

Kymerius snorted. "Where else? Not that you took that into consideration when you humiliated me in front of our entire company."

The resumed chatter of the inn stilled once again, and Ahmarahn felt every gaze latched onto him the way archers readied their shots. "Again, I'm sorry if I've done anything to offend you in the past. I was—"

"You were a fucking asshole, Zadel, and you knew it then. You knew it the first time you ate my rations, the first time you informed on me instead of waking me when I overslept, the first time you slipped sedare mushrooms into my soup so I'd hallucinate during a drill. It wasn't once. It wasn't an accident. It was intentional and repeated interference with my success for your pleasure."

Ahmarahn braced himself for a hit, one he probably deserved, but Kymerius's reddened face slowly returned to its milky white.

"I envied you," he continued. "Every day I fought to be better, and every time you outshone me. When you were sent off on your first assignment, I thought, 'Here it is. It's finally my moment to advance.' But I never did." Kymerius drained the last of the wine and slammed the bottle down on the table, rattling the drinks of those nearest him. "I fell into a pattern of sub-par service and finally deserted five years ago, and it was the best thing that could've happened to me. I'm a part of something greater than you ever were. What I do actually matters. And just when I thought my life couldn't get any better, you limp in here with your tail between your legs, reminding me that everyone gets what they're due."

"That's actually why I'm here," Ahmarahn said, unclenching his teeth. "I want to make things right. So many things. I've heard rumors this is the right part of the city for men seeking redemption."

Kymerius leaned in close enough that Ahmarahn could see his pores. "Not men like you," he growled. "But I'll let our leader decide."

JAKKI

The she-wolf lurked behind Jakki and Xaren while they gnawed at scrawny, spit-roasted hares, the little nourishment their captors allowed them. At least the meat was fresh, which was more than Jakki had hoped for, and the mountain spring water served alongside it rendered the meal extraordinary. Neharem was known for its pure water infused with therapeutic properties, but never in her life had she consumed something so full of vitality. Judging by the look of bliss on Xaren's face, she wasn't the only one affected by it.

"Hurry," the she-wolf growled. She paced outside the cells she'd returned them to, only this time, the brondite gate was left ajar, and Xaren allowed to share Jakki's cell while they ate.

"It's not good to gorge on a fasted stomach," Xaren replied in his dutiful, soldierly tone that made him sound like a child reciting his nation's creed. Most of the time, it made Jakki want to smack him, but given their circumstances, she offered him an approving wink instead.

Jakki examined the carcass she'd picked clean, then held it up to the she-wolf. "Should I dispose of this, or does your kind chew on bones like the tales say?"

The she-wolf's ears flattened against her head. She snatched the carcass from Jakki and shoved it into a woven bag hanging from her shoulder. "We consume everything eventually. This will feed our fungi, which in turn will feed us. I thought your kind had a similar way of being, but maybe you've become more like the Az Zarians as of late."

Jakki started to rise, but Xaren restrained her arm, interjecting with, "You eat the mushrooms? I thought skulmor were...you know..."

"Carnivorous?" The she-wolf kept her piercing green eyes trained on Jakki as she finished Xaren's question. "We are, when it's sustainable. Something that's becoming increasingly rare as our lands are seized." She briefly directed her glare to Xaren, as though he was solely responsible for generations of war between the skulmor and Az Zar. "Regardless, our fungi are more medicinal and supplementary than dietary."

"Like kinawa?" Jakki wasn't certain the skulmor were familiar with the psychoactive plant native to Neharem, but she had few other comparisons to offer.

For the first time since they'd crossed ill-fated paths with the she-wolf, she dropped her protective scowl in a moment of vulnerability. "I wouldn't know. We don't partake in the food or drink of your kind. If you survive your proving, I'll take you to see the fungi. Might even let you taste a few." Despite the harshness of her words, Jakki sensed the she-wolf softening to them.

An ally gained is an enemy lost. The voice of Jakki's mother echoed in her head, and she heeded it. "What's your name?" she asked as they departed the cells.

The she-wolf snorted and glanced over her shoulder as if questioning Jakki's authenticity. "I don't think your tongue can hold it."

Jakki glared daggers into her back as they marched up the stone stairwell.

She had enough allies, anyway.

"This is a fucking death sentence."

Xaren didn't object to Jakki's admission, nor did the color return to his already pale face in a timely manner. "You're strong, Jak. If anyone can—"

She silenced him with a look.

The she-wolf twitched her ears, but offered no condolences. She'd wound them up and out through the tunnels of Tyrgraak—the official name of the skulmor's mountain stronghold, and the only useful fact they'd pried out of their captor so far—before leading them out to a ledge above a small clearing near the tree line. The waning daylight soaked the forest in a crimson glow the shade of wildfire, accenting the deep shadows cutting into the Lesser Quentarri Mountains in the distance.

Despite the beauty, Jakki's gaze was wholly fixated on an impression left in the muddied snow not ten feet from their ledge. Five toes. Five claws. Four paw prints the size of a full-grown nyrian male.

All belonging to one tulek bear.

"If you want to kill me, you could just snap my spine and be done with it," Jakki said, fighting to keep the edge from her voice.

The she-wolf regarded her with a look that could've almost been mistaken for pity. In the sun's dying light, her silken fur looked a fiery cream, not unlike Lumira's, and Jakki found herself wishing the cat was with her. She could use the beridian's spite as motivation—not to mention another skilled in combat.

"The dominants offer you this opportunity to prove yourself," the she-wolf said, her eyes widening with excitement. The moment she'd pointed out the prints to Jakki, her attitude had shifted from irritation to anticipation. "They're allowing you temporary use of this." As the she-wolf dipped her hand into her satchel, Jakki could feel the parchment calling to her. "It is a great honor."

It took every bit of Jakki's restraint to not snatch it up and leap off the ledge as soon as it appeared. "And you trust me with it?" she asked, allowing her fingertips to kiss the edges of the parchment.

"I have orders to kill you if you try anything suspicious." The she-wolf gripped the parchment in her clawed hand a moment longer, as if to prove a point, then released it with a show of apathy. "But given your stormbird's ailment, I doubt you will."

"I wouldn't want to give your leaders the satisfaction of believing the parchment only answers to your kind, anyway." Jakki slipped the parchment into her tunic and practically shivered with delight. With it, she was whole.

"Jakki."

Fear gripped her heart upon hearing the brokenness in Xaren's voice. She scowled at the she-wolf and drew the boy soldier closer to her.

Xaren kept his gaze lowered as he covered a clenched fist with his other hand. "I can't reach him anymore."

Jakki whirled on the she-wolf. "I'll fight your bear, but you must let him go. Tell him how to cure Shadow."

"I'm sorry." The she-wolf pressed Jakki's staff into her hand and offered Xaren his bow. "The dominants said—"

A rage-filled scream poured from Jakki's throat, and a flock of birds dispersed from the forest, their black outlines stark against the crimson sky. "There's still time," she murmured to Xaren. "We're going to kill this thing, learn the cure, and make it back to him by dawn, alright? I need you to stay focused and strong to help me do that."

Whatever sorrow ate away at Xaren disappeared with a simple adjustment of his posture as he slung a nytak-hide quiver and his Az Zarian bow over his shoulders, then lowered himself over the ledge. She supposed his time spent serving Az Zar's military made the transition from mourner to soldier an easy one.

"I'll be back before dawn," Jakki told the she-wolf as she leaped down after him, the snow crunching beneath her boots.

She gritted her teeth as another *crunch* sounded beside her.

The she-wolf revealed her fangs in a bitter smile, then detached a small ax with a brondite head from her leather belt. "Not supposed to let you leave my sight."

Jakki adjusted her grip on her staff and gave it a good swing, coming dangerously close to the she-wolf, who, to her credit, didn't flinch. "I'm not going to lose any sleep over your death, as long as we don't end up in the same afterlife."

"I don't think that's possible."

They held each other's gazes as the last of the sunlight faded into a dusky glow, then Jakki vanished into the forest, a predator ahead of and behind her, and a once-enemy at her side. As she ran, she searched for Siren's essence.

If you can hear me, she pleaded as she trampled a bed of ice-crusted pine needles beneath her boots, *stay away, but tell Shadow to hold on just a bit longer. I'll let you know when it's safe to retrieve me.*

Extracting any information from the she-wolf proved to be as challenging as their upcoming task. However, based on what Jakki had learned earlier while they ascended from Tyrgraak's depths, this particular tulek bear had strayed far from its northern kin some moons prior. Whether driven by its age or food scarcity, it had made its home closer to the skulmor, destroying their preferred hunting grounds and picking them off when they dared to enter its newly claimed territory.

Jakki didn't know enough about the north to say with any certainty, but she could've sworn it was peculiar behavior for a tulek bear to appear south of the Greater Quentarris, where the prey was smaller and harder to catch. She hoped that meant it was sick or crazed.

Anything to increase her odds of survival, really.

They followed its tracks through the woods, an easy enough feat for even the most novice of trackers thanks to the bear's enormous size. It had practically carved a trail by tamping down the soil and snapping the limbs off (if not downright trampling) any tree in its path. As if that wasn't enough, they passed not one, but two massive piles of shit littered with undigested bones and roughage. All proper signs for an apex predator: nothing to fear, and no need to hide.

Until you meet me, Jakki thought, even if it was more wishful thinking than genuine confidence.

She was grateful for the little nourishment she'd consumed to sustain her on the trek, and even more so for the water sloshing in the pouch hanging off her belt. She was less grateful for her skulmor companion, but the she-wolf could function as bait, if nothing else.

Xaren halted abruptly, and Jakki followed his gaze through the thickly lined branches to the east. Her breath fogged the air just beyond her face, and with the three of them stopped, she could make out the yips of snow foxes scuffling in the distance. She closed her eyes and concentrated on the energy center of her mind, where Siren's voice usually stirred within her like a gentle breeze.

But this time, there was nothing.

Xaren gasped, and Jakki's eyes shot open.

"What is it?" she asked, no longer caring if the she-wolf discovered their ability to communicate with the birds. "Can you reach him?"

"I can, but it's darkness." Xaren's eyes were glassy, and Jakki sensed his struggle to remain composed. "It's like I can feel him, but he can't feel me. Like he's asleep. Or..." He bit down on his lip and kneeled to adjust his boots.

They didn't need adjusting.

Jakki's throat tightened. She jabbed the she-wolf in the chest with her staff. "How much further?"

The she-wolf bared her teeth but had the restraint to slowly lower the weapon instead of snapping it in two—a feat Jakki knew she was capable of. In fact, looking at her preferred weapon in the she-wolf's massive hand made her looming combat seem like suicide. What good was a simple staff against a bear larger than their two stormbirds combined? Even with

Xaren's well-trained arrows and the parchment, even with the benefit of surprise and their skulmor companion, it was suicide.

But one look at Xaren's face shattered her heart.

"Not long," the she-wolf replied. "It has slept near the same clearing for over a moon cycle. There's a cave entrance to an abandoned skulmor settlement that's just large enough for it to back into, minimizing the areas it needs to guard against."

Jakki's thoughts careened with opportunities. "Is there still tunnel access? Can we utilize them to sneak up on it?"

The she-wolf shook her head. "It was blocked off a long time ago. A rival pack caused a tunnel collapse, leaving them trapped and vulnerable. It would take a force greater than ours to unblock it."

"Then what's our plan when we reach the clearing?" Xaren asked, his voice dry and strained. "Does the bear have any weaknesses?"

The she-wolf's gaze went to Xaren's bow, and she cocked her head slightly. "How good is your aim?"

"He's near flawless," Jakki answered. A look of surprise crossed Xaren's face at the compliment. She shrugged it away.

That response seemed to satisfy the she-wolf. "I'd say aim for its eyes, then. We have no skilled archers among us, and it's resistant to our brondite weapons."

"What I wouldn't give for an Az Zarian blade right now," Jakki murmured, looking down at her staff with no shortage of apprehension. "Or their cursed—what did you call them, Xaren?"

The boy's deep brown eyes narrowed into slits. "Shieum."

"I'm familiar with them." The she-wolf touched her left shoulder, wincing at some unseen memory.

"We don't have time for this." Xaren started up the hill toward the tracks, but Jakki caught the edge of his hood.

"I won't formulate a plan or use the parchment until we see the clearing," she said, her voice low and commanding. "When we find it, get high, stay out of sight, and only shoot when I give the signal. Aim for the eyes, like the she-wolf said."

Xaren's lips disappeared into a thin line. "How does the magic work? How long does it work?"

No fucking idea.

But she couldn't say that, couldn't tell him that sometimes, like when she'd drowned Unleto, it'd lasted for what felt like hours, while on other occasions, it faded within minutes.

Or that there were rare times it hadn't worked at all.

"It makes my reflexes swifter, my thoughts faster, my impacts stronger. And it will last long enough."

And if not, we're dead, and I've contributed to the death of an endangered beast.

"This belongs to no bear." Jakki followed the she-wolf's voice a short distance from the path. She was bent over something dark, scenting the air around it.

Jakki crouched beside the wolf and peered down at yet another pile of shit, this one far smaller than the bear's leavings but still larger than anything else she'd come across. "It almost looks like nytak, but—"

A memory of the monstrous stags mounted by Atsukut warriors came back to Jakki in a rush of heat and twitching muscles. If they were close by, so were some of their riders. According to the information she'd gleaned from some of the Daruk in Agaas, the Atsukut bred and raised the stags themselves.

Hope flared in her chest. The three of them stood little chance against the bear, but alongside an encampment filled with lives she didn't mind sacrificing? Well..

Xaren caught Jakki's gaze, and there was understanding in his eyes. It almost felt like she communicated with a stormbird, as if she could reach up and cut a physical line that tethered their minds. He gave her a single affirmative nod.

"Do your people have bad blood with the Atsukut?" Jakki asked the she-wolf.

"We have bad blood with everyone because of Az Zar." She studied her non-skulmor companions with a wrinkled snout, then released a huff. "It matters not to me how you treat your own kind, as long as it's not traced back to us."

"If it goes the way I'm hoping, it won't be traceable to any-one." Jakki used her staff to gesture to the droppings left by the Atsukut's steeds, a trail far more subtle than the bear's, but only marginally more difficult to track. "I'm sure your scouts keep watch over all who enter your hunting grounds, not just mountainous bears. How close is the nearest Atsukut camp?"

The she-wolf's eyes glinted in the veiled moonlight drifting through the branches. "Just beyond the river. They've been mov-ing bands south, but that camp has remained stationary for several moon cycles."

"You don't interfere with each other?" There was no masking the suspicion in Xaren's voice.

"The river has functioned as an unspoken territory line," the she-wolf replied. "There's been no need to violate it."

Jakki crossed her arms. "And the tulek bear upholds this unspoken treaty?"

"Maybe it does." The she-wolf leveled a glare at Jakki as she snatched a stick from the ground. "Here are the Greater Quentarris and Tyrgraak," she said, drawing a mountain range in the dirt. She added some trees, then a long line just beyond them. "The woods, the Nipai River, and"—she drew a large cir-cle—"the Atsukut camp." She drew two short, intersecting lines just north of the river, then a smaller circle to the right. "And here's us and the bear. As to why it has left them alone, I can only assume it hasn't needed to go further south for resources yet, nor do I think it wants to."

"We'll give it a reason." Jakki smeared the makeshift map with her boot. "Xaren, find the encampment and position your-self high. You'll know when we're coming."

The boy's brow wrinkled. "You don't want to scout it out first?"

"Don't have time. Besides, I trust—"

Snap.

The trio fell silent, instinctively positioning themselves back-to-back to ensure the best defense against the intruder. Jakki couldn't afford to use the parchment before facing the bear, so she calmed her breathing and tightened her grip on her staff. For once, her mind was quiet.

The hare that dared to scamper by stood no chance against three warriors trained to kill. Jakki withheld her strike, but Xaren's arrow had already sailed into the brush it emerged from. It lay there, twitching, until the she-wolf snapped its neck and began tearing off its skin with her fangs.

"What?" she said, a chunk of raw meat in her mouth.

Xaren's eyes were wide as full moons. "You really don't cook it?"

The she-wolf gazed back at him in equal disbelief. "You really can't digest it raw?"

"Glad we've clarified our dietary preferences." Jakki rolled her eyes as she pulled Xaren aside. She gave him what she hoped was a look of motivation. Inside, she was hollow. "Be strong for Shadow."

He gave her a fierce nod, then vanished down an elusive path toward the river, leaving no tracks behind him.

"If you're quite finished with your hare," Jakki told the she-wolf as she stared after him, her heart pinched with worry. "We've got a bear to provoke."

Two things came to Jakki when they reached the clearing surrounding the tulek bear's cave. The first was how perfectly circular it was, hemmed in by thickly needled trees, as though the gods themselves had devised a naturally occurring arena and driven a monster down from the north to mulch up skulmor for their entertainment.

The second was that, of all the ways she'd entertained she might die, being mauled by a giant bear wasn't one of the expected outcomes.

Nor would it become one.

Before stepping into the clearing, Jakki brought the parchment to her nose and inhaled deeply of its must. She knew its every crease and wrinkle, the spots where it'd worn thin—had all but memorized the hard lines of its inscription. She whispered the first phrase so low that only she could hear, awakening bumps on her skin in anticipation. Despite the she-wolf being a good distance ahead, Jakki attuned to her silent breaths, to the way her heart quickened as her pupils constricted. She could even feel the hackles raise on the she-wolf's neck. Air rich with wetted grass and tree sap filled her nostrils, and the shrieks of a thousand creatures of the night rang in her ears. She dropped further into herself, yet expanded up and out, as though she could capture the entire world inside her essence and leaf through its layers like the pages of a book.

And now I'm truly alive, she thought—or maybe she spoke it aloud. It was never apparent in her awakened state.

The she-wolf bounded ahead toward a yawning cave at the foot of the mountains, its interior masked in shadows, concealing any forms hidden within. Jakki easily kept pace and soon overtook the skulmor, reaching the tulek bear's lair first. Bones were piled on either side of the cave mouth, whether as trophies or warnings. She could still sense the life in some of them, could trace the essence back to the creatures they once supported. A fox mourning its lost kit. A nytak buck on the cusp of sexual maturity. A skulmor who'd tried to prove himself to win a mate.

Jakki waited by the bones until the she-wolf rejoined her, and together, they entered the lair.

The stench of death was suffocating. A horrific combination of decay and fecal matter, of blood and decomposing flowers. And somewhere beneath it all, a hint of sweetness. Jakki's eyes adapted instantly, taking in the fullness of her surroundings with an adeptness not natural to her kind. The cave was larger than it looked from the outside. Despite the dryer climate of the north, the air felt thick with damp. And there, pulsating in the darkest corner, was the form of a giant beast. A hulking, smoldering monster with gore-encrusted claws.

The tulek bear's ears didn't so much as twitch as she slunk further in.

She took full advantage of what would likely be her one opportunity to assess her enemy's weaknesses. It slept curled on its side, its tree-trunk limbs drawn into its stomach with its head nestled between forepaws the size of Jakki. Its fur was a cream shade similar to that of the she-wolf's, only matted with enough blood and dirt to suggest otherwise. Something told her it was ancient, with an intelligence to rival the Great Beasts, and the realization tarnished the ease with which she hoped to make the kill. Deep, old scars ran like dry riverbeds above its right eye and along its snout, preventing the growth of new fur.

The bear huffed, stretching its limbs as if awakening.

Jakki held her breath, could sense the she-wolf slowly backing away. But the bear only rolled over to face the cave wall.

Again, Jakki's heart ached. It seemed the same as any other bear. Not vengeful or malicious. Almost endearing, was it not easily twice the size of its southern kin, with the appetite of a wildfire.

But Shadow. This, for Shadow. A life for a life. There was honor in that.

She had no choice but to believe it.

Jakki's beloved staff was no match for the bear, so she unsheathed her dagger to use as her primary weapon. Its lyvium blade glistened in the moonlight streaming through the cave. She'd always been skilled with her weapons of choice, but with the magic of the parchment coursing through her veins, the dagger was a true extension of her hand. Precise, potent, pure. Enough to wound the bear without causing significant damage, and enough to slow it down without stopping it all together.

She glanced over her shoulder at the still-retreating she-wolf and bade her to go with a lift of her jaw.

Are you certain? the she-wolf's eyes seemed to say.

Jakki gave a final nod, then turned back to the bear. Her footsteps were a mouse in the dirt; her breath a whisper of wind through the tall grasses; her hand a harbinger of death. She targeted one of the massive paws, lowering her dagger to the splayed claw nearest her. A claw twice the length of her dagger. The blade slipped through the bear's flesh with such ease that Jakki questioned if it was all a dream.

And then it roared.

Jakki's ears rang with a deep, vibrating bellow that sent her sprawling back, trophy in hand, the claw still attached to a chunk of bleeding flesh. But she was ready, half-crawling, half-scrambling away as she harnessed the full capacity of the parchment's magic. Her actions over the next few moments would determine her fate.

The tulek bear swiped blindly, its body a blur of matted fur and rage. But she was already out of the cave, running faster than the fastest skulmor, not daring to look back. The grass sprung beneath her feet, giving her traction as she dodged patches of mud with grace. She sensed the she-wolf well ahead of her, panting and pushing, felt the eyes of ravager birds watching from their perches, their heads cocked in anticipation.

Another roar echoed off the mountains. Thunder followed in the uneven cadence of a great, lumbering beast. Its footsteps rattled the ground, awakening every animal instinct Jakki possessed. She saw nothing but her path through the trees, heard nothing but the pulse of Quinaria, and trusted nothing but the guidance of her own heart.

It was all she needed.

Suddenly, the bear's breath was a hot wind on her back, the lapping tongues of a fire. She stumbled, making a quick recovery that meant the difference between life and death. Another rage-filled roar quickened her pace. Her hood slipped off, releasing a loosely woven braid that trailed behind her like a banner. She almost dared a glance behind her, then looked up instead. Clouds blanketed the sky. Though she couldn't see the form of a bird, she swore Siren was with her, tracking her every move.

Stay away, Jakki told her. *I can handle this.*

The bear's steps grew distant. She wove through the trees, a shrill laugh escaping her lips, a laugh that was as much the old man's as it was hers. The bear wouldn't catch her now. She was the forest incarnate; the very essence of Quorath itself.

And a world's essence never really died.

Instead of dwindling, the magic within Jakki surged as she leaped over fallen logs and clusters of hard-packed snow. The Atsukut camp was only a league from the bear's den—an easy enough run without the aid of the parchment. And with it? She'd likely have to slow her pace to keep it from abandoning pursuit.

As if confirming her suspicions, the bear let loose another roar as it smashed through the woods. The sound of snapping branches and splitting trunks filled the sparse silence the beast allowed, and Jakki slowed her sprint to a jog. She could regain momentum in an instant, if required. With the parchment's magic, she could determine the tulek bear's location based on sound alone.

The bear lagged as she delved deeper into the woods. As the roars and snaps grew further and further apart, her suspicions that the beast was old and lazy were all but confirmed.

No, you don't. Jakki gritted her teeth and came to a full stop. She could scent the mineral-laced river water not half a league away. If she lost the bear now, she'd never defeat it. And Shadow...

Something jabbed her leg. She looked down at the claw tucked in her belt, at its still bleeding stump staining her clothes. A plan sparked in her mind. She ran back in the direction of the bear, waving its claw in the air as she let loose a roar of her own.

"Want this?" she shouted. "I'll take another when next you sleep! I won't stop until I have them all and use your..." Jakki stopped as a thick cloak of shame enveloped her. "I'll..." She looked at the claw, horrified by the life she still sensed in it, at the pain she'd caused a creature who'd done nothing to harm her. "Please," she whispered. "Just come. I need you."

No roar answered her plea. Only the irregular thunder of a mighty beast favoring one paw.

And its pace was rapidly increasing.

Shit.

As Jakki neared the river, a throat-burning char began to overwhelm the crystalline essence of the water, until all she could smell was smoke. A flock of ravagers swarmed overhead, making for the north. As if she needed further confirmation of the fire, a nytak doe and two half-grown fawns galloped down her path, nearly knocking her over. Panic surged through her. She'd told Xaren to stay hidden, but if he'd started a fire, the camp would be awake, likely armed, ready for the she-wolf, the bear, and her.

Jakki cleared a patch of mud in a single leap, then sprinted up what she hoped would be the final hill. She could practically taste the water on her parched tongue. Whatever renewed energy the bear had harnessed forced her to push herself well past any limitations she'd ever set for her body, under the influence of the parchment or not. And for it to still pursue her despite the fire, well...that meant it had enough intelligence to hold a grudge.

A dangerous thing.

When she felt the first signs of her strength beginning to wane, the sound of rushing water and distant cries filled her ears. It was all the motivation she required. She emerged from the forest and half-sprinted, half-slid down the bank, crashing into icy currents that shielded her from the searing heat on the other side. Under normal circumstances, it would've been foolish to cross at a place where the river was so wide and wild. But for now, Jakki was the water, was Mother Itaso herself. The cold exhilarated her, awakened her blood. The unruly current beckoned her to lose herself to it.

But Shadow.

Recognition settled over Jakki like a gentle snowfall: the only way to prevent the parchment's magic from overtaking or abandoning her was to have a solid motivation to use it. The stormbird was her tether, her mission.

An arrow pierced the water, targeting the place Jakki's head had been seconds prior, before she sensed it approaching. She flinched as another took to the skies. But it sailed over her, heading straight for the forest.

The tulek bear was closer than she'd given it credit for. It burst through the trees, its golden eyes alight with flames. Jakki shrank into the water, mouth gaping as she took in its colossal frame. It easily stood twice the height of Grokhion, dwarfing the beridian's impressive eight-foot stature. But it was greater than that, towering beyond the height of the nazrath, the giants of the north. And why wouldn't it? The bear was as old as them, as old as the Great Beasts, and its size served as a testament.

Its mouth yawned open, revealing yellowed, crooked fangs, but before it could let loose another ground-shaking roar, an arrow struck the place just beneath its left eye. It snarled in pain. Jakki knew who'd made such a precise shot without laying eyes on the archer.

"Xaren," she screamed, unsure why she suddenly cared about the monster bear's wellbeing. "Don't hurt—"

She submerged just as another arrow glided across the water. She swam further downstream, holding her breath far beyond its natural limitations, then filtered the air in the water through her lungs as she had countless times prior. When she finally emerged, she'd cleared the border of the Atsukut camp, arriving at a cluster of thickly intertwined trees. It would've been the perfect place to flee, but she couldn't abandon Xaren. She pulled herself onto the bank and told herself she felt no cold. The magic waned, but it wasn't gone. Not until she'd squeezed out every last drop of it.

Screams rose above the rushing river and crackling fire, and Jakki knew the bear had made it across the river. She tore through the trees, its claw in one hand and her staff in the other, not allowing her mind to process a single thought until she reached the edge of the clearing.

Atsukut warriors darted about the encampment, their intimidating statures working to fend off both flames and bear. The fire had made quick work of their shelters; in fact, Jakki could only make out a few still standing. She crept out from the cover of the trees and ducked behind what remained of one of the larger lodgings comprised of sticks and skins. Not fifty feet away, the tulek bear faced off against a few dozen warriors, leveling groups of them with a swipe of its massive claws.

Jakki tuned out the screams of agony as she tiptoed through the rubble left in the fire's wake. She'd almost reached what remained of the poles marking the shelter's entrance when a growl sounded behind her.

Jakki spun, swinging her staff, but her enemy was quicker. Only, it wasn't an enemy; it was—

"Caution, nyrian," the she-wolf snarled. "We must leave. Your mate has lain waste to half the camp, and your bear torments the rest. But there will be survivors."

"Where's Xaren?" Jakki's gaze darted about the smoldering Atsukut encampment, feeling a brief surge of guilt. But they hadn't been innocent villagers. It was a Lawful Dominion war camp. The thought erased any trace of pity.

The she-wolf gestured to the opposite side of the river. "He waits. He watches. He's a shadow, that one."

A ghost of a smile pulled at the corner of Jakki's mouth. "Did they see you?"

"I, too, am a shadow." She motioned back to the woods. "Come. Let us be rid of this place."

Boom.

Jakki stopped in her tracks as a roar of anguish from the bear filled the camp.

Boom. Boom, boom.

No. Not on her land. Az Zar would not spread their poison here, would not claim the Atsukut as a weapon to wield against the few remaining wonders Quinaria had to offer.

If you can hear me, Jakki pleaded with the magic, with the old man, with whatever powers and goddesses had yet to abandon a world spiraling toward destruction. *Give me the strength to save this innocent creature. It knows not vengeance; it knows not prejudice. It simply wants to survive, and survival is not a crime.*

Jakki raced toward the bear. She lost sight of the warriors surrounding it, of the flames still ebbing in her peripherals. All she knew was the agony of its cry and the crimson staining its thick, matted fur. She'd never even seen a tulek bear before now. What if it was the last of its kind, and she responsible for its death?

She thought of Unleto, of Lumira, of every soul she'd wronged in her desperate climb for significance and approval, and she channeled all of it—the fear and doubt and self-loathing that simmered beneath her skin—into an internal fire.

One of the shieum wielders stood back from the others, reloading his weapon. Jakki attacked his seven-foot frame from behind with a crack of her staff to his skull. She snatched the Az Zarian weapon from his body, assessing its cold frame in her hands. She aimed it at the backs of the unsuspecting warriors in front of her and pulled the trigger.

A *boom* rattled her ears. She staggered back beneath its force, just barely maintaining her balance. The man she'd fired at crumpled before her, nothing but a bloodied hole in his back to hint at the cause of his demise. She pulled the trigger again and again, hitting each target with precision as if she'd been born to wield such a weapon.

She eliminated seven warriors before alerting the rest to her position, then brought down three more before the weapon stopped firing. There was no hesitation in her movements as she sprinted for the shieum of a fallen Atsukut, but another warrior was faster. They snatched up the weapon and aimed it at Jakki, who barreled on, regardless of the outcome.

If death wanted her, so be it.

But the she-wolf had other plans. She leaped from behind one of the charred structures, sinking her jaws into the unsuspecting assailant and giving Jakki a chance to rip the weapon away.

Jakki did her best to convey gratitude to the she-wolf before aiming the shieum at the incoming warriors with spears raised high. She pulled the trigger, savoring how it became more a part of her hand with each use, the projectiles an extension of her, like the arrows she'd never mastered. The bear roared again, but it sounded more enraged than in pain. Jakki hoped some part of the beast knew she was trying to make things right. She caught sight of its hulking form out of the corner of her eye as it crushed a warrior beneath one of its massive paws while sending another hurtling into the distance.

It had a chance now, Jakki knew. She could depart in good conscience.

She searched for the she-wolf, her gaze filtering through the mud and bodies and charred bits of fabric. A *click* responded to her attempt to pull the trigger and bring down an advancing warrior. Jakki tossed the weapon aside, retrieving her dagger just in time to fling it into her attacker's eye. He collapsed in the mud, landing on top of another body.

"She-wolf!" Jakki shouted as she made for the woods. The tulek bear was gone, and Jakki's heart lifted, hoping it had escaped.

And then it sank.

The she-wolf lay in the mud, a red streak spilling across her chest. Jakki sprinted to her, painfully aware of the Atsukut warriors encroaching on her. She kneeled beside the skulmor and tried to lift the wounded creature to no avail.

"Go," the she-wolf said through clenched fangs. "Tell my people I died with honor."

"No." Jakki snatched up an abandoned spear and launched it into the closest Atsukut.

The she-wolf closed her eyes. "You can't carry me." She pulled a ring off her finger, a simple lyvium band etched with runes. "Give them this. They'll believe you. They'll set you free."

"*I can carry her,*" a voice whispered in Jakki's mind.

She gasped and raised her head to the sky. There, illuminated by the first light of dawn, soared Siren. She swooped dangerously low, dodging incoming spears and arrows as she knocked dozens of Atsukut down with her outstretched wings. With her came rain and howling winds, and Jakki didn't doubt for a moment that she'd summoned them.

"Come on," Jakki grunted as she positioned the she-wolf's arm around her shoulders. "Looks like you get to show me your mushrooms after all."

The she-wolf's eyes widened as she took in Siren's magnificence, and she allowed Jakki to help her to a standing position. The stormbird careened toward them, and when she landed, ash swirled about like a veil, temporarily obscuring them from the enemy's view. Jakki climbed onto Siren's back, whispering silent blessings only the stormbird could hear. Once she'd secured the she-wolf in front of her, Siren flapped her massive wings, carrying them up and out of harm's way.

Xaren, Jakki thought, more to herself than the bird. But Siren heard all the same.

"He's safe," she replied. *"Already hidden deep in the woods."*

Jakki took her first genuine, shaky breath, free from the magic's essence. "We'll get you back to your people, wolf," she shouted over the wind.

"Uruuka," the she-wolf wheezed as her eyes fluttered closed. "My name's Uruuka."

ELAYSIA

A dozen pairs of eyes stared back at Elaysia as she paced around the gathering table. No one moved. No one spoke. No one had the answers she sought.

"Let me see it again," she said, making her way toward Kahana, the wood hard beneath her bare feet. The Moákun retrieved the tuross note from a small pouch on her belt and handed it over, her moss green eyes betraying the nyrian side of her heritage with their gleam.

Elaysia withdrew to the fire, her fingertips denting the parchment. No matter how many times she reread it, wishing the message away, it remained. Three words stood out every time. Three damning words, inked in blood.

Kelsia.

Captured.

Stormbird.

The rest were obsolete.

A glance back at the gathering table intensified the throbbing pain above Elaysia's left eye. She rubbed at it with fury. But it, too, like the message, was going nowhere.

Someone coughed as she reluctantly made her way back to the strained faces of her war council. What was left of it, anyhow. In some ways, she was thankful all that remained were her Stormriders, the head of her watchers, and three chiefs—one of whom had recently taken ill and been confined to his cot. Vahid and his head of kuza, Hallahd, helped fill the temporary gap left by Chief Arkuun, however. And Yerakai was more than capable of speaking on the Apáasutai leader's behalf.

"Perhaps we should allow ourselves a reprieve until tomorrow morning," Orandus suggested, leaning away from the table to stretch his arms and neck. "We've gone back and forth on this for hours, and our time would be better spent attending to other matters."

"Other *matters*?" Gibrund's empty drinking horn clattered to the floor. "Kelsia's life is not a matter, Chief. She is the leader of the Ni'anko and a woman who'd give everything for any person in this room, should it be asked of her." The Daruk chief's voice rose to a shout, and Elaysia wondered—not for the first time—if it would finally be the moment when he snapped.

"Be it so," Yerakai interjected, "it doesn't make us any closer to devising a solution." His perfectly collected tone was soothing enough to calm even Gibrund, who sat back in his cushion, grumbling. "No one is comfortable with the exchange proposed by Raynar, nor are we comfortable with the opposite outcome, should we do nothing."

Lumira leaned over the map carved into the center of the gathering table, her claw circling Lautei territory. "We don't have proof that they've captured her. She could've escaped."

"And not make for Agaas? Her only sanctuary and the place she sent what remained of her people to?" Gibrund cast his fur cloak onto the table, exposing arms coated in a variety of Daruk runes and imagery. He drew a hand down his face and the length of his beard. "Where else would she go?"

"We can't exclude it as a possibility," Mardus said, moving the cloak off the map with no shortage of irritation. "She might have plans unbeknown to us."

"And she might already be dead," Grokhion said. The beridian sat sullenly at the farthest end of the table, his ears pinned back, his pupils dilated.

Elaysia looked away before their gazes intersected. For no matter what words were exchanged, the war council would remain divided and trapped by indecision, because there was no logical answer. No way to win. And even though the questions weren't explicitly aimed at her, they were her burden to bear.

But she couldn't think clearly, not with them all staring, not with Gibrund repeatedly glancing at Kelsia's empty seat. Not with Grokhion looking the way he did.

"Out," Elaysia said quietly. Then louder, as she tried to assert the authority she never wanted, "We will proceed with Chief Orandus's suggestion and take the night to think on it."

Gibrund's blind eye seemed to pierce through her. "A night might be all she has left."

"Then pray to your gods she survives it." Elaysia meant it with the utmost sincerity, but the look on the Daruk chief's face made her regret her words.

No one spoke as the summit lodge emptied; though Yerakai acknowledged her with a fist to his heart, and Lumira offered an exhausted look of solidarity, one that said, *I see you.*

When the door finally closed, Elaysia found herself alone. With Vahid.

She gave him a curt nod as she stacked all the cushions by the fire, making something akin to a nest, then retrieved an open bottle of Cyan's wine left on the gathering table. Judging by the graying light she'd glimpsed as the war council departed, she maybe had the time it took to prepare an evening meal before the twins needed her to supplement theirs. She lay on the pile of cushions, wine in hand. Between the heat of the fire and the soothing aura given off by the nevethium crystal fused into the gathering table, her heavy eyelids seemed to close of their own accord.

"I hope you didn't find my silence off-putting."

Elaysia's eyes snapped open with a fierce glare. Vahid walked along the perimeter of the room, studying the various masks, ornamental headdresses, and retired weaponry adorning the walls amid the carvings.

She took a sip of wine, allowing the spiced notes to linger on her tongue. "Why would I?"

Vahid shrugged. "I just felt it inappropriate to offer advice on an issue whose stakes I can't fully speak to." He came to stand a respectable distance from her assortment of cushions. All that remained of his Orillon attire was his jewelry; he'd traded the rest for a pair of fitted leggings and a nytak-skin tunic the color of sand. "But if you'd like an opportunity to rid yourself of all the feelings you're holding back—free of judgment—I'm happy to lend an ear."

The beginnings of a retort formed in Elaysia's mind, but she caught herself before releasing it. Vahid wasn't the source of her troubles. In fact, he'd been nothing but supportive since arriving in Agaas. Taking turns with the babes, overseeing food distribution and lodging arrangements for refugees, training alongside Neharem warriors to find collaboration between them and his kuza army. He hadn't even asked once about moving in to her chambers.

Or fulfilling their union.

Guilt won out, and Elaysia made a peace offering of the wine, flinching as the warmth of his fingers brushed against her own. She scooted back, nestling further into the cushions.

She'd have none of that. *That* was the last thing she needed. Motherhood and leadership allowed no room for frivolous desires.

"No matter what I do, I'm going to upset half the war council and have blood on my hands," she said, securing her uncombed hair with a leather strap atop her head. "I can't sacrifice one of the stormbirds. They wouldn't go even if I commanded it. And Lumira's right: we don't have proof they've captured her. But if I willingly let a chief die..." Her nails dug into the tender flesh of her palms. "There has to be another way."

Vahid kept his attention on her as he sipped from the bottle. "Perhaps you need to stop looking at the situation through the eyes of a leader. What would you do if it was one of your children taken?"

The suggestion, even speculative, sent an icy spear through Elaysia's heart. Her body radiated with an energy so cold she could only describe it as a blue fire, so frigid it burned. She sat up, leaning toward him, driven by some primal force.

"I'd tear the world apart piece by piece until they were found," she whispered.

Vahid passed the bottle back to her. "Perhaps something similar should be done for this chief."

Elaysia took another drink, one much longer than the first. "I've considered it. Mardus even suggested something similar when we first received the message. But we don't know where they're holding her."

"I bet we can narrow it down." The way Vahid smiled at her was so reminiscent of Davier's wolfish grins that she had to look away. She'd fought so hard to push him from her mind. But she'd only felt her heart opening the way it was now once before, and the thought scared her more than the potential wrath of the war council.

"The tuross bearing the message was scaled, yes?" he asked, taking a seat beside her. "Not coated in the velvety skin of the northern varieties?"

She nodded.

"So the message came from somewhere south of Agaas."

Elaysia shrugged and took another sip as she studied his hands. They weren't the soft hands of a man of his nobility. Vahid had done everything he could to shed that association and carried himself with the humility of a true leader, even though she had suspicions he didn't believe himself worthy of that title.

"And wouldn't it be safe to assume," Vahid continued, "that they would keep such a valuable prisoner as close to their leader as possible, to prevent the spreading of their strongest forces?"

"It's a logical presumption, but we still don't know where Raynar's encampment is. Our scouts confirmed he isn't at the Lautei stronghold, but that's all we know." She passed the bottle back.

He refused with a shake of his head and gestured at her stormbird necklace. "You have the best eyes in Quinaria."

"Onitus and I couldn't even find Jakki and Xaren."

"The north is harder to scope out than the south."

"Have you nothing negative to say?" she asked, surprised at her flare of anger. "This is a war, a shit one at that, in the hands of a shit leader. Blissful optimism does nothing to help us."

"Neither does tunneled negativity."

They sat in silence, cross-legged before one another, their clothed knees touching ever so slightly. Elaysia's head still throbbed, and whether her eyes burned from lack of sleep or budding tears, she knew not. She took another drink, promising herself to stop after it. She couldn't afford the pains of over-drinking on top of everything else.

"I don't know how to be around you," she admitted, empowered by the wine. "You make everything clear and muddled at once."

"Do you want me to go?" Vahid's warm, brown eyes hinted at longing, at hope.

Yes, Elaysia thought. *And no.*

But she couldn't manage a response.

"I'm going to see if I can't track down Hallahd." The disappointment in Vahid's voice was blatant, yet not directed at her or filled with blame, the way others sometimes wielded guilt. "He told me Yerakai approached him about some Banaxa activity to the south. We'll gather enough kuza to provide ample reinforcements. I may go along with them to fight this time, if you have no need of my presence."

Elaysia nodded, unable to look him in the eyes. When the door closed behind him, she sprawled out on the cushions and stared at the figures carved into the ceiling. Her gaze lingered on the great bear, the goddess Chai'Tik. The Daughter. The messenger. The life-giver. She willed it to come alive, for it to speak to her the way the spirit walker had that fateful night in the forest. But the eyes remained wood, the body hardened into a mortal dream.

Maybe she hadn't even spoken to a spirit walker the night she'd found the eggs. It could've been a vision, a divine sight, like Konar said she had. Like her father had.

"Show me what to do," she whispered to the bear, not daring to let it become a prayer. Just a hope. "My people need strength. A sign. Something to show them we still stand a chance as our enemies close in around us like a herd of nytak backed against a cliff." Tears stained her lips with warm salt, and only then did she hear her own sobs.

"Show us," she begged. "Show me."

The sun was barely a dream on the horizon as she climbed onto Onitus's back the following morning. She'd protected her body from head to toe in thick layers of leather and skins, then filled her quiver with the finest lyvium arrows before slinging her bow across her chest and strapping her grandfather's dagger to her thigh. The latter was simple in design, its make bone, its handle wrapped in leather, but she felt its power and trusted the strength of her elders to guide her hands. It had served her family for countless generations, all the way back to when her grandfather's great-grandfather embraced Igtheos and his rebel stragglers from the east, creating an unlikely alliance that led to the unity of Neharem.

The dagger represented the hope of unity, of overcoming differences for a greater good. And today would not be the day it failed her.

Onitus flared his wings, fighting to remain grounded while the other birds and riders readied themselves. Rain soaked the training grounds around them, creating giant puddles the size of ponds and muffling the shrieks and flaps of eager stormbirds.

Elaysia thanked Quinaria itself for the gathering storm. Whether the birds had something to do with it or not, whether the gods cared or not, it was a fortuitous sign that validated her decision.

Which was exactly what she needed, given the raid she was about to lead hadn't been cleared by the war council.

Five of her most loyal supporters stood before her atop creatures more magnificent than life had a right to manifest. She could practically feel the power rippling from both birds and riders alike, could sense their spirits afire in the intangible realm that lay between the mortal plane and that of the deities.

And for once, she dared to hope.

"We'll follow the Nipai River east until it intersects with the Eraithos," she shouted over the wind. "From there, we'll split up, half of us approaching from the west while the rest attack from the east. Beridians with me."

Lumira gave an affirmative nod while Grokhion stared into the woods, his usual words of encouragement absent. Elaysia didn't envy any Lawful Dominion warriors who found themselves in his path.

Mardus stroked the top of an unruly Keera's snow-white head. "And I'm to lead from the east with Yerakai and Anahi."

"You know the land best, Brother," Elaysia said, looking to the human and nyrian flanking him. They both appeared calm, along with their birds, which was all she could ask for.

Elaysia brought her fist to her heart. "May your sunrises always hold promise."

"And may your sunsets always hold peace," the Stormriders echoed, each in their mother tongue, as they brought their fists to their own hearts.

The stormbirds shrieked, wings flapping as they took to the air in a flash of wind and feathers. They'd give everything they had to bring Kelsia home.

And the rest was up to the gods.

Elaysia scarcely noticed the land vanishing beneath her as she clung to Onitus, the rain pelting the exposed skin around her eyes. She didn't feel the damp sinking in through her layers, chilling her flesh. Didn't entertain the possibility of her returning injured. Or not returning at all. She'd harnessed a raw, primitive focus to make right everything the Lawful Dominion had wronged.

Starting with Kelsia.

Sleep had evaded Elaysia in the hours leading to her abrupt raid. She'd pored over maps and notes penned by the ever-studious Yerakai in Zavik's absence. Run through all potential outcomes with Lumira. Convinced Mardus to act without the council's leave. For Khiev-Tatamic's sake—she'd sought Konar's council, prying every bit of information he held about the Lautei and Banaxa out of his resistant, clutching fingers. She'd even made Maseeya promise to care for the babes in her stead, and appointed Orandus high chieftain, should she not return, leaving her desires in a sealed parchment at the foot of her cot.

Agaas was in good hands no matter the outcome, as it always had been. As long as its people believed in what Neharem stood for, someone worthy would rise to fill her role. And if they didn't, the land was beyond saving.

Elaysia relied on equal bouts of instinct and fact as they glided into Lautei territory. Vahid was right. It made sense for Raynar to keep Kelsia in a larger, fortified camp that didn't relocate as often as the smaller ones in the south and northeast. But she also trusted Onitus. While he didn't speak to her the same way the other stormbirds did with their riders, he had an intuition about him, an almost other-worldly awareness that delved well beyond her own understanding. The closer they drew to the heart of Lautei territory, the stronger the colors pulsated in her mind. Vivid flashes of crimson and sunset orange, of gold flecked with shimmering violet.

But instead of fading abruptly, as they usually did, they solidified into something else entirely.

A blurred room pulsating with fever. The woman, weak but steadfast as she clings to her silence. A flash of red as her cheek burns from a strike. The deep blue sobs rising from her chest.

The vision faded, leaving Elaysia to face the wind and rain of an angry sky. But for a moment, she'd tasted Kelsia's essence, had stepped into her body as if it were her own.

And now she understood the meaning of Onitus's messages, of his gifts. He could transcend thought, could stretch the very boundaries of reality itself. And through him, Elaysia could access it.

"Kelsia's alive!" she shouted into the wind.

Though no audible response came, she could sense Anadu's and Roth's reception of the message, could feel their warmth pulsating through Onitus.

Thank you, she told him. *Let's bring her home.*

The birds and their riders were one.

They knew no fear. They were gusts of wind and flashes of lightning as they dropped on the Lawful Dominion encampment like a hailstorm. All weapons and rage. All beak and bone.

Over a hundred shelters sprawled before them on a lush field the color of spilled wine. Lumira and Anadu dove first. The stormbird's sheer size sent warriors scattering for weapons and shelter. Some made for their steeds, but Grokhion and Roth beat them to it, his powerful talons uprooting the posts of the pen that held them. The horses trampled their handlers as they stampeded through the camp. People dashed helplessly from one space to the next as Mardus's flock bore down from the east, tearing up shelters as they went, their birds shrieking the battle cries of revenge. More and more warriors poured from the tents, like ants fleeing a flooded tunnel. Anadu snatched clusters of them, dragging them toward the clouds, until their fall meant certain death. Then she let go.

As Onitus began his descent, Elaysia forced herself to think of Kelsia and not the Lautei. Not the boy she'd shared a meal with as a child, while their fathers spoke of imports and wine. Not the old woman who'd braided her hair when her mother had taken ill on the eve of Novitae. Not the watcher who'd offered her a smile the day of her induction, when so many others had cast looks of disapproval upon her.

She couldn't allow herself to linger in the past. For the moment she remembered there were good people among the Lawful Dominion, was the moment her justification crumbled beneath her wavering feet.

Onitus flooded her mind with a rush of blue hues, each more intense than the last. She shut her eyes against the blinding rain as she followed his essence to the largest structure in the center of the encampment. A lodge of skins and bones.

Kelsia.

Elaysia pressed her face to Onitus's neck as his speed increased, trusting him to guide them safely. They were moments away from penetrating the fabric, from rescuing the Ni'anko leader, from securing a symbol of hope, a reason to keep fighting, a reminder that good things happened to good people, if they only tried hard enough.

Then the first shieum thundered.

Onitus arced, the projectile narrowly missing them. Elaysia's heart dropped as she lost her grip on his rain-slicked feathers, and then she was falling, limbs flailing wildly as she plummeted back-first toward the tent. A scream caught in her throat as she plunged into the fabric, only for it to rip beneath her, dropping her another few feet onto a table below. She lay there, stunned, ears ringing with the blasts of shieums intermingled with stormbird shrieks. A hot pain radiated through her right foot all the way up her tailbone. While she struggled to rise, hands clamped around her neck, cutting off her air.

Someone screamed. Elaysia thrashed at the rough hands pressing into her, squeezing tighter, harder, chasing away her consciousness. Just before she slipped into the dream world, she unsheathed the dagger from her hip and drove it into her assailant's neck. The breath that followed was almost euphoric. She pulled her dagger out and rolled off the table, her free hand rubbing the tender spots on her neck that were certain to bruise.

She backed up until she felt the security of the hide wall behind her, searching for enemies all the while. There were none. The tent she'd fallen into was no larger than her quarters back in Agaas. On the other side of the table lay a Lautei warrior, blood spurting from his neck and blending in with the crimson Az Zarian rug beneath him. Elaysia avoided looking at his face and guided her gaze to the reason for her mission: Kelsia.

The Ni'anko chief was tied to one of the tent's weight-bearing posts, hands bound above her head, her starved body dangling limply from her wrists. Her lustrous white hair had been crudely cropped in uneven patches, leaving scabs where the knife had come too close to her scalp. She wore nothing but a loincloth, exposing her emaciated frame and dulled, navy skin.

Elaysia feared she was too late. Then she recalled her own imprisonment, her depleted body upon returning to Agaas, and remembered just how fierce a woman could be. She limped on her good leg over to the pole and used her dagger to cut the bindings, catching the Ni'anko's featherlight frame as she crumpled down.

"Kelsia?"

The chief's eyes didn't open. For a moment that seemed to stretch into eternity, Elaysia lowered her ear to the nyrian's chest and waited for the reassuring beat of her heart.

It murmured, ever so gently. But it was there, promising life. Promising hope.

"I'm here," Elaysia whispered, stroking Kelsia's cheek. "We're—"

She gasped as the tent flap drew back, revealing two Lautei warriors. They glanced at their fallen brother, at their freed captive, and lunged for Elaysia, faces contorted by rage. In a flash, an arrow found its way from the quiver into her hand. A harsh exhale scraped against her throat as the arrowhead sunk into the broad-shouldered woman's eye socket. Meanwhile, a tall, hawk-eyed warrior aimed a shieum at Elaysia.

That was his fatal mistake.

Though powerful, the Az Zarian weapon's novelty was as harmful as it was helpful in the hands of Neharem warriors. Elaysia loosed a second arrow before he pulled the shieum's trigger. It tumbled from his hand as he dropped.

Elaysia snatched it up instinctively, slinging her bow across her chest so she could prop up Kelsia with her free arm.

"Water," the Ni'anko chief croaked.

Elaysia reached for her waterskin, only to find its usual spot on her beaded belt vacant. Had it become detached during her tumble from Onitus? She glanced around the room for water or wine—anything liquid—finding nothing but the rain pouring in from the torn hole of the tent. With reluctance, she approached the fallen warriors. There, on the woman's belt, was a waterskin. She whispered her thanks to Chai'Tik as she retrieved it from the body. The discovery provided another blessing: she didn't recognize the woman, nor the man, at least from what she could make out of their blood-soaked faces.

One less nightmare, she thought with ebbing guilt as she held the waterskin to Kelsia's cracked lips.

As the chief drank, Elaysia kept her gaze, and weapon, trained on the tent flap. The shieum felt cool in her hands; distant and other-worldly, as though it had a mind of its own.

"Can you walk?" she asked when Kelsia had had her fill.

The Ni'anko chief replied by placing a shaky foot forward. It did little to offset her weight—not that it was much to begin with. Still, Elaysia would have to make do with the shieum. It was impossible for her to fire a bow while simultaneously supporting Kelsia.

Onitus, she called from the depths of her mind. *I need you.*

He heard her. She sensed it. But beyond that, she knew without a doubt that he'd watched her fall and would make his way back to her when the time was right. Until then, she'd wait inside the tent, fending off enemies who dared to intrude. Only when she felt the undeniable rush of Onitus's imagery in her mind would she venture outside.

Crash.

Elaysia and Kelsia flinched in unison as a massive boulder careened through the tent, obliterating the entire left half in a single strike. It cracked two of the weight–bearing poles, narrowly missing Kelsia's still extended leg.

"Move!" Elaysia shouted, dragging the chief alongside her.

A wet cough rattled Kelsia's chest as Elaysia pushed through the hide covering to peer out. Several bodies lay paralyzed in the mud just beyond the tent, their faces forever frozen in anguish. The rain fell in sheets of silver, rinsing their blood off the ground. Upon finding no living threats, Elaysia retreated inside long enough to pull Kelsia out. But as soon as they emerged, a hulking Banaxa warrior raced toward them, club raised.

Onitus, she repeated in her mind like a prayer. She imagined the proud crest of his plume, his shimmering black beak. Intelligent eyes beyond her understanding. He'd come for her. She could depend on him even when everyone else failed her.

But she could also depend on herself.

She lowered Kelsia to the ground and, with both hands, guided the long end of the shieum toward the incoming Banaxa, her finger light but firm on its trigger.

Just like an arrow. Just like a target.

The weapon bucked in her hands, sending her tumbling backwards. A hollow ringing filled her ears. She'd never been so close to one when it fired and hadn't prepared for the bite of its force. Her hand flew to her dagger, but the Banaxa wasn't upon them. He'd collapsed a body's length away, blood spurting from a small hole in his chest. He pawed at it, his movements growing slower and more sporadic until he ceased moving altogether.

Elaysia stared at the shieum, filled with an unsettling mixture of awe and horror. How easy it'd been to pull the trigger, almost as if she'd done nothing at all. Almost as if it acted of its own accord. She clung onto it out of survival, only because she couldn't nock an arrow while supporting Kelsia.

The ground squelched beneath her boots as she maneuvered around the bodies. Another warrior sprinted past, his shieum trained on the sky. She followed his gaze to where Mardus and Keera soared overhead. The stormbird released two bodies destined to meet their deaths upon impact, then dove for another. Elaysia pulled the trigger before the warrior could, wincing as he crumpled beside the freshly fallen bodies, conflicted because Keera and Mardus flew away unharmed.

"On your left," Kelsia murmured.

Elaysia glanced over just as a Lautei warrior drew her bowstring taut. She had a clear shot and the element of surprise. But instead of launching her arrow, she met Elaysia's gaze. Recognition passed over the woman's face. She adjusted her aim, jaw set against the wind tangling the loose strands of her nyrian-white hair. But her eyes said it all. She lowered her bow with a rage filled cry and started for a cluster of warriors engaged in combat with an airborne Lumira.

"Wait!" Elaysia cried. "The woods!" She gestured desperately with her chin to the tree line a quick sprint away.

The woman shook her head and hurried toward the center of the encampment, determined to join her fellow warriors.

She didn't make it more than halfway before Roth swooped down, snatching the woman in his bone-crushing talons.

Elaysia's head swam. She wanted to scream, but her voice caught in her throat, twisted by guilt and regret. If she hadn't distracted the woman, if she'd just—

A jolt shook the ground. Elaysia lost her balance and fell onto Kelsia, nearly dropping the shieum. Another massive boulder careened through the sky, its arc targeting Yerakai and Wind Chaser. Dread filled her heart as she looked on, waiting for the inevitable collision, but the stormbird pulled up at the last moment, his wings fanning into a brilliant display of silver and onyx.

Relief flooded her body as she tightened her grip on Kelsia.

It vanished as something hard pressed into her back.

"Don't move, High Chieftain."

She stiffened, recognizing the threat and the shieum that would carry her sentence out should she not comply. She closed her eyes. Ignored the icy fear coursing through her veins.

Onitus.

A sudden burst of light shattered her perception, and in its wake, she found herself observing through the stormbird's eyes. She honed in on the Lautei warrior holding the weapon to her spine, and beyond him, Kelsia. And her. The rest of the world ripped by in a breath of wind, but there she was, clear as the present. Onitus's talons grasped the warrior tightly, as if they were an extension of her own hands, soaring higher and higher until there was no chance of survival. And together, they loosened their grip, sending the warrior to his death.

She could scarcely breathe as Onitus dove back toward the camp, his impeccable sight—now hers as well—catching even the subtlest of movements as he came to land beside her. It was surreal, almost dreamlike, to see herself there as she felt the ground shiver beneath her.

Her sight became her own as she heaved Kelsia onto the stormbird's back and surrounded her in a protective embrace. An arrow soared past her head, but she found solace in Onitus's presence as he took to the skies, her nagging fears and doubts washed away by the revelation.

She didn't need visions, at least not in the sense of divine interventions from the gods, of how and why to act. The power had been inside her all along, waiting for Onitus to unlock it. She just had to be still enough to listen, calm enough to receive, and strong enough to believe.

And now that she'd found it, she'd never let it extinguish.

KONAR

T'Vak proved to be every bit as mind-numbing as Konar remembered. It had scarcely been more than a fortnight, and already he'd considered shoving the backhander off one of the living tree platforms himself and framing the whole thing as an accident. He probably could've gotten away with it, but then he would've severed their last thread to Zavik, a sacrifice he was unwilling to make.

Yet.

If T'Vak wasn't telling stories, he was drinking. If he wasn't drinking, he was readying another batch of painfully elaborate stories regarding drinking—or worse, his various cot companions, of which Konar had lost count.

"Not picky at all in that regard," the backhander often slurred. "Living and breathing, not too old or too young, and that's my target fu—"

At which point Konar would quickly interject with an urgent request, even though the tasks he assigned were rarely urgent. T'Vak was most useful for procuring food and supplies, or occasionally sitting in on a war council gathering in Konar's stead. He'd yet to attend one himself, despite receiving multiple invitations from the high chieftain. She meant well, but his presence would only tarnish hers.

T'Vak had just returned from one such endeavor. He'd also helped himself to a drink on the way back, according to the stain on his lips. The Orillon man was undeniably a dependent consumer of the poison, but Konar could've sworn his consumption had increased since returning without Zavik.

And that guilt, unfortunately, was something Konar knew all too well.

"What did you learn?" he asked, closing one of his journals. He'd gotten much closer to unlocking the Prophet's code, but despite incorporating notes from the two scrolls in his possession, something remained amiss.

T'Vak leaned across the table covering the library's trap-door—it wasn't one of the secrets Konar had allowed him the privilege of—his filthy hands resting dangerously close to a full inkwell. "Same shit they're always going on about."

When it became clear he wasn't going to offer further explanation, Konar retrieved a bottle of Beridian Moonlight from his secret stash behind one of the shelves. He'd kept it there for years, waiting for a conversation that required a little more manipulation than usual.

He found himself in one of those times.

T'Vak's eyes widened as Konar set the bottle on the table, alongside a dusty but ornately carved chalice. He scratched at the stubble adorning his cheeks and cleft chin. "What's the occasion?"

"Death," Konar said mildly, as he poured the thick liquid into the cup. He wrinkled his nose at the stench of alcohol and shoved it toward T'Vak. "For she comes for us all, sooner than we'd like."

"Not you, though, eh?" The backhander studied Konar's empty hand. "The beridian stuff not good enough for you?"

"Oh, I hear it's the best in Quinaria." Konar returned to his seat, positioned with a clear view of the library door. The backhander hadn't bothered to bar it, and the vulnerability he felt in the room since Rajar's occupation had never fully gone away. "But drinking and I are old enemies."

"Rowdy years in your youth?"

Konar thought of his amma stumbling through their hut, cursing his appa's infidelity. "Something like that. Please"—he gestured to the cup in T'Vak's hand—"enjoy."

"Don't mind if I do."

Konar waited until T'Vak was two cups in before beginning his inquisition. He'd start with the simple questions, work his way to the scrolls, and then, hopefully, to Zavik.

"Is the kuza acquisition proving valuable?" he asked as he re-filled the backhander's drink. T'Vak's movements were relaxed, but his eyes were sharp as ever.

"Well enough. High Chieftain seemed more at ease tonight, especially with that scrawny blue nyrian tucked away safe. What was her name?"

Konar pursed his lips. "Kelsia."

"Right." T'Vak burped loudly. "Anyway, we haven't gained any ground, but the borders are holding fine and all that."

"Anything else?"

T'Vak drained the third cup and set it down with a clatter. "Successful smaller raids. I think they got their hands on some more of those slaver weapons, but they don't have many of the projectiles to go around. High Chieftain wants the riders to learn to use 'em. Thinks they'd be easier on bird back." He winked at Konar. "Council didn't like that."

"I imagine not." He followed T'Vak's gaze to the Beridian Moonlight and drew it closer to his chest. "Aside from a handful of raids and rescuing Kelsia, we've spent most of this war in a defensive stance. Was there any talk of an attack?"

"Big house man seems to think it's a good idea."

Konar rubbed his temples in frustration at the juvenile name T'Vak had assigned to Vahid. "Anyone else?"

"The northern chief with the impressive beard agreed. And the white cat. The others seem skeptical, and I don't think High Chieftain wants to take a side yet."

T'Vak held out his cup.

Konar reluctantly filled it halfway.

If Vahid, Gibrund, and Lumira wanted to make an offensive move, they could do so without Arkuun's and Orandus's war-riors—at least on a smaller scale. But Elaysia wouldn't want to make a decision that might distance her from half her army. If she waited until they were in full agreement, however, it would be too late.

T'Vak gestured at Konar's journal resting beside the bottle of Moonlight. "How's that coming along for you?"

"Stalled." He squeezed the doll in his pocket, wishing he could seek the person it represented for advice, but Karliah had made her choice long ago. As had he. "Something is missing."

"Like the rest of the scrolls?"

Konar regarded T'Vak with wary eyes. Perhaps a little more information would get him talking. "That's a glaring problem, yes. But not the only one." He retrieved the journal bearing the Prophets' emblem from the shelf nearest him, tracing his finger over the interwoven crescent moons on the cover. "The Prophets had a written code among them, one they used to explore their most heretical theories. Many think their knowledge and writings died along with them, but I discovered this journal in Az Zar many years ago."

"Whereabouts in slaver land?"

Konar swallowed. There was a fine line between gaining the backhander's trust and surrendering all the valuable information he had, and he wasn't going to cross it.

"It's been so long that I can't recall." He shoved the rest of the bottle toward T'Vak as a means of appeasement. "Living well beyond your natural lifespan does things to the memory."

T'Vak raised an eyebrow as he sipped directly from the bottle. "I'm sure Agaas appreciates your sacrifice."

Konar refused to acknowledge the sarcasm, instead cracking open the journal to one of the blank pages. "I've spent moon cycle after moon cycle experimenting with unique patterns and alphabets, hoping something would stand out. I've mixed languages, translated two of the scrolls, referenced every bit of writing in my possession, and it's all been futile. Sometimes, I wonder if..." He let his words trail off on purpose, smiling inwardly as T'Vak set the bottle aside. "Oh, never mind. Go on, enjoy the rest of your night."

"Wonder what?" the backhander pressed.

Konar derived some pleasure from putting on a show of re-luctance. "Call it an old man's premonition, but I sometimes wonder if Zavik did indeed find a third scroll. If so..." As he paused for effect the second time, T'Vak leaned forward, unde-niably intrigued. "What if there was something in it that finally allowed me to crack this code and learn the whereabouts of the remaining scrolls? The Prophet who hid them went to great lengths to do so, but she had to leave some hints and trails, especially knowing they couldn't be destroyed. She'd want them to fall into the right hands, were they to be found."

A deep-set frown blanketed T'Vak's face. "Zavvie boy found scrolls without a code. So did you, from what I've heard." He slid off the table and made for the door, bottle in hand. "Doesn't seem like the code is all that important."

Konar dropped all pretenses as rage flooded him. "Even if the code only leads to one scroll, it's still worth more than your waste of a life."

The backhander halted by the door. Konar couldn't tell if the man was amused by his loss of control or had actually taken offense. He didn't seem the sort to care about such things.

With a steadying breath, Konar stacked the journals and placed his hand atop them. "It'd be a shame if I moved on from this life before unlocking it. Especially with Zavik's fate unknown. I fear what might become of this world should the knowledge die with us."

"And the blood," T'Vak whispered.

It took all Konar's self-control to keep from grabbing the backhander and shaking him until he'd spilled every last drop of information. "The blood?"

T'Vak lifted his gaze from the floor. "Something Zavik would mutter in his sleep sometimes. 'The blood tells true.'" He swal-lowed, one hand on the door, the emotion in his voice undeniable. "Does that mean anything to you?"

Konar's eyes widened.

Why yes. That meant everything.

"Sit," he commanded, and the backhander obeyed. "I'm going to promise to spare your life, and you're going to tell me every secret you're harboring."

"Couldn't you just suck the blood of a baby rabbit or something to help you move faster?"

T'Vak didn't slow his pace as he tossed aside his latest insult like unwanted scraps, but he did take the time to peer over his shoulder and give Konar one of his vicious grins, a look that was caught somewhere between disdain and seduction. Whatever it was, it had no effect on Konar, other than to make him dislike the backhander even more. As if that were possible.

"Humans are ideal," he replied, slowing to catch his breath. Although the pain in his sides was almost unbearable, he was determined not to give T'Vak any more fuel for his fire. "Don't suppose you have a heart to spare."

"Lost the only one I ever had, unfortunately." T'Vak spun on his heel and strode toward Konar. "You're not missing much, though. Wasn't that big to begin with."

The swagger he exuded reminded Konar of the pirates his appa had associated with long ago. Perhaps T'Vak would've made a better pirate and son than he. The thought, coupled with his recent visitation from Karliah, made the ache in his chest hollower than ever. It was all he could do to keep his thoughts from his amma as well.

Konar adjusted his bag to his opposite shoulder, then resumed walking. "I've found people who say such things to have the biggest hearts," he said as he passed the backhander. To his surprise, T'Vak didn't contradict him.

They bore the rest of the journey in silence, trudging uphill, then down, needle-crusted topsoil turning up beneath their boots, the harsh coastal wind drying the sweat Konar had built up since departing Agaas. Even after innumerable trips west to Sunset Bay—his preferred sanctuary over hundreds of years—he still had to stop and appreciate the point where the army of trees parted for a horizon of water, where foliage and ocean became one. Nothing was more surreal than hiding in the depths of the forest and rich undergrowth while witnessing the untamed power of the waves. Only in their company did he feel truly seen; timeless beings out of touch and time, their presence too primal, their motives unclear. To know such a divine existence was to know peace. Of that, Konar was certain. He clung to the hope that, one day, his essence might be remade anew in the likeness of theirs. Offenses washed clean by the water. Wasted purpose transformed into a life-giving giant of fir or pine. The best and worst bits of him dissolved into something worthwhile, without his tainted memories to influence it.

T'Vak let out a shrill whistle as he came to stand beside Konar. "No wonder the All-Sovereign wants this place, eh? I never saw so much green before coming here." He planted his boot on a stump to adjust his laces, keeping his gaze on the ocean. "I think, if I could choose my death, I'd just have someone stab me in the back right here, while I'm looking at all this."

"That could be arranged."

"Anyone ever tell you you're a snarky old shit?"

"Probably the same number of times people have told you you're a cocksure alcoholic."

The backhander responded by uncorking his drink and raising it in a mock toast, which Konar ignored as he continued down the path, using his staff to steady his descent. When the first signs of sand began to intermix with the fallen needles and moss, he removed his boots and walked barefoot across the beach. It was never too hot to do so on the Apáasutai coastline—unlike his island home, back on Zelos. He found a spot where the golden sand turned a deep brown and seated himself there, backside on the dry spot and bare feet slipping into the wetted bits.

T'Vak eyed Konar suspiciously as he approached, his curved sword swinging at his hip. "Thought you said you needed something from the Igtheos place."

Konar feigned shock, following it with an exasperated groan for good measure. "Oh, how foolish of me. I wish you'd reminded me sooner. These hips of mine won't be ready for another hike for some time. If only—"

"Shut it." T'Vak drained whatever was left of his wineskin and dropped it into the sand beside Konar. "I'll get your gods-cursed boat, but I don't wanna hear another complaint about my person for at least a fortnight."

Konar raised an eyebrow.

"Fine." The backhander swatted his arm in the air as though he shooed a massive fly. "Give me a few days, then."

"One."

T'Vak trailed off in a sea of curses that soon blended in with the crashing of waves. Though a small part of him had wanted to retaliate against the backhander for a myriad of wrongdoings, that hadn't been his driving force in sending him to complete the task alone. No, what Konar really wanted—needed—was some uninterrupted silence.

It'd only been a few days since his suspicions had been confirmed, and that confirmation had unraveled a torrent of research and endless pacing about the library while T'Vak alternated bouts of sullen drinking with frenzied weapon sharpening. The truth of Zavik's blood was unexpected, at least in terms of what Konar had been trying to fish out of T'Vak. He'd known Zavik must have done something special to not only gain an audience with the shaktar, but to also walk away with scrolls—especially after Konar had tried multiple times himself, alongside Karliah, Rykahl, and countless other scroll hunters.

He just hadn't believed that special something was the lad's mere existence.

Considering his newfound knowledge, however, he was now all but certain Zavik was a descendent of Elize, and that she'd cursed or convinced the shaktar to guard the scrolls until someone of her blood requested access. A foolish risk, with there being no guarantee of her line's continuation, nor any way to determine the hearts of her future descendants. In fact, everyone thought her line *had* died out with her daughter, Zaria, over two thousand years ago during the Siege of Cadar.

But maybe she'd known. Known she would die, but her daughter, a nyman born of her and Igtheos, would survive with her mother's wit and her father's spirit in a city marred by war. That she'd not only survive, but thrive, and as one final slap in the face of their enemy, manage to conceive. And somehow, in the oppressed districts of a land that had never stopped hating humans, a near fully human boy was born with the same fiery hair of his ancestor.

And that boy, that single surviving thread to Elize, was in the clutches of those who could do him the greatest harm. Konar only prayed they knew, and that the knowledge might spare Zavik's life. For if three scrolls had been sealed with Elize's blood, what was to say the undiscovered two hadn't been?

None of that was what drove him to Sunset Bay, however. It was T'Vak's second admission that had been the real motivation. Once Konar had cracked the confession out of him regarding Zavik's betrayal by his former master and the exchange of the lad, alongside a scroll, for the merchant's amnesty, it didn't take long to scrape the rest of the meat from the shell. T'Vak hadn't come empty-handed to Agaas. The portions of the scroll Lanston had copied onto parchment were a wealth of knowledge, enough so that Konar made good on his promise to spare T'Vak's life, despite his confession of involvement in the abduction of what might be the single most important soul alive in Quinaria.

With that, Konar had set to work, scouring the other two scrolls in his possession alongside the newfound information from the pieces T'Vak had smuggled. Unfortunately, the old merchant's handwriting left much to be desired, and his notes were also choppy, often abbreviated, and riddled with personal asides. Still, Konar managed to glean some information, one of the most valuable bits being the alleged ritual for resurrection, a concept that intrigued as much as terrified him. Part of him hoped it wouldn't work without the scroll, that way he wouldn't have to hide it from the council or try to dissuade Elaysia and the Stormriders from using it. But such limitations were unlikely. Hadn't he survived for years using a ritual detached from its origin scroll? There was Karliah's theory, that it had to be done in the scroll's presence the first time, that there was a sanction in a Caman's touch, or whatever immortal being arose to bestow the gift.

It would take an attempted ritual to know for certain.

T'Vak disturbed Konar's musings with a needlessly loud groan as he dropped the yasaaka and its accompanying paddle onto the sand. He plopped beside it, breathless. "What's this fancy little vessel, then? Board or boat?"

"A little of both." Konar ran his hand over the well-sanded wood. He'd made it ages ago, back when he'd take it out on the ocean in search of the famed myrem settlements. It hadn't seen use in years. "It's called a yasaaka. They were common back on Zelos in my youth. We used them to fish and travel around or between islands."

"Uh huh." T'Vak's brow furrowed. "And you want to take this out there. Now."

They both looked out at the graying waves. Since T'Vak had departed half an hour prior, the sky had changed from a milky blue to a canvas of shadows. Though rain had yet to fall, the ocean already danced in anticipation, its white foam cresting and falling more rapidly as the shoreline crept closer to them.

"Yes," Konar said with genuine determination. "Yes, I do." He studied the sky for a moment to solidify his confidence. "I've seen enough storms in my time to know the dangerous ones. This will be mild at best."

"Sure it will."

But T'Vak offered his hand to help Konar rise, a gesture so disarming that he at first hesitated to take it. Had Zavik's betrayal truly triggered some empathy in a hardened criminal? Or was there something more there, a forgotten compassion that had simply been barricaded time and time again to shield from the pain?

The backhander looked warily at the yasaaka. "So we just stand on it?"

Konar removed his sandals and tossed them further up the beach onto a hill of boulders, then gestured to T'Vak's boots. "You won't want those."

The backhander grumbled as he threw his footwear in the same direction.

With practiced hands, Konar tied up his hair and eased the yasaaka into the water until the waves lapped over his knees. He held it in place as the tide tried to pull it in. T'Vak stepped gingerly into the waves, nearly losing his balance as he climbed atop the board, fingers and toes gripping the wood.

Konar fought back a smile as he recalled his own first attempt to balance. Only he'd been four, and the situation had been far less humorous.

"Take a few deep breaths to relax your muscles," he told T'Vak, as his amma had once told him. "Keep your weight centered and your movements calm. I'll sit in front and try to guide you as best I can."

The brief rest on the beach had done Konar good. He not only maintained flawless balance, but even found the strength to help paddle with his left hand. At first, T'Vak struggled to maneuver through the more aggressive waves nearest the shore, but once he broke free of the barrier, he moved to a standing position, which allowed him to cover twice the distance with the same effort. Konar directed him to follow the coastline, his destination more instinctual than a confirmed heading, for it'd been a long time since he'd ventured there.

Not so unlike the first time I found a scroll, he reflected.

Although he wouldn't find a scroll. Not in Neharem. He'd spent enough time over the past few hundred years scouring the land, and with three of the seven turning up in Orillon, deep within the belly of the Shaktar Caverns, Konar doubted Elize would've put the people of Neharem at risk. But she had come to their land and stayed long enough to do something of value.

Konar intended to find out what that was before making his eventual departure to Az Zar.

The sky remained gray but calm as the pair guided the yasaaka south, following the crescent coastline, cutting past rocky cliffs and areas otherwise inaccessible without a solid length of rope and obscene upper body strength. T'Vak's movements grew more fluid with each stroke, a talent Konar attributed to beginner's luck. He offered to paddle a few times—or attempt it one-handed, rather—an offer T'Vak declined, but kindly. As they passed the small island where Elaysia had found the stormbird eggs nearly two years prior, he pointed out the landmark. T'Vak seemed skeptical at best.

"Doesn't it strike you as odd that ancient eggs were just re-laxing inside a sea-weathered cliff too small for a full-grown stormbird to access?" he said with an air of arrogance. "And that they didn't die off as soon as the body heat left them? I'm no baby expert, but..." Konar peered over his shoulder just as T'Vak took a sip from a small flask he'd tucked inside his low-cut tunic. "Seems like babies need things." Another sip. "To survive. Even bird babies."

Konar prayed the backhander's tolerance for drink was as high as he thought; maybe higher. "Yes, T'Vak. Even fertilized eggs need 'things' to survive. However, stormbirds are an excep-tion." A gigantic wave coasted toward them, and T'Vak respond-ed by dropping to his knees to better brace for impact. Konar allowed his body to flow with it, hardly feeling the disturbance. "It's a widely held belief that all Great Beasts were as divine as the gods themselves. The deathstalkers, stormbirds, and seaser-pents all hatched from eggs, but no one knows how the first eggs came to be. However, it's been documented by countless scholars that Great Beast eggs can remain dormant for an undetermined amount of time, especially when under threat."

T'Vak groaned as another wave slammed into the yasaaka, but to his credit, he held strong. "So the little fuckers are survivors."

"Crass, but in essence, yes. Whoever laid those stormbird eggs—and I have every reason to believe it was Igtheos's bird, Araynia—could've used the assistance of her rider to position them."

"And we're paddling into the ocean because…" A hiccup interrupted the rest of T'Vak's thoughts, though Konar doubted he had anything of value left to say.

"Because," he replied, scanning the rocky coastline, "there was something in your stolen parchments that indicated the water held the secrets required to fulfill this quest. And not for the first time."

Another hiccup. "Come again?"

Konar reluctantly dredged up long-buried memories. "My family discovered the first of the scrolls many years ago, in a place not so unlike the one I'm taking you to. I've yet to fully uncover this sanctum's secrets, but I'm hoping your stolen bits of parchment will change that."

A look of intrigue flashed across T'Vak's face, triggering a flare of suspicion in Konar's heart. It was risky taking a treacherous man to a sacred place he'd never breathed a word about. But he needed T'Vak on his side for the time being, and the best way to do that was to convince the drunkard he was wholly safe in Konar's company.

And if things got out of hand, the sea was the best place to dispose of a body.

"No shit." T'Vak's tone was one of sincere astonishment. "You think there's a scroll here?"

Konar kept his attention on the water. "No. I think there's something even better."

A few yards ahead, peeking through the dissipating morning fog, towered a sheer cliff that looked entirely inconspicuous from afar. Even close up, one had to search for the narrow entrance cut into the rock face at water level, for the shadows played tricks. Konar motioned for T'Vak to angle the nose of the yasaaka toward the dark cut across the otherwise shale-gray cliffside.

If T'Vak felt unease as they drifted closer to the quickly approaching rock face, he kept it to himself, only letting out a whistle of relief as they coasted into the narrow cave entrance just large enough for a vessel like the yasaaka to access. Elize must've used something of a similar size, perhaps one of the Apáasutai's canoes or Ni'anko's fishing boats. Konar liked to think that over the years, he'd come to better understand—even idolize—her. And if he'd learned one thing about the prophetess, it was that her actions were understated, much as she'd been. So much divine intelligence wrapped in the unassuming flesh of a mortal human.

The cave inside was only a few feet longer than the yasaaka and lacking a single dry surface to set foot upon. Before T'Vak could make one of his sarcastic remarks, Konar retrieved a small nevethium crystal from within his tunic and held it up to illuminate the space. The cave ceiling was merely an extension of the walls, save for a small cutaway toward the top, a good twenty feet above them. It had been decades since Konar had made the climb, but there were still solid footholds, and the Daruk pickax he'd made T'Vak bring along would certainly help.

T'Vak's voice couldn't have been flatter as he probed Konar with a knowing gaze. "You want us to climb?"

"Well, *you* climb." Konar retrieved the rope he'd wrapped around his waist several times over before departing Agaas and passed it to the backhander.

T'Vak dropped it onto the yasaaka as though it were poisoned. "You're not serious."

A golden-shelled mussel made a popping sound as Konar pulled it off one of the many clusters along the cave walls. He used his dagger to crack it open so he could suck out the salty meat inside. "I'll hang on as best I can."

"Sure you will."

At first, Konar tried to help, but about halfway up, when his arm gave out and the rope cut into his midsection, he settled for trying to distribute his weight in a way that minimized T'Vak's strain. Still, the backhander spewed profanity after profanity, a thick sheen of sweat building on his face and taut arm muscles as they ascended one groan-filled heave at a time. When they reached the top, Konar freed his arm from T'Vak's neck long enough to help pull them over, then they sprawled face-first on the cool rock. Despite doing less than his share of the work, every muscle in Konar's body throbbed. He lifted a trembling hand to unfasten the knot and untangled his body from the backhander's, then crawled to the edge of the space so he could support himself against the wall.

The small cave hadn't changed since he'd first laid eyes on it. Back then, he'd been a younger man, still within the lifespan afforded to most nyrians. He'd successfully gained a reputable position in Agaas by becoming the high chieftain's primary advisor and was in the process of hollowing out the space beneath the library to conduct his most important research. He'd often gone on quests throughout Apáasutai territory, disguising them as sabbaticals to meditate and reflect—not entirely a lie. He would've gone mad without them.

But time and time again, he'd hit a wall. Discovered the location of a scroll only to be unworthy of retrieving it. Translated part of what he thought had finally been a cracked code, only to find it incorrect. Discovered a new use for nevethium only to find it unsustainable. On and on it went until the passion died during what should've been his final years. But then things overseas took a turn for the worse, and with an inevitable war on the horizon, he'd thrown himself into the one thing he'd known he could do with absolute certainty: protect. Protect the scrolls, protect his knowledge, protect the people of Neharem.

And protection meant ignorance.

He'd never forgotten about this place, however. Especially when he'd paddle out on his yasaaka and reminisce about simpler times. Times when his parents' love was at least predictable in their instability, and when Karliah looked up to him, believing their world would break were they ever separated.

Oh, Karliah, he thought, recalling the childlike wonder in her eyes, a look he'd never seen again after their discovery of the first scroll. *If only we'd known we'd break more than our world.*

"I fucking hate you," T'Vak growled.

The backhander dangled his feet over the ledge, his expression unreadable because Konar had closed his hands around the crystal in his grief. When he once again allowed it to illuminate the space, T'Vak looked as irritated as he'd sounded. He'd sobered up, if nothing else.

"I'm accustomed to people feeling that way about me," Konar said with a shrug.

T'Vak reached for his wineskin, then stared at it for a moment before tossing it aside. "Must be lonely. I wouldn't live this life over once. Definitely not ten times like you."

"Two times for my kind, actually. Though I understand your sentiment." Konar reached for the doll in his robes, only to find it missing. A burst of fear rippled through his gut until he remembered he'd purposefully removed it before departing Agaas. "Truthfully," he admitted, perhaps because he was too tired to keep secrets anymore. Perhaps because he knew, deep down, that loneliness was life's cruelest poison. "I've always known I was meant to be alone. It's the least I deserve. I survive it by constantly imagining my life as though the worst of my fears have taken place."

T'Vak grimaced. "Sounds comforting."

"It is, in a way." Konar forced himself into a standing position and followed along the wall with his hand. "When you can lie with the monsters at night and wake up the next morning broken but no less alive, you remove that fear. You've already faced it in your mind. When it comes, you're ready."

"You know this from experience?"

Konar's hand located the notch in the stone and lingered just above it. "I experienced it for the first time when my parents died, then again years later when I abandoned my sister. I've lost count since."

The backhander had no sarcastic quip to combat the heaviness Konar exuded between them, which was fine. He sought no comfort. The nevethium crystal hummed lightly as Konar held it up to his ear.

Then he plunged it into the small notch in the stone.

"Do try to remain calm," he said, stepping back.

"I'm not scared so easily, old man. I don't know how much Zavvie boy's told you about our past, but I, for one—"

T'Vak's words died on his lips as the cave trembled, sending small bits of rock raining down from the ceiling. Even though Konar had witnessed what was about to unfold countless times, the scholar in him practically clapped with anticipation as a swirled pattern, not unlike a maze, appeared on the wall where he'd inserted the crystal. It flashed as the ground split beneath them, revealing a set of lyvium stairs illuminated by the glow of nevethium.

"Are you summoning demons? Because I want none of that, thank you." T'Vak's tone was as strained as the nervous laughter that followed, and Konar felt that damning sense of pity that had ruined his plans time and time again. But perhaps pity was warranted. T'Vak was just a child, after all. What was a quarter century but a blink in a lifetime that had spanned over a thousand years?

"Not today, no." Konar lowered a foot on the stairs, then motioned for T'Vak to follow. "Today, we're revisiting history."

T'VAK

T'Vak hesitated at the top of the stairs. He hadn't consumed enough wine to prepare for whatever it was the crusty curmudgeon was about to ruin his day with. Sands of time—there wasn't a drink or drug out there that could prepare him for another day with Konar.

He'd known going back to Agaas would mean facing Zavik's mentor, hence why he'd filched Lanston's scroll scraps before departing. A little farewell punishment for his old master; a little peace offering for his new. What he didn't count on was just how much surrendering those parchments to the ancient nyrian would alter *his* future. T'Vak was fine with a little work and a lot of bloodshed, but the realm of the arcane wasn't something he liked to trifle with. Better to be ignorant and blameless. Better not to piss off something that could eradicate him with a breath.

And he was starting to wonder if Konar didn't have such powers himself.

"T'Vak." The nyrian's booming voice echoed from where he waited further down the stairwell. "I promise there's nothing dangerous awaiting us. It's smooth sailing from here on out." Konar laughed at his terrible joke, voice receding as he descended, not bothering to ensure T'Vak followed.

Well, T'Vak was a lot of things, but a coward wasn't one of them.

Was it not cowardly to abandon your friend in his time of need? his conscience whispered.

The pain in his chest, this sense of regret and longing, was foreign to him. Nearly suffocating. He leaped down the stairs, taking the curved steps two at a time, hoping the shock of what lay beyond was enough to stifle his nagging guilt.

Konar waited at the bottom, his stance the definition of calm and collected. T'Vak's attention didn't linger on him for more than a moment, however, for it was snatched away by what lay beyond the nyrian. Walls of lyvium covered the room from floor to ceiling, creating a cold, sterile presence despite the golden-green glow lighting a space roughly the size of the summit lodge. He searched for the nevethium source but found nothing that resembled the sacred crystal, save for the similarly colored tubes running about the walls and across the floor. They all converged on a single object in the center of the room: an altar. At least, that's what T'Vak took it to be, but it was unlike any architecture he'd ever seen. Geometric patterns covered the surface of its spider-like structure. Eight legs like curved pillars upheld three overlapping rings that formed something akin to a cage, inside which floated a translucent black crystal.

T'Vak rubbed his eyes. The crystal didn't cease floating.

A celestial pattern encircled the ground beneath the altar's legs. Some sort of moon cycle chart, each specimen showcasing a phase of the moons alternated with clusters of stars. It spiraled inward, concluding in a large circle directly beneath the crystal. It was shaped like a moon, but the markings on it suggested it represented something else. Directly above the altar, connected to the ceiling, was a thick metal ring the size of T'Vak's arm span. It, too, seemed to feed off whatever power coursed through the tubes, but it looked otherwise ornamental, if not bland compared to the rest of the structure.

T'Vak fought his urge to race back up the stairs. He didn't like how cold the room was. Didn't like how it smelled of nothing; how he could hear nothing but the hum of the crystal. And he couldn't shake the feeling he'd stepped into a different world.

One he didn't belong in.

"What is this place?" he said hoarsely.

Konar walked past him to the altar. He ran his hand over the cage surrounding the crystal, then looked back at T'Vak, almost gleefully. "I used to think it was a sanctuary created by Prophetess Elize, but I've spent enough time here to learn this is beyond any one person's handiwork, especially in the brief span of a human's life." The nyrian circled the altar, keeping his gaze firmly fixed on the crystal. "I began to wonder if it was a temple. A way for the ancient ones to feel closer to the gods. But then I asked myself, 'Why hide it away here? Why hide a place of worship at all?'"

T'Vak didn't realize he'd been backing up until his heel brushed the cool lyvium steps. "Because someone deemed it unlawful?"

"Perhaps. But religions are easily manipulated by those in power to serve their needs. This is something grander. Something evolved, yet ancient." The crystal flickered as Konar swiped his hand just above it, then faded again. "Ask yourself: what, by its very nature, is irreversible and uncontrollable?"

A lump had formed in T'Vak's throat, and no amount of swallowing would rid him of it. "A revolution?"

The ex-high elder wasn't impressed. "But what ignites a revolution?"

T'Vak shook his head. He could hardly think straight.

"A revelation." Konar answered his own question with no shortage of exasperation. "The realization that nothing is what you thought it was. That's what this place is to me. But, as far as your line of questioning goes, I believe it's a doorway."

"To where?" T'Vak's voice was scarcely a whisper.

"Perhaps the better question is, 'to what?'" The look in Konar's eyes sent chills rippling down T'Vak's spine. As he turned his gaze upward, his lips pulled back, revealing teeth that appeared unnaturally white in the odd light of the room. He held up his hand in warning. "Don't speak again until I tell you to."

T'Vak nodded.

"Requesting entrance," Konar said slowly in Ancient Nyrinian.

The tubes brightened in response, rapidly alternating from gold to green as the light migrated toward the altar in pulsating waves. It illuminated the moons and stars on the ground, then made its way up the geometric patterning of the altar, climbing higher, glowing brighter, until the crystal itself came to life with a burst of light. The sound of a stone door grinding echoed through the chamber. T'Vak raced up the stairs, reaching the top just as it thudded into place.

"No," he moaned, shoving against it to no avail. "Kona—"

"Welcome to bunker eleven," a monotone voice said in Ancient Nyrinian. T'Vak was no expert in the archaic form of the Vysilliam language—the modern form was hard enough—but he'd picked enough up from his time with Zavik to learn the more common bits. *"Please speak the access code."* The voice seemed to come from everywhere. It sounded feminine, but unnatural, almost as though it were a...well, T'Vak, didn't know. Did ghosts sound so detached? Was it the voice of gods?

T'Vak creeped back down the stairs, sword drawn, but the room remained empty—save for Konar. The ex-high elder stood beside the altar, which looked to be alive with the rotating cage of rings and the pulsating crystal inside. In his hand were T'Vak's smuggled parchments. He read something aloud, though T'Vak couldn't interpret the archaic dialect.

"Access denied," the entity's voice replied when Konar finished. It didn't sound angry, at least. *"You have two more attempts."*

Konar slammed his fist against one of the altar's legs. He studied the parchment a few moments longer, then tossed out another phrase—the meaning of which was still lost on T'Vak.

"Access denied. One attempt remaining. Would you like to enter an alternate form of identification?"

T'Vak's heart raced. He pointed the tip of his blade at the altar. "The fuck is it talking about? Is it a god?"

The glare that burned in Konar's eyes could have killed. T'Vak belatedly registered his error, but it was too late.

"Access denied. Zero attempts remaining. The emergency protocol has been activated and will remain in effect for eight hours. Shutting down."

Konar stepped away from the altar, and the crystal dulled in response. He turned to T'Vak, seething. "I gave you one command."

"You could've warned me."

"I thought I did."

They stood toe-to-toe, their foreheads perfectly aligned. As T'Vak's rage abated, frustration took its place. He hadn't intended to ruin whatever it was the old man was trying to concoct, but the bastard could've been clearer. No one ever took the time to explain things to him. Not Konar, not Lanston, not even Zavik. Everyone grazed over the finer details, leaving him with the simple tasks. Kill. Maim. Steal.

"I can handle sensitive information," he said, retreating to the foot of the stairs. "Just tell me next time, and I'll make sure whatever you need done gets done."

Konar's lips thinned, but he joined T'Vak at the stairs. "I am sorry. I should've told you. Trusting people doesn't come easily to me."

"Are we trapped in here?" T'Vak failed to keep the guilt from creeping into his voice.

Konar sighed. "Yes. At least for the next eight hours."

"Splendid." T'Vak reached inside his tunic for his wineskin. It wasn't there.

Of course not. Because he'd thrown it aside thirty feet up in some vain show of sobriety.

"For fuck's sake," he grumbled.

"Perhaps this might be a worthy substitute?" Konar held out his pipe and a small drawstring pouch, both of which T'Vak accepted reluctantly.

"I'd take anything right now," he admitted.

After several attempts, he successfully lit the pipe. He offered it to Konar first, a show of respect that seemed to please the old nyrian. When it was T'Vak's turn, the smoke burned his lungs and sent him into a coughing fit that drew water from his eyes. The sense of ease and clarity that followed, though…

Utterly worth it.

"So, how many times have you tried that?" he asked Konar, pointing at the altar.

The ex-high elder took another draw, then set the pipe on the stairs between them, smoke still curling up from its bowl. "I've lost count. I've tried dozens of words in all the languages I can speak, but nothing's worked. I'd hoped that there'd be something on the parchments you brought, but my attempts are all well-educated guesses at this point."

T'Vak studied the crystal through narrowed eyes. He didn't like how it came alive at will instead of constantly glowing like regular nevethium. Didn't like its lack of luster despite the way it hummed louder than any crystal he'd ever heard. It was unnatural, like the room that held it.

"What about that?" He gestured to the dormant crystal with his chin. "If that's the key to whatever you're trying to unlock, couldn't you just take it out? Maybe replace it with another nevethium crystal from Agaas?"

Konar shook his head. "I tried to remove it once. The shock it administered sent me flying into the wall. When I awoke, I couldn't move for hours, and when I finally left here, I didn't feel like myself for many moons. That is no ordinary nevethium. If it ever was, it's far removed from its original state."

"Ah." T'Vak genuinely tried to work his mind for a solution. Anything was preferable to sitting until his ass merged with the lyvium stairs. And really, it was the least he could do to make amends for causing their imprisonment. "What was the other thing it said to you?"

Konar's bushy white brows met at the center, then relaxed. "Ah, the bit about the alternate form of identification?"

T'Vak nodded and picked up the pipe. His second inhale only cost him half as many coughs. And the feeling was twice as good. He could get used to this.

"I've tried that route a few times," Konar continued. "A light, almost like that of the rippled auras in the northernmost skies of Morotôk territory, radiates from the crystal and slides over my body from head to toe. It always ends the same way."

"The same way it does when you touch the crystal?"

Konar nodded. He took another draw from the pipe, glaring at the altar all the while.

T'Vak thought of Zavik's allegedly sacred blood. "You think it would work on old Zavvie boy?"

"I'm not sure." Konar smoothed the coarse hairs of his beard. "Even if Elize discovered this place, I'm certain she didn't have a hand in its construction. She would've only been able to enter with a code." He retrieved two scrolls from the folds of his tunic and laid them out on the lyvium floor, unrolling and aligning them until their bordered edges seamlessly touched. "I'm certain there's something in the third scroll from the shaktar caverns, something that can only be seen when they're all together. Why else would she have hidden them as a trio when she went to such great lengths to split the rest apart?"

T'Vak shrugged and brought the pipe to his lips. Just one more inhale. Wasn't like he needed to be on guard in the cell he shared with the high lecturer himself.

As if to prove the point, Konar rambled on, once again in Ancient Nyrinian, with no encouragement on T'Vak's part:

"If it says...it must show us...translates the code...Prophets...might contain the code...activate this crystal."

Something Konar said made the crystal come to life again.

T'Vak retrieved his sword. Just in case. He searched the room with heightened focus, finding nothing but shadows in the breaths between the pulsating lights from the tubes.

"Gods, old man, can you not—"

"Hush, you fool! Look!" Konar pointed to the scrolls still spread out on the ground.

T'Vak was about to suggest the ex–high elder ease up on the pipe weed when a luminescent white writing danced on the parchments. The markings and coloring were the same on both scrolls, written above the permanent writings vertically instead of horizontally. They meant nothing to T'Vak, but the look in Konar's eyes suggested they meant everything to him.

The crystal flickered out as fast as it'd come, subjecting them to the remainder of their eight-hour confinement. That did little to dampen Konar's spirits as he practically danced about the room, clutching the scrolls to his chest and laughing a deep–bellied laugh T'Vak didn't know he was capable of making.

"I knew it," Konar cried as he rejoined T'Vak near the stairs. "I knew this room and the scrolls were tied somehow. Whether by the Ancient Ones or the Prophets remains to be seen, but at least this old man can die a little happier." He began rolling the scrolls back up with a gentleness most reserved for lovers.

T'Vak scowled at the scrolls. "Want me to give you three some privacy?"

Konar's violet eyes intensified. "I want you to help me retrieve Zavik and the Nyrinian scroll."

Nervous laughter tumbled out of T'Vak's mouth. "Us and what army?"

"No army. Our tactic would be discretion." With the scrolls secured back in their cases, Konar rose, fingers steepling together as he paced. "I know the layout of Cadar exceedingly well, including the inner workings of the palace."

"I thought you were from Zelos."

"Don't interrupt until I'm finished." Then, as if some ghost of a conscience still plagued the ex–high elder, he added, "Please."

T'Vak acknowledged it with a tight–lipped nod.

"I lived there longer than I did in Zelos, believe it or not. Though not by choice." Konar's attention drifted elsewhere, to some embittered memory. T'Vak knew the look. He'd looked that way himself more times than he could count. "If you can keep us safe, I'm certain we can locate Zavik and the scroll *and* smuggle them out."

"Right. Just the simple task of keeping us safe in Quinaria's most heavily fortified city when neither of us passes for locals. You'll walk us through the gates, pick the lock to Zavik's cell, snatch the scroll from beneath the All-Sovereign's arm while he sleeps, and if things start to go to shit—because they will—I'll just swing my sword overhead a few times to scare them away."

If Konar was rattled by the sarcasm, or the truth of the picture T'Vak had painted, he didn't show it. He simply stared, his body well-postured but calm, his jaw relaxed. This was, after all, a being who'd waited nearly a dozen of T'Vak's lifetimes to get the answers he sought.

And then he revealed the comment that forced T'Vak's hand.

"And wouldn't you like a chance to rectify your mistakes by rescuing him?" Konar said, almost absent-mindedly. "It might be your only chance to make it up to him. He very well may still go on hating you for the rest of his life, but—speaking from experience—I can promise you a life of misery and regret should you *not* take this opportunity."

A pit formed in T'Vak's stomach. He thought of Zavik and him as children, running through the streets of Munskahan, of the stolen scraps of food they'd shared. Of the days following the nights spent in service to Lanston's real source of wealth, the way they'd just sit together and watch the sunset, no need for words between them. Just someone who understood without judgment.

"I suppose you're right." He looked down so Konar couldn't pick up the pain in his eyes. "I'd rather die trying to make it right than live a long life knowing I've ruined his. He"—T'Vak fought for control over his voice, over emotions he usually subdued with drink—"he deserves better."

A warm hand gripped his shoulder. It was all he could do to hold back the tears.

"We'll right our wrongs yet, backhander." Konar's calming voice washed over him like a Gathering Moon breeze. "Or we'll die trying."

JAKKI

When Jakki returned to Tyrgraak with a badly wounded Uruuka and one bear shy of her mission, she feared the skulmor would kill her as soon as she set foot in the mountain; that Xaren, in his grief, would forfeit his life trying to avenge her, inadvertently killing Shadow by never finding a cure.

Several skulmor waited outside one of the tunnel entrances upon their arrival, the rising sun shielding their expressions. Jakki's jaw clenched. She could practically feel the Az Zarian boy's heart thudding against her back as Siren arced down, massive wings flared for landing. Xaren wouldn't release his death grip on her waist until she pried him free. When she glanced back at him as she heaved a blood-soaked Uruuka down from Siren and into the care of her pack, he didn't even acknowledge her. His eyes were vacant, his dried lips parted in a daze.

"Shadow?" she whispered, not wanting to ask, but knowing she had no choice.

"I can't feel him."

The words, so hollow and detached, pierced Jakki's core. She grabbed the arm of the first skulmor she found and yanked him toward her.

"The cure," she snarled. "What is the cure for brondite poisoning?"

The skulmor's yellow eyes widened. He glanced over his shoulder as if seeking permission.

"The bear's dead. Here's your proof." Jakki yanked the claw from her belt and hurled it into the cluster of wolves bent over an unconscious Uruuka. "Now give me the goddess's cursed cure!"

A few of them exchanged whispers, then one hurried back inside, its thick tail flaring behind it like a banner. The rest followed, carrying Uruuka on their shoulders. The she-wolf's head lolled to the side, revealing sharp fangs and the limp tongue caught between them. As she disappeared into the tunnel, Jakki offered a silent prayer that she might live. Her blood loss was substantial, but whether she'd been scathed or mortally wounded by the shieum projectiles remained to be seen.

The skulmor delivering the claw and Jakki's demands returned within a quarter hour, bearing a small bag slung over his brown furred shoulder. It was roughly the size of her head, but so lightweight that she had a fleeting fear it might be empty.

"It's medicine," he explained. "Mushrooms that fruit near brondite act as an antidote to its poison. Give it all to the stormbird now. We aren't certain of his weight, but this should be close enough to the right ratio."

"It better be," Jakki snapped. She almost felt bad, but then she remembered it was the skulmor's collective fault Shadow waited at the entrance to Everworld.

The skulmor pointed at the bag. "He'll need to consume this daily for at least the next fortnight. We'll provide more tomorrow during your audience with the dominants." He bowed his head, then disappeared back into the tunnel.

Siren soared with newfound energy toward the top of the mountains. Jakki glanced behind her more than once as they flew, fearful Xaren might tumble off in his grief.

But the boy held strong.

Shadow had chosen the tallest peak of the Lesser Quentarri Mountains as his deathbed: Mount Bongaiyo, named after the mother of all stormbirds. The wind howled, ruffling his splayed feathers that were tinged with an unfamiliar, icy-blue frost.

For a moment, Jakki feared they were too late.

But then Siren was hopping over, nudging his head with her beak, and his eyes shot open. Xaren tumbled down, crying the stormbird's name as he stroked his frost-bitten feathers, and Jakki hurriedly opened the sack. An assortment of mushrooms and mosses greeted her. She didn't allow herself to question their authenticity as she fed them to Shadow. The bird didn't resist. He even helped a little by tipping his head back in the swallowing motion common to birds.

Then they waited.

Relentless wind slammed into Jakki's back, sapping the last bit of battle heat from her limbs and chest. If Xaren felt the cold, he showed no signs of it. Jakki nestled against him, draping the edges of her cloak over his shoulders, pressing close enough to share what little warmth radiated from her. The absence of the parchment's powers left her body—as it always did—feeling far worse than before she'd summoned them. Her heart seemed to beat irregularly, and though she'd exerted ample energy running through the woods and fighting her way into the Atsukut en-campment, she felt as though she'd been starved for days.

She was about to suggest they take turns watching Shadow when the stormbird lifted his head. For the first time, his eyes seemed to focus on Xaren with clarity, and then the boy was gripping her arm and shouting in her ear even louder than necessary with the gusting wind.

"I can't understand you," Jakki said as a spark of hope ignited in her chest. "Stop speaking Zarith."

The look of wonder on his face said it all. Still, he took a breath to steady himself and took both her hands in his. "I said it's working, Jak! He's warming!"

Xaren was on Shadow in a heartbeat, his arms wrapped about the bird's thick, ebony neck. The tips of the stormbird's feathers still remained frosted, but there was a vitality about him again.

"He will live," Siren whispered in her mind. *"We will require more of the skulmor medicine, and the echoes of the ice poison will remain with him always. But he lives."*

Jakki lay down, almost lightheaded with relief. At that moment, everything was perfect in the world. No pain. No cold. No hunger, wars, or death. Just blissful, raw life.

She didn't notice the tears freezing on her cheeks until Xaren brushed them away with warm thumbs. "I owe you everything, Jakki."

"You owe me nothing. The fault was mine, and I've made right my wrongdoing. I can ask for no more." And she meant it.

"What about the skulmor?" Xaren asked.

Her outlook darkened as she recalled the command to see the dominants. She had no choice. They still controlled Shadow's recovery. "I'll go. Stay with Shadow. Siren will bring me to them."

"What if they take you captive again?" The concern in Xaren's eyes was so palpable that she had to look away.

"At least you and the birds will be safe." She approached Siren, who was already lowering her head for Jakki to mount. "Besides, I have things to bargain with now."

Xaren cocked his head, awaiting her answer.

"I killed their bear. I saved their warrior."

Siren screeched as she took to the skies, battling the wind.

"But most importantly," Jakki shouted, "I can wield their magic. They have no choice but to honor me."

Jakki felt less certain of her words as she approached the tunnel entrance into the mountains that had almost been her tomb. Only, unlike earlier that morning, there was no entrance.

Siren agreed to keep a distant watch as Jakki scouted the mountainside for an entry point. There was the same crooked tree leaning away from the mountain, the same ledge where she'd received instruction from Uruuka. She kneeled to inspect the ground, confirming her suspicions. Skulmor prints.

A sound like boulders grinding together had her whirling around, staff in hand. The opening had reappeared, and in it stood two hulking males rivaling Grokhion's ferocity.

There must be a release somewhere, she mused as they guided her into the mountain. She would search for it on her way out. Such knowledge could prove helpful in times of scarcity.

Her skulmor escorts didn't speak until they entered the spacious cavern with the statues and crystalline waterfall. When they did, it was mostly grunts and snarls, and it took her a moment to realize they were offering her food.

"Please," Jakki replied, her stomach growling. "And some for my...companion as well. If you have someone put it outside, my bird will take it to him. And we need more medicine. Shadow is healing, but—"

"Too many questions," the skulmor snapped in broken Nyrinian, his yellowed fangs bared. "The dominants will see you, but first, food and health."

Jakki didn't protest as they led her down to the lower levels, but as they walked, she asked, "What of Uruuka? Were her wounds beyond the reach of your healers?"

Her questions were met with silence. Fiery anger raged inside Jakki, making her forget her hunger and thirst and the gnawing emptiness of the parchment's magic that seemed to get worse with each use. "I'm familiar with the weapons the Atsukut used. If she was struck by one, there's not much time to—"

The snarl that emerged from the previously silent skulmor caused Jakki to leap back, fingers itching for the staff they'd once again taken from her. He bared his teeth in a predatory fashion, then prowled forward on all fours, his patched gray tail lashing.

Jakki kept a respectful distance from him for the rest of the journey, her boots absently sinking into puddles as she studied every inch of his body. Memorizing. Remembering.

He was not a friend.

Luminescent fungi weren't a scarcity in the skulmor caves; they covered nearly every surface of the cavern her escorts led her to. Some grew clustered in small bunches no larger than Jakki's hand, while others sprouted directly from the underground stream, towering well above her and the skulmor, their caps adorned with long, stringy tentacles not unlike those of the sea phantoms common to the reef near her island home. The tentacles seemed to sway despite the lack of a breeze, as if they danced to the high-pitched melody of the brondite.

Jakki reached to touch one, but the surly male snatched her hand away at the last moment.

"That one will kill you," he growled. "You have not grown accustomed to its toxins and wouldn't survive the night."

"Just show me the ones that will help Shadow," Jakki snapped back. She alternated her glare between both skulmor, ready to fight them with her bare hands, if it came to that. But then she felt a gentle touch on her shoulder. She glanced behind her, almost expecting to see Xaren, then sucked in a breath as she took in the golden-cream fur of Uruuka.

"I'll show her the ones that cure brondite poisoning," Uruuka told the other skulmor. "Thank you for bringing her to me."

"But Uruuka, she is not to be trusted," the patchy gray male said, fixing Jakki with a cold gaze.

"I will determine whose company I keep," Uruuka growled. When they didn't make a move to leave, she lunged at them, jaws snapping.

Whatever position Jakki's newfound skulmor companion held, it was greater than that of her escorts. They scattered, tails between their legs, but not before the surly male gave Jakki one final snarl.

"Don't mind them," Uruuka said, clutching her side. "We rarely converse with outsiders, and we never bring them below." The fight seemed to drain out of her as she spoke, and only then did Jakki see the red bloom beneath the bandage wrapped about her chest.

"You should be abed with your wounds," Jakki said, offering an arm to support her. Uruuka didn't refuse it. The weight of the skulmor was twice that of any nyrian, but Jakki did her best to stand strong.

Uruuka directed Jakki to an enormous mushroom sprouting low to the ground. It was as large as four cots pushed together, and when Jakki pressed into its spongy surface, she found it springy yet firm. Uruuka lay down, wincing.

"It's not as bad as it looks," she said after a few painful breaths. "Just a spearhead. And our medicine is good. We might not have much in the way of nevethium in these mountains, but our crystals provide their own healing methods by way of the mushrooms."

Jakki considered this. Nevethium, too, could be dangerous when misused. Perhaps it wasn't so unlike brondite after all.

"I'm happy to see you alive," she said, lying beside the skulmor. The mushroom was cool and soft beneath her, and already the pain in her joints seemed to drip from her body like melting ice.

Uruuka waited so long to reply that Jakki swore she'd fallen asleep, but then, with dutiful reluctance, she whispered, "I owe you my life."

"No," Jakki said quickly. She didn't need that, and certainly didn't want it. "I assume you've kept my secret of not killing the tulek bear, and for that, I thank you. Though I believe it's truly gone, I'm sure your leaders wouldn't be so gracious if they knew the truth." She propped herself up on her elbows so she could look into Uruuka's green eyes. "We're even."

The skulmor considered this. Jakki saw it in her eyes as she gazed up at the luminescent tentacles dangling from the ceiling mushrooms. She feared Uruuka wouldn't accept, or worse, that she-wolf would decide it was better to turn Jakki over to her dominants, removing any need for an exchange of services. But then her lips pulled back in a toothy grin, only slightly marred by pain.

"So we are. But I'll still consider you a friend, nyrian. If you'll have me."

Jakki stroked the velvety surface of the mushroom and nodded her consent. "I find myself in need of friends, as of late." She extended her hand to the skulmor. "Friend?"

Uruuka pressed her forehead into Jakki's hand, an exchange not entirely unlike what she'd witnessed of beridian culture from Lumira and Grokhion. "Until the moons rest forever," the she-wolf replied. "Now, let's harvest some more medicine for your bird. You've a ceremony to prepare for."

"What ceremony?" Jakki instinctively pressed the hidden pocket inside her cloak, the place she'd stored the parchment before returning to the skulmor stronghold.

The glint in Uruuka's eyes was unmistakable. "The one that makes you an honorary member of our pack."

It took great convincing on Jakki's part to summon Xaren down from the peak. He didn't want to leave Shadow's side, nor did he want to risk his life venturing below. Only when Jakki suggested she didn't feel entirely safe without him did he comply. Even then, he insisted on remaining armed, which meant he wasn't allowed in the inner sanctum occupied by the dominants. She conceded to that. All she wanted was for him to get proper rest and nourishment, anyway. He couldn't spend the next fortnight freezing on a peak.

Jakki had no need for anyone's protection. In fact, she'd realized soon after her interaction with Uruuka that she'd achieved a deity-like status among the skulmor—with a few outliers like her escorts, of course. She wasn't certain if the newfound respect had more to do with the assumed death of the tulek bear or her use of their sacred parchment, but everywhere in Tyrgraak she went, she drew gazes, summoned whispers, and even garnered the occasional gift of meat or fungi.

Olunkah Murtive, they called her.

"What does it mean?" Jakki asked Uruuka, as they approached the sanctum of the dominants. "Slayer of monsters? Magic user?"

"Fate-shaper," the she-wolf replied. "It means the gods have bestowed some of their life-altering powers upon you, allowing you to shape outcomes that were once set in stone."

Jakki puzzled at the explanation. The way she saw it, everyone held the power to shape their futures. But she'd let the skulmor think what they would. No need to lessen her position in their eyes; not when she'd literally fought for her life and those of her companions to get it.

As they approached the rune-covered doors barring entrance to the dominants' sanctum, the skulmor on guard lowered their heads. Jakki looked to Uruuka for insight on what greeting to return, but the she-wolf just walked through the doors without casting so much as a glance at them. It felt odd to stride by with no acknowledgment, but then again, it wasn't any different from how her own chief mother carried herself about their island.

The blue flames within the sanctum weren't lit, creating a tomb of near darkness save for the brondite altar near the dominants' thrones. As the doors shut behind Jakki and Uruuka, extinguishing the external light, glowing markings slowly pulsed into clarity like stars in the night. The skulmor in attendance had painted their fur with some sort of luminescent paste, accenting their necks, backs, and tails, as well as encircling their eyes and trailing down their snouts. Jakki looked down at her own near-naked body and found the paint Uruuka had slathered on her consisted of the same ingredients. Markings like the ones found on the skulmor architecture and on the parchment covered her stomach, running up and down her thighs, calves, and forearms, banding around her upper arms, and painted on her face. They'd drawn her long hair back in a tight tail—not unlike a skulmor's—and strapped to her hip was the tulek bear claw. It'd been fashioned into a dagger, the hilt made from a cool metal she didn't recognize.

As she drew nearer to the thrones, low, slow drums began echoing through the chamber. A cold light, almost like a moonbeam, suddenly streamed down, bathing the brondite altar. The sconces surrounding it came alive with blue fire, sending chills down Jakki's spine. She'd tucked the parchment into the waistband of her newly gifted fur skirt, and it pulsed against her skin the closer she drew to the altar. Almost as if it wanted to be there.

The dominants approached the altar at the same time as she and Uruuka. They wore cloaks of nytak skin embellished with tails and bones of other creatures, and Jakki guessed they must've easily weighed thirty pounds apiece. She kept her gaze low, as instructed by Uruuka, and watched as a thin adolescent approached the dominants with a brondite bowl filled with long-stemmed mushrooms flecked with luminescent violet. The female dominant retrieved four, then held them before the male's snout for him to inspect. Meanwhile, the drums grew louder, the air thicker, and Jakki's eyes wider.

A gnarled speech rose from the male dominant's lips. He plucked a mushroom from the female's hand and held it up high. The female took one and held the remaining two out to Jakki and Uruuka. Jakki took hers tenderly, twisting the thin stem between her thumb and forefinger. Uruuka warned it would bring visions, but not the kind she'd expect. Emotions, but unlike the ones she'd felt. And the greatest awakening she'd ever known. It would be near-instant, the she-wolf had warned. Be ready. Be open.

Jakki popped hers into her mouth along with the others, wincing at the bitter, moldy taste. As she chewed, the dominants broke into low howls that vibrated the cavern walls. After a few moments, the rest of the skulmor in attendance joined in, their howls a symphony, a prayer.

Jakki had never beheld something so enrapturing. At first, she was content to listen. But soon she found herself adding to the night music with her own cry as her heart pulsated with a deep sense of belonging she'd never experienced, not even with her own tribe. The roots of the mountain ran deeper, uniting everyone and everything it touched. Not even the boundaries of species mattered any longer. She was as much rock as nyrian, as much a goddess as a moon. There was a profound sense of interconnectedness, as though an invisible web tethered every single being's soul to all the rest.

She found herself on the cave floor, leaning against a skulmor she couldn't quite place—not caring that she couldn't. The ground rippled around her, shifting like water, laughing and dancing.

See? it seemed to say. *It is all the same. We are all the same.*

The howling ceased along with the drums, but from somewhere in the sanctum, Jakki heard a distinct singing, almost like chimes. It was the sound she'd first heard when passing the altar before battling the tulek bear, but now it was louder and longer, its melody without question. She didn't know if it was the crystals or the tentacle mushrooms. Maybe both.

Or perhaps it was the song of Quinaria; an enchanting melody that had always been there for those willing to listen.

And she'd finally torn down enough barriers to hear it.

ZAVIK

"We'd be twice as far ahead if you worked half as much as you slept."

Yikos accompanied her insult with a yank of the sheets, exposing Zavik's curled frame. Cool morning air creeped over his body, which—in his defense—was still covered with his palace-dictated clothes from the day prior. Contrary to the ghastly old nyrian's claim, he had *not* been sleeping excessively. In fact, Zavik's rest pattern would be considered insufficient by most. It wasn't his fault she was ancient and in pain and prone to taking cat naps scattered throughout the day instead of sleeping several hours straight, like a sane person.

He opened his eyes to an irritatingly sunny morning and fumbled for his seers on the table next to his bed. The palace had issued him a pair far superior to the ones he'd constructed for himself, though he liked to think he could've done an equally impressive job had he access to such fine materials. The glass had improved strength and enhanced quality, while the frames were made of lyvium with silk-wrapped arms that fit comfortably around his ears. However, what he enjoyed most were the smaller lenses he could easily slide over the primary ones to read finer prints and capture even the tiniest details. That little modification, he'd added himself. Well, with the guidance of an impatient Yikos. She liked to remind him of it daily, lest he forget how much he owed her.

"We'd be twice as far ahead if you moved a little faster," Zavik replied, as he swung his legs out of bed and pressed his bare feet to the plush carpet beneath. The room he'd first awoken in turned out to be his permanent lodging—a space shared with his nyrian elder with the piercing golden eyes. It might have been awkward, were she not ancient and easily one of the most unsettling people he had the pleasure of working in close quarters with.

Yikos's eyes narrowed as she drew up the hood of her cloak. "You'll have to break your fast in the arcanum."

It was the same thing she'd told him every morning for the past fortnight, to which he always replied, "Nothing I'm not used to."

And then they'd glare at each other all the way to the doors, where one of them would rap twice, signaling the guards without that they were ready to be escorted.

A particularly unpleasant one answered that morning. His golden skin gleamed in the light of the nevethium sconces lining the hallway, but he offered no smile. Not even a softening of the lines formed around his mouth and eyes.

"You're late," he growled. His partner, a shorter but no less bulky (or armed) nyrian standing beside him, echoed the sentiment with his crossed arms and permanent scowl.

"Our apologies to His Holiness," Yikos said, somehow managing to convey her apathy without being perceived as insulting.

Zavik didn't say a word. Never did. He learned the first day that communication with anyone aside from Yikos resulted in a worsened outcome, be it a genuine threat or merely a worsened mental state.

They followed their escorts down the hallway, past doors that were never opened and portraits that always frowned. There was never much life about the palace as they ventured to and from their chambers. Maybe the occasional run-in with a servant bearing a tray full of steaming buns, or a side-eyed glare from the dwarf who always seemed to be everywhere with little predictability to his timing or location. Zavik swore the bastard was watching him, perhaps on special order from the All-Sovereign.

Unlike most of the rooms, the arcanum was accessible by only one door and situated in the palace's absolute center—at least, according to Yikos. It was one of the oldest chambers, along with the library, and had withstood the test of time by surviving the structure's transformation from a place of learning to a palace, as well as the devastating fire that accompanied the Siege of Cadar.

Yikos and Zavik waited outside the door while the guards maneuvered into the first stage of unlocking it. Whoever had built the arcanum secured it with a mechanism unlike any he'd ever seen. Various carvings and symbols foreign to Az Zarian architecture decorated the arch surrounding it, and with no visible handle, it gave the illusion that the stone door was purely ornamental. Taking up most of its center were three rotatable rings, each nestled within the previous, and each one featuring the moons in different phases. The guards always made them turn the opposite way as they slid the puzzle into alignment—an unnecessary precaution, for even though Zavik didn't doubt he could crack the pattern given ten minutes alone, he couldn't employ the final step of inserting both three-pronged, talon-shaped keys at opposite ends of the door and turning them simultaneously, as the guards seemed to do.

The groan of the mechanism working drew his gaze to Yikos. She ignored him, like usual, but they'd spent enough time together now that he perceived the slight softening of the wrinkles around her eyes as something akin to acceptance.

"We'll be back with the midday meal," the apathetic guard said as his partner shoved them into the arcanum.

Zavik didn't bother with questions, for he had none left they could answer. No, he wouldn't be allowed leave to relieve his bowls in private—there was a pot in the room for that. No, they wouldn't pass along any of his questions to their superiors unless Yikos deemed it necessary—which she never did. No, he couldn't have a stroll about the grounds during the day—only nights, and only for fifteen minute, heavily escorted, intervals. And no, he wasn't to be briefed on any matters regarding Neharem, Orillon, or anything of actual importance. If it wasn't relevant to his work, it wasn't approved.

Oh, and should he pull a stunt like he did in his first two days (also known as refusal to take part in the empire's plans), they'd employ T'Vak to murder Elaysia's twins. Or her. When he'd suggested even T'Vak couldn't stoop so low—a claim he wasn't entirely certain of—he was informed they had multiple people in Neharem willing to perform the duty. To prove it, the dwarf, Dalgus, had shown him tuross messages exchanged between Rajar and the All-Sovereign, rendering him complicit in the attack on Agaas the day of Elaysia's induction, among other offenses. Az Zar had its teeth sunk in Neharem's neck for longer than Zavik had been alive. If he had any reason to doubt they were behind the Lawful Dominion, such suspicions were now crystallized, which summoned new fears of just how much they were helping Raynar's campaign. What weapons had been distributed? Were they lending soldiers as well as aid? And did Raynar so foolishly think he'd get the reward of ruling Neharem, as they'd likely promised him?

"You going to stand there all day?" Yikos muttered as the door sealed behind them.

"Perhaps I will. I did more than my fair share of the efforts yesterday." Zavik made his way to the octagonal table made of sun-blood wood that served as their shared workstation. He began sliding half-full vials and wells of dried ink out of the way as he listed his achievements. "Determined the right materials needed to manipulate deathstalker shells into armor. Adjusted the firing mechanism for the shieum to prevent future deaths of our beloved soldiers. Convinced the guards to allow us moskuto for performance enhancement." He made a show of retrieving the cast-iron pot from the fireplace beside their workstation and offered the first cup to Yikos. "Am I forgetting anything?"

Yikos wrinkled her nose but clutched the steaming mug greedily. Even she could find nothing negative to say about it.

"And one more thing," Zavik continued, not ready to re-linquish her torment quite yet. "I made you a salve out of those—how did you put it? 'Pagan herbs'? Slept better last night, did you?"

The scowl might as well have been permanently fixed to Yikos's face, so rarely did she soften it. But one sip of the moskuto, and there the ghost of a smile was. "I never said pagan. Pagan would imply I believed in a proper religion to begin with, or any religion at all, for that matter."

Zavik smirked as he dumped his meager ration of syrup into his moskuto. He was fully aware he'd misquoted her. That was half the fun with Yikos: making her explain things repeatedly and watching her limited patience slip away like the sands in the hourglass fixed to the center of their workstation.

"But yes, your tribal remedies seem to have relieved some of the pain in these ancient joints, and for that, you have my respect." Yikos took another sip, then set her mug aside in favor of the tome adjacent to it. "It's not my respect you need to secure, though."

All the lightheartedness Zavik had garnered from exchanging jabs with Yikos seeped out in an instant. No matter how much he grew to enjoy her company or appreciated the wealth of resources at his disposal, it didn't change the circumstances under which such benefits occurred. He was a prisoner, one wrong action away from causing the death of his loved ones, working to unveil discoveries that would be used to tear the world apart.

No pressure.

Zavik unrolled the plan he'd first started working on in Neharem. T'Vak had been nice enough to pass it along to Lanston, who'd been thoughtful enough to send it along with Zavik's pirate escorts. Between the work he'd done in Orillon and his time spent studying The Scroll of Crystals in Neharem—alongside Yikos's years of research—they had a working theory in place. But that's all it was. A theory. Just like Yikos's crazed rantings about the Trimoon Ascendance, her favorite (and entirely speculatory) celestial phenomenon that had little more than her scattered notes backing it. The All-Sovereign didn't care about any of that, though. He wanted new weapons, better armor, and above all else, nevethium-powered means of conveyance.

Or their heads.

"I don't know how else to look at this," Zavik groaned as he ran his fingers through the remnants of his hair. They'd seen to it most of his curls were sheared upon arrival to better conform to the neat look kept by those in the capital. He missed the weight of it, the way he'd gotten used to hiding behind his locks like a mask.

Yikos didn't glance up from her tome. "Keep working at it. Something will reveal itself to you. It always does."

"Does it?" Zavik's fingers began to shake; the result of too much moskuto on an empty stomach. "Then why haven't you figured it out yet? You're what, four hundred years old?"

"Four hundred and twenty. Only been at it the past few, though. The All-Sovereign doesn't like people knowing much for long. We have a deadline for success, and if you don't have the answers..." She drew a gnarled finger over her throat.

Zavik grabbed his own.

"Each of us is apprenticed to the former scholar, and once your knowledge supersedes theirs, it means their end is nigh." The look she cast upon Zavik was one of indifference.

"I'm sorry," Zavik said, realization washing over him. He didn't want to replace her. He didn't want to be part of whatever havoc the All-Sovereign intended to wreak upon Quinaria. "What was your life before this?" He hoped moving the focus to his mentor would ease some of her pain.

"Does it matter?" The lengths of Yikos's robe dragged along the stone floor as she circled the room, pausing every so often to inspect a vial or readjust one of the books on the shelves. "We are but insects waiting to respond to our master's call. I've never been so foolish as to believe life was mine."

Perhaps that was where Zavik had gone wrong.

They worked the rest of the morning in silence, hardly glancing up when the guards entered to bring them the midday meal and exchange their waste pots for fresh ones. Sometimes they'd both sit, hunched over their various tomes and scrolls, ink-stained fingers poised over their quills, should inspiration strike. Other times, they'd take turns pacing about the room, perhaps stopping to examine one of the many crystals entrusted to them or to slip a fragment of deathstalker under the magnifying glass to test how it held up against certain elements. Every so often, Zavik would simply stop to admire the most complete map of Quorath he'd even seen. It had been carved into an orb the size of a large gourd and made from a wood he couldn't quite trace the origin of. While he'd long since speculated the world was round due to how shadows fell, or how ships seemed to emerge from beneath the sea, the arcanum's map confirmed his theories and suggested the knowledge wasn't as newfound as he'd believed.

But as it drew near the time the guards were to collect them, the gnawing uncertainty of his future and Elaysia's choked any pleasure out of his observations. He glanced at his sketches for a flying vessel and fought the urge to tear them up and toss them into the fire. No matter how they threatened him, he couldn't make sense of something senseless. The plans for the underwater contraption were even more disjointed. These he did snatch up, dimpling the parchment beneath his clammy fingers.

"I can understand the military advantage of a flying vessel," he told Yikos, awakening her from her doze. "But why does the All-Sovereign want to go below?"

Her parchment-thin lips practically vanished in her frown. "You said yourself there's a wealth of nevethium below, according to your scroll back in Neharem. My research says no different."

Zavik dropped the plans in front of her as if to wash his hands of the matter. "And that's all?"

She scooted them aside with the tip of her quill. "Speculation of a scroll abounds. You've already found one of myrem make. Why not another? It would be one of the best guarded in Quinaria. He thinks it might be the one that binds them all."

"Be it so, what he wants is impossible." Zavik retrieved more sketches from his station and held them up to the light of the nevethium sconce. "I don't know how much Beridian Moonlight he's been consuming to believe this is anything more than a fever-dream, but I'm telling you it's not happening. Not in your lifetime, and certainly not in mine. There's simply no way to harness the energy from the crystals and turn it into a source that lasts long enough to give something life. Every time we successfully manipulate it, the result is short-lived and highly unsustainable. We wouldn't even be able to store enough crystals to travel anywhere worthwhile at the rate they'd expire. Just look how much nevethium the arkthanax consume." He thrust the plans for the monstrous drilling mechanism into the air, and when he received no response, glanced over his shoulder to find Yikos's eyes closed again. It took the better part of his self-control to keep from shouting. "Did you hear anything I just said?"

Her eyes fluttered open. "I never stop hearing you, even in my deepest slumbers. One of the less desirable effects of aging." She reached for her unfinished moskuto, which she usually made last throughout the day, and took several sips. "The All-Sovereign wouldn't believe it was possible if his awskada whore didn't think it was, and she doesn't place her faith lightly."

"Then we need to know what makes them so certain this can transform from theory to reality."

A sickly cackle emerged from Yikos's throat. "They'll never tell us."

"Then they'll never have these vessels. I can't create light if I've only ever known darkness." Zavik was surprised at the disappointment taking hold of him. Did he actually want this just as badly?

Yikos shoved a parchment and quill into his hand faster than he thought she was capable of moving. "Write that down," she rasped.

"Write what down?"

"Everything you just told me, in those exact words. Especially the bit about not being able to create light if you've only known darkness."

"But you said—"

"Abyss take what I said. If you convinced me, you might stand a chance reasoning with the All-Sovereign."

Zavik's excitement showed through the sloppiness of his penmanship as he hurried to do just that. Not only did the premise of hidden knowledge tantalize him, Elaysia's and the twins' lives depended on it. When he finished, Yikos folded it and secured it with her seal.

"There." She placed it on the table, right in the line of sight for when the guards entered the arcanum. "If you've any gods, best pray to them now."

A memory of T'Vak outside the Shaktar Caverns flickered in Zavik's mind. "Funny. A friend said the same thing to me at a precipice of equal importance."

"What did you tell him?"

"That I thought we were alone."

"And now?"

Zavik glanced around the room most didn't know existed, nestled inside a palace he thought he'd never set foot in, protected within a country he spent the better part of his life denying citizenship to. All he knew for certain, in that moment, was how uncertain he was of everything.

"I don't know," he replied honestly. "And I'm alright with that."

Yikos patted him on the back, a first in terms of both support and physical touch. "That's the ideal place to be, seeing as how this request will either grant us the wisdom our predecessors so craved or find us dead within a day."

Whether persuaded by Zavik's words or merely overcome by desperation, the All-Sovereign not only granted the request, he also coordinated an expedition for his scholars to witness whatever knowledge he held firsthand.

At least, that's what Zavik and Yikos were told. They hadn't charmed His Holiness so much as to deserve an audience with him, a condition Zavik was perfectly fine accepting as he didn't want to dedicate an entire day to making himself physically and spiritually worthy, as dictated by law. Instead, they were given one day to prepare themselves for the journey, packing any equipment or notes they thought might be of use. A private squadron was to accompany them to their unknown destination, and exactly one night after Yikos had handed off the note, they found themselves blindfolded and transported in an enclosed litter—the type used by highborns for traveling through less desirable districts. By the time they stopped to let Yikos relieve herself, they were well past the limits of Cadar with the Tsabian Desert spanning in all directions. They waited at a makeshift campsite just long enough to stretch their legs before a soldier rode up, leading a small herd of horses, at which Yikos scoffed and made a comment about refusing to subject herself to such harsh conditions at her age. If the soldiers overheard, they didn't care.

Zavik had never been the best at tracking something as menial as days when in the throes of research, and though the mission had a life-threatening quality about it, he still found time folding in on itself. Each day was much like the one before it: the terrain unchanging, the soldiers stoic, the food rubbish. He wasn't even allowed access to his journals when traveling. Staring off into nothingness it was. That, or attempting to engage in conversation with Yikos in between her bouts of moans and groans. It was rarely rewarding, but it helped to pass the time.

The further into the red desert they delved, the harder packed the ground became. Villages grew scarce, greenery more so. Zavik was thankful they'd brought ample rations to last the journey, for game was non-existent, save for small rodents scurrying between shrubs and the infrequent hawks swooping down to catch them. He didn't even witness a single sandcat. According to his research, they'd once been Az Zar's apex predators alongside the deathstalkers. Their absence certainly meant nothing good for the land's future, just as the extinction of the laazah, Az Zar's native herd creatures that had acted as the nation's primary source of meat in centuries past, had forced the people to turn to alternative protein sources. In fact, he was certain that was what drove Az Zarian acquisition of the human lands to the north and east. Not just new labor, but a wealth of resources.

And Neharem was next.

The chill that ran through Zavik's spine at first sight of the Caman Altars was a sensation he'd only experienced once before, at the Shaktar Caverns. Both sites carried a sense of the arcane, of the ancient, the timeless, and—dare he say it—the supernatural. According to Elaysia, the stairs leading up to the plateau were guarded by nothing other than two crumbling statues ten times the size of a human, along with smaller, more grotesque creatures perched along the path. If that was true for her, the All-Sovereign had since increased security measures. Several sentries stood watch beneath the statues, blocking the entrance to the ghost of a path leading to the stairs. Though they shared a similar look with the standard military, they wore white robes instead of uniforms, along with various pieces of lyvium armor protecting their arms, legs, and chest. The fiery eye of Mavet was embroidered along the sides of their hoods, and shrouded beneath were lyvium masks hiding their faces—eyes included.

Zavik lowered his gaze as they were ushered beneath the statues and along the path. Due to his now mostly sedentary lifestyle, he was ready to beg for a rest halfway up the crumbling staircase. But Yikos came to his rescue, insisting they stop on her behalf, else she'd die right then and there—and what would the All-Sovereign think of that? They sat knee-to-bony-knee, gnawing on jerky and staring off at the sea of red. It was actually beautiful, Zavik decided. From afar. He tried to imagine rolling fields of green speckled with flowers, rich with thick-branched trees, fertilized by herds of laazah, and crawling with sandcats which, he supposed, hadn't always been called that name.

He couldn't visualize any of it, though. Az Zar was so far removed from its original setting that he doubted anyone could. Even the oldest texts were nothing more than speculations of what it'd once been, based on the surrounding patches of land to the north and east that had yet to see utter annihilation. From where he sat, it almost seemed like death and decay spread from the Altars themselves; an observation that only slightly dampened his desire to go in. If this was the root of the disease, then this was the area that needed the most observation.

The guards jabbed the noses of their shieums into Zavik's and Yikos's backs, signaling the end of their respite. After a final, painful push, they stood at the top of the stairs, red-faced and panting. Zavik felt the beginning of a sunburn setting into his skin and sought shelter within shadows cast by the remnants of ancient structures. The guards didn't let him linger long. Yikos had stopped beside a cluster of unsettling statues situated at the front of what appeared to be an open-air temple of sorts—one not entirely unlike the illustrations he'd seen of Mavist temples. Agony and aggression contorted what remained of the statue's weathered faces, and despite their dormancy, Zavik got the sense they were, in fact, alive. Thankfully, the guards didn't entertain Yikos's fancies for long either, and they soon found themselves led through the temple courtyard and into one of the more intact structures.

Dust drifted through the air and had accumulated on all surfaces inside, but it was otherwise clean, free of filth and debris. Any creature that had once made a home there had long since died out, and all the accompanying signs of life, such as fecal matter or the scent of oils, had vanished as well. It was almost alarming how little it smelled like anything. Before Zavik could get a good lay of the room—the design of which was far too spacious to be anything but a gathering hall—a pair of altar guards began tinkering with a door in which was inset a puzzle, its make akin to the one barring the arcanum back at the palace.

Zavik nearly cried out with glee as he spun to inform his master, but one look from Yikos reminded him of the company they kept. The puzzle door clicked and whirred as they approached it, then groaned open, stirring the dust as a breeze rippled through the passageway. Darkness swallowed the path leading beyond the threshold, likely arcing down and around into the depths below.

"All yours," one of their Az Zarian military escorts grumbled, and then more rough hands were grabbing Zavik's shoulders and shoving him into the tunnel.

"My research," he protested, as the altar guards blocked his view of the departing soldiers. A satchel hit him squarely in the face. He would've fallen had Yikos's spindly, yet surprisingly strong, hands not planted on his back just in time.

"You better hope nothing in there is broken," she hissed at the soldiers.

"You'll make do if it is," came the curt reply. "Don't think His Holiness much cares about your trinkets."

The descent was steep but smooth, with a cool metal handle providing guidance until a green glow illuminated their path further on. Zavik wasn't certain if the walls were actually getting narrower the deeper they delved, or if it was just the effect of going underground. Either way, he already hated the feeling of being trapped.

Nevethium sconces appeared along the path, highlighting geometric markings on the walls and ceilings that were unlike those of any civilization he'd studied. So flawless were their forms that Zavik questioned whether a mortal hand, no matter how steady and skilled, could've carved them with such precision. One glance at Yikos's wide eyes and slack jaw told him she too was taken aback by the intricacy of the design.

They passed several places where the tunnel branched off, but the guards forced them onward, wending further and deeper, Zavik's hands growing rigid with cold as the temperature dropped with their descent. There were no sounds but the echoes of footsteps and Yikos's labored breathing. As they walked, Zavik recalled Elaysia's account of the horrific scene she'd witnessed at the Caman Altars, the location of which may have very well been accessible by a tunnel they'd already passed. She, along with the beridians, Jörd, and the traitorous Davier, had stumbled upon some obscene ritual with a handful of bone-masked priests, one involving blood and cannibalism. His stomach turned at the thought, and he did his best to guide his mind to the mysteries that awaited them.

When, what felt like an eternity later, they finally arrived at their destination, Zavik stumbled back into their escorts, his heart pounding in his chest. They'd halted outside a door—one he could've gone through the rest of his life without seeing and slept better for it. For it didn't look so much like a door as it did a gateway to the damned. A prison for immortals.

It was the eyes that troubled him the most. They glowed a rich golden color that flickered like fire and seemed to follow him no matter where he stood. The face was equally disturbing, with its elongated, skeletal form and spiked antlers that creeped up the door and onto the ceiling. He couldn't help but notice its similarities to the extinct laazah—albeit a sinister interpretation. According to surviving documentation, the Az Zarian version of the nytak had been larger and fiercer than their Neharem cousins, but he'd never seen them depicted so...ferociously. Carved hands grasped at the doorframe, appearing as if desperate victims struggled to escape from the mysterious entity locked inside. There were clawed hands of the beridians and skulmor; well-formed fingers of the nyrians and humans; the thick joints of the shaktar and the webbed phalanges of myrem.

Zavik jolted as the door split down the middle horizontally, half sinking into the ground while the rest disappeared into the ceiling. He glanced over his shoulder in time to see a guard removing a gloved hand from somewhere in the wall. He made note of it, then dared the first step inside, another gust of wind swirling about his feet and sending chills down his spine.

Something told him what lay within would change every-thing he'd come to know about the world.

ELAYSIA

R ain slammed into the roof, its cadence soothing to both babes and women alike as they huddled around the fire, drinking in the heat of the flames as though it were life itself.

"Explain it again," Maseeya said, her voice just a whisper to avoid waking the sleeping Elaron on her chest.

Kahana stood guard at the door, but her whalebone club hung lax at her hip, her eyes alive with wonder. "Yes, the part where you saw what he saw."

Elaysia smiled at the nyman's rare display of emotion. She slowly unlatched Dytana, who'd fallen asleep suckling, but remained in the cot beside her. It felt good to just lie, free of demands, of prying eyes, of plans that needed to be evaluated and disputes in need of settlement. Since she'd returned to Agaas with a malnourished, but very much alive, Kelsia a week prior, there'd been incessant disturbances and people vying for her attention. She'd managed to delay the war council gathering, but she'd have to face it on the morrow. The chiefs and their elders were eager to take offensive positions, especially with all the stormbirds now battle seasoned and Vahid's kuza army fighting alongside Neharem warriors.

Best to strike now, Gibrund had said when he caught up with her outside her quarters. *While the people are confident and our spirits high.*

He was right, of course. But it didn't make her any more eager for what would come. For despite their successful mission to rescue the Ni'anko chief, Elaysia's preparedness for battle spoke nothing of her stomach for it.

"Unless you'd rather not, High Chieftain," Kahana said, resuming her more stoic stance. "I don't mean to pry."

Elaysia shook her head apologetically, her long braids swaying with the motion. "Forgive me, my thoughts weigh heavy as of late."

She proceeded to tell them what it had felt like the moment she exchanged her vision for Onitus's; how she never imagined the colors she'd seen instead of hearing his thoughts like the others could mean something so wondrous. How the hues had slowly sharpened into focus, revealing the battle. How she not only saw what he saw, but *felt* what he felt, as though for a moment they both shared a body and mind.

"Were you frightened?" Maseeya asked, grabbing her cooled mug of tea with her free hand.

"I'd fear for my body," Kahana added before Elaysia could answer. "If you weren't in control of yourself, even for a moment, anything could happen. How would you know if you were in danger? Would you transition back instinctively if threatened?"

The thought had crossed Elaysia's mind, but she hadn't lingered on her fears in the moment. "I'm not sure," she admitted, brushing her fingers across Dytana's fine silver wisps of hair. "It was so brief. I suppose I won't know until I try it again."

Kahana chewed her tattooed lip. "I suggest you do. Better to find out in the company of allies."

Elaysia didn't protest.

"Kelsia is already showing signs of improvement," Maseeya said, skillfully changing the subject. "I tended to her myself this evening. She'll have some scarring, but she's been keeping liquids down. We'll try more substantial food tomorrow."

Kahana's eyes darkened as Maseeya spoke. "The Lautei should pay. They'd no right to treat a chief so, especially not one as peaceful as Kelsia."

"They did pay," Elaysia said quickly. Visions of the blood-soaked encampment filled her mind—already far too many familiar faces for her liking. "And justice will continue to be served. But we need to think beyond petty retaliation."

"What did you have in mind?" Kahana seemed genuinely interested, but Elaysia was not ready to discuss such matters. There would be enough of that in the morning.

"I think we'll save such talk for tomorrow, yes?" Maseeya suggested, swooping down like the mother bird she'd always been. "For now, let us enjoy a calm moment, for we never know how many we have left."

Kahana raised her waterskin. "I'll drink to that."

Elaysia raised her own—though it contained some of Cyan's anderberry wine—and Maseeya her tea. Together, they toasted to the hope of long and fulfilling lives, free of war and hardship.

When Kahana excused herself to make her rounds, Elaysia lay back on her cot and shut her eyes. But instead of being greeted with sweet sleep, the memories came.

Only they weren't memories, but more visions of the haunting world filled with fog and distraught voices. The cries of anguish. Screams of loss. And somewhere deep in the mist, two spheres of golden-green. Suns?

Or eyes?

She sat up after an hour of stirring and found Maseeya watching her from the fireside. "Bad dreams?" she asked, handing over a stirring Elaron, who reached eagerly for Elaysia's breasts.

"I'm not sure anymore." Elaysia attached the babe and watched, satisfied, as his starlight eyes closed. "I used to think that's all they were, but Konar says visions run in my family. He said my father had them, and that they increased in severity the closer he got to..." She shut her eyes and swallowed the lump forming in her throat. "I don't want them, Maseeya. Sometimes I still don't want any of this. If I'd just kept riding the night I turned back and discovered the eggs, or if I'd tried to protect Annonitus the day Kayrune—"

"None of that," Maseeya said, cutting her off gently but firmly. "Nothing in your life is a mistake, do you hear me? Without all the moments that have shaped you, you wouldn't be who you are today, and neither would the world."

"What if I could've been better?" The question hung in the air, haunting her now that she'd spoken it aloud. "What if the world would've been better?"

"If you live in the past, you can't be present and make better the future." Maseeya shrugged as though the matter was settled. "You are exactly who you need to be for the life given to you. No more, no less."

Elaysia wasn't so certain, but she inhaled deeply of the babes' sweet heads, clutching them tightly as though they might be torn away from her at a moment's notice. "My little moons," she whispered. "You reflect the little light left in a world full of darkness."

"Little moons they are indeed." Maseeya rose and kissed Elaysia on the forehead before making her way to her cot on the opposite side of the room. "And you are their sun."

"You know," Elaysia said as Maseeya nestled beneath her blankets. "I don't know how Eumma did it. It's scary to look at someone and know they hold so much power over you. To know your world would break without them." Once again, emotion threatened to choke her words. Once again, she tamed it. "I thought I was vulnerable before. Now I'm utterly tethered to lives beyond my own."

Maseeya yawned. "It is a good thing. You will always have a heart where others do not. Only love will fix things, girl. Remember that."

As the fire faded to embers, Elaysia turned Maseeya's words over in her mind again and again. She believed almost all of it. All but one nagging detail.

She only had a heart as long as the ones of those she loved remained beating.

As soon as the last chief departed the summit lodge—it was, of course, the ever-slowing Arkuun who seemed to appear more ancient by the day—Elaysia gathered her cloak and hurried out onto the platform. The crowds were thick with morning chaos. Hopeful new warriors readied themselves to march south, brushing shoulders with more seasoned fighters and dedicated kuza who'd just completed their rotations guarding the Apáasutai borders. Meanwhile, civilians bustled about with tasks that never seemed to end. Growing more food. Hunting and fishing. Repairing weaknesses in architecture, rationing resources, tending to the sickness plaguing those who weren't used to Agaas's climate and the unique diseases of her region. And that said nothing of their biggest concerns, such as forging weapons and providing shelter to warriors who journeyed beyond the shrinking perimeter of their land.

Elaysia shut her eyes to all it, just for a moment. She peered between the colorful robes and nytak-skin boots, around the golden-plated armor and leather tunics, until she located Vahid's thick, dark hair hanging about his shoulders. He was easy enough to find, especially with Hallahd and Anahi by his side. They stood in a tight circle just outside the lodge, curved swords hanging from their hips. It wasn't until Elaysia approached the pond they lingered beside that she realized she'd been avoiding it since her induction day. It was there she'd received the first critique of her leadership from her most trusted advisor, not an hour after her ceremony.

If only he'd known the insecurities he'd seed.

"High Chieftain," Anahi said, bringing her fist to her heart. "I was just telling my brother it was bold of him to suggest tactics without first conferring with you in private. Our faja taught us better than that." She directed a jagged look at Vahid with her fiery brown eyes, and Elaysia couldn't help but smile.

"My apologies," Vahid said. There was no sarcasm or reluctance in his voice. There never was. "I crossed paths with Maseeya on my way to break my fast this morning, and she mentioned you had an unsettling night. I promise, my intentions were pure." He ran a thumb over his ring as he looked to Hallahd. The older man avoided his gaze. "If you disagree with my suggestion but felt unable to refute it under the scrutiny of the war council, I'd be happy to recant my words to everyone in private."

Elaysia touched the top of Anahi's arm and locked eyes with Hallahd. "Would you two mind giving us a moment?"

"Of course not, High Chieftain. I'll be at the training grounds, should you need me." Anahi bowed and vanished into the thickening crowd.

Hallahd wasn't so easily convinced. He rarely left Vahid's side, even in the safety of the holy city. Elaysia didn't take it personally. There were undoubtedly spies and assassins burrowed in their midst, and she could see Kahana not twenty feet away, pretending to inspect the railing when she was, in fact, doing the same; keeping an eye on the leader she'd sworn to protect.

"You don't have to go far," Elaysia told Vahid's guardian. "It won't take long."

Hallahd's face softened into something reminiscent of understanding. "Forgive me, my lady—High Chieftain. It is not you, or your people, I fear." He gave Vahid a parting nod and melted into the background. At least a few feet away.

"Walk with me?" Elaysia asked, offering Vahid her arm. Surprise rippled through his features, but by the time he'd linked his arm in hers, he'd returned to his collected self.

"An honor."

They crossed a bridge leading away from the High Tree and descended several levels by means of the ramps. When they reached a mostly abandoned platform dedicated to lofts, Elaysia led them to a bench and unraveled her arm from his. It felt so cold, absent from the heat of his body, but she didn't dare try to sneak it back in again. It wouldn't bode well for the conversation she needed to have, anyway.

"I owe you my gratitude for inspiring my mission to rescue Kelsia. I also understand you and your kuza were single-handedly responsible for holding off a Banaxa attack on our southernmost border. It's not much, but I'd like to show my appreciation by supplying extra wine rations to those who fought alongside you." She kept her gaze fixed on his eyes long enough to convey her sincerity before letting them rest on something far less unnerving: the living trees across the way. "As for today, Maseeya shouldn't have felt the need to burden you with my troubles, but I appreciate what you said at the gathering all the same."

"It's never a burden to say the right thing." Vahid rose from the bench and draped his forearms over the railings. His tunic was rolled up to his elbows, exposing a still-healing cut running up his inner right arm. "As for the Banaxa, the wine is not needed, though I admire the gesture. Truthfully, I don't like being idle, and seeing as how I can only read a handful of the books in your possession, I find release busying myself with the war efforts. It helps my men see me in a different light, too."

Elaysia scrubbed a bit of hardened sap off the bench with her thumbnail. "I can't fathom that. I hate it all so much. The war, the endless gatherings, the problems that never seem to be resolved. I thought it would be easier embracing my duties as high chieftain this time. I earned the position. The people wanted me. I've sat on the steps of Haeshol itself. But I'm still..."

Me, she wanted to tell him. *I'm still a scared little girl, it's just that now I've been bit. Now everything's a serpent waiting to strike. A dagger in an embrace. Poison in wine.*

Something flared in her, a warning that she neared the point of being too vulnerable, a line she'd crossed with haste in her past. Never again, she'd promised herself. But she craved the release that accompanied such honesty, and Vahid had proven himself worthy ten times over. Surely, she could trust him now.

No, her gut whispered. It would never be enough. No amount of goodness could smooth over the scars others had left.

"Still?" Vahid prodded gently, keeping his attention on the sprawling forest of vibrant greens and rich browns.

Elaysia joined him, inhaling deeply of the soil's musk and the sweet spice of the needles, of the trace of salt intermingled with it all. "Just exhausted, I suppose." Before he could pry further, she added, "Anyway, I do think it's a brilliant plan. I'm glad you have spies in Az Zar who can confirm when they'll send their next shipment of supplies aiding the Lawful Dominion. And you're right that the birds provide the perfect airborne attack to catch the sailors off guard upon docking in Moákun territory. I do fear it could be a trap, though."

"I'm expecting one." He grimaced, then shrugged his shoulders. "But I don't think we have a choice. Your war council is eager for a grand offensive move, and though we've been holding our own on small-scale attacks, we still don't stand a chance to defeat the full-strength of the Lawful Dominion army head-on. This might be our only opportunity." Vahid turned from her abruptly, and a chill gripped Elaysia's spine.

"Why might this be our only opportunity?"

"I didn't want to say anything, especially in front of the war council, because it's only hearsay, but..."

Elaysia clenched her teeth as she grabbed his arm, careful to avoid his wound. "Tell me."

"One of my contacts said he heard rumors that this shipment would bring weapons capable of eradicating Agaas."

"Like the ones we saw rescuing Kelsia? The ones capable of propelling boulders?" Even as she asked, she knew it was something worse. Perhaps something akin to what caused the annihilation of the Igtheos Tree on her first induction day. "We can't let whatever it is on Neharem soil," she said, tightening her grip on his arm.

"We'll be prepared. With a dual attack coming from land and sky, they'll be caught off guard. I don't think they expect us to be so careless in leading with nearly half our forces, either."

"And you're certain you want it to only be your foot soldiers sent to deal with the ground skirmishes?" The guilt gnawed at her, no matter how much she wanted to spare Neharem lives.

Vahid's warm gaze radiated confidence. "It's the least I can do. Your warriors are better suited to defend their land, and my kuza would love the chance to visit a warmer climate, no matter how briefly."

Elaysia considered Orandus's apprehension in the gathering. "You should take at least some Moákun warriors with you. They know their land the best and where the Lawful Dominion might make use of traps within it."

"I agree. But just a handful. No need to risk unnecessary Neharem lives."

No lives are unnecessary, she thought. Instead, she offered the more light-hearted, "Good luck convincing Mardus of that."

He gave a knowing chuckle.

It wasn't long before the silence between them grew uncomfortable, at least to Elaysia. There were few people she could sit in stillness with and not feel the need to perform or entertain, and Vahid wasn't one of them. Not yet. Perhaps not ever. With Zavik gone, only Maseeya could provide such solace, but the poor woman did enough already.

"Something else weighs on your mind," Vahid said, smoothing the mustache of his beard. "If you want to talk about it, I'm happy to listen. I can also leave you to your musings."

"Clarity doesn't surface in your absence, unfortunately." Elaysia gathered the knotted strands of hair she hadn't found time to untangle that morning and fastened them atop her head with a length of leather cord. "Aside from the war, I fear for Zavik, wondering whose hands he's in. But I worry for Jakki and Xaren, too. No discord with the Morotôk should've taken this long, but I also don't believe Chief Amkah lied in saying she sent them off in good health. Jakki must've tried something again. She's always—"

Trying to help, Elaysia realized. The guilt gnawing inside of her turned into a gnashing of teeth, and it was all she could do to keep her feet rooted to the platform.

"If something had happened to them or the stormbirds, do you think you'd feel it?"

Vahid's question took her aback. Normal people didn't ask such things. They liked to feign belief in the supernatural without actually trusting it, especially when they weren't on the receiving end of divine interaction.

"I don't know." She draped her shawl over the railing, exposing her sleeveless tunic. Vahid never so much as raised an eyebrow at the patched markings on her skin. "I'd like to think so. We're all connected, especially the birds. There was a moment where, when asked about Shadow, Onitus would show me no colors at all. But now it's a gentle darkness again, as it's always been."

"Lumira told you something similar when she flew north to search, didn't she?"

"Yes." It was the only thing that had stilled Elaysia's nightmares of Jakki's death. "She said Anadu didn't fear for them, and neither did she. Not that Lumira and Jakki are the greatest of allies, so perhaps she wasn't the most reliable source."

Vahid had the kindness to smile despite not knowing the extent of their rivalry.

"If you have a little more time to spare," he said, stretching both arms overhead. "I'd love to show you something. It won't take long."

"Please." Elaysia motioned for Vahid to lead the way. She was quite alright with him taking up as much of her morning as possible. Konar had been pestering her to speak with him—alone—for several days now.

And she'd nearly run out of excuses to avoid him.

Whatever Vahid wanted to show her required a journey to base camp, where the kuza had constructed a myriad of tents and other temporary enclosures. She recognized his prized steed, brought over from Orillon, hitched to a tree beside one of the larger tents and stopped to rub his velvety pink muzzle.

"He likes you," Vahid said, combing through a tangle in the horse's snow-white mane. The stallion tossed his head as if to confirm, then huffed his sweet breath into their faces.

Elaysia followed him inside the tent, stepping over thickly padded blankets strewn around the entrance. Such sleeping arrangements weren't uncommon with the influx of refugees and kuza in Agaas, but seeing Vahid's meager belongings lying there, without so much as a basket to store them in, clouded her chest with guilt. If she'd just insisted he stay with her, it wouldn't be so.

Maybe it wasn't too late.

She quickly averted her gaze and followed him across the dirt-crusted rug to a long table. Several objects bulged beneath the thin sheet that had been cast over them, and the way Vahid shifted his attention from her to the table, eyes sparkling like a child at play, gave her an odd mixture of intrigue and suspicion.

Without warning, Vahid removed the sheet with the flair of a performer. Eight helmets—no, masks—stared back at her, each one unique and fashioned with care. Elaysia took a hesitant step toward the table, and when Vahid nodded, she picked up the one nearest her. It was light yet durable, structured yet soft. Some sort of leather dyed a brilliant teal with crimson accents, but it had been cured in a way she wasn't familiar with, creating a hardened exterior. There were large holes shaped like eyes and filled with glass, allowing protection from the elements while not obscuring vision. She tapped it a few times and found it of solid, almost flexible make. The mask had been crafted with elegant, sweeping sections that extended from the cheeks to the forehead, resembling feathers as they fanned out at the edges.

Stormbird feathers.

It was specifically designed for a nyrian (or nyman), with additional space to accommodate elongated ears, and someone with long hair, at that, for there was room for lengths of hair to come out the top or bottom.

"You have a keen eye. That one's yours." Vahid retrieved it from her hands and tentatively held it before her face. "May I?"

Elaysia nodded. She couldn't find her voice. It was more beautiful than anything she'd imagined, even more ornate than some of Zavik's early sketches. In it, she felt protected and powerful. Hidden yet known.

And in it, she'd do mighty things.

The mask smelled of leather and spices, along with hints of smoke from Agaasian fires. Their smoke had a distinct scent of foliage; there was almost a refreshing essence about the wood found in Apáasutai territory. As Vahid secured the mask behind her, his fingers brushed the exposed skin of her neck. She was both exhilarated and unsettled by the sensation that followed.

"What do you think?" he asked, stepping back. "Oh, wait." There was a rustling behind her, then he reemerged with a small, reflective oval supported by a handle. In Neharem, they used reflective bits of water or crystals—if anything. But there was a name for what the wealthy used in Orillon and Az Zar: an imitation glass.

Elaysia held her breath as she stared at her reflection. The woman looking back was something to behold. Hints of two-toned, luminescent eyes peering beneath the mask. A tangle of hair falling behind the feathers from where she'd loosed it from the tie. Strong shoulders held upright, commanding respect. A storm waiting to be unleashed.

Vahid appeared in the reflection behind her, and she fought to not get lost in his eyes. "I hope it's alright," he said, adjusting the mask ever so slightly. "You mentioned Zavik had planned to fashion masks, and when he was taken from you, I wanted to do my part to help alleviate the loss. I know it's not his handiwork, but I hope you and the Stormriders will find these sufficient."

"You made these yourself?" Elaysia's voice was all rocks and grit; a crumbling dam fighting to hold back the waters.

He lifted his shoulder as he dropped his gaze. "Not entirely. Zavik had already done the hard part of designing them. I added some of my own modifications to the plans and collaborated with my best armorers to ensure quality. Hallahd works with glass in his spare time, so the lenses are all his handiwork."

"Then I owe you and your men all my gratitude." Elaysia slipped the mask off and pivoted away from him, so he couldn't read the mess of emotions on her face. "They're perfectly suited to each rider. This one is Jakki's, yes?" she asked, picking up an icy-blue mask. Her opposite hand lifted a smaller one that shimmered gold. "And Anahi's?"

"Right on both accounts. The beridians posed a challenge, but we found a way to allow their ears full movement while still keeping them protected and the design streamlined." He picked up the largest mask, bearing stripes as well as feathers, the coloring a deep maroon. "For Grokhion."

Elaysia traced her fingertips over the rest: a shadowy mask for Xaren; cream with fired edges for Lumira; subtle browns inlaid with vine work for Yerakai; a bold red for Mardus. Each one perfect.

Each one cracking her frozen heart just a bit more.

She stopped after the last one and gripped the table, as though it were the only thing keeping her from tumbling into oblivion. It was all fear. She knew that, knew better. But something in her wouldn't let go. The longer she spent in Vahid's presence, the more such feelings arose. She couldn't let him in. Not now. Not with everything at stake.

"I have to go," she muttered, whisking past him.

She only made it halfway to the tent flap before he intercepted her. His sudden movement seemed to shock him just as much. He stood there, not blocking, but not moving, lips parted in some unspoken question.

"Would you rather me go?" For the first time, she heard the notes of uncertainty in his voice.

"No, it's nothing you've done. I just need to head back up to—"

"I mean, would you rather me just go back to Orillon." He interlaced his fingers, squeezing them tightly as he tried to hook her wandering gaze. "If I'm not helping you and your people, then there's no point in me being here. My faja doesn't need to know that I've returned, and you can be at peace, if indeed I'm causing you strain."

Of all the thoughts tumbling about Elaysia's mind, she couldn't harness a single coherent one. She knew she needed to say something affirmative, but it felt like admitting defeat.

She watched, helpless, as Vahid grabbed his possessions and set them gently into a thin blanket, then tied it in a knot and slung it over his shoulder. He turned his gaze on her one last time as he lifted the tent flap.

"Tell me to stay, and I'll stay. Otherwise, I'll assume I bring you more harm than help. The last thing I wish is to be a burden to you, High Chieftain." The formality with which he said 'High Chieftain' rang flat and cold.

Still, the words wouldn't come. They were trapped in the deepest pit of her soul, as they'd been after Annonitus died. All smoke and shadow.

"My kuza will take orders from Hallahd. You're in good hands."

And then he was gone.

Elaysia stood frozen as painful memory after painful memory hurled by like a flock of nightmares. And when they, too, departed, and the hollowness set in, she was left with one thought.

Don't leave me too.

When she drew back the tent flap, Vahid was nowhere to be seen. His steed, too, was missing. Elaysia's heart sank as she raced to the Agaasian pens with newfound desperation. Baudier, her ever-loyal stallion, whinnied at the gate, and within moments she was on his back and clearing the meager fence that never truly held him against his will. Together, they tore through base camp and into the woods, following the still fresh tracks of the other pair.

Vahid hadn't gotten far. He pulled his mount to a stop and regarded Elaysia with cautious eyes. "Did I forget something?"

"Yes," Elaysia said, drawing her horse alongside his. "Agaas needs you in this war. Your men need you. And I..." She knotted strands of Baudier's mane between her fingers and inhaled slowly. She wanted to mean it, to not rush it or glaze over it as she had with so much as of late. "I need you. I think you're one of the few true friends I have left in this city, and I'd be a fool to let you leave now."

Their knees brushed, and the warmth that filled Elaysia's body as a result was undeniable.

Vahid moved the hair from her face with strong, dexterous fingers. "And as long as you need me, I shall remain."

AHMARAHN

K ymerius led Ahmarahn between the two long tables and their accompanying patrons, most of whom whispered as he was paraded by them. One was kind enough to send his drink toppling off the table, where it splattered all over the ground and a sizable section of Ahmarahn's pant leg. The muffled laughter that followed confirmed his suspicion the act was intentional. He collected himself with a breath, ignoring the scathing gazes as they approached a dimly lit table in the far corner. Only one person occupied it, and their back was turned to the rest, masking their identity. Their figure was slight, their dark hair knotted at the base of their neck, their clothes as neutral and ill-fitted as everyone else's.

If this was their leader, Ahmarahn had little to fear.

He strode forward, ready to introduce himself and perform his rehearsed speech, when Kymerius unsheathed a knife from his thigh and brought it to Ahmarahn's throat.

"Don't try anything," the former soldier grunted. "You so much as look at her the wrong way, and I'll put this through one of your starry little eyes, you hear me?"

Her. Curious.

Ahmarahn considered the sharpness of Kymerius's lyvium blade and the hard set of his jaw, recognizing the sincerity of the threat. The grudge the man held from their mutual initiate training years past had only festered with time, and Ahmarahn could practically feel the hatred seething out of his pores. There was little doubt in his mind that Kymerius would exact his revenge, given the chance.

And that was going to make things a little more complicated.

Ahmarahn slowly lowered the blade. "Thank you for the grotesque imagery. It's extinguished my lust for blood."

The vein on Kymerius's forehead bulged, and Ahmarahn silently cursed himself for letting some of Davier's sarcasm slip out.

"Wanna try that again?" Kymerius growled.

"I won't harm a soul in this building," Ahmarahn said, mustering his most sincere tone. "You have my word."

"Everyone knows you have the lips of an adulterer, Zadel. I'm watching you."

Ahmarahn bowed his head long enough to send his resentment into the floorboards, and when he looked up, the woman seated at the table was gone.

Before he could ask questions, Kymerius jerked him left, dragging him down a dark hallway. It reeked of a trap, and Ahmarahn prepared himself accordingly. Instead of being confronted by hostile rebels, however, he was greeted with the pleasant aroma of baking bread wafting from a small kitchen. A robust woman glanced up as they entered, her cheeks a vibrant pink as she worked at kneading some dough into submission. She regarded Ahmarahn with a raised eyebrow.

"New recruit?" she asked, adding a handful of nuts to the mixture.

Kymerius looked as though he'd been asked to drink his own piss. "Hardly."

The woman shrugged and gestured to a round lump covered in a simple white cloth on the counter. "Bread if you want it. The scavengers scored a bounty today."

Ahmarahn's mouth watered. He couldn't remember the last time he had fresh food, much less bread.

Kymerius jerked Ahmarahn toward an open trapdoor, ruining any hopes of such a luxury. "I'm saving room for your sun-blood cakes later, Eumma," he told the woman as he forced Ahmarahn down the wooden steps. Something told him the woman wasn't actually his mother.

A single lantern illuminated the cellar. Dried herbs hung from the ceiling, partially obscuring a wall lined with shelves on which were various jars of flours, grains, and preserved fruits and vegetables. A table hosted a pitiful display of cheese, and beyond that loomed a cupboard, one of its doors ajar, showcasing the wines tucked inside.

The trapdoor thudded closed above him. As Kymerius descended, Ahmarahn's fear that he'd walked into a trap set for any would-be informants of the empire resurfaced. But if they wanted him dead, why not just kill him in the inn, in front of their most loyal supporters? Why go through the trouble of introducing him to the leader of their rebellion?

Kymerius frisked Ahmarahn for any hidden weapons, then wrinkled his nose after finding none. Ahmarahn turned his palms upward in an apologetic gesture, only this time, he didn't stifle the sarcasm in his expression.

A growl rumbled in Kymerius's throat as he reached behind the cupboard, revealing it wasn't flush against the wall. He fixed Ahmarahn with one final glare.

"I mean it. You do anything I perceive as a threat, and you'll be dead before you realize where you went wrong."

The threat was so void of humor, so intense and posturing, that it took all Ahmarahn's focus to subdue the grin attempting to claw its way across his mouth. "Gentle as a fawn," was all he managed.

A *click* filled the silence, followed by the sound of wood sliding against wood. Ahmarahn's footsteps creaked across the floor as he approached the false wall, its entrance mostly masked by the cupboard. Kymerius motioned him down a dark tunnel as he slid the wall back into place behind them.

A mixture of stone and clay made up the tunnel floor, and as Ahmarahn marched on, the occasional poke from Kymerius's blade a reminder to keep moving, he found the system broadened instead of narrowing. The further in they ventured, the more it wound about, and the taller the tunnel got, the more frequent the appearance of giant wooden beams supporting the structure.

They broke from the main path at the first divergence, where it spilled into a cavern roughly the size of the great feasting hall in the All-Sovereign's palace. Rectangular shelves were cut directly into the rock and lined most of the room, and cracked vases and urns littered the floor. Ahmarahn's eyes widened as he took in the crumbled remains of a headless statue at the center, its body kneeling and swathed in stone robes. The woman from the inn leaned against it, her arms crossed and an unsheathed dagger gleaming at her hip.

"And who is this man who riles you so, Kymerius?" The woman's tone was guarded but curious.

"He is a ghost," Kymerius replied curtly. He shoved Ahmarahn into the room. Upon closer inspection, the rectangular shelves were not regular shelves at all, but open-faced coffins containing mummified corpses. The room smelled of dust and stale incense, bringing with it an air of malaise, likely caused by the bodies.

Up close, Ahmarahn could make out the faint freckling on the woman's cheeks and nose, the roundness of her lips, the small hoops of lyvium pierced through her earlobes. Two strands of hair were pulled free of her knot, framing her face. They accented the sharpness of her eyes, which contrasted with her otherwise soft features. Despite her beauty, there was a fierceness, a subtle warning much like the ones exuded by a sandcat's fangs or a viper's patterning.

The woman tilted her head, raising her chin. "Ghosts can be helpful to our cause."

Kymerius, evidently eager to dispel what little interest she'd shown, added, "He's the All-Sovereign's dog. A favored soldier sent abroad to exact riches for the empire, no matter the cost. He tried to betray both the people of Neharem and the All-Sovereign, and when he got caught, he gave up his family in exchange for his life, content to serve the empire in the bowels of the slave district."

The room throbbed around Ahmarahn, pulsating with each beat of his heart. He could feel Kymerius's taunting gaze hot on his back.

He still saw Ahmarahn as his nemesis, and if he allowed this man to get a rise out of him, his mission would fail before it'd even begun. The leader would see him as a rageful, volatile ex-soldier, too unstable to serve the cause. He needed to remind himself of what was at stake.

Ahmarahn thought of Xi until his heartbeat slowed. He glanced up at the woman, expecting to find her face twisted with disgust, but he was met with attentive, dark brown eyes, her expression as collected as it'd been the moment prior.

Kymerius gripped Ahmarahn's arm. "We can't trust him, but we might be able to use him if—"

"Enough," the woman said, silencing him with a glare. "I will be the judge of his heart." She returned her attention to Ahmarahn, peering up at him through long, dark eyelashes. "Who are you, and what do you seek?"

"I wish to be a humble servant of the rebellion," he began, reciting the speech Zhia had given him. "I tried to overthrow the All-Sovereign, and I paid for it with my family's lives and my eternal enslavement. But now, he trusts me enough to once again conduct the matters he'd rather not dirty his hands with. And I seek vengeance." It came out so easily, so authentic, that Ahmarahn himself believed it.

Only for a moment.

For although he craved vengeance, everything paled in comparison to protecting Xi. Only once she was out of harm's way could he do something brash. But the rebels wouldn't be able to tell the difference, and he'd make sure they never would.

The woman's brow furrowed. "You're not being fully honest with me or yourself." She pressed away from the statue, circling Ahmarahn with the curiosity of a predator sizing up its competition. "I'll only ask you once more: who are you, and what do you seek?"

Ahmarahn turned the question over in his mind. Though he'd given Kymerius his newly adopted name, something about it felt wrong for the journey he was about to embark on. Ahmarahn wasn't capable of the dedication the rebel leader sought. He was tired, jaded, and wholly fixated on protecting Xi. But Davier...

Perhaps this was what Davier was meant for all along.

"My name is Davier," he replied, keenly aware of Kymerius snorting in the background. "And I seek vengeance."

The corner of the woman's mouth quirked for the briefest of moments. "Joining our cause will not provide the vengeance you seek, but it may prevent others from desiring it also." She moved to the perimeter of the room, pausing in front of a coffin to brush a blanket of dust from its side. "If you want revenge, that is yours, and yours alone. Return to the palace and slit as many throats as you can before they take you down. You'll feel a rush of power and a sense of rightness before you die."

Though the woman continued to study the coffin, Ahmarahn could feel her attention fully fixed on him.

"But if you want to die knowing you left the world better than you found it, I can help you find that meaning." She glanced up, and he found himself crossing the room to join her beside the coffin. He used his thumb to rub away more of the dust and uncovered an ancient, symbol-based language unknown to him.

"How old are these catacombs?" he asked, gently working to brush more of the dust away. "This must predate Az Zar, back to the days when the city had no walls, and the palace was an institute of learning."

"All your questions will be answered in time, after we assess your loyalty." Her gaze flitted to the brand on his forehead. "First, you must commit yourself to the rebellion. You are under no obligation to do so, and can walk away freely, should you choose. But if you elect to join us, there's no abandoning the cause. Do you understand?"

Kymerius appeared in the periphery of Ahmarahn's vision, the glint of his knife catching the light from the flaming sconces.

"I understand," he replied, trying to give the commitment as little thought as possible. The less real it was, the less of a betrayal it would feel like in the end. This time, there'd be no runaway feelings or swirling bouts of contradictory motives. All that mattered was Xi. "Is there something I need to say to make it official?"

"We require no public declaration here," she said, shaking her head. "No abducted firstborns, forced temple attendance, or required donations. That's the exact thing we fight against."

Ahmarahn couldn't argue with that. "And what may I call you, rebel leader?"

"We have no leaders. I'm merely a coordinator, one who knows what needs to be known, one who does what needs to be done." The woman smiled at him for the first time. A small, closed-mouth gesture, but a smile, nonetheless. "But you can call me Nanjiya."

That evening, Ahmarahn was afforded some necessities that, to him, delved into the territory of luxuries. First, he was assigned his own bunk, and though it was in a room shared with six other rebels, the fact that it wasn't stained with excrement and crawling with bugs made his privacy a non-issue. Second, he was issued knee-high boots with split-toed soles made from leather, a pair of black form-fitting leggings, and a similarly made tunic with a hooded cowl to match. The outfit wasn't a far cry from his military uniform, and it showed the rebels were both aware of the clothing's benefits *and* were consciously using it to blend in with empire soldiers when sneaking about at night. As if the new clothes and sleeping arrangements weren't enough, they allowed him two daggers, one of which desperately needed a good oiling and a visit to the grindstone. When he broached the subject of swords, however, he was met with bloodshot glares. He silently resolved to seek a pair of blades on his own.

The third and most valuable benefit to joining the rebels was, quite simply, the food. Asha, the woman he'd met briefly in the kitchen when Kymerius marched him down to the tunnels, cooked a hearty kuba grain gruel with a side of fermented vegetables and smoked fish for the evening meal. Though filling and wholesome, the main course was outshone by her sun-blood cakes that followed. The citrus-infused sponge cakes embodied a delicate and moist texture with the essence of terredon woven throughout, all wrapped in a thick coating of honey-kissed cream. Ahmarahn could only stomach one; his body wasn't used to such rich food after a year of eating bland scraps tossed out by the palace servants. Even in his glory years, he was rarely exposed to such delicacies. But he vowed to work his way up to three in a sitting by the end of the moon cycle.

During the meal, an ordeal involving at least thirty other rebels disguised as the inn's patrons, Ahmarahn tried a new tactic: listening. He was in no hurry to discuss his past for fear of Davier's ghosts coming back to haunt him, nor was he eager to bond with anyone in the room. The last thing he needed was a repeat of Davier's mistakes in Neharem. No relationships meant no loss. Thankfully, most of the rebels were too fixated on their meals, booze, and personal exploits to pay him much mind.

Not so unlike my time in the military, he mused.

He was just pushing aside his spotless plate, ready to excuse himself for the night, when Kymerius stabbed the tip of his knife into the table.

Right between Ahmarahn's thumb and forefinger.

"Was it something I said?" he asked, slipping his hand off the table and placing it on his thigh, where he'd strapped one of his new daggers.

Kymerius leaned in uncomfortably close, his nostrils flaring. "You might have the others convinced with your pity-me-because-the-All-Sovereign-murdered-my-family-and-stole-my-love act. I, however, am no fool."

"I used to think the same thing," Ahmarahn replied, recalling how he'd believed those very words as he set sail for Neharem, and how desperately wrong he'd been. "But we all become fools the moment we love something more than ourselves."

The wrinkles of confusion on Kymerius's brow nearly made Ahmarahn smirk, rescuing him from the grasping claws of remorse that consumed most of his waking hours.

And Kymerius's spite.

"Am I excused?" Ahmarahn asked.

Kymerius yanked his knife from the table and waved it at Ahmarahn as if he shooed livestock into a pen. "Actually, no. You're to accompany Nanjiya on a mission tonight. Her idea. Just a little test to prove your commitment to the rebellion before we waste any more of our precious resources on you." He prodded Ahmarahn in the back with the tip of his blade, forcing him across the room and out onto the back porch.

A cold silence greeted them, made more ominous by the thick blanket of fog rolling in from the coast. The rear courtyard was abandoned, an empty dirt patch no larger than the inn's common room with only a few dust-laden benches to hint that it had likely once been a beautiful place to linger. The door slammed shut behind them, leaving Ahmarahn alone with his favorite person.

"Now listen," Kymerius said, pressing the tip of his knife into Ahmarahn's chest. "If you fail to impress, we kill you. If you try to betray us, we kill you. If you look at me the wrong way again—"

"Yes, yes, you kill me. Your redundancies are impeccable."

There was a fleeting moment where Ahmarahn feared he'd pushed the ex-soldier too far, that Kymerius would happily slit his throat then and there, willing to suffer whatever consequences landed upon him. No one would shed any tears at Ahmarahn's abrupt and untimely death. No one but Xi.

"Sorry." He needed his apology—and false confession—to appear genuine, so he adopted a gentler demeanor and averted his gaze. "To be completely honest, the reality of being here and facing the empire again scares me shitless. I believe in the rebellion, but I'm afraid of what will happen if I get caught a second time."

Kymerius considered this, lowered his knife, and gave what could've been mistaken for a heartfelt shrug. "I'd say you're better off than most. What do you have left to lose? They'd probably give you a painful death and be done with it."

"Can't argue with that," Ahmarahn said quietly.

"Let us not talk of failure and death prior to a mission. It poisons the mind against itself, making it too focused on what can be lost instead of what can be gained."

They turned in unison toward the left side of the porch where a feminine figure cloaked head to toe in black leaned against the railing. Nanjiya must've possessed the agility of a beridian to approach without alerting them, and Ahmarahn found himself admiring her far too quickly for his liking. He tried to shake the feeling as he approached her.

"Have you briefed him on tonight's mission?" Nanjiya's gaze remained fixed on Ahmarahn, though she directed the question at Kymerius.

Kymerius glared at Ahmarahn, as though the fault for the failed briefing was his. "I was under the impression my only task was to make sure he was properly outfitted for tonight."

"One might presume the most important part of 'outfitting' is an awareness of the stakes and the mission at hand. But no matter. I will fill him in on the way." There was an aloofness to Nanjiya that wasn't overtly arrogant, but Ahmarahn got the sense that the protective layers masking her true self ran far deeper than the tunnels beneath the inn. "Goodnight, Kymerius. Defy the silence of oppression."

"And ignite the thunder of rebellion." Kymerius trudged back to the door, sulking. He made an audible, exasperated inhale, then shook his head as he released it, his storm-cloud eyes trained on Ahmarahn. "Are you certain you don't want me to follow, in the likely chance things go wrong? He could be leading you into a trap, Nan."

"If you treat everything as a trap, you're always prepared," she replied.

Kymerius's jaw ticked. While he offered no further rebuttal, he didn't appear keen on returning to the inn, either.

Ahmarahn lifted his gaze to the sky, aware that even a single look could reveal too much. Somewhere in the distance, a pack of street dogs snarled and yelped, probably caught up in a battle for whatever unfortunate carcass they'd discovered in the alleys. The cool, damp air clung to his skin, carrying with it whispers of rain, and he thought of the sea, of his long-lost dreams of voyaging and freedom, and his heart ached with longing.

Maybe it wasn't too late. If he could just get Xi out, they could start life anew in a foreign land, far beyond Quinaria's rotting corpse.

"Put this on," Nanjiya said, holding Ahmarahn's cowl out to him. Her voice was deceptively light, as was the touch she'd used to slip the head garment from his waistband without him noticing. She hopped over the porch railing and disappeared around the side of the building, not once looking back to ensure Ahmarahn followed.

He started down the stairs only to catch a foot from Kymerius that would've sent him sprawling, had his hand not connected with the railing in time.

"Miss me already?" Ahmarahn asked through clenched teeth.

Kymerius's chest puffed out a notch more than usual. "I make no idle threats, Zadel."

"We'll see." Ahmarahn was off the porch and around the corner before the ex-soldier could react.

Piles of dung and trampled, decaying leaves littered the path wrapping around the side of the inn. It flowed into the court-yard, where the shadows remained unhindered by motion, and the street beyond lay equally still, signifying the last warning gong had long since sounded. Even the dogs had ceased their quarreling.

Ahmarahn closed his eyes and tried to reconnect with the useful parts of Davier's past. When he opened them again, his gaze instinctively turned up, finding a pair of deep brown eyes searching his own. Nanjiya motioned him up with one finger to where she sat perched atop the roof like a cat. The climb to join her on the second story wasn't as easy as it looked, but the curved architecture of the roofs did work to his advantage. It'd been too long, Ahmarahn realized as he struggled to find purchase, since he'd used his muscles for tasks outside hauling large sacks and wheelbarrows to and from the palace grounds or swinging a pick into the core of Quinaria. While his strength hadn't withered entirely, he wasn't used to the variety of motion, nor the acceleration of his heart brought upon by endurance-driven activity.

When he joined Nanjiya on the rooftop, the view nearly took his breath away. From where they sat, Cadar unfurled before them in rings of splendor; each district nestled inside the prior, the perimeters getting smaller but the walls becoming grander, reaching higher and higher until the city culminated in the pinnacle of its glory: the Sun-blood District. It looked so beautiful from a distance. Radiant in nevethium glow, a testament to the architecture of ancient beings. But Ahmarahn could no longer behold it with pure eyes. What happened within that protected district was far worse than in the seediest alleys of Or Zahal.

"Once we go below, there's no coming back." Nanjiya's voice was so low that Ahmarahn could barely register her words. "Do you understand?"

Ahmarahn nodded. Yes, he was well aware that once given access to the tunnel system used by the rebels, he couldn't be allowed to return to the palace without just cause. Yes, he was aware this was the final step before he once again became a weapon against a people deemed lesser. Yes, he was aware this betrayed his last shred of humanity, that whatever happened next would likely lead to Nanjiya's death, and worse, the death of the rebellion.

But what choice did he have? Though he harbored no hate for her, she was just another fleeting body taking up precious resources, another face in the sea of the empire's oppressed, while Xi...Xi was life itself. She was Ahmarahn's past, present, and future.

And he'd kill for her a thousand times over if it meant sparing her from even a bit of the world's hatred.

Nanjiya touched his arm, and Ahmarahn flinched. Her eyes widened, more out of surprise than offense. "We will talk in the tunnels," she whispered, "but not a word until then."

She pranced across the rooftops, and Ahmarahn followed, desperately wishing he had a drink to drown out the cacophony of feelings threatening to spill over from deep inside his soul.

"No attachments," he murmured aloud as a reminder to himself as he pulled on the mask and cowl. "Only for you, Xi."

The tunnels that ran beneath Cadar sprawled beyond Ahmarahn's wildest dreams. He'd been underground a few times as a soldier, and even more as a slave, but none of that had prepared him for the catacombs built by Cadar's founders millennia prior.

He'd followed Nanjiya across several tightly stacked rooftops in the Old Nyzar District, then watched with a furrowed brow as she dropped into a sliver of an alleyway tucked between an illegal brothel and an abandoned mercantile. Behind a seemingly unassuming collection of compost barrels lay a grate identical to those used by the waste chute systems. She then proceeded to shove the barrels aside and used the tip of her military–issued sword—Ahmarahn made a note to ask her about how she'd acquired it later—to pry it open.

Then she lowered herself in, feet-first.

Ahmarahn prepared himself for the grotesque stench of excrement, only to find the cavity below tinged with dust and decay, similar to how the cavern he met Nanjiya in had smelled. A brilliant disguise, he reflected, as they wove through a cramped tunnel illuminated by the glow of a nevethium crystal Nanjiya had retrieved from her boot. Highborn and patrols would steer clear of the city drains, even if they knew rumors of an ancient tunnel system existed.

"How far does this reach?" Ahmarahn asked after they'd walked a good distance.

"To the end of Cadar."

Ahmarahn's gait faltered as he processed her words. "You think this will be the key to the city's downfall?"

"Instrumental, not key." She didn't slow her pace, nor glance over her shoulder. "Based on what we've ascertained from stolen logbooks, only one system leads fully out of the city, and one directly into the palace. But the founders did put them here to create an opportunity."

"For people to escape?"

"For people to bring down a corrupt system."

Ahmarahn wasn't so certain that'd been their plan, but such discussions were better suited for another time. Like when he wasn't trying to win over the rebel leader.

"You mentioned briefing me on tonight's mission?" he asked a few minutes later. Sweat had already built up from his exertion, prompting him to take off his cowl and mask.

"It's simple." She stopped abruptly and gave him her full attention. "We will emerge directly inside the Sun-blood District. There, you will obtain a high-ranking officer capable of providing valuable intelligence to the rebellion. Someone only you could gain access to. You will bring them down here, then help me bind and transport them for interrogation."

Ahmarahn's arms instinctively folded across his chest. "That's it?"

Nanjiya continued down the tunnel without another word.

"Nanjiya, wait. I..."

The sound of her fading footsteps echoed throughout the tunnels. Ahmarahn shadowed his face with the cowl, then set off after her, albeit slower, the drag of his feet echoing that of his heart.

A face had appeared in his mind the moment she'd laid out the conditions, and despite having previously fantasized about killing the wearer of that face, the urge to do so had vanished along with the opportunity. He didn't want to be a pawn for the rebellion any more than he wanted to be used by the empire.

But good soldiers followed orders. Besides, Nanjiya had said nothing about killing. Bind, transport, interrogate.

And that was the least General Zhia deserved.

Only once did Ahmarahn have the pleasure of visiting General Zhia's miniature palace, but once was enough to sear the location into his memory. Near the center of the Sun-blood District, beyond the merchants and lower-ranking highborns, lay a coveted neighborhood lined with nevethium lamps, water features, and homes containing a minimum of three levels, each with their own balconies. The All-Sovereign liked to keep his high-ranking military advisors close, but not so close as to give them unlimited access to the palace itself. They were still granted free rein of the grounds, of course. Who else would oversee initiate training? But their accommodations were far superior to barracks, leaving the generals, financial advisors, and war council with little want for anything outside the occasional escapade to the lesser districts for prohibited frivolities.

Nanjiya's chosen access point lay beneath a waste closet—a luxury only found within the Sun-blood District. While the rest of the city had to carry buckets of excrement to their quarter's communal waste chutes, the highborn frequented public waste closets that dropped the filth directly into the tunnels below. The wealthiest had them *in* their homes. Despite using waste closets with some frequency during his time in Cadar, it had never occurred to Ahmarahn that the chutes might connect with secret passageways. The more he thought about it, the more he realized how brilliantly the system was designed.

The brilliance made utilizing it no less miserable, though. Ahmarahn smelled the putrid odor of the waste chute long before they arrived at the grate barring it, and his evening meal threatened to come back up more than once.

"You can't be serious," he groaned as Nanjiya pushed open a cross-hatched gate to a lower tunnel filled with water and...

He didn't want to think about what else.

Even breathing strictly through his mouth, the stench was enough to make his eyes water. He looked down at his absorbent outfit and imagined the feces and urine clinging to every crevice and fiber.

Nanjiya whisked past him and lowered herself down onto a wooden ladder that didn't appear to be part of the original architecture; a little way down the shit creek rested another, leading up to a small tunnel in the ceiling. "It's not so bad," Nanjiya said as she descended. "Only comes halfway up my calves, and Asha has a concoction that will remove any stains and traces of odor."

A *splash* sounded as she landed in the stream and waded up to the next ladder.

"Perfect." Ahmarahn held his breath as he lowered himself after her, trying not to stare too long at any of the brownish buildup clinging to the spots where water met stone.

Nanjiya motioned for him to hurry, and he joined her on the next ladder, careful to keep his body as far from the rungs as possible in case any lingering feces dripped from her boots. She waited a moment, ensuring no one was using the chute for its intended purpose, then peered down at him.

"We will not speak again until we return," she whispered.

Ahmarahn shrugged. "Just get me out of this literal shit hole."

The second ladder was embedded in the wall, running alongside the open chute. Nanjiya reached for the handle attached to the lyvium chute's exterior. She hung there for a moment, then kicked her legs up and inside, presumably knocking open the interior cover and heaving herself into the closet.

Ahmarahn was glad he went second. Not only did he nearly lose his grip connecting with the handle, his first attempt to kick his legs up and inside bashed his shin against the edge. He cursed silently, making a clean transition on the second try.

Well, not literally clean. The filth on his pant legs confirmed otherwise.

Nanjiya was already peering through the cracked door when he emerged, and together they scampered across the street into the shelter of vines overhanging one of the second-level balconies. Thanks to the ever-glowing nevethium lanterns, darkness was scarce in the Sun-blood District, and thanks to the cleanliness of the streets, there were few places to hide.

But fate hadn't forgotten Ahmarahn and the few good deeds left to his name, for it had deposited them not two streets over from Zhia's home. If they climbed up the balconies and moved across the tightly packed rooftops, they could avoid any potential interaction with patrols.

Ahmarahn pointed up, then used the vines to scale the first floor. They did the same for the following two balconies, reaching the roof without even a hint of disturbance. From above the gilded eaves, they could perfectly see the streets of the Sun-blood District and the soldiers patrolling it. They waited until those closest to them made several rounds, memorizing their patterns and assessing the proper window in which to act. Ahmarahn determined they had just under ten minutes to cross three roofs, break into Zhia's home, secure her, and make their way to and down the waste chute.

Not ideal, but not impossible.

Crossing the nearly overlapping rooftops was the easiest feat he'd tackled in moons, and slicing through the sliding screen of Zhia's third-story balcony was equally effortless. Crime was practically non-existent in the Sun-blood District, and as a result, the homes were almost boastfully accessible. Furthermore, Zhia was renowned for her reclusive and arrogant nature, both of which increased the likelihood that she would live and sleep alone. Ahmarahn anticipated the rest of the mission to proceed flawlessly.

What he hadn't planned for was the sandcat.

The All-Sovereign was known for collecting an array of rare, foreign, or dangerous animals and plant life, so it wasn't surprising the hobby had spread to those seeking to emulate His Holiness. Still, Ahmarahn would've never presumed anyone in their right mind would try to domesticate one of the most dangerous nuisances indigenous to Az Zar.

He reached for the larger of his two daggers, testing its weight in his hand as he assessed the length of the lyvium chain securing the beast to a column at the room's center. Their options were limited. The sandcat could easily maneuver across the carpet and around the columns, then make its way over the lounges and past the potted plants to where he stood at the railing.

He'd settled on backing away quietly and trying another entrance when a growl rumbled in the beast's throat. Its mouth opened to reveal a set of yellowed, smaller fangs alongside the two massive tusks that stretched long past its jaw. Ahmarahn had seen the look in its eyes enough to know it had no intention of letting them pass.

The sandcat sprang, clearing half the room with the grace of an assassin. Ahmarahn crouched, both daggers drawn, his gaze trained on the soft cream fur beneath its barrel-thick neck. He knew its weakness, knew that, for a moment, it would risk exposing its heart to his lyvium blades when it went for the kill. It leaped again, this time from a lounge the size of a table, its mouth yawning wide. Ahmarahn angled his blade, his heart pounding in his ears. He willed his aim to be true.

He never found out.

Nanjiya slammed into him, knocking them both out of the beast's path. Ahmarahn shoved her off, desperate to regain his footing before the sandcat lunged again. He scrambled, gaze scouring the room. But there was no longer a threat. The beast lay still on the floor, limbs lazily stretched out to the side, tongue lolling in its mouth.

Ahmarahn creeped closer, his daggers still held defensively in front of him. The sandcat's ribs rose and fell with shallow breaths. He nudged it with the toe of his boot. Nothing.

"Our quarrel doesn't lie with this poor creature," Nanjiya whispered as she kneeled to pluck a small dart from its neck. "He is a prisoner as much as we are. There was no need to take an innocent life."

"A lot of innocent lives are going to be lost if this goes the way you want it to," Ahmarahn whispered back. "You don't get to play favorites in war."

"That doesn't mean we shouldn't give grace when given the opportunity." She pocketed the dart and hurried out of the room and down a hallway.

The urge to stroke the sandcat's golden coat was too strong. Ahmarahn ran his fingers over the length of its substantial body, pausing as his skin encountered the cool chain. He spared a few more moments to pick the lock securing the collar to the sandcat's neck, then stroked the place where the lyvium had worn down its fur into patches of bloodied skin.

"My debt is repaid," he told it, thinking of the night the sandcats had happened upon the camp where he and Elaysia were imprisoned, effectively causing a disturbance that allowed them to flee. "Get out of here when you wake, if you can."

Ahmarahn's head buzzed as he made his way after Nanjiya. The ordeal with the sandcat sent a wave of emotions and memories crashing through his mind, ones he'd fought to bury, along with Davier. They clawed their way back into his consciousness, endangering the false reality he'd constructed to maintain his sanity.

A *thud* sounded from further down the hallway, followed by a muffled cry. Ahmarahn sprinted toward it, smashing through a crack in the sliding screen that sealed the bed chamber. Inside, Nanjiya wrestled Zhia to the floor, pressing a cloth to her mouth. By the time Ahmarahn cleared the massive bed filling nearly half the room, the general had ceased struggling. Nanjiya lowered her ear to the thin, silk fabric covering Zhia's breasts, then folded the cloth and slipped it into her boot.

"Is she…" Ahmarahn didn't want to say 'dead,' didn't want to appear like he cared about her wellbeing, lest it come back to bite him.

Nanjiya shook her head. "Asleep, like the sandcat." She peered out the window and studied the streets below, then turned back to Ahmarahn with a glint in her eyes. "For now."

He rolled Zhia over with the edge of his boot, testing the strength of whatever drug Nanjiya had stained the cloth with. "Not sure why you brought me along. It seems like you have this handled well enough."

Nanjiya gestured to the bedchamber. "All the homes look the same here. I wouldn't have known which to target, or whose mind was the most valuable. And for all my notable talents, lifting heavy things isn't one of them." She looked pointedly at Ahmarahn, then used her chin to gesture to Zhia.

"Always the fucking pack mule," Ahmarahn grumbled as he hefted Zhia's sizeable frame into his arms. She was tall even for a nyrian, and unlike some of the higher-ranking military leaders, she worked to maintain a muscled physique that would've challenged him in his prime. Still, his time spent in the mines had prepared him for hauling heavy shit, if nothing else.

They escaped through the front door, sticking to the sides of buildings and avoiding the warm green glow cast by the nevethium lanterns. Ahmarahn's assessment proved true, and they slipped into the shelter of the waste closet mere moments before the patrol rounded the corner. The soldiers wouldn't know until dawn that something was wrong, when Zhia didn't show up for drills. Unless the sandcat woke and wreaked havoc first. Ahmarahn smiled at the thought of it stalking highborns as they strolled about in their silks, in full disbelief anything so beastly could penetrate their sanctuary. He almost hoped it would.

Aside from struggling to lower Zhia down the waste chute and into the stream of filth below, transporting their prize was an uneventful—if not exhausting—venture. When they emerged from the grate just outside the rebel's inn, they were met with the all-too-eager hands of Kymerius, who also looked to be sorely disappointed that Ahmarahn had returned in one piece.

They snuck Zhia in through the back door just before the golden rays of dawn pierced the sky, then secured her in the cellar below, binding her arms and legs to a chair. Ahmarahn noted they didn't bother to blindfold her, a choice that secured her fate. As she came to, he reminded himself that this was the woman who threatened to cut off his sister's fingers, the one who carried out the greatest number of the All-Sovereign's wicked deeds, the one who'd likely given the command to kill the rest of his family. Assuming she hadn't done it herself.

But seeing her thrash and strain, her luminescent eyes bulging with fear as she took in the armed rebels surrounding her, Ahmarahn's traitorous heart faltered. He lingered in the far corner of the cellar near the stairs. Out of her line of sight.

"You won't get anything out of me," Zhia spat as Nanjiya removed her gag. "I'm trained to withstand tortures far worse than your infantile brains could ever conjure, and I will take any and all military secrets to Mavet's eternal realms."

The corner of Nanjiya's lip quirked. "You all say that, but eventually, you talk."

Zhia tightened her lips, as if determined to prove her resolution.

Kymerius glanced at Nanjiya, who gave him a single nod. The blow he delivered to Zhia's face sent her chair toppling over. She wiggled helpless fingers as she coughed up a mouthful of blood, then spat two teeth onto the floor.

It's what she deserves, Ahmarahn reminded himself. *Think of Xi.*

And Xi was all that stilled his hand.

Zhia proved steadfast in her promise to remain silent. In the minutes that ticked by, Kymerius beat her to the point where she slipped beyond consciousness, only to coax her back awake to deliver the same treatment. Ahmarahn fought to keep quiet; to keep from admiring the commitment to her cause, no matter how misplaced her loyalties.

After one particularly cruel revival, in which Kymerius submerged her head in freezing water until she awoke, she registered Ahmarahn's presence in the room. Half-dazed, with an eye swollen shut and blood dripping down her snow-white skin, a gurgle escaped her throat.

"I told His Holiness you'd betray us," she rasped. "What do you think he'll do when he finds I'm dead and traces it back to you?" She choked on a laugh, spewing more blood onto her silk night shift. "Your sister will be dead before nightfall."

Ahmarahn's heart skipped a beat as all eyes turned on him. Nanjiya, from where she sat on the table, her legs dangling, raised an eyebrow. Ahmarahn swallowed. His gut told him everyone in the room wanted him dead. But as he reached for his dagger, he realized Zhia's admission had done the one thing he couldn't have done for himself.

It reaffirmed him as an enemy of the empire. And if he could gain the rebels' trust, make up a believable story for Zhia's death, and sneak away long enough to converse with the All-Sovereign, he could win this game yet.

Ahmarahn emerged from the corner, taking Zhia's bloodied face in his hand. He thought of Xi as he dug out the nyrian's still open eye, then flung it toward Kymerius. The whimpering sound that came from the general nearly broke Ahmarahn's resolve. But she was no hero, and neither was he.

"There's little you can tell me that I don't already know, Zhia," he lied, "but if you want to make your death more succinct, I'm happy to provide that relief." He grabbed a sharp grater from the shelf and kept Xi's face clear in his mind as he used it to shave off the smooth flesh of the general's right forearm.

Snot bubbled in Zhia's nostrils. "Please," she mouthed. Then, a little clearer, "I'll tell you what I know. Just please, kill me quickly after."

Ahmarahn lowered the grater. He looked back to Nanjiya, who studied him with unreadable eyes. She nodded.

"There, there." Ahmarahn stroked her blood matted hair. "Quickly now. Mavet's eternal realms await."

JAKKI

J akki would've stayed with the skulmor for moons, had it not been for Xaren's forlorn gazes and unspoken pleas. She'd only just begun learning the art of cultivating their sacred mushrooms, and which crystalline reservoirs were used for bathing versus ceremonies; to crack the ice of their culture and explore the endless caverns running deep beneath their mountains.

After her ceremony concluded, she'd become more than a part of the pack. She'd been awakened. Everything she'd once held as important seemed to fade in the blueish light of their underground world, yet the smallest things had gained significance. Something as simple as her breath was, when she focused on it, sacred. No longer did she take for granted rising in the mornings or resting in the evenings. How wrong she'd been to assume the skulmor were lesser than the other races. That was what Orillon thought of Neharem, and what Az Zar thought of Orillon.

No more. Never again. She'd see to it the world was made right before she exhaled her final breath.

When Uruuka had asked Jakki the morning after the ceremony what she'd thought of it, Jakki had replied that nothing would ever be the same again. That it had been as though she were a part of everything, and everything a part of her. That she knew she was merely self-contained for the span of her life, and that upon her death, she'd spill back out into the ether, back to the source. That she finally understood her sense of longing to be a part of something bigger and greater. That her homesickness had never been about her Yustano island home.

Uruuka had smiled her fierce wolfish grin in response. She said the skulmor believed that even the gods were made of stardust, and that while everything ended, nothing truly ceased to exist. Life simply returned to the source of its manifestation.

The day Shadow took to the skies in full health was bittersweet. There was nothing to keep Jakki and Xaren in Tyrgraak after, especially since they'd already stayed a full moon cycle. Jakki couldn't keep Elaysia waiting any longer. She'd undoubtedly returned from Orillon with her new mate and was likely drowning in gatherings and sleepless nights. Still, Jakki was surprised to find no urge to return to her, at least not in the way she had. But duty was duty, and Elaysia was still her friend and High Chieftain, and Jakki would be damned if the Lawful Dominion went down without her contributing to the fight.

The morning of their departure, Jakki found herself sitting beside the great crystalline pool in the center of the main cavern. Some pups splashed nearby, occasionally peering up with big, round eyes, intrigued by the woman dangling her furless feet in the water. One of them was bold enough to approach, and Jakki rewarded the effort with a bead from her tunic.

"He will be the envy of his litter," Uruuka said, taking a seat beside her. "Pups aren't given gifts until their fifth year, and even then, it's usually something the pack deems useful."

Jakki bit back a grin as the pup scampered off, trailing at least a dozen more behind it. "There's much more where that comes from up top."

Uruuka rubbed a spot just below her ribs, where her newly formed scar prevented the regrowth of fur. She'd healed quickly—far faster than Jakki had witnessed with Neharem remedies. In fact, it wasn't entirely unlike the nazrath treatment she'd received for her own wounds a year past.

"How long has your pack lived beneath the mountains?" Jakki asked.

Uruuka glanced over her shoulder at the great skulmor statues supporting the bridge. "The elders say all skulmor were born beneath the mountains. Throughout our existence, we've risen to the surface and spread out among the tundras and forests. But when things grow too dangerous, we again seek shelter below."

"Are you connected with the packs still above ground?" Jakki rubbed her own scarred leg. Though covered by fabric and well beyond healed, it seemed to throb beneath her touch.

Uruuka's ears pinned back. "Hardly. There's no unity among the packs. Tolerance, at best. Our brethren occupying the sur-face lands grew too complacent. They tried to imitate the ways of foreigners and established permanent communities, which made them vulnerable. It was only a matter of time before Nyzar beat them back."

"Nyzar?" Jakki took a moment to place Az Zar's old name. "That means you've been down here for over two thousand years."

"Forever," Uruuka said with a shrug.

"How many villages do the skulmor have underground?" It was a question Jakki hadn't wanted to ask until now, for fear they'd think she intended them harm. But a moon cycle had been enough time to gain their trust.

Uruuka eased herself into the pool, sighing as the waters lapped over her chest. "Only the moons know. There are at least two other strongholds in the north, one to the south, two to the east. Probably more, but whether or not they are occupied is another matter." She studied Jakki with guarded, green eyes. "My kind has never been well loved by the other races of land."

"The loss is theirs."

The silence that followed was calming. Jakki hummed a song of Mother Itaso, one that told the story of how she'd formed Quinaria from water, giving life to the star seeds that speckled the dead ground. When she finished, she found Uruuka looking up at her, wolven features etched with worry.

"You must be careful," the skulmor said, her tone nearly a growl. "The dominants have been documenting moon cycles and ingesting different combinations of mushrooms to gain visions for years. They believe everything is about to change, and that your stormbirds are the harbingers of it."

Jakki was on her feet in an instant, unsettled by the mention of Siren and Shadow. "I thank you for your kindness, Uruuka of Tyrgraak. I understand I cannot visit your dominants again before departing, so please let them know when you have an audience with them next that I will return when our war is over."

"No need to wait that long." Uruuka emerged from the pool. Her frame towered over Jakki's, but not in the threatening way of the skulmor that had knocked her to the ground in Gohla. "If you find yourself in need, I will do whatever I can to rally my people to yours. You are part of the pack now. Your wellbeing is ours."

"And yours mine." Jakki started to go, then turned at the last moment, ripping the nevethium pendant from her neck. "To keep and guide you," she said, holding it out to Uruuka.

The she-wolf refused. "It is too great a gift."

"That it is, but it is a gift available to all. At least, that's what we're fighting for." She shoved it into Uruuka's hand, folding her silken fingers over it. "Take it. I can get another. Nevethium is plentiful in Agaas. At least for now."

"I will protect it with my life."

Jakki hurried away before she could register the emotion on the skulmor's face. As she sprinted up the tunnel leading from the city, a single, mournful howl echoed off the walls, chilling her bones.

But also warming her heart.

Siren and Shadow deposited Jakki and Xaren at a cliff overlooking Sunset Bay—the shoreline nearest Agaas. They walked through the woods in silence, their footsteps light, their movements brisk. It smelled of damp soil and lush trees, and the air was refreshingly thick and cool—not frigid and harsh like the air of the Far North. Jakki stopped to pluck a few anderberries from the spike-leaved bushes on which they grew, then offered a few to Xaren before popping some in her mouth.

Xaren refused them, eyeing her warily. "Is there anything I'm not to speak of when we arrive?"

His question came so unexpectedly that Jakki halted, dropping the berries. "What is that supposed to imply?"

The boy frowned. "Nothing. You just have so many secrets. You're as hard as stone and twice as guarded."

Jakki bristled. "Is this about the skulmor? It's not my fault you spent most of your time hidden away, freezing on the peak, when you could've been below with me, learning more about their culture."

Xaren scowled. "I had to look after Shadow. But that's not what I mean." He pointed at her torso, and though the parchment was tucked safe inside, nestled in the layers of her furs, she knew it was what he gestured to. "You haven't said a word about it since the tulek bear, and despite it being sacred to the skulmor, they let you keep it. Just how powerful is it, Jak? What does it really do? And why have you told no one about it?"

The look he gave reminded her so of her chief mother that she felt a spontaneous urge to explain everything. How she'd found it, why she'd hidden it, and the way it made her feel. But doing so would be admitting to Unleto's death, and she wasn't ready to confess to that, no matter how it might expel the nightmares that plagued her.

No matter. She could omit the incriminating parts.

"I'll tell you, but this will stay between us until a time of my choosing. Understand?"

Xaren nodded and took a seat on a porous log that was nearly as spongy as the mushrooms of Tyrgraak. Jakki recounted everything from the moment she found the old man in the woods up to when she faced the tulek bear, adjusting where necessary to avoid Unleto and all the times she'd used the parchment simply for her own pleasure. She especially didn't mention her fear that she'd become addicted to its powers, that it seemed to leave her more ravaged after each use. That sometimes she feared the old man could step into her body *without* her permission.

Xaren's eyes widened with each confession. By the time she finished, he was pacing in front of the log, clutching a fallen branch as though it grounded him.

"And your skulmor friend didn't tell you more about this old man, as you call him?" he asked, pointing the branch at Jakki.

She swiped it away. "I didn't want to ask too many questions. They seemed convinced I'd killed the bear because of the parchment and that it had chosen me. Asking questions about it would've made me seem undeserving."

"*Not* asking questions about it makes you undeserving." Xaren's face twisted with disapproval. "This creature who gave it to you is not an old man, but an entity."

"I've concluded as much," Jakki said defensively.

"How do you know he's not an evil spirit? What if he's a Caman? You can't keep giving him access to your soul, Jakki. It's too dangerous." He glanced at her, side-eyed. "Has the parchment given you any ill effects?"

"No." Jakki hoped she'd answered slowly and firmly enough to seem sincere. "I'm worn out after, but that's no different from any other physical or mental exertion. Bodies and minds always need time to recover."

Xaren shook his head as he bent to adjust the fabric of his Az Zarian boots. He'd traded most of his old uniform for Agaasian wear, but the silent boots remained.

Jakki circled him slowly. "Are you still good on your promise to keep all this to yourself?"

"I'm no skirvin. I'll keep quiet."

She didn't know what a skirvin was, but she understood the implication all the same. Xaren didn't like secrets, but he'd keep hers. He'd proven himself trustworthy more than once—and that said nothing of the fact that she'd saved his stormbird's life. He wouldn't speak unless he truly felt there were lives at stake.

Jakki would make sure it didn't come to that.

She tried to make banter with him the rest of their hike to Agaas, but he would only force a laugh at best and ignore her altogether at worst. Something between them had changed. Only then did she realize how much she'd come to enjoy his company. He'd given her a chance when no one else had, had genuinely believed in her—looked up to her, even.

She'd win him back. She had to.

"Well, it's decided," Elaysia said, taking another sip of mead. "You are hereby forbidden from venturing into the north without me to accompany you."

Jakki took a drink from her own cup, relishing the sweeter notes of the Daruk beverage. It was thicker than wine and twice as intoxicating. "Because you fear for my life?"

Elaysia snorted. "Because I'm jealous of your life."

"I don't recommend the near-death experiences, but otherwise, I suppose it's envy-worthy."

"I've had a few too many of those myself."

Elaysia stared into the fire, lost in some distant memory. It occurred to Jakki just how much they'd missed of each other's lives since Elaysia had assumed her role as high chieftain. There had been a time when they shared nearly every moment, exchanging secrets to fill the gaps caused by temporary separation. Now, she was no longer certain the gap between them was bridgeable. Not while Elaysia had worries of rations and war. And maybe not ever.

"It seems like what I thought I knew about the world changes every day," Elaysia said, rising from the cushions they'd piled beside the summit lodge fire. She'd ordered the war council out as soon as Jakki heaved open the heavy doors, demanding to be left alone with her long-absent Stormrider. Then she'd wrapped Jakki in a hug that felt like longing and belonging all at once.

Elaysia leaned over the map carved into the gathering table, her white streaked hair shielding her face. "It makes you wonder if anything was ever true."

"Or if anything ever will be," Jakki finished. Their gazes met, and for once, Jakki looked away first. "How is everything here? The twins? Your union? Konar? The war?"

Elaysia held up a finger for each question as she answered it. "Surviving. Fattening. Surprising. Aggravating. And…" She chewed her lip as she made her way back to the fire. "There's not an encompassing word that describes the state of the war. Even with Vahid's kuza, we're still outnumbered, especially since we've lost another tribal alliance instead of gaining more, as I'd hoped."

Jakki had a feeling she knew which tribe had been lost, but she wasn't ready to bring up her mother.

"The stormbirds have provided some advantages," Elaysia continued, "and the council is mostly in agreement to use them on the offensive now that we've tested them in battle."

"You sound unsure." Jakki refilled her cup, then offered some more to Elaysia, who refused.

"I don't like putting them at risk before they've come into their powers. But I see few other options at our disposal. Our territory shrinks by the day, and the Lawful Dominion has shown they aren't above punishing even the neutral tribes for non-allegiance." She drank the rest of her cup, then held it out to Jakki, apparently regretting the refusal she'd made moments prior. "I wish Raynar would heed my request for a peace treaty, at least long enough for us to convene. If he could be made to see how he's a pawn for Az Zar, how there will be no victors in this war if we tear each other apart, then we'd stand a chance."

"He won't listen." Jakki refilled Elaysia's cup and took another drink. It was the first alcohol she'd consumed since being captured by the skulmor, and to her disappointment, the effect didn't seem as pleasurable as it'd once been. "He's too like his father, only weaker. It's a dangerous combination."

Elaysia glanced at the door, as if confirming they were truly alone, then turned an intense gaze on Jakki. "If he were gone—if all his advisors were gone—would his people turn to our leadership?"

Jakki studied the woman before her, the set of her jaw, the confidence of her posture. The coldness in her eyes.

"I think," she said carefully, "it's the only way."

"Perhaps our next attack will target more than supplies and whatever weapons they plan to annihilate us with." Elaysia gripped the cup so tightly Jakki feared it would crack. "Speak of this to no one. In the meantime, I'll send one final tuross message to Raynar, begging for an audience. His reply will determine his fate."

Jakki was grateful to sleep in her cot that night, tangled in blankets that smelled of smoke and herbs and love-making. But no matter how relaxed she got, sleep wouldn't come. There were too many unanswered questions.

And too much guilt.

When she finally nodded off, nightmares were waiting to greet her. They'd lessened since returning from Az Zar, but her venture north seemed to have unlocked the chest she'd buried them in.

The first two dreams ended almost as quickly as they'd begun. They were more feelings than visions, more smoke than reality. She'd shaken them off with the blankets and soothed her throbbing head with water.

But when *that* one came, there was no escaping it.

She felt the rocks first, cool and sharp against her skin. Then her ears filled with the merciless caws of ravager birds. Her body ached. Lips cracked. She forced her dream eyes open and stifled a scream. Unleto's empty eyes stared back at her, his body gashed and broken upon the rocks. A flurry of ravager birds tore into him. They cawed and cackled as they made off with chunks of the boy's flesh. She screamed and shooed them away. They responded by calling more of their kind, swarming Unleto's body until they covered him entirely in their crimson wings. Jakki hurled a rock at them, crushing one, then another. One by one, she smashed the black blood out from their crimson feathers until they'd all died or retreated. But there was no Unleto left to save; only his skeleton remained. She reached out to touch it, unsure of why she did, and found it warm. The hollow blackness of its empty eyes flashed open. Not Unleto's eyes. They belonged to...

Elaysia.

K onar withdrew his hand just as a serrated beak lunged for the small fish in his fingers, dropping it into the bottom of the cage. The tuross narrowed its multi-hued eye at him, then dove swiftly into the fray with its brethren. They emitted no sounds—at least not in a frequency humans or nyrians could pick up. It was rumored the skulmor could hear their pitch, but he'd never confirmed it. That, among other things, such as durability and intelligence, made the turosses ideal message carriers.

The tuross breed kept in Neharem were of the most common in Quinaria: scaled torsos with webbed wings that allowed them to navigate both sky and water, even though they didn't need to deliver messages to myrem settlements any longer. Assuming they ever did. There were some more colorful varieties in the south, even a few breeds that boasted feathers and were strictly airborne. The turosses of the north had thick, almost velvety skin, allowing them to survive the harsh weather so prevalent in the region.

What turosses didn't like was being trapped for too long. Half the battle in keeping them was ensuring they were sent out in the proper order, so they didn't go mad. A caged tuross was a bitey tuross, and the one Konar just fed had nearly severed his finger. Their size made them unassuming; adorable, even. That was the last mistake many new tuross handlers made.

Konar, however, wasn't new to such tasks. It'd been one of his earliest duties when he'd first been enslaved at the palace in

Cadar centuries prior, and like many things, he'd never forgotten.

"They've always liked you," a silken voice said.

Konar shrugged and closed the cage door. It was as tall as he was and stretched the length of the room, housing anywhere from one to three dozen turosses at a time. The numbers had dwindled since the start of the war, however. He needed to retrieve new eggs from the beach soon.

"I don't know about that," he said, facing Maseeya. She wore her usual colorful robe atop a neutral tunic and leggings, and her hair was fastened with a handcrafted pin she'd brought over with her from Az Zar.

"I do." Her round lips parted in a smile. "If they don't like someone, they refuse to eat until that person's left their presence. They must trust you."

"They're terrible judges of character, then." Konar eyed the litter levels, making a mental note to replace it with more dried moss and wood shavings the following day, then wiped his hands on a rag lying beside the empty bucket he'd used to bring their water. "But I do enjoy their company. It's nice to be needed, even if I can't hear their thanks."

"Sometimes the most important things are never spoken." Maseeya cocked her head in the way she always did when waiting to see how he'd react.

He had no words for her that day. He never did when it mattered most.

They walked out onto the main platform of the High Tree, taking their time in the late evening calm. It was one of the rare nights where the mist and branches allowed stars to wink through the trees, illuminating the bridges and platforms alongside the glow of the nevethium hearts. The air warmed in anticipation of the Feasting Moons, and Konar was comfortable walking about without his thick robe. The nytak life he'd taken earlier that day had likely helped as well, but he didn't want to linger on that. It was getting to be painful even with the animals now. So many unnecessary deaths.

"How does Kelsia fare?" he asked as they strolled past the pond, practically bursting with plump fish. Whoever had taken over feeding them during his absence had done a more than adequate job.

"She'll make a full recovery. Physically." The way Maseeya emphasized that last word told Konar all he needed to know. "Her people take turns trying to visit her, but she turns them away. Even Grokhion hasn't been allowed an audience."

"Give her time. I can only imagine the burden she carries." Actually, he could well imagine it, but going into depth would benefit no one. "And Elaysia?"

Maseeya sat beside the pond and trailed her finger through the water, dragging along the bits of leaves and branches trapped there. "Tired. Guarded." She looked at Konar with lively brown eyes, the creases in their corners even more pronounced than usual. "But today, I thought she seemed hopeful. It's the first time I've seen it since she came back to us."

"How so?" Konar took a seat beside her, giving his full attention.

"It's several things, I'm sure. Jakki's return. Rescuing Kelsia. Her connection with Onitus. The twins getting older and alleviating some of the stress from the early months. But there's something else, too."

Konar knew what—rather, who—she meant. He'd hardly spent any time around Vahid, but he'd seen and heard enough to know the Orillon man had proven more loyal and helpful in his short time in Agaas than half the council had since the declaration of war. Even T'Vak had nothing ill to say about him, other than jabbing at his privileged upbringing. Konar had spent much of his life sorting the good people from the bad, and though it never got easier, and though the lines blurred more and more the older he got, he still trusted his instincts when it came to assessing character.

He'd assessed nothing but good in Vahid.

"Good for her," he whispered. "She deserves to devour happiness in the rare occurrences it presents itself."

"And what about you? Do you devour happiness when she winks at you from across the fire?" Maseeya imitated this with her own wink, an action so atypical of her, yet so utterly convincing, that he looked away to hide the effect it had on him.

"That's never been one of my skill sets, I'm afraid."

"I'm sorry to hear that. Life is only so long. Well, for most of us."

He looked back, expecting to find her warmth replaced by a stony mask of judgment, but all he saw was unadulterated compassion. Something in him stirred, and he fought desperately to fight it. He'd done so for over a quarter century, and he wouldn't let one night ruin it all. Maseeya deserved better than that. Than him.

Konar cleared his throat. "Life is always too long and never long enough. It's no wonder most of us welcome death by the end."

"Death will have to drag me by my ankles. I love that girl and her babes too much to go without a fight." She balled up her fists in mock battle, then suddenly loosened them, her lips parted, as though she had a revelation. "It must be so hard for you to live without your son. Elaysia's not even mine, and my heart breaks at the thought of..." Her voice trailed off as she shifted uncomfortably and made to leave.

"Wait," Konar reached for her hand—offering, not taking. Hardly a day passed without thoughts of Kayrune; though, hardly a day passed without all his wrongdoings coming back to haunt him. "I've not heard his name spoken aloud in years."

"That tends to be the fate of those responsible for such atrocities." She wouldn't take his hand, but she remained beside the pond. "Still, it does not change the fact he was your son. I wouldn't wish that fate on anyone, especially not the way you had to take part in it."

Konar thought of the little babe he'd taken in all those years ago, an act of both mercy and convenience. Before Kayrune, he'd been quite satisfied with his childless state. Having witnessed the destructive nature of his parents' toxic relationship, he'd chosen to refrain from seeking love and pleasure, which naturally lent itself to no offspring. Research was his passion; the scrolls his love. The times he felt stirrings of longing, he'd throw himself into his work or allow himself release with a stranger he was certain to never cross paths with again.

But on his second and final voyage back to his island home, a trip he'd hoped to derive a sense of closure from, he'd come across an orphaned boy at the inn his father used to frequent. The Siren's Song had been run down beyond repair and all the people he'd associated with the establishment long dead, but there, at the bar, had been a squalling babe nestled in a woven basket.

His amma died in childbearing, the barkeep had told him. *I was out peeling bark from the zidel trees when I heard 'im crying. No sooner than I had 'im in my arms, I heard the bloodthirsty screech of a gwanei. He's lucky to be crying here instead of shredded by them razor teeth.*

Konar had found it odd that a woman gave birth in the middle of the jungle alone, and he said as much.

She was awskada, she was, the barkeep had replied. *I could scent it on her. Her kind isn't supposed to have babes without sanction, especially not a baby boy.*

That was all the convincing Konar had needed. The boy was as much his blood as any child ever would be. For all he knew, they *were* related. Awskada women were tightly knit, their lineages traceable back to the earliest histories of Zelos.

It hadn't taken more than a request for the barkeep to surrender the babe to him. By that time, the rujpati had seen to it that the Zelosi people were under absolute Az Zarian control, turning over more than half what they caught, earned, and grew to the mainland. Extra mouths to feed were enough of a hassle if they were kin, and an unclaimed child was as good as dead.

Careful of that one, the barkeep had said with a solemn face as Konar departed, woven basket in hand. *Awskada boys are bad luck, so they are.*

So they were.

But Konar had cared for the child as if he were his own, eventually giving him a name that linked Konar's past and present: Kayrune. The boy had a wild streak and a sharp mind, a dangerous combination that proved beyond brilliant when he cooperated and detrimental when he did not. Konar was careful to hide most of his past from the boy, but as he grew, he found it harder and harder to keep things secret while still training him to pursue the cause in his stead. And he could've seen—should've seen—Kayrune's passion for their shared dream and how it spawned his hatred and jealousy of Elishon. But Konar hadn't wanted to extinguish the lad's flame.

For that, he paid the greatest price.

But Konar wouldn't tell Maseeya any of that. Only the parts pertaining to Kayrune. And even that might prove to be too much honesty for her to swallow. People always said they wanted the truth, but rarely could they handle it.

Maseeya listened with rapt attention as he told the tale of discovering Kayrune back on Zelos and the lives they'd led over the next few decades, culminating in the fateful day the Moon-rider bloodline fell solely on Elaysia's shoulders. Along with everything else.

"I never knew," she said hoarsely when he finished. "Regardless, you loved him as though he was yours, and your pain is no less worthy. The fault also lies with you, and for that, I'm sorry. I'm starting to think your continued existence is a far worse punishment than death would've been."

A dark laugh rumbled in Konar's throat. She was right on all accounts. The love, the pain, the fault. And yes, if only she knew just how much he longed for death's embrace. He'd so naively assumed it was just around the corner after Elaysia's induction. How wrong he'd been.

How wrong he'd always been.

"Could you ever find it in your heart to tolerate me again, Maseeya?" He kneaded the fabric of his tunic, unable to bring his eyes to meet hers. "I don't expect you—anyone, for that matter—to ever fully forgive me. But sometimes, I dare to hope we could have more conversations like these. I miss it."

Maseeya waited for something. He could sense it pulsing from her core, could feel her gaze probing his face.

His throat tightened as his stomach clenched. It was so difficult. Why was it so difficult? What did he have to lose?

Only her, the quieter, more intelligent voice within him, whispered. *She's all you have left.*

"I miss you." Speaking the words aloud felt like ripping an arrow from his body. The silence that followed was agony. Half of him wanted to flee, the other half wanted to retract his confession or smother it with excuses, rendering it obsolete. But he forced himself to be fully present with the pain and tension. It was the least he deserved, and the least he could give her.

When he felt the warmth of her lips against his cheek, he knew he'd been undone. All the years of scheming, all the time spent rehearsing conversations and barring against unwanted outcomes, were truly lost. The final thread unraveled. But it felt good to let it all go, at least the parts concerning her.

And for once, he didn't regret his choice.

"I must see to Elaysia and the babes," she said, rising. "Join me tomorrow? After we break our fasts?"

"I wouldn't miss it for anything."

"I know."

The parting smile she gave melted the last layer of ice surrounding his heart. In its stead arose fear. Now, there was something to lose. Now, more than ever, he needed to uncover the last of the secrets before it was too late.

Upon returning from his conversation with Maseeya, Konar found T'Vak sitting at the library table. The backhander had been assigned his own temporary loft, but since returning from

Orillon without Zavik, he'd slept everywhere but there. As of late, his chamber of choice had been the library.

"Took you a bit longer than usual, didn't it?" he asked in the tone of a parent questioning their irresponsible offspring. "Flappers extra hungry tonight?"

Konar shook his head at the ridiculous name T'Vak had assigned to the turosses. "Not any longer than usual. I crossed paths with someone I've been meaning to catch up with, and way led to way. You know how it goes."

T'Vak raised a dark eyebrow and lowered the bottle that hadn't quite made its way to his lips. "Don't think I do. Care to enlighten me?" The twinkle in his eyes confirmed he needed no enlightening.

"Nothing that concerns you," Konar said quickly. "I just spoke to Maseeya again about getting an audience with the high chieftain. I need to inform her about our discovery and get her approval to rescue Zavik from Cadar."

"Maseeya." T'Vak savored her name, maintaining eye contact with Konar. "Nice for you two to get some alone time, I bet."

Konar's cheeks burned, a sensation he'd not experienced since he'd been very young. "I'm sorry?"

"No need to be sorry." T'Vak took a pull from the bottle and set it back on the table with a hollow *thud.* "If anything, I'm sorry it's taken you so long to get a little bit of—"

"If you'd like your tongue to remain in your mouth, I suggest you hold it."

T'Vak complied, though he didn't lose the sloppy grin plastered to his face. "Didn't mean to offend. It just seemed pretty obvious to me there was something kindling between you two. The looks she gives you, the way you go out of your way to avoid her. In fact, you hardly ever mention her when you won't shut up about everyone and everything else."

Konar didn't deny it. The backhander was smarter than he looked, after all. "I don't deserve her," he said, retrieving his pipe. He didn't have to ask for help any longer. The act of him revealing it prompted T'Vak to help him light it—as long as he got a few draws himself.

"Eh, we don't deserve anyone, the lot of us." He let Konar take the first inhale, then followed with one half as deep. "So maybe we really do deserve each other. If that makes any sense."

"T'Vak, you rarely make any sense," Konar said after another deep inhale. He relaxed into his chair, refusing T'Vak's offer of a third. "But I understand your intent. Broken people deserve broken people, yes?"

"Yeah." He smiled dumbly and kicked his boots up on the table. "That's some poetic shit right there. Maybe you were a story weaver in another life."

Konar didn't even feel an urge to swipe his boots off the table. For the moment, life was good. And considering how rare an occurrence it was, he forced himself to simply enjoy it, even if it was choosing ignorance over reality.

"Maybe I was," he murmured, closing his eyes. "Or maybe I have yet to be."

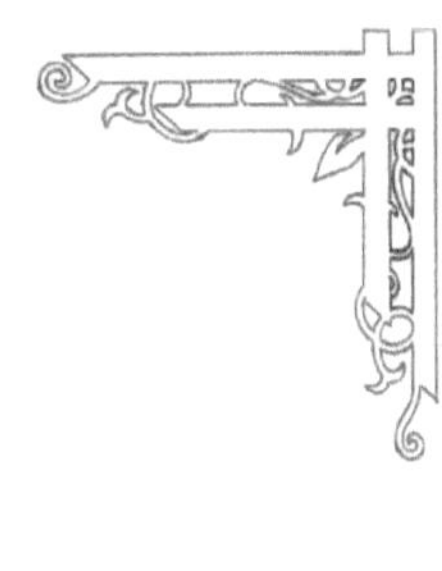

ELAYSIA

E laysia found Vahid sitting beside the river, the same one she'd taken refuge beside time and time again, both before her journey to Az Zar and after. He leaned against the trunk of a pocoaon tree, partially hidden beneath its veil of limber branches and silver leaves. As far as she knew, it was the furthest north one had been found. Just a little out of place. Just a little unexpected.

Not unlike him.

He greeted her with a warm smile when she drew back the curtain of branches, softly closing his book and laying it beside him on the blanket he'd spread. "High Chieftain." He started to rise, to greet her formally in the way of her people or his, but she held out a hand to stop him. It was the first thing that needed to change between them.

She dared a step closer, wanting to sit, but not wanting to be so bold. "I've been looking everywhere for you. Hallahd said I might find you here doing your late afternoon reading."

Perhaps puzzled by her act of seeking him out, his lips formed into a frown. "Is something wrong?" He again started to rise, so she quickly took a seat—against her better instincts. The blanket was small, no more than a few feet wide, and her legs touched his as she sat cross-legged beside him.

"Not anymore." She winced at the bits of her old awkwardness slipping out. "I haven't thanked you enough for the work you put into the masks you made for the Stormriders. Everyone is taken with them. Lumira and Mardus have already worn them into battle."

Vahid rested his hands on his knees. "The look on your face that day was thanks enough." They locked gazes for a moment that was entirely too long and not long enough. "You should know everyone has approached me privately to say something of the like. Even Jakki and Xaren—who I know are still exhausted from their time in the north—made it a point to come and see me, bearing small gifts."

Elaysia's heart warmed at hearing this. It was good to see those dearest to her coming together over something, no matter how small. And, according to the trial flights they'd all taken with the masks, the work Vahid had done was no small thing.

"I haven't given you anything to show my appreciation yet," she admitted. It would've been the perfect way to lead to her next proposition, the thing she hoped to share with him.

Vahid had other plans.

"I disagree." He plucked a small leaf from her hair and laid it on her knee, letting his hand linger a moment longer than necessary before removing it. "You've given me everything. I've always wanted to travel, but my father had other plans. You've freed me, shown me a lush world outside my own, rich with culture and life. You've allowed me to find purpose by putting all my training and knowledge to use, given me the chance to lead my men, to step out from my father's shadow. You've reunited me with my sister; brought honor to my family." He stroked one of the branches tenderly, running his thumb over one of the silken leaves, never once dropping his gaze from her. "Truly, what more could I ask for?"

Elaysia thought she knew, for it was the one thing she longed for but would never speak aloud. Unfortunately, even a moment of such pure vulnerability couldn't possess her to throw what was left of her heart on the table.

Still, she'd come for a reason.

"I wanted to see if you'd join me for a flight."

The look of shock on Vahid's face so contrasted with his usually softened features that she had to fight to keep from laughing. "On Onitus?"

"Unless you have a stormbird you've been keeping from me."

He jumped up, slipping the book beneath his arm as he playfully tugged the blanket from under her. "Turns out I was wrong," he said, beaming. "There was one thing, after all."

Elaysia's plan was twofold.

One, she did want to repay Vahid's kindness, and given how few alive had even seen—much less ridden—a stormbird, she thought it a decent offer. Not that it would entirely make up for, well...her. But still.

Second, she wanted to try seeing through Onitus's eyes again. But Kahana's inquiry as to whether or not she would still feel her own body while in his mind had haunted her. She needed to test it, to see how quickly she could shift back. Or if it was within her power at all.

They departed from Agaas as the sun began its descent—an ideal time, as the birds were usually well satiated by their hunts over the sea. As they approached the hill overlooking the training grounds, she caught sight of Anadu gliding in the distance, a massive fish in her talons. Actually—she squinted and edged out from the cover of the trees—it was far too large to be a fish.

"Is that a shark?" Vahid asked, lifting his hand to block what remained of the sun's rays.

"If so, the Lawful Dominion is in for more trouble than we are."

It wasn't entirely true. Despite the birds' size rapidly increasing, the ability to pick up large objects was only so much of an advantage. Still, they might evoke fear, if nothing else. Fear could do more than move mountains. It could destroy them.

"How do you summon him?" Vahid asked as they jogged through the knee-high grasses surrounding the training grounds.

"I don't," Elaysia said with a laugh. She could sense Onitus's incoming presence, though. He likely returned with his final kill of the day. "I ask, and if his desires align with mine, he comes."

Vahid slowed his pace to bind his thick hair with some leather cords, as Elaysia had recommended. She'd made the mistake of flying with her hair free only once, and it had cost her the better part of an evening to untangle all the knots.

"Is it often the case that they do?" he asked.

Elaysia nodded. "Yes. Khiev-Tatamic be praised." The turn of phrase once common to her felt foreign on her lips. It wasn't that she believed in the gods any less, but how she viewed them had changed. They seemed less definable, less powerful, and more distant. Perhaps one day she'd again find the time to reflect on it. If only she could be so lucky.

They came to a stop at the top of an adjacent hill, the one she'd climbed the day she'd almost confronted Konar but had not yet found the courage. She liked to think she'd found it since, but some days she could still feel that malnourished, frightened girl stirring inside her.

"Khiev-Tatamic?" Vahid pronounced the words slowly, the Nyrinian rolling off his tongue as though he'd been born to it. "That is your god?"

Elaysia plucked a small wildflower and twisted its fuzzy stem between her thumb and forefinger. "He—or she, or they, depending on how you view gods—is the most widely worshipped in Neharem. Most of the tribes acknowledge his existence, and many consider him the Creator of Quorath."

"Do you?"

"I don't pretend to understand the ways of gods. I treat their world with respect and hope it appeases them."

"A wise answer."

His eyes took on an almost golden glow in the fading sunlight. So warm and vibrant, filled with countless tones like the deserts of his homeland. Elaysia felt it again. That tingling pull. She was near certain by now that there wasn't a kinder man alive.

And it still frightened her; the thought of losing something, someone, so good.

"He's coming," Elaysia said, turning her gaze to the horizon. She thanked Onitus for his impeccable sense of timing.

She felt Vahid tense beside her as Onitus's silhouette came into view. It wasn't the reaction of someone fearful, but someone wild with anticipation. His lips parted, revealing the slight gap in his flawless white teeth. He touched her shoulder, squeezing it ever so slightly.

Elaysia had warned Onitus of her plans, so when the great stormbird landed beside them, he folded his silken wings and pressed his body to the grass. It wouldn't be long before she'd have to do some maneuvering to secure herself on his back. She slipped on her mask, instantly feeling protected beneath it, as though it not only guarded her face but also her mind. Vahid had refused her offer to borrow one of the other riders' and used his head wrap to cover everything but his eyes. Elaysia climbed up, Onitus's feathers firm but yielding beneath her. Once seated, she offered her hand to Vahid, and he accepted, even though he didn't really need her help to get on.

The feeling of his hands around her waist set off sensations that had long been dormant, as if her own inner workings were as the stormbird eggs had been. Alive, but waiting.

"Are you ready?" she asked, her tongue clumsy in her mouth.

Vahid leaned in close. "I was born ready."

When Onitus took to the skies, it filled Elaysia with the same sense of awe it always did, like the feeling of staring out at the ocean, or looking down from the peak of a mountain. She hoped the wonder would never fade. She needed something to remind her of life's miracles.

Vahid's grip on her was firm as Onitus soared higher, past the clouds and into the thinner air above. As he transitioned to a glide, the heir of House Undali eased with him, even getting emboldened enough to free a hand and hold it out in the air, is if he could catch the clouds slipping through his fingers.

Elaysia waited a while before attempting her feat. She wanted to give Vahid as much time as possible to revel in his ecstasy before making yet another request of him. When his hand slipped back around her waist, locking into his other across her abdomen, she straightened, pulling just slightly away.

"I'm going to try something," she shouted, turning her head back to catch his gaze.

Vahid's eyes widened. "I imagine there are only so many things you can try this high up."

"I'm not going to jump," she said with a nervous laugh. *At least, I hope not.* "But I'm going to try to enter his mind again, the way I did when rescuing Kelsia. I'm afraid I won't have control over my body when airborne, so I was hoping you'd..." It seemed so hard to ask it of him now. Why hadn't she said something earlier?

But Vahid, as always, was more attuned to her than she'd thought. "I assumed you wanted to do more than give me a bird's-eye tour of Neharem."

That hurt, even though she could tell he hadn't intended for it to do so.

"I won't let you fall," he continued. "I consider it a privilege that you trust your life in my hands."

Could nothing aggravate him? She forced out a guilt-laden "thank you," then moved Vahid as far from her mind as possible as she reached out to Onitus.

The colors all came at once, in a blur. It got easier each time, strengthened by their bond.

Show me, she told Onitus, pressing her masked face to his neck. *I am ready.*

Slowly, the colors took on shape, forming into the soft, golden rays and magenta-stained clouds of the sunset. She could feel the wind in her wings and her beak cutting through the air, could feel the warmth of the bodies nestled into her back.

Too much, she thought. She could still sense her body in the distance, almost like a dream. She tried to call to it, to keep both bodies balanced perfectly in her mind, but the second she focused too much on her true form, her glimpse into Onitus's eyes faded. It also took far too long to transition. By the time she was fully in control of her body, she would've fallen, had she ridden alone, or been killed, had she been on the ground in a battle.

She tried over and over, each time falling too far into one mind or the other, unable to hold them both in balance, to split his sight with her body. Once, she felt herself jerk, but Vahid's hold was firm, keeping her steady. The more she tried, the longer the transitions seemed to take, as though her mind couldn't handle going from one to the other repeatedly.

Help me, she begged Onitus. She felt his energy rippling around her. She had all his support, and dare she say it, love.

But it wasn't enough.

In a burst of frustration, she told Vahid to let go, hoping that the genuine threat to her life would allow her to return to herself as quickly as she needed. When she felt herself falling, she put all her focus on her body, desperately willing her arms to grab hold.

She came back to herself just as she slipped off his sleek feathers, a sick puff of air filling her stomach.

Vahid's reflexes were strong. He gripped her forearm, heaving her back onto Onitus. He didn't scold. He didn't laugh. He just held her tighter than ever before, his face pressed against her neck.

It gave Elaysia permission to let go. She'd tried enough for one day. There was no guarantee she'd ever have the control she wanted, and she knew she'd do well to allow herself that acceptance. She looked up at the star-speckled sky surrounding her and felt an overwhelming sense of love. She didn't know where or who it radiated from most, but something about Onitus and Vahid and a boundless sky created a trinity of security, exhilaration, and freedom that she knew she'd be a fool to lose.

When Onitus deposited them safely at the edge of the forest, Vahid took Elaysia's hands in his. It was a formal enough gesture—she'd seen hands held and kisses exchanged in Orillon as freely as air—but there was also something else there, beneath the surface.

"That was life-changing," he said softly. "Forgive me my plain words, but I seem to be at a loss for them."

"Onitus has a way of doing that."

"It wasn't Onitus."

Their bodies were dangerously close, so much so that she could feel his warmth. The desire to press her lips to his was more than overwhelming. Something in her still pulled back, even while every inch of her body screamed for it.

"Join me for a drink?" she asked, leading him into the woods. She hoped their maintained body contact would make up for her awkward departure. "I have an unopened bottle of Beridian Moonlight."

He tightened his grip on her hand, just for a moment. "I wouldn't miss it for all the treasures of Quinaria."

The room seemed smaller with him inside.

Even though Vahid was considerably tall as far as humans went, the idea was solely born of Elaysia's mind and the fact that she felt immensely exposed and confined within the four walls that were usually her sanctuary. When she couldn't escape into the sanctuary of nature—which was more often than not—her quarters provided her with that relief. Since having the babes, her security in and longing for the place had only intensified. And now, as he swept the space with his gaze, lingering every so often on a particular item like her father's last painting or her mother's sword, she felt naked.

"Sit wherever you'd like," she said hurriedly, gesturing to the chair that had been hand-made to rock the twins—a rarity in Neharem—then to the secondary cot that had been brought in for Maseeya. Thank the Daughter the woman she held as a mother wasn't around to witness her atrocious display of hospitality.

To her dismay, she made a complete fool of herself trying to open the bottle. The beridians sealed their precious Moonlight with spongy wooden inserts called corks instead of wax like the rest of Quinaria, and the one she was trying to wrangle out was giving her a cursed time.

"Can I help?" Vahid asked. She could feel him standing directly behind her, and her fingers fumbled more in response.

"I can handle it," she replied, albeit too quickly to be convincing. The cork came free with a final tug, and her hand jerked with it, nearly smacking Vahid in the face. "I'm so sorry," she said breathlessly. As if she needed anything else tallied against her.

"If I'd been hit, the fault would've been mine. I shouldn't have been standing so close."

No. You should've been standing closer. The thought came so quickly and unbidden that it frightened her. What had she been thinking to bring him to the one place she felt most vulnerable?

Nothing a drink wouldn't fix. But no, there was the old Elaysia talking again. The foolish Elaysia who made brash decisions and was a terrible judge of character. Better to make no decisions. Better to trust no one.

"I'll get chalices," Vahid said, stepping over piles of blankets and discarded bits of armor Elaysia had yet to return to the community stores. He wasn't going to find what he searched for. Maseeya had collected her dirty cups and plates in a quiet rage earlier that morning, muttering in Zarith under her breath about how Elaysia wouldn't have the excuse of early motherhood and war forever. Little muttering huffs were about as mad as Maseeya ever got, and Elaysia found them endearing even when directed at her.

"I don't have any in my loft, I'm afraid," she said, holding up the bottle. "If you don't find it too off-putting, we can drink straight from this?"

"I've never done such a thing." Vahid's face was stoic, save for his wide eyes and furrowed brow, and for a moment, Elaysia feared he was being genuine. He couldn't hold his performance for long, though. "Sorry, that was a shitty attempt at levity. My whole family's devoid of it, I'm afraid."

"That makes two of us."

Elaysia offered the bottle to him first, which he refused, as she'd known he would. The Moonlight hit her within the first sip. She wasn't certain of its fermentation process as the beridians guarded the secrets of their primary export with their lives. It was rumored, however, that the alcohol was infused with some local plant or flower, doubling the effect while also providing increased energy and alertness. Not to be mistaken for mental acuity.

Vahid let out a whistle after he took a drink, setting the bottle on the table with suspicious eyes.

"Have you not tried it before?" Elaysia asked, eyeing the bottle, fighting the urge to reach for a second drink so soon. She wanted—no, needed—more of the relaxation it provided to sit comfortably alone in a small room with a man she both wanted to order away and crawl into bed with.

"Oh, I've tried it," Vahid said, testing out the rocking chair and smiling at the motion. "I just don't drink all that much. Don't care for the way I feel after."

And Elaysia didn't care for the sudden wave of shame washing over her. He'd meant nothing by it, surely, but—

"For clarity's sake," he added, interrupting her thoughts. "I don't like drinking to drink. But I'm not above drinking for celebratory occasions."

Elaysia raised her eyebrow. "Is this a"—she took another drink to bolster her confidence—"celebratory occasion?"

"I just rode a sands-blessed stormbird, so I'd say it is." He took the bottle from her and gulped the syrupy liquid down in the most shamelessly un-highborn manner she'd ever witnessed from him.

The whole situation was so unlike him, in fact, that she could barely hold back her laughter. Her smirk had a mind of its own, though. "Debauchery and cursing, Vahid? Whatever shall I do with you?"

"Whatever it is, don't send me back home." His face turned solemn; his eyes distant.

"Is it so bad for you there?"

"Not in a way I'd ever complain about to my men." He took another sip, then passed the bottle back to Elaysia. "But Anahi left for a reason. I didn't understand why when I was younger. I even hated her for it. But the older I grew, the more I saw the world my parents were imprisoned by, and the less I wanted of it."

"But you couldn't let them down," Elaysia whispered, only belatedly realizing she'd spoken the thought aloud. She took another drink, then, in a bold move of the desire to simply sit near another being, motioned to the open space on her cot. "It's much more comfortable than that chair," she added, perhaps as a remaining layer of defense.

"I'll be the judge of that." He slipped off his Agaas-made boots and set them beside hers.

They sat, sharing one more drink between them. When they both spoke, it was all at once, words tumbling over one another's.

"I hate the circumstances under which we met," he began.

"I'm sorry I've been so cold to you," she said at the same time.

They paused, and Elaysia's heart raced as she considered the weight of his words—of her words, for The Daughter's sake.

Vahid took on the burden of clarity first. "Would you like to…"

"You first, please." Elaysia eyed the bottle, then decided against it. She wanted some coherence and control regarding whatever happened next.

"What I meant was…" Vahid drew a long breath as if to steady himself. "I think you're one of the most fascinating and brilliant people I've ever met. You have the mind of a scholar, the heart of a warrior, and the impulses of a child."

Elaysia snorted at that bit and nearly reached for the Beridian Moonlight, but then he gently took her hand in his.

"Do you know why people seem to love or hate you?" he asked.

"No." Her voice was dry and rough. She wanted to pull away, but she forced herself to stay present and strong.

"Because you surprise them."

She stared dumbly at him, not knowing how to take his observation, much less respond.

"Some people find you rash and unsettling, while others find you refreshing and exciting."

"And which group do you find yourself aligned with?" She didn't realize how badly she needed to know the answer until she'd spoken the words aloud. She also didn't realize how closely she'd leaned in until she felt the heat of his breath on her face.

"Both."

She almost kissed him then, just for his honesty, which was a treat she so rarely received. Instead, she lay back on her cot, taking another sip that dribbled down her chin.

"You can sleep here," she said, wiping her mouth. She was fully aware of the weight of her words despite the Moonlight working its wonders on her body.

Vahid's gaze trailed down her figure, something he'd been highborn enough to refrain from prior. "The tent I share with Hallahd is more than suitable. I respect your desire for privacy and know you like to have someone more helpful with the babes nearby."

"This isn't Munskahan," Elaysia said, setting the bottle on the table beside her cot after he refused another drink. "We're over-flowing with refugees, and I scarcely have the space to house them. It's illogical to keep you in separate quarters. Besides, I..."

I want you here. But she still couldn't say it aloud. By keeping it dormant, she kept it under control. To speak it was to free it, and once it was free, her heart would follow.

"I think it would do the people good to see us unified," she said finally. Even to her own ears, it sounded weak.

Vahid rose from the cot, the disappointment evident on his face. "If you only want me here to appease the curiosities of bystanders, then your request is no different than any made back home, and I'll have to politely refuse you." He started for the door.

Elaysia nearly tripped as she flung herself out of the cot. Her mind was a battle of longing and fear, of desire and deprivation. "Vahid, wait." She gripped his arm and pulled him to her in an unexpected embrace.

He didn't fight her, but he didn't lean into her either. He was waiting.

She swallowed, forced herself to meet his gaze. "I want you to stay here because *I* want you." The rest of it came out in a breathless rush of repressed emotions and unmet desires. "I've made a mess of so much of my life already, and you just seem like a dream. As though the gods themselves took everything I need-ed from another person and formed it into you. It's—you're—too good for anyone. For me." She swallowed a lump in her throat as her gaze dropped to the floor. "But I want to try. I'm broken and unpredictable, but if that doesn't frighten you, maybe there's hope for us."

Vahid's embrace both soothed and lit a flame within her. "You don't know how long I've waited to hear those words," he whispered into her hair.

"All of those exactly?" she said, laughing through the tears.

"Close enough." He pulled away, though his smile was as warm as ever. And there was a new glint in his eyes. Some darker, more alluring side of him he'd kept hidden.

Or maybe she just hadn't wanted to see it.

"I'll return in the morning with my things," he said, reaching for the door. "We can take it slow—"

His words cut off at the sight of her tunic slipping over her head. She didn't want to live in denial of anything anymore, to wait for it to be too late.

"If the suddenness isn't too much for you," she said, feeling the cool night air on her exposed breasts.

Vahid removed his hand from the door handle. "I wouldn't dare refuse the high chieftain." He slipped off his tunic, baring his own chest which had the look of a warrior's despite his highborn status.

Elaysia kept her attention on him despite the burning in her cheeks. She wouldn't look away, wouldn't feel shame or regret in her own chambers, in the great heights of her homeland. Besides, who was she guarding her heart for? She belonged to no one but her babes, and the man who'd once held her heart and gifted her them was dead. Even if he wasn't, he was dead to her. Love could outlast the bounds of time, could move mountains and calm seas, could survive the worst terrors conjured by gods and mortal beings alike. But betrayal? Betrayal was the antithesis of love. It was worse than hate because it meant that there had once been love, had once been something genuine and pure, however small. It killed love.

And there was no resurrecting it.

"Elaysia? Are you alright?"

Something tickled her cheek. A tear, warm and telling. She swiped at it and turned from Vahid, but he'd already seen her despair, was working his way to her and wrapping her in warm arms that felt like home. And despite herself, she fell into them, her walls crumbling, her chest heaving, her heart exhausted from denying the comfort she so desperately craved.

"What do you need?" he whispered.

"Hold me. Like this. But there." She pointed to the cot, and he picked her up without another word, nestling her body into his.

It was everything she needed.

And when they made love in the morning that followed, she swore she'd never known such ecstasy.

LUMIRA

Lumira stood poised to unleash her fury at dawn's first light.

She'd stayed up all night preparing for their attack on the Az Zarian ship, pacing and thinking, sharpening her spear head, running through less-than-optimal scenarios that might befall them—anything, really, other than sleeping. She trusted her nerves to carry her through the day, as they so often had, knowing that her body would succumb to a long and healing rest upon return.

She sprang from her loft and sprinted down two platforms to reach the bridge leading to the High Tree. Few were awake, especially after the previous night's revelries intended to send the Stormriders off in good spirits. Lumira hadn't touched a drop, not even of her people's Moonlight, which had been offered to her several times by well-meaning Agaasians. She'd only eaten because she'd known she'd regret skipping nourishment, especially since her body burned through food as though it were no more than kindling. Still, she'd hardly tasted the smoked fish and hunks of roasted nytak she'd forced down.

And she hadn't been the only one.

The war council had decided that only half the riders would go. Despite perceiving the mission as having low risks and high rewards, it was deemed too dangerous to launch a unified attack with all birds and riders, especially since they hadn't fully come into their powers. The council suggested drawing sticks, but Elaysia was adamant they chose amongst themselves.

It was all but unanimous that the high chieftain remain in Neharem, much to Elaysia's dismay. Something had blossomed between her and Vahid, and Lumira saw the pain in her eyes when he departed with his band of kuza nearly a fortnight prior to the Stormriders. Still, she saw wisdom in their reasoning. Neharem couldn't risk its leader so carelessly, and the council was still angry with Elaysia regarding her mission to rescue Kelsia—something they had never formally approved.

Lumira volunteered first, only beating Mardus's declaration by mere seconds. Grokhion was next, and though Jakki tried to offer herself up, Elaysia thought it unfair she and Xaren be sent off again when they'd only just returned. That left Anahi and Yerakai, and while the Apáasutai was more than willing, Anahi refused to let her brother see battle without her. No one argued with her.

The Stormriders were supposed to be sent off properly with love and blessings from the people, but Lumira had already obtained Elaysia's consent to depart discreetly at dawn, to maximize both time and emotional stability. On one condition, anyway.

Lumira knocked quietly on the door leading to Elaysia's quarters in hopes she wouldn't wake the babes. A sleep-tousled Maseeya answered in a robe as sheer as water. She tilted her head in confusion, then nodded to herself as though a reaffirming thought had entered her mind.

"She isn't here," the Az Zarian woman whispered. "You are to meet her at the cliff side."

Lumira nodded. She didn't need to confirm which cliff. There were countless access points to the jagged cliffs spearing out from the forests overlooking the ocean, but only one that Elaysia seemed to find herself at time and time again.

"Thank you," Lumira said, bowing her head.

She made to leave, but Maseeya grabbed her wrist and murmured something in a language Lumira didn't recognize, her silver-streaked hair masking her face as she bowed her head. When she finished, she looked up and smiled.

"It is a blessing," she explained, lifting her gaze to the sky. "An ancient one from a time when my people weren't under Cadar's control, when we lived freely in the east, much like the tribes of Neharem. I wasn't lucky enough to see such days, but my family carries traditions from the remnants of our culture, and I share them with you now."

"I'm honored," Lumira said, touched by the woman's kindness. She'd had only brief interactions with Maseeya, and most of them were in Elaysia's presence. It was comforting to know beridian hate hadn't contaminated all Az Zarian hearts. "What does it mean?"

"It means the winds take you. We believe wind is the essence of life, for it is breath itself. Wind first pushes air into our lungs, and when we die, it reabsorbs our spirits. When you are in the care of the wind, you are never alone, for you are always home."

Lumira held the words close to her heart as she made her way down the circling ramps of the living trees into the forested ground below. Perhaps she'd let wind be her guide in the looming attack. It seemed fitting for the stormbirds, and the beridians, too, cared much for the wind. It powered their sails, after all.

When Lumira broke through the last trees fencing off the cliff side, Elaysia greeted her, clad in a simple tunic and leggings. Lumira exhaled relief upon seeing her. She'd feared the high chieftain had taken it upon herself to join the attack against the wishes of the council. A year ago, she probably would've. But something had changed in her. There was a veil of skepticism wrapped around a weary heart. Lumira knew the look well. She'd been bearing it more years than she could count.

"Thank you for meeting me," Elaysia said, hooking a wild strand of hair behind her pointed ear.

Lumira brought her fist to her heart. "I wouldn't miss the opportunity."

"I'd go with you, if I could." She held something in her right hand, clutching it fiercely. "I need you to promise me something."

Lumira swallowed. She didn't want to make any empty promises, but neither did she want to be the one to pour ashes on Elaysia's embers. "If I can."

"A fair answer."

The cries of seahawks filled the air, and they both looked down to find a flock of them swarming the cliffs below. Lumira leaned as far out as the cliff would allow, peering through the fray of feathers and beaks until she located the creature they feasted on: a half-grown seapup with velvety skin the color of sand.

Something cold squeezed her heart. Not quite fear, but a sick anticipation of the losses she would soon face. If not this battle, then the next. If not the next, then the one after. As long as there was war, there would be death.

No one could avoid its gnarled clutches forever.

"What would you ask of me?" Lumira said, voice thick as she ripped her gaze away from the seapup.

Elaysia watched her intently, her two-toned eyes narrowed, her right fist still clenched. "I need you to promise to abandon the mission if the situation deteriorates."

"Those are vague terms," Lumira said, straightening. "But I'll do my best. I always try to pull back when I sense an impending loss."

"And you've done beautifully." Elaysia opened her fist, revealing a spiral shell the color of freshly spilled blood. "You've played a significant role in our victories, and I feel like I haven't thanked you enough for your leadership in my stead. This isn't much, but I hope you'll take it until I can properly repay you. It was my mother's."

Lumira turned the shell over in her hand, marveling at the way it transitioned from a matte surface to a shimmering interior. "It's beautiful. Would you do me the honor of guarding it until I return?"

"As long as you promise to return."

"The moons will keep me."

They sat side by side on the cliff, legs dangling from the edge, no need for words between them. It wasn't, Lumira imagined, how other leaders would send off their favored war generals. But it was how a friend would send off another friend.

And it meant so much more.

When Anadu appeared, Elaysia retreated to the edge of the forest to give them space. Lumira slipped on the mask made by Vahid, still in awe of how perfectly it protected her ears while still giving them mobility.

"I am ready." Anadu's words filled Lumira's mind, and she mounted, spear in hand, her body sheathed in the leather armor she'd conceded to wear.

"Shadow Chieftain!"

She glanced over her shoulder at Elaysia leaning out from the woods, one arm secured around a trunk.

"High Chieftain?"

"Bring him home."

Lumira's head told her to promise no such thing. But her heart had other plans.

"My life for his," she shouted as the stormbird took to the skies. "I'll see to it he returns on Anadu with me."

She didn't look back as the ground vanished beneath her.

All that mattered was what lay ahead.

Their strategy was to maintain a high altitude to avoid detection, relying on the excellent eyesight of the stormbirds to confirm the approaching ship. If anything, the riders hoped to be early, perhaps catching it at sea and sending the kuza away unscathed. They could've gone out days prior and tried to sink it far from land, but the council wanted the kuza reinforcements to assist in the rare chance that whatever weapon they harbored aboard was fully functional.

The Stormriders also had a special, land-locked mission to fulfill.

Elaysia had given them the order in private, without council sanction. Capture Raynar and any other high-ranking members of the Lawful Dominion. And if they couldn't catch him, death would do. The high chieftain believed that intercepting the shipment, although a proactive move, would only shift so much power in the war. But capturing the enemy leader, whose pride and desire to prove himself worthy to Az Zar had him overseeing all incoming shipments himself? Well, that was grounds for ending the war altogether, or at least strongly influencing it.

If everything went as planned, there would be no one left alive from the Az Zarian ship, and with Raynar captured or killed, and his seal obtained, they could place the blame of the attack on him, ending the Lawful Dominion's alliance with Az Zar. And then maybe, just maybe, there would be enough motivation for a treaty of the tribes once again.

The plan was gaping with holes and countless places where it could branch off in the opposite direction of their intended goal, but Lumira agreed they had little choice. Bold moves were all that was left to a losing side who hadn't the numbers or resources to hold off a larger army forever. Otherwise—as Elaysia had reiterated more than once—they'd soon find themselves in their own Siege of Cadar.

And Igtheos at least had fortified walls and a mature stormbird at his disposal, Lumira thought, glimpsing the first sight of the eastern coastline.

Anadu jerked to the right, a reminder to Lumira that she could perceive most of her thoughts when they flew together, whether she intended to send them or not.

I meant no offense, Lumira offered.

"I'll forgive you on account of the looming attack," the bird returned. *"Your kind can only handle so much stress."*

They flew a few miles over Skyfall Sea before cutting south toward the Moákun bay most favored for Az Zarian trade. Lumira had only been there once, back when they'd first set sail for Az Zar on account of Elaysia's irrational quest for answers. This time, the quest had merit.

It made the execution no easier.

Grokhion and Roth had followed them closely since departing Agaas, and once at sea, they came alongside Lumira and Anadu until the birds were evenly paced a few hundred feet abreast. Mardus approached rapidly from the west on Keera, Anahi and Corvax on their literal tail. They all looked impressive, she thought, in their new armor and masks. All that remained was determining their quality.

Lumira lifted her hand, and they broke into a diamond formation with Grokhion in the back and the humans on either side. They'd be approaching the bay within a few minutes, and according to the last tuross they received from Vahid, he and his kuza would be just outside the camp, awaiting the signal—the signal being cries of anguish from the Lawful Dominion as the stormbirds picked off clusters of their men and tore holes in their sails.

A prayer to the moon mothers found its way to Lumira's lips as she readied her spear. It wouldn't do her much good from the skies, but she'd brought it for the inevitable moment she was grounded and retrieving the target. Part of her wondered if she should've done more to encourage the undecided council to put the few Az Zarian weapons in their possession to use. Just the sight of their cold, shiny tubes made her angry, but on stormbird back, even Elaysia, Yerakai, and Xaren would struggle to wield their bows. With ranged weapons that could be used one-handed, they'd greatly improve their welfare and effectiveness—at least until the birds came into power. Hopefully next time.

Lumira just had to make sure there was a next time.

Whatever wind blessing Maseeya whispered must've worked, for the cloud coverage was thick over the ocean, spreading its tentacles over the beach and the deciduous forest that lay beyond it. The mast of the ship wasn't visible out on the water, however, and Lumira's heart sank as Anadu poured the fated words into her mind.

"It is there, at the docks," she said. *"Corvax spotted several pockets of reinforcements lined up along the beach, guarding the ship from all sides."*

She climbed higher and the other stormbirds followed. With the Az Zarian ship already docked, they'd change tactics, flying well above the clouds to remain unnoticed, then dispersing to initiate the attack from multiple directions. Lumira and Anadu would lead, followed by Mardus and Keera, then Grokhion and Roth, both from different directions. Anahi would go back to warn her brother and the kuza by flying low over them, then join the attack.

Lumira clenched her arrowhead necklace as the air cooled with altitude. It was the last moment of peace she'd receive before the world erupted around her like the fire mountains back home. Anadu spread her wings to glide, aligning her graceful form with the direction of the boat.

Then she dove.

Because of the mask's quality, Lumira no longer had to shut her eyes during the descent. She could hardly process the speed with which Anadu careened down, cutting through the clouds like a knife through butter, and as the ship appeared, she braced herself. The stormbird flared her wings and talons at the last moment, causing a jerking motion that would've thrown an unprepared rider from her back. The first mast gave with a *crack* as Anadu knocked it sideways, splintering the wood, and Lumira scoured the deck for any sign of a new weapon. Alarmed cries filled the air as the ship's crew scurried about like ants. Nothing appeared abnormal. Anadu didn't waste any time in moving on to the next mast, disabling it as she had the first. Lumira turned her gaze to the beach just as an arrow sailed past her head. Another *crack* sounded, then Anadu was climbing out of weapon rage, a victory shriek erupting from her lungs.

Before the beach disappeared from view, Lumira caught sight of Keera's moon-colored feathers hurtling toward the boat, ready to destroy the third and final mast. Screams filled the beach. Lumira had a strong feeling it was Grokhion directing

Roth to attack the foot soldiers. The rage in her kin's eyes hadn't fully faded since the Lawful Dominion attack on the Ni'anko. She hoped he'd have the sense to protect his life and that of his stormbird's, but she feared he'd be quick to dismount and join the fray well before the kuza reinforcements arrived.

And she should be down there with him.

"Where shall I drop you?" Anadu asked, perceiving Lumira's thoughts.

Lumira's gaze probed the beach, locating the recently unloaded crates and barrels of supplies. The clashing of metal and war cries filled the air, and she knew the first of the kuza had arrived.

There, she thought, still looking at the poorly guarded supplies. Only a few soldiers surrounded the goods. *Let's sink their provisions. Start bringing them to the water.*

Anadu replied with another shriek. When she came within twenty feet of the sand, Lumira back flipped off her, spear ready, claws extended. Anadu was the perfect distraction, temporarily commanding all attention as Lumira prowled toward the guards, slitting their throats. Remorse rippled through her heart as she noted their brightly colored clothing and tri-cornered headwear. They were Zelosi pirates, not Az Zarian soldiers. The empire never personally handled its dirtiest deeds.

Anadu snatched up a crate and carried it away from the beach. She didn't make it far before the sound of a shieum echoed, and the crate burst open, spilling weapons into the water.

Lumira stalled, a crumpled Zelosi body at her feet. A sudden urge to gather the goods for Agaas overtook her. Why should they waste perfectly good weapons and food when the people of Neharem would soon be in dire need?

Anadu, she practically screamed in her mind. *Stop! Leave the supplies. Sink the boat and kill as many enemies as you can.*

The stormbird soared back to the beach, snatching up a fleeing sailor. Lumira sensed someone coming up behind her, ducking just as a blade cut through the air where her head had been. She slashed through the sailor's thinly clothed stomach, then lowered herself, growling and protecting her hoard like a wolf guarding a fresh kill. A few yards away, Grokhion cut through Lawful Dominion soldiers, prowling on all fours, his fangs bared, his eyes darkened. There was no sign of *Belzaith*, his favored ax, though Lumira imagined it embedded in some unfortunate body, spilling blood onto the sand.

She worked her way through the remaining sailors in a matter of minutes. It was almost too easy. They hadn't seemed ready for battle. Most weren't even armed. Guilt threatened to slow her until she reminded herself that they knew what they'd signed up for. They'd chosen to serve Az Zar, and she wouldn't pity them for their poor decisions.

Further up the beach unfolded a commotion of swinging weapons and firing shieum, of rage-filled bodies and battle cries. It was easy to differentiate the opposing sides. The kuza wore golden armor atop billowing pants and had helmet-encased heads. The Lawful Dominion had adopted a style of their own, one quite unlike the tribes they'd originated from. They wore dark gray from head to toe and bore emblems attached to their armbands—a style similar to the Az Zarian military and far more uniform than they'd been in during previous encounters. From what she could make out, only the higher-ranking people wore lyvium armor, and from there it trickled down to steels and bronze and leather. Some wore no armor at all. Still, they were far better outfitted for battle than most of the warriors in Neharem. Perhaps sleeping with monsters had its privileges.

Lumira prowled along the edge of the battleground, making quick work of any soldier who made the unfortunate decision to attack her. She dodged most of the shieum projectiles with ease. Most of the Lawful Dominion warriors were still unfamiliar with the weapons and clumsy in their handling. The time they sacrificed taking proper aim gave her more than enough opportunity to get out of harm's way. Often, there was little harm to avoid if she kept her distance. Except for the one that burst the crate in Anadu's talons, most of the shieum seemed more effective up close, at least in the Lawful Dominion's untrained hands. Their aim left much to be desired.

Lumira trod silently through the sand and used her spear to pierce the exposed neck of a commanding warrior, smiling as the blood spurted from his throat. After him, however, she couldn't locate any familiar faces, much less anyone who looked important. If Raynar was among his soldiers, as Elaysia had hoped, he'd done a brilliant job of disguising himself. A quick look at the water confirmed that they had, at the very least, accomplished their main objective. The sunken ship peeked out of the waves like driftwood, bobbing helplessly beyond repair as it bumped into the dock.

As the stormbirds entered the fray, Lawful Dominion soldiers scattered with each talon-spread dive. Some retaliated with arrows, but they never stuck. Lumira wasn't certain, but she swore the stormbird feathers had a unique quality to them, one that almost seemed to repel the arrowheads in the way of good armor. The shieum projectiles were likely the exception, but Lumira and the other Stormriders were ready each time the birds came near land and rushed to remove any threats.

"I'm diving now," Anadu whispered in Lumira's mind.

Lumira quickly located the stormbird's form, then directed her attention to the cluster of warriors she careened toward. Most would be taken out before they could ready their weapons, but Lumira caught sight of one slinking beneath the cover of trees, loading his shieum. She snatched up a spear from a fallen warrior and launched it toward the Lawful Dominion attacker before he could take aim. It missed; she'd been too far out of range. But the intrusion broke his focus long enough for Anadu to soar well out of the weapon's range.

Pride threatened to swell within Lumira as she surveyed the Lawful Dominion bodies littering the beach. Every so often, she'd find a kuza among them, but the deaths were at least ten to one in their favor. Even without Raynar, the mission was a success—one with minimal loss. What more could Elaysia ask for? By the moons, with the recovered supplies and warriors high on victory, they could even follow up with another attack, this time bringing in Neharem warriors. The tide would turn yet.

The ground shook beneath Lumira, shattering her hopes. She crouched instinctively, body pressed against the sand. Debris rained down from the air in bits of char and flame. A few chunks fell beside her, smelling of burned flesh. Her eyes widened as she followed the damage further up the beach. The place where a victorious cluster of kuza had stood moments prior, defeating what remained of the Lawful Dominion soldiers, was now a ring of darkened sand. Moans arose, and Lumira looked on with horror as her mind pieced together what the debris was.

Bodies, she thought, stomach turning. *Dismembered bodies.*

"Retreat to the—" a commanding Orillon voice began.

Another *boom* silenced it.

Lumira recalled Elaysia's description of the attack on Agaas the day of her induction. There'd been a sound as loud as a groundshake, and they'd found entire platforms decimated, resulting in piles of burning ash and bodies. The tree had been compromised and eventually collapsed, taking connecting bridges with it. Belatedly, she realized what the recent shipment must've contained.

The key to Agaas's destruction.

"Anadu!" Lumira shouted. "Go! And take the other birds with you!" She didn't know how great the range of the ground-shaking weapons was, and she didn't want the stormbirds risking their lives near the beach. Not even for their riders.

A screech filled the sky, but Anadu's reply formed in her mind. *"We will pull back, but I am not leaving you."*

Before Lumira could formulate a response, the ground shook again, this time much closer. Bodies flew through the sky, leaving a thick, greenish smoke in their place. It blanketed the beach, making it harder to locate the kuza and her fellow riders. She prowled forward, coughing as the smoke entered her lungs.

Someone had to be activating the weapons, launching them into the kuza. She made for the trees, her vision throbbing with rage. She'd find the death makers and turn their weapons on them.

She was only halfway there when a blinding pain rattled her torso. She clutched at her ribs and found the leather armor torn away, leaving blood in its stead. The sand seized her as she melted into it, keeping her wound angled away from the aggravating abrasions.

There was no projectile she could find. It burned like fire, but the blood was already beginning to clot, thanks to her kind's superior healing. She pressed on, trusting the wound to take care of itself.

The lush ferns and ribbed trees surrounding the coastline absorbed her, and then she was prowling through their green, sheltering leaves. Another *boom* sounded further up the beach. The attacks were too dispersed for any one person. How many soldiers—

A blade plunged into Lumira's calf, dropping her to the matted carpet of fallen leaves and twigs. She rolled away from the direction of the attack, swiping her claws in defense at any pursuer. They snagged something, and she blindly clawed again and again until her slashes would've killed even a skulmor. She scoured her surroundings, ensuring no one else approached, then inspected her kill.

The shredded form before her had once been nyrian. Not that she could tell by the hair, for its head had been shaved. Nor its eyes, for their glow had faded with death. Only the pointed ears remained. Its skin was painted with the colors of the surrounding forest to blend in. The Lawful Dominion warriors must've been lying in wait, hidden from the eyes of kuza rushing past them onto the beach, waiting for an opportune moment to unleash death. She drew her claw across its throat, more out of rage than necessity, then began her hunt for the rest.

It was for naught. The groundshake weapon erupted faster than she could locate the warriors wielding it. Soon, the hollow moans of the wounded replaced the booming thunder. Lumira returned to the beach, to her fellow riders, knowing in her heart there was no more she could do.

She found Grokhion first, his mouth slick with blood, carrying two wounded kuza over his shoulders. The ones he'd chosen looked capable of survival, unlike the countless dismembered bodies wriggling in the sand like beached fish. His eyes carried so much hatred and rage that she shied away from his gaze.

Mardus turned up next, blood blooming across his arm. "We must leave," he shouted as he kneeled to assess one of the wounded kuza. The man's legs were missing below his thighs, and the Moákun whispered something before drawing a knife over the man's throat.

Lumira winced, knowing she needed to do the same. They couldn't save most of the wounded clinging to life on the beach. The least they could do was end their pain.

"Where's Anahi?" she asked, searching the bodies. Then, suddenly fearful of the answer, she added, "How many wounded do you think we can carry back on the birds?"

Mardus shook his head as he kneeled by a kuza with blood gurgling in his mouth. "I don't think there are enough for it to be a problem."

"This isn't all the kuza," Grokhion said, laying his still surviving men on the sand. Roth dropped toward him like a sea-hawk, his wings curled beneath him. "Maybe two-thirds of their forces, no more."

"I bet Vahid and Anahi are with them," Mardus said, wiping his dagger. "Further inland."

Lumira waved to Anadu, beckoning her down. "You two finish looking for survivors. I'll—"

Another *boom* echoed in this distance. It came from further inland.

When Anadu landed on the beach, Lumira didn't waste one moment before taking to the skies. Elaysia had given her a final command before departing, and Lumira wasn't returning to Agaas with it unfulfilled.

"Where are you going?" Mardus shouted as his figure shrunk beneath her.

"I'm bringing Vahid home," she replied. "Don't follow me. Gather what supplies and wounded you can and make for Agaas."

The rest of the kuza army wasn't hard to locate. The trees had been brought down along with the men, creating a clearing that was nearly perfectly circular. As Anadu bore them closer, Corvax's silhouette appeared. Her heart dared to lighten. If he still lingered nearby, that meant Anahi did as well.

"Corvax says Anahi waits below, unharmed," Anadu confirmed, breathing relief into Lumira's tightened chest. *"She was airborne when it happened."*

Lumira glanced down at her still-clotting wound. For now, the pain in her side was subdued by the battle vigor coursing through her. "Bring me down."

Anadu landed, remaining on the ground against her rider's wishes. She swore she sensed no more enemies lying in wait. Lumira dismounted, cautious of the countless kuza and trees strewn about the clearing. The situation appeared similar to that of the beach; the kuza achieving the illusion of success, only to be caught off guard with the blasts. A heavy weight pressed on her shoulders. She could've prevented the loss had she just been more aware, more prepared. A real shadow chieftain.

Not some foreigner playing at it.

Anahi didn't look up as Lumira approached. She cradled a body in her arms, silent sobs rattling her shoulders.

A burning sensation filled Lumira's throat. She turned to the side to wretch, wincing as it triggered a pain in her side. The world buzzed around her as she succumbed to exhaustion. She wanted to crumple into the sea of bodies and never awake again. Anything was better than confirming the identity of the body Anahi clutched to her chest. Anything was better than being the one to bring word to Elaysia. She stepped back to give Anahi privacy, averting her gaze to the woods beyond.

That was when she saw them.

A pair of eyes the color of embers peered through the trees. Lumira's mind raced back to the night of the Atsukut ambush, to the impenetrable being lurking amid the battle with a mighty blade. It hadn't appeared again, outside of her dreams. Not through the countless battles and skirmishes she'd fought her way through.

Not until now.

She sprinted into the woods, ready to confront the entity at whatever cost it required of her. But when she reached the trees, there was nothing waiting for her.

Nothing but her broken spearhead.

AHMARAHN

A hmarahn's heart pounded in his ears as he approached the stairs leading to the citadel gates. He wore the clothing loaned to him by the rebels but had removed the mask to ensure that none of the bloodthirsty sentries had a reason to harm him—the hooded demon in the night. There were at least two times the number of soldiers patrolling Cadar's streets since he'd been decommissioned, and though the final gong of the night had yet to sound, he hadn't passed a single civilian as he worked his way to the innermost districts. More and more, the city had come to resemble the offspring of the military and the temple, whose roles had increasingly blurred in recent years.

As Ahmarahn drew within the green ring of light cast by the nevethium pots positioned on either side of the guard-house, a sentry shifted from his statuesque stance. His gloved hands flicked to his blades, only returning to his side when he saw Ahmarahn was unarmed. Their uniforms, too, had changed. Though still bearing echoes of the previous style with the head-to-toe armor masking the soldier's identity, the color had changed from a solid black to a deep, dark red, the shade of dried blood. It was a bold move, one suggesting the military no longer felt the need for stealth, that they had the numbers to act on sheer force alone. And where the fiery eye of Mavet, the sigil of the Mavist Temple, had once been embroidered onto the cowl, it was now seared directly into the lyvium armor adorning the soldiers' torsos, forearms, and shins. In fact, even their head coverings had been replaced with newly forged lyvium masks reminiscent of the temple guards and priests.

"Victory in solidarity; strength in order," he muttered condescendingly.

"That's close enough," the sentry barked as Ahmarahn reached the foot of the nevethium-flecked stairs. "Who goes there, and what's your purpose?"

A shiver rippled across Ahmarahn's skin. It was too early for his report, nearly a fortnight so. Only two suns had set since Zhia had escorted him from the palace, but her death, while strengthening his position with the rebels, had potentially cost him his good standing with the empire.

Mavet almighty. He could still see her battered face, swollen beyond recognition. Had he known that, in less than a day's time, he'd be the one delivering her to the rebellion and ending her life, would he have gone?

It was a stupid question. He'd do anything to anyone to save Xi. But perhaps he would've said kinder parting words to the general. Still, things happened as life intended. He needed to trust that, to stop speculating all the ways his present would be different had he not made the mistakes of his past.

"It's Ah—" He caught himself mid-speech and begrudgingly retrieved the name the All-Sovereign preferred. "Davier. San Zadel. I'm supposed to report in."

The sentry disappeared inside the guard tower, likely to converse with a superior. He returned a few moments later, his magenta eyes narrowing beneath his mask.

"It's early," he said, posture as rigid as the walls he protected.

"Guess my task was too easy."

Ahmarahn waited for the moment where he regretted his words, but it never came. He followed the sentry up the stairs, stopping outside the polished jade of the gated archway. It took the strength of several men to heave one of the doors open, and then—after a quick search to ensure he carried no weapons—he found himself alone in the courtyard. Or was given that illusion, rather. Sentries undoubtedly looked down from the ramparts and from within the shadows.

Dalgus, the All-Sovereign's most trusted servant, greeted him at the palace door; though, greeted was too pleasant a word for the way the nyrian dwarf handled such exchanges. He wore the same ruby pendant he had the first time Davier visited the palace, bringing with it a wave of memories Ahmarahn was never ready to face.

"What do you want, Zadel?" Dalgus said as he led him through a long hallway adorned with Zal Drusa lineage portraits on either side. "I have an evening meal of steamed kuba and seared eel that I'm most eager to return to."

Ahmarahn made a face of disgust behind the dwarf's back as they entered a large hall once used for feasting—or so he'd been told in military history lessons. There were no tables or benches, only cobwebs and the ghosts of rebels who'd died in that very room over two millennia prior. In fact, despite the palace's size, it was relatively quiet and empty. It always was, at least the handful of times he'd been allowed entry. The All-Sovereign's arrogance and paranoia kept everyone but his most trusted advisors from accessing his fortress.

"I bring word," he said, running his hand along the gold-rimmed edges of a fire pot as wide as he was tall.

"Impossible." Dalgus studied him, his short arms planted on his thick waistline. "It's not been two days. What could you possibly have to tell us?"

I need to know Xi is safe, you little shit, Ahmarahn thought. But he didn't dare allude to his fear or anything else that might connect him to Zhia's death.

"I've already found their den and their leader," he said, hoping the information was enough. "And they've allowed me to join their cause. See?" He pointed to his clothes, then pulled the mask out from his belt. "I thought His Holiness would be glad to hear how smoothly the infiltration is going."

Dalgus yawned. "You thought wrong. None of that is worth his time. I'll spare you his wrath by *not* telling him you dared to give away your presence—and his—by coming back so soon." He pointed Ahmarahn to the door and shuffled past the fire pot.

"Wait," Ahmarahn pleaded, fighting to keep the desperation from his voice. He rubbed the scar on his forehead, and it was enough to fill him with rage-driven boldness. "I want to see Xi. Tell the All-Sovereign I won't return to the rebels until I get a moment with her."

The dwarf whirled around, seething. "Are you a fool?" He closed the distance between them faster than Ahmarahn had ever seen him move. "If you want your sister to remain safe, I suggest you don't return until you've something of value to offer."

"She's alive?" Ahmarahn's throat tightened with anticipation. "You know for certain?"

"Alive and well." Dalgus's gaze flitted around the room. He motioned Ahmarahn near, and Ahmarahn complied by taking a knee. The dwarf's lips were inches from his ear. "But that won't last long if you keep killing off those closest to His Holiness."

Ahmarahn's breath caught in his throat. His hands went clammy as the room blurred around him, and it took every bit of his will to remain rooted. How did the dwarf know? And why hadn't he put out an order for Ahmarahn's head?

Dalgus's bushy, white brows stitched together, their appearance made more shocking by the contrast of his bald head. From the look in his eyes, he seemed to enjoy Ahmarahn's vulnerability—even savored it.

"Who are you?" Ahmarahn's words came out in a growl. He still wasn't above snapping the dwarf's neck.

"A nuisance, a headache, an ugliness to be masked." Dalgus listed the offenses with no shortage of disgust. "A quirk in a flawless bloodline above all, I suppose."

Ahmarahn frowned. "You're related to the All-Sovereign?"

"Distant cousin. Distant enough to keep my identity hidden, but not so far from the line that he felt he could dispose of me." Dalgus rubbed the ruby dangling from his neck with both thumbs. "Which is fine with me, really. I can stomach his pretentious requests and insults in exchange for luxury. It allows me the opportunity to fulfill my heart's desires."

"Which are?"

Footsteps echoed into the room, and they both looked up as a young serving maid peered in. She bore a tray filled with nicely folded rags, the kind highborns used for cleansing after taking a shit. Dalgus's expression shifted from one of apprehension to warmth. He waved at the girl, and she nodded back, eyeing Ahmarahn as she vacated the room.

"She's fine," Dalgus said quietly. "But you best get out of here before someone else sees us talking. If any of the soldiers report your visit to the All-Sovereign, I'll tell him you brought me something of actual importance. Gods know I have enough secrets to barter with."

Ahmarahn couldn't bring himself to move. He had too many questions, and one screamed louder than all the rest. "Why are you helping me?"

"Couldn't care less about you, Zadel. Always found you to be an arrogant shit. Looks like that finally did you in." He pointed to Ahmarahn's scar, then led him out of the hall and back through the palace. Only when they reached the doors did he pause. "Remember that not everything is as it seems. You shouldn't trust anyone—no matter what side you're on."

Ahmarahn pressed his palm into the hard woodgrain, fingers lingering on the nevethium inlay. "And who do you side with?"

Dalgus flashed a gold-toothed smile. "Why, myself, of course. Ask your rebels about me, if it vexes you so. Just whatever you do, stay away from the palace until the time is right. Do you understand?"

Ahmarahn nodded. Even if he disagreed, he'd get nothing more from the dwarf that night.

"Good." Dalgus patted his back like a dog. "We don't want to upset His Holiness, after all. He's rather unstable. And unstable men are the most dangerous of all."

Ahmarahn found Nanjiya outside, in the inn's rear courtyard, a roaring fire highlighting her soft silhouette in the golden glow of its flames. She turned as he approached, somehow sensing him despite the discretion of his footsteps. Her round lips pressed together in indifference, but there was a glint in her eyes, a slight crease in the corners, and a relaxing of her brow. She was relieved, if not happy, to see him return safely.

It made the rock in his gut sink that much lower.

"Did you find your sister?" she asked as he joined her beside the fire.

Ahmarahn chewed the inside of his cheek. He could tell her yes, that he'd used the tunnel systems, broken into all the dungeons until he found the one that held Xi, then left her with a promise of his return—all without alerting a single guard to his presence. She might even believe it, given his performance the night prior. It'd be all too easy, just like it had been with Elaysia.

Or not.

A lump formed in Ahmarahn's throat. He shut his eyes and sifted through the sea of voices in his head, drawing them out and silencing them one by one. The All-Sovereign's threats. His father's judgment. Zhia's disgust. Kymerius's resentment. Grokhion's rage.

Elaysia's pain.

Everything negative in his life could be traced back to him blindly following orders. It had begun with small, simple demands. A drill here, a commitment there. But greed knew no bounds, and those in command always wanted more. More money, more death, more control. It was an insatiable pit of soul-sucking despair, and until he stopped being a good soldier, those in power would consume him bit by bit until he'd nothing left to give. For what good was Xi's freedom in a world void of hope? Ahmarahn could see the rest of his meaningless life unfolding in a rut of servitude, one that ended prematurely and unfulfilled.

No longer.

An honorable death, his father had said—one of the few valuable sentiments he'd passed on—*is better than a spineless life.*

Ahmarahn faced Nanjiya, taking her warm hands in his. Her lips parted as her eyes widened, but she didn't look away.

"I need to tell you something," he said, his voice low and steady. "I made a grave mistake once, and I'll not die knowing I've repeated it."

Her face showed no fear, no judgment, no anger. "I'll always hear the words of an honest man."

And there, in the city that bespoke his greatest fears and pains, Ahmarahn shed the lies and secrets he'd worn like armor. He exposed his past wrongs, his missteps and betrayals, everything from inadvertently ruining Kymerius's military future to pledging allegiance to the All-Sovereign to crush the rebellion.

He waited for Nanjiya to run, to attack, to summon her allies so they might do to Ahmarahn what he'd done to Zhia. He almost wanted it. He deserved to be punished for the pain he caused others, for the ripples of his actions still spreading out, out, out, cursing countless lives on account of his ambition.

But when he finished, his throat raw with emotion, Nanjiya did the one thing he thought impossible. She gathered all his shame and rage, absorbing it in a single embrace, and Ahmarahn clung to her as though she were life itself. And in that moment, she was. This woman, who he'd only just met, had given him the one thing he'd never managed for himself.

Forgiveness.

"Are you still that same man?" she asked, pulling back enough to look up at him.

"No," he replied. "That man died, and a ghost took his place."

"And where is he now?"

He found himself in her deep brown eyes and the faint freckles that surrounded them. "The ghost gave him the opportunity to rise from ashes, renewed and reborn. And now, he has one final chance to truly make things right."

"Good." Nanjiya's lips lingered dangerously close to his, her brow set with determination. "I'll ask you again: who are you, and what do you seek?"

"Davier," he replied. The weight of the name settled over him. "I'm Davier. And I'll be the death of this empire."

ZAVIK

"**A**ren't you sworn to stalk our every move?" Yikos said as the altar guards shoved her through the doors behind Zavik. He would've been slapped for such a remark, but she usually escaped repercussions for her subtly condescending insults, probably due to her age.

The groan of the split doors closing was their response, the altar guards apparently not allowed to witness what lay beyond the grasping hands and glowing eyes protecting the innermost sanctum. While this pleased Zavik to a certain extent—he preferred to work without someone breathing down his back—it raised questions as to why.

Don't be foolish, he told himself as he followed Yikos down a widening hallway into the golden-green glow that lay beyond. *They wouldn't let you in here alone with anything dangerous. They need you alive.*

But not unharmed.

Zavik reached for his knife, remembering only as he slipped his hand into his boot that it hadn't been in his possession since Lanston's betrayal.

"You going to leave an old woman to fend for herself?" Yikos huffed from where she waited a few steps ahead. "Don't get soft-bellied on me now, boy. This was your idea."

"Sorry." Zavik gave one last glance at the door, which looked far less terrifying from the inside, and hurried to meet her. He offered his arm, which Yikos accepted with guarded approval, and together, they ventured into the unknown.

Lights brightened the tunnel as they walked, filling the enigmatic patterns with a golden glow, as though the walls sensed their presence. They flickered out after they passed through a section, illuminating the next, further strengthening Zavik's theory. He couldn't stop the beads of cold sweat from trickling down his back, sending shivers through his body, but he could persevere in spite of it. He wanted to be strong for Yikos, if nothing else.

As they progressed, cage-like fixtures began to occupy the wall spaces where the illuminated patterns had existed just moments before. They were large enough to contain a crouched human, and locked inside were metal structures that Zavik could only liken to ovens—despite his intuitive understanding that their design, and purpose, was more intricate. Back at the arcanum, Yikos had shown him the plans and model gears for the arkthanax. They paled in comparison to the ones attached to the oven-structures, displaying a variety of levers and tubes that disappeared into the ceiling. They, too, seemed to awaken as Zavik and Yikos passed, only to fall quiet soon after.

"How can this place feel so dead and alive at once?" the elderly nyrian mused, as she stopped to inspect one of the lower-hanging cages. There were no locks on the bars, no handles or latches.

Zavik shook his head. He felt it, too, but couldn't place how or why. It was cold below, a drastic change from the warmth they'd experienced the past few days, but that can't have been enough to trigger the sense of dread overwhelming him.

At the end of the hallway—which had grown to an impressive height of twenty feet—lay a cleanly carved archway of nevethium-inlaid stone. At least, Zavik presumed it to be nevethium. It didn't have the warm, pure green he was used to seeing. The crystals adorning the door were more golden, and despite the warmth of their coloring, he swore he felt a chill rolling off them. The doors themselves were ajar, cracked just enough for a single person to fit through. A good thing, because Zavik doubted he and Yikos could heave them open alone.

He rested his hand on the lyvium handle, wincing as it sapped what little seemed to remain of his body heat. "Are you ready?"

Yikos gave an irritated shrug of her shoulders, and Zavik found himself emboldened by her apathy. He drew the deepest breath his unsteady lungs would allow and squeezed himself through the opening.

The room pulsated with bursts of greenish gold as soon as he stepped inside. It would've been frightening enough on its own, but the voice that accompanied it nearly loosened his bowels.

"Power sources at fifteen percent. Speak the passcode to proceed."

Zavik held up a hand to shield himself from the lights piercing through his seers. "Hello?" he shouted. It wasn't the first time he'd witnessed an otherworldly voice, nor his first time experiencing the sensation that it came from everywhere at once. The tone of this one, though; something about it was unnatural.

The lights flashed brighter. *"Incorrect passcode. Two attempts remaining. Power sources at fifteen percent. Speak the passcode to proceed."*

"For the love of Quinaria," Yikos murmured. She squeezed his elbow as she slipped past him.

Panic gripped Zavik's chest. "Yikos, wait! We don't know—"

"Incorrect passcode. One attempt remaining. Power sources at fifteen percent. Speak the passcode to proceed."

Faint whirs and grinding noises filled his ears in the voice's absence. He walked forward on unsteady feet, careful to avoid the pulsating tubes fused into the ground. Whatever lay at the chamber's center seemed to be drawing their energy, and as his eyes adjusted to the lights, he registered fleeting glimpses of a giant metal structure.

"Yikos?" Zavik's voice cracked as he willed his legs forward. He caught her slight form just as the lights went out.

"Incorrect passcode. Entering preservation mode. Units on standby."

The sounds ceased as abruptly as they'd begun. For a moment, darkness engulfed Zavik. Then a low hum vibrated the room, bringing with it a familiar green glow. Suspended from the ceiling was an enormous crystal that had been meticulously cut and polished, resulting in a near flawless orb instead of the usual sharp and uneven edges found in nature. Zavik hadn't even known it was possible to shape nevethium without compromising its power.

Unless it wasn't really nevethium.

His speculations subsided as his gaze wandered from the crystal to the monstrosity it illuminated. Sweat formed on his hands. His mouth was a desert. Despite sensing Yikos returning to his side, he couldn't turn his head away long enough to regard her.

It's not alive, he told himself as his legs trembled beneath him. *At least, it's not right now.*

In the center of the room, a colossal metal figure towered like a sentinel. An arch of deep onyx held its eighteen-foot frame captive at the wrists and ankles, though Zavik wasn't certain how effective the lightly fused lyvium bands acting as chains would be against such a being. Its form was wrought from the same metal, the surface of which was etched with lines and shapes that seemed to writhe in the shifting shadows. Though its face was sculpted to resemble a human's or nyrian's, its colorless eyes and mouth lacked any hint of warmth or emotion. Despite having no eyebrows, it looked angry. At least as angry as an inorganic thing could look.

A hushed stillness pervaded as Zavik and Yikos approached the metal giant, made worse by the unsettling energy in the air, as though too loud a breath would awaken it. In fact, he half expected it to. He assumed that's why the All-Sovereign had allowed them access in the first place. To prove that, at least at one point in time, nevethium had done more than heal wounds and help nurture the land.

It had powered gods.

They stopped a few paces away from the edge of the rune-etched ring encircling the ground beneath it. Close enough to inspect it, but far enough to flee. Its joints and connective metals were exposed, each part meticulously crafted and intended to function with efficiency. It had even been constructed to give the illusion of armor—though Zavik doubted it needed it. A helmet-encased head. Flared, protective pieces around the arms and legs. And its seamless torso looked impenetrable.

"The gods do exist," Yikos said, startling Zavik. He lurched back, just in case the thing decided to move.

It didn't.

Yikos regarded him with a mix of exasperation and disdain. "Oh, come now."

Zavik reluctantly rejoined her. "It's not a god," he muttered, still afraid his voice might awaken the metal giant.

"What's more godlike than this?" Yikos's tone was sharp as she walked within feet of the giant, her hood slipping off her head and revealing her pointed ears as she inclined her chin upward. "It's an all-powerful, immortal, larger than life being. Or is that not what you see before you?"

"I see it just fine." Zavik's irritation began to surpass his anxiety. "But this is mortal-made."

"So?" She gave an apathetic shrug. "The gods were constructed like the beliefs built around them. It's not a new phenomenon."

Breath caught in Zavik's throat as Yikos reached a bony hand to touch the armored leg. He waited for it to illuminate, to crush them with one stomp. But it remained still. Perhaps it was nothing more than a lifelike statue of metal and dread.

A frown deepened the wrinkles on Yikos's face. She huffed and began following one of the dim tubes that ran from the giant to the wall, only stopping long enough to motion for Zavik to do the same.

He blinked before tearing his gaze away from the metal giant. He doubted much else could prove half as fascinating as what towered above him, but he needed more than shock and awe to find the answers the All-Sovereign demanded.

The octagonal room was lined with various workbenches and shelves on which were jars and metal pots, sheets of lyvium, and various—if not odd—tools. He had the feeling there'd been far more stored there in the past, and that it had been plundered more than once. Something like an altar stood to the left of the metal giant, and when Zavik waved his hand over it, it glowed, revealing an abstract lettering unlike any language he'd translated. It was closest to Ancient Nyrinian, but the forms were wrong. As soon as he removed his hands, the glowing lettering vanished along with it.

"Boy, here," Yikos croaked.

Zavik shuffled over to the table where the elderly nyrian was hunched over, inspecting an assortment of gears. Strewn among the cogs and other bits was a peculiar device featuring a central crystal encased in a web of intricate obsidian gears. It didn't glow, and it had an almost depleted look about it, so pale was its greenish hue. Delicate mechanical arms extended from the crystal, frozen in place, as though waiting to be set in motion. Zavik picked it up cautiously, half-expecting the thing to come to life in his hands.

When it didn't, he allowed himself a breath and held it out to Yikos. "Do you think this…"

"I do," she replied, looking from it to the metal monster. "Theories are forming in my mind faster than I can process them."

Zavik understood, for he felt the same. He pointed to another table, this one containing a smaller, but no less terrifying, metallic head. "Looks like the gods come in all shapes and sizes."

Yikos eased the pack off her back as she gestured for Zavik to do the same. "Get your things. We've much to do and not enough lifetimes to do it."

Unfortunately, Yikos proved to be right. They worked quickly, with little drink and no food, for the better part of a day, tinkering with the newfound devices, taking notes, and theorizing aloud as they worked. Zavik had to stop sketching plans more than once due to hand cramps, and by the time a cloaked figure came to collect them, he found it difficult to straighten out his spine. They scrambled to fill their satchels with as many trinkets and devices as they could carry, the most prized of which were some of the more ornately fashioned gears, the spinning crystal device, and Zavik's sketch of the words that had appeared over the altar.

Their masked escort wore the robes of a temple priest—at least, that's what Yikos whispered to him as a spear tip prodded them out of the chamber and back down the hallway—but Zavik didn't recall the skulls of dead creatures being standard Mavist Temple wear. The unnerving figure marched them silently back up to the surface, then promptly shoved them into the care of the soldiers awaiting them.

The trip back to Cadar was far worse than the journey from it. In part, because Zavik's backside hadn't recovered from the first stint on horseback, but also because the soldiers wouldn't allow him to take anything out of his satchels for fear of 'loss or decay.' More like the soldiers weren't happy with their assigned task to begin with and wanted to exact what vengeance their lowly stations allowed. Zavik didn't press the issue. He worked from the confines of his mind, which allowed some progress, at least in the realm of theory.

As they rode, Zavik's head threatened to burst from the newfound knowledge turning over in it. The metal giant beneath the Caman Altars changed everything for everyone. Not only did it confirm the All-Sovereign's theory that nevethium had powered something akin to life, but it also meant that minds far more brilliant than his own had achieved such feats long ago, likely before Cadar was even a thought. But what had happened to such a civilization, and why? Were there other artifacts scattered throughout Quinaria, or had they been lost to time and land in the great floods and fire of legend? Zavik had the feeling any such discoveries would have to be on his own time—assuming he ever crawled out from under the All-Sovereign's thumb.

Upon returning to the palace, Dalgus awaited Zavik and Yikos in their chambers. The nyrian dwarf's nose was up-turned in his usual way, his eyes squinted tightly to give the appearance he was entirely above being disturbed by grievances.

"To what do we owe this pleasure?" Zavik asked as he deposited his bags gently on the floor. "If you're here to report our findings to the All-Sovereign, I'm afraid we're going to need more time. We weren't aware of the scope of—"

"Tell His Holiness a day was hardly enough time to take a proper shit, much less uncover the answers he seeks," Yikos snapped. "There's a nyrian lifetime of knowledge to dig up beneath those ruins, and your allowance barely gave us opportunity to scratch the surface." She planted her bony hands on her non-existent hips—as if her message needed further emphasis.

Dalgus opened one eye wide enough to level Yikos with a squinted glare. "It's hardly His Holiness's fault you didn't make good use of your time. You were given the privilege of accessing a restricted site for the purpose of your research. Nothing else. A full day was more than enough time to deduce what's needed to move forward with production."

"It was, and we are ever so grateful for the All-Sovereign's generosity," Zavik answered before Yikos could fire off another insult. She'd grown surlier during their journey back to the capital, and between that and her age—not to mention the fact she'd considered herself dead upon their return—she was a flame waiting to ignite.

Dalgus scowled at them both, thick thumbs stroking his pendant. "I am happy to hear it, for your sakes. Come." He spun on slippered heels toward the door, rapping twice for the guards without to open them, lest he exude any unnecessary energy.

"Um, could we have a moment?" Zavik asked, his gaze darting to the bags strewn on the floor. "It's just that..."

The doors swung open. Though visibly aggravated, Dalgus held up a hand to keep the guards at bay. Zavik looked at Yikos with pleading eyes magnified behind his seers, something that usually worked in his favor.

The elderly nyrian gave Zavik a knowing look, then raised a filthy, dirt-crusted boot for the dwarf to inspect. "We wouldn't dare insult the All-Sovereign with the stench of our travel. Perhaps he'd be so kind as to allow us the evening to rest and refresh."

Dalgus let loose a frustrated sigh as his glare roved from one scholar to the other. "Fine. I'll send for you at dawn. Don't keep him waiting."

"Thank—" Zavik began, but the door was already closing.

When they were truly alone, Yikos dropped her pretense of piousness and spat on the plush carpet where the dwarf had stood moments prior. Zavik squeaked something akin to laughter at the outburst. But after the humor of the obscenity faded, the fear of what awaited them dulled all else.

"He'll expect answers tomorrow," Yikos said, easing herself into the lounge. "Not just insights, but actual solutions. He took a risk letting us see that, and he won't settle for anything but significant progress."

Zavik forced his saddle-sore legs toward the table holding the water basin. "We have enough now. I can see the pieces fitting together in my mind. It's just a matter of getting them on parchment and into the workshops." He splashed his face with the tepid water, once again fighting the sensation of being simultaneously horrified by and fascinated with his discoveries.

"That's good, for your sake."

The hollowness in Yikos's voice sent a wave of panic rippling through Zavik's stomach. He blotted his face with his bed sheets instead of locating one of the towels, then hurried over to his mentor, who lay on the lounge with her eyes closed, her hands clasped over her stomach.

"I'm as good as dead now," she murmured. "I've taught you everything I can, and I don't have scroll-unveiling blood flowing through my veins. Just this old mind." She pointed at her temples, then gave a sad little laugh. "Truth be told, it was never that brilliant to begin with."

"Stop that." Zavik urged her into a seated position and retrieved a bottle of unopened wine resting on the adjacent table. "We'll figure something out. I'll convince him I need you to see the work through to completion."

Her wily eyebrows met at the center, but she didn't dissuade his schemes as she'd done in the past. "You really want the burden of keeping a pet crone alongside everything else you have to worry about?" She eyed the glass Zavik held out to her, not accepting it, but not refusing it either.

"You're like this wine, Yikos. Better with age and increasing in value every day." He traced his thumb over the braided lyvium rim before nestling it into his mentor's now willing hands. "You just need to work on the feel-good part."

The cackle that followed made him smile. She patted him on the back with the comradery of one soldier to another. "So I do, young apprentice. So I do." Her face gradually regained a grave expression. "Speak with such intent to the All-Sovereign tomorrow, and you might survive this world yet."

Zavik set his jaw. "I don't plan on dying until my sense of hope outweighs my sense of despair."

"Hope you've got some god's blood flowing through you too, then." Yikos lay back on the lounge, body positioned for sleep. "I've lived nearly five-hundred years, and the world's only gotten worse each day."

Zavik didn't sleep that night. He made a good effort to: finishing Yikos's wine alongside a hot meal; allowing the servants to draw him a bath to wash off the grime of travel; tucking himself tightly beneath the sheets. But no amount of comfort could keep his mind from imagining all the things that might go wrong during his discord with the All-Sovereign.

He threw off his bedcovers sometime after midnight and began unpacking the satchels of notes and relics he'd taken from the Caman Altars, starting with the mechanisms that made the...

The *what* work, exactly?

He studied the plates of blackened lyvium that comprised the mortal-made being's shell. Spun the device containing the dull bit of crystal that, although appearing lifeless, must've been something akin to a heart. Did it have a brain somewhere up in that metal dome, too? If so, then it was undeniably a new race, one with the efficiency of the arkthanax and the mobility of a mortal. A tool, a helper, a...

A weapon.

The pieces slipped from Zavik's hands, their fall cushioned by the carpet. Whoever made the beings of metal and crystal wasn't creating gods, as Yikos suggested, nor assistants, as Zavik had thought. Even if they had begun that way, the one beneath the Caman Altars was armored, one of its arms hollow, like the end of a shieum.

Zavik nearly woke Yikos up, then thought better of it. What could she do? What could he even do? Even if he refused to help build the All-Sovereign an immortal army, progress would be made eventually. Better for him to have a hand in it. He could learn and do the same for Neharem, should he ever escape. He could even make theirs better.

He could even make the ones in Az Zar flawed.

"There's more than one way to win a war," he whispered to himself as he flipped through his journal. "And you'll regret ever making me a part of it."

When dawn finally came, Zavik found most of his nerves subdued by sheer exhaustion. As Yikos choked down her morning concoction of various tree saps, spices, and sun-blood fruit extract, he organized the last of the notes he planned to bring before the All-Sovereign. These were separate from the ones he'd hidden in the sliver of space between the wall and his bed. Those were for his eyes only. He wasn't even certain he could trust the old woman with his plan yet.

"Get your beauty rest, did you?" Yikos asked as she clunked the empty mug onto the table. There were several dents surrounding the spot, and Zavik imagined she derived no shortage of pleasure from her destruction of palace property.

"None, actually." He chugged the last of his moskuto, setting the mug carefully beside Yikos's. What he had planned would leave far more damage than a few dents on a table.

If he didn't die first.

The door swung open without so much as a warning knock. They scarcely had time to rise before they were inspected and pinched, adjusted and smoothed, and forced into the hallway. No words were exchanged between them and their escorts as their footsteps echoed off the palace walls. Though Zavik hadn't found the time that morning to discuss their looming audience with Yikos, he got the feeling she trusted him to present their findings. Or maybe she just didn't care. She still seemed convinced her death lingered just around the corner.

Dalgus joined them in one of the larger halls, a sprawling room drowning in Mavist tapestries. The dwarf wore the same clothes he always did: a thin white robe that ran to the tops of his woven sandals, and his beloved pendant.

"His Holiness will see you now. Once we enter his quarters, you are not permitted to gaze upon him until he's bestowed his gift of acceptance, nor are you permitted to speak until spoken to." Dalgus produced a small, folded section of silk from his robes and handed it to Zavik. "Suck on these until we reach our destination."

The silk contained a pinch of cloves. Zavik recalled Davier complaining about such practices and winced as he popped the fragrant spice into his mouth. At least he'd been spared the slathering of oils, accompanied by a day-long fast to 'cleanse the soul and mind.'

When he offered a clove to Yikos, Dalgus snatched it from his hand. "Not for her."

Yikos and Zavik exchanged wide-eyed glances.

"There's been a change of plans," Dalgus continued. "She's to remain here while you present your findings to the All-Sovereign."

A knot formed in Zavik's stomach. This meant nothing good for Yikos. Were they going to kill her as soon as he cleared the hall? Or wait until they were satisfied with his report before removing the redundant scholar? He thought—hoped—the latter. They'd need to be certain they could afford to lose her, after all.

He squeezed Yikos's bony hand and tried to comfort her with a look, letting her know he'd do everything in his power to keep her alive. Her expression was a peaceful one, her golden eyes suggesting she'd accepted their fate, that anything beyond the next few breaths was a gift.

The soldiers remained with Yikos as Zavik and Dalgus departed the hall. He thought nothing of it until they were truly alone, walking side by side through dimly lit passages, not a sound to be heard beyond the swishing of the dwarf's robes.

Zavik nearly ran. He'd have no trouble escaping Dalgus, and though the palace was a maze, he'd pieced together much of its layout from various plans and journals in the arcanum. If he slipped into the clothes of a servant and removed his seers at the first sign of trouble, he might even make it beyond the courtyard and into the city. He'd all but decided to risk it—they couldn't kill him, after all—when it occurred to him that the circumstances in which he found himself were oddly ideal. He'd never been allowed to wander the palace without the shadows of guards looming over him. Why change precedence now? He should have ten times the escorts to enter His Holiness's domain. Unless the dwarf had arranged it as such.

"What do you want?" Zavik whispered as they passed through a hallway lined with Az Zarian armor at its various stages of evolution.

Dalgus didn't so much as glance at him. "Good lad. I was beginning to worry you weren't as intelligent as they say."

"And what do they say?"

"Oh, a great number of things. That you're a performer, a cursed soul, an awskada's bastard. That you killed the actual person who retrieved the scrolls and assumed their identity." An evil grin slithered across the dwarf's face. "Some simply place bets on whether His Holiness will just kill you and use a jar of your blood to gain access to whatever secrets it might unlock."

Zavik's heart thudded in his chest. "That's foolish. There's no guarantee it would—"

"I say it in jest, lad. He wouldn't dare. *She* won't let him. She doesn't like to take risks." Dalgus's lips retreated into a hard line as they started up a flight of stairs. Climbing them took great effort on the dwarf's part, and Zavik felt the stirrings of pity for him.

"Why have you arranged for us to be alone?" he asked from where he waited a few steps ahead.

Dalgus kept his attention on the polished marble steps as he climbed. "How long will it take?"

Zavik's brow furrowed. "How long will what take?"

"Don't be dense now," the nyrian dwarf snapped. "The inventions. The vessels, the army. How long?"

Zavik wasn't certain he could trust the All-Sovereign's favored servant, but then again, the information he requested wouldn't be secret for long. "The time needed to complete the work has many variables," he said, offering Dalgus his hand, which the dwarf promptly refused. "It depends on the skill and number of laborers, the ease of accessing materials, and how long the All-Sovereign will allow for tests. Actually, much of it boils down to how he wants to prioritize, because the metal soldiers will be far more complicated than flying—"

"Just give me a worst-case scenario." Dalgus stopped to catch his breath, then snapped his fingers. "Quickly, quickly!"

Zavik glanced up and down the stairs. It could be a trap to test his loyalty; to see if the answer he gave the dwarf was different than the one he'd give the All-Sovereign. But despite Dalgus's abrasive and condescending demeanor, Zavik sensed his opposition to his master was genuine. He was going to find out, at any rate.

"We could potentially have operational flying vessels within a few moon cycles. Their underwater counterparts, however, will take twice as long at best. As far as the metal soldiers..." Zavik wracked his mind for an estimate, finding none. "I don't have enough to go on yet. No timeline until I can determine how they function without someone steering them, so to speak."

"Then we're almost out of time." This Dalgus muttered to himself, as if no one else were present. He stroked the ruby with his thumb as he fixed Zavik with his crimson gaze. "Speak of this to no one and don't try to contact me. We may never speak again."

Zavik stared dumbfounded as the dwarf resumed climbing the stairs. "Who are you?" he protested, hurrying after him. "You can't just take my knowledge and give me nothing in return. Or are you as unfair as your master?"

Dalgus's cheeks flushed as red as his eyes. "I'm giving you more than you know. Just promise me you'll do what you can to delay progress. And be ready. You'll receive a signal when it's time."

"Time for what?"

"Your freedom."

Zavik fought for control of his thoughts as the doors to the All-Sovereign's private feasting hall swung open. As soon as he'd deposited Zavik with the guards, putting on a great show of disdain at having been the one to escort him, Dalgus had departed. The dwarf's absence struck Zavik like a blow. He'd only just learned the identity of the man who was likely his most valuable ally within the palace walls, and he had no way of contacting him again.

All thoughts surrounding Dalgus vanished as the door slammed shut behind him, sealing him inside the All-Sovereign's domain. The entire room had been painted a vibrant red that was as unsettling to look at as it was distracting. The rug beneath his feet was no better, and even the table had been painted with crimson sun-blood blossoms—as if the color of choice hadn't been pronounced enough.

Zavik recalled Dalgus's instructions to avert his gaze as two figures emerged from behind the curtain separating the balcony from the feasting room. He lowered his head, then bent fully at the waist, just to be safe. For a painfully long moment, he heard nothing but his own heavy breathing, smelled nothing but the overpowering scent of cloves wafting from his breath.

Then he felt a light touch on his head. Still, he didn't dare lift it.

"Rise, young scholar, heir of the Prophets and protector of the scrolls."

The words sounded false, coming from the All-Sovereign's mouth. Almost comedic. Zavik tightened his lips as he met the silver-skinned nyrian's gaze. His silken white hair was pulled back in a military-style bun, but the rest of his ensemble seemed to suggest more of a temple association than a royal one. He wore a tunic of plated lyvium, the sections of which were lightly overlapped, resembling scales. Beneath it was a long-sleeved robe of velvet, each shoulder embroidered with the eye of Mavet and accompanying filigree.

The woman beside him was dressed nearly identically, save for her tunic being more fitted at the waist and tapered about her breasts. She couldn't have been more than thirty, or its equivalent in nyrian years—same for the All-Sovereign, actually—and she had the most piercing violet eyes set against dark brown skin. Violet was the rarest eye color in Quinaria, found only in nyrians hailing from the Isles of Zelos.

Eyes like Konar's, Zavik realized, studying her. In fact, the closer he looked—

"I hope your time at the Caman Altars proved insightful, for your sake," the All-Sovereign said, shattering his thoughts.

"Insightful is an understatement, Your Holiness," Zavik admitted.

The woman—who he presumed was none either than the Lord Priestess—gestured to his satchel. "Please, enlighten us." Her unrelenting gaze made him feel as though she could pluck all his secrets out with a look.

Zavik eased the satchel off his shoulder and clutched it to his chest. "Before I begin, you should know that, for now, these are all just theories, but I—"

The All-Sovereign silenced Zavik with an upraised hand. "You have until this runs out"—he turned over an hourglass filled with light pink sand—"to convince me your time there was well spent. Otherwise, I'll be tempted to remove your legs below the thighs. I doubt you'll need them to complete your work."

"I, uh..." Zavik's gaze locked on the rapidly decreasing sand. Where to begin? "The trip proved to be...what I mean is Yikos and I...we believe..."

His mouth was drier than it'd been on the ship to Az Zar. He could feel the All-Sovereign's stare burning into his skin, could see the guards dragging a blade across a helpless Yikos's throat, could predict Elaysia's horror when she learned that he'd failed her, yet again, and it gave him an overwhelming sense of despair, one that made him feel helpless, like things would never—

No. Not helpless. It enraged him, above all else. It was all wrong. So wrong. He focused on that, allowing the anger to give him clarity.

"I'll try to put this as simply as possible," he began, surprising himself with the steadiness of his voice, "starting with the vessels. We believe nevethium can create a substantial energy current when exposed to controlled vibrations. In theory, the flying ships you desire would use advanced systems to induce these vibrations, employing mechanical devices that cause back-and-forth movements and harness changes in air pressure."

"Advanced systems?" the All-Sovereign asked, his manicured eyebrow raised.

The Lord Priestess shot him down with a glare, then motioned for Zavik to continue. "Go on."

"If I can direct your attention to a diagram I've sketched," Zavik said, retrieving one of the larger parchments from his satchel and unrolling it on the table. "As the crystals vibrate, they generate a significant energy current, which is then stored onboard here." He pointed to the inner workings of the flying vessel he'd designed. "This stored energy powers the vessel's propulsion mechanisms, almost like energy-driven propellers. I believe these directed vibrations can also impact aerodynamics, aiding in lift and stability. The shape of the vessels and construction materials will also have to help induce flight, but again, entirely possible."

The Lord Priestess leaned over the plans, lips parted in a blend of excitement and disbelief. She smelled both spicy and sweet, an aroma he couldn't quite put his finger on. "How soon can we have a working model?" she asked.

"A few moon cycles?" Zavik stammered. *Lie, you fool. You're supposed to lie.* "Actually, probably closer to half a year. Maybe even longer. I mean, we don't want to rush something like this. The slightest error could cost us a fortune—not to mention lives."

"Coin and lives are of little importance to me." The All-Sovereign retrieved a bottle from one of the ornately carved cabinets and set it on the table with a thud. "And what of the underwater vessels?"

Zavik supplied another diagram from his satchel, unrolling it atop the other. Every bit of him screamed to keep it hidden. While the plans for the flying vessel had been made at Az Zar's prompting, the plans for a water-resistant means of conveyance that could grant them passage to the alleged myrem settlements were something he'd been working on since long before his capture.

"With underwater transport," he said through clenched teeth, "instead of air pressure differentials or similar mechanical devices, we might be able to utilize water currents or the acoustics of waves. We'll also need to look into waterproofing to prevent corrosion, and perhaps some sort of sealant around the lyvium made from naturally water-resistant substances. I've already begun itemizing things in nature we can learn from."

"No need to learn," the All-Sovereign said. He took a drink straight from the bottle, and Zavik caught the Lord Priestess rolling her eyes in disgust. "We'll just take what we can't replicate."

A cold, slim hand covered Zavik's own. He couldn't bring himself to look the nyrian woman in the eyes, and it wasn't solely because of her beauty.

"And the metal giants?" she asked breathlessly. "What of them?"

Zavik chewed the inside of his cheek until he tasted blood. "I found this in the chamber," he said, pulling out the spherical device with the faded crystal in the center. "I think it helps them balance, maybe move. And, in theory, the mechanics used to power the vessels could power them. But something's missing."

A groan escaped the All-Sovereign's lips. "What more could you possibly need? I've given you charts, tools, books, a seasoned assistant, and most of all, access to a sanctum you shouldn't even know exists." He was almost shouting and Zavik found himself shirking away from the table.

"I'm forever grateful for your kindness," he said, his hands folded in a plea. "And I will find the answer, I promise. If I had more knowledge, perhaps, of the scrolls in your possession, maybe I could—"

"How dare you demand such a thing!" The bottle trembled in the All-Sovereign's hand. "I needed these answers a fortnight ago. My life depends on"—he clenched his fist as if to halt the violent show of emotion, and then, in a much smoother cadence, corrected himself—"the lives of my people depend on it."

The Lord Priestess's lips curved upward as she studied Zavik, awaiting his reaction.

He wanted to call out the bald-faced lie. Snatch the bottle of Beridian Moonlight from His Holiness's hands and dump it all over the plans. Maybe make a run for the balcony and fling himself over it, dutifully ending his life before they could misuse it any longer. But he forced a smile, the same one he'd seen Elaysia force again and again during council meetings and otherwise strenuous affairs.

"Then you will get me access to the scrolls."

Both the nyrians leveled looks at him; the woman's one of devilish enjoyment; the man's one that bordered on murderous.

"Why?" the Lord Priestess asked calmly.

"Because I don't know how the metal giant ever functioned autonomously. I can't find anything in my research or experiments that would allow a non-organic being to act of their own accord."

The All-Sovereign's perfect forehead wrinkled, but the Lord Priestess nodded slowly. "I've wondered myself if they weren't powered by magic or the gods."

"It might not even be of the supernatural," Zavik added. "Often, logic and science in infancy are mislabeled as the work of the divine. Regardless, I've seen two of the scrolls and am familiar with their contents, for the most part. If you allowed me access to the ones in your possession, there's a chance they hold the secrets needed to power your metal army."

"I doubt it," the All-Sovereign scoffed.

"You have a brilliant mind not usually found in your kind," the Lord Priestess said, ignoring the naysaying of her companion as she rose. "I will allow you to pore over them in the arcanum. But don't make a fool out of me for giving you this chance, eh?" Her accent slipped, just a bit, revealing her Zelosi roots.

Zavik didn't realize until they were halfway to the door that his audience had ended. "Wait!" he called out, abandoning his diagrams on the table, at least for the moment. "Yikos!" How could he have forgotten Yikos?

Brilliant, Zav. Just brilliant.

The Lord Priestess didn't turn to address him, but he could almost sense her wicked smile as she said, "Yes, you may keep your pet a while longer. Companionship is good for the soul."

The doors slammed behind them. Zavik melted to the floor at the sudden release of tension, both from his mind and muscles.

"I hope your plan for my escape is well underway," he whispered to a non-present Dalgus. "I won't be able to stall them much longer now."

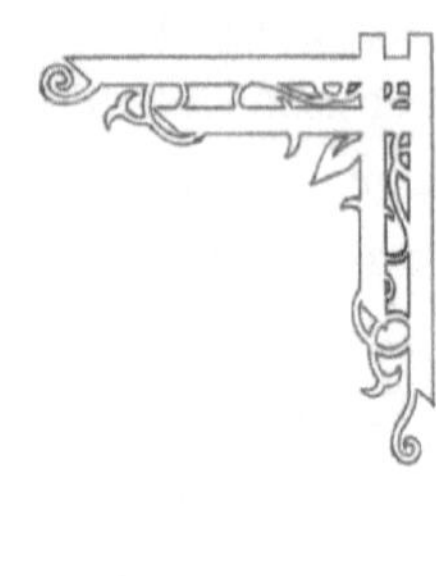

ELAYSIA

The vision engulfed her as she swung her mother's sword atop a cliff overlooking Sunset Bay. She'd been practicing some of Hallahd's forms, ones he'd shown her in the handful of lessons they'd had together before he and Vahid marched east with their kuza. One moment, she saw the flash of her lyvium blade against a flawless blue sky; the next, a brilliant, throbbing red.

At first, she thought she'd tapped into Onitus's mind accidentally, even though he'd been gone hunting for well over an hour. Then the same enveloping fog present in all her visions, her accursed gift passed down from her father, choked the sky, and she understood what transpired.

She stood at the cliff's edge, anticipating the voice that would call from beyond the fog, the one that sometimes sounded like Zavik, or Jakki—or even rarer, a stranger. But instead of a single voice slowly increasing in clarity, a storm of unintelligible moans clawed for her attention. She sifted through the chaos for coherent words, for just one of the cries to resemble a language, only to realize they already spoke in a tongue known by all mortals.

Pain.

The screams were hauntingly melodious in their anguish, hitting eerie, blood-chilling notes she'd never forget. She covered her ears, and the act only seemed to magnify the sound, sending it vibrating down into the depths of her soul.

The cries stopped abruptly, as though something had cut them off. When Elaysia thought the terror was over, two suns appeared in the distance, slowly descending into the dark waters below. But their coloring wasn't right. Instead of the reddish orange of a sun setting, they were a deep brown streaked with warm notes, like honey. Like sand.

Like Vahid's eyes.

Another scream filled her ears, but this time, it was her own. A guttural, deep-chested cry that tore at her throat. She wasn't certain when the vision faded, nor did she realize she'd been crying until her chest and shoulders ached from heaving, until her cheek had practically fused with the stone upon which she lay, the salt of hear tears blending with that of the sea. Her heart felt the same inside her chest; twisted, broken, crumpled on the cold rock, waiting for the seahawks to devour what scraps remained of it.

She never saw his face beyond the sunset eyes. There was no confirmation of his voice; no reenactment of the moment he was violently ripped from existence. No comforting revelation, where a spirit from beyond told her he was gone, but safe, flourishing in a new world. It was a silent breeze; a change in the waves; an echo in her heart.

But most of all, it was emptiness.

Elaysia remained at the cliff side the rest of the day, feeling neither hunger nor thirst, nor the ache in her bones as her back grew stiff from sitting on the rocky edge, bare feet pulled by the wind. Twice, her milk tried to come in. Twice, she ignored it, trusting Maseeya to make do with the babes. They were beginning to eat solid foods, and it wouldn't be long before they were fully capable of surviving without her.

A good thing. The fewer people that relied on her, the better.

Keera's white figure soared over the cliff first, just as the sun slipped beneath the horizon. If Mardus saw Elaysia, he made no attempt to double back. She didn't blame him for not wanting to be the bearer of bad tidings.

Lumira came next, riding Anadu. A red streak ran down the stormbird's neck, and for a moment, Elaysia forgot all else. She pushed herself up from the cliff, standing on her toes to inspect Anadu as she approached. But as she backed up, giving bird and rider ample room to land, she noted the blood trail came from something resting atop Anadu's neck, rather than from a wound on the bird herself. Someone lay in front of Lumira. The arm sticking out from behind Anadu's head was stiff, almost like a spear, rather than hanging limply the way an injured or unconscious person's might.

Elaysia swallowed the bile forming in the back of her throat. All the pieces had settled into place, all the initial shock over with. All that remained was confirmation and acceptance. She could handle that much. At least it wasn't a betrayal.

Or was it? Wasn't death the ultimate betrayal, the one thing people always anticipated, yet no one was ever ready for? The thief in the night who could pick any lock. The serpent who could slither through any barrier. A disease-bearing gift that mortals just couldn't stop spreading, hoping, thinking, praying that this time, just this once, just for them and their love, they'd be pardoned, given an antidote. Cured. Because everyone thought, deep down, they might be the one to look death in the eye and tell it not them, not today. Not ever. And sometimes, death was kind enough to wait, to eat away at a life slowly. Other times, it ended one before it had even begun.

But it always came, and it never forgot.

Lumira's mask remained on as she dismounted, but Elaysia sensed the apprehension in her. The beridian angled herself toward Anadu as she lifted the body free, as though she didn't want to meet Elaysia's gaze any sooner than necessary. Dried blood matted the fur on her side, and her new armor had already been damaged beyond repair—save for the mask, which was unharmed, despite the layer of grime covering it.

Elaysia clung to her mother's sword as Lumira approached with the body. It gave her courage, rooting her to the part of her past that had been through death before. She'd survived then, barely a wisp of a child when word of her parents' murders had arrived. She'd witnessed the slaughter of her brother as she cowered in the corner, a toy sword extended, waiting to be next. She'd watched warriors crumble under the weight of her poor decision-making; had been forced to observe someone writhing before her, veins alight with nevethium poisoning. She'd nearly died on a foreign altar while the crowds cheered on, then taken the life of a chief she'd known since her birth.

No, death was no new adversary. It simply took on fresh forms, challenging her in new ways when she thought she'd grown numb to its attacks. And, as always, it'd found a new hole in her armor, and pierced clean through.

She didn't look directly at Vahid's body as the beridian limped toward her. Anadu lingered near the ledge, her plumage raised, as though she feared Elaysia was reckless enough to take out her aggression on Lumira. An unnecessary caution.

Elaysia wouldn't contest her own instability, especially given the circumstance. But for the bird to fear she was careless enough to destroy one of the few allies she had left?

No such insanity would ever befall her.

"As you requested, High Chieftain." Emotion had such a hold on Lumira's voice that Elaysia struggled to make out her words over the roaring waves. The unharmed patches of her fur shone, brightened by the moonlight reflecting off Vahid's armor. She kneeled, laying the body upon the stone. She didn't rise as she slipped the mask off her face, but she lifted her chin so her gaze could meet Elaysia's with apologetic humility.

"I promised to bring him to you..." Her words faltered as she drew a sharp breath. She clutched her arrowhead necklace and looked at the moons before continuing. "This isn't what you meant. It's certainly not what you wanted. But I thought you should have him all the same. I couldn't leave him there in the clearing, surrounded by—"

"Enough." Elaysia intended her tone to be gentler, more understanding, but all that came out was a rage-filled hiss. It wasn't directed at Lumira; it wasn't her fault. But she couldn't find the words to convey it. "I appreciate your efforts."

The look in Lumira's eyes told Elaysia she'd only worsened her guilt. Part of her regretted it, but a greater part of her didn't care. Lumira likely hadn't tasted half as much death. Killing? Sure. It was part of a backhander's code. But the loss of loved ones? She doubted the beridian had ever carved much room in her heart for such things.

"Does Anahi know?" Elaysia asked in a thick monotone.

Lumira rose, revealing a second wound freshly clotted on her leg. "She was there when it happened. She's gone home to tell her parents. She wanted to bring the body with her, but I... I told her I promised you." Despite her increasingly evident discomfort, Lumira held Elaysia's gaze. "She's also going to see about keeping the few kuza still present in Agaas."

"Good." An icy edge seeped into Elaysia's tone. "We'll need to retain every fighter we can. How great are our losses?"

Lumira's face told all before her words confirmed it. "Only a handful survived."

A strong desire to protect usurped Elaysia's sadness. And on its tail, anger. "My Stormriders?"

"We're fine. The birds are well, too." She glanced over her shoulder as Anadu took flight. Elaysia could tell the movement pained her. "Perhaps the gods haven't abandoned us yet."

"No," Elaysia said through gritted teeth as she stormed toward the forest. "They're just taking their time."

Vahid was to be buried in Orillon, in the tomb of his family nestled in the hills that lay just beyond Munskahan. So said the tuross message they received from Anahi.

Elaysia didn't want to attend the ceremony. She still hadn't placed eyes on his body—at least not consciously—and didn't care to surround herself with his mourning family and friends. They had far more reason to be heartbroken than she, who'd only known him a few moon cycles. Then again, it was almost as long as she'd known Davier.

Perhaps she'd not grown as much as she'd thought. Or perhaps some things were rooted to her person, just like her two-toned flesh, hair, and eyes. How had she heard it put so often?

A body at war with itself, destined to tear itself apart.

Perhaps no one was better suited to lead her war-torn nation than she.

Maseeya was the one who finally convinced her to go. *For Anahi's sake, if nothing else, Elaysia,* the most trusted person in her life had told her. And she'd been right, so Elaysia reluctantly climbed onto Onitus and—with Maseeya's assurance it would be the perfect time to wean the twins—soared toward Orillon on Siren's tailwind. Jakki had understood Elaysia's unspoken desire to *not* be the one carrying Vahid's body back to the family he'd been taken from, so she'd volunteered, leaving Hallahd to ride with Elaysia. The head kuza remained silent during the flights, as well as when they landed briefly to rest. She was grateful for such a gift.

No one else accompanied them to Orillon. Every able-bodied warrior had been assigned to training and preparing Agaas for a siege. Tightening perimeters, rationing food, and fortifying the holy city and its surrounding encampments were top priority. However, with Chief Arkuun's blessing, Yerakai had held a small ceremony on sacred Apáasutai grounds, in a small clearing beside a waterfall. The Stormriders and war council were all in attendance, along with Hallahd and the surviving kuza. It was beautiful, but empty, like the pyre they built for him. Elaysia didn't cry during the ceremony, nor did she speak.

She planned to approach the one in Munskahan similarly. Stay strong, perform, return home.

Sayetta Undali greeted them with tear-swollen eyes at the gates of House Undali. Anahi and the saya waited inside at a long table covered with sun-kisses, honeyed insects, and many other such delicacies Elaysia had enjoyed during her brief stay in Munskahan. Hallahd ran to Anahi, who practically leaped up from the table to meet him. Elaysia had to look away from their tear-streaked faces and was grateful for Jakki's strong arms embracing her from behind as they stood at the edge of the room like outsiders peering through courtyard gates.

It was Orillon, or at least the Great Houses of Munskahan, tradition to bury the dead as quickly as possible. Saya Undali, furious that they'd already waited several days, immediately set his servants to washing and preparing the body. As they walked through the fields the next afternoon, Anahi explained that they would sew up wounds and groom Vahid—even going so far as to liven pasty skin with tinted powders and salves. Then he would be garbed in a simple tunic of neutral color and placed in a box custom made to house it.

The death ceremony, unlike the unity ceremony, was held at dawn, signifying the spirit's departure to the next life. Though Az Zar had begun to weave Mavism into Orillon by erecting an excessive number of temples, the people still clung to their ways. There was no one god or goddess; rather, they believed in the manifestation of divinity through people and beasts. The sand especially was sacred, for it carried memory, the essence of intelligence itself.

Sleighs and zaka-zakas carried all members of House Undali across the sand, a trip during which the saya reminded Elaysia that their arrangement was now obsolete. What remained of his private military was to be escorted back to him upon their return to Agaas, and Anahi along with them. She was now the sole surviving heir.

"And don't forget the nevethium," he'd added sharply. "It's the least you can do to compensate for the loss of my son and kuza."

Anahi and Elaysia exchanged knowing glances. There was no point in telling the saya none of his requests could be fulfilled right away, if ever.

As they approached the burial site, the weather in Munskahan took an unusual turn. Dark clouds rolled in, casting a shadow over the tomb. Elaysia was grateful for the white shroud she'd been required to wear, for it shielded her face from inquiring minds. She lined up with the others—though toward the front, at a place of honor—while Anahi, Hallahd, the saya, and the sayetta carried the coffin through the sand to the entrance of the tomb. Friends and family took turns speaking over him, wishing his spirit safe passage to its new body. A few sang songs. Meanwhile, the winds picked up, and thunder rumbled in the distance.

Elaysia focused on Neharem throughout the ceremony, doing everything in her power to keep her attention off what was actively occurring around her. If she didn't acknowledge it, didn't acknowledge *him*, it couldn't hurt her. Not fully.

The stormbirds circling overhead helped to distract her, as did her growling stomach. She'd barely eaten since arriving in Munskahan two days prior, save for politely nibbling on food when offered and drinking small glasses of wine. When it came her turn to approach the ornamentally carved coffin, Elaysia nearly collapsed, saved only by Jakki's ready arms. It was the heat, she told herself. It was the hunger.

It wasn't him.

But when she reached the body and forced herself to truly lay eyes on him for the first time, everything changed.

Vahid's lifeless eyes were closed, as though he were sleeping. His beard had been finely trimmed, his hair pulled back, his skin powdered into a semblance of its former glow. He wore his family ring, whose line had now ended, as Anahi was beyond the age of bearing children. His mouth almost seemed to quirk up in the corners, hinting at a smile. But that's all it was. A hint. A trace of his former self.

Vahid was gone, and no beautification of his body could mask that. Even if he returned, as the Undalis believed, in a new form worthy of the life he'd led, it still wouldn't be him any more than a plant fed by the rich soil of a carcass was the nytak it had absorbed.

A deep, painful sob caught in her throat. She barely got clear of the gathering before it spilled out of her lungs in a tired, heaving moan just as a bolt of lightning struck the ground nearby. The onlookers shrieked, but the release Elaysia felt was as refreshing as the gentle rain that followed.

Upon returning to the Undali home, Elaysia expressed her plan to leave immediately to Anahi and the sayetta.

"I don't want to intrude," she said through cracked lips. "And I fear I have much demanding my attention back in Neharem."

Sayetta Undali took Elaysia's face in her hands. Her fingers were soft and comforting, not unlike her own mother's had once been. "Anahi says you made him happy, and I can never thank you enough for that."

"If I thanked you a thousand times over, it would never be enough to express what he meant to our people. To me." Elaysia fought to hold the older woman's gaze. "May this be your last sorrow," she whispered, head bowed.

"And may our next meeting be in times of happiness," the sayetta returned.

Anahi followed Elaysia out to the courtyard, where the storm-birds soared above like ravagers circling a kill. She'd maintained better composure than the rest of her house, but Elaysia knew the dam holding her tears back had nearly reached its breaking point.

"I'll understand if you wish to remain here," Elaysia said, taking Anahi's hand in hers. "I hereby free you of any commitments to Agaas. Corvax as well."

"I'm sworn to your cause, High Chieftain," was the Orillon woman's dutiful reply. "I'm long past the age where my faja rules me. I will return to my family permanently when the time is right. Until then, I'm yours."

"Then take some time, at least. Mourn with your loved ones, then send a tuross when you're ready."

Anahi's brown eyes narrowed. "Are you certain?"

Jakki's expression suggested that she, too, thought it to be a bad idea, but she had the decency to hold her tongue.

"We'll be fine. It's probably better if we don't have all the stormbirds clustered together, anyway." Elaysia knew her excuse was a flimsy one, but she also couldn't force House Undali's only heir to leave her family at their time of need.

"I will return," Anahi said, pulling her in for a tight embrace. "Thank you, Elaysia," she whispered into her ear.

Elaysia's throat tightened. "I am the one who should be thanking you for introducing me to your beloved brother." She pulled away, holding Anahi's hand until the last moment.

Jakki didn't try to lift Elaysia's spirits as they waited for the stormbirds to descend. She knew better than that. A drink was what Elaysia wanted in that moment, and knowing it wouldn't be wise to imbibe before a flight, she simply tried to stand as straight as her friend as they donned their masks, bodies silhouetted in the sunset.

As Elaysia clung to Onitus, no colors filled the cavern of her mind. It was all numb, sludge-filled darkness. A drowsy poison trickling down into her flickering soul. All she could focus on, all that kept her hanging on, not throwing herself to the mercy of the ground racing beneath her, was her resolve to never love again. No one else would be allowed access to the thick walls of her heart, and of those already barricaded inside, only one remained outside of her control, of her arc of protection.

And she'd do everything within her power to bring Zavik home.

PART FOUR

DAVIER

The rebels didn't so much as breathe as they leaned across the table, attention wholly fixated on Nanjiya's map of Cadar's underbelly. It wasn't an original copy, at least from what Davier could tell. But despite its patchwork design, they seemed to have compiled a decent guide to the catacombs running deep beneath the city.

"If you look here," Nanjiya said, her finger hovering over a spider web of passages near the eastern half of the Labor District, "we have multiple escape routes to choose from."

Kymerius snorted before knocking back whatever thick ale Asha had brewed in her secret vault beneath the stables. Her drinks weren't palatable—Davier found them downright impossible to stomach sometimes—but they accomplished their job of taking the edge off frazzled rebels after a day of terrorizing the Sun-blood District. And since Davier and Nanjiya's capture of General Zhia, that's all they'd been doing. Targeting a city official here, threatening a highborn there. Painting the doors of government shops with the rebel sigil. Defacing a Mavist banner. On a better day, they'd steal large quantities of food and distribute it to the working-class districts, or even gather more weapons and uniforms to be used in a large-scale attack.

Davier liked those missions the most; the ones where he felt like he'd actually done something that mattered. Much of his life had been spent following meaningless or destructive orders, so when he saw his actions positively impacting lives, it almost gave him hope for redemption. Still, the rebels would never get far if they continued to think small. He'd said as much to Nanjiya the day prior, and apparently, it'd stuck, because she'd spent the rest of the day in solitude, only emerging at night to summon Davier to her room to discuss plans. The look Kymerius had given him as he'd gone in suggested his old military rival thought other things were afoot, but that was because he, too, thought small. What Davier and Nanjiya wanted for the rebellion was lasting change, and if anything happened between them in the aftermath, so be it. But that was not at the forefront of his mind, nor hers.

"Do you," Kymerius said, plopping his empty mug on the table, "have any idea how dangerous this plan is? Even if we got into the mines safely, there's no way we're getting dozens of sickly children out alive."

A retort flew to the tip of Davier's tongue, but he held it back. He'd not been made privy to Nanjiya and Kymerius's history, but whatever relationship they'd once held had all but disintegrated since Davier joined the rebels over a moon cycle prior. Just another reason for Kymerius to hate him.

Always the victim, Davier thought, studying Kymerius's storm-cloud eyes.

Nanjiya threw up her hands in exasperation. "What would you have us do? Continue throwing pebbles at a sandcat? We're only further provoking the beast. We received word not two days past that they're cutting rations by a third in the working-class districts. One can only imagine how much worse the slaves are faring." Her dark gaze cut through the fifteen rebels gathered at the rectangular table, their faces a mixture of exhaustion and avoidance. "If anyone has other suggestions, speak now, please."

Kymerius stretched his arms overhead, flexing them in his short-sleeved tunic as he lowered them back down. Davier forced himself to drink some of the sludgy ale instead of commenting on the pretentious display. His old physique had been resurfacing thanks to his now varied activity and mostly bland but nourishing diet afforded to the rebel leaders, but he'd never be caught posturing as Kymerius did everywhere he went.

"Are you afraid of causing actual change?" Davier asked, emboldened by the ale.

"Of course not," the ex-soldier replied. His face took on a pink tinge as he angled his body toward Davier, who sat across and to the left of him. "I just don't have a death wish. If we all perish in some ill-planned raid, then our cause is lost."

Davier set his drink down carefully, hoping someone—ideally Nan—would note how his actions were far more controlled than Kymerius's. "If our cause is lost on account of us perishing, then we never had a cause to begin with."

"Well said." Nanjiya squeezed his forearm.

Davier tensed at the sensation radiating from her touch, then relaxed as it spread through his body. Life was too short to ignore its rare pleasures.

"Shouldn't we try something that poses less of a risk to our fighters? Maybe a larger attack on the Sun-blood District?" The questions came from a man whose face was almost as expressionless as his tone. He carried himself as though he'd been in the military and kept his hair cut close to the scalp, like Kymerius. Davier could never recall his name—probably because he always referred to him as 'Kymerius the Lesser,' in his mind.

A fiery, sturdy woman named Lox splayed her fingers on the table as though she intended to pounce. "So they can retaliate by stringing up more suspected rebel sympathizers alongside the nevethium lanterns? Are you hearing nothing Nanjiya is saying?"

"It's alright, Lox," Nanjiya said, holding up her hand to quiet the growing murmurs around the table.

Lox crossed her arms. "With respect, Nan, it *isn't* alright. Eumma overheard today when collecting her rations that the All-Sovereign is almost ready to reopen the arena."

Nanjiya's eyes widened. "Is this true, Asha?"

The mother of the rebels, or just 'Eumma,' as Davier had so often heard her called, stopped ladling second helpings of stew and gave a slow nod. "I'm 'fraid so. She's behind it, his awskada whore. Rumors are they want to make Cadar as it was when Ashaat ruled, and his arena battles were the height of entertainment back then."

"And control." Nanjiya let her night-black hair down from its knot atop her head. It cascaded around her shoulders, soft as silk.

The room took on a sour note, as though death itself poisoned the air. Davier rubbed his forehead, anger rising at the touch of the brand seared into his flesh.

"All the more reason to get the children out of there," he said, sliding the map out from beneath Nanjiya's fingers. "I spent much of my enslavement in service to the mines, and I've seen what happens to them." His stomach turned at the memory of soot-covered children reaching skeletal limbs into the arkthanax, responsible for maintaining the parts adults couldn't access. He recalled the hollowness of their eyes, the trembling of their fingers as they crawled about the floor, gathering every shard, sweeping up dust with their sweaty arms and brushing the residue into pots. Thin bodies descending into holes with pickaxes half their size, not allowed to come up for drink or rest until they had a prize worthy of it.

Nanjiya looked deep into his eyes. He'd already told her the horrors of what happened below, and she wouldn't make him relive it now.

"We have a few allies among the sentries below," she said, directing her attention back to the table. "They will help us when the time comes, but we'll need to create a diversion to draw the others away."

"We've recovered two of their groundshakers," Davier said. "We could use those not just for distractions, but to bring down an arkthanax to slow production."

"Assuming we get them out, what are we going to do with a boatload of whelps?" Kymerius leaned across the table, attention on the map, his body invading Nanjiya's space. She drew back subtly, and Davier felt a flicker of rage spark inside him.

"Get them a boat, of course," he answered coolly.

Kymerius took a half-full mug from Kymerius the Lesser, who didn't protest as he tossed it back. "So." He wiped the froth from his puffy lips. "Not only do you want to break into the mines and rescue children, you want to smuggle them out of the city and onto boats—headed where, might I ask?"

"That is for me and those supporting that directive to know." Nanjiya offered no smile to lighten his exclusion. She'd told Davier ahead of time that they'd managed to secure the children passage to Orillon, hoping they'd take pity on the human young fleeing an oppressive empire. Allegedly, some wealthy merchant named Lanston had agreed to feed and house them in exchange for work.

Kymerius rose from the table with an air of disgust. "Seems like there's no point in this meeting, then. You've already made up your minds. If you care to fill me in on the details before we depart, you know where to find me."

The inn door slammed shut behind him.

They crept into the mines at dusk the following day. It was a shift change for the sentries, but more importantly, it was when the weekly services held at Mavist temples took place. Attendance was mandatory to any citizen not on duty or at work, but the rebels chosen to infiltrate had disguised themselves in the uniforms of soldiers assigned to the mines.

The uniforms alone weren't enough. They also needed papers disclosing their duties, if asked. But cooking wasn't Asha's only skill, and the rebel mother had forged documents and carefully reapplied military seals stolen from others. With them, Nanjiya, Davier, Kymerius, Lox, and a pair of twins known simply as the brother and the sister, worked their way through the tunnels, popping out in the Labor District just outside the mines.

Davier carried a basket overflowing with day-old bread rations supplied to the military. Beneath the bread was a thin cloth, and beneath that cloth, the groundshaker. Nanjiya carried one as well, and as they approached the sentries guarding the entrance to the main access tunnel, she cast an apprehensive glance his way. Baskets or sacks of rations weren't uncommon accessories for soldiers beginning a shift, but anything was subject to inspection by any guard who deemed it necessary. As the shifty eyes of the sentry on the left lingered on Davier's basket, he realized he still hadn't settled on a convincing excuse to keep them from searching it, should they demand it of him.

Kymerius and the sister entered without question. When Nanjiya approached, the sentries asked to see her papers, then waved her through with a scathing comment about her slight frame—it was assumed all human soldiers were male. The brother and Lox entered with another glance at their papers, and then it was Davier's turn. His heart thudded in his chest. He was unsure whether his fear stemmed from the upcoming inspection or from the equally daunting prospect of facing his personal demons in the mines. Probably both.

Instead of asking for his papers, the sentry jabbed Davier's basket with the butt of his spear. "Your friend had a basket, too. I haven't seen but one other today, so two in a matter of seconds is a bit unusual. Wouldn't be smuggling in extra rations to punished soldiers, would you?"

Davier chewed the inside of his cheek, thankful the uniform revealed nothing but his eyes. He hadn't considered such reasoning. Punishment by ration reduction was nothing new, but he hadn't known soldiers had grown so desperate as to smuggle food in for their friends. Just how bad was the resource crisis getting in Az Zar?

"I'm afraid you've caught me," Davier said, hoping the admittance of something trivial would keep the more damning evidence hidden. "My mate got caught sending rations home, and I had extra, on account of my parents' passing." He swallowed, trying to get his bearings on the wave of sadness sweeping through him. He'd never properly mourned his family. Just adopted a new identity like a coward in hopes of forgetting everything.

Even them.

The sentry seemed to soften, giving Davier hope their rebellion might still sway others to join. "I was in a similar place myself a few moon cycles ago. Alas, I can't allow it. Not on my watch." He motioned for Davier to hand over the basket. "Give it here, and I'll let your friend already inside keep his."

Davier's grip on the basket was lyvium. "Take some." He retrieved one of the small loaves and held it out to the sentry. "You as well," he said, directing his attention to the other.

They eyed the bread greedily. It was something so small, a hardened loaf of bread. But the empire would rather see it go to waste than distributed outside their controlling methods. The thought angered Davier, and he let it seep into his words.

"Who are they, sitting on their cushioned lounges with more food than they could ever eat, to decide what we do with the scraps they toss us? This isn't even stolen. It's hard-earned food that I've every right to distribute as I see fit."

The words were treason. Davier had put it all on the line, trusting that the mistreatment of the sentries would instill injustice in their minds, allowing them to overlook his minor infraction. But they could just as easily turn him in. Or worse, open the basket right there, ruining the plan and trapping some of the most important rebels inside.

The sentries exchanged glances with each other as their feet shifted uneasily. The one on the left peered around Davier, taking in the abandoned clearing and the fact that no one waited behind him. Their timing had been good, if nothing else. The rebels were the last to enter.

"Two loaves," the sentry said, almost indiscernibly, as though ears within listened.

"For both of us," his partner clarified, sticking out a gloved hand.

Davier handed the loaves over without a word, leaving only one on the top layer of his basket. He walked inside as if the exchange had never happened and didn't stop to catch his breath until he'd rounded the corner.

"What took so long?" Lox hissed, gaze flicking to his basket.

Nanjiya shook her head and pointed down the tunnel. Davier had made it inside safely, and how he'd done so wasn't pertinent to discuss immediately, if at all. Kymerius leveled a glare at him all the same, then they were marching down the tunnel, hands on the wooden railing as they descended shoddy steps fashioned from dirt and planks. Flaming sconces cast dancing shadows on the walls, and the occasional skirvin skittered by, their poison spikes gleaming.

The sight of the rodents turned Davier's stomach. He'd experienced more than one incident with skirvin while imprisoned—had once even awoken to a bite as one tried to nibble its way through his food-stained fingers. He slept with all limbs tucked firmly in after that. Thankfully, he'd never been poisoned, but he'd witnessed multiple instances of fellow slaves being taken out of labor for as long as a week, as well as children and elderly who didn't survive it.

The tunnel they followed widened, branching off into separate passageways. Already, the air grew thick and stuffy, the tunnels filled with the sounds of hissing arkthanax and clanging tools. Davier frowned as he took in his surroundings. The mine they'd entered was much larger and more elaborate than what he was accustomed to, filled with little coves furnished with temporary cots and small tables. Some even boasted shelves lined with non-perishable foods. He wouldn't be much help navigating, but he could hopefully make up for it in other ways, as he had with getting the basket by the sentries. He doubted Kymerius would've sailed through without bloodshed.

They straightened as another pair of soldiers passed by, then Nanjiya motioned them to the side, pulling out a roughly copied section of the map she'd brought with her. She pointed to where they were, then traced a path leading to where they needed to go. It wasn't far from what Davier could tell. She slid her hands into his basket to ensure the groundshaker was still nestled below, brushing her gloved fingers over his in the process. The look in her eyes was alluring despite the vengeful fire he could sense burning beneath it. What they were about to do lit Nanjiya with a passion she rarely displayed otherwise. In fact, he'd only witnessed it at such times.

The party broke into two groups. Nanjiya took the twins down a passage to the right while Davier led Lox and Kymerius left. He hadn't realized how much he would dislike the feeling of being separated from her until it happened. But as much as it worried him, he knew the twins worshipped her and would protect her with their lives. With luck, they'd all be back together within an hour, meeting up outside the city under the cover of night.

Davier slowed his pace as he entered the cavern. A massive arkthanax roared and groaned at the far end of the room, its great lyvium pick boring into the rock, dislodging massive chunks that slaves hurried in to remove before it plunged again. Their sources had proven accurate: there were at least thirty children at work, alongside another twenty or so adults. It was a blessing, having so many grown people. If they didn't crumple in panic when the groundshaker went off, they could help guide and even carry some of the smaller children.

A soldier stationed next to the arkthanax waved an arm in greeting. Davier waved back, cursing under his breath as the soldier made his way over, likely curious as to why three more of his comrades had entered when there were already twenty on duty. Davier used the thirty seconds remaining between him and his approaching doom to assess the room. The soldiers were stationed in evenly spaced pairs every twenty or so feet. Having just assumed post, they were fresh and assembled, ready for anything. Nanjiya's source had said patrols passed through the halls every half hour, and they'd just passed one a few minutes back, making the nearest interference at least ten minutes away. There was only one entrance to the cavern, but multiple options for escape lay without if they could funnel all the slaves through.

"Lost?" the soldier said when he reached Davier. His tone wasn't suspicious so much as irritated.

Davier used it to his advantage.

"I believe that description belongs to you, my friend," he said, shoving past the soldier with all the authority he could summon. "Now, run along back to your proper duty station, and I'll see to it your commanding officer doesn't hear of this." Davier motioned for Kymerius and Lox to follow, which they did without question.

It took the soldier a moment to gather his bearings before rushing after him. Four of the other soldiers joined, and together, they formed a semi-circle around Davier's rebels.

Davier shook his head as though he didn't have the time. "I'm not above a good brawl," he said through a yawn, "but this is neither the time nor the place."

"Let me see your orders," an impressively large soldier grunted.

Davier handed his papers over without protest. As the soldiers crowded around to read them, he passed the basket to Kymerius. The ex-soldier may have hated him—probably awaited the opportunity to kill him—but his hatred for the empire was stronger. He nudged Lox, and together they made for the arkthanax.

The first soldier's eyes narrowed as the papers crumpled beneath his fingers. "A sudden change in duty stations? How come I received no word of this?"

Davier shrugged. Inaccurate orders were rare, but not unheard of. "Why don't you take the evening off and sort it out with your superiors in the morning? Services are just getting started, after all. Surely you have something to seek penance for."

He regretted the final remark as soon as it left his lips. The soldier's eyes darkened.

"We'll take it to our superiors right now," he said, shoving the orders against Davier's chest.

"Be my guest." Davier bowed, sweeping his hand toward the entrance. It was going better than planned. With some of the soldiers gone, their odds of success increased, and by the time they returned with their commanding officer, the rebels and slaves would be long gone.

A jerk on his uniform squashed his premature celebrations.

"You're coming with us," the soldier snarled. "And so are your friends tinkering with the arkthanax."

Davier looked past the soldiers to where Lox was holding up her hands defensively, blocking two burly soldiers' paths to Kymerius. The fool somehow managed to look suspicious even in uniform as he stepped out from behind the machine, basket-free and a hand on a child's back to guide them away.

Away from the groundshaker.

Fuck.

Kymerius had lit the fuse. If they were lucky, they had a minute before it laid waste to the cavern.

Everything slowed. Davier's heartbeat was a distant echo, the shouting a dream. The arkthanax's deafening roar faded in his ears. He unsheathed his swords, drawing them swiftly across two of the soldiers' throats.

The blades felt like family. Like home. They were lovers in his hands, sighing beneath his touch, bending to his will. He gutted the next two before they could draw, then was onto the next, lyvium meeting lyvium in an eerie crystalline ring. In the distance, he could make out Kymerius and Lox whipping out their own blades, nearly as formidable as he in rage, if not in practice.

The soldiers on guard hadn't been as ready as he'd thought. The survivors stared dumbly for a moment, processing the severity of the situation. They rushed forward, as good soldiers did, blades raised above their heads as they came down on the rebels. Only one had been smart enough to grab a child, holding his blade across the tiny throat as he barked his terms.

"Stand down!" he screamed, inching toward the entrance. "If you come near me, he dies." The boy in his arms didn't whimper but looked fiercely at Davier with a rage and understanding well beyond his years.

Do it, his face screamed.

Before Davier could decide whether to spare the last soldier standing, and therefore the boy, a *boom* rattled through the cavern, bringing everyone to their knees as chunks of rock and stalactites fell from the ceiling. Davier dropped and buried his head, hoping the boy in the soldier's arms had done the same. When the smoke cleared, he looked there first, nearly tripping over his feet as he ran.

The soldier had been pinned beneath a chunk of rock nearly as big as Davier was tall. The boy stood over him, a distant look in his eyes, his thin arms trembling in his threadbare tunic. He didn't look for help as he picked up a jagged stone from the ground and held it over the soldier's head.

Davier called out to him. The boy didn't need to bear the weight of murder on top of his already stolen life. But he raised the rock over his head and, despite the soldier's pleas, brought it down on the masked face. Hard. Blood gushed from the wound, and by the time Davier reached them, the boy was already three strikes in, and the soldier's head concave. He pulled the boy away, dropping the bloodied rock onto the stone with a clatter.

"Zadel!"

Davier's head jerked to where Kymerius and Lox had rounded up all the slaves by the entrance.

"Grab the boy and let's go!" Kymerius shouted, then he disappeared into the tunnel, a dozen slaves at his heels. To their credit, they hadn't so much as protested. Lox carried two smaller children on her hips, glancing back at Davier with wide eyes before vanishing along with the others.

"Come on, boy," Davier said, yanking the stunned child by the arm. He couldn't have been more than ten, and just like that, his innocence had been lost.

Or maybe it had already been absent for some time.

Before they abandoned the cavern, Davier cast a final look back at the arkthanax, grinning as he took in its destruction.

Where once had stood a formidable monster of metal and gases, was now a pile of rubble. Steam still hissed, and nevethium still glinted, but the arkthanax was no more. Somewhere further in the tunnels, another blast rang out.

Nan.

Good. Her groundshaker had gone off as well. He gathered a shieum from a fallen soldier, as they'd planned, and sprinted toward freedom.

The boy wasn't moving fast enough, so Davier scooped him up in his arms, rushing him down the tunnels as his footsteps sounded like gongs in the darkness. It wasn't until they'd cleared the cavern that the boy began to whimper. Davier clutched him tighter to his chest, whispering promises into his shaved head, the sorts he would tell his sisters.

"I'm here," he reassured the boy. "You are safe. You are loved." And in that moment, he felt nothing but the giver of those things. Presence. Safety. Love.

And in it, he found purpose.

Footsteps reverberated in the tunnels behind him. He increased his pace, hardly feeling the wisp of the boy against his chest, nor his weight in his arms. Kymerius and his pack were well ahead, and Nanjiya and her group even further along, much closer to their means of escape. There was hope, Davier thought. As long as he could keep up his current pace—

Shieum thunder sent him skidding.

It was close. Too close.

The boy's sharp fingernails dug into his collarbone as he pushed through the pains in his side and barreled down the tunnel. No matter how close the footsteps and shieum fire got, he pressed on, refusing to look back, not daring to even acknowledge the possibility of failure, lest he give it the advantage it needed to swallow him whole.

Kymerius waited at the end of the tunnel, his silhouette nearly indiscernible against the dark sky. If Nanjiya's contacts had done their job, they'd be met with no resistance, at least at the tunnel mouth.

A shieum projectile whizzed by Davier's head, its heat close enough to register. As he escaped into the small clearing that had once been a courtyard, Kymerius guarded his flank, firing a shieum he'd snagged from the cavern into the dark tunnel. A cry of anguish sounded in response, but before Kymerius could get in another shot, Lox was pulling him out of the way while Nanjiya raced toward the tunnel, a third groundshaker sparking in her hands. Davier set the boy down, fighting back tears of joy. Had her contacts tucked away another groundshaker on top of securing their path to freedom?

A blast of rubble and grit flew from the tunnel mouth as thunder exploded within. Davier forced the boy to duck with him. They kept their faces pressed to the dirt as debris rained down on their heads. Smoke burned Davier's throat, and he tucked the boy closer, hoping to prevent some of the poison air from seeping into his lungs.

"Hurry!" Nanjiya shouted as soon as the dust settled.

Davier jumped to his feet, surveying the damage. The tunnel mouth was sealed, leaving them in a small ruin of a courtyard crusted with dirt and scraggly plants reaching up through cracks in the stone. All the rebels were accounted for, along with at least fifty slaves. Mostly children. Mostly weak. But alive, breathing clean air.

And now, they had a chance.

They fled the courtyard as quickly as the smallest and oldest ones would allow, two rebels at the front, two in the middle, two at the end. Davier brought up the rear with Lox, and they spent most of their time walking backwards, their shieum trained on whatever might arise from the shadows.

A gong sounded in the distance, alerting all citizens that services had ended, and it was time to make their way home. It only rang once, meaning word hadn't made its way to the palace yet. Or, if it had, the All-Sovereign wasn't keen on letting the people know. Fear seized Davier as he thought of Xi, of what might happen to her if the All-Sovereign realized he was genuinely helping the rebels, had murdered Zhia himself. But he couldn't linger on it, not with so much at stake.

He would get Xi next, rebel support or not.

Since services had only just ended, the streets were mostly clear, as they'd hoped. Still, they stuck to alleys, moving as silently as possible. They'd nearly reached an entrance to the catacombs when footsteps and shouting sounded close by. Davier cursed beneath his breath and climbed atop one of the curled roofs, pressing against it as he'd seen the beridians do so long ago. There, three streets up and to the left, marched a small squadron. Their weapons were drawn and their movements brisk. Davier's heart sank as he looked from the slaves to the soldiers, finally turning his gaze on their escape. The catacomb entrance was only a street ahead, tucked behind the waste bins of an abandoned inn. But they wouldn't get everyone inside before the soldiers advanced on them.

Davier willed his mind to produce a solution.

A thundering boom echoed in response.

The blast sounded a few streets away from the incoming squadron. Davier blinked, shocked, then remembered a rebel sympathizer had agreed to create a diversion in the city, should they need it. He'd never learned who, and right then, didn't care. The soldiers ducked, shouting, then sprinted away from the slaves, toward the wreckage.

Davier lowered himself down from the roof and gave Nanjiya a sign that it was alright to proceed as planned. In the next few minutes, they'd secured all the slaves in the waste tunnels below.

It wasn't a moment too soon, for as Davier closed the grate, footsteps marched around the corner.

The boy didn't let go of Davier's uniform as they wended their way through the passages beneath the city, though it seemed as much out of loyalty as fear. The slaves, he reflected as he watched them move through the darkness with ease, were used to being so much further beneath ground that the catacombs must've felt like a taste of the surface.

Since Nanjiya had only confirmed one route leading out of the city, it took the better part of the night to guide the slaves to freedom. They didn't have the time or resources to pack food and drink, but Davier stopped once to discreetly share his waterskin with the boy and those closest to him. As he did, he caught Kymerius watching, but with no venomous words or hateful looks. Drunk on adrenaline or not, Davier swore something changed between him and his old rival in that moment.

The docks of Cadar were well-guarded even in peacetime, and with word of the mine rescue likely spreading like wildfire, Nanjiya had arranged a means of passage for the slaves through carts loaded with trade goods for Orillon. A thick bearded man with kohl-lined eyes greeted them a good distance from the city walls, motioning quickly for the slaves to board one of the three wagons he'd readied beneath a grove of trees.

As the slaves climbed in, Lox and the twins spoke with the other two drivers while Nanjiya approached the kohl-eyed man.

"Your payment," she said quickly, retrieving several empire notes. Davier knew they'd come from Zhia's home before her death, and he consoled himself with the thought that her wealth was now benefiting a worthy cause.

The kohl-eyed man rubbed his thumb across them, then held them up to the moonlight, ensuring they revealed the hidden ink marking them as genuine. Davier didn't like that they were paying the man up front. Even good men could be tempted to run off with the profit. Why would he still risk his life taking three wagons filled with fugitives down Az Zar's desolate southern coast, with soldiers on his heels?

"How do we know your word is good?" Kymerius asked, arms folded as he leveled one of his stormy glares at the man.

Davier smirked. If Kymerius kept down this path, he was going to have no choice but to tolerate him.

"Because your lady here isn't sending the second half of my payment until the cargo is safe in Munskahan," the kohl-eyed man said in a thick Orillon accent. He shrugged, then slipped the notes inside his boot.

"It's always a pleasure, Nahiim," Nanjiya said, helping a small girl into the wagon. "Join me for a drink when you're in town next, yes?"

Nahiim flashed a golden grin. "Would if I could, my love. Don't think I'll be coming back to your nation. Not with wars brewing everywhere but home. Seems Munskahan is the safest place to be."

"You better hurry," Davier said as he tried, unsuccessfully, to pry the boy's fingers from his arm. "Our people should've taken care of the guards on the bridge, but it won't be long before reinforcements arrive."

"Tell that to your little friend." Nahiim raised an eyebrow at the boy, then climbed atop his wagon with a sigh. "Next stop, freedom. Or as close as you'll get to it, anyhow."

"You'll feed them?" Nanjiya said, grabbing the reins of the thick hooved horses hitched to the wagon. "They haven't had water all night, and—"

"All a part of the payment, Nan," Nahiim said, jerking the reins back from her. "Be off with you now, or it'll be your heads spiked in the marketplace next."

The wagons had already begun rolling out by the time Davier detached the boy from his body. "You have to go with them," he said, hoisting him into the wagon. "There's a new life waiting for you. Take it."

The boy only remained in the wagon because the hands of elder slaves held him firm. He didn't take his gaze off Davier, and before his figure faded into the darkness, Davier caught sight of a single tear glistening down his cheek.

KONAR

Konar paced in the main hall of the Igtheos refuge, desperately wishing he had a way to light his own pipe. The two scrolls, along with T'Vak's pilfered parchment, lay on the table, illuminated by the flame from a single dripping candle. He'd also brought out two wooden chalices he'd discovered during his initial stay and taken the liberty of filling them with Cyan's anderberry wine. He'd given himself just a sampling—nothing that would give him any of the ill effects of alcohol, but enough that Elaysia wouldn't feel like she was drinking alone. A necessary sacrifice, he told himself, given how often he'd chastised her habits in the past.

There were no windows in the main hall of the refuge, but by his internal measure, she had to have been a half hour late. Was she punishing him by not attending the gathering she'd finally agreed to? Or had something called her attention away, as it had multiple times over the past moon cycle since she'd returned from burying her dead mate? She couldn't have gotten lost. Not unless someone...

Konar could no longer live with the scenarios unfolding in his mind. He hurried to the door, throwing it open only to find Elaysia standing there, her cloak drenched from the rain he'd not registered pattering against the roof in his distracted state.

"High Chieftain," he said, bringing his fist to his heart. It was the wrong fist, and the motion felt awkward. But how else was he to show his allegiance? "You're soaked. Come inside, I can start a fire."

"Can you?" Elaysia asked, shutting the door behind her. Her question was tinged with sarcasm, although just a hint. Almost as if a bit of their old banter had survived.

"I'd need some help," Konar admitted.

She removed her cloak in a sweeping motion and laid it at the far end of the table to dry. "It's alright. It's a warm, Feasting Moons' rain."

Konar eyed the chalices, uncertain if he should offer them as a peace treaty prior to the discussion beginning. It was the least venom she'd displayed toward him since their reckoning on the beach the day of her second induction, now almost a year past. He wasn't quick to perceive her depressed and distracted state as acceptance of his wrongdoings, though. She'd not forgotten them yet. She never would.

"Is this for me?" Elaysia lifted a chalice to her nose and inhaled deeply. "Ah, Cyan. You know, a lot of the people have been storing up his wine in their lofts, treasuring it even above food."

"I'd wager it's worthy of that. It provides relief, after all."

"But not for you." Elaysia looked from the second chalice to Konar, still holding hers just beneath her lips.

He retrieved his chalice with a steady hand, holding it up to hers. "Times such as these call for it."

"I appreciate the gesture, but you don't have to."

Elaysia tipped the violet liquid into her mouth, her gaze never leaving his. When he raised his chalice to do the same, not so much as wincing when the drink hit his lips, she cocked her head, the corners of her mouth curving upward.

"I think someone could spend a lifetime with you and never unravel your secrets," she said, setting the unfinished chalice down.

The second sip hit Konar easier than the first. He set his drink aside, too, not wanting to be tempted by it further. "Would you be so different, were your circumstances mine?"

Whatever humor she'd momentarily allowed dissipated, replaced by the stoic face of a leader, arms crossed over her stomach in defense. "That's a dangerous game I don't care to play."

She gestured to the scrolls with her chin. "You said you had important things to discuss."

Thunder rumbled in the distance.

"Yes. Where to start." A forced chuckle made its way out of Konar's throat. He reached for the parchment, then stopped as his fingertips grazed the edges.

He couldn't go on with the division between them any longer. It all felt so wrong, so forced, like they spat rehearsed speeches at each other again and again, all while the resentment continued to simmer below the surface. If she didn't want to make peace with him, that was more than fair. But he couldn't continue to step gingerly around her, over analyzing everything she said and didn't say, everything she did and didn't do.

"Ellie." He hesitated, waiting for her to react to the name she'd forbidden him from using.

Her eyes glistened, but she didn't rebuke him. "What?" The words were gravelly, almost as if she'd taken sick.

Konar drew a long breath, relying on it in the absence of his pipe. "I have much to tell you, and my time is short. I still don't expect you to ever forgive me for what I've done, much less trust me again. But if you can be stronger than I and put aside your grievances long enough to hear me out, I've spent a lifetime acquiring knowledge that needs to be passed on."

She remained silent as he walked barefoot to a small chest where he'd stored his journals from the library. T'Vak had helped him bring them over earlier that day. All his research, all his musings. And a special book just for her.

"I'd hoped to train Zavik, and I still do. I trust you'll keep these safe until his return." With the exception of the journal he'd written for her, he piled all the books in front of her. He'd considered giving it along with the others, but had since decided it would be better received after he departed for Az Zar. Maseeya would look after it until then.

Tears continued to well in Elaysia's eyes. Still, she said nothing. She hugged the journals to her chest, stroking them gently as if they were her own babes.

Konar cleared his throat. "The information contained in those is for the two of you. I didn't know it as I wrote them, but they were always meant for you, for your minds. Your heritage."

"We can't abandon him over there," Elaysia said, voice breaking. "It's been so long already. What if they...what if he..." She buried her face in her hands, not sobbing, but breathing loud and slow, as if to gain focus.

"We'll bring him home," Konar said, placing his hand on her shoulder. When she looked up at him, eyes brimming with cautious hope, it gave him the courage he needed to proceed. "I have every reason to believe he's alive, and I'll tell you why."

For the first time in his life, Konar held nothing back.

He started from the beginning, working his way from his broken childhood plagued by piracy to his first encounter with one of the scrolls. How he and Karliah survived in the palace by their wits, how they made a particularly useful friend whose desire to overthrow his father aligned well with their pursuit of the scrolls. How they'd grown apart in the years to come, as he began to see the world differently than his sister and her sometimes lover, and of the fateful night that had separated them forever.

Next it was all about the scrolls, about Neharem, about every little plot he'd hatched and why he'd done so. About his pursuit of the scrolls to keep them safe, turning into a quest to keep them hidden. About the sanctum located in the cliffs of Sunset Bay, and the mysterious voices inside. About the lives he'd taken to sustain his unnatural one, and the guilt that haunted him—all of which culminated in the adoption of Kayrune and his inevitable desecration.

He didn't linger on Elaysia's family. Didn't need to. It had been spoken of once, and he wouldn't force her to relive it unless she asked it of him.

They nibbled on some nytak jerky as he tried to break down exactly what he knew of the scrolls. Yes, there were seven according to most legends, though the occasional one mentioned an eighth. No, he still wasn't certain where they all were, though he believed at least one to be with the myrem, and possibly one in the uncharted north.

And then, noticing the fire in her eyes as he spoke of them, he begged her to use them wisely. If at all.

"They are more addictive than any drink or drug," Konar warned as she studied the myrem scroll with interest. "Do not underestimate their power."

Elaysia barreled on, as though she hadn't heard him. "What happens when they're all recovered? Is it just a power move? Or do they…" She rubbed her fingers together, searching for the word. "Unlock something? Summon something?"

Konar set his half-gnawed jerky aside. "The more I learn about them, the less sense they make. It's a jumble of pieces that never seem to fit perfectly together. Every time I think I have the answers, a new piece enters the equation, and I have to start all over again."

"You're holding something back." Elaysia reached for—and finished—Konar's barely touched chalice. "What happens when all the scrolls are in someone's power?"

No more lies, he reminded himself. *Only truth.*

"The scroll my sister and I first discovered, the one currently in hers and Rykahl's—sorry, the All-Sovereign's—possession, contains a ritual that releases Mavet, if one holds all the required items. The entire collection of scrolls is one such requirement."

A mixture of disgust and horror painted Elaysia's face. "It's true, then." She pushed away from the table and paced. "Why would the Prophets do that? Create a way to release an ancient evil that was obviously locked away for a reason?"

"If I've learned anything through my years of obsession," Konar answered calmly, "it's that nothing is as simple as it seems."

"You said one of the scrolls here mentioned a reawakening of Quinaria, almost like a, a..." Her hands clawed at the air as the words continued to evade her.

"Resurgence?" he offered.

"Thank you." The look she offered him was so genuinely grateful that he struggled to withhold further pursuit of her approval. "And that's why you think the Great Beasts have returned and why the wars are starting."

Konar didn't want to claim anything as fact, especially not with Elaysia, not when she was torn between grief and vengeance. "It could all be coincidence. Wars are inevitable. With the way Az Zar exploits resources, namely nevethium, it was only a matter of time."

Elaysia completed another circle in silence before taking the seat directly beside Konar. He nearly flinched when she reached for his remaining hand, taking it in hers.

"What were my father's visions about?" The look in her eyes was beyond commanding. It was inspiring.

"Ellie..."

"I know he told you. I know they were..." She swallowed, gaze low, nails digging into his hand. "Part of the reason you had him killed."

A sick sensation stirred in Konar's stomach. He couldn't stop with the truths now, no matter how much it hurt to proceed. This was what she needed to heal, what he needed to die in peace, and perhaps what the world needed to go on.

"Many of them were pure chaos," he began. "Elishon struggled to put them into words in the first place, and I fear much was lost in translation. But he said he saw a world that was like our world, but not our world. That it was too far removed from our time. He believed he was receiving visions of what Quorath would eventually become. He saw gods walking among mortals, saw unity, heightened intelligence, times of great prosperity and knowledge."

Elaysia squeezed his hand, urging him to go on.

Konar tried to recall Elishon's precise descriptions, but all he could see was the wonder and horror in his eyes. "The visions would always transform halfway through. It was never clean, never clear, but he would begin to see wars and famine, fires and floods. There were weapons like the shieum, only much larger and more powerful, and the glow of nevethium always filled the edges of the visions, sometimes flickering to a sickly yellow."

Elaysia's words tripped over themselves. "Did he say why it was happening? What happened at the end? Did he see our fates—"

"You, of all people, know visions don't work like that. And, truth be told"—he pulled away from her hand and eased his aching body out of the chair—"I don't think he shared them all with me. Toward the end, before he set sail for Az Zar, he hardly slept. I think they took a turn for the worse, but we'll never know."

"Just that he wanted to see the Caman Altars." Elaysia massaged her temples with a groan. "I wish I'd had more time to explore. I sensed something there, Konar. Something ancient and evil."

"I'll spend some time there when I return."

A scowl formed on Elaysia's face, and Konar winced. He hadn't intended to announce his plan to rescue Zavik in such a fashion, but there it was.

"It's one of the main reasons I've wanted to meet with you," Konar explained. "To apologize, to share knowledge, but also to announce my plans to leave with T'Vak within a fortnight."

A dark, cruel laugh slipped from Elaysia's lips. "With the backhander, the man who had a hand in Zavik's betrayal?"

"But not for his own gain. He's quite torn up about it himself." Konar bit his lip. Defending T'Vak wouldn't win over what remained of Elaysia's favor.

She folded her arms, chin jutted out ever so slightly. "I'm coming with you. We'll gather some warriors and—"

"Elaysia, you cannot risk yourself or your people while contending with a rebellion." She grunted, but he could already sense her relenting. "It's better for everyone that T'Vak and I go alone. It will be easier for us to move about unnoticed, and I know Cadar better than anyone here."

"Not Maseeya," she said defiantly.

"Not Maseeya," Konar conceded, despite it not being true. "Still, this is best for everyone." He waited until he held her gaze, then poured all his dedication into that moment, as though he wielded the weapon of his soul. "Let me do this for you. Let me make things right."

"A fortnight," she whispered, voice thick with emotion.

"One fortnight."

She wiped away a stray tear and straightened her back as she made her way to the door. "I'll expect several more gatherings like these. I won't allow you to set off on some suicidal quest without harvesting all the wisdom in your extraordinary—if not aggravating—mind. Can you agree to that?"

"Nothing would make me happier."

She nodded, slipping through the door before her face crumbled. Konar knew this, for he was sure his face looked the same. A fragile fortress of false confidence waiting to shatter.

Just like his heart.

ZAVIK

Zavik awoke to a boot in his side.

He cried out as he rolled over, tucking himself into a fetal position, mind scrambling for what he'd done to deserve such a painful awakening.

"You so much as touch me with your filthy boot, and I'll rip it off and forcefully insert it into your anus."

Zavik's eyes shot open at the sound of Yikos's voice. He peered from beneath spread fingers as the old nyrian pressed up from the makeshift cot they'd brought along especially for her. The soldier standing over her—the one who'd presumably kicked Zavik—wore the standard issue uniform of the military, albeit in its newer, more heavily armored form.

"If His Holiness hadn't said you were to be protected at all costs..."

The soldier let Yikos fill in whatever he dreamed of doing with her imagination; not that she'd likely even entertain such scenarios. He lifted his knee as if he intended to kick again, but upon seeing Zavik flinch, seemed satisfied. At least for the moment. He withdrew some hardened bean cakes and a waterskin, dropping it between them.

"Eat and dress. The ritual begins in one hour." The soldier stormed from the room, leaving Zavik and Yikos alone with a gaping hole where a door had once stood.

They made no attempt to escape. Door or not, several guards were stationed outside, ready to intercept an old woman and a sleep-deprived scholar with moskuto jitters.

Zavik wiped the sleep from his eyes, then cleaned his seers as the fog lifted from his mind. They were back at the Caman Altars; had arrived late two nights prior. The ruined building they'd been cast into smelled of dust and crawled with insects hearty enough to survive the desert, and Zavik had spent the better part of both nights holding a nevethium shard out to the darkest corners of the room, fearing what creeped in the shadows.

"Big day today," Yikos said as she inspected one of the cakes with a frown.

The ease with which she said 'big day,' picking at the hardened bits of cake and flinging them into the corners, hardly conveyed the stakes that lay before them.

"I know apathy is what keeps you sane," Zavik said, stretching his aching limbs, "but is this really the time for it? The All-Sovereign and Lord Priestess have come out with us this time and intend to watch our experiment—"

"Ritual," Yikos corrected.

"Whatever." Zavik snatched the remaining bean cake, which was as hard as a rock. "Look, we've stalled as much as we could this past moon cycle, but they won't wait any longer. If they don't see tangible proof today..." A vision of Elaysia and the babes filled his mind. He shoved some of the cake in his mouth, forcing himself to focus on the texture as he chewed.

Yikos hurled her mostly untouched cake at the door, an attempt that only resulted in it landing a few feet beyond her cot. "Just think of it this way: if you succeed, they'll probably kill me. If you fail, they'll still kill me, and probably torture you. Either way, you're rid of me."

Zavik's throat tightened at the thought of the old woman's death. He hadn't exactly gone out of his way to avoid becoming attached to her, but neither had he anticipated just how much he'd come to care for her. She, like so many in Cadar, was just another weapon for the All-Sovereign to wield. Another piece in his game.

"It's not humorous, Yikos," he said, coming to sit beside her. "You don't deserve the life they've given you."

She took his hand in her wrinkled ones and gave it a gentle pat. "It's been given to me all the same. I have no regrets, boy. Can't afford to. All we really get to choose at the end of the day is how we work with what we've been allotted. I like to think I've done well, despite my circumstances."

"I think you've done more than well." He squeezed her hand gently, then retrieved the waterskin, offering it to her before taking his own drink and cleansing his face. "For better or worse, I fear it will go as planned today."

"As do I."

The hour crawled by. Yikos napped; Zavik paced. Over the past few weeks, all their notes and theories had been put into practice, and into the hands of those who could apply it. They'd been sent to the factories and mines themselves to oversee the work, which (to Zavik's great dismay) was progressing much faster than he'd hoped. As the All-Sovereign had said, the empire had a wealth of resources and laborers at its disposal. Some of Az Zar's most brilliant minds, alongside a horde of soldiers, servants, and slaves, worked all hours of the day and night. When they'd left Cadar for the Caman Altars a few days prior, the flying vessel was nearly halfway to its first test stages. Once that happened, Zavik mused, they wouldn't be able to hide the experiments from the civilians any longer.

Most likely, some already knew.

Zavik overheard chatter from the soldiers on occasion, detailing the resurgence of a rebellion—one the All-Sovereign seemed to think he had under control despite evidence suggesting otherwise. In fact, shortly before they'd departed, he'd learned of an attack in one of the more profitable mines, one that resulted in the destruction of two arkthanax and the loss of fifty slaves. Dalgus had come to his quarters the night it happened, warning Zavik that the time for his escape was near. He needed to be alert. He needed to be ready.

And he needed to secure the scrolls.

Zavik had spent most of the journey to the Caman Altars wondering exactly how he was going to pull off such a feat. He had access to all four scrolls, yes. But never for long. Never alone. And certainly not outside the arcanum. Except for the purpose of summoning an ancient magic by means of ritual, of course. Because even a person whose bravado replaced all logic wouldn't risk running through the desert with the empire's best soldiers at the ready.

He didn't have time for such thoughts at the moment, anyway. All that mattered was giving life to the metal giant and ensuring Yikos kept hers.

Guards marched in without warning. They were outfitted in the haunting robes of the temple guards, and by now Zavik had learned that they answered to the Lord Priestess while the regular soldiers took orders from the All-Sovereign. The arrangement struck him as odd, and he wondered just how things were between the two most powerful people in Cadar—if not in all of Quinaria.

The temple guards weren't nearly as brutish and waited for Yikos and Zavik to shuffle out on their own instead of kicking or yanking them to their feet. Zavik caught a fleeting glimpse of sunlight before they were ushered into the tunnels and the enveloping cold.

As they walked, the light of nevethium torches guiding their steps, Zavik tried to prepare himself for what he was about to witness. He recalled the scene Elaysia had described, the eerie robes and masks, the cannibalistic practice, the way the blood made the floors come to life. Then he thought of Konar's own confession of his life-prolonging ritual, and of the things he'd read in the scrolls. They all had three things in common: a sacrifice, a visitation, and a blessing.

Or a curse.

Pulsing lights came to life on the walls, streaming down from the tubes and signaling their approach to the hall containing the metal giant. Zavik steadied his trembling hands by shoving them into his pockets and looked over to find Yikos had done the same. They'd spent the better part of the day prior in the secret chamber, working to restore the spherical device and replace the crystal within. The tools Zavik and Yikos had invented to work on the flying vessels worked on the metal giant as well, and he was glad he'd brought some of the newly minted, spiral bits that held pieces of metal together without heat. The giant was filled with such bits—it was where he'd gotten the idea for some of the mechanisms in the first place. But when they'd left the hall the previous evening, Zavik swore he heard something whirring deep inside the giant's chest.

Now, they'd find out.

For the first time since they'd first laid eyes on the hall, it wasn't void of life. A vibrating hum spilled out from the cracked doors, increasing in volume as they drew near. It had an ancient sound, one filled with minor notes and deep resonance. It both soothed and worried Zavik, as though he was being sedated for a kill. The guards stopped just outside the great door as they had the time prior, leaving Yikos and Zavik to squeeze in through the crack. Unlike the last time, however, the room within wasn't empty. Six figures in heavy robes and bone masks stood in a semi-circle around a table that had been scooted away from the wall. The Lord Priestess lurked at the head with the All-Sovereign just off to her left. The tube lights pulsated around them, making the shadows darker, the angles of the masks more intense.

On the table lay a scroll Zavik had only read once, but it'd been enough. It was written in ancient Nyrinian, and while its most damning content was a ritual for releasing Mavet—a section he tried to retain while simultaneously detaching from—it also listed other rituals for summoning the lesser Caman. From what he'd gathered, the Caman could be called upon at the site of their origin, presumably the Caman Altars, and have any request made of them. Sacrifice was required to summon them, but there was no guarantee the ancient deities would comply with the request. Zavik wasn't certain what the Lord Priestess intended to offer in exchange for giving life to her metal giant, but he tried to comfort himself with the fact it wouldn't be him.

Not until they had all the scrolls.

The Lord Priestess's lips curled into a smile that didn't reach her eyes. She motioned Zavik and Yikos closer with a hand that just barely peeked out beneath the length of her flowing white sleeve, then pulled her own bone mask down over her face. The All-Sovereign wore a simpler robe of muted colors, but his mask was identical to hers. It almost looked like a nytak, but it was far larger, and a large rack of antlers sprouted from the mask, the ends of their prongs stained red.

Zavik had been so transfixed by the Lord Priestess that he didn't notice one of the other cloaked figures had creeped behind him until he felt cool hands slipping something over his face.

"To protect your identity," the man whispered in a slithering voice. "Caman are known to haunt those who summon them."

No protest escaped Zavik's lips. He ran his hands over the mask, then let them fall to his sides. It was better not to know, he thought. He didn't want to think of himself as a part of this order.

Whatever it was.

Yikos grumbled beside him as the priest did the same to her before falling back in line with the rest of his kind. The Lord Priestess held up her palms, muttering something unintelligible, while one of the priests unrolled the scroll. The All-Sovereign stepped back, and Zavik got the sense he didn't like whatever was about to unfold.

The Lord Priestess's voice rose, her incantations reverberating through the cavernous depths like the mournful wails of the damned, each syllable dripping with ancient power and malignant intent. Zavik couldn't place the language, only that it sounded ancient. Angry. The priests joined in with their own chants, creating a cacophony of twisted tongues, a blasphemous melody that seemed to twist and contort reality itself with its otherworldly resonance. It was as if the words clawed their way from the Lord Priestess's throat like the anguished cries of a dying soul, while the priests hissed and spat like serpents in the darkness. Some syllables seemed to linger in the air like a foul fog, while others echoed and reverberated with a chilling clarity that sent shivers down his spine.

And beneath it all, there was a primal rhythm, a pulsating beat that seemed to echo the very heartbeat of Quinaria itself.

The lights flashed brighter and faster, increasing in intensity along with the incantations until they suddenly went out. The great hall lay shrouded in an oppressive darkness, suffocating and thick. Even the Lord Priestess's nevethium pendant hanging at her breasts faded.

A muffled cry broke the silence, followed by a *thump.* Zavik's stomach twisted in response. It was time for the offering. No amount of preparation had readied him for the sound of metal scraping against a scabbard. The dagger in the Lord Priestess's hand glowed a deep red, almost the color of Elaysia's eye. It flickered feebly, casting twisted shadows that worked their way around the room in a macabre dance. As the Lord Priestess whispered the final syllables of the incantation, a chilling wind swept through the chamber, carrying with it the faint echo of distant screams and hollow laughter.

Zavik made the mistake of looking at the victim as the crimson blade drew across their throat, spilling blood like a waterfall. He'd expected a slave or a servant—even one of the guards—but the sacrifice atop the table wore the mask of a priest. He reached for Yikos's hand, instinctively pulling her near.

There was no hand to grab.

The ground seemed to shift beneath him with a sickening lurch. Tears stung his eyes as he looked from the body to the priests and their leader, their demonic figures materializing before him in the returning light of the nevethium pendant. He tried to shout, but the words caught deep in his throat. Blindly, he stumbled forward, reaching for her body as though he could save her, but with a deafening crack, the very fabric of reality seemed to tear asunder. A creature emerged from the abyss just above the table, its form twisted and grotesque, its eyes burning with a hunger that could never be sated. With a voice like razors upon flesh, it growled, stepping onto Yikos's body, gnarled talons digging into her flesh.

Zavik stumbled back, landing on his rear. He wanted to make for the door, to race into the desert and take his chances with the elements. But he'd never make it past the guards. And he'd regret leaving without the answers, without the scrolls. It was no way to act with the debt of Yikos's life already paid.

The Caman's jagged ribs rose and fell with an unnatural rhythm, as if it drew breath from the very shadows themselves. Its elongated limbs moved with an unsettling grace; each movement accompanied by the sound of bones grinding against bone. A pair of hollow sockets glowed with malevolent fire, casting a baleful gaze upon the Lord Priestess. From its hand dangled a lantern, gleaming with an ethereal luminescence, casting an eerie glow that illuminated the hall with a sickly pallor.

As it approached the Lord Priestess, a suffocating stench of decay filled the air. All the priests and the All-Sovereign had fallen to the ground in a bowing motion, their hands outstretched above their heads like beggars. Zavik held firm, not fleeing nor mimicking their positions as the Lord Priestess pointed to the metal giant behind her, her head bowed. A yellowish hue overtook the nevethium pendant on her neck, the shade nearly identical to that of the tubes prior to the Caman's summoning. The creature slowly craned its head in the direction of the metal giant, and Zavik swore it smiled in response, its mouth full of serrated, rotted teeth. It glided to the cold, dead thing and placed an open hand on its leg.

For a long moment, nothing seemed to happen. Perhaps the Caman was playing tricks on them, or maybe the Lord Priestess hadn't been worthy enough to make such a request, or hadn't sacrificed enough. Maybe the metal giant had never been more than a statue, a tool of intimidation, an idol.

Then the ground shook.

It jostled Zavik so harshly that his seers slipped off the bridge of his nose. He clutched them to his chest as the priests' nervous cries filled the air. An ear-splitting *crack* drowned out their pleas, followed by the smashes of falling rock. Zavik scrambled toward the entrance and wedged himself between the crack in the doors, trusting their strength to protect him. He slipped his seers back on just in time to see a priest running toward him—right before their body disappeared beneath a chunk of the ceiling. Everyone cowered and fled, save for the Lord Priestess, who stood in the center of the hall, unharmed, a deep cackling resonating from her throat.

The ground split before her, a chasm bursting with golden-green luminescence that nearly ran the length of the room. One of the priests fell in as it opened, his scream lasting several moments before ending abruptly. The Lord Priestess hardly noticed. She continued to laugh, her arms reaching higher and wider as loud whirring sounds emitted from the metal giant. Meanwhile, the All-Sovereign curled up beneath a table, arms wrapped around his legs as he rocked and moaned like a child.

Despite everything, Zavik's eyes widened. He leaned out of his shelter long enough to get a better view. The metal giant remained still, but the cracked ceiling above it revealed a dark sky—an odd occurrence, for as far as he knew, it was still morning. When he dared a glance at the newly formed chasm, he half-expected more Caman to come crawling out. None did.

For now.

Another groan drew his attention, and he looked to the left of the doors, where a priest had been skewered by a fragment of rock. His mask lay broken a few feet away. In the fading golden-green glow of the chasm, Zavik could still make out the dribble of blood dripping down the snow-white nyrian's cheek. He felt an urge to help, to put the man out of his misery if nothing else. But then he thought of Yikos. No death would be painful or long enough for the twisted beings gathered in the hall of the metal giant.

When the ground ceased shaking, Zavik emerged from his shelter. The Lord Priestess didn't take her eyes off the metal giant. She walked around its legs, tracing her fingers over it like a lover, whispering something beneath her breath. It continued to groan and whir, but it didn't move.

With the All-Sovereign still huddled beneath the table and all the priests dead, Zavik crept toward the end of the chasm closest to him. A stale, metallic odor drifted up from the abyss. He braced himself, then peered over the edge.

It took a moment for his eyes to adjust to the sight. The chasm yawned at least a hundred feet below him, its depths illuminated by a faint glow. At first, he thought the ground was uneven, broken up by jagged rock formations. But as his vision solidified, a chill ran down his spine. Lining the bottom of the cavern were figures, neither flesh nor bone, but crafted of metal and mystery, just like the giant the Lord Priestess had failed to awaken. They stood silent and still, their metallic frames reflecting the faint light. The chasm seemed to stretch on endlessly; the figures lining its edge fading into obscurity.

A thud reverberated behind Zavik, jolting him from his reverie. He whirled around and found himself staring up into the glowing golden eyes of the metal giant. It took another step, then another, its massive frame moving with an unsettling precision, each step echoing ominously against the stone floor.

The Lord Priestess hurried after it, struggling to keep pace. Zavik couldn't move, couldn't so much as cry out as the metal giant's foot came down on the table, crushing Yikos beneath its behemoth frame. As it approached Zavik, a sense of dread threatened to drown him. In the presence of the monstrous creation, spawned from whatever magic the scrolls possessed, he knew something in the world had changed forever. Or rather, it already had, long ago.

The question was how long ago, and how. And why.

Before he could speculate further, the chasm once again flashed a brilliant golden-green. This time, the groans and whirs of hundreds of metal soldiers followed, and Zavik knew without looking that they, too, had awakened.

Heart pounding, he braced himself for whatever fate awaited him in the darkness, in the glow of the metal giant's eyes blazing in the shadows.

LUMIRA

*T*he *ember-colored eyes bear down on her.*

Lumira swings at the entity, dragging her claws through its empty cloak again and again, never catching flesh or bone. All the while, the eyes seem to laugh, sparkling with intrigue at her predicament. She growls at it, lunging as it steps just out of reach and fades into the darkness until all she can see are its fiery eyes.

It treads upon a carpet of bodies. Most are nameless Neharem warriors, but some are faces she knows all too well. Jörd. Vahid. And...

A scream scrapes her throat.

Then she's falling into the darkness, into the bodies, their cold hands grasping, their bodies bloated with death.

And still, the eyes come ever closer.

Lumira sprung awake, clawing at the darkness.

Her vision adapted rapidly as she searched her loft, finding nothing out of the ordinary. She inspected her perfectly made cot, wondering why she'd never even bothered to sleep in it. Must've passed out on the floor after finally losing her battle with exhaustion.

Moonlight streamed in beneath her door. She flung it open, almost expecting to find the monster lying in wait. Instead, she was met with a baffled Jakki who lingered a few feet away, bottle in hand, garbed in a simple chest wrap and flowing pants, not unlike Lumira's usual wear.

They stared at each other, frowning. Lumira didn't know why the nyrian was creeping about in the dark, especially near her loft. She'd chosen one on the far end of the High Tree's upmost platform to avoid such situations.

She was about to slam the door in Jakki's face when the nyrian forced something that resembled a smile and gestured inside. "Is everything alright? I heard you crying out."

"I fell out of my cot," Lumira replied curtly.

Jakki twisted a lock of silken hair with her free hand. "Did you land on your spear?"

The door swung fast under Lumira's force, but Jakki slipped her boot in just before it latched. "I'm sorry," she said, even though it seemed like the admission pained her. "Given our history, I wasn't sure how to begin this conversation."

Lumira wanted to slam the door—on Jakki's foot if necessary—and attempt at least a few more hours' sleep before dawn. But sleep hadn't been her friend in some time, and moons be cursed if she wasn't at least a little interested in whatever inspired the nyrian to seek her out in the dead of the night.

"Insult me one more time, and you're gone," Lumira muttered, opening the door wide enough for Jakki to squeeze through.

Inside, Lumira curled up on her cot, taking no shortage of pleasure in the fact that she'd no seating to offer the nyrian. As usual, she also had no food or drink to offer, but was it really her fault the people of Neharem kept choosing to visit in the middle of the night?

"Can't sleep?" Jakki asked, gaze flicking about her barren loft.

Even by Neharem standards, Lumira's possessions were minimal. Her spear, her necklace (which she never took off), her cuff earring (which she also never took off), and some bones left over from a rabbit carcass she'd picked clean earlier that evening. It was the only way to be. Live light, travel light.

Nothing to lose.

"My wounds ail me," she said, gingerly touching the scar on her calf. It'd fully healed, but Jakki didn't know that.

Apparently, she wasn't convinced. "I thought your kind healed fast."

Lumira glared at Jakki, then looked at the door, prompting the nyrian to hold out her drink as a peace offering. She refused with a shake of her head. Cyan's wine was little more than water to her, but she was not in the mood for drinking with enemies. Not that Jakki was truly an enemy—she had enough of those in the war—but she wasn't exactly a friend, either.

"What do you want, Jakki?"

For the first time since Lumira had known her, Jakki seemed to shed her defenses. She set the bottle down gently and sat on the floor beside it, legs crossed. "I'm worried about Elaysia."

Lumira frowned. This wasn't the conversation she'd expected. Actually, she wasn't certain what she *had* expected, but given their—how had Jakki put it? History?—she'd anticipated veiled threats, at the very least.

"A just concern," she finally answered, still unsure of how to respond. "I'm worried about everything. Our high chieftain's mood is a part of it, but so is our weakening defenses, the remnants of our restless kuza, our vanishing borders. Not to mention the complete lack of support from any of the neutral tribes."

It hit Lumira then, part of the reason for Jakki's general aloofness since returning from the north. Her chief mother had vanished at the first signs of doom, demanding her daughter to be sent back to the island as soon as she returned.

"My mother's self-preservation knows no bounds," Jakki said with a shrug. "She's sent me at least a dozen tuross messages since I told her I wasn't returning until Agaas was no longer at risk of attack. She's threatening to take the chiefdom away from me. I told her she can keep it."

The shock on Lumira's face must've been evident, for Jakki nodded as if to acknowledge the surprising nature of her own actions. She gathered her hair on the side of her face and began braiding it in intricate sections.

"Do you worry for her and your people? If the Lawful Dominion—"

"They wouldn't dare," Jakki said quickly, dropping a strand. "Everyone knows Jattai Rain-Bringer's island is fiercely protected." She returned her attention to the braid and fastened it with a thick strand of beaded leather. "Besides, I'm sure they'd rather have her as an ally, should Agaas fall."

It made sense. Only the Moákun and Daruk had been voyagers in recent history. The Lawful Dominion wouldn't waste the time mounting a waterborne attack when a much greater prize lay in the holy city. Still, Lumira found it hard to believe Jakki could so easily set aside the fates of her mother and people. Then again, according to Elaysia, Jakki had spent her most formative years in Agaas, and therefore probably felt more at home here than on her island.

"I saw some of the kuza packing up this afternoon during my base camp fortification inspection," Jakki continued, as though uncomfortable with Lumira's silence. "I thought Anahi and that old general would be enough to keep them here, but more desert every day."

"Hallahd," Lumira clarified. "That's the 'old general's' name."

Jakki took a drink, masking the irritation on her face. "Right. I meant no offense. I've just spent so little time with them."

Lumira wasn't eager to hear any more of Jakki's excuses. "None taken." She took a small sip from the bottle to show it, then sat back on the cot in a more rigid fashion. "You're right. Nearly a third of the surviving kuza have either died in battle or snuck home since Vahid's passing. I'd wager we'll lose another third within a fortnight, especially if we have any more ambushes like that nightmare up north."

Jakki winced. Neither of them had been present for the horrendous massacre of a small hunting party two day's ride north of Agaas. Yerakai had been the only rider nearby, and had he not been airborne on Wind Chaser at the time it happened, he likely would've perished along with the twenty other warriors. The effect it had on the people was undeniable, not to mention the loss of potential food. Already, the Apáasutai forests had begun to empty. It was gradual, and nothing near urgent, but the increase of bodies and the confines of the hunting grounds seemed to make the game both scarcer and more aware. Some people even complained the birds depleted the food sources, even though they did nearly all their hunting over the sea.

Lumira thought the cause was something else entirely, though. Something in the groundshake attacks seemed to have unsettled even the smallest of creatures, and she couldn't help but wonder if the Lawful Dominion was using their new weapons, amongst other things, to drive the game north and south, out of Apáasutai territory. Whether or not her theory had any merit, it didn't change the very real situation that the people of Agaas wouldn't last endless moon cycles holed up in their overcrowded land. Whether by force of Lawful Dominion armies or lack of resources, they'd have to act soon.

"I don't think we'll last much longer," Jakki said, as if reading her thoughts. "If the Lawful Dominion choose to bring their full strength down upon us now, we'd put up a good fight, but ultimately lose. I think they've only held off as long as they have to see how much more they can increase their odds. Each week brings more people abandoning the cause, more small-scale attacks, and more infighting."

Lumira shut her eyes. None of what Jakki said was a revelation. The war council had debated as much earlier that day after Arkuun relinquished his chiefdom to a reluctant Yerakai. The dying Apáasutai chief had no heirs, and Yerakai had long been a favorite of the people—so the old nyrian had said—and he wanted to ensure they were in good hands before he passed into the beyond. Given the circumstances, the change in roles had been quick and unceremonious. Then conversation had turned to the usual points of contention, which all seemed to connect one way or another to whether they should fight or flee. Chief Kelsia, whose voice had slowly returned, pleaded escape, not wanting to endanger any more lives, for hadn't there been enough death already? But Chief Orandus had countered with the equally important issue of where it was they were to run off to. The neutral tribes, as far as they knew, were under Lawful Dominion control, and therefore no longer neutral. Anahi and Hallahd suggested Orillon, but it was quickly determined the Great Houses wouldn't be welcoming to a horde of refugees. Jakki had then mentioned her new skulmor alliance—something that still didn't sit well with Lumira—but the similar problem remained that there were just too many Agaasian allies to dump in one place.

"Did you see how detached Elaysia was during the gathering?" Jakki asked, drawing Lumira's attention back to the intruder in her loft. "I've seen her go through plenty of emotions; everything from fear to frustration to pride. But this apathy, her utter lack of engagement..." She frowned, chewing her lip. "She's been spending most of her free time with Konar at the old Igtheos refuge, and I'm worried about what lies he's spinning now."

"I don't think he has any lies left." Lumira leaned back in her cot, claws puncturing the cloth beneath her.

"And what *do* you think?" There was a slight edge to Jakki's voice, but one born more of frustration regarding the situation than anger toward Lumira. "I understand we aren't exactly friends, and I know I came here uninvited, but I think you're"—she took a deep breath and let it out with a huff—"one of the few with their head on straight."

A smirk tried to surface on Lumira's face. "Was that a compliment, Nyrian?"

"Don't get used to it, Cat." Jakki huffed again, but her change in attitude wasn't lost on Lumira. "Anyway, you didn't speak much in the gathering, either. I'm sure it's been a lot for you, enduring the burden here in Agaas with the rest of us spread all over. What does your gut tell you?"

Just what had the skulmor done to Jakki? She was hardly the same backstabbing wench who'd tried to have Lumira killed or imprisoned on at least three separate occasions.

"The stormbirds need to be the priority," she said, deeming it safe to share her thoughts with Jakki. "They play a greater role in this than any of us, save for the high chieftain. I know Elaysia doesn't want to abandon her home, but we're fools to stay here while they take their time picking us off and honing their new weapons."

Jakki rubbed her neck, feeling around it for a moment before dropping her hand slowly back into her lap. Come to think of it, she usually wore a nevethium pendant there. Had the skulmor taken it?

"What do you suggest?" Jakki asked.

"That we put several ideas into motion." Lumira sat up, drawing lines across a ghost map in the air. "We send as many civilians as we can south to Orillon—ideally the humans—then hope your skulmor will take the rest. Some will choose to remain or return to their ancestral lands, and that's their choice. We can't force them to flee if they want to fight or surrender."

Their gazes met as Jakki digested the weight of what Lumira suggested. "It naturally lessens the number of people we have to worry about."

"We're not sentencing them to death." Lumira's voice was low, almost indiscernible. "They could come."

"But you know some won't," the nyrian said, rising. She walked to the door and peered out, as if suspicious of eavesdroppers. "I agree with you. Just startled to hear someone else voice my own thoughts."

An odd sensation spread through Lumira's body, one that was pleased to finally be accepted by a former enemy, but also sickened to find similarities between them. "As to the Stormriders," she added, eager to change the subject, "once the civilians are free of Neharem, we can regroup in one of the neutral territories and determine who will pursue which targets."

Jakki raised an eyebrow. "Targets?"

"We need to get back to the bigger tasks at hand: securing the remaining scrolls, forming new alliances, and keeping an eye on Az Zar."

"And how might we do that?"

"Elaysia and Konar should have some insight into the scrolls' locations. Maintaining awareness of Az Zar's advancements will probably require a spy, along with aerial observation. As to the alliances…" Lumira swallowed. She knew the answer, had known it since Anahi first spoke up, suggesting an alliance with Orillon. She just hadn't expected that one to crumble so quickly. "I've considered returning to the Beridian Isles." It wasn't the grandest plan Lumira had formulated, but it had merit. It was certainly better than waiting to die in the trees.

Jakki came to stand at the foot of Lumira's cot. "You'd go back? Do you have many allies there?"

"I'm not sure. But I don't know what else to do."

"If you go, I'll do what I can to gain support from the skulmor. They've come to"—Jakki looked away, and Lumira wasn't certain if she was searching for the proper words or hiding something—"respect me. They also have some powerful resources that could prove useful."

Lumira rose to meet her, staring deep into the nyrian's luminescent eyes as she tried to probe through what veiled them. "You're many things, Rain-Bringer, and while I don't like some of them, I'd never speak ill of your cunning."

"Nor I of your ferocity." She extended her hand to Lumira. "Allies?"

Lumira took her hand, gripping it firmly. "Allies."

"Let us speak of this to no one. I want to pull Elaysia aside one more time before we bring this to the war council."

"Agreed."

Jakki slipped out onto the platform. As she closed the door behind her, she peered over her shoulder, her gaze not quite connecting with Lumira's.

"She was right to choose you, Cat."

Lumira couldn't sleep after Jakki's disturbance, so she ventured outside a few hours shy of dawn. She didn't know she was headed to Grokhion's loft until she was standing right outside it, and when she knocked, he opened the door immediately, as though he'd been waiting for her. There was still an odd haze to his eyes, a distance that had never fully vanished since the massacre of the Ni'anko people. He'd gone back more than once to mourn, but Lumira had hoped the rescue of Kelsia would be enough to heal his wounds, or at least call him back to himself. But her return had only deepened the chasm in his eyes.

"Lumira. Come." He stepped back, motioning her inside.

"I thought we might inspect the perimeter," she suggested. In truth, she just couldn't stand sitting in another stuffy loft, even for a moment.

Grokhion considered, then disappeared inside, returning a moment later with *Belzaith* and a waterskin. The ax rarely left his side—in case anyone questioned whether he still adhered to his former pacifist ways.

They descended the ramps in silence, then ventured out into the forest. Coughs rattled the silence of base camp, and Lumira feared the rumors of the kuza taking sick were true. Most of them had never set foot outside Orillon prior to Elaysia and Vahid's union ceremony, and they had no natural immunity to the diseases of the north. With the cluster of bodies from varying tribes and regions, illness had taken its toll on everyone, but what was a runny nose to a Daruk or Apáasutai was a heavy, wet cough and fever to a kuza.

All the more reason for them to desert, Lumira thought.

A shriek drew their attention overhead. The stormbirds made regular rounds over what remained of Apáasutai territory and were quick to warn their riders when they noticed an encroachment on any of the camps. When Lumira and Xaren had made their patrols a few days prior, the Atsukut had all but secured Ethoos Lake, and the Lautei possessed nearly everything south of the Osupahpah River. There were still some relatively safe passages along the far western coastline, but it wouldn't be long before those, too, were under Lawful Dominion control.

They stopped to drink water and share strips of nytak jerky that Lumira hardly tasted as she swallowed. She debated sharing the plan with Grokhion. Not that she didn't trust him, but she knew he'd never agree to a tactic that left people behind, even if it was of their choosing. He and Elaysia would've been the hardest to reason with even before they'd suffered losses. Now they were both one bad tuross message away from going on a suicide mission.

"I'm thinking of returning to the Isles," Lumira said indifferently, as though she suggested she might go for another walk later.

Grokhion looked up from inspecting his ax handle, his brow furrowed. "You want to run again?"

"No." His assumption made her ears flatten. Hadn't she proven her loyalty ten times over? "We need help. We need allies, we need sanctuary, and we need the wisdom of our mothers."

Grokhion shook his head. "We've abandoned our mothers. Their wisdom is no longer ours."

"Do you have a better idea?" All of Lumira's anger toward Grokhion for drawing into himself, essentially abandoning her, seemed to overflow at once. "These people you've come to love as your own are in dire need, Grokhion. They will not win this war. We need to convince them to leave and find help wherever it may lie, and we need to humble ourselves and face our ghosts. I will return home if it means helping Elaysia, no matter how it pains me."

Grokhion leaped up in a rage, roaring as he swung his ax into a tree. He swung again and again until the ancient being toppled over with a *crack*. Then he dropped his ax to the ground, shoulders heaving.

Lumira didn't dare touch him, but she picked up his ax, clutching it to her chest. "Whatever you've done," she whispered, "it can be made better."

He shook his mighty mane, releasing another roar. "Nothing can be made better. What is broken is broken forever. You cannot undo pain. You cannot undo death."

"Then don't ruin this, too," Lumira pleaded. "This situation is not beyond saving. You always tell me knowledge is of the past, but wisdom begets the future. Where is your wisdom?"

A joyless smile spread across his face as he turned to Lumira, but the pride in his eyes was undeniable. "Why, I think you've gone and stolen it from me."

"About time. I've heard enough of your lectures." She gripped his arm, bringing her forehead to his. "Just do this one thing for me, and I'll repay you a thousand times over. I swear it by the moons."

Grokhion released a sigh that carried a thousand secrets as she pulled away. "I will go wherever you go, Lumira, even back to the life I wish to forget. But you must promise not to lose yourself there. And we must talk. Soon."

She tossed the ax back to him—not an easy feat, given its size—and started back toward Agaas, not wanting him to see the emotion on her face. "We'll have much time to talk on our voyage to the Isles. Let's just get out of Neharem alive first."

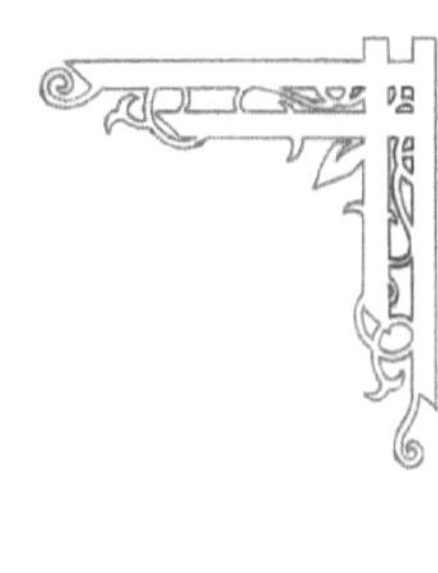

ELAYSIA

E laysia eyed the vibrant plumes cascading like a sunset waterfall. The feathered headdress had once belonged to Rajar, abandoned after his death and never retrieved by his son, who'd refused to set foot in Agaas even once as an ally. She stroked the feathers, recalling the last time she'd seen it. It had still been flecked with dirt. Still stained with his blood.

"You're certain this will work?" she asked, recoiling from it.

Konar lifted his shoulders. "I don't claim to be certain of anything. But I've had the unfortunate experience of utilizing two of the scrolls, not to mention witnessing my own mother's rituals firsthand." He set the headdress on the table beside the Shaktari scroll and faced the dying fire. "Magic is a fickle thing, Ellie. It's not so unlike the weather. You can learn to predict it, what to prepare for, and know when to press on or take shelter. But never assume it can be controlled."

A shiver coursed through Elaysia's body, raising bumps on her arms. "This was never in Raynar's possession, though. It's not a part of him."

"Shaktari is difficult to translate directly to Nyrinian," Konar said, poking the embers with the bottom of his staff. "It actually means something more along the lines of 'belonging to.' It's true Raynar likely never had the privilege of wearing his father's headdress, but I don't think that's necessary. What matters is that the headdress symbolizes his position as chief, something he inherited with the death of Rajar. Regardless if he's worn it, that belongs to him."

Elaysia followed his gaze to the headdress. The uncertainty was enough to drive her mad, but what choice did she have? They were out of time and options, and the war council wouldn't last more than a few days without action. Even her own Stormriders whispered behind her back—judging, making plans, taking matters into their own hands.

Let them try. She was the only true Agaasian among them, the only one who'd been crushed beneath the boot of the war, the one who assumed all responsibility for the lives lost and those still hanging in the balance.

"I trust your judgment," she said. When Konar's eyes widened, she added, "At least in matters such as these." She walked past her armor and mask on the far end of the table and swung open the door, making her way around the Igtheos refuge to the cliff side. The sun hung just above the horizon, blazing a brilliant red.

Just a few more hours until justice.

"Ellie." Konar's calm voice washed over her, and she allowed herself to accept all that it was—all that he was. There was evil and pain, arrogance and cruelty, but she could no longer deny his love, his desire to remake things anew, and his bold ambition. Things weren't as simple as she'd believed them to be, and neither were people. To deem anything tarnished with evil as tainted and unworthy of life—to strip it from all goodness—was to set the whole world afire. For who could stand and claim themselves unblemished by wrongdoings?

No. There weren't any bad people. Just those who forever lost the battle with their own goodness.

"I understand if you don't wish to come," she said, keeping her gaze on the ocean. How satisfying it was to watch the waves crash against each other, to behold the juxtaposition of something so deadly and yet calming.

Bury me in the waves, she thought. *Let the ocean dissolve me, let it numb my pain, let it—*

"We both know I can't let you go alone," Konar said, coming to stand beside her. "You can't read Shaktari yet, and I'd have no choice but to cast myself into the sea if something happened to you."

A dark chuckle emerged from Elaysia's throat. "I've spent so much of my life trying to be everything you're not, but you've raised me in your likeness all the same." She narrowed her eyes as she picked up the faintest dot on the horizon. Onitus. And his color burned red. "I'll be glad for the company. Are you ready to fly, though?" She glanced at his bent frame, the hollowness of his cheeks, the tremble in his hand. "When was the last time you..."

Murdered something. There was no hiding Konar's deeds, but it still felt odd to call them out so plainly.

His lips drew thin. "I'll be fine a while longer. I don't know if I could even handle two summonings in one day."

"You won't be doing it," Elaysia insisted. "It's my decision to use the scroll, and I will pay the price."

"Elaysia—"

"You said yourself we don't know how this one works. It doesn't say how much life it takes in exchange for the possession, and seeing as how you're already living on literal borrowed time, we can't risk you doing it. I have at least two hundred years ahead of me to gamble with."

Konar looked anything but convinced, but he didn't press the issue further. "I'll have T'Vuk head back to Aguas and let them know we'll be spending the night here."

As Elaysia returned inside to slip into her armor and mask, she swore she heard whispers drifting through the refuge like wind. It seemed to emanate from the Shaktari scroll, and when she hovered her hand above the case to retrieve it, it illuminated for a fleeting moment.

She shoved it into her bag before it could dissuade her. Then, headdress in hand, bow and quiver slung over her shoulder, she hurried outside to meet Onitus.

It was time for the war to tip in their favor. With Raynar in captivity, lured away by the scroll's powers, his people would have no choice but to surrender.

Konar did well on the flight.

She shouldn't have been surprised. According to the stories he'd entrusted to her as of late, he'd lived through a seaserpent attack, witnessed the brutal murder of his parents, and been betrayed by his own sister. As if they didn't already have enough in common.

Elaysia's eyes widened as the mighty stronghold of the Lautei appeared on the horizon. It had no name, for they believed adorning it with one would curse it. If it was named, it was alive. And living things could be killed.

From what she could see, they had nothing to fear. At the center of the village, a massive stone fortress rose, made iconic by its four triangular sides meeting in a single point at the top. Each side of the structure sloped upward, forming a sharp angle toward the apex, and each layer of blocks was carefully stacked one upon another, gradually narrowing as it reached the summit. It was, Elaysia thought, almost like a geometrically precise mountain, but one formed by the hands of mortals.

And how was she, scroll or not, to draw their leader out from his stone halls, past his guards and civilians, and into the forest in the middle of the night without so much as a batted eye?

Onitus kept his distance from the Lautei fortress, dropping them off a few miles beyond it. There was a chance he'd been seen, but Elaysia hoped the stormbird's regular inspections of enemy territory would make the Lawful Dominion assume his presence was nothing unusual. At any rate, by the time someone located them, the deed would—in theory—be done, and Onitus would be ready to carry them back to safety.

The moons shone full and bright, both a blessing and a curse. Their light glinted off Raynoos Lake like sunlight upon lyvium, and Elaysia hoped their lack of attacks had made the Lawful

Dominion careless, especially with regard to their best-defended stronghold. The most recent tuross message Elaysia received from her scouts confirmed Raynar still resided within the comfort of his walls, and she wondered if he'd fought alongside his people even once. They'd received countless reports of his bravery in battle, but not one of her warriors had ever seen him. It was just as likely he'd inherited all of his father's arrogance, but none of his valor.

The thought made what was about to transpire a little easier.

"How close do we need to be for it to work?" Elaysia asked when they paused a mile west from the lake for Konar to rest. She hadn't noticed any signs of patrols or watchers, but the odds of them remaining undisturbed decreased with each step.

Konar bent forward, hands on his knees, as he drew a shaky breath. "It's all speculation at this point."

"Then make an informed guess." The fear stirring inside Elaysia made her tone harsher than she'd intended. "I'm not trying to put us at risk unnecessarily, but this has to work."

"We should've brought T'Vak," Konar said, peering into the darkness. "He could've watched our backs. The rituals make one—"

"I don't trust him, and I don't care." Visions of Elaron and Dytana formed in her mind. The more she tried not to think of them, the more panicked she grew. She couldn't leave them alone in such a cruel world.

Konar retrieved a stick from the ground and began drawing in the dirt. Elaysia recognized the symbol from the Shaktari scroll. Three circles interlinked, with a triangle at their mutual center, and a diamond fully encasing them.

"From what I've seen, each scroll has a unique sigil used to summon, and a unique sacrifice required. You'll have to be the one to speak the invocations aloud, but I'll whisper it into your ear to ensure accuracy." He rose, seemingly satisfied with his handiwork, and cast a final wary glance around the small clearing. The golden-trunked, spindly trees of the Lautei lands towered around them like sentinels, their grasping branches beckoning. "Once the final words are spoken, I'll retreat just out of sight. Unlike the scroll and ritual I've been using to keep myself alive, I don't believe this one can affect more than the invoker and the invoker's target. But I'd rather be safe, and I want to protect you, should it come to that. Whatever you do, stay focused on your intention. The Caman like to play tricks, and I'm uncertain which one this will summon."

Konar handed her the headdress and slowly unrolled the scroll, holding it up to catch the moonlight. An owl screeched as it glided overhead, its shadow shrinking as it honed in on a mouse skittering through the fallen leaves. It dove without warning and crushed the small creature in its talons. The skirmish caught Konar's attention, and he lowered the scroll in response.

"We don't have to do this," he said in a grave voice. "There are other ways to survive."

"But no other ways to win." Elaysia inhaled deeply of rich, musty lake water, thankful there was at least something nearby to remind her of home as she clutched the headdress in antici-pation. It was time to act now, before her rage was extinguished by fear. "I'm ready."

Konar stood behind her right shoulder, his beard tickling her ear as the Shaktari speech left his lips. She repeated the words as he spoke them, doing her best to match his intonations. Shak-tari flowed surprisingly smooth—much in contrast to how she envisioned the beings it originated from. It was almost haunt-ingly musical, calming. Though most of the words were lost on her, she noted one that had stood out when Konar first read the rough translation to her: *aakŭlah.*

Surrender.

A coldness enveloped Elaysia, one that seemed to come from within her instead of being brought by the elements. It started in her stomach and spread outward, tentacles reaching into her limbs, spreading up her neck, and finally, into her head. With it came a clarity that dimmed the world around her. The awareness of the blood rushing through her veins, fed by her beating heart, was suddenly so tangible, so real. She traced the path of the air brought in through her nose, reveling in the way it was so cold upon entry and as warm as life upon departure. There was an emptiness on her right side as Konar vanished into the trees, but no fear came to take his place.

Only anticipation.

A thick, dark fog set in over the sigil, spreading out until it encompassed Elaysia entirely. It smelled sickly sweet, and she gagged as it entered her lungs. But once inside, an even deeper calmness settled over her. Her hands just barely clung to the headdress. She wanted to shut her eyes and fall back into the darkness; had every sense the fog would somehow catch her and deposit her gently on the ground. Or maybe it would just hold her as the spirit walker had in the woods, the night she'd been shown the eggs.

Stay awake, she told herself. *Konar said...*

Actually, she couldn't recall. She was supposed to be afraid, wasn't she? But she hadn't slept well in so long, hadn't known such peace since...

When? How long had she been in there, in the bliss? She should leave, shouldn't she?

Who even was she?

She grabbed for memories and found them as fleeting and insubstantial as the fog. There must've been a reason she was there. Everything had a reason. Everything had a purpose. Didn't it?

Something dangled from her hand. Feathers. They were so heavy. Why?

She brought them to her face, staring dumbly at the plumes, running her fingers across the frayed edges. Despite the softness, it brought her pain, pooled tears in the corner of her eyes that threatened to spill over. It was important. She could sense that much. She needed to, to...

Revenge.

"Show yourself!" she shouted into the darkness, still not fully aware of who she called out to.

A figure manifested in the shadows. It had six heads and countless limbs that moved forward in a gyrating, jerking motion. Some limbs just hung there, bent at odd angles and useless to the mass from which they spawned. The eyes were worse, some of them glowing, tracking her as it approached, while others dangled lifelessly from their sockets. It didn't fully consist of humans or nyrians, but included parts of beridians, and what she guessed to be skulmor, shaktar, and...myrem?

The writhing mess moved closer, teeth gnashing.

It wants to frighten me, she thought, forcing herself to stand tall. She held the headdress—that's what it was—out like a shield as the monster approached. The closer it got, the more the calm drained from her body, replaced by ripples of fear.

But with the fear came memory.

"I offer my life for control of his," she shouted at the monster. "I just need him for a moment."

The creature shrieked and hissed as it approached, stopping just shy of the headdress. "A moment is an hour, is a day, is a year," a chorus of voices called out, each vying to be louder than the rest. "There is no time. Only what you fear."

"I don't understand." Her arms trembled under the weight of the headdress. "I brought an item belonging to the soul I wish to possess."

Several of the arms snatched it from her grasp, drawing it into the chaos of limbs and heads. They curled in on it, still shrieking, and then it was gone. "We grant your request," the voices hissed. "His life merits no worth to us."

Before Elaysia could respond, could ask them how long she had him for, and how much life they demanded from her in return—what it would *feel* like—they sunk their fangs into her flesh. The bites came fast and furious, attacking her from every direction. Pain pulsed through her, filling her body with a piercing heat. Release followed almost immediately, like waves lapping over her skin. Despite her eyes remaining open, darkness flooded her vision. She was falling, falling, careening rapidly into...

Him.

RAYNAR

Raynar, Son of Rajar, Descendent of Rayanti, Chief of the Lautei, High Chieftain of the Lawful Dominion, sat on the edge of his great stone bed, bare feet dangling as he lifted the cup to his lips. The wine had long since soured, but he didn't want to alert his watchers by leaving his chambers at such an hour. Already, they whispered about the bodies he demanded be brought to him after his public sacrifices made to their god, Rayanti, once a moon cycle. He told them it was to consume the blood, to drink the very essence of their vitality, as his father had, as his father's father had. How else was he to ascend into the land of eternal triumph like his ancestors?

But Raynar couldn't stomach drinking the blood. Couldn't stomach blood at all, actually. It was why he'd made excuses to avoid battles again and again, much to the dismay of his elders. He wouldn't be able to avoid it much longer. Not with the victories on their side. There was hardly any risk in accompanying his ever-growing army of warriors, armed with the weapons of the emperor across the sea. It was almost too easy. His father would've been so ashamed.

Good thing the pompous blood-luster was dead.

And in his death, he'd given Raynar more than he ever dreamed. Aside from the threat of his chiefdom being denied, his father's absence had created opportunities the Lautei had never even considered. His father's ambitions had been too small. Why settle for ruling Agaas when one could rule Neharem? Any fool could've seen the tribes' alliances were weak, that the independence of their leaders posed a risk, that they needed a central governing ruler just as in the model executed so flawlessly in Az Zar. And what gifts that union had brought.

Such a small sacrifice, answering to the foreign emperor. A shipment of nevethium every moon cycle? He could mine the lands for his entire lifetime and still have more to spare. Beneath their great fortress alone lay a treasure trove. And agreeing to help with the acquisition of Orillon? Again, he had more than enough warriors; he still would even after the civil war.

The humans in the south meant nothing to him. It was their fault, really, for remaining on the wrong side of progress. They cared too much for simple pleasures when their focus should've been elsewhere. Not that he could blame them entirely.

Raynar finished the rest of his wine and, tossing the cup to the floor with a clatter, slipped off his bed and strode toward the naked corpse slumped on his floor. It was a nyrian woman, a little older than he would've preferred based on the sag of her breasts, but she'd do. They always did.

He dragged the corpse to his bed and hoisted his tunic above his waist. But before he could ready himself, an odd sensation flooded his mind. His vision blurred, as though he was seeing both his room and the cold light of the moons shining down on him. Even though he didn't command his body to do so, it stumbled back, holding his hands before him as if to shield himself from the corpse lying on his bed.

Rage sprouted in his mind, though it didn't come from him, not truly. His heart raced as he scrambled about his room, on his hands and knees now, peering beneath the bed, searching the chests for something, something—

No. Not that.

Every part of Raynar's spirit resisted as he drew the sacrificial dagger from its display rack on the wall. He held the blade in front of his face, hands trembling.

Please, he protested to whatever possessed him. *I'll stop, I won't ever do it again, I—*

But he was heaving open the stone door, running past his watchers to the edge of the platform at the top of his fortress. Concerned voices called out after him, but he could hardly hear them over the pounding in his ears. Beneath him, his city sprawled in a configuration of perfectly constructed buildings alit with nevethium, like the eyes of a dozen stone gods. Though he'd only consumed one cup of wine, he stumbled toward the stone altar and climbed upon it.

"High Chieftain!" someone cried out.

"For Agaas!" he shouted back. "Long live the true high chieftain, may her sunrises always hold promise." The voice was his. The words were not.

Footsteps raced toward him as he pressed the lyvium blade to his throat, but it was too late. He drew it across his tender flesh with a steady hand.

His body returned to him as something warm trickled down his neck. He grabbed at it, trying to rise, but succumbing to the darkness engulfing him.

As the final embers of his life faded, words in another voice filled his mind.

And may your sunsets hold nothing but despair.

KONAR

K onar waited for the demon to come.

He never kept watch for the ones summoned during his own rituals. He'd grown so accustomed to the process that he simply shut his eyes after the deed was done and the words were spoken, not wanting to subject himself to the entity that bestowed unnatural life upon him again and again.

Circumstances were different for Elaysia's first ritual, however. Even if he hadn't raised and loved her as his own child, even if he didn't owe her his undying commitment, he still would've been compelled to observe whatever being emerged. He'd looked enough times during his life-extending ritual to know the same Caman—or at least the same form—appeared each time. And though he'd only attended one summoning at the Caman Altars, that creature had looked at least related to the first. Now, he needed to know if the pattern continued.

He never found out.

Elaysia stood there, frozen, unflinching, for what felt like a quarter hour. Konar began to worry the ritual hadn't worked. Perhaps they hadn't been close enough. Perhaps the headdress wasn't enough to prove a connection to Raynar. Perhaps he'd mistranslated the scroll, or worse, misread it aloud to Elaysia, ruining the summoning before it even began.

He called out to her, asking if she saw or heard anything. When he received no reply, he approached, apologies ready on his tongue. She still didn't respond. Not to his words; not to his touch. Suspicion seeded itself deep in his mind, but he held it at bay, hoping her non-response was brought about by frustration or meditation.

It was her eyes that gave it away.

They stared straight ahead, unblinking, their usual crimson and green replaced by a pupil-less, luminescent iridescence. He shook her, shouting her name, begging Chai'Tik to intervene on her behalf. Elaysia remained statuesque. Konar even tried to pick her up, but it was as if she was made of stone.

What felt like another quarter hour passed by, though he was no longer certain of his ability to perceive the passage of time. He stroked her arm, reassuring her he was there, that she could come back whenever she wanted. If anyone was strong enough, it was her.

His anxiety had nearly become unmanageable when she let out a small cry, crumpling in his arms. He lowered her to the ground, lips moving in a silent prayer he wasn't certain mattered.

"Ellie?" he whispered. "Can you hear me? Keep fighting. I'm here, waiting for you." He dropped his ear to her chest, and relief flooded his body. A steady beat thudded.

When a small groan escaped her lips, he drew her to his chest, as though she were his child come back to life.

Maybe she was.

"Konar?" she murmured in a groggy voice.

"I'm here." He helped her sit up, then offered her water, which she refused. "What happened? Did you have a vision?"

Elaysia's brow furrowed. "I... I don't know." She ran her fingers across her throat as if she expected to find something there.

"Tell me everything," he said, helping her to her feet.

"Not here," she croaked. "I've called to Onitus, he's coming, he's—"

Her legs buckled beneath her. Konar kept her from collapsing fully, wondering if she'd even be able to stay upright on the stormbird. He opened his mouth to suggest they rest a moment longer, for both their sakes.

Then the moaning began. A chorus of cries carrying on the night air like a mist. Only one thing would cause the entire village to erupt in such a melancholy melody all at once, and any lingering doubts were extinguished as the drums joined in.

He practically dragged Elaysia to the clearing where Onitus waited. Whatever she'd seen had drastically affected her, whether conjured in her mind or not. Onitus eyed Konar with suspicion as he helped his rider on, but he allowed him to mount—more likely to protect Elaysia, than out of care for Konar's wellbeing.

By the time they landed on the cliff overlooking Sunset Bay, they were both on the verge of collapse. Onitus stood guard until T'Vak roused himself from whatever stupor he'd fallen into and escorted them both back into the safety of the old Igtheos refuge. Once settled in cots, with plenty of food and drink at their sides that neither of them could stomach much of, he left them alone.

Elaysia's eyelids drifted closed as soon as the backhander departed, but Konar couldn't relax, not until he knew exactly what had happened to her during the ritual. When he had no success in rousing her, however, he leaned back on his own cot, desperately wishing he'd asked T'Vak to light his pipe.

Then she moaned.

"Konar," she whispered, her voice thick with emotion. "I murdered him."

DAVIER

Davier stared off as the rest of the rebel leaders celebrated, raising mugs of Asha's ale and bragging about acts of violence and liberation against the empire. Only Nanjiya seemed to notice him sitting in the darkest corner, an untouched mug at his feet. He offered a weak smile from across the room, then slipped out onto the back deck so she didn't feel the need to come over and check on him. They had every right to celebrate, after all. The liberation of the mine was their greatest accomplished feat yet.

But something about it felt off. Davier couldn't quite put his finger on it, but their recent success seemed almost undeserved. Even though the rebels had fought back against the empire's tyranny for over a year, and though Az Zar's leaders were distracted with larger, looming problems overseas, was it really enough for the hardened military he'd once served to become so careless? And even if it was all genuine, a brilliant mixture of luck, timing, and connections, how long could it last? The rebels were getting ballsy, too public with their actions, too bold with their symbols, and while they remained mostly untouched, the empire still took out its rage on the civilians. It would take a full-fledged attack against their enemy to truly weaken them, and he wasn't certain that was something they were capable of.

Or something he wanted to be a part of.

"Not feeling celebratory?" a deep voice inquired.

Davier peered into the darkness, past the fire pit and into the shroud of dead trees beyond. A figure loomed in the courtyard—rather, they sat, leaning against a tree in a non-threatening manner. Davier reached for his daggers, only letting his hands fall back to his sides upon recognizing the intruder.

"Kymerius?" he asked, kneeling beside him so they were eye-level. "What are you doing out here?"

The ex-soldier shrugged and tipped back his mug, then placed it next to two empty ones on the ground beside him. "Same as you." He gazed at Davier with startling clarity. "Guess we're not that different after all. We're the only ones who know what the empire is truly capable of, what wrath the All-Sovereign can unleash with the snap of his fingers."

A coldness seized Davier, and he wrapped his arms around his chest to rid himself of it. "Maybe we're too jaded. The rebels have done things I never would've dreamed possible. Last night was a—"

"Come on, Zadel." Kymerius glared down at his empty mugs, then leaned his head back against the tree. "Last night should've been a death sentence for us all. I hoped I'd maybe go out with glory, finally feeling like I'd earned the right to die. I don't know what happened, and I sure as fuck don't know why you're still here."

Davier wanted to counter his observations with a convincing rebuttal, but he found none. They should've suffered some casualties, and hearing Kymerius's confession of craving a good death contradicted the pompous nature he had cultivated. But the last comment unsettled him the most.

"I told you and the other leaders of my mission," he said guardedly.

"'Course you did. Yet, you're still here, thriving well past your deadline, and last you checked, your sister as well, yes?" Kymerius stared pointedly at Davier with his storm-blue eyes. There was no malice in them. Just unfettered apprehension.

The apprehension didn't take long to find a home in Davier. "I last checked in a week ago. I didn't meet directly with the All-Sovereign, just his dwarf servant. He told me she was fine, and..." He bit his lip as he broke from Kymerius's gaze. Dalgus had told him to be ready, that he was arranging the release of

Xi in exchange for Davier's role in helping another prisoner escape. He was to speak of it to no one and await the word, and even though he didn't fully trust the dwarf, he didn't want to endanger any chance to run away with Xi, no matter how unlikely.

"And?" Kymerius pressed.

"And to be ready, is all."

Kymerius frowned. He rose from the tree and gestured to the nevethium–lit inner districts towering at the city center. "I think they're playing us for fools, Zadel. Nan means well, but she's too hopeful. Whether or not they allowed us to destroy that mine, they'll retaliate with full force because of the public embarrassment. We need to act fast; try to disrupt whatever they're plotting."

"Quite the change of heart you've had, considering not two days past you were against our little mine rescue." Davier came to stand beside him, hands once again itching for his blades.

"Our little mine rescue is what's prompting this." The moon-light cut harshly against Kymerius's already sharp features as he stroked his cleft chin. "Throwing rocks at the sandcat—as Nan so beautifully put it—was one thing, but now we've aggra-vated it by taking its food." He shrugged. "We can't stand idle, waiting for it to massacre us."

Davier had no rebuttal. The empire was certainly provoked now if it hadn't been already. But could he really risk an even bigger strike? The mine incident may have already put Xi's life in danger. Anything more extreme would all but guarantee her death.

"My sister," he began, but found the tightening of his throat too intense to continue.

In a moment of unprecedented kindness, Kymerius placed his hand on Davier's shoulder, giving it a firm squeeze. "The right attack might be exactly what you need to get her out. Let's draw Nanjiya away from the others, and I'll share my idea with you both."

Kymerius's plan was so outrageously dangerous and bold that it just might work.

At least, that's what Nanjiya expressed to Davier as they lounged on her bed, a bottle of stolen wine between them. Kymerius had coerced them all to her room, then departed shortly after detailing his ideas for an attack—one that involved many pockets of rebels rising simultaneously over the city in a chorus of destruction. He'd told them to take the night to think it over, then winked at Davier as he closed the door; a show of comradery Davier still wasn't certain how to take. Not a week past, he could've sworn Kymerius wanted to kill him. Now, it seemed they were one night of drinking away from a friendship.

"You've hardly said a word tonight," Nanjiya said, turning her back to him as she slipped out of her stolen uniform and into a sun-blood-colored silk robe.

There was nothing meek about the rebel leader, but her bold act caught Davier off guard and he looked away, blushing like an adolescent caught peering through a window. She reached for the bottle as though nothing had happened, red lips parted in anticipation.

"Life has made me wary of being quick to share my thoughts," he said, glancing at his blades leaning against the wall. The room was small, and it smelled of stale food and smoke from the inn below, but there was also an underlying musk that was almost alluring. "But I think Kymerius's plan has merit. We can't stop now because the empire won't stop. Better to use the momentum provided by our recent successes."

"And you'll do anything for a chance to save your sister?" she asked, cocking her head. She freed her hair from its knot at the base of her skull, sending it cascading in a silken black waterfall over her thinly clothed shoulders.

"Almost." He noticed his breath growing increasingly shallow but couldn't determine if it was because of the rebels' circumstances or Nanjiya's forwardness. "I think I've proven I have morals."

"I think you've proven many things." She reached across him for the rolled-up map resting on the small table at the foot of her bed, lingering longer than necessary for its retrieval. "If we're to do this," she said as she eased back over to her side, "there's no going back. Not for you, not for me, not for any of the rebels, and certainly not for Az Zar."

"I don't look back anymore. There's nothing for me there." Davier resisted the sensation stirring inside him as the edge of her robe slipped off one of her shoulders, revealing the moon-toned skin beneath.

She set the wine down on the floor and leaned in until her face rested inches from his. "And what does your life mean to you?"

Nothing, he thought. But that wasn't wholly true. It meant revenge, it meant redemption. And it meant hope.

"Everything," he whispered.

Nanjiya brushed the hair out of his eyes and traced her thumb over his scar. With her so close, he could hardly keep the thought of kissing her from his mind. He'd found her comely enough at their first meeting, but he hadn't given something so frivolous as sexual attraction much thought—if any—since his capture. What was love-making in the throes of a rebellion, with his own sister's life hanging in the balance? And he was the last one to deserve such things, even something as fleeting as lust.

But when she moved her thumb along the stubble of his cheek and danced it across his lips, he made no move to stop her. Her eyes were both hurt and hungry. Maybe she felt the same, too undeserving of love, too overwhelmed with the evildoings of others to grant herself even the most basic of comforts.

"I think," she whispered, lips hovering dangerously close to his. "Life is so overrun with pain that it's our responsibility to steal snatches of happiness wherever we can. We've earned that much, yes?"

Davier let his kiss be the response.

Nanjiya dropped her robe and lay back on her bed, legs spread, eyes fiery yet beckoning. For a fleeting moment, a vision of Elaysia danced across his mind. He'd fought hard to avoid thinking of her, but the situation spawned nothing but memories of their coupling.

She'd never have him again, though. And he didn't deserve her.

He didn't deserve Nanjiya either—didn't deserve anyone—but at least they seemed to have an unspoken agreement regarding what was about to unfold.

Comfort. Passion. Release.

"I'm not the man you think I am," he protested, even as he removed his uniform to join her. "I'm not worthy of love. I'm not a good person."

She crawled toward him and brought his face down to meet hers, their lips just brushing as she spoke. "No one really is. And I'm not asking for love or you. Just tonight; just in case my time is near."

As she slipped her tongue into his mouth, any sign of resistance vanished as waves of pleasure pulsed through his body.

He didn't love Nanjiya, no.

But as their bodies met and the nightmares of rebellion and moon cycles of imprisonment were washed away in moans of release, he no longer cared. Love was a luxury he'd never be able to afford.

He wouldn't let life take his snatches of happiness, too.

Davier awoke to the patter of rain against the inn's roof. Nanjiya had already slipped away, likely to meet with some of her contacts as Kymerius had mentioned the night before. When they met later that day to discuss the plans with the rest of the rebels, he was happy to find that nothing had changed between them. It was one thing he'd feared—an unraveling of the fragile stability he clung to—but other than the gleam in her eyes when their gazes met, there were no changes, no expectations.

Exactly what he needed.

His mood was dampened, however, when he learned exactly what she planned to do, and how soon. She'd already gone and made arrangements with several contacts, the biggest of which included trading half their rations and all their capital notes for two dozen groundshakers. She also informed them that her contact in the palace—whom Davier couldn't help but assume to be Dalgus—was in the process of arranging for them some highly flammable liquid that could start a raging fire in a matter of minutes. It was allegedly still in its testing stages, but the palace's famed prisoner was something of a miracle worker when it came to destruction. According to Nanjiya.

"I don't know where they got him from or why," she said, between bites of Asha's stew consisting of an unidentifiable meat, "but there are rumors within the palace that he's creating vessels that will allow the empire to fly."

Kymerius snorted at the ridiculous claim. "And the All-Sovereign is a god."

Davier considered telling him the nyrian was at least immortal, if nothing else, but there was little value in winning such an argument. "Well, if we make our moves as quickly as Nan suggests, they won't have a chance to find out."

"How quickly are we thinking, Nan?" Kymerius glanced back and forth between them with a wicked grin, drawing the attention of the rebels sitting closest to them at the long table. "Weeks? Days? Hours?"

Nanjiya slid her empty bowl aside to unroll the map. "Everyone, please lean in as close as you can and ask any questions you may have. It will be your job to relay this information to your soldiers within the day, and to have them fully supplied and ready to act within a week's time."

A hush fell over the room as Nanjiya explained a plan similar to Kymerius's, yet far more elaborate.

Everything centered on the All-Sovereign's recent announcement of the revival of the arena games. With it, he hoped to distract the civilians and punish the rebels and slaves who sought to disrupt his peace. Enemies of the empire had been rounded up along with opponents and creatures for them to face, and a date for the grand reopening had been announced—a date that was less than a fortnight away. They'd considered wreaking havoc on the city *during* the reopening, but then quickly decided they wouldn't allow such a spectacle to even start taking place, nor sacrifice their friends already taken prisoner. They'd act a week from now.

Next, Nanjiya circled areas throughout the city where the attacks were to take place. They'd focus on the innermost districts and save over half their groundshakers for the palace itself. They'd pose as soldiers, as servants, as highborns and slaves, planting themselves all across Cadar like the invasive weeds the empire believed them to be. The groundshakers would go off simultaneously, hopefully triggering hysteria and giving those near the palace the opportunity to infiltrate. A small group led by Nanjiya would capture the All-Sovereign, while another, led by Kymerius, would locate the Lord Priestess. During this time, Davier would free Xi, then aid in the burning of the palace and Sun-blood District while other pockets of rebels destroyed the entrances to the mines.

Yes, some would die. Yes, it would be worth the few civilian and rebel lives lost to throw the city into irreparable destruction.

Without leaders and a palace, the military would turn on itself, and the people would look to those who at least resembled a lyvium fist of order: the rebels. The symbol of liberation.

As Davier watched the bright eyes and eager faces of the rebel leaders listening, he tried to mimic their confidence and excitement. It could, after all, be the answer to everything.

Or his worst nightmare yet.

Unlike typical rebel activity, their blow to the empire was planned for high noon, in hopes it would gain the most attention, make the biggest impact, and strike the highest death count.

Not civilian lives, of course, as Nanjiya had reminded everyone the night prior. They weren't to stop or alter the attacks based on civilians, but they weren't to target them, either. Not even the highborn. The military, though...

They wouldn't be so lucky.

Davier was ill-rested, and it was only partly because of his most recent turn in the cot with Nan. Being with her was already starting to feel like a drink, a way to numb the pain, a way to forget. He felt guilty for thinking of her in such a way, but he suspected their lovemaking was the same for her. The way she came at him, all hunger and passion, retreating to an almost detached state afterwards, all but confirmed it.

It was funny, he thought, that he had to join a legion of bloodthirsty rebels to find all the people just like him. Perhaps that was what made a true rebel. Someone who could no longer tolerate abuse, whether directed at them or others. They just never spoke about how their hearts were lost along the way.

The uniform Davier wore wasn't entirely unlike his old one. He hated that he still felt at home in the masking layers of empire-issued wear, but it was helpful in such times. Nan surprised him by giving him a lingering kiss in front of the other rebel leaders, an act that elicited countless eye rolls from the others and mocking expressions from Kymerius. Before his fellow ex-soldier departed for his duty, Davier pulled him aside in the courtyard.

"I just wanted to tell you," he began, wishing his mask was already on, "and I know you might not believe it, but I'm genuinely sorry for the pain I caused you during our initiation. I was...unkind." He could've mentioned again how it had been unintentional, how Davier had quite forgotten Kymerius's existence until joining the rebels, but that would've lessened the weight of his apology.

He held his tongue.

Kymerius saluted him, a quick right fist to the air, the first of its kind Davier had witnessed in ages. The suddenness of it, the comradery of it, stirred something in his chest. "As the commanding officers always used to say, Zadel: nothing is personal if you don't let it be."

Davier thought there was more there, hidden in the words, but before he got the chance to inquire further, the twins were whisking Kymerius away to get outfitted. Lox was with Nanjiya, among others, but Davier's mission was his and his alone.

He preferred it that way.

As he disappeared into one of the many catacomb entrances, he focused solely on Xi. She was still the reason, the prize. He'd do everything in his power to aid the rebellion, use every bit of his strength and cunning to overthrow the people who'd picked his life apart, piece by piece, until it resembled little more than the Abyss, but not at the expense of Xi. She was everything. The only thing.

Dalgus had informed him—curtly so—at their prior meeting that Xi was being held in the palace prison, a place intended to keep people of great value who also demanded a sufficiently high standard of accommodation. Xi was a far cry from the pompous lords and captured leaders they probably intended it for, but it comforted him, knowing she wasn't thrown in with the rapists and murderers who likely wouldn't have let her live past the first night.

They didn't think twice before throwing Elaysia into the worst prison, he thought, heaving open the grate.

He smacked the side of his head as though it would rid him of the thought. Ever since he'd started sleeping with Nanjiya, thoughts of Elaysia plagued him all hours of the day. But the dreams were worse. In the past two nights alone, he'd had three nightmares, each featuring Elaysia amid some new horror. He watched her tumble from the back of a great bird; saw her take fatal wounds in battle. But the worst had been the one where she'd died in childbirth, especially when he couldn't shake the dreadful thought that the babe might've been his.

Bad things, nerves. That's all it was. The sooner he found Xi and escaped, the better.

Davier positioned himself beneath the grate nearest the servants' entrance to the palace. Between Nan's maps, Dalgus's hints, and his own recollection of the layout, he had a decent idea where he'd find his sister.

The wait seemed to take ages, even though it couldn't have been more than an hour. More than once, fears of finding Xi dead—or worse, not finding her at all—filled his mind. He beat them away as best he could with fantasies alternating between his next meeting with Nan and any of the variety of ways he might torture the All-Sovereign and his controlling priestess. He had a few favorites, namely weighted drowning, mutilation, and slow death by sandcat. They were all so petty and short, though, and the more he thought about it, the more he felt no death would be good enough. What they really needed was to be forced to live out their miserable lives, powerless and feeble, void of all pleasure and comfort—isolated, abandoned, hated.

And forgotten.

Before Davier could devise exactly how that might be achieved, the reverberations of the first groundshaker going off rattled the ground above him. Screams followed, but they were almost immediately drowned out by another, then another, until he swore the catacombs wouldn't hold against the impact. He pressed against the wall, using his arm to shield himself from the falling debris, but little more than pebbles grazed his head.

When the shakes faded, he hurried up the broken rungs of the ladder leading to the surface.

Despite the overcast day, the sunlight was near blinding. He stopped, the grate cracked, until he had better command of his vision, then slipped out after a pair of footsteps raced by away from the palace.

Good. If people were fleeing, he might have a chance.

He did his best to resume a pace that was urgent, but not overly so, and was pleasantly surprised when the courtyard turned out to be the one he'd been marched through the night the All-Sovereign first threatened him with his sister's life. He skirted around the frightened servants, pretending to help guide them to safety, then slipped up the stairs without so much as a question.

There were no screams inside the palace, further verifying his theory that the All-Sovereign lived alone, surrounded by nothing but servants and paintings. It took every bit of his self-restraint to keep from sprinting down the hallways. His caution, however, proved to be wisdom, for he came upon not one or two, but at least half a dozen soldiers in his search for the descending staircase that led to Xi. Most of them passed him by with a nod, but one, a higher-ranking officer, pulled him aside.

"Wrong way," the officer barked. "I need you outside, soldier."

Davier tried the first excuse that came to him. "I've been given special orders to—"

"Fuck your orders. The All-Sovereign wants everyone out. Now."

Before Davier could unsheathe his blades, a nasal voice stilled his hand.

"I gave him the orders," Dalgus said, hurrying up to them. "Or would you defy His Holiness's greatest servant?"

Davier could've kissed the damn dwarf.

"I..." Another *boom*, followed by screams, was enough to nip in the bud any suspicions the officer had. He gave Davier a final glare, then hurried down the hall.

When the officer disappeared, Dalgus shot Davier a look that could kill. "What are you and your friends doing, Zadel?"

Davier blinked. Did he not know? Was he not Nan's contact in the palace?

"I told you all I was arranging something the night of the games!" Dalgus snapped, his gaze darting about the halls. "This could ruin everything. How am I supposed to free him now?"

"Where's Xi?" Davier managed to eke out. "I can't find—"

The dwarf's face turned bright red. "I don't give a skirvin's ass about your pathetic little sister! You can't leave without *him*. I've prepared nearly everything for that lad's escape, and I won't let your eager little cause ruin it." Dalgus grabbed Davier's uniform, his crimson eyes flashing. "Do you not understand what's at stake? He is the key to the scrolls. The key!"

"Who?"

Shouts echoed through the halls, and in a panicked fury, Dalgus shoved him away. "Be gone with you. I'll find another way. Your sister can be found through the tunnels accessible by the Zal Drusa lineage paintings. Feel the wall beneath the sickly looking one. It will give beneath your touch."

"Wait, I..." but the dwarf was already gone, shuffling down the hall and vanishing around a corner.

Davier didn't waste any time in rushing to the place mentioned. As Dalgus had said, one of the stones beneath a sickly looking fellow about halfway down the line gave, and he found himself in a dark tunnel. He shoved thoughts of skirvin from his mind as he found the inner mechanism to close the door, then hurried down the steps, taking them two at a time. When he reached a dead end, he cursed and swatted blindly until one of the stones blessedly gave beneath his touch.

The door slid open and, for a fleeting moment, he caught Xi's wide eyes peering through the bars of her cage.

Then a *crack* rang in his ears, and the world faded around him.

JAKKI

All hope of discreet, well-timed retreats vanished upon the high chieftain's return.

Jakki had suspected something was afoot with Elaysia's abrupt reattachment to Konar and the excessive time they spent at the Igtheos refuge in the wake of Vahid's death. She'd ignored it, telling herself that Elaysia was merely trying to restore old relationships in the light of the one she'd lost. It was perfectly logical to desire the comfort of a parental figure, even one as fucked up as Konar. And when Konar's pet backhander came with word that the high chieftain wouldn't be returning to Agaas one night, no one so much as batted an eye. Well, no one but Maseeya who'd become more and more the babes' mother, as of late. But Jakki hadn't even once considered they were plotting to use the scrolls, not when Elaysia had promised there was to be consensus among the Stormriders before doing so.

Then again, the woman was nothing if not rash.

That didn't stop Jakki from letting the dread and anger dance across her face when Elaysia approached her the morning after the incident, an equally shaky Konar in tow. They looked like guilty children recounting a tale of broken pottery, not two adults who'd taken it upon themselves to murder an enemy leader in the most gruesome way possible.

"What in the name of Mother Itaso were you trying to achieve?" Jakki had asked in hushed tones, her attention darting about the High Tree platform that already bustled with morning activity.

The high chieftain's hands were shaking, her lips chapped, her eyes distant—almost crazed. "Peace," she'd replied, though so uncertainly that it had sounded like a question. "I thought I could bring him back here to...bargain with him."

"And you did what, exactly?"

Konar had stepped forward, almost placing himself between Elaysia and Jakki. "It was my idea. I told her—"

"I didn't ask you," Jakki snapped, keeping her attention on Elaysia's tear-streaked face.

Elaysia had squinted and looked down, as though she couldn't quite process the events. "I made him kill himself. I didn't mean to, Jak. He was just so...and the watchers were too many. There was no way to get him out. I..." Then she'd held her two-toned hands in front of her face, studying them intently. "Do I look like me to you?"

"An exhausted you, but undeniably you, Ellie." Jakki swallowed back a frustrated sigh. "Come on."

She'd helped Elaysia to her chambers and saw to it she'd changed, eaten, and fallen asleep before seeking Lumira. They tried to keep it a secret, but Elaysia insisted on telling the war council later that day, feeling they deserved to be ready for whatever fallout might come. Reactions ranged from shock to horror, and even though Gibrund was fully in support of the vengeful slaughter, he didn't approve of the secrecy.

"And now chaos ensues," Lumira had muttered under her breath as the war council departed, each chief and advisor at conflict with one another about what was best to do.

A good third wanted to stay and fight, or at least die in their holy city. Others wanted to make peace and accept the Lawful Dominion as the ruling government of Neharem, at least long enough for them to regroup. At least half were ready to flee, but of those wanting to start new lives, few liked the idea of doing so in Orillon—or worse, with the skulmor. The council seemed to only be unified on one front: they were out of time.

Given the publicness of his...execution...word of Raynar's death had likely already spread to all pockets of Lawful Dominion forces overnight. Even camps stationed in the Far North and deep south would find out within a matter of days. The closest forces, however, namely the Atsukut and Lautei, could be ready to take their revenge on Agaas within three nights at the most.

With no agreement in sight, it was decided that all chiefs would lead their people as they saw fit. Elaysia might've had some sway if she hadn't been as conflicted herself. No part of her wanted to surrender—Jakki could see that much—but whether to stay and fight or flee with what remained of her loved ones, she knew not.

The first day raced by in bouts of paranoia and distress. A fight broke out at base camp over some refugees taking more supplies for their journey than the ones staying thought necessary. Up in Agaas, it wasn't much better. The people who called the living trees home seemed even more torn over what to do, no doubt feeling a powerful alliance to their city in contrast to their own lives. But as she walked through the platforms, she found as many people departing with bundles as those staying.

Jakki didn't blame them. Even with the stormbirds, they stood little chance against the Lawful Dominion forces who outnumbered them ten to one. Besides, it'd been all but confirmed they took their orders from Az Zar instead of the insipid deviant Elaysia had removed at the cost of some of her own life—however that worked. The high chieftain had apparently caught sight of an Az Zarian seal on a parchment in Raynar's chambers, and there was little doubt as to whom it belonged to.

Jakki tried not to think of her own mother as she sought each remaining chief individually, hoping to turn them one by one to the plan she and Lumira had concocted. Thoughts of her mother brought upon equal measures of guilt and rage, which was a deadly combination, given the circumstances. She told herself the Yustano would be alright until the Agaasian people and their allies were relocated, and then she could fly back to her island home to check on them. Maybe even sway her chief mother to join her beneath the mountains with the wolves.

Highly unlikely, but entertaining to imagine, nonetheless.

The sway she had over the chiefs was little, and despite Lumira's increased contact with them, her odds fared even worse. No one wanted to go to Orillon, and no one trusted the skulmor to not rip their throats out while they slept. Couldn't the stormbirds protect Agaas? Couldn't the remaining warriors form an impenetrable line around the city? Fire off that crateful of shieums they'd confiscated?

When the Stormriders met that first night, at the training grounds under the cover of darkness, their gathering hardly fared better. The birds, not yet two years old, still hadn't come fully into their powers. And though they could provide aerial attacks on the armies as they approached the thick Apáasutai forests, once the enemies made it safely into the shelter of the trees, their people would be on their own.

"We don't know what other weapons they've acquired," Mardus said, rubbing his face vigorously as though he could massage away their pains. "But we should probably assume they at least have more of the groundshake weapons."

"We should probably assume they have unlimited resources and warriors." The remark came from a stoic Anahi, who Jakki hadn't seen smile since the death of her brother.

Lumira poked at the coals with a long stick, her nightstalker eyes glittering in the firelight. "The northerners will be riding those monstrous stags, and they'll navigate our forests with ease."

"Then we should all leave while there's still time, regardless of what the people do," Xaren said, setting aside his newly sharpened arrowheads. "If the odds aren't in our favor, it doesn't make sense to have all the birds exposed to—"

"But it makes sense to leave those who stay to fight unprotected?" Grokhion snapped, his emerald eyes flashing with terrifying intensity. He muttered something in the language of the beridians—Jakki couldn't remember what it was called—and marched a few feet away, his back turned to them.

"I understand your concern, my friend," Yerakai said, placing a hand on the Az Zarian boy's shoulder. "I, too, think some of the birds should be sent away, along with the scrolls and those crucial to our cause."

He seemed older than ever, aged by his chief's recent passing and the new responsibilities bestowed upon him because of it. Jakki no longer craved a chiefdom as she once had, and she'd nothing but sympathy for her fellow nyrian.

Elaysia folded her arms across her chest as she gave her head a slight shake. "I'm not leaving until all hope is lost. This is my doing, and I won't abandon my people in their time of need."

"How about when they need a living high chieftain?" Jakki said, fighting to keep some semblance of calm in her voice. She couldn't stand to listen to the circular conversations any longer. "Do your babes mean anything to you?"

Elaysia's nostrils flared as she locked gazes with Jakki. "They mean *everything.*"

"Then leave now with them and Maseeya on Onitus," Jakki said. "Half of us can stay to help ward off the incoming armies, but once they're in the safety of the trees, we need to send all the birds away from here."

"Are you going to cower in the mountains with your wolves?" Mardus asked, his tone slick with judgment. "They'd just as soon kill you and Siren. The way you told it, they almost did."

"But they didn't," Jakki said through clenched teeth. "And I've earned their respect. But I don't have the time to educate you on your prejudices right now, Brother."

Mardus seethed with rage, but he held his tongue.

"Anahi," Elaysia asked the Orillon woman. She spoke in a lower voice, as though the others weren't even there. "You and the kuza should return to Orillon at the very least. They won't be targeting those fleeing along the coast right away. Their focus is Agaas and the crystals she harbors."

Anahi's kohl-lined eyes narrowed. She'd outlined them like that daily since returning from Orillon, and while Jakki first thought it a mourning custom of her people, she now speculated it was more the woman's own ritual, be it for remembrance or resilience.

"I mean it," Elaysia insisted. "You can even look into arranging temporary lodging and work for those choosing to seek refuge in Orillon."

"If you require it of me, I'll have no choice but to comply." Anahi's intent was clear: she didn't like the idea of abandoning Elaysia and would only flee to Orillon under strict orders to do so.

"I agree with the high chieftain," Jakki said, hoping it would give Elaysia the affirmation she needed to proceed with the command. "You and the kuza can even escort any refugees already willing to depart Agaas and ensure they arrive safely."

The corner of the Orillon woman's mouth quirked, and Jakki thanked herself for rebranding the mission as one of protection instead of one of cowardice.

"I'll go with her," Xaren said, slinging his quiver over his shoulder as though he was already set to leave. "It provides better protection and removes another stormbird from Agaas. I have no people here in need of my show of confidence for battle, and I'll be more readily accepted in Orillon than some."

By some, he meant nyrians and beridians, both of which held similarly lower status in the human-dominated nation to the south. When no one openly disagreed with him, Elaysia nodded to both humans, giving them her blessing.

"Leave first thing in the morning," she said, rising. She brought her right fist to her heart as she fixed them both with a stern gaze. "Is there a blessing common to your lands I can send you off with, should we not meet again?"

"Speak no such words," Anahi said, almost scoldingly. "You give them power." She softened her expression, then took Elaysia's hands in her own. "But back home, we say, 'May the sands of time ever shift in your favor.'"

Xaren frowned when Elaysia's gaze turned to him. "Az Zar is filled with pompous decrees of allegiance to Mavet."

"But what of your people to the east?" Elaysia asked. "Your traditions before Az Zar occupied your lands by force?"

The boy's brown eyes lit up. "There is a saying, 'Even death brings peace.'"

Charming, Jakki thought.

But Elaysia offered him a sad smile. "So it does." The high chieftain embraced them both, then ordered them to make for Agaas.

As Jakki watched them go, a crisp Gathering Moon wind pulling at her hair, she couldn't rid herself of the gnawing feeling that she should go with them. That they all should. But there was no way to convince the rest of those already committed to stay.

Or was there?

While Lumira and the other riders spent the better part of the next day preparing for battle, Jakki spent every moment trying to convince Elaysia to let her use a scroll.

"They could be here as early as tomorrow," she insisted as Elaysia prepared bags of supplies for Maseeya and the babes. At eight moons, they were both crawling about on the floor, pulling themselves up on furniture, and getting into everything but what they'd been given to play with. "If you let me do the ritual on one of the influential chiefs, we could convince another third of the people to abandon this suicidal hope of protecting Agaas."

Elaysia spun, spilling the contents of her sack onto the floor. "It is *not* suicidal. There is hope unless you stop believing in it." Elaron began to fuss at Elaysia's harsh tone, and she scooped him up, bouncing him gently on her hip as she hushed him. "Besides, they would never forgive us if we used it against our own," she said, far quieter, in the sing-song voice of a parent soothing a child. "They might even be aware of the ritual as it happens, and what then? Another civil war?"

"Fine," Jakki said, throwing up her hands. "I'm tired of trying to fix things. Will you at least come with me to the north? I understand that Yerakai and Mardus feel a need to stay for their people, and the beridians have no ties, but you and I can go to the skulmor and make arrangements for refugees. Like Anahi and Xaren in Orillon."

Elaysia let out a small shriek, and Jakki followed her gaze to Dytana, who'd managed to slip a knife from the sack and was holding it dangerously close to her smooth infant skin. Jakki snatched it away in a blur, then picked up the girl to compensate for the pleasure she'd been deprived of.

"Take this, you little tyrant," Jakki said, slipping off one of her bracelets to hand to the babe.

Elaysia's face softened. "I plan to send the babes and Maseeya with you, Jak. Konar and the scrolls, too. They'll be in excellent hands."

"Send?" Cold tendrils of fear coiled in Jakki's stomach. "Ellie, you can't stay here. You'll be their primary target next to the nevethium and—"

"That's why I have to stay." Her lips hardened into a thin line, but her eyes were wet with unshed tears. "My life might be the only offering they'd accept to let any survivors go free. And I can't have them following me, putting the scrolls at risk."

Jakki's head throbbed from clenching her teeth. "The scrolls are at risk without you. And if you think for a moment they are going to spare a single life for yours, you're—"

The door to the high chieftain's chambers burst open, revealing a wide-eyed, breathless Kahana.

Jakki knew the meaning of her visit before the Moákun opened her mouth.

The Lawful Dominion had come.

LUMIRA

They came from the north, south, and east, only sparing the west because they'd yet to learn the ways of water or seduce the myrem to their side.

A blessing, Lumira wondered, *or a curse?*

It wasn't as though everyone loyal to Agaas could dive off the cliffs in hopes of saving themselves. At best, the boats in the Apáasutai's possession could hold maybe a quarter of the holy city's occupants. Would the rest drown? Be run off the cliffs and bash their heads upon the jagged rock below, the waves sweeping any traces of violence clean in a simple exhale of salt and sea?

No. They'd be lucky to escape their tomb of a city unharmed, if at all.

But now wasn't the time for further musing. Anadu was already arcing down, closing in on the place where a flock of birds had emerged from the shelter of the forest just moments prior. They'd gone up like a cloud of smoke, all caws and shrieks, and in their absence was an eerie silence only further intensified by the thick fog that rolled in from the coast.

Lumira had been assigned to the northern watch that night, but she hadn't expected anything so soon. Except for small attacks to test the borders, the Atsukut had been dormant for the past moon cycle, almost as if they took the time to rest while the Lautei and their southern allies hemmed in the bottom half of Neharem. Jakki thought they'd been busy with the tulek bear, then resumed fighting over land with the skulmor.

Lumira knew otherwise.

Resting they were. Lying in wait. Ember eyes boring into their monster steeds' backs. It had all been a game, just as she'd imagined. Hunters toying with their prey.

She peered into the dark canopy of trees interspersed with scattered glimmers of moonlight, but her vision was all but lost in the fog and the thickness of the branches. They were there, though. The enemy. She could sense them moving; could almost hear the hoof falls of the great stags they rode. But most of all, she could feel those eyes.

Anadu glided just above the treetops, her gaze piercing the shield of branches, catching things even a beridian would miss.

"Can you see anything?" Lumira asked.

"Many things," the stormbird said, flooding Lumira's mind with her own thoughts. *"I can try to find where the hoard ends or begins. Already there are too many to count. They are moving fast. Agaas will be overrun in a matter of—"*

Anadu banked left as an arrow sailed from the trees, arcing through the air where the stormbird's wing had been a moment prior. Several more were launched on its tail, one just narrowly missing Lumira's leg.

"We've seen enough," she growled, glaring into the woods. "Go south. We need to check on Mardus and Grokhion."

Anadu complied. She'd already established limited contact with her nestmate, at least long enough to confirm that an attack to the south unfolded simultaneously. Then their connection had been lost abruptly, as though something had diverted the other stormbirds' attention. Lumira's and Anadu's thoughts on the matter were unanimous.

Something had gone wrong.

As they raced south, hoping to intercept the intruders coming from what was once a territory shared by the Ni'anko and Apáasutai, Lumira's thoughts kept circling back to the eyes that haunted her dreams. No longer would she cower, letting them cripple her clarity and confidence. Should she see them again in battle, she'd face them head-on, glad to die confronting her fears rather than slowly being consumed by them.

They hadn't yet made it out of the thick forest surrounding Agaas when Lumira picked up on the steady thud of war drums, accompanied by deep, resonating horns. The closer they flew, the louder the declaration of war became, the more each beat and blow shook her to her core. Lumira pressed against Anadu's neck, her stiff, silken feathers giving her the briefest sensation of protection.

The field beyond the forest's southern tip was alight with green and orange, as if hundreds of oddly colored stars dotted the landscape. Rows of warriors stretched beyond her vision, far more than the Lautei ever had. Even with the contribution of the Banaxa, the numbers still outnumbered that of both tribes, and Lumira's heart sank, knowing the Moatiwe and Tangeesh likely marched with them. They bore great banners and flags of many colors, ranging from beige to black, from red to blue.

Apáasutai warriors launched arrows from the shelter of the trees. Up on the northern borders, the Daruk likely did the same, as did the Moákun to the east.

None of them would hold the line for long.

Lumira readied the shieum she'd brought on patrol, taking aim as Anadu began plucking warriors from the field. She fired a few shots, taking a life with each one. It made no more difference than spooning water from the ocean. As she stopped to reload, she beheld a colossal wooden behemoth amidst the chaos of marching warriors. Its weight-bearing arm was dangerously low to the ground, connected to its body with intricate ropes and pulleys. In its grasp was a massive boulder. Before Lumira could fully process what was happening, the counterweight plummeted, the ground trembling beneath its weight. Its mighty arm swung, a pendulum of destruction releasing the massive boulder. She followed its intended trajectory, and her stomach dropped. Keera was flying right toward the incoming boulder, her attention focused on the Lawful Dominion warriors that Mardus had begun picking off with a shieum. The boulder had already reached its zenith, and they wouldn't see it coming, wouldn't—

"Mardus!" she roared.

But it was too late. Her heart leaped to her throat as Keera dropped from the sky, like a sparrow that had struck a tree while fleeing a falcon. A ghost of a scream tried to claw its way from Lumira's throat, but no sound came out. Nothing she could hear over the war cries and drums.

Anadu, Lumira managed in her thoughts, but the bird was already making for her fallen kin.

Keera twitched on the ground, wings spread at odd angles, white feathers spread around her like snow. Mardus was on his feet, his club swinging at any who dared attack his bird.

He wouldn't last long. Warriors closed in, and Lumira roared with fury as an arrow found its way into the Moákun's arm. Shieum thunder filled the air, and she knew she only had moments to act before both bird and rider were lost forever.

"I can carry her," Anadu said, stretching out her great talons. *"I will take her to our island. She will be safe. You and Mardus can ride on my back."*

"No," Lumira shouted, taking aim at a warrior who'd drawn too close to Keera. "I can't leave Elaysia and Grokhion."

The stormbird didn't protest further as she landed, spreading her wings over her fallen sister like a shield. She let out a piercing shriek that gave the Lawful Dominion warriors nearest her cause to stop. Mardus took advantage of the moment and Lumira's protection of his flank to approach Keera. He threw his arms over her neck, muttering something in the tongue of his people. A shieum projectile glanced off Lumira's mask. She sprang back to Mardus, yanking him off Keera with a single jerk.

"Get on Anadu!" Lumira cried as she shoved a stunned and wounded Mardus toward her bird. "She will take you and Keera to refuge."

"I can't," he began, words breaking off as he clutched the blood spurting from the wound on his upper arm.

Lumira ducked as an arrow whizzed past, then heaved Mardus onto a wide-eyed Anadu, snatching his shieum in the process. "You're no use to us dead, and neither is Keera."

As Anadu grasped her nestmate's talons in her own, Lumira ran into the fray, both shieums loaded and ready, taking aim. One of the warriors—their tribal affiliations were obscured by their Lawful Dominion uniforms—rushed at her, shouting, a massive flag trailing from a pole in his hands. Lumira brought him down with a single shot, then fired another at the warrior trailing behind. She dropped to her knee to reload, stopping beside the fallen flag. Something was odd about it, a patchwork of colors, uneven stitching, and odd textures.

She stopped mid-load, blood cold in her veins. Her mind raced back to the attack on the beach, to the massacre of the Ni'anko, to the countless other Neharem lives lost during the war.

It was a flag of flesh.

A blinding rage seized Lumira as she rushed into the sea of enemy soldiers, firing the shieums, then casting them aside for a spear when they emptied. She was hardly aware of the contact she made with the bodies, of the cries filling the air, of the sensation of her claws tearing into the tender flesh of necks. The world was a blur, her body sea and storm. She was unstoppable.

She was death itself.

As she approached the behemoth weapon that had plucked Keera from the sky, she realized it had moved closer to the tree line. Dozens of half-naked nyrians and humans were bound to the construct, heaving it through the field, their bodies bloodied by the chains. They were, Lumira realized with horror as she inspected their slight frames and colorful tattoos, Ni'anko and Kahaloán. She attacked the guards whipping them, then tried to free them from their chains. It didn't work. She had nothing that would break lyvium.

With a sorrowful look, she raced on, cresting the hill, taking more lives with her as she went. A shriek filled the skies as she ran, and she looked back to see Wind Chaser and Yerakai barreling down on the behemoth contraption. The stormbird gripped the wooden arm in his talons, yanking it onto its side. She hurried on, trusting they'd destroy it. Its absence would save many lives. When she reached the top of the hill, however, she froze. At least a dozen more of the behemoth contraptions made their way forward in the valley below.

And their projectiles were alive with fire.

She glanced back toward Agaas, knowing she belonged there, only for her breath to catch in her throat.

There, amid the Lawful Dominion laying waste to the Apáa-sutai brave enough to emerge from the tree line, was the looming, cloaked figure with the ember eyes. Lumira couldn't move, couldn't breathe, as its hateful gaze bore into her.

As her body fought to respond to her command, her mind wandered to the first time she'd witnessed the shieum the night of Elaysia's capture, then to the attack in Daruk territory, and finally, the massacre on the Moákun beach. The three terrors became undistinguishable, a warped nightmare of past and present. And at the center of it all, those ember-colored, pupilless eyes.

She drew a sharp breath. That's what all the memories had in common. Those eyes.

Caman eyes.

Lumira shook her head, forcing herself to remain present as she snatched up a fallen weapon. It was an Az Zarian sword, of all things. But she had no time to trade it. She sprinted back down the hill, blade catching in the collarbone of a would-be attacker. She yanked it free, barreling on.

It wasn't until she'd made it halfway that she realized the entity, the Caman, was moving in the opposite direction, away from her, its arms raised toward the sky. Darkness spawned from its hands, a swirling black cloud thicker than smoke and faster flowing than water. It climbed up, spreading across the sky like a blanket of death, shielding the field from the moon-light.

Lumira ran faster, pushing until her lungs burst, searching the skies for Grokhion and Roth. She hadn't seen her kin since arriving at the battle, but they had to be close by. If Anadu had sensed it, surely—

She just glimpsed a flash of Roth's outstretched wings, as an arrow as long as she was tall and a third as thick careened toward them.

Then darkness swallowed the moons.

ELAYSIA

E laysia was distantly aware of the commotion whirling around her, but it was like something from a dream.

Or a nightmare.

She clutched Dytana to her chest as she followed Jakki, who held Elaron, through the swarms of people clogging the bridges and platforms. Kahana led the way, despite Elaysia knowing she longed to make her way to the edge of the forest, where the battle reportedly raged.

"We'll head for the Igtheos refuge," Jakki said, moving Elaron to her left hip. "But first, I need—"

She halted abruptly as a horde of Apáasutai archers sprinted by, angling for good lookout points over the platforms.

"Fools," she muttered under her breath, grabbing Elaysia's arm with her free hand. "I need to stop by my loft. My staff is there, and so is"—she swallowed, her gaze a little too focused on an elderly woman hobbling by with the aid of a cane—"something personal."

"Your loft is in the opposite direction of the nearest ramp," Kahana shouted, a little too loudly. "We must get the high chieftain out as quickly as possible."

Elaysia was already pulling Elaron from Jakki's arms, already anticipating the way her friend would feel torn between duty and whatever it was she needed. For all she knew, it was a special token from Jak's mother, or a note from a lover since passed on.

And she couldn't have anyone torn in such a manner responsible for the lives of her babes.

"Go, Jak," she said, when the Yustano woman's lips parted in protest. "You can find us again. Or better, get as many people out of here alive as you can."

Jakki's luminescent golden eyes darted from her to the living tree across the way. "Ellie…"

"I need to find Maseeya."

Elaysia broke away before fear could convince her otherwise. They had time. They had plenty of time. The Stormriders would do everything they could to hold off the Lawful Dominion as long as possible. She just needed to find Maseeya, who was at the summit lodge. Or was it the library, retrieving something for Konar? Surely she hadn't gone down to base camp so late in the—

Boom.

A sick, burning knot twisted in Elaysia's stomach. She'd heard that same sound in Agaas nearly two years past, the day of her first induction. The day the Igtheos Tree had been damaged beyond repair.

The day its heart had been stolen.

She took an unsteady step forward, struggling under the weight of both babes.

"High Chieftain," Kahana began, but her voice was drowned out by another *boom.*

Then another.

And another.

And another.

They happened in such rapid succession that the sounds of their destruction were one prolonged roar. An endless thunder. Before Elaysia could get a word in, several more went off, these closer and closer, until she felt the very platform she stood on tremble beneath her feet.

When the booming stopped, a high-pitched ringing deafened her ears. She could feel the babies squirming, could see the tears wetting their cheeks, their mouths wide and howling with fear. Someone grabbed at her elbow, and she swung her leg, kicking a shocked Kahana in the stomach.

The Moákun warrior clutched her midsection, face contorted in a grimace.

"I'm sorry," Elaysia rasped, though she could still hardly hear her own voice. "Are you alright?"

Kahana held up her hand and nodded. Elaysia swore she heard another muffled *boom*. The ground trembled, confirming it.

"We need to find Maseeya," she shouted, hurrying toward the summit lodge.

"We need to leave," Kahana called after her, her voice distant, as though it were under water.

Elaysia fell to her knees as another tremble shook the High Tree platform. The darkness was illuminated by an odd, greenish-yellow smoke rising around the living trees and their platforms. There was no more denying it. Agaas was under siege.

The summit lodge doors swung open and Maseeya stumbled out like a spirit walker, two wraps and a bag in her hands. She was all calm and precision as she fastened one of the wraps to her back and slipped Dytana inside. Even as the smoke grew thicker and the booming nearer, she helped Elaysia into her wrap and placed Elaron snug against her back.

Kahana herded them both across the platform, trying to secure a clear path between the battle-crazed warriors and panicking civilians. It was only when they'd started down a ramp that Elaysia realized what she'd left.

"My mother's sword," she said, digging in her heels. Her dagger was strapped to her thigh, where it always was, and she'd left her bow with Konar at the Igtheos refuge. But that sword was all she had of her mother; the only bit of her Az Zarian heritage she'd been brave enough to cling to.

Kahana yanked her forward. "We can't turn back now."

"No need!"

All three women spun to find Jakki right behind them, her staff and Elaysia's sword in hand. "Missing this?" she asked with one of her winning grins.

"How'd you..." Elaysia couldn't find the words as she wrapped her fingers around the smooth hilt.

"No time for thanks," Jakki said, urging her to follow an increasingly stressed Kahana. "You and Maseeya stay between us. I'll watch the flank."

"How are they here already?" Elaysia asked as she jogged down the ramp, coughing as smoke filled her lungs. "Kahana received the tuross message only a few minutes before we departed my loft." Her ears still buzzed with the aftermath of the groundshakes, but she could hear well enough to make out the words of those closest to her.

Jakki peered over the edge of the ramp as she ran, frowning. "It's impossible. Even if they crossed into the forest at the same time as the tuross, they couldn't have reached Agaas yet. Turosses are four times faster than any race of land."

"Then they were already here." The chilling conclusion came from Kahana. She slowed long enough to glance over her shoulder, face hard as stone. "They must've snuck in spies."

"No one new has come in ages," Maseeya said, pausing for breath. She was in good health and mobile for a human her age, but running with a twenty-pound babe was clearly taking its toll.

Jakki's eyes darkened as she helped the Az Zarian woman away from the railing. "Then we've been played for fools."

They hurried down the ramps, pausing to rest when Maseeya needed it, Jakki and Kahana standing sentinel, weapons at the ready. They were only a few minutes from base camp when cries erupted from above, followed by a sickening *crack*. Elaysia knew without looking that one of the living trees was about to fall. The following snaps and cracks confirmed it, and then there was a bone-chilling chorus of shrieks filling the air as the tree succumbed to its fate.

Kahana jerked Elaysia forward, dragging her to solid ground, while Jakki did the same with Maseeya. They didn't look back, not even as the ramp shuddered beneath the weight of the living tree as it fell into it, destroying the chance of escape for those still trapped above. Elaron's tiny hands gripped the fine hairs on Elaysia's neck as she plowed forward, keeping pace with Kahana, her other hand pulling Maseeya and Dytana along with her.

No sooner had they reached base camp than the groan of another living tree snapping free of its roots filled the night. Elaysia could hardly discern the screams from the cracking and snapping. Only the rumble of groundshakes thundered above all else. It wasn't until they'd cleared the mostly abandoned base camp that she heard the undeniable shriek of a stormbird, followed by the chilling beats of the war drums.

Elaysia glanced up as they ran through the woods, looking to the moons for comfort, for their winking celestial faces peering between the branches. But when she looked up the third time, well away from the glowing green of the fallen city, the moons were no more. A thick darkness settled over them, blotting out all the light in the sky, as though it had never existed.

And then the sound of shieums firing filled the night.

T'VAK

"**S**omething's wrong," T'Vak said, storming back into the refuge.

Konar looked up from the scrolls, entirely unmoved by T'Vak's extreme show of distress. "When isn't something wrong?" the ex-high elder muttered, returning his attention to the rolls of parchment as he took another pull from his pipe.

T'Vak snatched the scroll away, wrinkling it in the process. The look in Konar's eyes suggested he would've considered that grounds to kill him, were he not a crippled old man clearly outmatched in strength.

"This better be important," the nyrian said through gritted teeth, his luminescent eyes flashing.

"Have a look yourself." T'Vak pointed to the open door with his sword. "Something's wrong with the fucking sky."

This proved to be enough for Konar to not only peel himself away from his research, but to do so quickly, almost sprinting for the door. As fast as the crusty old man could, anyway.

T'Vak followed him into the night, squinting to find his way in the scant spear of light coming from the open door. Just a few minutes prior, he'd been pacing outside, waiting for Konar to discharge him so he could grab the last of the wine he'd hidden in Agaas. But as he'd looked up at the sky, making shapes in the stars as he often did, they vanished. It was almost as if a thick, black fog had swallowed them and the moons. He thought he'd maybe overdone it on the kinawa that night, but according to the gaping ex-high elder beside him, he wasn't *that* crazy.

That, and neither of them could ignore the roaring thunder, despite no signs of rain.

"Khiev-Tatamic help us," Konar whispered. "Quick, back inside."

They hurried into the refuge and rolled up the scrolls and the parchment, securing them in a satchel over the nyrian's shoulder. T'Vak attached every blade at his disposal, leaving both his sword and favorite dagger unsheathed and in his hands.

"Do you think this has anything to do with the Lawful Dominion?" he asked as Konar pulled a nevethium pendant out of his robes, extinguishing the candle on the table with a breath. A green glow replaced the orange one, and for the first time, T'Vak found himself unsettled by it.

"Without a doubt," was the ex-high elder's reply.

T'Vak pointed to the stairs leading to the rooms on the second level. "You. Hide now."

"Excuse me?" Konar straightened to his full height, which was admittedly a touch taller than T'Vak.

"Don't be like that. You claim those things are so sacred, so why risk the enemy getting them?"

"I need to find Elaysia. She and Maseeya and the babes are all in Agaas. If they—"

"And how much help would you be? Gonna swing a pipe at them with your awkward left hand?" T'Vak let his words sink in before starting for the door. "How many people know about this place?"

Konar sat despondently at the table. "Maybe a handful of the Apáasutai. It hadn't even been inhabited in years prior to Zavik rediscovering it."

"Good." T'Vak paused in the doorway, inhaling deeply to clear his head. "Then it's where you'll stay, and where I'll bring whatever survivors I can find."

"And if someone comes?" Konar asked as T'Vak closed the door.

"You'll use your poison tongue on them. It's gotten you away with murder, after all."

The door clicked shut before Konar could reply.

T'Vak retrieved his own crystal, something he'd pilfered from the holy city on his first visit, if he could recall properly. He didn't like using it. Didn't want to be a beacon in the night, giving away his position for anyone looking to send an arrow through his heart. But he couldn't very well proceed without it. Not with the sky dark as a tomb.

Eventually, he was able to slip it back into his tunic. A green–yellow smoke rose in the distance, and a few miles south was the unmistakable glow of firelight against the sky. Neither was a good sign, nor were the steady drumbeats. He almost made for the training grounds, the area that seemed to be the source of the flames, but Konar would never let him live if he didn't go directly to Agaas as promised.

He slowed to a prowl as he slipped into the woods. His feet were less clumsy around the foliage than they'd been a year prior, but he was still careful to mind his footing and stop every so often to listen. It paid off sooner than he expected.

He ducked behind a trunk as war cries filled the air, followed by screams. A few shieum fired, and the voices fell silent. T'Vak grimaced. The weapons born of Az Zar were perfect for such spineless fighting, launching blindly into the darkness and massacring whoever lay in their path.

It didn't take long for him to discover the first body. The lack of light wasn't doing him any favors, so he kneeled, hands probing, checking for signs of life. His fingers sunk into a cavity in the skull. He yanked his hand away, fighting down the bile rising in his throat as he shook the blood and brains from his fingers.

A cowardly weapon indeed.

After finding two more bodies which had succumbed to similar fates, T'Vak stopped kneeling to check for survivors. He knew the look of Elaysia well enough to know when it wasn't her at a glance. With her unique appearance and the twins to confirm it, she would be hard to miss.

Unless they already had her.

The ground shook as he neared Agaas, but there was no thunder preceding it. He realized, belatedly, one of the trees must've fallen, and winced as wails filled the air in the aftermath. Scattered shieum fire sounded to his right, and he instinctively ducked each time, wondering if his thinly plated armor would even matter against the projectiles.

As he scurried through the brush, the crisp night air filling his lungs, he sensed something following him. He dove behind the next thick trunk, dousing the light of the nevethium in his tunic, blades drawn.

He waited. Listened. The conflict was distant enough that he could pick up the faint sound of a branch snapping just a few feet from his hiding place. He shut his eyes, thinking of Zavik alone in some Az Zarian prison, and let the guilt of knowing he'd put him there be the confidence he needed. Another snap, and T'Vak was leaping out, sword cutting down in a clean arc.

It met no resistance.

Before T'Vak could take another swing, something sharp pricked the skin of his neck. But there was something soft attached, just above his chest. Then his captor growled.

"Drunken fool," a thick beridian accent hissed. "I could smell you a mile away."

"I doubt that," T'Vak said, slipping free of Lumira's grasp. "But I'm glad I'm so memorable to you."

Lumira growled again, then inserted her hand in his tunic without warning, exposing the top part of the crystal. For a brief moment, their faces came into focus, then she slipped it into her own wrap, leaving only a veiled green warmth about her chest. Her breathing was labored, and there were at least half a dozen cuts on her body, though none looked life-threatening.

More shieum fire sounded, followed by more screams.

"They've made it to Agaas," Lumira said, dropping to a crouch. "I don't know where any of the Stormriders are, except for Mardus. Before it went dark, I saw Grokhion and Roth. They'd launched a massive arrow at him, but I didn't hear any shrieks.

I think they got away." She flattened herself against a fallen log, ears twitching.

T'Vak mimicked her, taking shelter behind the log. "Massive arrow? What's happening out there?"

"They attacked from the north and south. The Atsukut came down on those monstrous stags, and the rest of the Lawful Dominion forces came from the south. They have new weapons that can launch larger projectiles than I've ever seen. Not just huge arrows, but great boulders." She pawed at his clothes until she found his wine skin. "They mean to bring down Agaas with them."

He didn't protest as she finished what remained of his wine. "And the darkness?"

She tossed the empty skin back to him. He couldn't quite make out her face, but her tone said everything. "They have a Caman with them. One walking about seemingly of its own accord."

"Is that—" T'Vak swallowed. "Normal? I thought they had to be summoned?"

Lumira shrugged. "Ask Konar. He's the only one who seems to know much about them. We'd do well to learn more before we cross paths with one again."

T'Vak didn't think it was the best time to mention he'd left said nyrian to his own defense. "Well, at least the darkness affects their fighters, too. They'll be taking down some of their own in the crossfire." He squinted into the woods, then stiffened. There was movement in the shadows.

Lumira matched his readiness, her superior gaze tracing his. "They don't care. The loss of a few lives is nothing to them in exchange for the living tree hearts. That's why they've wanted Agaas so badly. It's the only source of crystals that large above ground." She elbowed him, then held up her fingers.

Three.

Two.

One.

They leaped in unison, coming at the intruder from both sides. T'Vak's blade met flesh, and the victim's cry was cut short by Lumira's claws to his throat. They froze, listening, ensuring he was alone. When no more sounds came, she held the nevethium out to inspect the body. Blood poured from the wounds on his neck and stomach. T'Vak didn't recognize the body, but Lumira must have, for she stumbled back, cursing in her native tongue.

"Who is it?" T'Vak asked.

Lumira refused to look at the body. "A Daruk warrior and one of Chief Gibrund's primary advisors."

"Oh..." T'Vak tried to think of what Zavik or Konar would say in response. He wasn't known for his words of wisdom. "If he's made it this far, that means others might've escaped from Agaas, too. Where would the high chieftain go, if she made it out?"

"She made it out," Lumira snapped. "She'll head for a place where Onitus can retrieve her. All the Stormriders were told to meet up at the Igtheos refuge if things took a turn for the worse."

"Then to the coast we go." T'Vak wiped the blood from his blade. "Unless you want to head back into that."

The sound of Shieum fire filled the woods in response.

Lumira hissed, then sprinted west toward the coast. T'Vak followed, but not without pausing every few feet to glance behind him.

The woods, unlike the sand, were deceitful.

JAKKI

J akki shoved the other women to the ground as soon as the world went dark.

It wasn't a moment too soon, for the sound of shieum fire filled the air just as she secured Elaysia beneath her. They lay there, unmoving, the babes' cries drowned out by the fighting and screaming. When it lessened, and the wails of the babes increased, Jakki forced everyone to their feet and blindly stumbled forward, holding her staff out to intercept incoming branches. She'd summoned the parchment's magic and could easily find her way through the woods, even in the darkness. But there was no way everyone else could keep up.

"I have nevethium to light our way," Elaysia whispered—a measure of caution that was rendered futile by the babes' cries.

"They'll see us," Kahana protested.

Jakki shook her head—not that anyone could see it. "Bring it out, Ellie. We'll risk it if it means getting us closer to the refuge. But as soon as it's out, everyone move as quickly as you can. I'll take the lead. Kahana, the flank. Maseeya, give me the babe."

No one protested as the woods around them glowed into green focus. Elaysia had Elaron off Maseeya and strapped to Jakki in under a minute, then they ran swiftly through the clawing ferns. Even Maseeya held her own with the weight of the babe lifted from her shoulders.

Siren and Onitus glided above them, following their movements through the woods. Even though the stormbird could do little to aid her through the thick canopy of the trees, Jakki was comforted knowing she was near. And soon enough, not even the woods could hinder the bird's powers.

Can you see anything? Jakki asked, reaching for Siren's mind.

Warmth radiated through her body as Siren replied. *"We can see what the fires and crystals illuminate. The forest south of Agaas is aflame, and several of the living trees have fallen, creating an opening above Agaas. Would you like us to fly over and look for survivors?"*

Jakki shook her head, adjusting Elaron's wrap as she perched atop a log. *Don't risk it. We don't know what kind of weapons they have alongside the groundshakers. Can you and Onitus sense the others?*

"Shadow and Corvax have been out of reach since Xaren and Anahi left for Orillon. We saw Anadu carrying Keera to the nest island."

Good. At least six were accounted for. But...

What about Roth and Wind Chaser? Grokhion and Yerakai would've been patrolling when the fighting broke out.

A wave of uncertainty flooded Jakki's mind as Siren replied, *"We were helping Roth and Wind Chaser bring down the be-hemoth boulder-heavers on the battlefield. Onitus drew their attention while I dragged one to the sea. We haven't seen or heard from Roth since the darkness. Wind Chaser, too, has been distant, though I thought I sensed his presence near Agaas."*

Jakki glanced at Elaysia, thankful she couldn't perceive such clear thoughts from her bird. *Stay with us, Siren. We'll get everyone to shelter and decide what to do after.*

"I sense Onitus," Elaysia said as they slowed their pace ever so slightly. The sound of crashing waves competed with the distant shieum fire, signaling they were almost out of harm's way. "He's above us."

"And Siren," Jakki replied, hurrying ahead before Elaysia could inquire about the others.

Dawn pierced the darkness, lighting the woods with golden streaks. Jakki winced at the sudden intrusion, wishing it had held off just a bit longer. Whatever magic the Lawful Dominion had evoked had lost its hold, and she couldn't help but wonder if it was intentional. They would certainly have reached Agaas by now, and the light would make picking off survivors as easy as plucking wildflowers.

When they arrived at the refuge half an hour later, T'Vak and Lumira waited out front. They lowered their weapons upon recognizing who approached and ushered them inside. Before entering the refuge, Jakki cast a glance at the sky and counted three stormbird silhouettes.

Fly east, she told Siren. *Use caution, and stay well out of range, but see if you can spot Roth or Wind Chaser.*

The stormbird replied by breaking off from the group.

Inside, everyone had gathered around a long table. T'Vak stared off, Maseeya attended to the babes, and Kahana paced. Elaysia fussed over a wounded Lumira, who didn't look as though she wanted to be bothered with such attention. Only Konar acknowledged Jakki with a nod. She gave him one back, then eased her aching body onto the bench. There was no more denying it. The magic wore off faster with each use, and the pains it left in its stead increased in severity.

As Konar prepared tea and served them wild berries and fish, they pieced together what had transpired. The Lawful Dominion implanted spies long before the attack. They'd likely been waiting for such a moment and had only needed a tuross message to call them to action. While Elaysia's murder of Raynar probably forced their hand, it would've happened eventually, they assured her.

She didn't seem convinced.

Lumira described the boulder–launchers in great detail, to which Elaysia reminded her they'd seen something of the like when rescuing Kelsia. Just not quite as large, nor on fire. But when the beridian spoke of the Caman who'd blotted out the moons and stars, Konar's brow furrowed. He wasn't convinced summoning one was possible without a scroll, but T'Vak swore the rest of the discovered scrolls were in Az Zar, with Zavik.

This only made the ex-high elder more paranoid, and he ceased commenting on the alleged Caman.

When Lumira recounted her final moments of sight, right as a massive spear careened toward Roth, the room fell silent.

"But you didn't hear any shrieks or roars?" Maseeya offered, being the hopeful light she'd always been.

Lumira shook her head. "I think they got away. They must've."

"Grokhion knows to meet us here," Elaysia said, dread creeping into her voice. "Has anyone seen Yerakai or Wind Chaser? He was patrolling too, no?"

"I sent Siren to search over Agaas and the fields," Jakki said gently. "If they're there, she'll sense them. She'll bring them home."

"And what of my cousin?" Kahana asked in a rare display of emotion. She hadn't set her club down since entering the refuge, and Jakki didn't think she was going to anytime soon.

"He's safe," Lumira reassured her. "He's with Keera on the island where Elaysia found the eggs. Anadu brought them there, and I've since visited them myself with supplies. They're wounded, but I think Keera will be able to fly in a few days."

"We don't have a few days," Elaysia said through clenched teeth. "We'll be lucky to have one before this refuge is crawling with Lawful Dominion warriors."

Kahana frowned. "I thought they didn't know of this place?"

"They won't have to torture too many survivors to find out."

The ominous realization came from Konar. No one refuted him.

"We need to leave by nightfall," Jakki said, rising from the table. Her braid had come loose in the chaos of battle, and dried blood knotted her hair. "I'll start gathering supplies."

Elaysia blocked her from going upstairs. "We can't leave without looking for survivors."

"What survivors?" Jakki said, voice rising. With the rush of battle and the magic gone, she could no longer hold back the fear swirling inside her. "The Lawful Dominion will kill everyone they find. They've surrounded Agaas and cut through what remained of our warriors to do so. It's not worth risking our lives and the birds for a handful of stragglers."

Elaysia's eyes flashed with intensity. "It's always worth saving more lives."

They stood, gazes locked, fists clenched. Jakki tried to calm herself enough to reason with Elaysia.

She didn't get the chance.

The door to the refuge swung open. Jakki leaped for her staff—they'd forgotten to post someone on watch. But her weapon wasn't needed. In the doorway stood a bloodied Yerakai, holding a broken arm against his chest.

"Come," the Apáasutai said, ushering them with his good hand. "Grokhion is outside; I can't carry him in." He swallowed, chin dimpling. "I don't think he has long."

LUMIRA

L umira leaped from the bench and barreled past the others. She danced around the wounded Apáasutai, telling herself she could make it up to him later. All she saw, all she felt, were killer waves rising around her, their white foamed peaks ready to crash upon the one person who reminded her most of the father she'd lost all those years ago.

Not again, she prayed as she sprinted up the sandy path leading around the edge of the Igtheos refuge. Before she reached the cliff, where the stormbirds often perched, she heard the high-pitched, soft whistle of a bird. She knew it well, for she'd heard a similar sound emitted by Keera not an hour prior. But this... It sounded far weaker, less pained. Almost like mourning.

Lumira funneled all of her strength into the last stretch of her run. When she reached the top of the hill where the cliff jutted out over the sea, she skidded to a halt.

There, lying atop the shiny black rock, was Roth. His head was cocked at an odd angle, his fog-colored wings splayed and bloodied, his body motionless. The massive arrow was still lodged in his side. Anadu perched above him, her plumage raised to ward off would-be attackers, but Lumira could already sense the action's futility. There were no words in Anadu's mind, nothing to translate the utter rage and loss her stormbird felt. Lumira knew it all too well.

The tears came without warning. She blinked them back, sucking air into her tightening throat. The sound of footsteps echoed on the path behind her, but no one approached. She wanted to run back down the path, to not see what lay beneath the cover of Roth's broken wing. If she didn't look, then she didn't have to know. She could keep living her life in the liminal space between love and loss, refusing to acknowledge either as true.

But then he called her name. It was a garbled, weak sound, no more than a gruff whisper, but it was meant for her. And she came.

One of Grokhion's eyes was crusted shut and swollen twice beyond its usual size. A deep cut ran down the side of his face, splitting his orange fur and revealing the bloodied skin beneath. Another cut had gone all the way to the bone of his right arm. The skin around the wound had blackened, and Lumira felt a growl rumble in her throat. They'd used poisoned blades; moons knew what else. He could still recover, though, even if he had to lose the arm. He could still have a good life, he could—

Lumira's hopes died as her gaze trailed down his mid-section. He'd been shot at least half a dozen times from stomach to leg with shieum projectiles, and from the way he clutched at his ribs with his good hand, she knew they'd been shattered. Someone had applied a shoddy tourniquet to his left calf where his leg had been severed—no, it wasn't a clean cut; it was torn and jagged, with loose bits of bone and flesh protruding.

The groundshake weapons.

Lumira took Grokhion's unharmed cheek in her hand, fighting back the sobs as she reconciled the broken beridian before her with the great cat she'd come to idolize.

It can't be, she prayed again. *Please, not like this. Not a ghost of his true self.*

Grokhion's mouth opened, revealing blood-stained fangs. No words came out.

"It's alright," Lumira said in a voice that was far more pleading than soothing. "You're going to be alright. Konar is here. He knows medicine. And Yerakai." She snapped her head back, glaring at the others who lingered just out of reach. What were they doing? Giving her time alone to say goodbye? There would be no goodbyes if they could just fix him, just...

"Help him!" Lumira roared.

Yerakai hadn't come with the others, was likely nursing his own wounds inside. But Konar kneeled beside her, his face twisted into a frown.

Lumira gripped the nyrian's arm. "Can you save him?"

The violet eyes that met hers narrowed. "I don't know, Lumira. Your kind is strong, but his wounds are great."

He turned back to the others, taking Jakki and Elaysia aside. Lumira half-listened as he explained what plants to look for and sent them into the forest, then he directed Lumira, T'Vak, and Kahana to help him bring the great beridian inside. Even between the four of them, he was nearly impossible to carry. They paused three times on the way back to the refuge, and each time they set him down, more blood seeped from his wounds. By the time they got him inside, he was no longer conscious.

Or breathing.

A white heat seized Lumira. "Heal him!" she screamed at Konar, grabbing him by the front of his tunic and thrusting him against the table where Grokhion lay motionless. "Do it now, or I'll have your head!"

Kahana tried to pull Lumira back, but she shoved the Moákun against the wall. T'Vak looked on dumbly as Konar pressed his ear to Grokhion's chest. "Lumira..." He shook his head.

Lumira shook her own. "No." The room ebbed around her. She couldn't get air into her lungs, just as she hadn't been able to the day she learned she lost her papa. Her claws shot out on instinct, and she dropped to the floor, digging them in. She was a cub again. Frightened. Helpless. Weak.

Or was she?

The scrolls flashed through her mind. The ones Elaysia had decided against using. The ones she'd gone and used anyway, behind their backs.

Now, it was her turn.

"Where are the scrolls?" she said, leaping toward Konar, claws still extended. "There's one that can save him. A new one Zavik's backhander brought."

Konar's mouth hardened. "Lumira, I don't think it will work. It's just a parchment; just a copy of the writing from the original scroll. And even if it did, we have no idea what repercussions—"

"Exactly," Lumira hissed. "So let's find out. Blame me. I'll bear the weight of it all for him."

ZAVIK

"**Y**ikos!"

Zavik sat up, panting. He reached blindly for his seers, his body refusing to regulate until he'd untangled himself from the memory posing as a nightmare.

When he came fully to, he found himself surrounded by the hateful red walls of his new chambers. He wiped the stray tear from his cheek and curled into a fetal position on the bed, facing the hideous wall. A growl rumbled in his stomach, but he hardly noticed it. He'd lost track of time since they'd returned from the Caman Altars a week prior. With Yikos gone and the All-Sovereign having no further need of Zavik's services outside his heritage, he'd been moved from his old chambers and thrown into a room serving as a glorified cell.

It could've been worse. While there were no windows, it was warm and dry, furnished with a simple bed, chair, and table. He was fed three times a day and provided a fresh pot to do his business in with every meal. No one harassed him or beat him, and he'd even been offered moskuto on more than one occasion, which he'd promptly turned down. He had no need for it.

It also couldn't have been much worse. He hardly had space to stretch his legs and spent most of his days and nights lying in bed, glaring at the bright red walls. The lack of physical exertion would've been fine as a solitary issue, but combined with the fact he had nothing to do, it was all but unmanageable. He begged for something to read the first few days. Anything. Poetry, songs, some poorly written accounts of history. When that failed, he asked for scraps of parchment and a quill, that he might further his research or write his own story to entertain himself.

When his requests went unanswered, Zavik knew it was only a small taste of the fate that awaited him. He'd remain the All-Sovereign's pet, his little researcher that he brought out in times of great need. Then it would be back into the cage, like a good lad. And eat enough to stay alive, won't you?

Zavik had tried a hunger strike a few days back, but it didn't last long. One of the guards came in with a sinister smile and said how they'd hate to shove it down his throat, should he continue to misbehave. He hadn't liked the sound of it. Or the look in the guard's eyes.

The loss of Yikos was far worse than any punishment they could subject him to, anyway. When the shock of the discovery beneath the Altars wore off, all that was left was a dull ache. She'd been old, yes. A bit of an ass. Had said herself she'd lived a long enough life and was happy to leave it. But that didn't make it any better, didn't make the horrid way she'd perished any less brutal, didn't erase the rawness of her screams as she'd gone painfully into the night. She deserved better. The Lord Priestess could've used anyone for her ritual. Yikos, she'd...she'd been a reminder. A warning. For now, Zavik was untouchable, but that wouldn't stop them from using anyone to motivate him.

Or punish him.

And he was only alive until all the scrolls were recovered, anyway. Just a pile of sand slipping through the narrow neck of the glass, waiting to run its course. As were they all.

Zavik wasn't aware he'd fallen asleep again until the sound of a key turning in the lock made his eyelids flutter open. He didn't move from his fetal position atop the bed. It was probably mealtime. Or shit time. Shitty mealtime. He snorted to himself, undeniably amused at his own mental instability as the door opened, wafting in the cooler air of the hallway. It reeked of sweet incense, and the room stunk of it long after his food bearers departed.

"Five minutes," a gruff voice said.

The door latched closed.

Zavik's interest was piqued at this. They never spoke when they brought his meals. In fact, they'd gone out of their way to avoid making eye contact when he asked questions. Hence his sullen posture on the bed.

Still, he wasn't ready to give in so easily.

"Is this how you greet all your guests?" a nasal voice asked in Nyrinian.

Zavik tumbled out of the bed as he clumsily slid his seers on. Even without the Nyrinian—a telltale sign it was someone above the standard intelligence of the Zarith-speaking guards—he'd only heard one person who spoke with enough disdain to rival the All-Sovereign's.

"Dalgus!" Zavik said, then, realizing they were likely being listened to, added, "You impish miscreant. Have you come to hurl insults at me, too?"

The dwarf wrinkled his nose. "Charmed. No need for that, though. Kreeus is on duty. He's an idiot, but a trustworthy one. I would've come sooner, but they had him on sentry duty at the mines the past few days." He twisted his ruby pendant as he inspected Zavik's living conditions with a frown. "I trust you've been well taken care of."

"They murdered Yikos," Zavik said, the wound reopening as though it'd just happened. "I thought I could—"

Dalgus silenced Zavik with a waggle of his finger. "They were never going to let her live. She served her purpose long ago, preparing the way for you. I am sorry, though. She deserved better." For a moment, the dwarf almost appeared genuinely moved by the injustice. But then he rubbed his hands together as if washing them of the matter. "We don't have much time, so let's be done with the inflated speech, yes?"

Zavik gritted his teeth but managed a nod. He tried to remind himself that the dwarf had presented himself as his friend, perhaps the only one he had left in Cadar.

"Our hand has been forced on account of your underground discovery and the rebels' ill-timed attacks." Dalgus climbed onto the chair and leaned back in it as though he recounted a hard day's work to a friend. "I was hoping to move you under less uncertain circumstances, but we've no choice but to act immediately."

"Rebels?" Zavik asked, curiosity replacing some of his bitterness. "What rebels? What have they done?"

"Something foolish. I gave them tools to use at a specific date to free *you*, but they've gone and acted of their own accord. Left to me to clean up the mess, as always."

"I heard about the slaves freed from the mines, is that—"

"We don't have time for this!" Dalgus said, eyes widening. Zavik was so used to seeing them half open at most that the result was quite alarming. The dwarf's pupils were oval instead of round. "The mines, the rebels, they're all just aphids in the garden. Understand this."

"Sorry," Zavik mumbled, scooting further back on his bed.

"What matters is getting you and the scrolls out of here in one piece. Everything hinges on it."

"Everything?"

The vein on Dalgus's forehead throbbed. Zavik knew his voice sounded anything but convinced, but he no longer cared to put on an act, especially for a dwarf who was maybe his friend and maybe a fanatic. He no longer doubted the power of the scrolls, but they almost seemed minuscule when compared to the power he'd just helped unleash beneath the Caman Altars. Between the metal soldiers and the new vessels he'd helped design, there was little chance of resisting the future that the All-Sovereign—or rather, his Lord Priestess—had set into motion.

But there was still a chance to help Elaysia and at least some of the Neharem people. That had to count for something. He could still fight back for Yikos, for the world. Anything was better than playing dead until Az Zar no longer had use for him.

He sat upright in the bed and squared his shoulders. "Tell me what I need to do."

"There's a good lad," Dalgus said, his reddened face softening back to its milky tone. "Tonight. Be ready. The guards will come to switch out your meal, but it won't be your usual guards."

"Who—"

Dalgus made a hissing sound that raised the hairs on the back of Zavik's neck. He didn't interrupt again.

"You'll be given an officer's uniform and guided to the central part of the palace. From there, it will be up to you to secure entry to the arcanum." He must've noted the worry in Zavik's eyes, for he added, "Someone will be there to help you trigger the locks, but it is your responsibility to solve the puzzle."

Zavik wondered who that someone might be, though he didn't dare speak his concerns aloud.

A soft rapping sounded on the door. Dalgus shot it a glare as he slid down from the seat. "I doubt all three scrolls will be there as the Lord Priestess talked some sense into His Holiness as of late, advising they be stored separately. But seeing as how—thanks to you—they've wanted them kept close by for research, we hope at least one is inside."

We? Zavik wondered. Just how deep did the conspiracy against the empire run?

"Your life matters above all," Dalgus continued, hand hovering above the handle. "If there's nothing in the arcanum, so be it. Your guide will see you out of the palace through the catacombs that run beneath the city. The grand reopening of the arena tonight should provide ample distraction, along with something else I have planned. Still, you must leave Cadar with haste."

"I have special parchments hidden in my old chambers between the wall and my bed," Zavik said, suddenly remembering them. "Can you retrieve them? They might be of use."

"Fine." The handle creaked. "Tonight. Be—"

"But how will I stay in touch with you?" Zavik pressed, suddenly fearful of never seeing the dwarf again. "Do you have contacts in Neharem?"

Dalgus bared his teeth in a grimace. "I have contacts everywhere, but after tonight, I will cease to exist." Before Zavik could ask what he meant by that, the dwarf emitted a forced sigh, saying, "I'm afraid there will be no Neharem to return to. Not the Neharem you know, at least."

"But... I..." Zavik stammered, his mind concocting a slew of scenarios that rivaled his worst nightmares.

"You'll go north to the nazrath. It's long been believed your ancestor hid her most valued scroll up there: her own."

Zavik's mouth worked, but no words would come out.

"Oh hush," Dalgus said with a wave of his hand. The door opened, and he paused in the doorway, looking over Zavik as if he'd been given the stalest bit of bread but would make do to avoid starvation. "The fate of our world lies in no one person's hands, but you, unfortunately, hold more sway than most. Do well by it." The door latched behind him with a *click*.

And Zavik had never felt so alone.

DAVIER

A z Zar had achieved a great number of things since its foundation, the least of which wasn't its formidable prisons. From the island stronghold that had held Elaysia captive to the underground cells that locked him away for countless moon cycles, Davier thought he'd seen the worst of them.

He'd been wrong.

The holes in the ground encircling the outer edge of the arena were just that: holes. Deep, impossible to climb out of, and sealed with lyvium bars should its inhabitants somehow manage to scale the stone with bare hands. But holes all the same. The bars secured the prisoners while also letting in the elements, the creatures, and those who wished to taunt from above. Davier had been locked up for less than a week, and he'd already experienced bone-chilling rain, a bold skirvin (who'd died upon impact), and two streams of piss from juveniles looking for a thrill. The guards posted hadn't stopped them. They'd just as likely encouraged it.

He'd been given just enough water and day-old steamed kuba grain to stay alive, and he expected nothing more. He'd known the moment Xi faded from view that his second chance at life had ended, and despite his attempts to live better, he only felt worse. He'd never know the fate of his sister, never avenge his family. And though it mattered little, he'd never truly redeem himself.

"Davier?" Nan's voice was hoarse, but still audible. Just enough.

"I'm here," he replied, sinking against the wall.

There wasn't enough room to stretch his legs, so he drew his knees to his chest and shut his eyes in a vain attempt to block out the scorching sun beating down through the bars. From what he could tell, she was in the hole directly next to his. They'd spoken a few times, but it was hard to carry on any proper conversation with the yelling, especially when the soldiers on guard interfered. She'd been able to make contact with one of the twins in the hole next to hers, but beyond that, the chain was broken, the next occupant either dead or too injured to reply. Davier doubted many of the rebels survived the failed attack. They'd been expected. Somehow, the All–Sovereign was always one step ahead, everyone a player in his games.

And tonight was his grand finale.

"Who is she?" Nanjiya asked. "The woman you think of when we make love?"

Davier's breath caught in his throat. He was grateful she couldn't see his face. Despite his attempt to muster an excuse, none would come. He'd denied Elaysia's existence for so long. In the darkest times of his imprisonment, he'd nearly convinced himself she was nothing but a fever dream. But the thoughts of her never ceased to come. Memories of her touch, of the looks she'd given him. Of her kiss. It was deeper than desire, deeper even than love. It'd almost felt like destiny, though he wasn't certain he believed in such things. Still, something tethered his spirit to hers, despite their brief time spent together and the horrific way it'd ended.

And yes, each time he'd been with Nan, his thoughts had wandered to Elaysia.

"It's alright," Nanjiya said when the silence had gone on too long. It made Davier want to sink even lower. "Our stars weren't meant to align. At least we eased one another's pain." He could almost see her smile when she added, "I think, in another life, we might've been happy."

"Maybe next time," he replied, though there was little hope in his voice. He believed no more in a good life after death than he believed the All–Sovereign to be a real deity. "I'm sorry this happened, Nan. You don't deserve to die. None of you do."

Tears stained his cheeks. The real blessing would be if he didn't wake up the next morning. He couldn't bear the weight of any more lives brought down due to his actions. Everything he touched turned to poison. To dust.

He was, after all, a corrupted, little moth.

Once again, Nanjiya's voice was mercy itself. "I've been ready to die a long time. It will be a blessing to join my family, who've gone on before me." One of the guards called for her silence, but she paid them no mind. "They wait in the lands beyond this one, and they will reward me for my bravery." Her voice grew louder, shouting for anyone nearing the arena pavilion in anticipation of the games to hear. "My sorrow is for the ones who must remain after we're gone. The true punishment is theirs."

Nanjiya cried out in pain, and Davier leaped to his feet, fists balled at his sides. "Leave her alone! Nan, are you alright?" He waited for a response. "Nanjiya!"

Only silence greeted him.

Davier pounded on the wooden door to his cell until his arms gave out, then collapsed back against the wall. His head pounded, and his lips were rough and cracked when he ran his drying tongue over them.

Just a few more hours, he told himself. When they came to drag him to the arena, he wouldn't even fight. He'd just lie down and die, allowing whatever creature came first to trample him or tear him to shreds. He wouldn't give the All–Sovereign and the highborns the satisfaction of an entertaining death.

It would be his final stand.

The sun sank from its perch over his cell. When darkness began to dim the scrape marks on the wall, where countless other prisoners had tried to claw their way to escape in delusional desperation, someone jostled the sliding lock of his door. A gong sounded. The commotion of shoes slapping against stone took over as the ringing faded. The crowds were gathering.

It was almost time.

The lock slid out, and the door swung open, revealing another nameless, faceless soldier. Given the new drafting laws, Davier estimated at least one in six people in Az Zar now served in the empire's proliferating legion. Worse still, over half were likely enslaved or indentured servants. But soon enough, none of it would matter. Not to him, at least.

He didn't fight as the soldiers marched him down halls lined with stone the same reddish brown as the Tsabian Desert, past countless other cells that looked identical to the one he'd been in. He didn't protest as he was shoved into a horde of rebels and slaves at a gated entrance to the arena, even though he recognized over half of their faces. He didn't even shed a single tear when he found Nan, and she took his filthy hand in hers, pulling him close and planting a kiss with her rough lips.

"For luck?" he asked, when she pulled away.

"To send you off well," she replied.

Still, Davier held it together, determined to let whatever unfolded glance off him like sunlight on a snowbank.

But when another soldier approached, a small body thrashing behind him, Davier's stomach clenched.

When the soldier said, "One more for the arena," his throat tightened.

And when they pulled the hood off, revealing a terrified Xi, he roared.

ZAVIK

Something must have gone wrong.

Zavik stared at the ceiling, hands twitching nervously at his side as he went over the calculations in his head. Aside from speculating about the code to the puzzle mechanism barring entrance to the arcanum, he'd nothing better to do than count down the hours since Dalgus's departure. Even if he'd overshot his estimates, a minimum of seven hours had transpired, making it at least one hour past when his final meal of the day should've been served. Due to the windowless room, he had no other way to track the passage of time, but he trusted his instincts. Something was wrong. Or...

He'd gone crazy. Had he imagined the whole conversation with Dalgus? Had he imagined Dalgus? He'd been closed off from the outside world an awful lot the past few moon cycles. Maybe with the loss of Yikos, it'd finally proven too much too—

The lock on the door came alive with a *click*.

Zavik sprang out of bed, wearing nothing but a loincloth. He thought it would make it easier to change into the uniform, but the sudden thought of the whole thing being a delusion he created nagged at the back of his mind. He glanced at his tunic folded at the foot of the bed and reached for it, just in case.

The door swung open before he could secure the protective fabric.

A soldier stood in the doorway. High ranking by the look of his badges—though Zavik wasn't exactly knowledgeable of such things. Luminescent teal eyes flicked over his body with a mixture of shock and irritation.

"What kind of services have you been providing His Holiness, exactly?" the soldier asked, tossing a uniform to Zavik.

"Ah, none of that," Zavik stammered, catching the clothes in mid-air so he could drape them over his body. "I just thought I'd be ready. Dalgus said there wouldn't be a lot of time, so—"

"Who?" the soldier asked, his teal eyes narrowing as he handed over two sleek Az Zarian swords.

Realization washed over Zavik like cool rain. The dwarf's involvement was not to be discussed. Not even in the presence of allies.

Brilliant, Zav. Just brilliant.

"Uh, no one. Nothing." Zavik pulled on the uniform, surprised to find it fit him perfectly. The mask would take some getting used to, but he liked the anonymity it provided, especially given he'd had so little of it lately. The swords, however, weighed him down, and he wasn't certain he could even draw them if his life depended on it.

"How do I look?" he asked when he'd finished dressing.

The soldier cocked his head and gave a brief shrug. "With luck, half the city will be too drunk to notice. The All-Sovereign is sloshing up everyone up for free so they're less apprehensive about the arena reopening. Here." He reached into a small bag and retrieved a shieum. It was smaller than the ones Zavik had seen, and he realized, belatedly, it was modified with his and Yikos's suggestions.

He shook his head. "I don't want that. I don't even know how to use one."

"I doubt that, seeing as how you helped design it." When Zavik refused to take it, the soldier shoved it into his hands. "This is no time for moral stances, my friend. An officer of your rank carries one of these now alongside his blades. Besides, it might prove itself useful yet."

Zavik awkwardly slipped the shieum into the holder on his belt that appeared to be custom made for it. He started for the door, but the soldier held up his gloved hand, blocking his escape.

"Once we leave here, we don't speak a word unless it is dire. Are we clear?"

Zavik nodded to prove he understood. He could be a man of few words when it was required of him, which—thank Quinaria—wasn't often.

He followed the nameless, supposedly friendly soldier out of his prison and down a hallway that was fairly barren compared to some of the palace corridors he'd seen. He got the feeling they were up rather high, a suspicion that was confirmed when the soldier released a secret panel in the wall and brought them down several flights of cobweb-ridden stairs. When they emerged into an incense-laden hallway, he was surprised to find they were only a few twists and turns from the arcanum entrance.

Zavik braced himself for interference. Every time he'd been escorted to the arcanum, he'd gone past at least three different pairs of guards leading to the sealed door. There was no way around them. No secret entrance, no back door. But when they approached the place where the first pair normally waited, at the start of the long, stone hallway, there was no one there.

He desperately wanted to ask the soldier where they were, or if he was even aware there was normally someone standing sentry there—if they were walking into a trap—but he held true to his promise and remained silent. It was a good thing, too, for when they reached the spot where the second pair usually waited, and found guards actually there, they exchanged nods with Zavik's escort and waved them through.

Probably being disposed of, Zavik considered, then decided he didn't want to linger on such thoughts.

The final pair of guards, the ones usually posted right outside the arcanum, were also missing. Zavik took no time to assess their fates and immediately set to work on the puzzled door.

It was a mechanism comprised of interlocking rings, each one capable of fully rotating both ways.

"Make sure you're certain before we activate the lock," his soldier escort whispered. "The wrong combination triggers a release of toxic gas."

"I'm sorry, a what?" Zavik said, shirking away from the puzzle.

"That's what they say." The soldier shrugged. "They replace the guards with knowledge of the puzzle every fortnight. His Holiness doesn't like loose ends."

"Lovely." Zavik took a step back, studying the rings. There were four of them in all, each with all the phases of the moons. It couldn't be so simple as their regular cycles. It had to be—

"I'd hurry if I were you," the soldier said, with no shortage of gruffness. "The games are about to start, and I've heard what His Holiness has waiting for the rebels. They won't last long."

Zavik gritted his teeth. "If I could have some silence?"

"Right. Sorry."

The rings glared back at Zavik, daring him to misalign them. There were countless patterns and important dates they could point to. A time of year, an important holiday, an ancient religion. But why the four? Some in Neharem believed there'd once been four moons, but that wasn't common in Az Zar.

Unless one of them *wasn't* a moon.

The sun? What was it Yikos had always gone on about when she'd had too much wine? Her prized research? It was the ascending—no, the tri-ascending—no, the...

"The Trimoon Ascendance," Zavik blurted.

The soldier raised an eyebrow.

"It's a phenomenon where all three moons align in a specific configuration relative to each other and to the sun. It allegedly only occurs once every thousand years, but of course, no one alive can confirm that." Well, Konar could. And the All-Sovereign. But never mind that. "If I'm right, and we align the moons as such"—he slid the rings into alignment so the full phases perfectly overlapped one another—"then it should..." He stepped back, satisfied with his work. "Do you have the keys?"

The soldier retrieved them from his bag, handing one of the talon-shaped tools to Zavik.

"On three," Zavik said, sliding the talons into the keyholes. "One. Two. Three."

The mechanism shifted.

And the door groaned open.

Only one scroll was hidden in the secret compartment located beneath the floor of the arcanum, but it was enough. Zavik tucked it under his arm as discreetly as he could manage, not even bothering to peek at which one was hidden beneath the generic lyvium case. He did stop on his way out, however, to snatch a few more of his older plans. Not being complete, they had been overlooked.

But he could still make use of them.

"Hurry up, then," the soldier whispered. He shifted anxiously in the doorway, hand on his shieum.

Zavik joined him in the hallway, and together they sealed the door and hurried away from the arcanum. Once back inside the safety of the hidden passageway, the soldier slowed his pace, leading them up crumbling staircases and around sharp corners until they reached a dead end.

"This is where we part ways," the man said in a gruff voice as he gave Zavik the bag slung over his shoulder. "Inside, you'll find a partial map of the catacombs running beneath the city, as well as the parchments you requested." He pushed one of the stones in the wall, and it gave, sliding open to reveal a courtyard illuminated by the moonlight and nevethium-flecked pathways.

"Thank you," Zavik said, slipping the scroll inside the bag. It clinked against something, and Zavik's brow furrowed as he retrieved three cylindrical tubes holding a dark liquid.

The soldier gestured to the tubes. "Oh, those are in case you run into trouble. Something Yikos was working on before you got here, to elevate the groundshakers."

Zavik gingerly placed the vials back inside the bag. "What do they do?"

"Make groundshakes? Make fires? Maybe both?" The soldier shrugged and shoved Zavik into the courtyard. "They don't tell me everything. Just throw it if you're in trouble and get far away. I'm sorry I can't go with you," he added, almost remorsefully. "I'm needed here. We'd arranged for an ex-soldier to escort you from Cadar, but he was compromised."

"An ex-soldier?" Zavik asked, a name rising from the depths of his mind. But it couldn't be. He was dead.

The panel began to slide closed, but before it secured, the soldier said, "Zadel. Davier San Zadel. Used to be one of His Holiness's favorites, but I wager he's already bleeding out in the arena."

The door became a wall.

Zavik pulled out the map and saw a catacomb entrance was only a few blocks away from his current position. From there, it was easy enough to escape the city. But the arena wasn't far. He could hear the roars of the crowds and the beating of the drums. He swallowed, body angling toward escape while his heart pulled him further into the city.

He didn't owe Davier anything. Like the soldier said, he was probably already dead. But he owed it to Elaysia to know for certain.

And he owed it to Yikos to disrupt the All-Sovereign's games.

DAVIER

Davier's heart was regulated only by the drums. Without their steady, haunting beat, it surely would've rammed itself clean out of his chest.

Or stopped beating altogether.

He lurched toward the soldiers. His fist connected with the jaw of the one holding Xi, resulting in a satisfying crack. The others were on him before he could get another hit in. One seized a thick chunk of his hair, snapping his head back and slamming him against the stone. Kicks rained down from all angles. His stomach. Ribs. Arms and legs. Not wanting to lose clarity right before the fight for his life—for Xi's life—he protected his head. When the soldier in charge called the others off, he rose, bloodied and in pain, but more alive than he'd felt in days.

"Xi?" he croaked, peering through the crowd of dirty rebels and half-starved slaves.

A waifish figure with golden hair slipped between two large men. Her silver eyes widened as she approached, and she stopped a few feet away, as if in disbelief. "Davier?"

Davier's arms worked faster than his words. He scooped the girl up, holding her in an embrace stronger than lyvium. She stiffened at first, then melted into his touch, tiny hands wrapping around his neck.

"She said they killed you," Xi whispered.

Davier could feel the gazes of everyone gathered, along with their silence. He didn't care. "They've certainly tried. And they would've succeeded, had they not given me the thing I needed to survive."

"What's that?"

A warm laugh tickled his throat as tears welled in his eyes. "You, Xianna. You."

She pulled back enough to study his face, and for the first time in almost two years, he got a good look at her. A little older, a little larger, and certainly much wiser. But she was the same defiant little girl with wild eyes. He almost wished he believed in the gods so he could thank them for protecting her innocence.

"Hello, Xi," Nanjiya said, approaching with a half-smile. "Davier's told me much about you."

The girl's eyes lit up, but before she could open her mouth to reply, the gates began to rise. Something that sounded eerily like the chanting from Mavist temples rippled through the arena, and the drums quickened in response. Davier gripped Xi tighter. He didn't want to set her down ever again, but he'd have to if they stood a chance at survival. More soldiers filed in behind them, ushering them into the arena with the sharp points of their spears.

Davier walked boldly into the night. While most of the others followed suit, a few desperate individuals began to shriek and wail, some even collapsing to the ground or trying to find a weakness in the spear wall. Their defiance gave them an early death by spear, and though what waited within likely would prove to be a far worse death, the sight and sounds of the fallen broke everyone into a run.

"Wait along the walls until the gong sounds!" a soldier shouted after them.

As the gate lowered behind them, its rusty creaks counting down the moments until the bloodbath, Davier took in the surroundings. Despite the darkness, the moons shone brightly, and chunks of nevethium illuminated the areas their cool light couldn't penetrate. The crystals were infused throughout the arena, creating an eerie battlefield of shadow and light. It was, in itself, a spectacle.

The arena had been closed for centuries—maybe well over a millennium, for all Davier knew—but the All-Sovereign must've been planning to reopen it for a while. Sections of the walls and seating had been refurbished and strengthened, and Davier was fairly certain the central platform was a recent addition, as were the randomly placed platforms and towers scattered throughout the arena. The platform almost looked promising. Sitting about two spear lengths from the ground and piled with weapons, its only deterrent was the four sandcats staked to poles with tethers running the length of the surface. Davier made quick note of the other gates, the most obvious being the one nestled inside the mouth of a giant stone deathstalker with nevethium eyes. Similar, albeit smaller, gates were placed every twenty feet or so after that.

They'd all yet to be opened.

The gate thudded shut behind them, and the drums and chanting fell silent. Davier scoured the spectator seating for any weakness. The walls ran at least forty feet high to the lowest levels, and none of the makeshift towers and platforms came close enough to assist with escape. He kissed the top of Xi's head, then looked to Nan, who'd joined up with the twins, Lox and Kymerius.

"One last drill, eh?" his fellow ex-soldier said, stern face overcompensating for the fear he likely felt.

Davier offered a weak smile. "They never could get enough of those in."

"I'm going for the weapons," Nan said, clenching her fists.

Lox's thick fingers gripped her arm. "That's a death sentence."

Nan's dark eyes flashed. "Staying weaponless is a death sentence."

"She's right," Davier said, setting Xi down. He lifted her chin tenderly. "I'm going to get us out of here, alright? I need you to stay right next to me and do everything I tell you. Can you promise me that?"

Xi's lip quivered, but she nodded, straightening.

"I don't think any of us are making it out of here," Kymerius said with a frown. "But I'll fight like there's a chance. Better than waiting to die with my head in my hands." He strode toward a spectator section that was set apart from the rest, its walls higher, its gem-laden roof jutting out like a shroud. "You hear that, you sick old fuck of a ruler?"

"Kymerius," Nan hissed, gaze darting from him to the gate behind them, but he kept walking, flinging insults like rocks.

"Brought this back to entertain the people, did you? Anything to keep them distracted from the utter misery you've created for them."

Davier wanted to pull him back, or better, to join him. But he had Xi to think about. He lowered his gaze instead, showing he was a compliant participant.

"But it's also to remind them, isn't it? To flex your power? Today, it's us pesky rebels. But tomorrow…" Kymerius laughed wildly, pointing toward the crowds in a grand swooping motion. "Tomorrow, it's whoever pisses him off. Or thinks too loud. Or doesn't hand over half their aspar to the temples and all their baby boys to the capital. You're fools. You're all big fuc—"

An arrow pierced Kymerius's skull. He dropped to his knees, then fell over, eyes wide, mouth still parted in a bloody smile.

Xi let out a little gasp, and Davier pressed her face into his tunic. He ignored the sensations stirring in his stomach and activated what remained of his training.

Survival.

There were fifty or so rebels, slaves, and criminals in the arena. If he and Xi kept their heads down, they stood a chance. He just needed to wait for one of the gates to open, then slip inside after the beast it held was out but before it went down. If he was armed, he stood a chance at fighting his way through the guards. It was a small chance, but it was the only one he had. He couldn't take the others, but he hoped they'd understand. Want it, even.

Nan would never agree to leaving the others, though.

He caught her gaze, trying to say goodbye with a look, to convey how much he'd cared for her, that things could've been different, but really, she deserved better, she—

The deep ring of the gong echoed through the arena.

Nan was off before he could stop her, racing toward the platform and the sandcats that guarded it. About a third of the combatants followed her, the rest scampering up the platforms or crumpling into sobbing heaps on the ground.

Davier needed a weapon. He didn't want Xi near the sandcats, though, nor so exposed. But if they worked together...

"Run," Davier shouted, jerking her toward the platform, and not a moment too soon, for a gate nearby slowly creaked open. "And don't look back."

The spectators shrieked as whatever had been locked behind emerged, triggering screams of anguish for the unfortunate souls caught in its path. Davier kept his gaze on the prize, watching with anticipation as Nan reached the platform first. She waited until one of the twins caught up with her, then motioned for them to give her a boost. Davier's breathing grew shallow as Nan slipped onto the ledge, snatching the sword and spear closest to her. By the time the sandcats caught wind of her, she was leaping down, just out of reach of their swiping claws. When the next pair tried, some rebels Davier recognized but couldn't name, the sandcats were ready.

The one meant to retrieve the weapons fell off the platform, clutching her neck. She didn't get up again.

Davier and Xi were twenty feet from the platform when a bellow filled the arena. He dared a glance over his shoulder and saw a massive hairy beast standing roughly as tall as the platform. It charged on all fours, propelling its elongated and stocky frame toward a cluster of cowering slaves. It would've been formidable in size alone, but the sharp horn protruding from its leathery face was nearly as tall as Davier.

Xi screamed, and Davier's gaze darted back to the platform where the sandcats were making quick work of a brawny man who'd managed to secure three weapons. He dropped them over the side for an eager duo of rebels as more screams arose from the giant horned beast's latest trampling. It bellowed into the night, then propelled itself toward another cluster of rebels.

Davier's mind raced with his gaze as it darted about the arena. He located a treacherous-looking tower that was impossible for the average person to scale alone, then dragged Xi to it. She protested as he climbed up with her, shoving her onto the top, a narrow space only just wide enough for her to crouch.

"Don't leave me!" she screamed.

"Don't move!" he yelled back, making for the weapons.

An idea formed as he ran, one that involved fighting his way to the platform, retrieving a pair of swords, then perching on a tower near Xi's while he waited for the next gate to open. When he reached the platform, however, there was no one left to give him a boost. He leaped toward the top in vain, only earning himself a snarl from a sandcat. Before he could figure something else out, the horned beast charged toward him on thundering feet. He rolled out of the way as it rammed into the side of the platform, enraging the already agitated sandcats.

The platform cracked.

A roar erupted from the crowd, one mixed with cheers and horrified screams. It gave Davier hope. At least some refused to enjoy the All-Sovereign's game.

Davier was about to retreat when he noticed an ax lying on the ground, likely knocked down during the impact. He scrambled toward it. The ax wasn't his weapon of choice, but what choice did he have? The horned beast shook its head as if stunned, then charged toward one of the smaller towers. It was far from the one he'd nestled Xi in, but it meant she was no longer safe. He scrambled back to her, trying to locate Nan as he ran.

He wasn't ready when two more gates groaned open at once. He cocked his head toward the furthest one, wincing as half a dozen deathstalkers crawled into the arena. Their wings had been removed, rendering them flightless, but no less deadly. The sharp barbs on their legs would still allow them to climb, and their poison-tipped stingers would still kill with a single strike. Davier pushed harder against the cramps in his sides.

Xi's tower was only a spear's throw away when the occupants of the second gate were ushered into the arena, stopping

Davier mid-stride. It was a horde of sickly children cowering together in a giant pack. He could've kept with his plan, and would've, had he not recognized a child in the front. The only one standing defiant with his fist raised high.

It was the boy he'd rescued from the mines.

ZAVIK

Zavik considered using the catacombs to approach the arena, but the city was all but dead because of the games. He raced down the empty streets, gaze sweeping the ornate architecture, the gilded gables, the bright red roofs with curved edges. The air smelled of blossoms mixed with salty ocean air, and he understood at once why Cadar was such a prized city.

Or rather, why it once had been.

For all the city's beauty, it was tainted by banners on nearly every building, some Mavist propaganda, others long parchments plastered with new rules and regulations. *Meat rations restricted to three times a week,* one said. *All nevethium must now be reported to the authorities,* said another. From what Zavik could tell, he was in one of the nicer districts. He could only imagine what the others looked like—or worse, what had become of those living outside Cadar altogether.

The arena was a massive structure at the edge of the district. Its deep-red stone walls towered above the other buildings, nearly rivaling the height of the palace. Two giant deathstalker statues stood at attention at the gated entrance, which was wide enough for whole crowds to pass through at once. Their nevethium eyes peered down at him, and he tried not to imagine meeting the creatures they were modeled after. Reflective panels directed moonlight into the dome and illuminated the sides of the arena in a ghostly glow. It didn't help Zavik's nerves that there were ominous beings carved directly into the walls, nor did the fact that they looked unnervingly similar to the Caman that had appeared the day they awakened the metal giants.

Few guards remained on post as he slipped through the gates, and the ones still adhering to their duties didn't pay any mind to another soldier vying for a look at the games within. Merchant stalls lined the path inside leading to one of the balcony-seating entrances. Most had been abandoned, but one man beckoned Zavik closer, promising a little kuba wine would make the massacres far more enjoyable. This was accented with a particularly shrill scream coming from the arena, a noise that chilled Zavik to his core. He ignored the merchant and walked beneath the archway separating the covered part of the building from the open arena seating. No one seemed to notice as he inched his way closer to the railing, dodging sloshing drinks and fist-pumping soldiers, clutching the bag closer and closer to his chest. He wouldn't have a repeat of what happened in Amiren.

Zavik peered over the balcony and found it surprisingly well-lit despite the hour. The reflective devices provided ample moonlight, and the glow of nevethium further transmuted the shadows, creating a vivid show of color amongst the actual spectacle. Any awe he held, however, vanished as a large northern beast collided with one of the towers scattered about the arena, knocking a contestant from a significant height before trampling them underfoot. Zavik dropped a secondary lens down over his seers, allowing him to see better than the average human. He searched the arena for Davier, wondering if he'd even recognize him among the other contestants scattered about.

A cry sounded at the far end, and Zavik squinted, pinpointing a figure rushing toward what looked like a handful of human-sized insects with thrashing stingers. They were identical to the statues posted at the arena entrance, save for the wings, which had been removed. Zavik looked on with horror as the deathstalkers fell on a gaggle of small bodies that could've only been children, shutting his eyes as their screams filled the arena. Even the surrounding spectators quieted in response. The lone figure reached the deathstalkers and began hacking at them with an ax, skillfully dodging their stingers and amputating their limbs one by one. A thick fluid oozed out and piled around their bodies, and several people cheered as the hero cut through one of the insects before it slaughtered another handful of children.

Across the arena, some of the other contestants were taunting the great northern beast, leading it to the large central platform where a handful of sandcats were tethered. Zavik's heart raced as a woman climbed atop, boosted by another, and began to slice the ropes tethering the sandcats to the platform. She danced away, freeing one after another, and when they gained on her, she leaped down, landing in the arms of another contestant. The northern horned beast rammed the platform, and the cats rained down on it, sinking their sharp fangs into its flesh.

Clever, Zavik thought, redirecting his attention to the children's champion dueling the deathstalkers. The victor had successfully slain all the bugs, and though over two-thirds of the children lay strewn in the sand, he stood on guard in front of those remaining. He snatched a fallen spear and launched it toward the large, covered balcony positioned above one of the gates. It penetrated the netting and pierced a guard, who fell back into a shrieking pile of highborns. A silver nyrian rose from his seat in the shadows, coming to stand at the edge of the balcony. He raised his hand as if motioning for something, then dropped the spear back into the arena.

The gong sounded.

As the victor sprinted to retrieve the spear, Zavik got a better look at him. His stomach twisted even as his heart rejoiced, for there was no mistaking the figure now.

Davier.

One of the gates groaned open, and Zavik held his breath, waiting to see what beast would emerge. But it wasn't a beast at all. It was a monster.

A monster of his making.

Zavik gripped the railing as a dozen metal soldiers marched into the arena. Some spectators shrieked with horror, pointing and grabbing each other's clothes, while others praised Mavet and the All-Sovereign for their miracle. There was no praising within the arena, only screams and shouts as what remained of the contestants scurried to high ground, most congregating on the central, cracked platform. Davier shoved the children away from the metal soldiers, head snapping this way and that. Zavik could practically taste his despair. Despite his best efforts, their lives were soon to be lost. They all were. No height would protect them from the metal soldiers' weapons. Zavik hadn't yet seen them in action, but from what he'd assessed, they carried no ordinary projectiles.

The metal soldiers were shaky at first, almost like toddlers learning to walk. But then they picked up speed, breaking into something that resembled a jog. One raised its arm, taking aim at an older contestant who hadn't been able to keep up with the rest. A burst of yellow-green shot from its arm.

The contestant dropped dead, smoke rising from his body.

The arena became a blur of bodies, making it hard for Zavik to track Davier through the chaos. He clutched the bag tighter to his chest, registering the hard outline of one of the vials. It was his only chance. Blood of Elize or not, he was still mortal, but he believed she'd want him to be brave now, even at the cost of his own life.

Zavik snatched a long scarf from a nearby observer who hardly noticed its disappearance. He tied it around one of the decorative mini spires adorning the railing, then gave it a tug. It wouldn't get him all the way down, but it would have to do.

"For you, Yikos," Zavik whispered.

Then he dropped into the arena.

DAVIER

The boy's hand was slick in Davier's as he dragged him toward the tower holding Xi. He was distantly aware of a storm of feelings brewing beneath his exertion, but he didn't have the capacity to bear the weight of the burden at present. Defeating the deathstalkers had depleted most of his strength, and it took all his focus just to will his legs forward, still dragging the boy toward his sister. He didn't know what sorcery had made the metal monsters marching behind him, nor did he want to find out. A burst of yellow green glanced off the wall beside him, and he looked over his shoulder to find a freshly collapsed body, smoke rising from it as though it'd been burned.

"Faster," he shouted, jerking the boy's arm. He wasn't even certain why he felt any need to protect the boy—not with Xi to worry about. But as he scooped the boy up and forced his bare feet through the sand, he knew why. The boy was him. The boy was Xi. The boy was everything wrong with Az Zar wrapped into a tiny, malnourished flesh package of brittle bones, and he'd be damned if he stood idly by.

Xi leaped into Davier's arms as soon as he reached the tower, forcing him to momentarily drop the boy. The three of them stood there, breathless, stunned as rabbits before wolves. They were further away from the metal monsters than the rest, and some of the rebels had even taken to fighting the intruders, but it wouldn't last long. Their weapons appeared to do little to the monsters' lyvium exteriors, and one by one the contestants dropped to the sand, their bodies smoke signals in the night.

Nan glanced Davier's way as she headed into the fray. She raised her hand to him, and he lifted his chin in response. He wanted to beg her to come to him, to not waste her life so frivolously. But who was he to say her life had been wasted? She'd started a rebellion and made her stand against the empire. Davier could live a thousand lives and never be so worthy.

It didn't make it any easier to process the hole in her head as she crumpled beside the metal monster that'd ended her life.

Davier looked away, despair burning his eyes as he buried Xi's and the boy's faces into his chest. He searched for a way to comfort them in the face of their looming deaths. To comfort himself. There would be no more opening gates, no more chances for escape. He raised his ax, jaw set as the metal monsters made their way toward him. In the corner of his eye, he caught sight of a soldier stumbling toward him.

A soldier?

Davier blinked the grit and sweat from his eyes to rid himself of the illusion. Only the soldier had drawn closer, was pulling something out of a bag, motioning for him to get down. Davier dropped to the ground, taking the children with him, just as a groundshake rattled the arena.

Whatever the soldier used hadn't been the standard groundshakers pilfered by the rebels. In the aftermath, black flames rose from the ground, licking the sky and spreading to nearby structures. Spectators on the balconies began to scream, at least from what Davier could make out. It was hard to hear much through the ringing in his ears. Xi and the boy grabbed at his tunic, and he pulled them up, dragging them away from the flames.

The soldier emerged from the smoke like an angel, motioning Davier to follow him.

Having no choice but to trust him, Davier did as commanded, following the soldier to the gate the horned beast had emerged from. The soldier pulled something else from his bag and hurled it at the gate. This time, the impact not only shattered the gate, it rattled the very structure of the arena. The stone wall began to crumble, bringing down a large section of seating. Someone grabbed Davier's arm, and he looked up from his daze to find the soldier pulling him toward the smoldering rubble of the gate. The destruction had extinguished some of the flames, but those that survived grew in intensity.

They crawled over the smoking stone just as the black fire engulfed the opening behind them. More cries filled Davier's ears as he and the soldier dragged the children down the empty hallways and up the stairs leading to the common entrance. A guard emerged from around a corner, but Davier's soldier escort fired a shieum, dropping him like a bird. He peeled the guard's mask off and handed it and the shieum to Davier.

"Put this on," the soldier hissed. "It won't fool people for more than a few seconds, but that time could be the difference between life and death."

Davier recognized the voice, but he couldn't place from where. Another ex-soldier? It was the only thing that made sense, but—

Xi screamed as more guards rounded the corner.

Davier and his soldier escort fought their way through in a blur. The soldier was clearly inexperienced, but he got in a few impressive shots. Davier didn't like the feel of the new weapon and quickly tossed it aside in favor of one of the fallen soldier's swords.

A dozen bodies and a few minutes later, the quartet found themselves in the courtyard outside the arena, temporarily hidden in a sea of civilians and soldiers fleeing the smoldering arena.

The soldier motioned Davier to follow him down an alleyway. He tried to get the soldiers' attention to tell him about the secret passages beneath the city, but when he finally caught up, he realized that was exactly where they were headed.

He must be a rebel, Davier thought as the soldier struggled to lift the grate.

They maintained silence as they worked their way through the catacombs and waste tunnels. The soldier, clearly more knowledgeable regarding the routes than Davier, led them down several new pathways, ultimately leading them to a gate that smelled of salt and sea. The sight and sound of the ocean nearly brought tears to Davier's eyes. They stood a chance. He, Xi, and the boy finally stood a chance.

"Who are you?" Davier asked the soldier, voice cracking. "I owe you a thousand life debts, my friend."

"I don't want you owing me anything," the familiar voice said. "I still don't trust you." The soldier pulled off his mask, revealing a mess of red curls.

Davier stared in disbelief. Memories rushed back of the Az Zarian boy born in Orillon, yet who called Neharem home. The one clearly taken with Elaysia. The scholar. The skeptic. The one who'd first smelled Davier's deceit.

The one who'd probably been told every horrid thing he'd done.

"Zavik?" he said shakily. "How are you here? How did you, how could you…"

"No time," Zavik said sharply. "We need to get north as quickly as possible, and you're going to help me get there."

All Davier's bottled-up emotions threatened to burst, but he couldn't let them out. Not yet. They had to get far away from the city, then farther still. But he needed to know one thing first, especially if Zavik was here instead of there.

"Elaysia. How is she?"

Zavik frowned. "I don't know for certain. But if you want to see her or your children ever again, you better fix that lip tremble and fall back on whatever soldier spirit still resides within you."

Davier choked back a sob. "Children."

The dreams were real then, at least in part. Once more, Davier felt his life torn at the seams, ripped away to make room for something—for someone—new.

And this time, this version of himself, he let the tears fall.

KONAR

I t was wrong.

There was no doubt in Konar's mind. Even if the ritual worked, the state Grokhion returned in would likely not be the one they'd come to know and love. And when the ritual didn't work, because it wouldn't, because they didn't have the scroll the ritual originated from, the Stormriders would have to process his death all over again, convinced as they were that he wasn't lost. It was foolish, unnecessarily painful, and time-consuming.

But there was no dissuading Lumira—or several of the other Stormriders, for that matter. Yerakai had been the most vocal opposition, but he was hardly in any condition to put up much of a fight about it. And while Mardus didn't seem overly pleased, he offered little resistance beyond disapproving, dark glares. Xaren and Anahi likely would've protested, but they weren't around to have their say, leaving Jakki, Lumira, and Elaysia to make the final decision.

Konar didn't think there was a more dangerous trio.

They'd gathered on the small island Elaysia had discovered the eggs on, all in agreement the Igtheos refuge wouldn't remain safe for long. Their two scouting flights over the mainland had proven fruitless anyway. Konar doubted there were many survivors, and the few that might've escaped the siege of Agaas likely didn't know the refuge existed. They'd scatter, seeking sanctuary in the solace of the north or in the anonymity of Orillon. Once a plan had been settled on, there was a chance the Stormriders might locate a few on the way to their new destinations, but what then? Take them where, exactly? Whoever remained was better off without their company, in Konar's humble opinion. Besides, Elaysia and her band of loyalists could do with less weight. The journey ahead would not be an easy one.

The sound of footsteps pulled Konar out of his musings, and he looked over his shoulder to find Jakki emerging from the scraggly conifers clustered on the island. She wore a hybrid outfit with elements of island flair, such as the vibrant silk sashes, but she was predominately clothed in the leathers and furs of the north. Despite her southern heritage, it suited her. She looked at him with a firm jaw, and though he could see her throat working, no sounds came out.

He replied with a single nod, then drew his legs back in from over the cliff edge. The air rolling off the ocean at sunset was chilling, but if not for the telltale bumps on his forearms, he wouldn't have known it. Already, he'd slipped into the state that consumed him prior to a ritual. It was as if nothing else mattered. Nothing ever had, and nothing ever would.

T'Vak pulled himself back from the cliff as well. He'd given Konar the space he required, but always kept him within earshot, if not within eyesight. To the backhander's credit, he'd managed to remain sober since the attack. That was likely because alcohol wasn't readily available, but still.

"You want this?" T'Vak said, holding Konar's robe out awkwardly.

No, Konar thought, *otherwise I would've brought it.* But he took it, anyway, even allowing the backhander to help him slip into it. T'Vak was trying to prove himself, and Konar would give him ample opportunity to do so in the coming moons.

They walked the hundred or so feet to the center of the island where everyone else had gathered—everyone, that was, except for Maseeya, who'd gotten the twins to sleep in the small cave beneath their feet, an irony that wasn't lost on Konar. Elaysia now sheltered her babes in the place the eggs had taken shelter in before she'd discovered them. Konar tried to catch her gaze as he joined the circle, but she kept her attention on the great beridian lying on the ground between them.

Grokhion was nestled in piles of furs from the refuge. Yerakai had done decent work of cleaning and tending to the wounds, but there was only so much one could do. There was no way to make a blood-drained and battle-marred body lifelike again, no way to restore the missing patches of fur, or regrow lost limbs. Konar knew that better than most.

He held the parchment in a firm grip as he addressed everyone in attendance. He was wary of performing the ritual with such a large gathering, but the love for Grokhion was great, and there was no dissuading them. All he could hope was that they wouldn't take it too harshly when it didn't work.

"I advise you to look away once the ritual begins," he said in a low voice, trying and failing to catch any of their gazes. "Looking upon a Caman when you don't intend to access its powers is rumored to be"—he breathed deeply through his nose, trying to find a word that would enforce his wishes without frightening them with tales of Caman hauntings—"perilous."

Elaysia drew her cloak tighter about her shoulders. "Where's the offering?"

Despite the deepening darkness, Konar felt all eyes on him as clear as day. "According to the copied parchment, none is required. Just the body of who you wish to resurrect, and the symbol that I'll draw in a moment." It was his first sign that something had been lost in translation with T'Vak's master's parchment, rendering the ritual unusable. "Would you like me to begin?"

Elaysia held his gaze with the most intensity he'd experienced since she'd first confronted him on the beach, the evening of her second induction, what must've been nearly a year to the day. Only this time, it wasn't challenging, but determined.

Konar drew directly on the dirt, outlining the symbol the merchant had crudely drawn on the parchment. It was something akin to an intricately woven knot. Or maybe a heart. Maybe both.

When he finished, he forced everyone out of his mind and began reading aloud the ancient Nyrinian dialect scrawled on the parchment. It wasn't masterful calligraphy as he was used to seeing on the scrolls, and with each imperfection, he became more and more certain nothing would happen. The words themselves were jumbled, not words at all really, and almost impossible to pronounce. He was familiar with their structure, but not their meaning. It was only when he finished that he realized it.

They *were* scrambled. Jumbled. No, backwards.

Konar pored over the page, deciphering the code, but he didn't get far before a familiar chilling wind rustled his robe. He fell to his knees, praying the others did the same, just as a gust began to swirl around Grokhion. Before he lowered his gaze, he caught sight of a pair of eyes that were as endlessly colorful as they were eternal voids.

His heart thudded against his chest as he knelt there, waiting, still in shock the ritual had worked without the original scroll. The realization changed everything. It went far beyond Grokhion, far beyond the potential to resurrect the dead. If the scrolls weren't the source of the power, but mere conduits, what was? And what was the significance of having all seven? Everything in his research had led him to believe that they, together, could make or break the world, but now, he wasn't so certain. As far as he knew, Karliah was still adamant in her pursuit. Would she stop if she knew the powers weren't restricted to the scrolls?

The swirling gust surrounding Grokhion's body ceased far too soon for Konar's liking, but he pushed himself up all the same, curious to see what magic the demon had wrought. Lumira, Elaysia, and Jakki were already huddled around his head, blocking it from Konar's view. From what he could see, nothing had changed. Still a missing lower leg. Still a battered body. Still a lifeless shell.

He took a few cautious steps closer, and sensed T'Vak creeping behind him, eager to do the same. Grokhion's face was just as he'd last seen it. Peaceful, but empty.

Elaysia glanced up at him, her brow wrinkled with a mixture of defeat and confusion. Lumira looked as though she would turn on them all in a moment. A dozen condolences came to Konar's mind, ones he'd used successfully in the past. None were fitting.

He'd settled on a simple, 'may he thrive in Everworld,' a common enough Agaasian offering, when the great cat's eye shot open.

But the eye was not his.

JAKKI

Jakki didn't like the way Grokhion stared at nothing. It didn't help that it was only one eye, the vibrant green replaced by a murky white that focused nowhere and everywhere all at once. His right arm dangled helplessly at his side, which was still better than his missing foot that gave him a lurching limp. Elaysia had insisted they wrap the stub, not that it mattered much. Grokhion didn't seem to feel pain.

He didn't seem to feel much of anything at all.

Lumira hadn't left his side in the twelve or so hours he'd been awake, but Jakki saw her resolve melting with each passing moment. Grokhion moved about, stared off at the ocean from the nearby ledges, and even offered the occasional huff or sigh. But whatever Konar's parchment had done, it hadn't brought him back. Several of the riders had tried to get him to eat or drink, but he had no hunger or thirst. They offered him a blanket, a place by the fire, but he felt no cold. He hadn't stepped away to relieve himself, hadn't twitched a single muscle in his face, didn't even seem to recognize Lumira, no matter how much she doted on him, singing lullabies in their tongue and telling him stories of their homeland.

Jakki was fairly certain that if she pressed her head to his chest, there'd be no heartbeat.

"I think he just needs more time," Lumira said that evening as they all gathered around the fire for a dinner of fish and mussels. Grokhion had refused to join them and remained by the cliff, staring at the thrashing waves with his empty, one-eyed stare. "We have healers on our isles," she continued, her face at war with her unruly emotions. From what Jakki could tell, she'd soon lose that battle.

Elaysia placed a squirming Dytana on a blanket a safe distance away from the flames. "You wish to return home?"

Lumira's gaze strayed to Grokhion before returning to Elaysia. "It would be a multi-purposed journey. I want to take him home, yes. But I also thought I'd try to find you more warriors. There are plenty of beridians who hate Az Zar—"

"Warriors for what purpose?" Mardus bellowed. Kahana placed a hand on his forearm to still him, but he shirked away from her touch. "We've lost everything. Even if you returned with an entire beridian fleet, we wouldn't stand a chance against the empire."

"We might yet be able to turn the Lawful Dominion to our side," Yerakai said, setting aside his needle-brew tea. His ashen-violet cheeks were hollow, the bags beneath his eyes heavy. "Once the All-Sovereign implements his new government, I'm certain those who joined with Raynar will grow restless. They wanted to be on the winning side of Neharem; not ruled by a foreign dictator."

"Then they shouldn't have been such cowards!" Mardus kicked a stray cone into the fire before storming into the woods, likely to check on Keera's wounds. She'd taken several trial flights, but was still weakened.

One of the stormbird's cries cut through the night. The volume suggested Onitus.

"We mustn't lose hope," Konar said, and Jakki had to stifle the cynical laughter trying to escape her throat. He couldn't have sounded more disingenuous if he tried. "The scrolls are still the priority, as is protecting the stormbirds. T'Vak and I will go to Az Zar as planned and secure Zavik."

Jakki's gaze darted to Elaysia. It was the first she'd heard of such a plan, but Elaysia didn't look surprised. Elaron yanked a lock of his mother's hair, and she hardly seemed to notice. Her two-toned eyes just stared into the fire, distant. Guarded.

"Unless the All-Sovereign is bringing him here," Yerakai said, inspecting his blood-soaked bandage.

Kahana shrugged as though she didn't see the problem, nor any need for discourse regarding their next steps. "Then we split up as planned. Anahi and Xaren will soon arrive in Orillon with the last of the kuza if they haven't already. They probably don't even know what's happened."

"What of your relationship with the skulmor, Jakki?" Elaysia still didn't tear her gaze away from the fire. "Do you really trust them?"

"Perhaps the better question," Konar interrupted, "is what benefit do they serve?"

Jakki bristled. He couldn't have known about the parchment, but she still disliked how he insinuated that her connection to them went beyond just an alliance. Elaysia and the others might have welcomed the murderous traitor back with open arms, but she'd never trust the ex-high elder again.

"They have every reason to hate Az Zar and could be our strongest allies yet," she replied coolly. "There are also rare crystals that form in their mountains that could prove useful, should they deem us worthy of them."

Elaysia glanced up from the flames, brow furrowed. "These are the same crystals that almost killed Shadow?"

"Yes." Jakki could feel herself becoming flustered, and it only shortened what little remained of her patience. "But that could be used against our enemies. The skulmor are a thriving civilization. There is much to be learned from them."

More than you know. But she couldn't say that aloud. Not in front of cautious Yerakai and vengeful Kahana. And Konar would likely oppose it just for the sake of opposing Jakki. She'd tell Elaysia about the parchment, of course. When it was the right time.

Elaysia retrieved a stick from the ground and began to draw in the dirt beside her babes. Four circles, each at equidistant points with a line to connect them. North and south. East and west. "This will be the most spread out we've been," she whispered. "We'll need to have a plan in place for communication, as we no longer have access to Agaas's turosses."

"We have them on the Isles," Lumira offered. "And Anahi has them in Orillon."

"I don't think the skulmor rely on them," Jakki admitted. "But it wouldn't be impossible for one of us to fly south or west to bring word."

T'Vak forced himself up from where he'd sprawled out next to the fire. Jakki thought he'd been asleep, struggling against his withdrawal symptoms, but he looked undeniably sober, if not distraught. "Don't think All-Sovvy's going to let us borrow his turosses out of the kindness of his heart, but me and the old man will find a way. Won't we, old man?"

Konar glared daggers at the backhander, but he gave Elaysia a reaffirming nod. "There won't be much to report. We'll either come back with Zavik, or we won't."

Elaysia looked as though she had more to say on the matter, but didn't want it aired in front of the others. She returned to her drawing and began adding tallies to each region. "Anahi and Xaren are already in the south. Kahana and Mardus will join them."

Kahana placed one hand on her club. "High Chieftain, I shouldn't leave your side."

Elaysia ignored her. "Lumira and Grokhion will return to their Isles in the west and see who will join us in the fight for Quinaria."

A nice way to put it, Jakki thought, though she felt no animosity toward the beridians any longer. She pitied them, hated seeing such powerful warriors brought so low.

"High Chieftain," Kahana protested.

"I won't have more than three birds in one place," Elaysia snapped. "We can't lose another. Do you understand what's at risk? Orillon is our safest option, and as humans, you and Mardus will be welcome there."

Kahana squatted beside the fire, her eyes smoldering.

"Konar and T'Vak will retrieve Zavik from the East, and upon their return, we will bring Zavik down to the sanctum Konar discovered. Hopefully, he can unlock what lies within." Elaysia looked away for a moment, and Jakki could sense her fighting back waves of emotion. "Yerakai and I will visit Jakki's skulmor allies in the north. The babes and Maseeya will come with us. If you trust them as much as you say you do," she said, directing her attention to Jakki, "it is the safest place for them."

"It is," Jakki said, meaning it wholeheartedly. The skulmor were violent, but they weren't conniving or backstabbing. Who knew how many Az Zarian spies lay in wait in the south? Zavik was proof of the dangers of Orillon. "Their fortress is strong, and I'm certain their leaders would like to meet you."

"Then it's decided." Elaysia brushed the dirt off her hands and scooped up Elaron. "We'll perform one more flyover of the refuge to ensure there are no stragglers, then depart at dawn. And"—she scooped up Dytana, her back still turned to the flames—"all scrolls and parchments will stay in my possession from now on. We'll arrive at our destinations and convene within a moon cycle at a place I've yet to determine, save for Konar and T'Vak, who will arguably have a difficult time making impromptu arrangements without a stormbird."

Elaysia took a few steps away from the fire, then faced them. The moonlight glinted off the ocean, cutting a stark silhouette of her and the babes against the silver, thrashing waves, her cloak and hair blowing in the wind like banners. Jakki had never witnessed her rooted so strongly, so assured of herself and her actions.

Or so jaded.

"The battle for Agaas is lost," Elaysia said, speaking in the same tone she'd used during her speech after her second induction. "But the war for Quinaria has just begun. I truly believe we are all that stands in the empire's way. Protect yourselves and the stormbirds above all. Promise me that."

They all nodded, some bringing their right fists to their hearts.

Elaysia looked out at the ocean, at the husk that was Grokhion, then back at them. "And one last thing: I'm no longer your high chieftain. I never wanted that, and it was never meant to be mine. Follow me if you will, but see to it those words never leave your lips again."

As she walked away, Jakki couldn't help but mourn the innocent young girl that was lost.

But it happened to everyone, eventually.

LUMIRA

Lumira called to Anadu under the cover of night.

They were to leave at dawn with the others, but she couldn't stand the thought of any more goodbyes, nor the sorrowful looks everyone cast upon Grokhion as though he were an old man on his deathbed. That wasn't how they departed life on the Isles, and she wouldn't have them look that way at him again.

Lumira waited at the cliff, hoping Anadu wouldn't cause too much of a commotion when she arrived. She'd wanted to leave from the opposite end of the island to ensure no one awoke, but there was no way for her to move Roth, even with Grokhion's help. They'd wrapped the stormbird's head in a blanket from the refuge, then used fishing nets to secure his wings to his body. Elaysia wanted to burn the body on the island, but Lumira stood firm against it. Grokhion had the right to decide what became of his bird.

As Anadu's silhouette appeared in the night sky, Lumira's stomach growled. She ignored it, had taken no supplies for herself, feeling as though a little hunger was the least of the pain she could carry alongside her kin. Grokhion remained stoic beside her, his single, milky eye unblinking.

"We'll find someone back home who can cure you," Lumira whispered, taking his hand in hers. It was cold and limp. She fought the urge to drop it. "They know little of moon magic here."

Anadu landed as gracefully as a bird of her size could manage, perching beside Roth's body. She lowered her beak, nudging his wrapped head and emitting low, chirping sounds.

Lumira couldn't watch anymore.

When she'd finished, Anadu hopped toward her rider, a motion that had once been adorable and was now a bit unnerving, then lowered her body so Lumira and Grokhion could climb on. The elder beridian had yet to acknowledge the large birds frequenting their island refuge, hadn't so much as flinched when Anadu landed. Lumira told herself it was because he grieved. He'd come back to himself in time, would take up arms with her and seek to avenge Roth.

Unless it wasn't Grokhion who'd come back.

Lumira clawed anxiously at her necklace, wishing away the thought that had come unbidden. Of course, it was him. He was just stunned, probably experiencing something akin to being born again. He'd return to himself with time. Even if he could no longer fight, he had wisdom to share, could live another thirty years or more at home with his people.

She guided him to Anadu and, after much instruction, got him safely atop the bird's back. Hopefully, he'd have the basic instinct to keep himself balanced. If he started to topple, there wasn't much she could do.

"Reverting to your old ways?" a weary voice asked.

Lumira kept one hand on Anadu as she faced Elaysia. The high—no, the warrior mother—stood in a thin shift with tousled hair. The wind pressed it against her body, outlining the effects of her recent training. The softness of childbearing was gone, replaced with something hard and resilient.

"What do you mean?" Lumira asked, though she already knew the answer. She just didn't want to admit it.

Elaysia gestured to Anadu with her chin. "Alone. Running off without warning. You know, Konar always thought you were only in it for the egg."

If Lumira's fur could've blushed like the skin of pale nyrians and humans, it would have then. "I didn't want anyone to see us off. I thought it would be easier this way."

Anadu chirped as Elaysia approached and placed her hand on the bird's beak. She was the only one all the stormbirds tolerated outside their own riders. It was as if they knew she was the one who'd freed them from the cliff in the first place.

"Promise you'll come back," Elaysia whispered as she stroked the place between Anadu's eyes. "I need you more than ever now."

"You have my word." Lumira reached for the clasp securing her necklace and freed it from her neck. She fingered the bone beads, running her thumb over the five arrowheads adorning the jewelry, then held it out to the former high chieftain. "Hold on to this for me, until my return."

Elaysia's eyes widened. "I'll do no such thing."

"I insist." Lumira pressed it into her reluctant hand. "On the Isles, we believe someone must return to you if you have something of theirs. The time my father didn't return to me, he hadn't given me a token, as he often did." She shut her eyes, fighting back the memories she'd have no choice but to face back home. "Just take it. Please."

Elaysia fastened it around her neck, and she looked fiercer than ever. "I'll protect it with my life."

"Then it's already doing its job." Lumira climbed atop Anadu, body trembling with fear and anticipation of what was to come.

"May your sunrises always hold promise," Elaysia said as Anadu's wings raised a cloud of dirt.

"And may your winds never cease," Lumira returned, combining a blessing of her people with that of Agaas. "When we meet next, there will be hope."

As Anadu soared into the night, her wings gliding just above the waves, the salty spray washing over Lumira like a mist, she tried to believe it.

She had no choice.

ZAVIK

They stopped to rest outside of Zorinthu, seeking refuge on its rocky coastline. Davier claimed the Az Zarian village was made up of fisherfolk and aging northerners, who'd decided the cold of the Far North was too harsh for their liking but didn't want to settle in the stuffy nyrian capital. They should be relatively safe, or at least the population would be indifferent to them. So the ex-soldier thought.

Zavik still didn't trust it. Besides, the beach lent shelter by means of old driftwood huts the locals used as fishing refuges when they couldn't make it home by nightfall. They had nothing to fish with, but Zavik's soldier friend had packed bean cakes and hunks of smoked fish in the bag, and along with the water-skin attached to his borrowed uniform, it was enough for one night. On the morrow, they'd have to venture into Talza to secure resources, but for the moment, Zavik wanted nothing more than to fall asleep next to their little driftwood fire and forget the world.

Xi had other plans.

"If you're not a soldier, then who are you? How do you know my brother?"

Zavik sighed and slipped his seers back over his eyes. He'd managed to avoid most of Xi's questions the past day. They'd stolen horses from an inn outside Cadar, and Zavik rode with the boy, whose name remained unspoken, while Davier rode with his sister. Whenever they stopped to stretch their legs or relieve themselves, however, the wisp of a girl hovered around Zavik like a fly. Poking at his seers, peeking in his bag—completely unaware of the concept of boundaries. Davier, on the other hand, had hardly spoken a word to Zavik since hearing the news of his progeny. It was probably just as well. Zavik wasn't too keen on discussing it himself, nor was he in a place to help Davier with whatever trauma he'd experienced as of late.

He had enough of his own to worry about.

"From Neharem," Zavik said, pressing up to his elbows.

Apparently, he'd been the only one trying to sleep in their little stick hovel. Davier faced the ocean, watching the rain spatter the rocks, giving their surfaces a glossy appearance. The boy leaned against his back, eyeing Zavik with no shortage of suspicion despite the hours they'd shared on horseback. It was the uniform, Zavik thought, but he couldn't discard it yet. Davier had spoken enough to tell him the boy was a slave, freed from the mines. He likely hadn't been outside of his assigned district before, let alone Cadar. Zavik tried to remind himself of this as the boy's dark eyes shot a look that could kill.

Xi, however, was completely unbothered by such notions and had positioned herself so close to Zavik that her boney little knee pressed against his. "You don't look like you're from Neharem," she said with a raised eyebrow. The suspicion evident in her tiny features was almost amusing, looking as though it belonged to a person who'd experienced far more in life.

But maybe she had.

"So they tell me." Zavik offered her the last bit of water from the skin, drinking it when she refused. "To be completely honest, I'm afraid I don't hail from anywhere. No one wants to claim me, and I'm uncertain that I want to be claimed any longer."

"I'll claim you." Xi flashed a grin, revealing her missing left incisor, and Zavik immediately regretted his previous shortness with her. She was just a child. He promised himself he would attempt to keep his frustrations from surfacing in front of either child.

"I'd like that," he said softly. "Are you happy to be reunited with your brother?"

"Yes..." Xi chewed her lip as her gaze drifted to Davier. They had the same eyes, Zavik noted. A blueish white, like the stars. She looked as though she wanted to say more, but not in front of her brother.

No matter. There'd be plenty of time for conversation in the coming days.

Zavik patted her back and offered the spot he'd warmed. "Get some rest. Tomorrow, I'll answer all your questions, alright?"

"Alright," she said through a yawn, as she lay down. In mere moments, her breathing became the heavy exhalations of someone asleep.

Zavik waited until the boy was snoring against Davier before creeping to the front of the shelter to address him. Davier's bare feet were bloodied from their escape, and he bore several cuts and bruises from the arena—none of which were as unsettling as the brand on his forehead. His golden hair covered most of it, but the sea wind had blown it back, fully exposing the mark.

He quickly averted his gaze.

"I said earlier that I wanted you to guide me north," Zavik began, almost regretting the words as he spoke them. But then he thought of Xi and found the resolve to push through. "But this is far enough. You have your sister and this boy to worry about. I don't want to risk their lives on my fool's errand. We can part ways here. I'll even give you half the aspar."

Davier looked disapprovingly at the lyvium coins in Zavik's palm. "Keep it. I'm coming with you, as agreed. It's the least I can do."

"I'm not returning to Elaysia," Zavik clarified, in case, in his despair, Davier had forgotten. "At least not yet. Dalgus made it sound as though she might no longer be in Neharem, anyway. I'm afraid the war's taken a turn for the worse, forcing them to—"

"Dalgus?" Davier's back straightened, and the boy slipped off him and onto the ground, mercifully sleeping through the ordeal. "You spoke with the dwarf?"

Zavik adjusted his seers. "Why yes, I—How do you know him?"

A ghost of a laugh escaped Davier's throat, and he rubbed the space between his eyes. "You were the valuable person I was meant to help escape. How fitting."

The conversation with the soldier at the palace came back to Zavik in a rush. "I learned it shortly before venturing to the arena. I was told to flee, but when I heard you were still alive, I had to..." *Ensure I had no guilt on my conscience, should I see Elaysia again.* But he cleared his throat and said, "See for myself. We all thought you were dead."

Davier touched the brand on his forehead, eyes narrowing. "I was."

Zavik tried to pluck one of the many thoughts swirling through his mind. There was much to tell Davier. But how, and when, were other matters entirely. He decided to start with what was essential, giving Davier bite-sized pieces he could digest to minimize any chance of overwhelming him.

"I believe in my heart," he began, "that Elaysia is alive and well, as are your children."

"Tell me about them," Davier said, voice thick with emotion.

"Uh, one boy. Elaron. He's named after Elaysia's family. He has her spirit, but your eyes."

The corner of Davier's lip started to turn up, but he covered his mouth with his hand, as though he didn't trust himself. "And the other?"

"A girl, Dytana, named for your family, I imagine. She looks a bit like Xi. Of course, I haven't seen them in moons."

Davier nodded rapidly as he looked away. The emotion he fought to hold back was so evident that Zavik almost left to give him privacy. But there was one more thing he needed to address.

"Davier, the reason I have to go north is because the scrolls are somehow tied to me." Zavik dug his forefinger into his thumb's cuticle, still resisting his connection to it all, still refusing to fully believe he could matter that much, if at all. "I'll tell you everything on our journey, should you choose to accompany me, but you should know returning to Elaysia is no longer my priority. And I have no idea what awaits us in the north."

Davier drew several steady breaths. "The thought of meeting my children fills me with awe and terror. I want to meet them. Truly, I do. But I'm not ready to face her. Not yet." He buried his face in his hands, then lifted his head slowly, staring back at the sea. "If I can prove myself right by you, then maybe I'll finally be worthy." He locked Zavik in a gaze as he offered his hand. "I'll go with you to the end, if you'll have me. It would be an honor."

Zavik gripped his hand in return, giving it a firm shake. "The honor is mine."

ELAYSIA

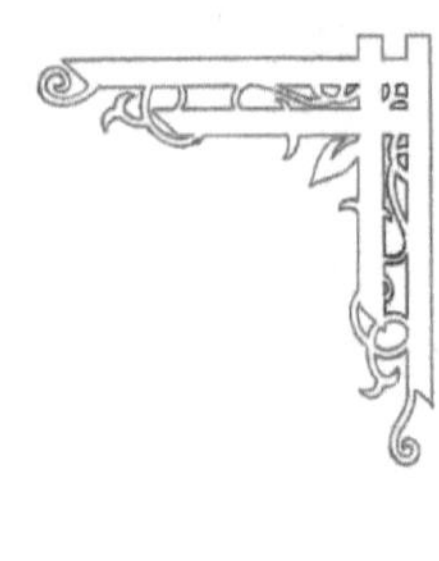

There was nothing more soothing, more endlessly enrapturing, yet utterly humbling, than the ocean. So long had it been a source of both comfort and power, something as dear as a friend and as terrifying as a god. And before she left it to find a new home in the mountains, she wanted to breathe in its very essence, so when life became too much, as it often did, she could sit with the waves crashing inside her, in awe of her own splendor.

She was a part of the ocean, after all. And it was a part of her.

Her legs dangled over the cliff side, as they had so many moons past. She'd felt a similar sense of despair then, the feeling that something was about to change, and that no matter how hard she fought it, it would transpire. She could either go rearing and screaming, or she could ride on the winds of uncertainty. Last time, she'd gone reluctantly; a filly broken and wary.

But this time? Well, she'd *lead* the change, and good luck to those standing in her way.

"Elaysia?"

The sound of Maseeya's voice flooded her soul with warmth. She patted the spot on the cliff beside her, and the older woman emitted a huff.

"You may enjoy sleeping with death," Maseeya said, her voice laced with genuine fear, "but I have no desire to even glance in its direction until it's my time."

Elaysia tucked her legs in, scooting just far enough inland that Maseeya would join her. "Are the twins alright?"

"Out like candles." Maseeya shivered and opened up half the blanket in offering. "Keep an old woman warm?"

Elaysia rolled her eyes. "Oh, stop. You wear your age with absolute dignity and beauty, Maseeya. I can only hope I age as gracefully." She slipped into the blanket and laid her head on the shoulder of the woman who was undoubtedly her mother, even if she never said it aloud.

"You'll have plenty more time to figure it out."

They shared a quiet laugh and warmth as they waited for the first signs of dawn to peek over the horizon. Elaysia cherished the silence like the calm before a storm.

And that's exactly what it was.

Eventually, however, stirrings of frustration and regret got the better of Elaysia. She lifted her head from Maseeya's shoulder and scowled as the waves of emotion slammed into her again, reviving negative feelings.

"All this could've been avoided if Raynar hadn't followed in his father's footsteps," she snapped. "I doubt he even wanted it. In fact, I *know* he didn't want it. They just expected it of him, and he didn't have the mind to think for himself."

Maseeya simply nodded as Elaysia struggled to untangle her thoughts from the emotions surrounding them.

"Actually," Elaysia continued, "it's not even fully his fault. It's just as much his father's, who couldn't stand to see me leading Agaas, and it's just as much the All-Sovereign's, who couldn't help but take advantage of a precarious situation." The more Elaysia detailed everyone responsible for the pain, the more enraged she became. "But it's also Konar's, for trying to manipulate everything. And before him, some dictator ancestor of the All-Sovereign wanted to eradicate a people and claim the scrolls for himself. It's just a mess of controlling, power-hungry, and discontent monsters whose selfish actions breed more of their kind."

"Men have always waged the wars, and women have been left to sift through the rubble." Maseeya's voice grew somber, almost defeated. The way she stared out at the water instead of Elaysia made her wonder just what her mother figure had been through prior to arriving in Neharem. "All we can do is be the voice of reason when allowed."

Elaysia clenched her fists. "Maybe they should be forced to listen."

"Don't you be too wild now, girl. No one is more feared or hated than a woman breaking free of the boundaries the world's set for her. This, I know. This, your mother knew." Maseeya rose, pulling Elaysia up with her. She grasped Elaysia's shoulders and held her there for a long moment before speaking again. "If you are going to defy those in power, no one will come to your aid until you've won your battle. I don't say this to dissuade you. Only to make you ready."

Elaysia considered this, then gave Maseeya her honest reply. "I'll never be ready, but I'll rise to the challenge, regardless."

"And I'll be by your side. Always."

Maseeya pulled Elaysia close, and together, they watched the sunrise.

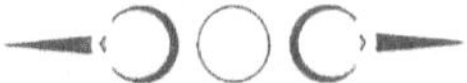

Kahana and Mardus left with strong, stoic faces, just as Elaysia anticipated. Before departing for Orillon, they were to complete one last flight over Agaas looking for survivors, namely a certain Moákun chief. Elaysia didn't protest, but she didn't dare hope, either. She knew the pain of losing a parent and understood Mardus was in the early stages of grief. Part of her hoped he'd find a body, so he could have that closure, if nothing else. She wished she'd had it all those years ago.

In the absence of the Moákuns, the population of the tiny island was largely reminiscent of her life prior to her induction. Konar and Maseeya, Jakki and Yerakai. Faces she'd known and come to love since she'd first opened her eyes. How fitting they were all together again. Only T'Vak and the twins were new. And the only absence...

No. She refused to see it as such. Zavik would return, and she'd never let him out of her sight again.

"Wind Chaser has returned with one of the Apáasutai boats," Konar said, joining her on the fallen log where she sharpened her arrowheads.

Elaysia couldn't bring herself to meet his gaze. There were too many expectations surrounding their looming parting, and she couldn't rid herself of the finality of it. Too many goodbyes as of late had been unexpectedly damning, and this one seemed the riskiest of all.

Konar cleared his throat. "It's a lot of boat for two people, but I'll make a sailor out of T'Vak yet."

"One of us could fly you over," Elaysia said, setting aside her arrows. "It would be faster and safer."

"Faster, yes, but the sense of security above would cost us down below. I'm certain the All-Sovereign has people who watch the skies night and day, lest you make any surprise attacks." He bent down to retrieve an unusual rock that was a translucent green and smooth as skin. "No one will expect an old man and backhander to be a source of trouble."

Elaysia had no stronger argument, so she rose and strode through the trees to where T'Vak was spinning tales for Maseeya and the twins by the fire. She had to admit they looked amused, if nothing else, then hurried on before they noticed her. Yerakai was performing his own final flyover of Agaas, and Jakki scoured the Igtheos refuge for supplies. Within a few hours, they'd all be gone, perhaps never returning to the little island again.

Perhaps never returning to Neharem again.

Elaysia let the thought sift from her mind like sand. She could only hold on to so much negativity if she was to stand any chance of climbing out from the pit she'd dug for herself.

As she approached the cliff one last time, the tread of footsteps signaled Konar's approach. This time, however, he simply stood beside her, for the first time in his life, not filling the space with his endless supply of words and wisdom.

Surprisingly, she missed it. She missed so many things.

"Life is never really going to be good, is it?" she asked him, keeping her gaze trained on the horizon. "I crave the blissful memories of my childhood, but the more I strive to recreate those sensations, the further away from me they get."

"I suppose that depends on what you mean by good," Konar replied, holding the translucent rock up to the murky sunlight. "If you mean perfect, flawless—a utopia—then no. I doubt we'll see that in our time. I've lived a thousand years and only watched the world descend further into madness. People are selfish and driven by fear. We'll likely remain broken forever."

"You always know what I need to hear."

"You've always craved the truth, Elaysia. I'm forever done lying to you." He sought her gaze, but she held firm. One genuine look, and she'd break. "But," he continued, "I think there's beauty to be found amid the brokenness. There will always be light in the darkness, and sometimes it shines so brightly that we forget there was ever night."

"Night still comes." Her voice, like her heart, was ice. And both were cracking.

"So it does."

"Then this is for nothing."

"Only if you choose to see it that way. Are your babes for nothing? Your Stormriders? What remains of your people? Even when the battle is uphill, when the winds and rains howl against you, when your enemies close in on all sides, you make a difference just by continuing to stand. And maybe, one day, love will overpower fear long enough to set a new world into motion."

He pressed the rock into her hand. She gripped it as though her life depended on it. A sharp gust slammed into them, and it was all Elaysia could do to maintain her stoic exterior.

"Do you truly believe that?" she asked when the wind died down.

"I'm starting to."

Their gaze met, and Elaysia inhaled sharply when she found Konar's eyes filled with tears. They triggered her own, and slowly, she tore down the last walls of her grudge against him. When she embraced him, he stiffened, as though he never thought such a thing would come to be again. And when he returned her embrace, she knew it had been a mistake.

Because now, she had to let him go.

"Don't do anything foolish over there," she whispered. "Just find Zav and bring him home. I need you both if we have any chance of turning this tide."

He gave her a final squeeze, then pulled back enough to look upon her face. "I will do everything in my power. But you must promise to trust yourself and guard those scrolls with your life. If the rituals aren't tied directly to them, they must hold some other importance we do not yet know of. Be cautious. Be wise."

Voices carried on the wind, followed by the crunching of footsteps. Their moment was almost over.

Elaysia gripped his forearms as she smiled through her tears. "Jakki's packing your journals as we speak. I will wait for you in the mountains and learn all I can."

"And I will find you there, one way or another."

A cloud of foreboding gnawed at Elaysia's heart once again, and she nearly mentioned it. But the others were already there, Dytana and Elaron reaching out their plump little arms, crying for her.

Within the hour, Konar and T'Vak were packed into the boat with their supplies, carried by Siren's strong talons as she safely deposited them into the sea. Elaysia fought the urge until they were nearly out of earshot, then she ran to the edge of the cliff and shouted as loud as her lungs would allow.

"Konar!" she screamed. "I will lose no one else in Az Zar, do you hear me?"

He moved to the side of the boat nearest her and waved his arm. "Elaysia," he shouted back. "I love you. Be strong."

And then he was gone.

EPILOGUE

The thirteenth of Mavalar, year 3039, N.W.

My Dearest Rykahl,

As the sun rises on a new era, I scribe these words to you, not out of malice but out of necessity. When you awake and find this letter, you will no longer be in the palace, nor even in your beloved Cadar, for that matter. You have outgrown your usefulness to me and the empire. I have yet to decide on where to banish you, but by the time you read this, your fate will have been decided. I should just kill you. It would be so clean, so simple. But despite your many faults, I have grown to tolerate you.

I would never claim our relationship was anything beyond lust, and even that was short–lived, but I do consider you an ally. Without you, I would not be where I am today, and for that, I will spare your life. You may do with it as you see fit, for you are no longer a threat. And now, whether abandoned at sea, cast into the desert, or deposited atop a mountain, you may find yourself wondering what transpired; questioning the winds of fate that have brought you to this moment.

Allow me to elucidate.

Our journey together has been one of ambition, of shared dreams and aspirations. Together, we sought to conquer and shape the very fabric of our nation. Of our world. Yet, as the tides of power ebb and flow, it becomes apparent that our paths must diverge. This, I have always known. I foresaw my brother by my side, but he, too, has failed me. Such is love.

You must know somewhere, deep down, that I have intentionally lingered in the shadows of your influence, biding my time, honing my craft. But now, as the fruits of our labor ripen, I find you no longer tethered to our Lord's vision. Nay, I have forged my own path, one that leads far beyond the piddly throne you once occupied.

This was never about Az Zar, Rykahl. Nor Quinaria, nor all of Quorath itself. You sought power and luxury, fine drink and partners. I sought to tear *the veil between realms. And you never wanted that, did you? Just your father out of the way, and the immortality offered by the scrolls. You were satisfied then, and you have remained so since.*

Do not lament the loss of your rule, for it was never truly yours to begin with. Perhaps, in time, you will come to thank me for bringing your meaningless life to an end. Surely, you could not have gone on as such forever. You have already wasted two life-times. Is that not wretched enough? If, however, you do not understand the necessity of my actions, the inevitability of change, you can always perform the ritual yourself. Keep prolonging your pathetic life if you wish. Just do so far from me.

Fear not, for when I am finished with this world, you will see the impact no matter where you reside. My light will shine so brightly that it will be visible from the highest peaks and the greatest depths. Rest assured knowing I am the leader you never could be. A goddess divine. Life and death itself.

For they, my tepid lover, are one and the same.

I have no wishes in parting; they are as fleeting as breath itself. Know that I appreciated you for what you once were. A tool. A step.

A gateway.

With love,

Karliah

AUTHOR'S NOTE

T hank you for reading *Of Love and Loss*. I hope it provided you an escape while giving you some thought-provoking moments to dwell on. If you can spare a few minutes, I'd be ever so honored if you left a review on Goodreads and on Amazon (or wherever you purchased the book from). Aside from purchasing a book, leaving a rating and review is one of the best ways to support an author. Your feedback is important to me and will help other readers both find the book and decide whether to read it.

If you'd like to stay up to date on my writing journey, upcoming releases, and be the first to receive exciting news, please sign up for my newsletter at bshgarcia.com/subscribe. When you sign up, you'll also receive exclusive access to a **free** prequel novelette, *From the Ashes*. Set over two thousand years prior to the events in *Of Thieves and Shadows*, this story follows Igtheos and Elize amid the Nyzarian civil war and the deadly Siege of Cadar.

Note: if you're having difficulties navigating to the subscribe link via your e-reader, it may be easiest to just type the website into your phone or computer. Not all of the e-reader browsers are up to date.

You can also interact with me on Instagram and Twitter (@bshgarcia), and follow me for important updates on Facebook, Threads, Goodreads, and TikTok (same handle).

Finally, I'd like to note that the fictional lands of Quinaria are inspired by events and legends from all over the world. None is intended as a faithful representation of any one country or culture at any point in history.

Thank you again for your support. I can't wait to thrust you into the next installment of this epic saga.

–B. S. H. Garcia

THE
STORY
SO
FAR

Foremost, this summary of events to date is solely a refresher and not intended as a substitute for reading preceding books in the series.

Second, if you're simply needing a reminder of characters, races, or words unique to Quinaria, you'll find those in the pages immediately following these.

While I've done my best to reference situations and histories mentioned in previous installments when the narrative calls for it, this is a sprawling epic fantasy with multiple characters and storylines. I'm aware some people read dozens of books (sometimes hundreds) in a year, and that the wait time between releases can be months (or years) on end. Being someone who rarely has time to reread a book before the next in series releases, and after lengthy discussions with those in online reading communities, I've concluded this addition does more help than harm.

If you're an expert in all things Quinaria, please skip ahead to the main course itself.

For the rest of you, enjoy this appetizer before diving in.

What we currently hold as truth...

The land of Quinaria relies on a finite resource: life-giving nevethium. From plants to beings, the crystals influenced the health and prosperity of all. When over-harvested and mis-used, the surrounding land became inhospitable. Three nations had maintained tumultuous peace for centuries, but as the crystal supply dwindled, tensions rose. One nation sought progress, another luxury, and the other peace. These conflicting world-views were destined for war.

Elaysia, the mixed-race daughter of a nyrian and a human, assumed the rule of her peace-seeking nation, Neharem, as the nevethium crisis reached a boiling point. Rumors of war abounded after a trade discrepancy, and on her induction day, the holy city was attacked, and a sacred crystal stolen. Terrified of responsibility, she fled, hoping her mentor and surrogate father, Konar, would lead in her stead. Her plans changed after a supernatural encounter guided her to stormbird eggs (Great Beasts previously thought extinct) and set her back on the path of her murdered parents. They'd died years prior in Az Zar, seeking solutions for the rapidly depleting nevethium and searching for ancient scrolls of power that would aid Neharem, should war arise.

The stormbirds were powerful creatures containing the minds of people and the power of gods. Combined with the Prophets' scrolls, they could be the key to saving Neharem. Stormbirds always bonded with a rider, so Elaysia returned home to Agaas with the eggs and gathered a disparate crew of allies to become her Stormriders. They also aided her in uncovering the mystery of the nevethium raids and the rumored experimentation overseas in Az Zar. Among this group were Jakki, Elaysia's lifelong friend and the daughter of a chief, and Lumira, a beridian mercenary caught thieving in the holy city.

Meanwhile, Az Zar's dictator, the All-Sovereign, plotted to capture Elaysia and the hatchling stormbirds to gain the upper hand in his nevethium conquest. He sent Davier, an undercover soldier, to lure Elaysia and the stormbirds to Az Zar with the promise of a military promotion as his reward. The All-Sovereign, along with his right hand, the Lord Priestess, had extended their lifespans by utilizing the scrolls in their possession. They seek to conquer the other nations and gain complete control of the nevethium supply. But most of all, they desire the Prophet's Scrolls, ancient artifacts said to contain the world's true history, secrets of the gods, and divine magic.

As nevethium raids increased and hostile skulmor of the north infringed on Neharem's borders, Elaysia, against the better judgment of the council, left at the height of the crisis and split up her crew. Jakki took a party north to investigate the local raids, and Elaysia sailed with some warriors (Lumira and Davier included) to Az Zar. She also sent Zavik, a dear friend and scholarly refugee, to his home nation of Orillon in search of the Prophets' Scrolls. Back in Agaas, Konar strived to settle the unrest in Elaysia's absence as a usurper rose. Meanwhile, he also faced the ghosts of his past: like the All-Sovereign, he had extended his life by unnatural means and overseen the puppeteering of Neharem's leaders for many years. He had to decide if he would renounce control in favor of supporting his loved ones, namely Elaysia.

Up north, Jakki, driven by jealousy and love for Elaysia, ventured beyond the scope of her initial orders. Aside from confirming the skulmor were indeed behind the nevethium raids, she encountered an ancient being who clouded her judgment with promises of justice and power. He guided her to a magic parchment of unknown origins. South, in Orillon, Zavik miraculously secured three of the Prophets' Scrolls, but one was stolen before he returned to Neharem.

In Az Zar, Davier foiled the Neharem party's plans by causing a scene that led to the separation of himself and Elaysia from the rest of their allies. As they journeyed to the capital, he wavered between his duty and his blossoming love for Elaysia. Davier's allegiance drifted in favor of Neharem, but he couldn't bring himself to be honest about his mission for fear of what Elaysia and the others would think of him—not to mention the threat his desertion would pose to his family. Back in Neharem, Zavik and Konar began translating the scrolls while a rival chief staged a coup.

Elsewhere in Az Zar, after witnessing a new nevethium-powered weapon, Lumira investigated local workshops where there were rumors of experimentation. She confirmed they sought war and had made significant nevethium advancements that would forever change the world. Jakki and her party journeyed to Az Zar to rejoin the others and share their discoveries. After another divine encounter, no one could dissuade Elaysia from entering the Az Zarian capital: Cadar. She was determined to learn the truth about her parents and the scrolls, and she didn't want to return home empty-handed. Lumira's party reunited with Elaysia and Davier, as well as Jakki's party. After exchanging information, they decided to capture the Lord Priestess for leverage, considering the looming war. Their attack was anticipated, however, and Elaysia was imprisoned. Davier's secret was exposed, and he was injured by the new nevethium-powered projectile weapons. The rest of the party escaped.

While imprisoned, Elaysia learned Konar orchestrated the murder of her parents to keep control of Neharem and ensure peace—peace meaning the scrolls remained hidden. She also learned she was pregnant with Davier's child and sank into depression. Jakki planned a rescue inspired by the new power she'd gleaned from her magic parchment. Davier recovered and, now outcast by the Stormriders, made plans of his own. The two rescues culminated in a confrontation in which Davier sacrificed himself so the others could escape with Elaysia. When they returned to Neharem, Elaysia found another chief had taken her place, and the people had lost faith in her. She contemplated suicide, but Zavik convinced her to fight for her home. She challenged the chief who'd unseated her and, after beating him in hoksanu, regained her rule. Though jaded, she'd found an inner strength and regained the respect of her people. She decided to keep the baby. Despite the whispers of war, she would fearlessly lead her people and fight to preserve Neharem. She had scrolls, stormbirds, and newfound confidence; though, there remained the matter of Konar's betrayal to address.

The All-Sovereign feared all was lost. He was behind the attack on Agaas and had bribed the chief to overthrow Elaysia. Az Zar was running out of local nevethium, and they didn't have the numbers to attack Orillon and the unified tribes of Neharem. Karliah, the Lord Priestess, reassured him, however. Weaponry advancements were well underway, and she believed they could still break Neharem from within, especially now that her brother, Konar, had been exposed. There was also the potential allegiance with Orillon. It would come down to who they allied with, and who uncovered the next scroll.

War is definite. Nevethium is finite.

The battle for Quinaria has just begun.

THE INHABITANTS OF QUINARIA

The Inhabitants of Quinaria

The Tribes of Neharem

AGAAS

- **Elaysia {ee-lay-zhuh}:** *nyman*. High chieftain of the twelve tribes of Neharem and a Stormrider.

- **Konar {ko-nar}:** *nyrian*. A former high elder of Agaas. Former guardian of Elaysia. Brother of Karliah.

- **Jakki {juh-key}:** *nyrian*. A Stormrider and next in line to become chief of the Yustano.

- **Zavik {zav-ick}:** *human*. A high elder in Agaas and advisor to the high chieftain. Former Orillon refugee. Former apprentice to Konar. • **Lumira {loo-meer-uh}:** *beridian*. A Stormrider and newly appointed shadow chieftain.

- **Maseeya {ma-see-uh}:** *human*. Once a handmaid to Annalee, Elaysia's mother, she now oversees food acquisition and distribution in Agaas. Co-guardian to Elaysia.

- **T'Vak {t-vaak}:** *human*. A backhander hired by Zavik. Normally resides Orillon.

- **Grokhion {grow-key-uhn}:** *beridian*. A Stormrider. Formerly resided with the Ni'anko and originally from the Beridian Isles.

- **Xaren** {zah-ren}: *human*. A Stormrider. Formerly an Az Zarian soldier.

- **Mardus** {mar-dus}: *human*. A Stormrider and next in line to become chief of the Moákun.

- **Anahi** {uh-naw-hee}: *human*. A Stormrider. An Orillon native who lived amongst the Tangeesh for several years.

- **Yerakai** {yer-uh-kye}: *nyrian*. A Stormrider and skilled Apáasutai tracker.

- **Elaron** {eh-lay-rohn}: *nyman*. Firstborn son of Elaysia and Davier. Twin brother of Dytana.

- **Dytana** {digh-tah-nuh}: *nyman*. Firstborn daughter of Elaysia and Davier. Twin sister of Elaron.

- **Kahana** {kah-ha-nah}: *nyman*. Recently appointed head of the watchers. Moákun by birth and cousin to Mardus.

- **Cyan** {sigh-an}: *nyrian*. Famed winemaker known for his anderberry wine.

- **Elishon** {ee-lye-shun}—(deceased): *nyrian*. Father of Elaysia and former high chieftain of Neharem.

- **Annalee** {ann-uh-lee}—(deceased): *human*. Mother of Elaysia and former citizen of Az Zar.

- **Annonitus** {an-non-eye-tis}—(deceased): *nyman*. Elder brother of Elaysia.

- **High Elder Sower** {so-er}: *human*. A high elder of Agaas.

- **Kayrune** {kay-roon}—(deceased): *nyrian*. Son of

Konar.

APáASUTAI {AH-PAW-SOO-TIE}: *a medium-sized tribe occupying the forests on the west coast, the Apáasutai are known for their hunting skills and bold-colored artforms.*

- **Arkuun {ar-koon}**: *nyrian.* Chief of the Apáasutai.

ATSUKUT {AT-SOO-CUUT}: *a small-sized tribe in the north, the Atsukut are said to have giants' blood giving them larger statures.*

- **Senai {say-nigh}**: *nyrian.* Chief of the Atsukut.

BANAXA {BUH-NOX-UH}: *the largest tribe in Neharem known for their predominantly human population, they occupy a large plains territory.*

- **Paska {pah-skah}**: *human.* Chief of the Banaxa.

DARUK {DUH-RUUK}: *known for their fierce warriors and inclination toward farming, this small northern tribe shares a border with the formidable Skulmor.*

- **Gibrund {jib-rund}**: *nyrian.* Chief of the Daruk.

- **Jörd {yerd}**—(deceased): *human.* Former Daruk warrior. Killed protecting Elaysia in Az Zar.

- **Hilför {hill-feeyor}**: *human.* War refugee residing in Agaas.

KAHALOÁN {KAH-HUH-LOW-UHN}: *a small coastal tribe reliant on fishing and weaving textiles for trade.*

- **Raenais {ruh-nayz}:** *nyrian.* Chief of the Kahaloán.

LAUTEI {L-OW-TAY}: *second only to the Banaxa in population and to the Atsukut in stature, they have a history of aggression and were the last to join Agaas in a united Neharem.*

- **Rajar {ruh-zhar}**—(deceased): *nyrian.* Chief of the Lautei. Killed during hoksanu.

- **Raynar {ray-nar}:** *nyrian.* Son of Rajar and leader of the Lawful Dominion. Former chief of the Lautei.

- **High Elder Strong-spear:** *nyrian:* Advisor to Raynar and high elder of the Lawful Dominion. A former high elder of Agaas.

MOÁKUN {MO-AH-KUN}: *a coastal tribe key to Neharem's trade alliance with Az Zar, they are skilled seafarers and boat-builders.*

- **Orandus {oh-ran-dus}:** *human.* Chief of the Moákun and father of Mardus.

- **Aleilah {ay-lay-lah}:** *human.* War refugee residing in Agaas.

MOATIWE {MO-AH-TEE-WAY}: *exclusively nyrian, they are known for their ice-white eyes and aloof, taciturn natures.*

- **Unleto {uhn-leht-o}**—(deceased): *nyrian.* A warrior. Killed accidentally by Jakki the first time she used her parchment.

. **Eeshta {ee-shta}**: *nyrian*. A warrior.

Morotôk {MO-ROH-TOKE}: *the smallest and northernmost tribe is comprised of hard-working individuals well acclimated to harsh weather and scarce resources.*

. **Amkah {ahm-kah}**: *human*. Chief of the Morotôk.

. **Nanotsuk {nah-noht-sook}**: *human*. A Morotôk elder.

Ni'anko {NEE-ON-KOH}: *pacifist and philosophical, this west coast tribe welcomes anyone who honors their ways, native or not.*

. **Kelsia {kel-see-uh}**: *nyrian*. Chief of the Ni'anko.

Tangeesh {TANG-EESH}: *the southernmost tribe has merged the neighboring nation of Orillon's lifestyle with their own, including interbreeding with them.*

Yustano {YOO-STAHN-OH}: *located on an island just off the southeastern coast of Neharem, they cultivate rare crops and place great value in artistic expression.*

. **Jattai {juh-tye}**: *nyrian*. Chief of the Yustano and mother of Jakki.

Orillon

House Undali

- **Vahid Undali {vah-heed}**: *human.* Heir to House Undali and brother of Anahi.

- **Saya Undali {sigh-uh oon-dah-lee}**: *human.* Head of House Undali. Father of Anahi and Vahid. Husband of Sayetta Undali.

- **Sayetta Undali {sigh-eh-tah oon-dah-lee}**: *human.* Head of House Undali. Mother of Anahi and Vahid. Wife of Saya Undali.

- **Hallahd {hah-lahd}**: *human.* Head of House Undali's kuza.

MUNSKAHAN

- **Lanston {lan-stun}**: *human.* A successful merchant. Formerly employed Zavik.

- **Nahiim {nah-heem}**: *human.* A smuggler.

Az Zar

CADAR

- **Davier {daav-ee-air}**—(deceased): *human.* A former decorated captain in the All-Sovereign's army. Presumed killed while helping Elaysia and the rest of the Neharem party flee Cadar.

- **The All-Sovereign**: *nyrian.* The supreme ruler of Az Zar and believed by many to be a god. Also known as Rykahl.

- **The Lord Priestess**: *nyrian*. The head of the Mavist order and right hand to the All-Sovereign. Also known as Karliah.

- **Dalgus {dal-gus}**: *nyrian*. A dwarf and distant cousin of All-Sovereign working as his servant and advisor.

- **Zhia {zee-uh}**: *nyrian*. A decorated general in the All-Sovereign's army.

- **Yikos {yee-kohs}**: *nyrian*. A scholar and researcher employed by the All-Sovereign.

- **Xianna {zee-ah-na}**—(deceased): *human*. Davier's younger sister. Also known as Xi. Killed by the All-Sovereign to punish Davier.

- **Kiska {kiss-kah}**—(deceased): *human*. Davier's younger sister. Killed by the All-Sovereign to punish Davier.

- **Dynah {digh-nah}**—(deceased): *human*. Davier's younger sister. Killed by the All-Sovereign to punish Davier.

- **Kyreena {kigh-ree-na}**—(deceased): *human*. Davier's mother. Killed by the All-Sovereign to punish Davier.

- **Davkahl {daav-call}**—(deceased): *human*. Davier's father, a war veteran. Killed by the All-Sovereign to punish Davier.

- **Rykahl {righ-call}**: *nyrian*. A part of the ruling line of Zal Drusa and a descendent of Ashaat the Victor. Also known as the All-Sovereign.

- **Karliah {kar-ligh-uh}**: *nyrian*. Advisor to Rykahl. Sister of Konar. Also known as the Lord Priestess.

- **Ryman {righ-mun}**—(deceased): *nyrian*. A part of the ruling line of Zal Drusa. Son of Rykahl.

- **Ireena {eye-ree-na}**—(deceased): *nyrian*. Wife of Rykahl.

- **Ashaat the Victor {uh-shaat}**—(deceased): *nyrian*. The first emperor of Az Zar and ancestor of House Zal Drusa.

- **Igtheos {ig-thee-ohs}**—(deceased): *nyrian*. The leader of the ancient Nyzarian rebellion and co-founder of Agaas. Life partner of Elize. Survived the Siege of Cadar.

- **Elize {ee-leeze}**—(deceased): *human*. A former member of the Prophets and responsible for hiding the Scrolls throughout Quinaria. Life partner of Igtheos. Perished during the Siege of Cadar.

- **Zaria {zah-rhee-uh}**—(deceased) *nyrian*. Daughter of Igtheos and Elize. Believed to have perished during the Siege of Cadar.

THE REBELLION

- **Nanjiya {nahn-jigh-ah}**: *human*. The leader of the rebellion in Cadar.

- **Kymerius {kigh-meer-ee-uhs}**: *human*. Second in command of the rebellion. Former Az Zarian soldier.

- **Asha {ah-sha}**: *human*. A cook. Fondly known as "Eumma" aka the mother of the rebels.

- **Ahmarahn {ah-ma-rahn}**: *human*. A slave sent to infiltrate the rebels. Formerly known as Davier.

. **Lox**: *human*. A rebel fighter.

Skulmor

TYRGRAAK

. **Uruuka** {uh-roo-kah}: *skulmor*. A warrior and respected member of the pack.

Other Important Figures

STORMBIRDS:

. **Onitus** {o-nigh-tus}: Largest of the males, reserved in demeanor but fiercely loyal and impulsive. Bonded to Elaysia.

. **Anadu** {uh-nah-doo}: Second only in size to Siren, she's the boldest of the bunch. Bonded with Lumira.

. **Siren** {sigh-ren}: The largest of the stormbirds, she's standoffish around outsiders and prone to aggression. Bonded to Jakki.

. **Wind Chaser**: Per his namesake, he's the fastest and quite intelligent. Bonded to Yerakai.

. **Shadow**: The smallest of the bunch, he's unnoticed (as stormbirds go) and sleek. Bonded to Xaren.

- **Keera {key-ruh}:** Looks intimidating but she's actually the kindest of the birds. Bonded to Mardus.

- **Corvax:** He's an excellent judge of character with a strong memory. Bonded to Anahi.

- **Roth:** He's the wisest and not easily triggered but will do anything to protect his own. Bonded to Grokhion.

DIVINITY:

- **Khiev-Tatamic {khey-ev-ta-tah-mec}:** The great Creator. Commonly worshiped in Neharem.

- **Mavet/The Son {mah-vet}:** The son of Khiev-Tatamic. Worshiped in Az Zar, demonized in Neharem.

- **Chai'Tik/The Daughter {shy-teek}:** The daughter of Khiev-Tatamic. Worshiped in Neharem, demonized in Az Zar.

- **Rayanti {ray-ahn-tee}:** The god of war. Worshiped by the Lautei.

- **Itaso {ee-taas-oh}:** The mother of water. Worshiped by the Yustano.

- **Minara {mee-nar-uh}:** The goddess of love. Worshiped by the Kahaloán.

- **Rash-Yaanah {raash-yah-nuh}:** The god of the harvest. Worshiped by the Daruk.

- **Moartea {mo-ar-tee}:** The goddess of death. Worshiped by the Moatiwe.

- **The Old Man in the Woods:** Origin and true name unknown. Frequently appears to Jakki and gave her a magic parchment. Worshiped by the skulmor.

GLOSSARY

*-please note this glossary incorporates all terms intro-
duced in The Heart of Quinaria series to date, therefore
it may include terms not present in this installment-*

abdano {ahb-dah-no}- a Zelosi dish comprised of wild hog
and pyanne.

Agaas {uh-gaas}- the capital of Neharem.

Akaesho {uh-kay-show}- a sacred tree in the Ni'anko lands.

amma {ah-ma}- Zelosi word for "mother."

anderberries- a sweet and salty berry that grows in the
forest near the Apáasutai coastline. Commonly used in baking
and for wines.

appa {ah-pa}- Zelosi word for "father."

arkthanax {arc-thuh-nax}- an Az Zarian invention capable of performing the work of a hundred men, much faster, and
with little to no breaks. Production includes textile weaving,
mining, etc.

arzok {ar-zock}- a nocturnal, flying mammal with sizeable
fangs and forelimbs adapted as wings. Native to Zelos.

aspar {as-per}- the basic monetary unit of Az Zar, also commonly used in Orillon. Made from lyvium (see definition) and
cast into coins of varying size and shape to denote value.

awskada {aw-ska-duh}- the Zelosi word for a person, most
often a woman, who professes or is supposed to practice magic
or sorcery. Also used in Az Zar.

backhander- someone for hire, usually for dangerous and/or
illegitimate work, such as brute force, smuggling, bodyguarding,
assassinating, etc.

belzaith {bell-zay-uth}- the Hispen word for "underworld
spirit." Also, the name of Grokhion's ax.

Beridian Moonlight- a strong, sweet, fortified wine made
from a rare fruit and a potent plant native to the Beridian Isles.

It is highly alcoholic yet surprisingly palatable, and the secret plant added during fermentation creates a unique high for the consumer. (Also just called Moonlight).

birth keeper– a skilled person who assists with childbirth, offering traditional knowledge, care, and support throughout pregnancy and delivery.

blue fever– a disease caused by nutrition deficiencies and characterized by swollen, bleeding gums, raging fevers, and the opening of previously healed wounds. Common to pirates and seafarers.

Bongaiyo {bong-eye-oh}– believed by many cultures to be the mother of all stormbirds; also a constellation used for navigation made up of ten stars that form the rudimentary shape of a stormbird. Contains the south star, Elonias.

bretata {bray-tah-ta}– Zelosi word for "brother."

brondite {brawn-dight}– icy-blue crystals found deep in the Quentarri mountains. Used by the skulmor for rituals, purification, and as a weapon. Origins unknown.

bugana {boo-gah-nuh}– a fibrous, stalky plant sacred to the Zelosi people. It is often harvested for its sugar and used in cooking or distilled into kolaash. Its stalks can also be dried out and hardened for building materials and tableware.

Cadar {cay-dar}– the capital of Az Zar.

Caman {cay-men}– immortal beings loyal to Mavet. Depending on one's belief system, they are said to be angels, demons, or myth.

Cassonith haya {kah-son-eeth-high-ah}– a Hispen phrase for parting in good company, roughly translated as "may the moons watch over you."

Chai'Tik {shy-teek}– a goddess of great power, she is revered, demonized, or considered farce, depending on one's belief system. Also called The Daughter.

deathdrop– a carnivorous plant that lures bugs and small birds to it by posing as if it has dew, when the little orbs are, in fact, sticky and poisonous. Native to Zelos.

deathstalker– giant insects equipped with stingers that release a deadly venom. One of the three orders of The Great Beasts of Old.

desert bite– a chronic disease caused by unclean water, leading to skin sores, nerve damage, and muscle weakness, often resulting in death. Only found in Orillon.

dominants, the– the leaders of a skulmor pack. There are always two.

Dzro Jiazin {zhro-jye-zin}– (also called The Cleansing) an Az Zarian holiday celebrating the foundation of Az Zar.

dzvadra {zhvah-dra}– the Zarith word for "deathstalker."

edoja {ee-doh-juh}– the Nyrinian word for "father."

Elonias {ee-lon-eye-uhs}– the south star, part of the Bongaiyo constellation.

endei {en-digh}– an Apáasutai word for "a bad omen."

Eskos {ess-kohs}– the smallest island of Zelos.

eudna {yood-nuh}– the Zarith word for "father."

eumma {yuum-muh}– the Zarith word for "mother."

Everworld– an eternal paradise that is key to the belief system of some tribes and peoples.

faja {fah-jah}– the Westmun word for "father."

Feasting Moons– summer. Contains the months Gryphar, sub-Gryphar, and Phoenal.

firebug– a flying insect that flashes a glowing light at night.

Gathering Moons– fall. Contains the months sub-Phoenal, Mavalar, and sub-Mavalar.

gidmörni tree {gid-meeorn-ee}– a species of tree that grows on the cliffs of the western Neharem coastline and produces rare blossoms that provide extreme clarity when consumed.

Great Beasts of Old– the first of the beasts, wise as the Vysilliam (see definition) and blessed with long life and special abilities. Includes stormbirds, seaserpents, and deathstalkers.

groundshaker– a powerful explosive made of lyvium and nevethium absorbed into a porous material like sawdust or wood pulp. (Also called groundshake weapons.)

groundshakes– a sudden and violent shaking of the ground, sometimes causing great destruction, as a result of movements within the land's crust or volcanic action.

gwanei {gwah-nay}– small, bipedal, carnivorous reptiles that travel in packs of thirty to fifty, using their razor beaks and toothed tongues to take down larger prey. Native to Zelos.

hal-eudna {haal-yood-nuh}– the Zarith word for "grandfather."

Haeshol {hay-sholl}– a torturous, eternal holding place that is key to the belief system of some tribes and peoples.

helgin {hell-gin}– a monstrous boar with four tusks.

highborn– a term used to describe persons belonging to Az Zar's elite class.

Hispen {hiss-pen}– the official language of The Beridian Isles.

hoksanu {hoke-saw-noo}– an ancient Neharem tradition allowing one to challenge a chief or the high chieftain for the right to lead. It consists of two to three trials between the leader and the challenger.

Khiev-Tatamic {khey-ev-ta-tah-mec}– the first god, the creator or discoverer of the world, he is revered, demonized, or considered farce based on the belief system of the character.

kinawa {key-naw-wah}– a stout, aromatic, erect annual herb native to Neharem. When smoked, its leaves release a psychoactive substance. It's believed to have therapeutic properties and enlighten one's mind.

kolaash {koh-lah-sh}– an alcoholic liquor distilled from bugana and sweetened with pyanne.

krizah {cree-zah}– solitary feline predators found in the north.

kuba {koob-uh}– a nutrient-dense grain native to Az Zar. It has a nutty aroma and is most often steamed. Sometimes used to make kuba wine.

kuza {koo-zuh}– private military used by the noble houses in Orillon.

laazah {lah-zah}– a large and hoofed grazing animal, with branched bony antlers that are shed annually and typically borne only by the male. Distantly related to the nytak and, though once found in Az Zar, believed to be extinct.

lightbursts– contraptions that light up the sky with bursts of greenish-yellow light for celebrations. Commonly found in Az Zar and Orillon.

living trees– giant trees found in northwestern Neharem. The citizens of Agaas live in them, and they are nurtured by large nevethium (see definition) crystals referred to as "hearts."

love-giver– a person who engages in sexual activity for payment. Commonly found in Orillon and considered an honorable profession, unlike the whores of Az Zar who are often slaves.

lyda {lye-duh}– the Nyrinian word for "demon."

lyvium {lye-vee-um}– native to Az Zar, it is stronger than any other metal, yet light and flexible, making it ideal for weapons.

maja {mah-jah}– the Westmun word for "mother."

Mavet {mah-vet}– a god of great power, he is revered, demonized, or considered farce, depending on one's belief system. Also called The Son.

Mavism {mah-viz-um}– the official religion of Az Zar, it contains rigid practices surrounding penance and the giving of one's self to Mavet, the savior, and the government.

mawsk {mauh-sk}– a small, desert-dwelling rodent with long hind legs for jumping, large eyes, and a long tail, known for its ability to survive without drinking water by getting moisture from seeds. Native to Orillon.

mizol {mye-zoll}– a crustacean that produces a fluorescent, waterproof ink.

moon cycle– roughly a month's time on Quorath.

moon dust– a naturally sweet powder imported from the Beridian Isles. Origin unknown.

mosku plant {moh-skoo}– shrubs native to Orillon. Their seeds are often used to make moskuto.

moskuto {moh-skoo-toh}– a hot drink made from the roasted and ground seeds of the mosku plant. Its flavor profile is bitter and acidic, and consuming it provides stimulation of the mind and body.

Munskahan {moon-ska-haan}– the capital of Orillon.

Myremese {meer-rem-eez}– a lost language once spoken by the myrem and retained by a handful of scholars.

nazrath– giants descended of the nyrian bloodline.

nevethium {nuh-veth-ee-um}– radiant green crystals whose absence, when overharvested and misused, renders the surrounding land inhospitable. Also referred to as "the heart of Quinaria."

Novitae {no-vee-tay}– a Neharem holiday celebrating the story of creation.

Nyrinian {nee-rin-ee-in}– the ancient tongue once spoken by all nyrians is the official language of Agaas. It is also spoken by upper-class citizens in Az Zar who choose to honor the ancient ways.

nytak {nigh-tack}– a deer-like creature native to Neharem with scaled hooves and a long, furry tail.

palano tree {puh-lah-noh}– tall, slender trees with a crown of long, feathery leaves. They are found in Orillon and often produce sunkisses.

plant guardian– someone assigned to tend to gardens and crops in Neharem.

pocoaon tree {poh-co-uhn}– a tree species found throughout Quinaria in generally cool areas. Most grow near rivers, lakes, or swamps, and have limber, dangling branches.

populum {pop-yoo-lum}– a hallucination-inducing root native to Orillon.

Prophets, the– a sacred order coinciding with Az Zar's foundation. They studied the natural world, kept records, explored alternate histories, and some believe they learned the powers of gods.

Prophets' Scrolls, the– parchments containing years of research, history, and philosophy, penned by the Prophets. Rumored to contain magic spells unlocking the power of gods.

pyanne {pigh-ann}– an acidic fruit with sugary and spicy notes, used in both sweet and savory cooking. Native to Zelos.

Quinaria {quee-narr-ee-uh}– the central landmass on which the story unfolds. Includes Neharem, Az Zar, and Orillon. See map for details.

Quorath {cor-rath}– the planet in which Quinaria resides. Includes all of the known and unknown world.

ravager bird {rav-uh-jer}– a carrion bird species with brilliant red feathers, found throughout Quinaria.

Resting Moons– winter. Contains the months Onelar, sub-Onelar, Vynar, and sub-Vynar.

rujpati {roozh-pah-tee}– Az Zarian appointed government officials of Zelosi provinces.

ryptan {rip-tin}– a large avian-reptilian hybrid with feathers and scales. They rely on large talons and fangs to hunt and defend. Native to Neharem.

sandcat– large felines with long fangs. Native to Az Zar.

saya {sigh-uh}– the head male of a noble house in Orillon.

sayetta {sigh-eh-tah}– the head female of a noble house in Orillon.

seapup– a carnivorous, fin-footed, semiaquatic, mostly marine mammal found throughout the oceans surrounding Quinaria.

seahawk– birds that are both aerial and aquatic.

seaserpent– giant serpents that live in the sea. One of the three orders of The Great Beasts of Old.

sedare {suh-dare}– a mushroom native to Az Zar and known for its medicinal properties, specifically pain relief.

seers {see-ers}– a contraption worn over the eyes to enhance poor eyesight.

setata {say-tah-ta}– Zelosi word for "sister."

Shaktari {shack-tar-ee}– a lost language once spoken by the shaktar and retained by a handful of scholars.

shieum {shee-um}– new weapons made of lyvium and nevethium that launch far deadlier projectiles than arrows and make a booming sound when used. (Also called thunder-makers).

siren– a nocturnal bird known for its eerily human/nyrian sounding music and its shimmering midnight blue feathers. Native to Zelos, but also found on the islands inhabited by the Yustano people.

skirvin {sker-vin}– large, vicious rodents with poisonous, sharp spines and impeccable hearing. Native to Az Zar and commonly found in large cities like Cadar and Or Zahal where they can burrow under homes, in tunnels, and crypts.

sleepstalk– a root native to Zelos that can induce sleep or render one unconscious. Too much can result in a painless death.

snatcher– a thief.

Sowing Moons– spring. Contains the months Chailar, sub-Chailar, Tiknal, and sub-Tiknal.

specter moth– ashen black moths with fluorescent green eyes patterning their wings. Highly toxic when consumed. Native to Az Zar.

spirit-scape– a supernatural plane that physical bodies cannot access. Entering it requires the use of magic, meditation, or the assistance of immortals.

spirit walkers– angels or demons, or lesser gods and goddesses, depending on one's belief system.

starflies– Zelosi word for a winged, soft-bodied beetle with luminescent organs.

stormbird– giant birds of prey capable of manipulating/channeling the weather. One of the three orders of The Great Beasts of Old.

Stormrider– an individual who has bonded with a stormbird and gained the privilege of approaching it, maintaining physical and emotional contact, and riding on its back.

sun-blood tree– a species of tree found in Az Zar that produces small, tangy citrus fruits. They have vibrant crimson blossoms and are found in much of Az Zar's architecture and general imagery.

sun butter- a paste made from the seeds of the palano tree. Often sweetened or salted. Native to Orillon.

sunkiss- an energy-dense fruit with a sweet, caramel-like flavor and chewy texture. Found on palano trees in Orillon.

terredon {tehr-eh-dawn}- a flowering plant whose rhizome is widely used as a spice. Native to Zelos and Az Zar.

toi {toy}- a fermented plant drink with fruity undertones common among the southern tribes of Neharem.

Tongura {tahn-goo-ruh}- the largest village on the main island of Zelos.

Trimoon Ascendence, the- a phenomenon where all three moons align in a specific configuration relative to each other and to the sun. Believed to occur once every thousand years.

tulek bear {too-lek}- giant bears of the north.

tungata root {toon-gah-tuh}- an earthy root located in northern Neharem that is often ground up into a powder and put in teas for energy.

tuross {ter-ross}- flying lizards bred from ancient times when messages needed to transcend water, land, and sky. They are still a primary form of long-distance communication.

Tyrgraak {teer-grahk}- a skulmor stronghold in the Quentarri Mountains.

Vysilliam {vye-sill-ee-um}- believed by some to be the three original races of Quinaria comprising a trinity of beings suited for sky, water, and land. Includes the shaktar, myrem, and nyrians.

watcher- someone who helps patrol or guard in Neharem.

water dancer- a short-lived, slender insect with delicate, transparent wings and two or three long filaments on the tail.

Westmun {west-muhn}- the official language of Orillon.

widow-maker- a venomous spider identifiable by its crimson coloring and dark crossed-bone marking on its back. Without consumption of antivenom, its bite results in death. Native to northern Neharem.

xyrong {zigh-wrong}– an Az Zarian strategy game consisting of an octagonal board and hand-carved tokens.

yasaaka {yuh-sah-kuh}– a small paddle boat/board used by Zelosi locals to fish and for easy travel around and between islands.

zaka-zaka {zah-kuh-zah-kuh}– a large marsupial serving as the primary form of transportation in Orillon deserts.

Zarith {zare-rith}– the official language of Az Zar.

Zelos {zell-ohs}– a collection of islands off the southwestern coast of Az Zar.

Zelosi {zell-oh-see}– referring to the various peoples inhabiting, and dialects spoken on, the islands of Zelos.

zidel tree {zai-dell}– a tree with an angular crown and erratic branches with large, fanned leaves. Its bark is often consumed or smoked for its clarity benefits and general feel-good sensations. Found in Zelos and southern Az Zar.

THE
RACES
OF
QUINARIA

The Races of Quinaria

Beridians {bur–rid–ee–in}
- Physical features: Feline–esque beings covered in fur instead of skin with the tails and ears of great cats, they stand six to eight feet tall and walk upright

- Lifespan: Average of 300 years

- Traits: Poisonous claws, nocturnal vision

- Location: Predominately their isles with the exception of a few backhanders and explorers

Humans
- Physical features: Standard human variations

- Lifespan: Average of 75 years

- Traits: Skilled with tools and weapons

- Location: Some in eastern Az Zar and Neharem, but Orillon consists predominantly of humans

Myrem {meer–rem} (*also classified as Vysilliam in some belief systems, one of the three original races comprising a trinity of beings suited for sky, water, and land*)
- Physical features: Unknown, but rumored to be amphibious

- Lifespan: Rumored to be 1000 years

- Traits: The ability to breathe underwater

- Location: Unknown as they've not surfaced in generations

Nazrath {naz-wrath}

- Physical features: Giants rumored to have been three times the size of a nyrian while still resembling their basic features

- Lifespan: Unknown

- Traits: Immense strength and intelligence

- Location: Once northern Az Zar, but rumored to have retreated to the Uncharted North where they died off

Nymans {nigh-men}

- Physical features: These rarely conceived human–nyrian hybrids tend to result in dual to tri-toned skin, hair, and eyes while retaining the nyrian pointed ears and luminescent eyes

- Lifespan: Average of 200 years

- Traits: While they tend to carry the superior health and intellect of the nyrian parent, most nymans struggle with infertility

- Location: Neharem and Orillon

Nyrians {neer-ree-in} *(also classified as Vysilliam in some belief systems, one of the three original races comprising a trinity of beings suited for sky, water, and land)*

- Physical features: Slightly taller than humans on average, white hair, pointed ears, and luminescent eyes

- Lifespan: Average of 500 years

- Traits: Strong immune systems, superior intelligence (due in part to the extended lifespan), better vision

- Location: Az Zar, Neharem (rarely found in Orillon)

Shaktar {shack-tar} *(also classified as Vysilliam in some belief systems, one of the three original races comprising a trinity of beings suited for sky, water, and land)*
- Physical features: Unknown, but legend says they could fly

- Lifespan: Rumored to have been eternal

- Traits: Unknown

- Location: Unknown, but legend says they occupy caverns in eastern Orillon

Skulmor {skull-mor}
- Physical features: Canine-esque beings covered in fur instead of skin with the tails and ears of wolves, they are roughly eight feet tall and prefer to move on all fours (though they can walk upright)

- Lifespan: Average of 40 years

- Traits: Hulking strength and powerful fangs

- Location: The Skulmor territory (nomadic)

ACKNOWLEDGMENTS

This book is long, so I'm going to keep this short and sweet.

I'm not exaggerating to say that *Of Love and Loss* literally wouldn't have happened without the support of some priceless individuals. While I've had people involved at various stages throughout my writing and publication, there are a select few who show up time and time again, and without them, you wouldn't be holding this book in your hands.

First, I want to thank my editor, Jon, for allowing me to alter my MS delivery schedule when we got hit with an unexpected move. It threw a wrench in my drafting plans, and the extra few weeks' worth of wiggle room you gave me meant everything.

Next, I want to thank my proofreader, Dom. I had to change some things last minute, and it's so reassuring to know you can catch the adjustments made between copy edits and proofreading. I'm in good hands.

And to my cover designer/artist, Jeff, thank you. Your vision for the second cover was just as glorious as the first. I'm so excited to see where the series goes.

There's always a disconnect between the author's brain and the readers', and you need early readers to help you close those gaps. Tim and Lisa: thank you a thousand times over for stepping up on such a tight schedule. You've been the most loyal readers and supporters, and I'm so grateful I have you to help sculpt the vision of Quinaria. Special thanks for your laugh-out-loud commentaries. I also want to thank Lindsey for being one of my most supportive readers and just an all-around lovely person to chat with. When you've got someone in your corner who markets your books better than you do, you know the universe has smiled on you.

Everlasting thanks to Kaylea, my critique partner, fellow writer, and friend. You are always an email away, ready to lend a hand and adjust your schedule to offer insight. You've contributed countless hours, discussed plot points and character decisions with me, and talked me down from my proverbial ledge more times than I can count. It's been an honor to walk through the journey of publishing with you and to call you my friend. Your writing inspires me as much as you do, and I can't wait to see where your career goes.

I'm forever grateful to my ARC readers for taking an early dive into the manuscript. An extra shout out to Elena for acting as secondary proofreader out of the kindness of her heart. Seriously, you're such a lifesaver, my friend.

To my family: Jared, Björn, and Éowyn (and the little fuzzy butts). Thank you for tolerating my absolute insanity. I'm sorry for covering the walls with plot notes and scene outlines, and I'm forever grateful for how much you all support my passion. I hope I've made you proud.

I also want to shout out Kelsey, Dad, and Ryan. Thank you for being my real-life people in support of my writing endeavors. I'm so happy to have you all nearby again.

There are so many others who've supported my journey so far, so many that I can't possibly begin to name you all. Just know that every read, review, share, and purchase means the world to me.

May your sunrises always hold promise, and may your sunsets always hold peace.

B. S. H. Garcia is the author of the epic fantasy series, *The Heart of Quinaria*. A household manager by day, writer by night, she graduated with honors from The University of Colorado with a bachelor's degree in English Writing. To get into character for her stories, she trudges through the woods in cosplay with a mead-filled drinking horn and has traveled from Oregon to New Zealand seeking inspiration. Visit her online at www.bshgarcia.com.